THE EPIMETHEUS TRIAL
BOOK ONE
ELDER BLOOD

I0741341

E. A. SETSER

"Elder Blood"

Book One of "The Epimetheus Trial"

©   Copyright 2012, 2017 Social Detriment Publishing

http://www.amazon.com/author/easetser

Cover Art by Joseph Yerka (Lights Out, God Help Me)

Editing by Celia Setser

The Epimetheus Trial

Elder Blood

Thanks to anyone who helped me with research questions.

Kris, Tim, Jillian, Connor, and anyone else I'm forgetting.

Also to Ja'Van, Bo, and Tavin

For letting me borrow your face, your hair, and your boots, respectively

Prologue

Worn and weary, a body on the brink of demise

Beneath a statue of a progenitor

An ancient leader

A voice, a whisper, carried on the wind

The voice of the elder

The bloodline must not end

No progeny, none to inherit the legacy

His spirit beckoned to the beyond

The whisper flows into the body

Breathing in new life

The life of the ancestor

The bloodline must not end

The embodied ancient spirit

The revived descendant body

Speak premiere words as one

So shall it begin once more

Chapter 1

With the rising sun shining through his window, he sat at the foot of the bed, rubbing the fatigue from his eyes. He glanced over his shoulder to find the bed otherwise empty. His wife had awoken unusually early, perhaps roused by their son. Upon the dresser sat a stack of folded clothing, and before it was a pair of boots. He meticulously unfolded each item, careful not to wrinkle them as he dressed himself. This was his uniform, save for the misplaced helmet.

"I must have left it in the living room," he mumbled to himself.

At well over two meters tall with broad shoulders, his stature was indisputably intimidating. Adding to the image were his thick black locks of hair, naturally matted in small patches. Despite looking to be something of a warlord, he was among the newest recruits in ArcNos's internationally renowned Military Guild. His name was CreSam.

His footsteps echoed throughout the stairwell as his heavy steel toed boots clomped against the carpeted wooden stairs. BeiLou waited at the bottom, beaming with pride at the sight of her husband in full fatigues on the morning of his first mission. From the direction of the living room, he heard a faint giggling.

"You're up awfully early," CreSam noted, kissing her on the cheek.

"I just wanted to make sure you had a good breakfast before you go," BeiLou explained sweetly, "There are biscuits in the oven and bacon and eggs on the stove."

As he rounded the corner into the kitchen, the laughter grew louder. He looked to the couch and saw his son's fingers curled over the top. Playfully, he crept to the back of the sofa and tapped the small child's digits. Like a spring loaded trap, MeiLom sprang from the front of the couch, arms outstretched, and clung to his father's neck. CreSam's comparably massive helmet spun around the three-year-old child's head.

"Oh, that's where I put it!" CreSam remarked, reclaiming his lost article, "Wait a minute, you're not the hat rack."

"No! I'm MeiLom!" his son protested through laughter.

"Oh, right, of course you are. But what were you doing with my helmet? We talked about this."

"Making sure you don't forget me!"

"MeiLom, you know I can't take you with me to Berinin."

"Actually, he needs to go with you," BeiLou interjected, "Chieftain Sage Gijin sent a letter asking you to bring a friend or relative. Custom dictates that a foreign visitor be present to witness the birth of his grandson."

"I can do it after I retrieve the parcel."

"He addressed that in the letter. It can't be anybody visiting on any official international business. It's the child's first connection to the outside world."

"Hm, well that's a new one on me," CreSam admitted, rubbing his stubble, "but I never was much on foreign customs. I guess that means you're coming with me, buddy."

MeiLom threw his hands up in delight and dropped from his father's shoulder. It was a long drop for his small body, but his legs sustained the impact quite well. He turned sharply, clapping his feet together, and saluted his father, nearly looking straight up to face him.

"Alright! Let's move out!" he announced as firmly as his young voice allowed.

"At least give me time to eat breakfast," CreSam laughed.

"I'll double check your bags while you eat," BeiLou offered.

"I'm not that forgetful, am I?"

"You forgot where your helmet was," MeiLom piped up, "but I didn't!"

"Okay, kid, that's enough out of you," CreSam said with a laugh, "Let's grab some grub and procure some pills."

After a heavy breakfast, the two of them left on foot for the southeastern coast, leaving the car for BeiLou. She proudly waved farewell to them, watching from the front porch until they disappeared behind the horizon. This was to be MeiLom's longest trip away from home without her.

CreSam walked in shortened strides, while MeiLom jogged alongside, his little legs trying to keep up with his father's. Despite the fairly long hike of five kilometers, he refused to tire. His father had become his role model since joining the military, and he already knew he had a tough act to follow.

"Hey Papa! What kind of place is Berinin?" MeiLom asked, breaking the long silence.

"Berinin hosts the Medicinal Guild, so they make and sell pills and immunity shots, that sort of thing," CreSam explained, "The culture depends on what area you visit, as does the sort of medicine they produce."

"What part are we going to?"

"We're going to the capitol, Masnethege. It's a small primitive village on the southeast coast. They practice herbal medicine, meaning they make it from plants."

"You mean they eat sticks when they get sick? That's weird!"

"Sometimes it can work wonders. You'd be surprised," CreSam said as they reached the docks, "Here we are. Can you untie the boat?"

A dinghy sat in the water, anchored by a rope. MeiLom fiddled with the knot for a moment, struggling to pull it apart. With persistence, he eventually pulled it loose and hopped into the boat.

"Come on, Papa!" he beckoned, "The boat's gonna leave without you."

CreSam reached down and gripped the end of the boat, holding it in place as he climbed into it. He flashed a grin and a consenting nod to his son, who returned both. With an oar in each hand, he pulled them away from the shore, sending them southward.

He continued paddling in long strokes, building momentum until he could no longer see the shore. Now in open sea, he raised the sail and let the boat drift. The wind blew in their favor, continuing to carry them in a general southward direction.

MeiLom perched himself at the bow like a gargoyle, the wind tossing his hair about. His eyes panned over the waters ahead, mentioning anything that fed his curiosity. Even the splash of the smallest fish caught his attention.

"Hey, pal, are you hungry?" CreSam asked, speaking for the first time in hours.

"I sure am," MeiLom answered, "Are we gonna catch some fish?"

"Well, I am," CreSam said with a laugh, "You're free to try if you want."

CreSam dug through his bag, searching for the fishing rod. Once he had found it, he held it in one hand and hoisted his son onto his knee with the other. He set both their hands on the rod and tipped it back and forth to demonstrate a basic casting motion.

"You see how it's done now?" CreSam asked, "Now watch."

MeiLom dropped his grip from the fishing rod. With a powerful thrust, CreSam cast the line far over the water, the bobber barely noticeable over the swishing waters. The two of them eyed it until, after a few silent minutes, the bobber sank. CreSam gave a firm tug and reeled it in until the fish hung over the water, a decently sized specimen of perhaps five kilograms.

"This should last us a while," CreSam commented, "Now we just need to gut it and cook it."

"I'll get the knife and the matches," MeiLom offered.

"No, I should get those. You're likely to hurt yourself."

CreSam drew a knife from his bag along with a travel sized grill. He began by decapitating the fish, then removing its tail. MeiLom tossed both back into the ocean. CreSam ran the knife along the back of the fish, and dug into it, gutting it. MeiLom promptly tossed the bloody scraps into the ocean.

His hands trembling anxiously, CreSam struck the match and pitched it into the grill. He cowered back into the rear of the boat, watching the flames catch from a distance. MeiLom sat beside the grill, bathing in its warmth.

"Why are you all the way over there, Papa?" he asked, confused by his father's cowardly actions.

"I'm pyrophobic," CreSam explained, "I don't know why, but fire frightens me."

"This one's warm," MeiLom said, "I like it."

MeiLom watched in awe at the flames rising between the bars and licking the fish's searing flesh. The fire delighted him as it warmed him with its heated glow and amused him with its dance. His father was the reverse, watching from a distance at an angle that shrouded most of the fire from view.

"Take that fish off and put the fire out," CreSam ordered after a few minutes, "Can you do that for me?"

"Sure thing Papa," MeiLom agreed.

With his bare hands, he snatched the fish and dropped it behind him. Recklessly, he grabbed the sides of the bowl, but drew them back quickly. CreSam watched in silence, waiting to see how MeiLom would handle the situation. After a moment of thought, he removed his shirt and wrapped it around his hands, using it in lieu of oven mitts. He hoisted it off the stand, careful not to pull it against his bare torso. Steadying himself on the swaying boat, he shuffled to the edge and pitched the whole thing overboard.

"It's easier to bring the water to the fire, MeiLom," CreSam said, laughing as he retrieved the soaked grill.

"My way works, too!" MeiLom remarked, "Now let's eat some fish."

Despite how thoroughly BeiLou had checked his bags, they had both neglected to pack forks. Not ones to be hung up on improper etiquette, they simply ate with their fingers instead.

After they ate, CreSam dipped his hands in the water to get clean. MeiLom leaned over the edge, teetering on his belly, but his arms could not reach the water. CreSam lifted him by the ankles, hanging him upside down.

"Ready?"

"Ready!"

All at once, CreSam dunked MeiLom into the water, up to his chest. He pulled him back out and set him down in the boat. MeiLom looked up at him with a sneer.

"You had some food on your cheek," CreSam said with a chuckle.

MeiLom spouted a stream of water at his father and laughed.

Once the meal was done and the mess cleaned, CreSam took the oars once again. He paddled without rest for an hour, finally stopping as the sky reddened with the setting sun. At that time, he hoisted the sail and pulled the oars into the boat for the night. Soon after, they both fell asleep as day faded into night.

The following two days carried out with minimal ado, much in the same way as the first. On the third dawn, they arrived in Masnethege.

"MeiLom. MeiLom," CreSam called to his sleeping son, his hand on his shoulder, "Wake up, MeiLom. We've made it to Berinin."

A young woman in animal hide clothing stood on the shore, looking over the guests.

"That you have," she said, "I assume by your uniform that you're from ArcNos."

"Yes, we are," he said as he picked up MeiLom, "I am Green Rookie CreSam of ArcNos, and this is my son, MeiLom."

"Oh, you brought your little boy with you," she noted with delight, "Are you sure that's okay with your commanding officer? I thought your guild was quite rigorous."

"Gijin asked me to bring him, apparently. By the way, could you hold him for a moment while I tie the boat?"

"Of course, I love children."

CreSam handed MeiLom to her, quickly latched the boat to a post on the shore, and reclaimed his son as he began to awaken. MeiLom lay across CreSam's arm, eyelids flickering under the sunlight. CreSam and the Berininite both watched, waiting for him to waken. Upon gaining full consciousness, his first sight was of the young woman. He jumped, obviously startled.

"Who are you?" he asked.

"We're in Berinin, MeiLom," CreSam said.

"This is Berinin?" MeiLom asked, "Why are all the houses made of sticks and leaves? I thought that's how they made their medicine."

"We use the land for many things. The land and the sea are our most valuable resources," the woman answered.

"By the way, where does the Chieftain Sage live?" CreSam asked, "I need to drop MeiLom off before I fetch the parcel."

"Gijin's house is on the north end of town, slightly larger than the surrounding homes. He's been unusually reclusive lately, but you may have some luck if he requested your presence."

MeiLom jumped from his father's shoulder, absorbing the impact of the landing. CreSam took his hand and led him north into the village. A dense forest sat slightly beyond it, the two coming within a few footsteps of overlapping

"Papa, how long have we been here?" MeiLom asked.

"We just got here before you woke up. Don't worry, you didn't miss anything," CreSam assured him.

A bit unexpectedly, the Chieftain Sage's hut didn't quite have a door as much as a grassy flap. Assertively, CreSam shook the flap. An elderly voice spoke out from within, asking of his purpose. After introductions and a brief exchange, Gijin's demeanor turned more welcoming as he invited the visitors inside.

CreSam pulled the curtain back, letting his son enter before him. Several streams of grey and white hair adorned the walls, some as long as the room was tall. Centered near the back wall was a copper statue of a man with four arms and windblown hair, within a shrine of brick and mud. Two of his hands each held a bowl of water above his head, while the second pair held forth a third bowl in offering, all three overflowing into the stone tub in which he stood.

Before it sat a frail diminutive old man, anatomically normal but dressed in garb better suited for the statue. His flowing white hair hung past his waist, the ends sprawled on the floor. He radiated an air of mingling power and benevolence.

"I see you brought your son, just as I asked," Gijin greeted, "Come forth child. Tell me what they call you."

MeiLom stepped out from behind his father's leg, and hesitantly approached the unusual old man. He stopped at a short table as their eyes locked. Gijin looked him over, peering into his wholly green eyes.

"He is one," Gijin exhaled inaudibly.

"Heh-hello," MeiLom stuttered, "My name is MeiLom."

"So it is. As you may know, I am Chieftain Sage Gijin," Gijin greeted, now smiling warmly upon MeiLom.

"So, where would I find this medicine?" CreSam asked.

"The parcel you seek is in the house next door, to the east," Gijin answered somewhat dismissively.

"Thank you, sir," CreSam said, "MeiLom, stay here."

"Okay, Papa. I'll just wait with the Cheepin' Safe," MeiLom agreed.

Gijin laughed quietly as CreSam left to fetch the shipment of herbal medicine.

"That's Chieftain Sage," he corrected, "I'm Chieftain Sage Gijin. Now, go on and make yourself comfortable. I may be of high standing, but you are my guest."

Though custom dictated it, such inviting behavior had recently become uncharacteristic of the once benevolent leader. Somewhat ironically, the change came about soon after he narrowly escaped the inevitable throes of death. Still, this sort of personal altruism was beyond even his former self.

MeiLom sat on the floor, watching Gijin intently as he lifted the bowl from the statue's offering hands. The crystal water sloshed over the sides a bit as he set it steadily upon the table.

"Hey, Gijin," MeiLom piped up, "What are you gonna do with that?"

"Watch, my child," Gijin insisted, "Just watch."

Gijin dug through one of his pockets and withdrew two vials of blood. He popped the cork out of each and poured the contents into the water. With a long fingernail, he nicked his finger and added two drops of his own blood.

The three crimson stains flowed together slowly into a single cloudy mass. Gijin dipped his finger in the bowl and swirled it a couple of times. The mixture of blood spiraled in the water. A warm blue glow formed on the surface, the bloody water

6

sloshing upward into it. The light swelled and lifted, slowly forming into a ball. It hovered over the bowl, the concoction of blood and water swirling within. Gijin held his upturned palms beneath the luminescent orb. MeiLom watched in mesmerization.

Gijin mumbled an incantation repeatedly. With each repetition, the blood swirled faster. As he fell silent, and blood slowed and pulled toward the center into a concentrated mass.

It appeared shapeless initially, but the form of a fetus slowly developed in the mystifying blood. A coating of flesh enveloped the bloody silhouette, detailed with a thin layer of black hair atop its head. From the water and the blood, a child had taken shape.

Gijin reached into the fading light and retrieved the silent newborn. With his free hand, he returned the bowl to the statue.

"My child, your name will be," Gijin said to the infant, "Galo."

"How did you do that?" MeiLom asked in amazement.

"Your eyes are better suited for explaining it than are my words," Gijin muddled, "However, I do have something for you."

MeiLom watched in confused anticipation as Gijin knelt beside the bed, the child still on his arm, and reached beneath it. Galo looked at MeiLom and managed a tiny chirp from his newborn throat. Gijin pulled his hand back, dragging a wooden box. He opened it and withdrew a silver medallion on a matching chain. Embedded in the medallion was a ruby star with four points and arced edges. MeiLom looked down and smiled as it was lowered into his hands.

"Keep this always, and wear it when at all possible," Gijin insisted.

"Thank you, Gijin. I'll take good care of it," MeiLom accepted, "Does it do anything?"

"For now, it is merely a gift. The rest will come in time, Sinkua."

A silent infant slept in her crib, a thin wall standing between her and the enraged discourse of her parents. Though he still took up residence with her and her mother, the man responsible for her conception refused to acknowledge such. Since birth, she had been fatherless by all other meanings of the word.

"What are we going to do with her?" Kabehl asked.

"We're going to keep her and raise her, because she's our child," Elemeno snapped, "regardless of how she looks."

"Elemeno, the girl is a freak! There is no way that that thing is my daughter!"

The child had been born with something of a birth defect, though calling it such was the topic of much debate both in her home and in the medical community. Her upper back was adorned with a pair of dark purple splotches, almost like bruises though that explanation was ruled out. Her doctor authoritatively declared them birthmarks, a statement which popular theory held as dismissive with any number of motives.

"That thing? That thing!? You say that like she's deformed! It's a birth mark, nothing more. So what if they're discolored? So what if she has two of them?" she argued.

"Oh, sure, that's perfectly normal!" he sarcastically retorted, "I'm telling you, she is not my daughter."

"Why? Because you don't have two purple birth marks? Well, in case you haven't searched me thoroughly enough, I don't have them either."

"What are you going on about?"

"If those are genetic, they probably came from recessive genes. Nobody in my family in the past five generations has had those markings. Does that mean she can't be my daughter?"

"I saw her come out of you! Of course she's your daughter! Besides, your family is full of nutcases and degenerates. Mine has long been upstanding and, quite frankly, normal."

"Normal this and normal that. What is your obsession with normality?"

"Normal is acceptable, plain and simple."

"Normal is boring, plain and boring. Would you rather Eytea be just as gray as the rest of the world or embrace her uniqueness?"

"Honestly, I don't give a shit what happens to Eytea! She is not my daughter, and that's the end of the argument."

Even reinforced by a physical wall, the wall of sleep fell to the sound of Kabehl's ranting. Eytea cried out as she awoke at such an undesirable hour.

"Oh, that was real good. You just woke her up. Are you proud of yourself, now?" Elemeno hissed in a sharp whisper.

"Like I said, I don't give a shit what happens to her!"

Eytea continued to cry out, now louder than before.

"Sounds like she could use a little father-daughter time," Elemeno suggested, hoping to push the father into a relationship with Eytea.

"Sounds to me like you need to find her real father."

"What are you implying? You know you're the only guy to ever get at my knickers.'

"You lying bitch! You've slept around, and everyone knows!"

"Now, you're just being ridiculous. Quit with your assumptions, and don't use that language around Eytea."

"I told you before; I don't give a shit what happens to Eytea, bitch!"

"Hold your tongue! I told you not to use that language around her."

"Bitch! Bitch! Bitch! I'll say whatever the hell I want, wherever the hell I want."

"Not in my house, you won't."

"This house is just as much mine as it is yours. You can't get by without me."

"And what makes you think you can stand on your own? We're stuck with each other, but that doesn't mean you should take it out on Eytea. She's just as much your daughter as she is mine."

"How many times do I have to say it? She's not my damn daughter, and I don't give a shit what happens to her!"

"She is your daughter. It's time you faced the truth."

"And what exactly is the truth, do you think?"

"The truth is that she's your daughter, like it or not. You and I are stuck with each other, and it would be best for Eytea if we didn't argue in front of her, and for you to watch your language."

"I am getting so damn sick of you telling me how it is."

"No, you're sick of always being wrong. And how many times do I have to tell you to watch your mouth?"

"Goddamn it, woman! Stop telling me what to do."

"Hypocrite," Elemeno muttered.

"I heard that! Don't think I didn't."

"Did you really, hypocrite? Are you proud of yourself, hypocrite?"

"Shut your damn mouth, woman!"

He drew his arm back across his shoulder and swept it forth in a powerful arc. The back of his hand slammed into Elemeno's temple, forcing itself across her face. The stout woman collapsed with a cry of pain.

Eytea cried louder, too loud for her abusive father to bear. He kicked Elemeno in the head to get her attention. She lay there playing opossum.

"Shut her up, woman," he demanded.

With that, he went outside to sleep in his car, too sickened by his wife and alleged daughter to spend the night in the same house. When she heard the door shut, Elemeno got to her feet. She had faked most of the pain for her own sake as well as Eytea's.

She slipped quietly into Eytea's room. Her cries waned when she saw her mother, but she seemed upset by the all too familiar red mark on her face. She scooped Eytea out of the crib, holding her in her arms, swaying back and forth. Eytea's cries slowly fell silent as she drifted back to sleep.

"Don't listen to what your father says. You're something special," she whispered reassuringly, "You're my Eytea."

An eight-year-old boy lay asleep, alone in his room. On the backs of his eyelids played dreams of glory days he was certain would come. In any number of ways, his every waking moment was spent pursuing his goal of joining the ArcNosian Military Guild as a soldier.

Beside his bed, he kept a tree branch, meticulously cleaned of offshoots and bark. What appeared as just a stick was, to his imaginative mind, a fierce quarterstaff. He trained daily, teaching himself as he shadow sparred with invisible foes.

Rather to his impatience, he was still seven years shy of the qualifying age. He frequently reminded himself that this would allow him more time to hone his admittedly ragged skills. If he were ever to stand with the greats, he would need to make a strong impression on the aging Brigadier General Elite HarEin.

He mumbled in his sleep, rolling around and tossing the sheets about. His quarterstaff danced and tapped across the wooden floor. When the bed began to shake, he sat up quickly, clutching the edges of the mattress as he took stock of the situation. Pieces of the roof dropped to the floor, and the window frame cracked.

The young boy tossed the sheets aside and rolled onto the unstable floor. Chips made by his bouncing quarterstaff nicked his bare feet and knuckles. He swiped the staff and ran to the hall.

The house shook more violently. Window frames buckled while more pieces of the ceiling broke away and plummeted to the ground. In the kitchen, dishes shattered against one another in both the sink and the cabinets. Light fixtures swung about while decorative candles fell with their stands and broke against the floor. From high above the fireplace, an antique candelabrum crashed and shattered against the brick hearth.

The child ran to his parents' room to awaken them. Unlike him, they were unusually heavy sleepers. He pushed their door to no avail. Desperately, he pounded on the door and began to shout.

"Ma! Pa! Ma! Pa! It's an earthquake! Wake up!" he yelled.

There was no answer. Time to play hero. He gripped his quarterstaff and slammed the wider end against the door. The door cracked a bit, but the house continued to crumble as the frame buckled in on itself. He hit it again and again, wearing away the wooden door. Finally, he busted through and peeked inside to find his parents still asleep.

"Wake up! Wake up! It's an earthquake! The house is falling apart!" he yelled.

They stirred a bit, mumbling incoherently, but remained dormant after all.

The wall between them began to deteriorate, small fragments of it breaking away. With its support diminishing, a large section of the ceiling collapsed, landing partially atop his parents, They looked around in panic, then to their son, who was still looking through a hole in the door.

"Spril! Get out of the house!" his father called out.

"It's about time you two woke up!" Spril remarked before running to the front door.

The earthquake grew in intensity, collapsing furniture. Every window frame had cracked and caved in on itself. The cracks in the walls spread like a plague. The ceiling sagged over the damaged walls, fragments of it dropping and shattering against the floor.

Spril shoved his entire weight against the front door, but it was jammed all the same. Once again, time for him to play the hero. He bashed upon the door with his quarterstaff, cracking the door slightly. A large section of the adjacent wall crumbled, dropping a piece of the ceiling with it. Panicked, Spril banged on the door again and again.

Another pounding noise resounded from outside. As he pulled back to strike the door again, it burst forth from the frame and knocked him to the floor. An arm reached in, grabbed him by the shirt, and dragged him out from under the door and out of the collapsing house.

The rest of the front wall collapsed. Large sections of roof dropped in, throwing up clouds of dust and debris as they shattered on the floor. The other perimeter walls followed in quick succession, taking much of the roof with them. Spril watched helplessly as his home sank in on itself, falling into a pile of rubble in the final seconds of the devastating earthquake.

With tears welling in his eyes, Spril ran to the back of the fallen house in search of his parents. He climbed over the rubble, pulling aside what he could lift in a desperate panic. The mysterious rescuer cut across the wreckage, once again coming to Spril's assistance.

The young man pulled larger pieces of debris aside, still thus far unacknowledged. Spril was too consumed by grief to pay mind to much else. The young man peered through a hole he had formed and caught a glimpse of Spril's parents. He turned an ear to the hole and heard nothing. Hesitantly, he reached in and touched their faces. They were lukewarm but perhaps a bit cooler than normal. Spril continued to dig, oblivious to all of this. The young man stretched his arm further and checked each for a radial pulse. Neither had one.

He pulled his arm out and looked over at Spril, who was still digging hopelessly. He reached out and set a hand upon Spril's shoulder. Spril jumped and looked up, finally seeing who had helped him save himself.

"Phylus?"

"Spril, I'm sorry," Phylus apologized.

"Sorry?" Spril asked, frightened by the implication, "Are my parents...?"

Phylus lowered his head and sighed heavily.

"They're... They didn't make it."

Spril cried out in anguish, the tears running faster down his face and blurring his vision. He threw himself on Phylus, who wrapped an arm around the crying dreamer, offering what comfort he could. His other hand ran over Spril's abnormally smooth scalp.

For years, Phylus had been Spril's babysitter, called upon when his parents wanted a night out alone. As luck would have it, this was one such night, placing Phylus in close proximity when local seismologists warned of what was likely approaching. Though, perhaps it was the fatigue of a long night out which kept his parents from waking.

In saddened reflection, they sat atop that heap of wreckage that had once been Spril's home. All that he had left was Phylus, his quarterstaff and a dream.

That night, they slept in Phylus's car. Phylus was scarcely in the right frame of mind to drive after what had transpired. Besides, Spril needed to sleep, and the car tended to keep him awake, unlike most children. Spril rolled onto his side and nudged him.

"Phylus, are you sure I can stay with you?" he asked sheepishly

"Well, of course I'm sure, buddy. Why wouldn't I be?" Phylus replied in a bit of surprise.

"I just know you and Malia are having money problems, and I don't wanna make more."

"No, you won't be a burden. Don't stress yourself over it."

"That's good. I know you were getting good money from my parents, but maybe now you'll have time to look for a better job."

"That's true. I mean, there's no way those nepotistic jerks I work for are ever going to give me a raise," Phylus ranted, ignoring Spril's callousness toward the loss of his parents.

"How's Malia doing with her catering business?"

"Not bad, but the money isn't steady. She's been talking about wanting a child lately, but I really don't think either of us is in a good position for that quite yet."

"Good thing you've got practice, though," Spril joked.

"That I do. You were quite the handful just a year ago," Phylus retorted as he rubbed Spril's scalp.

Spril laughed childishly, squirming in his seat and trying to catch his breath. Phylus watched him with a smile. He had watched this child grow up in irregular intervals, and the night's events were sure to bring them closer. He already saw him as kin, but what sort was debatable. The age difference was too narrow to consider him a son, but they had not been familiar enough to see him as a brother. Perhaps a cousin would be a suitable relation.

Spril, having finally caught his breath, rolled over onto his back. Phylus smiled and tipped back over to his back. He closed his eyes slowly.

"I think I'll try to sleep now. Goodnight, Spril."

"Goodnight, Phylus," Spril answered through a yawn born from fading consciousness

Malia knew not to worry. Phylus was to have reported for a temporary assignment that night, so she didn't expect him until morning. When warnings of an earthquake arose though, he cancelled his plans in anticipation that Spril would need him, neither to Malia's knowledge.

His intuition served him well, even though few children would have come as close to escaping that house unaided. Perhaps never knowing the limitations of his peers played a part in this. The few children he knew generally kept their distance, an ill sentiment he eventually came to reciprocate.

The rural region was sparsely populated as it was, which translated to fewer children. Being typical kids for the most part, they frequently mocked his scalp condition, sometimes referring to him as a tiny old man. At one point, he sought a cure or a toupee in lieu of such. Both ideas were promptly scrapped when he realized their acceptance wasn't worth living a lie. Following shortly after that epiphany was the birth of his dream.

When they arrived home the next morning, Phylus quietly opened the door and stepped inside. Spril followed close behind, dragging his quarterstaff over the front step.

"Malia? Malia!" Phylus called out, his voice echoing slightly.

Quite concerned for her absence, Phylus searched the small house thoroughly, checking rooms twice and thrice. Spril followed close behind, all the while getting acquainted with his new home, though Malia's absence was undeniably worrisome. In the kitchen, Phylus found his answer in the form of a note on the table.

Spril watched Phylus's every expression as he read the note. The outlook was grim. Phylus heaved a sigh of displeasure and let the note drop to the floor.

"She left me," he said flatly, "It seems that last night was too much for her, so she up and left. Crap."

"Oh, that's too bad. I thought you two had hit it off," Spril said in condolence.

"So did I. She just couldn't handle my being away at night on temporary assignments."

"If you want me to pick up a job cutting grass or something, I will. You know, so you don't have to work all those part time jobs at night."

"Like I told you last night, there's no need for you to worry yourself with that, but thank you anyway," Phylus reminded him, "By the way, are you hungry? I could whip something together for us."

"Now that you mention it, my belly is growling. What do we have?"

"Let's take a look in our refrigerator."

Phylus opened the refrigerator to the sight of two small sealed containers, each filled with a sickly substance. He held both up to the light as he tried to remember what they were. Spril tugged at the leg of his pants, curious as to what he had found.

That small event sparked his memory into clarity. He and Malia had developed a backup plan in case they could not conceive naturally. Two months ago, they stored their sperm and eggs for artificial insemination, but Phylus had never paid any mind to those cups. With Malia gone though, suddenly they caught his interest again.

He returned to his seat, setting the two cups in the middle of the table. He rested his elbows on the table and his head upon his overlapping hands. In deep contemplation, he stared at the two cups, weighing his options. Spril tugged at his arm but was ignored, overshadowed by Phylus's introspection.

After a few minutes, he silently returned the cups to the refrigerator, his decision finally made. He and Malia had decided they would bring a child into the world together, no matter the circumstances. Lately, he had grown curious about such a child, one composed from both their strengths and flaws. This and the fact that she left her eggs both cemented his decision. He reasoned that she would have thought to take the eggs if she had any objection to the notion. Sadly though, her only connection to the offspring would be genetic.

Spril patted Phylus's leg to get his attention. Phylus looked back over his shoulder and smiled down at him.

"I'm going to be a father."

Chapter 2

MeiLom's eyes flickered open as the sun shone upon them through the open blinds. Reflexively, he squinted as he turned his back to the window. He hopped down from the bed, his little feet thumping against the wooden floor, and made for the stairs.

CreSam cocked an ear as he heard the thump of little feet from upstairs. As had been customary on mornings of deployment for the past year, MeiLom rushed downstairs to see his father off. Quite atypically though, CreSam avoided eye contact.

MeiLom leapt from the stairs and was caught, spun, and set on the floor. CreSam patted his back and sent him on to the kitchen for breakfast. MeiLom climbed into his chair, then onto the table to watch his parents converse. Wise to his eavesdropping, they kept their voices low.

"How long will it be until you get back?" BeiLou asked nervously.

"Six days," CreSam answered quietly, "Keep an eye on MeiLom. He's behaving strangely."

"I hadn't noticed. Maybe he's just being a kid."

"BeiLou, he's been asking to go back to Berinin every day for the past year. He keeps saying he wants to see Grandpa Gijin and some kid named Galo. I don't know who this Galo is, and I especially don't like him calling someone we don't know Grandpa."

"Well, if I can find the means, perhaps I'll take him down to Berinin while you're away," BeiLou suggested.

"I'd rather you didn't, but I suppose I can't stop you while I'm away. Do as you wish," CreSam reluctantly agreed, his expression as flat as ever.

CreSam hoisted his pack onto his shoulders. He turned to MeiLom with a stern expression, a faint glimmer of compassion hidden within, and called to him. MeiLom jerked his head up and looked to his father as sternly as he could manage.

"I'll see you in six days," CreSam said plainly.

"Right!" MeiLom acknowledged with a firm nod, though CreSam's back was already turned to him.

Perhaps MeiLom had changed over the past year, as children are wont to do. As far as BeiLou was concerned, CreSam was the only one expressing any sort of qualm with it. She acknowledged that the military may have been taking too much of a toll. The stress of performance and being away from home were heavy burdens.

MeiLom tried to eat as his mother insisted, but the thought of it left him feeling ill. He sat and stared into his bowl, apathetically leaning his elbow on the table and his face against his hand.

He had always shown signs of separation anxiety during his father's absences, but this time they surfaced abnormally early. At any other time, his mother would have simply assumed he was taking the absence particularly hard, but CreSam's observation changed that. Now, she knew that anxious longing could just as easily have been for Grandpa Gijin or Galo.

Up in his room, MeiLom kept his necklace in a box beneath his bed, successfully hiding it from his parents. His father was blinded by his career ambitions and his mother by her unwavering support thereof. CreSam had never asked who Galo was, but it didn't seem too much to expect him to deduce an answer. As for Gijin, they had met briefly, but whether he remembered seemed doubtful if he couldn't figure out who Galo was.

Still with an empty stomach, MeiLom crawled under his bed and withdrew the box his parents never suspected. He sat on the floor with his back against a bedpost and the box on his lap. Quietly, he slid the lid back and stared deeply into the necklace bestowed on him by Gijin on the day of Galo's birth.

His eyes traced the serpentine path of the chain from one side of the medallion to the other. He scooped the medallion up in his hands, resting his arms on is legs to support the weight. Even if he needed not hide it from his parents, its mass was too great to wear anyway.

He ran his thumbs over opposing segments of silver, separated by the ruby star in the center. He gazed into that ruby. It shimmered red against his eyes, which shimmered green over the crystal, the exchange of light creating something of a tiny aurora. Looking longer, he began to see his reflection in the ruby with its reflection in his eyes, the cycle repeating with perceivably endless continuity.

"Rookie CreSam?" Captain SenRas called.

"Sir!" CreSam firmly answered.

"Infantryman DelRol?"

"Sir!" the understandably shorter man answered.

"You both recently received promotions. Congratulations to you both. This is your chance to either justify it or botch the whole thing" SenRas continued in varying tones, "North of Ferya, you will find the island of Kirts. A possible threat has established a base there. Their origins are as of yet unknown, so we cannot pin this on Kirts. A few days ago, a spy returned with intelligence on new age weapons development. As we all know, allowing such technology to outpace the technology of the rest of the world would inevitably lead to an arms race and force other research onto a back burner. Furthermore, the fact that they operate in seclusion suggests an aim to drive the Military Guild into obsolescence.

"They recently received a shipment which has been concluded to be for a homing device. Your mission is to stop it from being put into use, either via theft or destruction. You will be provided with a map of the building as drawn from the spy's memory as well as the knowledge that the workers leave by sundown. Good luck to the both of you. See you in six days."

With their orders and their map, they left on the duo mission, a Rookie and an Infantryman assigned to infiltrate an uprising and cut them off at the roots. Such missions were often reserved for soldiers of higher rank and longer track records. So the fact that either of them had been chosen was abnormally rare.

The expedition spanned roughly two and a half days. For this mission, they had been granted exclusive use of a dinghy. There being no room, or need for that matter, for an armory on board though, they had chosen their armaments before departure. From the vast array of weaponry, CreSam selected his usual broadsword, while DelRol naturally chose a pistol from the armory.

"Hey, Infantryman," CreSam said between breaths as they walked up the beach on the west coast of Kirts, "What sort of contraption do you think we're up against?"

"As I've told you at least a dozen times in the past sixty hours, my name is DelRol, and I prefer to be called by it," DelRol snapped, "But I have no idea what to expect. Captain SenRas said something about a homing device. I think that means it tracks its target, makes bullets and whatnot self-aiming."

"How would something like that work?" CreSam asked bewilderedly.

"How would I know?" DelRol snapped again.

"Well we're about to find out. Look up ahead."

Atop a hill roughly thirty meters ahead of them stood a broad short brick structure, the doors and windows lined with chrome. Charcoal gray smoke spewed from a series of pipes along the perimeter of the flat roof. CreSam found himself entranced by the whole experience as the smoke swarmed his olfactory.

He shook his head about, climbing out of the trance. With a quickened pace, he caught up with DelRol, who had passed him in impatience.

"About time you decided to come along. For a minute there, I thought you were just going to stand there and will the device to destroy itself," DelRol said sarcastically.

"That might be a good idea," CreSam suggested after a moment of thought, "If we can't destroy it, we could just set it to target itself."

"We don't know how to set the target, but it's good to see you finally using your brain for something other than holding your skull up," DelRol snarked, "Now then, what's my name? Let's see if you can get this one."

"Where's the map, Infantryman?"

"The door's right there. Turn the knob, and I'll bet it opens."

"Are there any other entrances? We'd be rather stupid to walk right in the front door."

"It's after sundown."

"I noticed that much. What's that have to do with this place?"

"You weren't listening to Captain SenRas, were you? He said they all leave by sundown. We've got a clear path to the device," DelRol reminded as he opened the front door.

It seemed suspicious that the door had not been locked. Perhaps, these unidentified insurgents thought the location secluded enough to not be stumbled upon. Despite his confidence in their solitude, DelRol kept one hand on his pistol. The corridor appeared empty when they looked inside though, so it seemed best to take advantage. DelRol pulled the map from his pocket and unfolded it, studying it as they slowly crept along in the dark. CreSam kept one hand on the hilt of his broadsword.

"Alright, if it's been built, it will be at the end of the hall in the room on the left," DelRol clarified, "Or, wait a minute. According to this map, there's a door going out on both ends of this hallway. Did we enter from the southwest or the northeast? Wait, is that entering from the southwest or heading southwest? I'm horrible with maps."

"Then why in the hell did you opt to carry it?" CreSam snapped, snatching the map, "We'll just check the room to the left of either entrance until we find . . ."

He stopped when he heard the door open at the other end of the hall. The silhouette standing within produced a small pistol. DelRol quickly drew his larger standard model. The two fired at each other as CreSam charged with his broadsword drawn, the sounds muffled by the echoing of the door shutting behind the guest. His bullet grazed DelRol's in flight, and both exploded, briefly illuminating the hall.

CreSam rapidly decelerated to a halt at the mesmerizing sight of the explosion. Military Guild bullets were propelled by a combination of air pressure and spring mechanisms, designed for high velocity puncturing and certainly not explosive impact. It had clearly been the work of that man in the shadows. Noticing the hypnosis gripping CreSam, the shadowed man tossed the gun to him. CreSam caught it with a reasonably puzzled expression.

"CreSam, don't take it! We're here to destroy the homing device, and that's it," DelRol boldly ordered

"Rid yourself of this nuisance and become one of us," the shadowed man muttered.

"Don't listen to him. You're a proudly accomplished ArcNosian soldier. You don't need these things. The risk of collateral damage is too great for any conceivable task."

"But what of the larger tasks? Small game like that homing device will likely not always be your prey," the shadowed man argued, "Take the shot, soldier. Take the shot."

"Take him down, and let's move on!" DelRol pleaded.

His mind made up, CreSam fired the new pistol. The target collapsed to his death as the bullet blasted a hole in his chest cavity upon impact with a rib.

A year had passed since the largely private birth of Galo, and custom dictated that only now was he to inherit the title of Chieftain Heir. In many generations past, newborn Chieftain Heirs had perished within the first year of life, making their ceremonies retrospectively macabre. It had since come to be believed that a child of the Chieftain Bloodline who survived the first year would lead a long and prosperous life. Though admittedly, much of this was to counter the fear of a curse that came with heirs dying in infancy.

Gijin made his way through a path that parted in the crowd as he walked. One hand clutched the head of his cane while on the other arm slept Galo. His robe dragged along the ground, sweeping sand over his footprints. Gijin laid Galo atop the podium, stepped behind it, and turned to face the audience. He braced the sides of it with both hands, as though to hold it steady for the sleeping infant. Gijin spoke, and for his stature, did so quite firmly.

"People of Berinin. My people. My children. My brethren. A few years ago, my family was stricken deathly ill. After the death of my son Gabdur and his wife Zheal, it seemed that I would pass without an heir. I feared that the Chieftain Bloodline that began with the construction of Masnethege would soon meet its final day. However, in the midst of my illness, something came over me and restored my health long enough that I was able to rectify things. The exact nature of it is still beyond my knowledge, but regardless, the next step was to restore someone else's health.

"When my daughter-in-law passed, she was pregnant but twelve weeks shy of her due date. It was a risky maneuver, but my only hope was to extract the fetus and restore the child's health. This child lies before me now, and we will all know him as..."

He bowed his head, took a deep breath, and then lifted it again.

"Chieftain Heir Galo!"

A roar of applause exploded from the small crowd. Galo was stirred awake by the noise. He giggled delightedly when he saw all the people looking up at him joyously.

Gijin withdrew a small robe from his pocket, similar in style to his own aside from only having two sleeves. He laid it across his grandson's shoulders and maneuvered his arms into the sleeves. This robe was a mark of a Chieftain Heir, the first of many with more coming as he outgrew each one.

Gijin lifted Galo and placed him on his shoulder, watching over the crowd with him. He raised a hand high, then swept it out over the podium. The crowd fell silent. Gijin paused for a moment before speaking.

"May the festivities begin!"

The people applauded exuberantly at the announcement. Galo pumped his arms and giggled at all the excitement. Most of the people had come to the ceremony purely out of respect for tradition, but this was the moment many of them had been awaiting all morning.

Men and women known as Tide Dancers donned gypsy garbs and slam danced near the shore, the tide lapping at their feet. Beads of water split the air in radiant patterns, refracting the sun's rays, as they kicked about with beautiful aggression. Others nearby slapped addicting rhythms on their drums, their music synchronizing with the movement of the ocean. Galo watched them with a great curiosity, his spongy young mind absorbing their every movement.

Near them, other residents swam and bathed in the shallows. Even their movements flowed melodically with the rhythms of the drums, which moved with the song of the sea. Every motion of every attendant of the festival was rooted in the sea.

It was their source of life. They worshipped the sea for all that it was, including a means of travel, communication, and nourishment as well as a representation of the ether of spirits. They were a people of the waters with every action and decision rooted in the ocean.

Gijin lowered Galo upon the platform, facing him. Now that the citizens were at play, he could concentrate his thoughts to find out what the child wanted as a gift. He placed his hand gently atop Galo's head and closed his eyes. Galo relaxed under Gijin's hand.

Visions of the child's thoughts passed across the elder's mind's eye, lined and marked by confusion and curiosity. His childish mind had been bathing in everything it encountered in this world still so new to him. As curious and fascinated as he was though, his thoughts often traced back to one subject. MeiLom. Galo had come to think of him as a brother and simply wanted to see him.

At that, it was settled. Though he knew the risk, Gijin decided they would set sail that afternoon on a trip to ArcNos to visit MeiLom. The weather was favorable enough, but that was prone to change with too little warning to avoid it once they were on the sea.

MeiLom sat staring out his bedroom window, watching the birds go by. He jumped slightly when his mother rapped upon his door before entering. She sat next to him on the bed, looking him over with deep concern.

"MeiLom," she said sweetly, "What's wrong? You haven't been yourself for quite some time now, but you always say it's nothing."

MeiLom sighed, then answered, "I know. I didn't wanna say anything with Papa around."

"Oh, are you afraid of what he might think?"

"Uh-huh. Do you remember when he took me to that country in the south,

Mama?"

"Berinin, yes. Do you miss it there? Is that why you've been so out of sorts?"

The child rubbed his head as he responded, "Yeah, um, I miss Galo and Gijin."

"Your Papa mentioned you were talking about somebody named Galo on the trip home, but he stopped talking about it."

"He didn't like me talking about it. I think he hates the people there. He was acting funny when we left. He wanted to leave real fast."

"Well, would you like for me to arrange for a boat to take you to see them the next time your father is away for more than six days?"

MeiLom's eyes lit up. "Yes, thank you. Sorry I didn't say anything sooner, Mama."

"That's okay, MeiLom," she excused, running her fingers once through his hair, "I'm just worried what your father will say, assuming you're right about his disliking those people."

"He won't find out," MeiLom chuckled, "I know how to be sneaky."

BeiLou laughed and nudged the child, toppling him into a fit of laughter. She tickled his belly, laughing at the sight of the small boy rolling about on the mattress. They both stopped suddenly when they heard a knock on the front door.

MeiLom agreed to stay in his room as his mother went downstairs to answer it. She opened it to find a small old man in a robe with four sleeves, who was holding a baby in a robe cut from similar cloth. She stepped back, eyeing the pair with intrigue.

"Are you BeiLou?" the old man inquired.

"Yes. Yes, I am," BeiLou answered.

The old man looked down at the child and beamed, "Hey, those directories worked better than we expected, didn't they?"

"Wait a moment, did you come here from Berinin?" she asked with a sudden grin, "Such dark complexions are rather scarce in this town."

"Why, yes we did, madam," the old man answered, "A tad unfortunate to hear about the lack of diversity here, but I suppose you could guess why we've come then."

"That depends. Are you the Chieftain Sage of Berinin?"

"Indeed, I am, and this child here is the Chieftain Heir. We're here to see…"

"Galo! Gijin!" a voice shouted from atop the stairs.

BeiLou jumped with a startle, as she thought the boy was still waiting in his room. He rushed down the stairs to greet his unexpected guests from across the ocean.

"MeiLom, your friends are here," BeiLou playfully announced as Gijin dropped his cane and scooped MeiLom off the floor.

BeiLou took MeiLom, insisting that Gijin needn't strain himself with the weight of both children. The two of them set their children on the floor, facing each other. Galo was just learning to walk. He hobbled toward MeiLom and opened his mouth, trying to push forth some kind of sound. The three of them watched as this tiny boy uttered a childish little peep resembling a hi. MeiLom's eyes lit up. His little brother still recognized him, despite having only seen him when he was born.

"Hey Galo!" MeiLom welcomed with delight, "This is my house! And that's my Mama. Really, it's her house. And my Papa's. They bought it. Not me. But they let me live here, too!"

BeiLou and Gijin both laughed. A draft reminded them that they were still standing in the foyer with the front door open. BeiLou invited them in to stay a while. Gijin accepted and pulled the door shut behind him before they headed for the living room.

"I can see now why MeiLom wanted so badly to go see you two, especially Galo," BeiLou remarked as they all found seats.

"Indeed. Even after all this time, Galo still sees him as his brother, and I would expect nothing less than a reciprocated feeling from Sin... eh MeiLom," Gijin agreed.

BeiLou looked at Gijin curiously, having caught his near slip of the tongue. MeiLom somehow knew it would be best for him to leave the room while Gijin explained the situation to his mother. He took Galo and led him out onto the lawn to play. The two of them had plenty of catching up to do.

"What did you say?" BeiLou asked as the door shut, scooting a bit closer on the sofa.

"Eh MeiLom?" Gijin answered uneasily.

"Before that."

Gijin drummed his fingers together uneasily as he answered, "Reciprocated feeling?"

"After that," BeiLou clarified with a sigh.

"Sin..." Gijin admitted, having been cornered, "I was about to say Sinkua."

"Sinkua? That's not my son's name. Why would you call him that? Are you not feeling well?"

"I'm well enough, and you're right. It isn't his name, not the name you gave him anyway. But it is still who he is."

"This isn't making any sense. He's MeiLom, just MeiLom. My son doesn't have multiple personalities. Even if he did, it's too early to notice such things."

"Once again, you're right. He doesn't now, nor does this mean that he ever will."

His hand opposite to her curled nervously, scratching the sofa cushion. His robe found itself pulled in by the scratching, the loose cloth bunching around his fingers. Anxiously, he searched his mind for some way to explain the situation to this caring mother without worrying her. She continued to study him inquisitively.

"I believe your son will grow up to be a noble man. He may not always show it, nor will he necessarily fit the description to those not aware of his reputation. He will be a man of great power, influence and fortitude, but only if he keeps on a righteous path. I felt it a proper alias for an hero of his lineage, perhaps because he reminds me so much of an old friend by that name."

"My son is going to be an hero?"

"That's right, madam." Gijin confirmed with a smile.

BeiLou sighed as she turned to watch the children from the window. She couldn't be bothered to ask what Gijin meant with his reference to MeiLom's lineage. Their ancestry was not a foreign subject to her, though the era to which he most likely referred was embedded a handful of millennia in ancient time, well beyond the extent of her studies in her days as an historian.

It was an age forgotten by time itself, ruins and relics entombed in the sediment of more recent bygone eras, history buried by more history. Though much had been lost, legends could still be found in stories and fireside conversations. At the shrouded height of society had stood a vast family of aristocrats, their myriad of talents granting them representations in all fields and aspects of culture and society. Like all great families, they inevitably fell from power, and in their death throes, one member had sworn that the house would rise again someday. Perhaps it would be her son to do just that.

"Galo, too, you know," Gijin added, interrupting her thoughts.

Her mind flickered suddenly, as did the decorative candles on the table beside her.

"Galo is a descendent of aristocrats?" she asked.

"Hmm, so you're that aware of your ancestry? Quite impressive. Most people don't know much more than the past five generations, if even that."

"My last job was as an historian, before I became a career mother. Now, about your grandson?"

"Ah, how interesting. No, he's not descended from aristocrats, but our family does have quite a fascinating history. What I was saying is that if he keeps on a righteous path, he too will grow up to be an hero just like your son. The two of them have astounding potential. I was delighted when I found many of Galo's thoughts to be associated with your son. Keeping this brotherly bond will surely help them in the future."

"This is really quite something," she exhaled as her eyes wandered to the window to watch the children play.

"By the way, if you don't mind my asking, where is CreSam?"

"Oh, he's on a trip to Kirts. Military business. He's not due back until tomorrow evening."

A few minutes passed as they exchanged pleasantries and watched the children on the lawn, until the door swung open violently. CreSam looked around, puzzled and agitated. His attention turned to the little old man sitting beside his wife.

"Who are you?" he bellowed.

"Sir, I'm…"

"Who are you? Unless you're some uncle I haven't met, you need get off that couch."

MeiLom came running in with Galo in tow and hugged CreSam's leg. He looked up at his father, smiling joyfully, though he was a bit confused. CreSam paid him no mind.

"Sir, I'm Chieftain Sage Gijin of Berinin. We met briefly," Gijin answered, "I brought my grandson here for his birthday to visit your son. Your wife and I were simply talking about our young ones. The two of them are really something, you know."

CreSam looked down at the two of them. He managed a grin for MeiLom, but was apathetic toward the toddling Galo. He scooped MeiLom off the floor and set him on his shoulder, leaving Galo by himself. Galo dropped to his butt and sat in the doorway.

"I think it's time for the two of you to go," CreSam announced firmly.

"Sir, I hope we haven't upset you, what with showing up unannounced and uninvited. It's just that, well you see…"

"Get out!"

"Papa!?" MeiLom snapped.

He jumped down from his father's shoulder, landing beside Galo and shielding him. He looked up at CreSam with confusion and a bit of disgust. This was not the father he had known. He had grown cold and harsh. Perhaps the military was changing him. In that moment, MeiLom silently swore to never enlist, no matter the cost or risk he might incur.

Gijin came over and scooped Galo off the floor, not the least bit hesitant under CreSam's massive frame. He simply looked up at the wall of a man and sighed in disdain.

"CreSam, my good man, I see not what it is you have against my family," Gijin spoke in a sagely tone, "but I pray that someday you will see that we are not so different as to regard us as your enemy."

CreSam snarled, staring down at the old man and the child, "I didn't ask you for a soliloquy. I said get out!"

Galo's eyes welled up, tears streaming down his reddened face. He curled up in the folds of Gijin's robe, trying to hide himself from the bellowing man as he bawled loudly. MeiLom looked up at him, sad and disappointed. A few tears trickled silently down his face. CreSam simply stood in silence, an unemotional wall of a man.

Gijin sighed and slipped past him, out the door with his grandson. Courteously, he shut the door behind himself before the two of them left for the southern shore. The trip was necessary, he knew, but he regretted the poor timing nonetheless.

Inside, MeiLom ran upstairs to his room to sit and gaze into the medallion, hoping it would calm his nerves. BeiLou stayed downstairs with CreSam. His pulse was still racing, but he had calmed a bit.

"Why did you do that?" BeiLou asked in the least accusing tone she could manage.

"I'm not sure," CreSam answered, trying to stay calm, "I'm just jumpy right now, and I didn't want any company. Especially not them."

"Do you have something against those two, honey? Because they really are nice people. They're not trying to take our son away from us. They just want to be a part of MeiLom's life and ours by extension. We should find ourselves lucky to have friends of such prestige."

"No. No, I don't, BeiLou. That's why I didn't want them here. I told you, I'm just on edge, and they threw me for a loop. I didn't want to do or say anything to really hurt them."

He dropped onto the sofa to relax. As BeiLou opened her mouth to speak, he anticipated what she had to say and interrupted her.

"The emotional scars will heal in time. Gijin is an understanding old man, I'm sure."

He rubbed his index finger over the curve at the base of his thumb. BeiLou peeked to see what had distracted him. It looked as though he'd been burnt, judging by the redness around the blister he'd found.

"Here, dear, speaking of scars, I'll get you a washcloth for yours."

"What? Oh, this is nothing," CreSam answered uneasily, "But, thank you anyway. That's, uh, quite nice of you."

BeiLou simply ignored the uneasiness of his answer as a side effect of his edginess. In the kitchen, she snatched a washcloth from the basket on the countertop. As she turned to run the tap over it, something odd caught her attention. The water in which the dishes were soaking was rippling as though from a splash.

The stout young woman hoisted a bag of grain onto her shoulder in the late Swelter's midday sun. Balancing it carefully, she made her way across the stable, a layer of straw and hay licking her bare ankles. She filled the trough for two and set the bag beside it, rolling her shoulder as she stood upright again.

Two horses, bred of champion quality, promptly trotted to the trough to feed. The woman sat upon a nearby bench to relax as she watched the two of them, satisfied

22

with their continuing good health and fortitude. What stood before her was her life's work.

A squirrelly little voice interrupted her thoughts. Beside her now stood the work of a lifetime, her two-year-old daughter.

"Hi!" the toddler remarked delightedly.

The tiny girl stood beside her mother, dressed in shorts and training pants, nothing more. Two dark purple splotches adorned her back in symmetrical form. Her hair reached her shoulders in a most peculiar array of colors. The roots were dark brown, and it faded through many shades into a light blonde at the tips.

"Hello Eytea," Elemeno replied happily, "What are you doing out here?"

"Came to see you," she said, climbing onto the bench, "And horses."

The two of them sat together, silently bonding as they watched the horses eat. One was of a slender frame with powerful haunches, bred for speed. Elemeno aimed to train her as a champion racehorse. Her brother was of a stout build, his body rippled with muscle definition. He would be a powerful workhorse and also able to protect his sister from large predators. The two of them were the result of Elemeno's years of research and breeding, and Eytea would have the pleasure of working with them when she was of an appropriate age.

"Eytea, why don't you go inside for a bit? It's too hot for you out here," Elemeno suggested.

"Okay mommy," Eytea willingly agreed.

She climbed off of the bench and headed to the door with a constant smile. For the nature of her childhood thus far, she was a peculiarly happy little girl. Of course, this was of little worry to Elemeno. To her it showed early signs of tolerance.

Back in her bedroom, Eytea stood with her back to the mirror, examining herself over her shoulder. Her tiny fingertips ran over her back, feeling the splotches that adorned it. The edges had the slightest ridge, not visible to the unknowing eye, but faintly tactile. She smiled at the feeling on her fingers and the tingle in her back. Her mother had horses. She had splotches.

Her mother had never bothered to raise any concern over it, but Eytea had developed at an accelerated rate. She spoke as eloquently as children a year her senior, sometimes even more so. Also, she walked as a small child would, rather than toddling as would be expected. She, of course, was oblivious to her gift because normal for her was normal to her. She did, however, seem to know the marks on her back were something special. Though she had not seen particularly many bare backs, none but hers featured such distinct markings.

Out in the stable, the two horses had finished their meal. Elemeno stood beside them on a stepstool of her own crafting, running a firm brush through their coats. With each stroke, the path left by the stiff bristles glistened in the stream of light angling its way into the stable.

This light was interrupted abruptly by a long shadow. Elemeno turned as she felt the shadow cast over her.

"May I help you sir?" she asked before returning to her task.

"Oh, I'm just visiting, madam," a soft voice answered as the man stepped into the stable.

"Here to see the champions in their youth, are you?" she asked, obviously proud of her noble young equines.

"Well, I suppose you could say that," he said with a smile in his voice, "How rude of me not to introduce myself. My name is Gijin."

Elemeno turned her head with a jolt, "Gijin? The Chieftain Sage of Berinin? I heard you were nearing your end."

"Ahh, but I found my health again. The gods had mercy on this old soul, I suppose."

"It's good to see you're back on your feet, sir," she complimented, getting to her own feet as well, "What brings you to this town and, more to the point, to my home?"

"As you said, I'm here to see the champion in her youth. I heard a very special child lives here."

Eytea watched from her window as the enigmatic old man slowly walked into the stable. She wasn't worried in the least. He appeared kind, and she knew her mother was strong enough should her intuition be faulty. Her curiosity, on the other hand, had been piqued.

She trotted eagerly across the wooden floor, her steps light and flowing. At times, Eytea seemed to glide as she walked. Of course, this was not something she had ever noticed about herself, not at that early of an age, but it was yet another quirk. Indeed, this girl was a curious specimen.

Gijin turned his head as he heard the door to the cottage open. He glanced back to Elemeno, who nodded, and the two of them headed out into the yard. There, they found Eytea standing in the open doorway.

"Hi!" she remarked when she saw Gijin.

"Come on out here, honey," Elemeno beckoned, "No reason to stand there with the door open, now."

"Hello," Gijin warmly greeted, waving to the little child.

Eytea jogged over to her mother and Gijin, curious about this old man's nature. Thousands of thoughts ran rampantly through her head, and she was about to get some answers.

"Who are you?" she asked quite boldly.

"Aha! Well, you get right to the point, don't you, little girl?" Gijin answered boisterously, "My name is Gijin. I'm from a land called Berinin. What's your name?"

He sat down on the grass to put himself more at level with her. She stepped closer to get a better look at him.

"I'm Eytea. That's my mom," she introduced, "Why'd you come here, huh?"

"You have a lovely name, Eytea. I came because I heard there was someone special here, and I think it might be you. Can I see your back?"

Eytea looked up at her mother for approval and, to some extent, an explanation. She knew her back was peculiar but couldn't fathom how word of it had spread so far. Nor could she think how it warranted a visit from this soft spoken old foreigner. Elemeno shrugged and motioned for her to turn around.

Eytea spun around and stood rubbing her head in confusion as Gijin examined her back. He simply looked over it for a moment, deeply intrigued by the markings on her back. He lightly placed his fingertip on one of them, brushing it along the edges. She jumped a bit, and he pulled back cautiously.

"Thank you for that," he nodded, "It's exactly what I was looking for."

"Why were you looking for me? What're those spots?" she asked.

"Those? Well, those just mean you're a very special girl," he loosely explained in a warm tone, "And well, a man of my age should get as much out of his final years as possible. So I'm traveling all over Ouristihra, meeting people with unique qualities. I heard you were here, and I knew you were someone I'd like to meet before I pass on."

"Thank you! I like them, too. I think they're neat."

Elemeno watched the two of them in awestruck silence. She wondered why her daughter trusted this man so much, as she had always been cautious with strangers, just as she had been taught. His benevolent and diplomatic reputation preceded him, but Eytea could not have known of such things. Besides that, his answers were conveniently vague and a touch too dodgy for her taste.

"Eytea, dear, why don't you head back inside? I'd like to talk to our guest alone," she ordered, directing her daughter back toward the cottage.

Eytea quietly agreed and walked back to the door, waving to Gijin as she stepped inside. Gijin waved back. As soon as the door closed, Elemeno began digging.

"Okay, so seriously, what are you doing here?"

"I am on a mission of the utmost importance, madam."

"A mission? What does it have to do with my Eytea?"

"Quite a bit, but it will come much later in her life. She will be ready for it. You are raising her splendidly, Elemeno."

"Thank you, sir. That means a lot from a man of such high repute, but I'm still not clear on everything. What's this mission you're on?"

"As I told your daughter, I am seeking people with unique qualities, but not just anyone, mind you. Your daughter, like others I have met, will be an hero someday if she keeps on a righteous path. I fear Ouristihra is heading into a great danger. United with others of her ilk, Eytea has the potential to steer us safely through this coming turmoil."

All Elemeno could manage was a puzzled stare.

"My daughter is going to be an hero? How can you tell this? Is it because of the markings on her back?"

"Precisely, madam. They are a mark of greatness, and as she grows as a person, so too shall they," he explained, "On that note, I have something I want you to give to her when she is older."

He turned and walked back to the stable. Throughout the entire conversation, she hadn't noticed what he had leaned next to the door, apparently upon his arrival. He carried it back and handed it to her. Despite the oddity of this gift, all she could do was silently accept it with a thanking nod. She had far too many questions to know which to ask now or at all.

He nodded back to her and walked away in silence, aided by his cane. She watched him as he walked toward the southern horizon, never meandering from his straight path. As he faded into the landscape, she looked down at what he had placed in her hands. Running two meters in length, it was a halberd with blades forged from an unimaginably sturdy yet lightweight metal. Looking it over, she began to understand a bit more of what Gijin had told her about her Eytea.

Although she took Gijin quite seriously, she still found it all hard to accept. It did, however, provide an explanation for Eytea's markings. She pondered what would become of them as she examined the blades of the halberd. She also contemplated what sort of evil Gijin spoke of and how her daughter would contend it as a young adult. This led to questions about timing and who else would be involved, which led to doubts of their readiness.

She shook her head, snapping herself out of her spiral of anxiety. This was no time to dwell on the future. The immediate order of business was to hide the halberd. That would be the easy part, though. Onward from that day, it would be her secret to keep but never to forget.

Behind the stable, she dug an elongated hole. She set the halberd gently in the bottom of the pit. After refilling the hole, she kicked some dirt about to cover the freshly overturned soil. Pausing for a moment, she considered the weight of the burden she had undertaken, knowing she could speak a word of this to no one for an indeterminate number of years.

As she collected her composure, she returned to the cottage to spend what remained of the day with her daughter. She knew it was only a matter of time until Eytea grew up and left home to become the hero Gijin foresaw. This was her time to urge her into the proper woman for the job.

"What did he say, Mama?" Eytea asked as her mother returned.

"Oh, he just asked where you got those lovely marks on your back. I told him you were just born special."

Eytea was sitting on the floor, leaning against the side of the couch and playing with one of her toys. Elemeno scooped her up on her arm and kissed her forehead. Eytea smiled at her lovingly.

"He was kinda silly, huh?" Eytea observed.

"Aha, now I wouldn't say that. Chieftain Sage Gijin is a very wise man. His family is even believed to have strange powers," Elemeno explained as she sat down on the couch, finding herself getting lost in her thoughts, "Some say he can even see the future."

She smiled at Eytea and wiggled her nose with her fingertip. Eytea giggled and squirmed on her mother's arm. In that moment, Elemeno knew that her daughter would surely grow up to be the person she needed to be. When whatever evil Gijin spoke of came into their lives, Eytea would be ready to confront it. It was admittedly absurd, but she was putting faith in her two-year-old daughter.

Late that night, a figure shrouded by the darkness set a hand atop a fencepost and flung his body over it and into the vast rural community. He radiated a pungent scent of the sea and left a trail of water as he walked toward a cottage in the east. As he made his way, he rolled his neck a couple of times to alleviate the cramps that had developed in his travels.

He pulled out the front of his shirt and twisted it, wringing out some of the water. The sea had been particularly unkind that day. He shuffled his feet, leaving tracks rather than footprints in the dirt. When he reached the fence around the cottage, he paused for a moment to listen to the still night air. They were asleep.

At the front door, he paused again. He looked down at the mess the sea had made of him and shook his head in disapproval. He looked forward again, sighed deeply and opened the door.

Kabehl stepped lightly into the cottage, careful not to stir anyone. He crept first to Elemeno's bedroom. Peeking inside, he found her fast asleep, just as he had hoped. The timing of his return was thus far perfect.

He eagerly tiptoed across the hall to Eytea's bedroom. Curling his fingers around the door, he peeked in to look for the aggravatingly strange little girl. Exactly as he hoped, she was in a deep slumber. He stepped into the room and stood over her.

She stirred a bit, and he stepped back cautiously. When she stopped and remained asleep, he returned to her bedside. She rolled onto her stomach as though to flaunt the marks on her back. They had become perfectly symmetrical since he last saw them.

His mind was thrown into a rapid panic. His chest heaved with heavy breath. Even though she was asleep, it seemed like she knew he was there. Not only that, but she apparently knew how uncomfortable the markings made him and was now taunting him. Just as he had planned, this was indeed the night to rid himself of this bastard burden.

When he reached for his pistol, however, he found his holster was empty.

A proud warrior stood barefoot in the field, the windblown grass lashing at his ankles. Staff in hand, he stared down a vast spread of rogues stretching on to the horizon. Behind him, his troops loyally awaited his command. The world stood still around them, as the wind slowed to a halt. The grass was stirred by neither rogue nor troop. All were locked in a standoff as they waited for orders from their commanders.

Silently, the warrior raised his staff above his head. The troops all clutched the hilts of their weapons. The young leader slammed the end of his staff against the ground with a thunderous crash, simultaneously sweeping his other arm outward to point over the field. At this moment, he closed his eyes.

Spril watched his mentally conjured troops rush around him to battle his imagined rogues at the other end of the field. They fought proudly and valiantly. Most importantly, they fought under his command. In the past year, his aspiration of enlisting as a soldier in the Military Guild had grown to being the first foreign-born Brigadier General Elite. He opened his eyes as a voice interrupted his thoughts.

"So the commander has come at last," the voice announced.

"General Phylus! So it's you," Spril shouted back, "It's time to end this. My quarterstaff and I will put an end to you!"

Phylus let out a deep bellowing laugh from across the field. He held a fist-sized rock in each hand, tossing and catching them repeatedly.

"But what will you do," he asked, "without your quarterstaff!?"

With that final word, he pitched both rocks at Spril at a blinding speed. Spril smiled at how much Phylus was getting into his battlefield game but managed to maintain his composure and his defensive stance. Before he could swat them from the air though, the rocks struck his hands. He jerked back reflexively and dropped the quarterstaff.

He rubbed his knuckles and reached for his weapon. When he looked up, Phylus was nearly upon him. In the moment of distraction, he had rushed across the field for a tactical direct strike. Phylus also carried a quarterstaff of similar design. Spril snatched his own staff and swiftly erected himself.

As Phylus closed in, Spril put his left foot forward to hold him at bay and leaned back on his right foot, narrowing parrying Phylus's attack. He held his staff only in his left hand now. His right hand moved back to catch himself as he leaned too far. Staring up at Phylus, he shoved off the ground and swung his quarterstaff. The middle of it collided with the side of Phylus's ribcage. Phylus fell to the ground. Spril righted himself and dropped his weapon.

"Hoo boy, that was good, Spril. You're really something," Phylus gasped, holding his side from both pain and laughter.

"Thanks, Phylus. It's fun playing battlefield with you," Spril beamed as he sat on the grass beside him.

"Oh am I that fun to beat up?"

"Haha, no! It's just none of the kids at school take the game seriously. Or me, now that I think about it."

"Or you? What do you mean?"

"Well, you know, they think it's ridiculous that I'd want to be a soldier. They say I'll never make it."

"Well Spril, you know what the best thing is to do about kids like that? Prove them wrong when you get the chance. If we can get to ArcNos six years from now, we both know you'll make the cut."

Spril shrugged and helped Phylus to his feet. While he was confident enough in his abilities, somehow he knew it wouldn't be enough to silence the naysayers. After all, being a child himself, he knew how they operated. They weren't ones to be proven wrong or, moreover, to admit it.

While the opinion of onlookers would scarcely be a factor in the validity of his accomplishments, he made it his prerogative to change their perspective of him. His greatest pleasure was derived from the idea that many of them could someday work for him. The rest would entrust him with their lives.

The two of them walked across the field, back to Phylus's car. Spril had walked out their alone earlier that afternoon. Such were his weekends, a long walk out to the fields followed by an intense training session which ended with one of his imagination war games. On that particular day, Phylus had decided to surprise him by showing up for the game. Phylus also had other business to tend to, and he saw it fitting for Spril to come along.

Spril sat quietly in the passenger's seat, his quarterstaff in the back, watching the scenery dash past in a green and grey blur. Phylus tapped his fingertips on the steering wheel in nervous anticipation. Once Spril realized the unfamiliarity of the area, the silence was broken.

"Hey Phylus, um, where are we going?" Spril asked.

"Heh, I was wondering when you were going to ask," Phylus mused, "We're going to the clinic."

"Clinic? Which one of us is sick?"

"Neither of us. We're going to visit the geneticist at the fertility clinic," Phylus clarified.

"The geneti-who at the fertili-what?"

"Ha ha, don't you remember? That's where they're incubating my daughter. She's due for release today."

"Oh, right. I forgot it was time for that."

Only a few other cars were in the lot when they arrived. It being the weekend, staffing was sparse. Phylus's doctor was waiting outside and out of uniform with a young girl standing beside her. Aside from his appointment, this was to have been her day off.

"Dr. Chekov, good to see you," Phylus greeted as he closed the car door.

"And you as well, Phylus," she welcomed, "Right this way."

Spril stepped out of the car. Immediately, his eyes fixed on the young girl. She looked him over and smiled shyly as their eyes met.

"Oh, you never told me you had a son already," Chekov observed.

"What? No, I'm just his guardian. I'm not old enough to be his biological father."

"Hm, well my daughter is about his age. Maybe they could get together sometime. I'd like her to make some friends around here."

"I think they're already ahead of you on that one," Phylus said, nodding toward them, "Spril, stay out here while the doctor and I go in to pick up Vielle."

Phylus and Chekov headed into the building while Spril and Chekov's daughter stayed out on the sidewalk. About a month earlier, Phylus had decided on

Vielle as a name for his test tube daughter. It carried an air of uniquity without excessive absurdity, and a flowing melodic air, suggesting finesse and strength of character.

Spril finally managed a smile through the surprise and dumbfounded feeling. Still silenced however, he simply absorbed what he saw before him. It was as though the two of them were getting to know one another simply through a stare and a smile. After what felt like hours, the young girl broke the silence.

"Hi," she peeped, trailing off, "I'm Yrlis. What's your name?"

"Hi. I'm Spril."

"Hehe, that guy lets you shave your head? That looks cool," Yrlis complimented.

"What, this? I didn't do this," Spril admitted, "But um, thank you. You're the first kid to tell me that."

Spril smiled warmly at Yrlis. For the first time, he didn't feel bitter when somebody mentioned his bare scalp. He deduced that her unique tastes must have been the reason for the lack of friends her mother mentioned.

"Oh? Well I'm sure I won't be the last," she insisted, smiling back at him, "So what is it, anyway? Are you sick?"

"I guess you could say that. I was born without hair follicles on my scalp. I can never grow any hair up there."

"That's weird. I've never heard of that condition."

"I've never heard it called a condition. Everyone else calls it a disease."

Yrlis leaned in and took Spril's hand. He gave her a puzzled look. When she squeezed his hand though, he gripped hers as well.

"You don't get along much with the other kids at school, do you?"

"No, but I have a feeling you don't either, after what your mother said."

"I just don't think like the crowd, so they shun me. I have different tastes; that's all. What's your story?"

"You mean other than my lack of hair?" he specified "Well, I'm training to enlist in the ArcNosian military when I turn fifteen. Everyone at school thinks it's a ridiculous idea."

"Wait. I knew your name sounded familiar. You're that Spril?" she gasped.

"I have a reputation now?"

"Well yeah. Everyone at school has heard of you. I had just never seen you before."

"If you'd heard of me, the scalp should've been your first clue."

"Believe it or not, I hadn't heard of your scalp condition. Just your dream to join the military. You're an inspiration to other outcasts, you know."

Inside, Phylus and Chekov stood before of the incubation chamber. Phylus drummed his fingertips on the side of his leg. Chekov could see his pulse racing on the side of his neck.

"Excited, are we?" she asked with a small laugh.

"Just a bit. This is a huge moment."

Chekov smiled and unlocked the hatch on the chamber. The frame hissed as she pulled the door open. Phylus's pupils dilated. She reached in and drew out a newborn baby. Ever so gently, she handed the child to her father. He accepted her with warm open arms.

"Hey Vielle," he welcomed with a smile, "I'm your father. I'm your daddy."

"I'll give you two a moment alone," Chekov offered as she walked to the door.

Phylus ran his fingers along the side of Vielle's head, admiring the smoothness of her skin. When he felt her ears though, he noticed something unusual. He tilted her head and cocked his own. Her ears were misshapen to resemble a pair of crescent moons.

"Dr. Chekov," he beckoned, "What is this?"

30

Chapter 3

The coastal waters washed up onto the shore, wrapping around the ankles of the two children. One stood in shorts and a sleeveless shirt, his naturally matted hair flattened by the moisture. The other, the younger of the two, stood beside him in tattered shorts, his thick dark hair running nearly to the small of his back. The two looked at each other and smirked.

They charged together into the surf. The elder pushed persistently through the crashing waves, refusing to let himself fall to them. The younger slipped smoothly through the waves, moving as though his body was designed for the aquatic. He crouched before a breaker and leapt clear over the churning water. He dipped behind the breaker, streamlining through the water like an eel. Popping his head out of the water, he turned to face his friend and smiled.

"Cool trick, Galo!" ten-year-old MeiLom called over.

"Heh, thanks brother," Galo called back, "Wait until you see what I can do next."

Galo stood upright in the water, letting the breakers crash around him. Nothing seemed unusual at first, until MeiLom noticed three pulsating slits on either side of Galo's neck. Simultaneously, all six of them slowly atrophied to vague reddish lines.

"Whoa. Were those gills?"

"Yeah, I think so. I can stay under water longer than anyone on the island."

MeiLom was puzzled and intrigued. He wondered how long his friend had possessed this odd growth. Then again, he thought, it was no more unusual than his fully green eyes. At least Galo's anatomical anomaly was more easily hidden. He recalled how Gijin had used the water from one of the fountain bowls when he manifested Galo. That water, he deduced, must have been connected to his having both gills and lungs.

Of course, that still left other quandary. The usefulness of Galo's abnormality was obvious enough, but he couldn't discern what advantage came of his unusual eyes. Granted, he could see more clearly than average through dense fog. His mother had come to use him as a navigator during trips through heavy storms. He never thought it to be anything special though. Perhaps, it was because his advantage over others in this regard was only slight. Or maybe it was rooted in his crumbling self esteem and relationship with his father. CreSam had been increasingly absent in the past six years, both physically and emotionally.

"Hey Sinkua, you know what I just thought of?" Galo asked, interrupting MeiLom's thoughts.

"Hm, oh what?" MeiLom answered, still not accustomed to Galo and Gijin calling him by that name.

"If we were one person, we could live underwater," he mused, "Well, if my gills stayed open forever. Because I can breathe like normal down there and you can see clearly."

MeiLom pondered this imaginative thought. It was almost as though Galo could sense his anxiety and doubts of self worth, what with how he presented their anomalies as equal and, moreover, as cooperative forces. He grinned at Galo.

"You're weird, little brother," he chuckled, "Us as one person. That's crazy."

"Haha! I know. But what do you expect? I'm a kid with gills. Of course I'm gonna be a little strange, Sinkua."

"Hey Galo, I have a question. Why do you and Grandpa Gijin call me that?"

"I don't know, really. I call you Sinkua because Grandpa does."

Apparently, both of them had secrets about each other that neither could explain. Galo had MeiLom's odd nickname, while MeiLom had Galo's origins. Galo was under the impression that his parents died before his first birthday. Gijin thought it best for him not to know the truth until adulthood. Knowledge of such an odd birthing could prove to be psychologically confusing and perhaps disfiguring.

"I'm going to ask him," MeiLom asserted, standing up in the water.

Beads of water dripped from his medallion. The wet chain shimmered in the daylight. The sun's rays reflected and refracted on and through the ruby. Nearby Masnethegeans turned their heads and watched as the foreign child marched across the sand to Chieftain Sage Gijin's hut. He boldly pulled the grassy flap aside and peered inside.

"Grandpa Gijin, I need to talk to you."

Gijin was meditating in front of the statue, his hands mimicking those held above its head. His eyes fluttered open with a bewildered look on his face. Once he saw who had interrupted him though, he smiled warmly.

"Come in, Sinkua. What brings you before me?"

"That's exactly it. That name. I think it's time you told me why you call me that. What does it mean?"

Gijin stood and walked toward MeiLom. MeiLom had made his way to the middle of the room as he posed his question. Gijin looked him over and lifted the medallion.

"Tell me child, do you feel any different when you wear this?"

"Um, a little. I get this sensation going through my body, like it's in my veins. I can't think how to describe it, except that it's kinda warm."

"Sinkua is the name for a person capable of wearing this for a long time, such as you can. For many, the sensation you get never occurs. It's simply jewelry. To a few others though, that sensation is dangerous. Their body consumes it but cannot withstand it. Do you understand?"

MeiLom took the medallion in his own hand, staring into the ruby and contemplating what Gijin had just told him.

"So I turn into Sinkua when I put this on?"

"No, not at all. You're always Sinkua, and you're always MeiLom as your mother named you at birth. Being Sinkua simply means you bear the emblem, and one who bears this emblem in this age is surely destined for greatness."

MeiLom looked deeper into the ruby until he could discern every color of his face through the myriad crimson tones. The medallion reflected in the surface of his eyes. Through deeper gazing, he could see the reflection of the ruby inside the reflection of his eyes in the ruby. His eyes shimmered a bit, and their glow meshed with the

32

shimmer of the ruby like a minute aurora. Just like the sensation it gave him when he wore it, he couldn't explain this sudden comprehension.

"I understand now, Grandpa Gijin. I was born MeiLom, but I wear the emblem. My name," he said, "is Sinkua."

The sound of the shutting door echoed through the chamber lined with pillars. A fit young man of fifteen boldly marched toward the center of the room. There, he was greeted by a wall of a man who simply nodded to him.

"Green Rookie Spril?" CreSam asked.

"Sir," Spril answered, saluting.

"Welcome to the preliminary arena," he greeted, "Here, we will test your existing combat skills to determine the appropriate position and field training for you as a soldier in the ArcNosian military."

"It's a pleasure to be here, sir. I won't let you down."

"I certainly hope not. I've heard great things about you, young man. Rumor has it, you have much potential."

CreSam grimaced at him. Spril felt as though those eyes could pierce his body. His massive size aside, this soldier carried a foreboding air about him. Spril made a mental note to never turn his back to him.

"Thank you, Colonel CreSam, sir," he replied flatly.

"Let's get on with this, then," CreSam said with a vague chuckle, "I will even give you the advantage of being second to choose your weapon."

"That won't be necessary, sir," Spril insisted, "I already know what weapon I want. The quarterstaff."

"That is precisely the sort of ignorance we wish to avoid. My weapon of choice is the broadsword," CreSam snapped, "Are you sure you don't want to change your selection?"

"Absolutely certain."

CreSam sneered at him. The two walked together, though a great distance existed between them, to the rack of weapons along the wall. Spril's eyes scanned the wall. Though he was a devoted advocate of the quarterstaff, he held an appreciation for all armaments.

CreSam drew a broadsword with a one meter blade from the sword section of the weapon rack. He looked it over with a sense of deep pride. Spril knew he was far from unfamiliar with this blade. Still, he had his own pride and something to prove as well. He silently pulled a two meter quarterstaff from the rack.

"You would pit a stick of wood against a solid metal blade?" CreSam asked bitterly.

"Of course," Spril nodded, "That's exactly my advantage."

"Such arrogance will not be tolerated in this military!" CreSam boomed.

CreSam charged and slammed the blade down at Spril. Spril sidestepped and pivoted out of the way, his staff held in one hand behind his back. The blade crashed into the floor with a thunderous clang. CreSam quickly lifted the blade, spun and slashed. Spril slid back, letting the blade pass in front of his chest. Still, he kept his staff behind him.

CreSam swiped again from the other direction, this time aiming at his neck. He bent backwards to dodge the attack. As he was righting himself again, CreSam drew back slightly and thrust the sword at Spril's chest in a quick following attack. Spril pulled the staff from behind his back and bludgeoned the side of the blade, knocking it off its trajectory and pulling CreSam's arm with it.

"Like I said, that's exactly my advantage," Spril repeated with the blade pinned, "Your hubris is my strength."

"So you countered one attack," CreSam somewhat conceded, "Don't get ahead of yourself."

CreSam spun the sword slowly in an hypnotic motion. Spril ignored the intended distraction and focused on CreSam's eyes instead. He poised himself in a combative stance, his staff drawn back and ready to strike or defend. The two stared at each other for a minute, each sizing up their opponent. Having timed the spinning of the blade, Spril thrust forth for the first attack and swung the staff from the side.

CreSam hastened the spin. Just as the blade struck the staff, Spril pulled downward and stepped aside, spinning around behind CreSam's back. Once there, he struck CreSam between the shoulder blades with the quarterstaff. CreSam bellowed in pain and frustration. Spril had taken the bait with bait of his own, and CreSam was made the fool. Infuriated, he swiftly pivoted to face Spril, who had stepped back and returned to his original stance. Spril smirked and invited CreSam to attack.

CreSam charged him with the force of a freight train, slashing his sword recklessly. Spril walked backwards, dodging a few strikes but blocking most with his staff. Rather than stop the blade directly, he struck the side of the blade to deflect it. CreSam grew increasingly angered with every countered swing and every missed blow. Tired of the game, Spril slammed the staff against his forearm with a swift but powerful single handed swing. CreSam's hand fell open and the sword dropped to the floor. His opportunity made, Spril lunged forth for the counter. CreSam reached for his sword, unmoved by Spril's technique.

Just before he struck, CreSam thrust the sword upward, plunging the tip through the staff. Spril clutched his weapon and held his ground. CreSam pushed a bit, and the blade pierced further through, nearing Spril's throat. CreSam drew back a bit and lunged forth. As he did, Spril pulled and stepped back. CreSam followed, still pushing. Spril began running backward to avoid the blade that was now wedged through the fibers of his wooden quarterstaff. CreSam laughed menacingly.

"What were you saying of hubris, boy?" he jeered.

"Don't get ahead of yourself."

Spril turned the quarterstaff at a slight angle as he passed between two pillars. When it was between them, he turned it perfectly horizontal, wedging it between the columns. He released the staff and fell into a crouch. Carried by his own momentum, CreSam continued forth, driving the blade through the staff down to its hilt. Spril lunged toward CreSam and, with one hand holding his staff, pounded his fist against CreSam's stomach.

He withdrew his fist and took hold of the other end of his quarterstaff. CreSam was red in the face with both anger and pain. He refused to let this Green Rookie teach him such a thing as humility. He jerked the sword back as Spril pulled his staff off of the blade. The two lunged at each other once more. Again, CreSam came down with a swift and fierce overhead strike.

The sound of the blade slashing through the air could faintly be heard resonating through the pillars. Spril parried the falling blade, and it slammed into the ground, shattering tiles and tossing ceramic shrapnel about. The cacophonous crash reverberated through the floor and up the pillars like stone drums.

With a deft pivot, Spril spun to CreSam's side, his staff held high as he positioned himself beyond the reach of the blade. He came down with great momentum and slammed the quarterstaff against the back of CreSam's neck. The staff snapped in two, and the severed end spun once, bounced off of CreSam's back, and fell to the floor. CreSam bellowed in pain as he dropped his sword and collapsed.

Spril picked up the sword and the other end of the staff and returned them to their respective racks. Silently, he exited the room, leaving CreSam to wallow in the defeat that he had brought upon himself with his own arrogance. After the door closed, CreSam slowly pulled himself to his feet. He dusted himself off and sighed in dissent.

BeiLou sat silently in the corner chair, alone in the house. Her husband was out for a few days, training new recruits after his recent promotion to Colonel. In his absence, she had sent MeiLom to Berinin to visit Galo and Gijin. Thanks to recent developments in aquatic travel by the Ivarians, the trip from ArcNos to Berinin now only took about a day and a half.

She sighed deeply, not for loneliness, but impending regret. CreSam was due home soon. She looked down at her open right hand and shook her head in disapproval. In it was a pistol she had found in her husband's pocket. As necessary as she knew it was to confront CreSam about it, she also knew the exchange would stay civil for a dismally brief moment. That had been her ulterior motive in sending MeiLom to Berinin.

While some soldiers did use guns, CreSam had never been one of them, so far as she knew. More suspiciously, this one displayed no insignia. Moreover, it was found in the pocket of his military fatigues. This unregistered foreign weapon had been with him on any number of missions. She worried what sort of corruption had befallen her husband.

The door opened abruptly, interrupting her thoughts. She quickly stuffed the gun between the seat and arm of the chair and got to her feet. As she turned to face the door, CreSam entered the house, still rubbing the back of his neck.

"We need to talk," BeiLou asserted.

"I have enough problems to deal with aside from you," CreSam muttered as he closed the door behind himself.

"What problems do you have?" she continued, "Working as a soldier? The man I married was man enough to handle a soldier's life and a family life. What happened to him?"

"Who are you to judge me? I'm out every day trying to better myself as a soldier, and you have the gall to speak like that to me?"

"Better yourself? CreSam, I know about your crutch. You're not bettering yourself. You're out for power."

"What?" he asked, walking toward her, "What did you say?"

"I know of your dealings with foreign agents. Weapon agents."

"Who told you this?"

BeiLou was trembling in fear, though she tried desperately to steady herself.

"It doesn't matter," she deflected, now on the verge of tears, "but I'm going to expose you. I'm sorry, but this can't go unnoticed. Your disloyalty needs to be known before it becomes a serious threat."

"Who are you to stop me from my mission? What do you think you can do?"

"I can do plenty, CreSam. Whatever you're up to with them, it can't be good for the country. I can't let history take that road. I'll do everything I can to keep it from happening, even if it means turning against my husband."

CreSam withdrew a pistol and aimed it at his wife. With tears streaming down her face, she crouched in front of the chair between them, digging for the other gun. CreSam walked toward her in long slow strides, his gun arm never wavering. Once she had fished the gun from the chair, she looked up to find the barrel of CreSam's pistol pressed against her forehead. Obstinately, she pointed the gun at his chest.

"Pull the trigger, and we both die," he barked, "See the mess you've gotten yourself into? If only you had stayed out of the way and let me do my job. I have big plans involving these agents, you see, and I don't need anybody getting in the way. History be damned."

"What's happened to you, CreSam? It didn't used to be like this."

"What's happened? The truth happened. I must rise to claim my rightful title. It is for them, for all they've given me."

The door opened again. BeiLou's eyes widened as she dropped the gun, and it bounced off the cushion and dropped to the floor. CreSam arched an eyebrow. BeiLou's focus turned to the door. CreSam glanced to the side, watching the door from the corner of his eye. A child's foot stepped into the foyer.

"MeiLom! No!" BeiLou cried out desperately.

"What!?"

Driven by overly delicate reflexes, his finger had already pulled the trigger. The remainder of the bullet bounced and rolled along the floor behind her, smoking from the explosion it had induced against the back of her skull. Seared fragments of bone and pieces of brain matter rained from the back of her head, soaked in blood. Smoke streamed from her mouth as blood pooled in her hollowed throat. She fell back on the floor. Her skull cracked and shattered further upon impact, bone shrapnel piercing through her flesh from within. She lay pale and motionless, a pool of blood forming around her.

Sinkua stood in the foyer, watching in mortified silence as his father murdered his mother.

"Phylus? Vielle? I'm home."

Spril walked proudly into the small house and hung his jacket upon the coat rack in the foyer. He was covered in sweat and his shoulders ached, but he carried himself as though the pain was of no concern.

"How did things go today, my man?" Phylus asked as he stood up from the couch.

"Well, I won the match against CreSam, but…" Spril trailed off.

"But what?"

"Uncle Spril!" a voice called out delightedly.

Little Vielle ran out of her room and leapt at Spril with open arms. He crouched and scooped her out of the air with both arms. She clung to one side of his body, sitting on his right arm, and kissed him on the cheek.

"Hey, little girl," he greeted, "You been taking good care of your Papa today."

"Uh-huh, you betcha," she answered with a wide smile, "I missed you today."

"Well, I missed you too, Vielle. But you know what?"

"What?"

"It helps keep me going, knowing I've got people like you to come home to. Now, I need to talk to your father alone. Could you go outside for a few minutes?"

She nodded and hopped off his arm. Spril and Phylus both watched as she ran to the door and out into the back yard to play. As soon as the door closed, they turned to face one another again.

"Any idea what's up with her ears?" Spril asked.

"None. I've given up on it. Aside from the shape, her doctor says there's nothing wrong with them," Phylus shrugged, "Now, what were you going to say about today?"

"My trainer worries me. He seems to think he's in charge."

"Well, he is in charge of you, Spril."

"No, I mean he talks like he's in charge of the entire military or of ArcNos itself."

"Probably just on a power trip."

"That's putting it lightly. He's got this hunger for power. I could feel it in the way he carried himself. He even tried to kill me."

"What? Are you certain?"

"Phylus, when a man tries twice to split your skull, several times to slice your torso open and once to drive a sword through your neck, you start to get the feeling that he wants you dead."

"I see why you wanted Vielle to go outside."

By now, they had made their way to the couch. Spril leaned his head back and heaved a deep sigh, staring up at the ceiling. Phylus leaned forward, his elbows resting on his knees. He shook his head in distress.

They both knew of the potential dangers of entering the military, Spril especially. Although, he hadn't anticipated a threat to his life from within the system. Were he to testify to HarEin, CreSam would go on trial. However, if the outcome was not in his favor, CreSam would remain free but with the knowledge that he tried to have him prosecuted and discharged.

On the other hand, resigning from the military was still a legally viable option. He could simply say he had decided it was not the life for him. But they would never believe it, as his reputation preceded him.

Perhaps his own pride was getting the best of him though. CreSam may have been right about his arrogance. He considered that maybe, in some way, his mind was making excuses not to leave, but he had made up his mind long before such dangers arose.

Phylus was buried in his own anxiety as well. He questioned his own actions as to whether bringing the three of them to ArcNos was a wise decision. Even with the age difference becoming less significant with each passing year, he felt something of a paternal instinct with Spril, one that had grown stronger since Vielle was born. They had come to be friends, but he was still a guardian to him. While he was able to provide food and shelter for the three of them, he felt helpless knowing that Spril's life could be in danger every time he went to work.

He was deeply worried for his daughter, as well. If what Spril said was true, and he trusted it was, all three of them could have been in danger. CreSam sounded like the type to disregard any legal ramifications tied to threatening either of them to get back at Spril. Though one carried himself with honor and the other with arrogance, both were proud soldiers. Their persistent clashing could be either one's undoing. If Spril was first to fall, he knew he could be next. Or worse, Vielle.

Then again, he could also pursue other soldiers. Phylus stood up from the couch and walked to the door.

"I'm going to work. I'll be home late tonight," he said as he put on his jacket.

Spril waved as Phylus walked out. When the door shut, he went to the back yard to spend some time with Vielle.

Shortly after arriving at work, Phylus walked down the center of a vast corridor. His dress shoe footsteps clapped against the tiles and echoed through the hollow chamber. Something about this hall felt like a crypt today. He paused for a moment and listened to the air. He shook his head to dismiss such thoughts, discerning that they were merely a product of his own worry.

At the end of the hall, he stood before a massive double door, wider than his arm span. He straightened his jacket and tie and knocked on the door.

"Yes? Who is it?" an elderly voice called from within.

"Negotiator Phylus, sir," he answered.

"Phylus? I don't recall sending for you."

"You didn't, sir. There's a matter I wish to discuss with you, sir, in private."

"Your tone worries me. Come on in."

He opened one of the doors and stepped in, courteously closing it behind him. Behind the desk sat Brigadier General Elite HarEin, a man well into his seventies if Phylus were to guess. He face was stern and noble. His torso filled his shirt well. He wore a uniform with a seemingly endless array of medals and badges.

"Sorry for the closed door policy, Phylus," HarEin apologized as Phylus took a seat, "It didn't used to be this way, you know."

"May I ask why the sudden change, sir?" Phylus asked.

"Well, I've been worried. I wouldn't dare tell this to the other soldiers, but in your position you need to be informed of such things," HarEin began, "I suspect there's a usurper in the area. After as many years as I've been an authority figure, you develop a nose for such a thing. Foreign agents have been around, according to one of our reconnaissance teams. Unregistered and unmarked weapons and other equipment have been found in the area. It's almost as though they're baiting us, whoever they are."

The situation was becoming clearer.

"Or maybe they're trying to distract us, sir. I mean, what with their equipment being unmarked and left lying around. They know the investigation would distract us and that you would be worried, creating the opportunity to strike. All respect intact, sir, a paranoid leader is a weakened leader. Whoever they are, they will expose themselves in time. But for now, I believe there's a more pressing matter," Phylus urged, "Though he isn't necessarily one of them, I believe their influence has already infiltrated the Military Guild."

"Go on," HarEin beckoned with raised eyebrows.

"As you know, I'm guardian to a new soldier, Green Rookie Spril. Well, he was in the preliminary arena with Colonel CreSam today, getting sized up for his training regiment and his placement. From what he told me, CreSam was trying to kill him. Now, I know the training is meant to be aggressive, but as Spril put it: When a man tries twice to split your skull, several times to slice your torso open and once to drive a sword through your neck, you start to get the feeling that he wants you dead. HarEin, sir, it was only a placement exercise, and the man was trying to slaughter him. This can't be standard policy."

HarEin heaved a deep sigh.

"No, Phylus, it isn't," HarEin agreed, "Thank you for bringing this to my attention. I'll have it investigated further. If you have anything more to report on this matter, do not hesitate to let me know."

"Thank you, sir. I'll be sure to keep you informed," Phylus said as he stood up from the chair, "Now if you will please excuse me, I have some papers to go through in my office."

"Very well, then. Do be careful, Phylus."

"Likewise, sir."

Eytea, now a child of eight years, sat outside the stable, studying her mother's movements. Elemeno was saddling the smaller of the two horses and trying to teach Eytea by demonstration. As she finished the job, Eytea fetched the step stool.

Thanking her mother promptly, she climbed onto the horse. Obediently, the horse remained still and waited for her signal to carry the child around the yard. Eytea sat proudly on its back. Elemeno admired her daughter's posture.

In her mind's eye, she pictured Eytea a decade older in the same position. In one hand, she held the reins. Her other gripped the halberd, glistening in the light of the three moons. Other young heroes were lined up beside her, all riding horses she had bred. Whatever adversity was coming, she knew her part in it would be to provide the best mounts for her daughter and her allies.

Eytea tugged the reins twice, and the horse began to trot along at a smooth pace. It stayed near the stable, walking laps around it. Eytea bounced with the impact of her hoof steps, just as her mother had always taught her.

Elemeno couldn't help but smile at the sight of it all. Her daughter was growing into a far better person than she thought possible during her infancy. Not only that, but she was continuing to learn and develop at an accelerated pace. Perhaps, it was connected to those markings, something to do with what Gijin had told her. No matter the reason, she knew that her daughter would grow up to be a great woman, one worthy of her pride.

Kabehl would have nothing to do with any of it, though. He sat alone in the living room, sifting through some files from his work. He spoke little of his job, the extent of it being to tell her he was leaving. He had been spending more time on the road lately, and that was perfectly fine with Elemeno.

On the table before him sat a pack of dossiers. He opened it and began reading over the roster. He set most of them aside to be discarded. Others, he marked and set aside in another stack. Toward the end though, he paused for a moment, his attention seized.

"Well what do we have here?" he asked himself as he read it, "Ah yes, him. Haven't heard anything in a couple of years."

He pulled a small portable phone from his pocket and called his workplace.

"Hey. It's Kab-... Excuse me. It's The Scout. I have a question," he began, "It's about Subject C151. How is he doing? . . . I thought so, too. . . Colonel now? . . . Right, he's getting close. We were right as always. . . For the arising. Goodbye."

He turned off the phone with a crooked smirk on his face. Without a second look, he merged everything else into one pile to throw away, leaving only Subject C151. To the left of the name, he wrote Colonel and penned the date on the other side. He returned it to the dossier folder, which he then slipped into his briefcase. He locked the briefcase and slid it under the couch.

The door opened abruptly, startling him. He grabbed his coat from behind him and hastily pulled it over his shoulders, covering his arms. Elemeno gave a confused look from the doorway.

"Kabehl, why so jumpy?" she asked softly, hoping her tone would avoid confrontation.

"Nothing. I was just lost in my work."

"What was that I saw on your arm? Are you hiding something?"

Of course, he was hiding plenty of things. She had stopped bothering to question his employment though, and that seemed to be the root of most of his secrets. For the time being, she had decided to remain ignorant. He was still providing monetarily for Eytea, even if he was still emotionally absent.

But Kabehl was now cornered into revealing one of them through a tattoo on his upper arm. He held his bicep with his left hand, avoiding eye contact with Elemeno. He concocted an alibi, then let down the coat.

On his right arm was a tattoo of a black x with three vertical lines running through it, the one in the center being notably longer than the two on the ends. Elemeno examined at it and furrowed her brow.

"What is it?" she asked.

"It's just something I got at work."

"Okay, but what is it?"

"It's a simplified diagram for a geometrical theorem we're developing and researching for some new excavation technology. Subterranean travel and such. Everybody on the crew has one."

"Why do I get the feeling you're lying to me, Kabehl?"

He was quickly offended by the accusation, his face doing little to hide his aggravation. Elemeno knew this to confirm her suspicion, but there was nothing she could do to expose him. All she knew was that he was hiding something, nothing more.

Kabehl sprang from his seat and walked assertively to the foyer where Elemeno stood. His eyes never left her, staring straight through her like a pair of spears. She stood her ground, refusing to flinch under Kabehl's menacing glare.

"Did you just call me a liar? Did you, bitch?"

"Yes. Yes I did. I know I can't prove it, but I just don't trust your answer."

He raised his hand and slammed the palm heel against her forehead. Her head snapped back for a flash of a moment and rolled forward again. Ignoring the pain, she stared up at him dauntingly.

"Do it again, you asshole," Elemeno taunted.

Outside, Eytea could hear the sound of flesh striking flesh. With no hesitation, she jumped from the horse, tumbling across the dirt as she landed. She ran to the cottage and burst through the door to find her father standing over her mother with his hand raised.

"Dad! No!" she cried.

She slipped between them, facing her father, with her arms spread. Though Elemeno was a decent bit taller than her, Eytea still tried to guard her. Ignoring his daughter, Kabehl slammed his hand down at Elemeno's forehead.

The back of Eytea's shirt ripped from within in two place. Tiny feathers were thrown about as a pair dark purple wings burst from her back, their span roughly equal to that of her arms. The two wings pulled upward, rising above her head. Kabehl's fist fell upon a thick sheet of purple feathers. He lowered his fist in awestruck and frightened silence.

Chapter 4

"Dear Galo,

As you and your grandfather both know, my fifteenth birthday is three days after the posting date on this letter, which means I'm three days from qualifying to enlist in the military. So, I'm afraid my father, now a General, plans to sign me up as a soldier. I swore long ago never to let that happen, ever since I saw him murder my mother.

ArcNos is rapidly evolving, and I don't like where it's heading. Weapons technology is increasing and just keeps building momentum. Sea travel research has allowed them to travel from here to Berinin in less than a day. Air travel is also under way, an achievement yet to be met by said Ivarians.

Also, the only things anyone has heard from Brigadier General Elite HarEin have been through messengers, and it's always about aggression and growing faster. I think he's trying to become independent of Ouristihra, but somehow I doubt it's even him. After living alone with him for five years, that sounds more like CreSam.

Honestly, I'm not certain which is growing faster, the military's power or CreSam's ego, but I want nothing to do with either. Any power that not only fails to punish a man for murder, but drives a man to do so, isn't to be trusted.

To get to the point though, I've decided I'm going to escape from all of it. You're the only person I'm telling, but you may not hear from me again for a long time. When you read this letter, I will be fifteen years old and on a dinghy heading south. I know what you're thinking, and no I won't be going to Berinin. I will be nearby on a small island about twelve kilometers to the east.

You're welcome to visit me, but please do so sparingly. I don't want you to be spotted and raise suspicion. Still, I do wish to see you on occasion, and I'm sure a twelve kilometer swim won't be much of a burden. I might also visit from time to time, provided my boat is in good enough condition after this trip. To be honest, I stole it from a military surplus heap. It was outdated, so it was going to be scrapped anyway. Either way, it's not in the best condition, but I'm confident it will survive the trip.

Your friend and brother,

Sinkua."

On the corner of the letter, he dripped a bit of fluid from a vial in his desk. It was Galo's scent, made from sweat and skin flaked. He rolled the paper into a tube and fastened it with a length of yarn.

Perched in the windowsill was a small grey bird. It had been watching Sinkua intently since he withdrew the vial from his desk. He offered it a taste of the scent on the corner before fastening the letter to the bird's leg. The bird then flew from the window in search of that scent, and Sinkua closed the window.

Though a postal service had been available for nearly a century, this archaic messaging technique was still practiced by a fair number of Ouristihrans. People exchanged vials of their scent, which were used to mark letters. Tracking pigeons, originally bred by an avian geneticist in Ferya, then delivered those letters to the person carrying that scent. As far as anyone knew, the system had never failed.

Sinkua had used the pigeons several times to keep in touch with Galo and Gijin, especially since the chance to visit them regularly died with his mother, but only now was he truly putting his faith in their reliability. If the letter failed to reach Galo, nobody would know of his whereabouts.

He lay in bed that night, staring at the ceiling and scarcely blinking. Although sleep eluded him, he did still dream. He dreamed of his life beyond the reaches of CreSam and the fetters of the military. He dreamed of his own freedom, but anxiety still was taking over.

"What if this is a bad idea?" he mumbled to himself, "Maybe things will be worse if I get caught than they would be if I stayed. Maybe I should just stay and enlist. But then, I'd just become a part of what I hate. What else can I do though? Nothing for now. I can't do anything from far away either, but at least I can be safe from them until I figure something out.

Is it really a good idea to move so close to Berinin though? What if they come looking for me? I'd hate to involve the Berininites. No, then again, no matter where I went, Galo would involve himself. That's just how he is."

He glanced down at the medallion on his chest. Since that afternoon in the foyer, he had never taken it off, but he did hide it under his shirt in CreSam's presence. In that time, he had grown accustomed to the warm sensation and now suspected that going without it would leave his blood feeling cold. He held the crystal in his hand. It was warm to the touch, warmer than the sensation he felt in his veins.

Since the day Gijin explained his name to him, he hadn't bothered to question the overall functionality of this gemstone or if there even was one. He could vaguely recall Gijin telling him that there was more to it, but it sounded like such a distant memory. Still, it had become a part of him. Its mysterious air was his solace in this time of chaos.

He rolled over on his side and watched the night sky through the open window. Off in the distance, he could still see the tracking pigeon, but its caw had become inaudible. The sky was as still as the dead and just as empty. Not a star could be seen for all the strain of his tired eyes. Below, the city was bustling even at this late hour. The noise sounded of disorder and incomprehensibility.

Sinkua rolled onto is other side to try to tune out the noise. In his mind, he plotted his escape. The boat was in place, and he had gathered most of the supplies he would need. Timing was still an issue though, as was his constant worry that he was forgetting something.

He turned once more to face the ceiling. Writing upon it with his mind's eye, he reviewed CreSam's schedule. He studied it for a while, trying to determine the best time to escape. Consumed in his thoughts, he was harshly startled by a loud noise outside.

It sounded like an explosion. A series of them followed, and they seemed to be hitting progressively closer to the house. He shot out of bed and threw on his jacket as he ran down the stairs and out the door.

Just a handful of meters away, a fiery military truck came screaming down from the sky and crashed into the ground. Shards of smoldering glass mixed with smoke and blood spewed out in a planar spray. He turned his head, using his forearm to shield his face. Knowing surviving such a fall would be impossible, he concerned himself instead with what caused it.

Off in the urban distance, buildings collapsed upon themselves. It looked as though they were buckling under their own weight. Sirens wailed, audible even from the suburbs. Screams and cries echoed through the smoky night air. Morbidly curious, Sinkua ran toward the wreckage. As he approached, the sirens grew deafeningly louder, and the screams grew more distinct.

Smoldering vehicles continued to rain down from the sky, military and civilian alike. Entire families were falling helplessly to grisly demises. Some leapt from their vehicles, only to have their bodies shatter against the asphalt in a sinewy mess. Sinkua just watched helplessly, but something still drove him onward.

As he entered the city, he could see cars leaving the ground as huge explosions scattered them into the searing wind. The shockwaves toppled nearby buildings. Cars frequently crashed into each other in midair, ricocheting and spinning chaotically.

Missiles sprayed forth from the darkness ahead, exploding violently against anything they touched. The night sky, choked by blood and smog, vomited the burning wreckage of the city upon itself. People ran from the falling buildings only to find themselves crushed under the deadweight of their fellow townspeople.

Sinkua paused in his tracks. Just ahead, a missile came screaming downward toward a nearby parked car. The driver, close enough to count the hairs on his chin, threw the door open and made a desperate run for safety. The explosion threw him forward, along with his car. He and Sinkua caught each other's eyes as he passed.

"Save us," he gasped almost breathlessly.

"What is this?" Sinkua asked.

The car slammed against the man's back and pinned him as it dropped upon the asphalt. He was crushed under the weight of it, his remains rapidly incinerated in the fire. Sinkua's pulse accelerated as blood laced with embers sprayed over his legs. His neck throbbed. His blood felt like it was boiling.

"What could be doing this?" he snarled, "What power is this? What kind of sick…….. I won't let this happen!"

In a fit of reckless rage, he charged into the darkness. Missiles sprayed around him, but he weaved to evade the onslaught. The sky spilled smoldering metal, blood crusted shards of bone, and half melted stone. Soon the screams and sirens could no longer be heard over the sound of fiery debris ripping through the air and crashing into the crumbling asphalt.

He stopped suddenly, his attention snagged by a new sound piercing the macabre air. On each side of the road, two chains with links bigger than his body burst forth from the darkness, each one equipped with a tripod hook at the end. They crashed through buildings, exiting with furniture, structural beams and even bodies hanging from their prongs. As they dropped to the ground, the hooks were driven into the concrete by their own momentum. The chains were pulled taut, and a huge shadow was cast over the street. Sinkua stepped back cautiously.

A massive metallic beast of a war machine tore through the bloodied smog and landed before him. This abomination towered over the city, armed with innumerable munitions. It fired a few shots past Sinkua, but he stared defiantly at the towering icon of hatred. It looked down at him and spoke in a gruff menacing voice.

"So it's you, MeiLom. Why not join us? You are the son of a soldier. You have a right to this sort of power," it beckoned.

"My name is Sinkua," Sinkua muttered, "and I am no soldier's son."

"What did you say, boy? Speak up!"

"I said you'll never have me!" he roared "And you'll never leave here alive!"

The warm sensation in his veins intensified. The ruby in his necklace began to glow, emitting a brilliant red light. His eyes flared for a moment, radiating with an ominous green light. They faded to a faint glow, and he charged the enemy.

Several barrels aimed downward. Missiles shot down like sleet, all aimed directly at him. As he ran, they tracked his motion and changed their trajectory to follow it. His own death impending, he still drove onwards. His heart battered his ribcage, either one feeling as though it could shatter at any moment. The ruby's shimmer swelled into a blinding crimson glow that swallowed the darkness around it.

When the light faded, Sinkua found himself alone. He looked around for a moment, carefully observing his surroundings. He was back in his bedroom, lying on top of the covers. Curiously, he went to the window.

Off in the distance, smoke spewed from a building. In a confused panic, he snatched his binoculars from atop the dresser. Upon closer scrutiny, he realized it was only a house fire. It was a tragedy nonetheless, but nothing like the destruction that had just occurred.

He set his hand over his heart, checking to see if his pulse had calmed at all. When his bare forearm touched the necklace, he jerked it back quickly. Lifting it with the bottom of his shirt wrapped around his hand, he looked down into the ruby. It was warmer than usual, hot to the touch even.

"This really is more than jewelry," he whispered.

By the time morning came, he still hadn't slept. The nightmare had left him too anxious to even try to rest again. Ever since his mother died, sleep had become a fleeting luxury, one that he missed terribly but was quickly growing accustomed to doing without. Instead, he spent the remainder of the night gathering a few last minute provisions.

Hanging from the handle on his closet door was a rope belt with a pouch hanging from the side. In it, he had stashed a vial of Galo's scent as well as one of Gijin's. He also stored some paper and a pen with an extra bottle of ink. To top it off, he added a handful of small candles and a pocket knife.

He had passed more of the time watching the city in quiet anticipation. The nightmare felt disturbingly real, perhaps as though he had been offered a glimpse of the future. But his behavior was rather peculiar as well. He had never seen himself as a fighter. It wasn't that he couldn't, but rather that he didn't seek it.

And the ruby seemed to behave on its own, as though it was protecting him. Sinkua thought it over, replaying the scene in his mind. Even though it had just been a dream and was several hours ago, every moment of it was still vivid. He was still uncertain as to what exactly the ruby was, but it seemed to be some sort of weapon.

There was one especially key factor that pointed to the nightmare portending a dark future for ArcNos. Most of the cars were powered by combustion engines, rather than the steam engines currently more common to the area. The military had a few combustion powered prototypes, though HarEin felt they would be a danger to the passengers in a combat situation. The highest concentration of combustion engine vehicles existed in Ivaria, and even there it wasn't particularly high. Environmental and safety concerns inhibited mass international distribution, despite generally higher top speeds and overall power.

With that in consideration, Sinkua knew the timing of the dream couldn't have been present day. Now the location was in question, though. Sure, he rose from his bed in his room in ArcNos, but the scene beyond that suggested Ivaria as a possible setting. Perhaps ArcNos had occupied and subjugated Ivaria, or as a less dire alternative, they may have stolen the technology.

Still, he found his mind wandering back to his own actions as well as those of the ruby. He was coming to accept that he may have to fight and even kill, especially if events such as those were ever to come to fruition. In fact, he took a bit of solace in knowing that he would be willing to at least try to fight back, but if he couldn't, the ruby behaved independently, protecting him as though it had a mind of its own. He looked down at it, contemplating it with greater depth than usual.

"What are you, really?" he muttered under his breath.

"MeiLom!" a voice boomed as the door swung open.

Sinkua jumped and hastily stuffed the medallion under his shirt before turning around.

"Y-yes, father? What is it?" he asked.

"You're jumpy, boy. What are you up to in here?"

"What? Oh nothing. Just bird watching."

"Eh? Well it's no matter. I was just coming up here to tell you I'm leaving on a mission. I'll be gone for three days, then I'm coming back on your birthday and taking a few days off to get you ready."

"Okay, father. I'll see you then. Good luck."

"And I expect the house to be clean when I get home."

"Yes, sir."

The door closed, and Sinkua turned back to the window. The farther CreSam advanced in the military, the less Sinkua felt like a son to him. And the less he felt like a son to him, the less he felt he had a place in ArcNos. With how emotionally bankrupt CreSam had become, any further sovereignty granted to him would undoubtedly have been detrimental. Yet, as obligated as Sinkua felt to try to change things, he knew he was helpless for now. He had spent nearly five years unsuccessfully trying to connect with CreSam, and once he joined the military, the formal hierarchy would make it all the more difficult.

The fact that CreSam planned to enlist him on his fifteenth birthday meant he would be on his way home the day before. As the front door closed, Sinkua realized this meant a considerable risk of crossing paths were he to set sail that day. Seeing CreSam heading down the front walk, he jerked the window open.

"Hey, father!" he called down.

CreSam stopped to look over his shoulder, up toward the window.

"Yeah, boy? What is it now?"

"Um, just wondering, but where are they sending you now?" he asked.

"Not that it's really your business, since you're not even a Green Rookie, but I'm going to Tanelen."

Without another word or acknowledgment, CreSam continued to his car. Sinkua had gotten what he was after though, and it was the best answer he could have hoped for. Tanelen was almost directly north of ArcNos, while Berinin was far to the south.

Now alone, he wandered around the house. The very air of it had felt different since that dreadful day five years prior. Still, he took time aside to take in every bit of it, without CreSam lurking over his shoulder, before he left it behind indefinitely. Regardless of it being an admittedly broken home, it was a home nonetheless.

Of course, he could just as easily have walked out the door and sailed off in the middle of the day. It wasn't as though he was trying to avoid anyone else but CreSam. Instead, he thought he would take some time to enjoy having the house to himself. The place always felt more comfortable when CreSam was away, those times perhaps being the only thing that kept him there.

Also, he worried that leaving in haste could have him leaving poorly equipped. This concern had been constant, but remembering those last minute provisions the night before had evolved the worry into anxiety.

In a way, he still felt obligated to clean the house before he left, too. CreSam was just crooked enough that Sinkua could imagine him tracking him down just to come home and finish the chores. Besides, he felt it best not to contest the man, at least not just yet. Even if he did, a petty thing like house chores was no affair over which to do so.

The day was mostly spent cleaning. He did stop to eat and rest periodically, but he kept busy to ward off anxiety. He was convincing himself that every possible snag, save for the largely unforeseeable weather, had been worked out of his escape plan. The letter would reach Galo as scheduled, and if the nightmare were to come true in any medium, he would be ready for it. Galo would stand alongside him, he was sure.

Throughout the day, a record player in his bedroom blasted out Masnethegean rhythms. Listening to it was forbidden while CreSam was home, as anything about Berinin made him irritable. For Sinkua though, the memories elicited by it were as close as he could get to happiness in that fractured home. It certainly made the house chores seem less of a burden and helped to silence the worry that his plan was in any way insufficient.

As one full moon and two crescents hung high over the city, Sinkua left home. His binoculars hung from his neck, over the medallion. From his side hung the pouch on the rope belt. Over one shoulder, he carried some last minute provisions wrapped in the blanket from his bed. This included several nonperishable foods, a long rope, a plastic tarp and a few metal bowls of various sizes.

After about an hour of walking, he reached the shore with sore shoulders and tired legs. He hoisted the bag up to his shoulder and launched it into the boat. It fell open upon landing and scattered the contents about the deck. With CreSam away, there was no need for a clandestine departure. He untied the rope from its post and climbed into the boat, thus beginning his long sail to freedom.

The boat was of moderate size, significantly larger than the one he and CreSam had traveled to Berinin on twelve years ago. There was ample room to walk about as well as small quarters with a bed and what could only be described as a scaled down kitchen. There was a miniature refrigerator, a sink, and a stove with just one eye. No oven, but it would still be enough to serve his purposes.

Also, below the deck was a storage cellar about twice the size of the quarters. On days prior, he had packed it with what supplies he could carry when the opportunity arose. He gathered up the last of it, rolled it in the blanket, and hauled it down the stairs. Off in the corner, something curious caught his eye, a wooden pole extending out from behind his supply heap. He reached for it and dragged out its full length of about a meter. At the end was a shiny metal chain. He got to his feet and lifted it as he continued to pull. When a length of chain a bit longer than the stick was revealed, it got hooked on a bag. With a strong jerk, he pulled it out, ripping through the bag. There at the end lay a metal ball covered in spikes, the full size of it about that of his head.

He lifted the ball from the floor and looked it over for a moment. It was a morningstar. He had heard of them, but he had never seen one. Given how awkward and dangerous they were to use, they had earned a reputation as one of the most difficult melee weapons to wield without injury.

Regardless, he thought it would be worth the challenge to try. At the very least, practicing with it would keep his body and mind sharp. Besides, once he reached his destination, he'd have little else but time. He smirked and shrugged.

"Could come in handy when I get there," he said.

He wrapped the chain around the handle and left it below deck when he returned to the surface. Up on the deck, he watched the night sky reflected on the sea, mottled patches of starlight scattered over calm waves.

The southward wind was strong and steady that night. He raised the sails and retired to his bunk for the night. The hours passed with the ship being tossed across the sea while he tossed across the bed.

The next morning, Sinkua found himself leaning on the starboard rail with an orange in hand, warding off both hunger and scurvy. What few seeds he found were extracted and dropped in his shirt pocket. He looked out toward the horizon, scanning the seascape.

He was far enough out that no land could be clearly distinguished. Even with his binoculars, he could only vaguely see a shoreline off in the distance, and that could just as well have been a sandbar. Assuming it was not though, that meant he was passing Ivaria. Presumably, he was making great time, better than he had when he traveled with CreSam.

When he finished the orange, he pitched the rind into the ocean. A fish surfaced and nipped at the scraps. This was the way out here, he pondered. Nobody is picky about what they're offered. Survival is the foremost priority with everything else being a luxury.

For him, surviving meant running from the military. While this was his only choice at the time, to uphold his principles would mean fighting back eventually. He wondered if he would ever be ready for it or if it would consume the land before he had a chance to try. His mind storming, he tried in vain to calm it by convincing himself that fighting back now would be a wasted effort. He had neither enough evidence nor allies. They would crush him in every conceivable way.

To distract himself, he turned his attention to the sky. Cumulus clouds were scattered about, one particular cluster covering the sun. The air was warm and humid. A gaggle of geese passed overhead, traveling almost exactly opposite the ship's path. Sinkua watched them for a moment, something about their direction seeming peculiar, perhaps even unsettling.

He went to the sails turned each one to catch the wind at a slightly different angle. Going by the geese's trajectory, the boat was heading directly south once again, back on course to Berinin. He had decided he would try to land there first to visit Galo and Gijin for a day.

Sick of listening to his anxious thoughts, he went below deck to find some sort of distraction. He was tired of trying to talk his subconscience into agreeing with his conscience that he would survive the trip. Beyond that, of course, there was the concern that it was the best way to approach the circumstance, or at least a good way.

Down in the storage cellar, he found that morningstar lying at the bottom of the steps. Sure, he had left it down there, but what seemed odd was that he hadn't left it in that spot. It was obviously done by the tossing of the ship, but he couldn't help but feel like it was some sort of sign. It was as though this weapon was presenting itself to him, beckoning him to wield it. He picked it up and looked it over.

He doubted that there would be any other way to contest ArcNos than to fight against its military. So when he was ready, this would mean launching an attack on his homeland, though it would be more on the source of the corruption to be more exact. What it all came down to was that if he didn't learn to fight back, he would have no chance of surviving. If he wanted to truly stand for his principles, he would have to learn to stand up for more than just himself, and as scattered and anxious as his thoughts were, he knew one thing for certain. If he could master this awkward weapon or at least wield it well, he would be more than a thorn in the side of the growing war machine. His decision was made, but in a way it was made for him. He would take up the morningstar and ready himself in case a war was to come.

On deck once again, he stood with his knees locked. His right hand clutched the handle of the morningstar. He swiveled his wrist, spinning the chain in a narrow circle. With a stiffening of the wrist, it slowed to a halt. He tried again, but this time he stiffened and flicked his wrist. The spinning stopped faster this time. Involving his forearm now, he widened the circles.

Though it wasn't his intent, the head nearly struck him in the knee. Improvising his training, he pivoted and pulled that leg back behind the other. He kept his arm steady, holding the morningstar in a fixed spot. He continued the spinning and returned to his original stance. When it came back around, he stepped to dodge again. For a several minutes, he continued this pattern, slowly accelerating.

He tried dodging the spin while moving his arm. It was difficult at first, so he started slowly. After some time though, he was just as comfortable dodging with his arm moving as he was with it still. With his right arm growing weary, he switched hands. Although he was predominantly right handed, he knew it best to train with both hands. Aside from the fact that his arms could become lopsided otherwise, being able to use either hand would prove useful. Besides, it was just another challenge to face, one that would make him a stronger opponent regardless of whether he succeeded.

The work with his left hand proceeded more slowly than with the right. Though it was partially due to confusion with mirroring his early movements, the delay stemmed more from a natural awkwardness in operating with his recessive arm. With time and persistence though, he was spinning and dodging just as well with the left as he could with the right.

Now it was time for a new challenge. He tossed the morningstar from one hand to the other. The throws were straight and precise at first. Catching was easy enough this way. He quickly moved up to arcing pitches, throwing higher with each catch. For a while, he had to watch it, but with more practice, he was able throw and catch while looking in any direction.

Combining the exercises, he spun the chain in a couple of circles, dodging the back swing each time. Without hesitance, he tossed it to his other hand and continued spinning and dodging. With each toss back and forth, he spun the chain little faster. His throws fluctuated sporadically from quick precise pitches to arcing tosses.

An accidental short throw looked of impending injury. Though he stiffened and flicked his wrist upon catching the morningstar, the spinning didn't decelerate quickly enough. He had put too wide a radius on the spin, and the ball careened toward his left leg. In a split second reaction, he jumped and tucked his knees. To his relief and surprise, he cleanly cleared the ball and chain without stopping his spin.

Yet another challenge was presented. He kept spinning it with his right hand, holding the weapon out in front of his body instead of off to the side. With each revolution, he jumped over the passing ball, careful to hold his position and keep his arm steady.

Aside from a couple of breaks to relax and eat, the rest of the day passed with little other than training with the morningstar. His primary focus was on dodging recoil, though he concerned himself some with precision of motion such as throwing and catching it while in use. y nightfall, he went to bed confident that he would come to wield it well, perhaps even master it.

Chapter 5

"Strong willed? Yes," a familiar voice said, "A good navigator? Not so much."

"Huh, what?" Sinkua mumbled in his sleep.

"Wake up, Sinkua," the voice ordered.

"Shut up and let me sleep," he groaned, burying his face in the pillow.

There was a brief pause. Sinkua began to think he had finally been left alone. He was too tired to even realize how odd it was to be hearing someone else's voice on the boat, much less to distinguish who it was. Ignoring the oddities of the morning, he began to fall back asleep.

"Hey, breakfast is almost ready," the voice announced suddenly.

Sinkua quickly rolled over and opened his eyes.

"Breakfast?" he asked.

"Morning," Galo welcomed, "I knew that would get your attention."

"Ha. Very funny, Galo," Sinkua muttered, sitting up in bed, "Wait a minute. How'd you get on my boat anyway?"

"Well, have you noticed how still the boat is? You drifted ashore a couple of hours ago."

Sinkua climbed out of bed and threw his shirt on. With a quick shake of the head, he threw his hair out of his eyes. It hung just past his ears in thick black spikes, just a bit longer than those on his morningstar.

"That's strange. I must have been thrown off course."

"The sea's got a mind of its own, Grandpa always tells me," Galo explained from the foot of the bed.

Sinkua dug through the fridge and pulled out an apple. He looked back and tossed it over his shoulder. Galo caught it and looked at Sinkua, puzzled.

"Thanks, but I wasn't lying about breakfast."

"I know. I can smell it from here. I'm just thanking you in advance."

"Thanking me for what?"

"Because you," Sinkua asserted as he put on his boots, "are going to help me get this boat back on the water."

Sinkua exited the cabin without another word. Galo watched him walk away with one eyebrow raised. After the door closed, he shrugged and took a bite of the apple.

"Well, of course I am," he agreed as he got to his feet, "That's the sort of thing friends do for each other."

Breakfast that morning was a meal for three. Gijin, Galo, and Sinkua sat on the floor around the table in the Chieftain Sage's hut, dining on grilled fish and fresh fruit. Sinkua pondered if the extra plate had been prepared because they anticipated his being on the boat that washed ashore or if the same would have been done as an act of kindness for a lost traveler. Either way, he was grateful.

Also, it spoke volumes of why the people looked up to Gijin so. This had nothing to do with lineage. Even without tradition, they would have praised and followed him just the same. Rather, they allowed him to lead for his sense of honor. He was a man of strong principles and endless benevolence.

Sinkua looked up from his plate and across the table. Gijin was thoroughly enjoying his fish as well as the company of his grandson and friend. Sinkua grinned at him and returned to his meal, his mind wandering once again.

He felt at home here. Ever since he was given his alternate name, that hut felt more like home than the house with his parents, despite his mother's best efforts. That shore was more inviting than his lawn. Berinin welcomed him while ArcNos scarcely acknowledged his existence. As he sat eating breakfast with their leader and his closest friend, part of him wished he was born a Berininite. It seemed so much more a fitting nationality for him.

"By the way, Sinkua," Gijin said, breaking the long silence, "We were hoping you would stay until tomorrow evening. We can prepare a second cot in Galo's room for you, if you would like."

"Well, I wasn't planning on it," Sinkua admitted, "but I'll take the invitation, thanks. Can I ask why though?"

"Sinkua," Galo chimed in, "did you really forget your own birthday?"

"Did you really think we would forget your birthday?" Gijin added with a hearty laugh, "This is the first chance we've had to spend it with you, so we want to take the opportunity."

Sinkua rubbed the back of his head. He had never expected anything like this. For the past five years, birthdays were nothing more than dreaded milestones. Happy birthdays were a concept long buried.

"Oh. Well um, thanks guys," he accepted, reaching for the right words, "That'll be nice."

"Hey brother, we know what you were expecting to come on your fifteenth birthday just a few days ago," Galo added, "So we thought we'd make it better for you than just getting out of joining the military."

Sinkua had hoped for something better every year, but he had never bothered to expect or even ask for it. Lately, it had been barely more than an afterthought. Even at the young age of eleven, Galo could sense that the thought of turning fifteen troubled him, and here he was offering companionship and camaraderie to ease his mind. Already, the boy was developing his grandfather's sense of hospitality.

The rest of the day was spent with the two of them in and out of the sea as well as on and off of the boat. The deck had not aged well and thus had suffered notable weather damage. What time wasn't spent in the surf was spent patching holes. Even though it left them both with sore backs, it didn't feel in the least like work.

It helped Sinkua to get his mind off of his affairs, as well. Oddly enough, working was helping him relax. For a few hours, he actually wasn't worried about CreSam pursuing him. Besides, as far as he was from ArcNos at that moment, he was even farther from CreSam.

This day cemented what he already thought to be true, as well. The farther he was from CreSam, the more comfortable he was. Knowing how great the distance between them was, Berinin felt more like home than it ever had on any previous visits. A part of him wished he could stay, but he knew it unwise to do so. The place that felt the most like home could never be such.

That night, he lay on a cot in Galo's room. He thought about the coming morning as he stared up at the ceiling. A week ago, he looked to this day with anxiety. Tonight however, he looked toward it with calmed anticipation.

The following morning, a thunderous crash resounded through the village. Again and again, metal clobbered wood, a spray of splinters showering across the sand. The two boys propped themselves up on their elbows, startled awake.

"The boat!" Galo shouted.

Galo and Sinkua threw their sheets off themselves and ran for the door. Sinkua threw his shirt over his torso as he ran, struggling to force his arms through the twisting sleeves.

Outside, the two were met with a spray of wooden shards coming from Sinkua's stolen vessel. It looked as though it had tangled with some savage beast. Whatever caused it sounded like it was inside the hull. Sinkua popped his neck and walked in long strides toward the ship. He held his left forearm in front of his face to shield it from the raining splinters.

"What kind of beast could do such a thing?" Galo asked, still standing in front of the hut.

"As soon as I find out, it'll wish it never did," Sinkua bellowed, "I've come too far to be stopped now."

Galo returned to the hut. Inside, he looked about in a panic for his grandfather. He wasn't meditating before the statue as he typically did in the morning. Galo stood in front of the shrine, trying to think where Gijin could have gone. After a few minutes, he decided there was no use in trying to predict the old man's actions and opted instead to search blindly.

Sinkua peered into a hole in the starboard side of the vessel. Nobody was in sight. He snickered, confident that he was getting the jump on whatever was ripping his boat asunder. Although as irritating as it was that they were interfering with his escape, the very idea of this assailant coming ashore and threatening the Berininites angered him even more so. He crawled into the hole and got to his feet. Standing his ground, he studied his surroundings. The hull was in shambles. Quite abruptly, he heard a loud creaking in the planks above. Before he could react, a great weight fell upon his shoulders and he was dropped to the ground.

Galo searched the remainder of the hut. Still, he found no sign of Gijin. He scratched his thick dark hair. Gijin rarely left the hut without making his departure known. Galo wondered if his absence could have been connected to the assault on Sinkua's ship, but he couldn't think what anyone would hope to gain from pursuing his grandfather. As unlikely as it seemed though, the thought of anyone coming after Gijin cut away at his fuse. He ran out of the hut and toward the shore.

Sinkua fell on his hands and knees. With a grunt and a shove, he rolled over, throwing aside what had fallen on him. He sprang to his feet and took a defensive stance as another body erected itself. In the dim light, the person's face was barely visible. It looked to be male, a few years older than Sinkua and a little shorter.

"You're only human," Sinkua noted.

The young man snickered as he walked backward into the shadows. Sinkua followed cautiously. The two of them never took their eyes from each other. Sinkua knew he was being led to a trap of this shadowed man's device, but there was no other way to catch him than to trigger it. The assailant disappeared in the darkness of the hull. Sinkua stopped.

"Peekaboo," the intruder hoarsely whispered, "I see you, little Hybrid."

"Little what?"

The assailant sprang forth from the darkness, holding a dagger in each hand. Thoughts of the strange nickname shattered, and his attention was back to the matter at hand. Sinkua stepped to the left, deftly dodging the surprise attack. He pulled his right arm back and clenched his fist. The sound of flesh and bone striking flesh and bone echoed in the hull as his pounded his fist against the back of the young man's neck. The assailant hit the floor with a thud. Sinkua stood with a foot between the man's shoulder blades.

"What do you think you're doing on my boat?" he barked.

"What? You don't even care who I am?" the man asked with a scoff.

"You've already sabotaged the ship. Your intentions mean more to me than your name."

"Oh, you only know the half of it, boy."

Sinkua looked him over, now able to study the man more thoroughly since he had the upper hand. He was dressed in street clothes, nothing unusual outside of Masnethege. Sinkua found only one distinguishing mark. Upon his right arm was a tattoo, two symmetrical triangles joined at the corners with a line bisecting the arrangement. He said nothing but made a mental note of it.

Galo jumped as a hand set upon his shoulder. Ready for the worst, he turned his head slowly. Both his fists were half clenched, prepared to strike with the heels of his palms.

"Galo my boy, calm yourself," Gijin insisted, "It's just me."

"Grandpa, you startled me. What are you doing out here anyway? Sinkua's boat is being sabotaged."

"That's exactly why I'm out here."

"You're not thinking of…?" Galo began to ask, concerned for his grandfather's safety.

"Oh no, not at all. I'm too far past my prime," Gijin admitted, "I was waiting for you so I could give you something. Wait here, my boy."

Without another word, Gijin walked behind the hut while Galo waited anxiously at the front. His attention was divided between Sinkua's boat and toward the back of the hut as his eyes darted between the two. A couple of loud crashes within the boat concerned him, but his attention was seized when Gijin returned

He approached with a weapon in his hands. The handle was made of oak and stretched nearly two meters. At the end was a wide curled blade with a slight hook in the end. The handle looked heavy and powerful, while the blade appeared light yet sturdy and aerodynamic.

"This is it, Galo. It's called a glaive. Many call it the sword of the sea, as with the right handling, it can slice through water as easily as a sword does through air," Gijin elucidated, handing him the weapon, "Whatever is on that boat may try to come ashore. Just as I did with this very weapon in my youth, it is time for you to defend our people and our home. With my blessing, I pass this inheritance to you."

Galo held the glaive in his hands and studied its structure. He looked his grandfather in the eyes and smiled. He had expected for the past year that he would someday have to defend the village and thus had been preparing for it. While he had been developing a sturdy body with his frequent swimming, he had also been undergoing agility training with the Tide Dancers.

They had taken great pride in teaching him their craft. Theirs was a beautiful and powerful art, pleasing to the eye yet with a great potential for lethal force. It was one requiring a fine balance of strength and grace

"Grandfather," Galo answered, holding the glaive upright, "With your blessing, I will not let Berinin down."

Sinkua pressed his foot into the man's back. He gritted his teach and grunted, refusing to cry out in pain.

"I'll ask you again," Sinkua continued, "What are you doing on my boat?"

"Well if you hadn't come in here and interfered," the man gasped, "I would have been gone already."

A couple of shards of wood dropped from the underside of the deck above him. Sinkua lifted his foot and stomped on the man's spine. This time, he bellowed a loud cry of pain. Sinkua stepped off of him, and the tattooed assailant pulled himself to his feet. He was shaky but still appeared cocky about the situation. Sinkua stood silently with his arms folded.

"Then go," he ordered, breaking the long silence.

The assailant took a few steps back, still cautiously watching Sinkua. Sinkua remained statuesque, never wavering or blinking. Hastily, the man turned and dashed for the port side of the boat. When he turned his back, Sinkua grabbed two support beams above his head.

He lowered his body, crouching until his arms were straight, and lowered his head. With a jump and a pull, he sprang upward with the force of all four limbs. His shoulders crashed against the underside of the deck, busting a hole in the tattered wood. Sinkua climbed through the hole and onto the deck.

The deck was in ruins, barely in better condition than the hull. The sails were shredded and the mast was cracked. The sink overflowed and the fridge sat open and empty. The door to the storage room had been ripped from its hinges. Inside, only a couple of bags of supplies remained. The intruder hadn't just wrecked the ship, but he was about to make off with most of Sinkua's belongings as well. The morningstar was missing, too. Below his feet, he heard wood break on the port side. He ran toward the water and leapt overboard.

He landed on a smaller boat hidden behind his own. On it were several bags and a pile of food, all of them his. The tattooed intruder emerged from a hole in the port side of Sinkua's boat, unaware of his presence. Sinkua crouched to bring himself to eye level.

"Peekaboo," he growled, grabbing the man by the collar of his shirt, "I see you, too!"

With a strong jerk, he pulled him the rest of the way through and pounded the man's face against his knee. The jagged wood shredded his shirt and lacerated his flesh, leaving vermilion stains on the side of the ship. His body was slumped over the side of his boat, his legs dangling overboard. Pained and infuriated, he pulled himself into the boat.

"Son of a bitch!" he shouted, "Don't think for a second that I'm going to let you stop me."

"You're persistent, I'll give you that," Sinkua conceded, "but at some point you crossed the line into just plain stupid."

"Really now? And how did you intend to stop me anyway?"

Sinkua stopped and stepped back. He actually hadn't thought about it, as he didn't expect to find the ship ransacked. He anticipated nothing more than destruction. Considering the crimes done, Sinkua couldn't justify killing him, not even to himself. Alone, he couldn't reclaim his belongings, as the thief would either get in his way or simply steal it again when he turned his back. It couldn't all be taken back in one trip. Sabotaging the ship would mean sacrificing his own supplies as well as subjecting the Berininites to this criminal. He decided to bluff.

"It'll be easy to reclaim my supplies and fix my boat after I watch the sea carry your carcass away."

"Don't make me laugh, boy," the man countered, "You'd sooner kill yourself with this clumsy bastard of a weapon."

The thief kneeled down and picked up the morningstar. Although his weapon was out of his hands, Sinkua felt no fear of the situation.

"Hah! And you think you would do any better?" Sinkua asked, "Go ahead. Try me."

Angered and cocky, the assailant swung the chain about clumsily. Sinkua dodged the flailing spiked ball quite easily, while the thief's concern soon turned more toward avoiding his own recoil than landing a hit on his victim. Sinkua laughed and shook his head. The man drew back, pulling into a reverse stance. He swung the morningstar overhead, the chain arcing high. The ball dropped over Sinkua's head, but he caught the chain just behind it. The ball settled against his forearm, the flesh wedged between two spikes. The assailant tried to pull back, but Sinkua tightened his grip.

"Sabotage, thievery, and now attempted murder," Sinkua began "I don't know or care where you're from, but you should've learned the punishment for such crimes before you came here to commit them."

"But Masnethege doesn't have a formal criminal law system," the man argued, though he was obviously frightened and baffled, "That's why I knew it…"

"Because we don't need one," a voice interrupted from above, "but we know how to improvise when we need to."

Galo leapt from the railing of the boat, his glaive held high. Sinkua stepped back, pulling the chain taut and the man's hand forth. Galo came down upon him, slashing the blade downward through meat and bone. In a bloody mess, a severed hand fell from the handle of the morningstar. Galo got to his feet and wiped the blade on the side of his shorts. The assailant screamed in pain, holding his bloody stump wrist with his remaining hand. Galo removed his shirt and threw it at him.

"Bandage your wrist with that," he offered.

"What are you…?"

"Wait here while Sinkua reloads his ship," Galo ordered with the tip of the blade near the intruder's throat, "When he's done, leave here alone and empty handed. We'll let you off this time, but if there's a next time, it'll be your head."

Sinkua took his time reclaiming his supplies. He was enjoying watching this assailant suffer, and he knew Galo was taking pleasure in watching him squirm while he defended his people. When all was done, the two of them returned to shore and watched the criminal sail away wounded and defeated.

Back in the hut, the two boys sat before Gijin, who sat in front of the shrine. He looked back and forth at the two of them. With a deep sigh, he smiled and finally spoke.

"You both make me proud," he boasted, "The two of you worked excellently together and you fought honorably. Thank you."

"That means a lot, Grandpa."

"Yes, it does," Sinkua agreed, "but I have a question. That man called me something when we were fighting in the hull. 'Little Hybrid.' What does that mean?"

"I suppose in this age, your type isn't common enough for you to know what you are," Gijin pondered, "Allow me to explain it. Galo, you need to hear this as well."

Sinkua and Galo both listened intently.

"Sinkua, your full green eyes are unique among your peers. They give you an advantage over others in that translucencies bear no visual obstruction to you. Galo, as you know, the marks on your neck are sealed gills. With them, you are welcome among the creatures of the sea for hours at a time. While you both are still essentially human, there is a name for people bearing advantageous genetic anomalies such as these. Hybrids."

"So we're... superhuman?" Galo asked.

"In some sense, yes," Gijin agreed, "There is more to your anomalies, however, but that will have to come on its own when the time is right."

"Gijin, I have to know," Sinkua interjected, "Is my condition the reason you welcomed me into your home twelve years ago?"

"Yes. I won't lie to you, that was exactly why," Gijin admitted, "You see, Hybrids are extraordinarily rare. They were once a bit more commonplace, but they have since come to have thought to be met with extinction. When I saw you, I saw a chance for recovery, and I knew I had to do everything I could to see to it that you grew up well."

"I understand, Gijin. But why such an interest in my upbringing?" Sinkua asked

"Because, when the human race is met with a sudden spike in development," Gijin explained, "it can only mean that trouble is afoot somewhere."

Throughout the remainder of the day, Sinkua and Galo worked on repairing the boat. The holes in the side were of lesser priority, as damage to the hull and the mast were considered more of a threat. It only needed to stay afloat for a few more kilometers. It didn't have to look good doing it.

As a way of giving thanks and praising their victory, many of the villagers offered assistance. Some helped with the repairs. Others gathered wood and sheets of fabric. Others still offered supplies and rations to replace what was lost in the scuffle. The food offerings were appreciated but politely turned down.

Repairs on the ship were slow and tedious. Fixing any one problem seemed to create two more. Apparently, the intruder had been at his task for quite a while before awakening anybody. Sinkua often found himself lost in thought, wondering what that man wanted with trashing his boat.

Perhaps, he thought, that tattoo had some significance. It seemed to be some sort of logo or emblem, maybe a symbol from an ancient language. He considered that his being an Hybrid could have something to do with it. Here he wasn't even fully aware of what he was, and he was already facing discrimination for it.

Being the only two Hybrids that either of them knew tightened the fraternal bond between Galo and Sinkua. After the attack, they both began pondering the notion of living with discrimination for their genetic anomalies. While lashing out at the rest of the world certainly would not have been the advisable solution, they knew they had to stick together. Both of them harbored faith that there were others like them in the world. As odd as they were, they couldn't have been alone.

56

The Masnethegeans still treated them with the same respect. Galo considered himself no different from the rest of them. They all loved the sea; he was just more equipped for it. He did blend in better than Sinkua though, who stood out with his shimmering green eyes, pronounced jaw line, and shaggy hair. He was also a good bit taller than the other teenagers on the island. The Berininites had a sadly unique knack for seeing people for their character rather than their appearance and thus welcomed Sinkua all the same.

As evening fell over the village, repairs on the boat were finally complete. With the help they received, rather than merely patching over the holes, they were able to restore it to its original state. Its grand reflection scattered across the liquid sky, accompanied by broken stars and three cracked moons.

Sinkua prepared to board the ship and set sail for the night. Galo and Gijin, as well as a handful of villagers, gathered around to see him off.

"Thank you, everybody," he said, "I couldn't have asked for better help than what I got today."

"We're glad to help you, Sinkua. It's wonderful to see you growing up into such a fine young man," a female villager called back.

Sinkua glanced over to her with a nod but paused for a moment when he caught eyes with her. He looked her over, sensing a distant familiarity about her. He studied her face, and as he blinked, his mind raced back twelve years. She was the woman who had greeted him and CreSam on the shore the day they came to get the crate of medicine. Even after all this time, she still remembered him.

"After what you did this morning, you're always welcome here, boy," another local added.

"Yeah, we worked pretty great together, huh?" Galo suggested, "We really showed that crook not to mess around in Berinin. Got your boat back and protected the village."

"Yeah, we did, Galo. We're a good team," Sinkua agreed.

Gijin cleared his throat and stepped forth with his hands in his pockets. The dull roar of the small crowd fell into silence. All heads turned toward the old Chieftain Sage, and Sinkua's attention fixed on him as well.

"Thus arises a question I wish to pose, Sinkua," Gijin began, "Why do you fight?"

"Well, um… Why do I or why did I?" Sinkua asked.

"Why do you? There are no right or wrong answers," Gijin clarified, "Just good answers, bad answers, and lies."

"Well, I never really thought about it, because this is the first time I really fought."

"Not true, my boy. I know you opposed your own father on countless occasions, especially after your mother's demise. Also, you've contended enlistment by fleeing ArcNos. Fighting is not always a physical struggle. So, I ask you once more, why do you fight?"

"I never thought about it that way, but as always you're right. All this time, I've been fighting to keep control of my life and my future. I suppose I fight to reclaim what's rightfully mine. But at the same time, my blood boiled at the thought of that man coming ashore. So I guess the best way to put it is that I fight to protect people I care about and to contend wrongdoings in my own life and to the world around me."

"Retribution, then? That and protection?"

Sinkua nodded.

"Good answer," Gijin said, "And an honest answer. That's actually more important. An honorable answer means nothing if it's a lie."

Sinkua smirked and nodded once again. Galo was watching the two of them intently. Upon hearing Sinkua's answer, a smile spread across his face. He felt great pride in knowing his lifelong friend was one of such strong conviction.

"Sinkua, I have something to give you for your travels," Gijin continued.

He pulled his left hand from his pocket, withdrawing a dagger. The handle was intricately carved with a fitted grip. The blade extended well over thirty centimeters and featured a runic inscription down the length of it. Gijin held it out, laid across both hands. Sinkua stepped forth and took it with both hands and bowed his head respectfully. Gijin also bowed his head.

"Thank you, Grandpa Gijin," Sinkua accepted graciously, "Now why do I have the feeling this is more than an ordinary dagger?"

"Because your intuition is strong," Gijin answered with a small chuckle, "This dagger holds a deep enchantment. Its true purpose will come when it is needed, but until then, it needs to be, well, let's say charged. It is not necessarily to be used for everyday functions, nor is it intended for battle. Instead, the blade is to be lined with that for which you fight and, when its purpose is set to pass, what drives you to fight. Before you ask, no, these are not the same thing. The answers will come to you in time and must do as such. You cannot simply be told and understand quite the same."

"I think I get it," Sinkua accepted, looking the blade over, "I'll keep this in a safe place."

"Grandpa had me pack a belt holster for it in the bag with your ropes and tarp," Galo interjected, "So you already have a place for it."

Sinkua snickered and thanked Galo.

"Well everybody, I'm off. Thanks again."

Before he could board the ship, Galo stopped him one more time. Galo raised his right arm, and Sinkua did the same. Galo pulled him into a one armed hug and patted him on the back.

"Stay alive, brother," Galo insisted

"You too, Galo."

Under a starry sky, Sinkua continued his voyage to the nearby island of refuge. Tired from the day's work, he set a course for the island and retired to the quarters for the night. There, he tossed about, greatly fatigued but sleeping all too little.

He awoke the next morning to find the boat still once again. He stepped out onto the deck, and, just as he had expected, learned he had hit land in his sleep. The sun was barely risen, peaking over the eastern horizon and stretching shadows far across the landscape. Reaching out, they seemed to beckon him. This was his new home now. He set out to find an ideal place to set up camp.

Part of him began to think the whole idea was ludicrous. He could hardly fathom what had possessed him to think surviving on his wits and the contents of a military surplus boat would accomplish anything worthwhile. No matter how he tried to shake it, that same thought came back over and over again. He wasn't strong enough to fight back. Perhaps Gijin's words had more weight to them than he originally thought, but he was never one to underestimate the old man's ramblings.

"I'm so much more certain of myself when I'm in Berinin," he muttered, speaking aloud to keep himself company, "but I guess I can't dwell on that now. I've got my own life here. I can't get them involved, especially not if CreSam comes after me."

In the middle of the forest, he found four sturdy trees, all with similar trunks, arranged in something close to a square. Between them was little foliage and minimal growth. With some tools he brought along, he cleared out the area. Several hours following were spent building a shelter using those trees as the corners of the framework.

Across the ground inside, he laid a large tarp and fastened it to the walls. With this in place, he was free to walk barefoot inside without worry of snakes and large bugs getting at his feet. Also, it was a bit easier on the ankles. Keeping that in mind, he devised a general plan to compile animal hides into a makeshift carpet.

In one corner, he kept a few changes of clothes in a crate that he had packed for just such a purpose. The morningstar leaned against the wall in yet another corner. Caddy-corner to that was the bed. The one in the boat was reasonably light, so he simply sawed the legs from the cabin floor and hauled it out to his shelter. Nobody was going to miss it. Most of the building material had come from scrap pieces of the ship anyway. Leaving it there would have been not only an eyesore, but a dead giveaway as well. In the last corner, he kept various tools and supplies, including cooking and eating utensils as well as vials of Galo's and Gijin's scents for the tracking pigeons.

Satisfied with his accomplishments in erecting a shelter in one day, he stepped outside to enjoy the evening air and admire his new environs. It was beginning to feel a bit more like home. Unlike the house he grew up in, here he was no longer frightened. He no longer worried about anyone losing their temper or about saying the wrong thing. The air was cleaner, both literally and figuratively. Here, he had found the peaceful surroundings he longed for, greatly contrasting the descent to madness in ArcNos.

He walked through the woods, both observing and admiring the trees around him. Out of the corner of his eye, something tantalizing caught his attention. Veering from his path, he went off in pursuit of it.

"Pomegranate," he said with a grin, "Just like I thought."

From a little ways beyond the fruitful shrub, he could hear running water. It was close enough that he could faintly feel the mist gathering on his bare forearm hairs. Pomegranate in hand, he hiked up over the ridge to find a sizable river at the bottom of the hill on the other side. He stood sideways to brace himself and shuffled his feet to control himself as gravity carried him to the bank at the bottom. Once he was within a couple meters, he sprang from the side of the hill and landed perched on a rock half on the shore and half in the water.

There he sat with his legs folded, watching the water pass by. It was teeming with fish. He looked down at the pomegranate in his hand. After tracking it down and carrying it down the hill, it occurred to him that he had nothing on him with which to split it, much less anything into which to empty the bits. Not being one to be set back by such petty details, he simply shrugged and took a big bite out of it, rind and all.

He scraped the rind with his teeth and spat the bare skin into the river, leaving himself with a mouthful of juicy bits of pomegranate. He rolled them around in his mouth, stripping each seed of its ruby encasement. When all were left bare, he spat a series of tiny seeds into the flowing water. A fish surfaced to pick at the discarded rind.

"You're dinner," Sinkua remarked as he got to his feet.

Such was his way for many more weeks to come. His water came directly from the river, as it was clean enough that he didn't have to construct a purification tent like he had planned. Fish and indigenous fruits were his staple foods. It was varied and flavorful enough to keep his palate interested, and it kept him healthy as well. Also, he was waiting for Harvest to come.

In his supplies, he had packed a wide variety of seeds. Over the course of the first few days, he made a large garden and planted them just outside of the forest. Enough of those were growing well enough to keep him fed when Frigid came.

During his plentiful free time, he often trained with his morningstar. His skills with it were developing rapidly. He had grown comfortable with it and no longer feared the flailing spiked ball. He felt as though he had control over it now. It couldn't hurt him without his approval.

Other time was spent either climbing in the trees or playing in the river. He would lie back, facing downstream, and let the water carry him where it may. Here, he was actually comfortable relinquishing control and letting his surroundings carry him on his path. It never led him to harm, and it was a good feeling to think that something could both overwhelm and guide him simultaneously.

He also spent a bit of time meditating each day. Gijin had taught him that it was a good way to relax, and Gijin's advice had always proven useful. Through this, he gradually developed control of his anxiety and was able to better focus thoughts of the reason for his escape.

The escape was a tactical one. It wasn't necessarily a matter of growing stronger but of realizing what role he needed to play regarding the descent of the governmental integrity of ArcNos. Thus far, he had not shunned them, and they had not shunned him. He and CreSam had shunned each other.

If ArcNos were led into corruption and ruin, for him to turn a blind eye would be to abandon his homeland. Though he had never been much a part of its society and hardly felt at home there, there was a still an evident trail of umbilical residue between himself and those cities. He felt it tugging deep within.

On top of that, if the problem were to spread from the shores and reach Berinin, turning a deaf ear to the problem would be to shun those who had helped when his father shunned him. Being an Hybrid, he knew it was his duty to use his advantageous anomalies to combat the corruption growing in ArcNos. Someday, perhaps years from now, he would have to return to defend the land he fled.

Someday, he suspected, CreSam would assume control of ArcNos. That appeared to be his aim. Sinkua knew that, when that time came, he could be the only one who could bring him down, because he may have been the only one left with any hope of reaching him.

Chapter 6

Kabehl walked silently through the corridor, his eyes fixed straight ahead. Though not in local uniform, his presence went unquestioned. He acknowledged nobody, and no one regarded him. Another walked to his right, a few steps behind him.

This comrade of his stood a bit taller and was mostly of a more muscular build, save for his arms. Those were long and lanky, rather contradictory to the rest of his body. His hair was short and his jaw line riddled with stubble. Upon each hip rested an automatic pistol along with two shotguns strapped to his back, crossed over each other.

Kabehl stopped and turned. His partner followed suit as though he had anticipated the move. Kabehl opened the door, and stepped aside. A female Colonel, perhaps a bit over thirty, pushed past them, her expression of frustration turning to one of disdain as she looked them over.

"After you, Amirione," Kabehl offered after the woman passed.

"Scout, you will refer to me as The Hunter in public."

"Yes of course, after you, Hunter."

Kabehl and Amirione, otherwise known as The Scout and The Hunter stepped into the room. It was a fairly large office, the walls strewn with various military decorations and marks of honor, most of them related to combat and field command. Each plaque and certificate shared a common name of CreSam.

CreSam pivoted his chair to face them. He now donned upon his chest the mark of Brigadier Elite. He had come to achieve the second highest rank in the ArcNosian military.

"Well well, if it isn't the man who got me started with you people," he greeted, "Tell me, Scout, what have you got for me today?"

"CreSam, I'd like you to meet another of our, eh, honorable guild," The Scout opened, "Introduce yourself, my brethren."

The Hunter stepped forward, but kept his hands out of reach and simply nodded.

"Call me The Hunter, CreSam."

"Adept with a pistol, I might assume," CreSam postulated, "So is this man going to teach me sharp shooting?"

"What? Oh god no, man," The Hunter refused, "There's a reason lab rats are only given small dosages, you know."

"Well good, I was worried you might go and waste your time. You look a bit young to teach a veteran like me much of anything with a pistol."

The Hunter stepped forth and swiftly withdrew his pistol, aiming it toward CreSam's head. In the middle of the draw, CreSam rose to his feet, changing the barrel's position to the middle of his torso, and withdrew a pistol of his own. He pressed the barrel against The Hunter's forehead. Neither wavered.

"Eight years ago, I took the life of a loved one in identical manner," CreSam muttered flatly, "Don't think you're so fucking special that I can't take yours, boy."

"Enough of this!" The Scout shouted, "Back to business."

"Yes of course. Business," The Hunter bitterly agreed, returning his pistol with one eye on CreSam, "I work for this guild of ours as a professional mercenary. I was sent here to assist you with a little, shall we say, inconvenience you're soon to have on your hands."

"You're talking about that bald boy, aren't you?" CreSam guessed as he returned his gun and sat again, "Spril, the other Brigadier Elite."

"Indeed I am."

"He worries me, too. He reached his status in only eight years of service. That's a record this century, and after enlisting at the minimum age, no less. Could he be working for another sect of outside agents?"

"I've traced his background," The Scout explained, "even deeper than military records are able to do. He's flying solo. Just an orphan from Ivaria with a strong conviction."

"So once he's out of the way, the problem is no more," The Hunter appended, "and that's where I come into the picture. Brigadier General Elite HarEin, rest his soul, was pronounced dead a couple of weeks ago. This leaves you and Brigadier Elite Spril as the coinciding highest ranking officials. By ArcNosian law, you and he are to take part in a competition of military and leadership skills. While we are confident in your abilities, I am here to, well, tip the playing field in your favor. Think of me as your trump card."

"Excellent. I'm looking forward to seeing just what you can do. In the meantime, I know a way to hurt Spril's pride before the match," CreSam proposed.

"Do as you wish," Kabehl accepted, "but don't do anything to compromise our plans for him."

"I wouldn't think of it," CreSam agreed with a smirk, "By the way, have a look in the closet. You stand out like a blister in these halls, and it's time something was done about it."

Phylus sat at his desk, sifting through stacks of papers. Since a competition for the rank of Brigadier General Elite had not arisen since before HarEin was even in service, the duties of filing the paperwork and combing over the details had to be assigned on the fly. Since it was a matter of coming to an agreement between two parties considered as equals, it was determined to be a matter of negotiation. This naturally left Phylus with the brunt of the labor.

The intercom speaker on his desk fizzled and clicked, startling him slightly and drawing his attention away from the documents. He turned to face the speaker and waited.

"Negotiator Phylus?" a static voice called.

"Reporting, sir."

"This is Brigadier Elite CreSam. Report to my office at once."

"Yes, right away, sir."

Phylus walked down the hall, avoiding eye contact with anyone. It wasn't that he wanted to shut them out, just that his mind was frantic at the moment. CreSam rarely summoned him personally, nor did Spril despite the fact that they were essentially family. Familial matters were left at home where they belonged. This summons was undoubtedly something of significance, but he couldn't think what it might have regarded. Nothing he had done lately was all that remarkable by his standards, just performing his job duties as per the usual standards

About ten meters from CreSam's office, he passed another man walking in the opposite direction. An air about this man drew Phylus to make brief eye contact with him. He wore the mark of Lieutenant First Class. The soldier nodded to Phylus, and Phylus returned the gesture.

"Evening, sir," The Scout said to him and continued walking.

Phylus pushed the door open and stepped inside. He let the door close behind him but did not approach the desk.

"Negotiator Phylus, reporting as per your request, Brigadier Elite CreSam, sir," he announced.

"Enough with the formalities, and from now on, you're just Phylus," CreSam dismissed.

"What are you getting at, sir?"

"Or if you're too accustomed to titles, we could try something like Freelance Phylus or..."

"Sir, again I ask, what are you...?"

"Oh, I know! Fired Phylus! That can be your new title."

"What!? You're firing me?" Phylus shouted, appalled at CreSam's decision, "I was in the middle of combing over the details of your competition with Spril. You can't fire me; I'm the only Negotiator this military has got."

"You used to be, yes, but now you've been replaced. Meet my new Negotiator," CreSam refuted, nodding toward The Hunter, "His style of negotiation is far more influential. Actions speak louder than words, you know, and his actions speak very loudly. Quite frankly, Phylus, you're obsolete."

Phylus looked Amirione over with disgust. His position of Negotiator was being handed to a trigger happy man child with compensation issues. He thought the situation over for any sort of flaw or scapegoat.

With both CreSam and Spril holding the title of Brigadier Elite and thus being of equally high authority, both held individual reign. Either could make such decisions without the counsel of the other, but at the same time, hiring, promoting and enlisting could also be done in identical fashion. However, once a soldier was dishonorably released or a worker fired, that person could not reenter in accordance with ArcNosian law. This left him not only unemployed but hard pressed to find employment anywhere in ArcNos, as privately owned companies were increasing in scarcity. CreSam had spoken, thus nothing could be done by Spril to counteract. Even if Spril could have anticipated the move, there was nothing he could have done to prevent it.

Phylus pulled the badge from his shirt and let it drop to the floor along with his self respect. CreSam and The Hunter watched in silence as he stepped out into the hall and let the door close behind him, still standing just outside of the office. He leaned back into the door and slamming the back of his head against it. He closed his eyes and sighed.

"Shit."

After gathering his effects from his office, he walked home under a deep grey sky, keeping against the side of buildings so as to take advantage of the awnings. Less of the rain fell on him there, though he was hardly concerned with keeping himself dry. The stress and frustration were too immense to be bothered by such a thing as mucky hair. His problem with it was that it kept dousing his cigarettes.

He sparked his fifth one since leaving the facility. It was only the third, however, that he had actually been able to smoke. One other kept losing its spark until he grew too irritated and pitched it at a passing vehicle, and the other's paper became too damp and crumbled between his fingers. His hand now carried odiferous traces of warm wet tobacco.

His smoking habit had worsened lately, ever since HarEin's death. No details were released on the matter. He made no final address at the feeling of his impending end. One day he was alive, the next he was dead. Though he dared not mention it to any soldiers or coworkers, he had theories of his own. Spril wisely kept his mouth shut as well, but he shared the same sentiments.

Standing on the front steps of his home, Phylus pulled the partially smoked cigarette from his lips. He looked it over for a moment, shrugged, and returned it to his lips. With a strong inhale, he took one last long drag off of it. Somewhat more satisfied with the use he had gotten out of it, he took what remained and doused it with a wet spot on his shirt. The lifeless butt was pitched into the hedge with so many others.

Spril was sitting in the dining room when Phylus walked in. He had slipped out of the facility in the commotion to head home and face his friend on more personal terms. CreSam's rash decision had created a bit of an uproar and everyone had their conspiracy theories.

"Phylus, I'm sorry I…" Spril began.

"I know who did it," Phylus interrupted.

"I know you do, I'm just trying to…"

"No, not that," he interrupted again, "I know who assassinated HarEin. You see that man with all guns and pistols and whatnot? Yeah, him. And the salt on the wound? The bastard took my job, too. "

"That guy with more firearms than a hunting trip is your replacement?" Spril asked, "CreSam has really outdone himself this time. What makes you so sure he's the assassin though?"

"We both know CreSam has been trying to take control of the ArcNosian military. All he needed was a way to free up the position without getting blood on his own hands. HarEin dies, and suddenly this guy shows up and starts working for CreSam," Phylus explained, "Besides, look at him."

"Very true," Spril agreed, "Not to mention, he has this unsettling familiarity that I just can't place."

"Any idea where you might recognize him from?"

"None, but his continued presence in ArcNos troubles me. Mercenaries operate on a for hire basis. Once a job is done, they take their pay and leave. His still being here means CreSam has further plans for him."

"You fear you're the next mark?"

"Exactly. I'm the only one standing in the way of his reign."

"But if his known mercenary were to kill you, surely the citizens would…"

"They would speculate, but that's it. Nobody can prove the nature of HarEin's death. They would continue to live under the rule of whoever ends up in control, even if it were CreSam. The only difference is that everyone would sleep with one eye open."

"You're so dismal Uncle Spril," a nearby feminine voice said, "Most people might turn a deaf ear out of intimidation, but many would refuse to live under the rule of a tyrant like CreSam. The rift in the populous would weaken his power and the revolutionaries would have a chance to overthrow him."

"How optimistic of you, Vielle," Spril noted, "but even though you make a good point, I'd rather not give him the opportunity to taste authority over ArcNos. Just smelling it has thrown him into a fit of megalomania."

Vielle's slim fingertips traced the banister as she descended the staircase. She wore a camisole and an unbuttoned cardigan to match. Her feet were bare and the bottom few centimeters of her shins exposed. She wore high water pants because she enjoyed the feeling of tall grass brushing against her skin. Her clothes were colored with earthly tones. A black skull cap with dark green lining adorned the top of her head, her deep brown hair hanging out of the back and sides a little past her jaw line.

At the age of fourteen, her body was well on its way to developing into that of a woman. She stood roughly a meter and a half tall, and it seemed she would not grow much taller. Her body was slim, mildly curvaceous, and a source of nightmares for her father.

Around others, she was terribly shy and rarely spoke unless spoken to. At home however, she was boldly outspoken. It was her outlet to vent her thoughts on the ArcNosian administration, and how convenient that it was in the presence of someone with such clout as Spril. Outside of their home however, she dared not speak such radical views. It was admittedly ironic, but she dismissed that fact with the idea that it was not yet time to act upon such sentiments. Preemptive action would be widely repudiated without better proof than theories of CreSam's motives.

"What do you plan to do then?" she asked, propping herself up on a stool in the corner of the dining room.

"Like I said, I'm the only thing keeping him from taking over ArcNos. The way I see it, my only choice is to fight back and take the title from him."

Days later in the auditorium, rafters shook under the clamorous stomping of the waiting onlookers. Scores of decibels reverberated through the seats in the accumulating uproar. The stage was empty now, but soon it would be occupied with a more earthmoving production than any theatre troupe could ever compose. Here the next Brigadier General Elite would be decided in a duel to surrender or death, in accordance with the decree of the newly hired Negotiator Amirione.

From a crowded balcony, the newly unemployed Phylus and his petite teenage daughter looked on with stadium binoculars. The grounds below were yet unoccupied, but people still shouted both cheers and hazes, most of them impersonal and simply calling for the event to begin. The excitement broke Vielle's inhibitions, and she found herself joining in the clamor.

"Come on, Spril!" she shouted, "Take him down!"

Phylus dropped his binoculars on his feet with a start. Nobody seemed to care that she was blatantly wishing to see the defeat of a specified contender. Everyone was consumed in the moment, but Phylus was feeling paranoid.

Spril would have lied horribly had he denied a similar feeling. Here he was about to once again face this wall named CreSam who had surely acquired strength yet to be seen in his ascent through the ranks, but also a trigger happy mercenary sitting inconspicuously among the crowd. He knew he was walking into an ambush, but no matter how much he tried to convince himself otherwise, this was his only choice. His path of resistance led him straight into the assault. He was the last line of defense against CreSam taking control of the nation, and this was his last chance to fight back. He looked over his quarterstaff, standing tall and proud beside him.

"We've done some great work together, and you've served me well," he said to his weapon, "but here is where all our work will matter the most. Everything up to this point has been to prepare for this day. Our performance today will define us for years to come and serve to shape a nation for even longer. Let's not falter."

His pocket watch buzzed against his thigh. He and CreSam had synchronized theirs earlier, and this was his signal to enter. Using his quarterstaff like a walking stick, he walked out into the concrete arena.

In the middle of the stone field, he and CreSam stood and observed the audience towering around them in the vast sea of stadium seating. To anyone else, it may have been overwhelming, but both of these soldiers found it empowering, albeit for different reasons. Their eyes caught each other and both nodded.

CreSam withdrew his broadsword and poised himself in a warrior's stance. Spril spun his quarterstaff around his hand a couple of times and stopped it with his forearm, drawing back into a defensive stance.

"Whenever you are ready, sir, let's begin this," Spril ordered, "I expect a clean fight out of a man from the same honor as myself."

"Do you now?" CreSam asked mockingly, "Well I expect a clean victory."

CreSam lunged forth with a great and sudden aggression. Caught off guard by the comment, Spril could not defend quickly enough. He dodged instead, jumping back to avoid what could easily have been a fatal strike.

In a blink of silence between cheers and hazes, a glimpse of calm within the clamor, a mechanical snap could be heard from beyond the rafters. What followed was a whistle so shrill it cut through all other sound and sliced open the air around it. In that critical blink, the entire audience unknowingly held its breath, their future carried on a bullet.

The bullet struck flesh and bore through to the first layers in an excruciatingly eternal nanosecond of pain. Blood sprayed from the back of his head as it dug into the base of his skull. His hands trembled, and his weapon fell to the ground. His competitor appeared statuesque. As he struggled to mutter a departing statement, the bullet exploded against the base of his skull. Shards of smoldering skull were spewed from the back of his head as agonizing cries of anguish were spewed from the front, both lined with streams of blood.

His legs grew weak, and he fell to his knees. Obstinately, he tried to support himself with his weapon, but his arms had become just as useless as his legs. He looked up to see his opponent's reaction to this macabre moment that would ascertain his position as Brigadier General Elite, leader of the ArcNosian military and government. The fellow soldier slowly lowered his weapon and looked on with unwavering sternness. This was his final site as his vision was consumed in black, and he collapsed face down on the concrete in a pool of his own blood.

The mayhem ensued as it had on many nights for the past three years. Smoke consumed the air with its choking grasp. Fiery debris rained from the nether reaches of the sky, pounding into the ground like localized meteorites. Buildings buckled under the pain of shattered foundations and crumbled to the ground. Bodies were burned, gnarled and otherwise destroyed in the most gruesome of manners.

All fled from the destruction, but inevitably found their lives washed away in the tides of this nigh unstoppable onslaught. All fled except one. This one walked into the assault, not for suicide but for purpose. A certain curiosity and conviction pulled him into the blood laced smog. Through him, others passing in the opposite direction found fleeting glimpses of solace in their final breaths of mortal existence.

Horrid as what transpired was, none of it was consciously familiar.

Eytea stirred awake and rubbed the fatigue from her eyes. She yawned and stretched, her dark purple wings spreading with her arms, mimicking them. Fishing a handful of scrunchies from atop the bedside table, she pulled her hair back into three ponytails, a style she had carried for about a year now.

Dreams such as these had begun when she was thirteen, and lately they had become increasingly common. The people and the locations were all too unfamiliar in her conscious state. In her dreams however, it felt as though she recognized them all, perhaps was even intimately cognizant, though lately her subconscience was developing its own lucidity and also questioning those elements.

In the past few months, the focus of her free time had turned to sketch artistry. She was naturally adept with a pencil, drawing only freehand and strictly from what she could imagine. The subject of her sketches most often came from her dreams, even when she attempted to draw otherwise. It was her way of trying to better envision them in a waking state so that she might gain a clearer understanding of them.

Her desk was riddled with papers both new and old. Borderline panic attacks, all triggered by the dreams, had driven her to rip the pages out of all of her notebooks in an outburst of frustration. Most had been drawn on, some at the extent of her abilities and others quick passing doodles. Others were written upon. She withdrew one on which she had already drawn a picture of a weatherworn copper humanoid with four arms and water overflowing out of bowls on his hands, and she laid it face down on the desk.

Despite her confusion and resulting frustration, her pencil moved smoothly over the page. The details were more becoming more vivid with each sketch. There existed implied colors within the shades of grey. Charred bricks exhibited a nigh tangible texture, and the heat of the flames could nearly be felt radiating from the page. If not for the edges of the paper, it would feel as though one was in the scene itself, even despite the chromatic limitations thereof.

When she finished, she looked over her work, satisfied with the quality though still baffled by it all. The walker felt oddly familiar, and not just from that particular dream. She felt, somehow, a connection to him. Perhaps, she thought, he was featured in other dreams.

She shuffled through her old sketches, checking the subject of each one. Last night's dream appeared at least thrice more in lower qualities and details. In some, the physique of the walker was barely even discernable, but now she could nearly count the hairs on the back of his head. Finally, near the bottom of the pile, she found it.

A tall sturdy man stood over a slim woman, holding a pistol to her open mouth. This drawing depicted a still frame a mere moment after the trigger had been pulled. The look on the woman's face was somewhere between one of unbearable agony and one of dying rest. The man's eyes were awash with anger, power and still a bit of confusion. It was as though he had longed to pull the trigger up until the moment it finally happened. Doubts came a moment too late.

This all appeared to take place in a living room or den. In the background stood a young boy in an open door. He appeared about ten years of age. She looked closely, comparing him to the walker of more recent dreams. Judging by the head structure, they appeared to perhaps be the same person, but only seeing the back of the walker's head, she wanted a second opinion. The child's face did resemble what she recalled of the walker's.

"Mother?" she called out toward the living room, "Can you come in here a moment? There's something I'd like to show you."

After a moment, Elemeno appeared in the doorway. She flipped her reading glasses open and set them upon her face. Having anticipated being shown a sketch of her daughter's creation, she had fetched them from the end table on her way to the room.

"Got another piece of art to show me, Eytea?" she asked proudly.

"Actually, I want a second opinion on something. Come look at this."

Elemeno stood beside Eytea's chair and looked over her shoulder. Eytea used half of the new drawing to cover the shooting in the old drawing and place the two subjects closer to one another. She pointed at each of them.

"Those two, take a good look at them," she instructed, "Do you think they're the same person? They're obviously a few years apart."

Elemeno scrutinized both for a few minutes. Before long, it was apparent that she was studying more than just the two boys but rather the sketches as a whole.

"Eytea, I need to ask you something. I want you to answer honestly," Elemeno insisted, "Have you ever snuck out and gone to ArcNos?"

"What? Of course not," Eytea countered, "If I were to sneak out, it wouldn't be to there, not with how things have been going lately. Why?"

"So you've never seen it?"

"I couldn't tell you the first thing about it, honestly."

"Well, apparently your dreams can," Elemeno noted, "This cityscape is clearly ArcNosian, and I know what this means. Today is the day I've awaited for fourteen years."

"It is? You do? What?"

"Follow me out to the stable, Eytea," Elemeno beckoned as she left Eytea's bedroom, "By the way, yes I think they are the same person."

Eytea appeared to glide across the floor as she walked, her violet wings tucked behind her for the sake of the decor. In her eagerness, Elemeno moved quickly while Eytea stayed a few steps behind. Out at the stable, Elemeno stopped just outside the door and waited for Eytea to catch up.

"Do you remember talking to Chieftain Sage Gijin when you were two?"

"No sorry, Mom. Toddler memory isn't in my repertoire of super powers," Eytea answered slyly.

"Hah, very funny," Elemeno scoffed, "Anyway, he told me that the marks on your back, now your wings, were a sign of greatness. He also said that you were to be some sort of hero once the time came. Well, your dream about the destruction of an ArcNosian city along with the recent shift of power over there seems like a sign that that time is drawing near. So, I need to pass something on to you. It's buried where I stand, has been for fourteen years."

The two of them each took a shovel from the stable and began digging. Eytea was silently absorbing all that had been said. Instinct had told her, from the day her wings sprouted, that she had been given them for some greater purpose. However, the knowledge that it involved the call of the Chieftain Sage of Berinin was overwhelming. That was not to mention the fact that he had sought her during her toddler years to ensure that she was not led astray at any point in her life. Whatever her calling, it was obviously one of an utmost importance. Her thoughts were interrupted when the shovel struck wood.

"There it is," Elemeno announced, "Take it out and have a look at it."

Eytea gripped the revealed cylindrical segment of wood. She pulled upward, thus forcing the rest of it through its earthen confines. As the dirt poured from it, its identity gradually became clear. Now fully exposed, she erected it by her side, shook the dirt from it, and looked it over.

"Is this a halberd?" she asked.

"Exactly that," Elemeno confirmed, "This is what Gijin wished me to give you when the time was right, and like I said, now seems perfect."

Eytea admired the craftsmanship of her new gift. The grip fit perfectly in her hands. The blades shimmered even after their years beneath the soil and exhibited edges and tips both graceful and fatal. The handle appeared as though it had nary aged a day in the oft trodden dirt, much less fourteen years.

"So then, this is my calling, is it?" she said, swinging the weapon and following with a thrust at the air, "I'm to be a warrior?"

"Apparently so, my dear."

Eytea swung the weapon about, showing an amateur status with latent expertise. This potential would come with practice, of course. Elemeno watched proudly, having already come to terms with the notion of her daughter running off into battle. She trusted her daughter would find the strength to be victorious, no matter the endeavor, and that the other heroes of which Gijin spoke would keep her alive. They would watch over each other as a tightly bound group of elite destined heroes.

"You know, something just occurred to me," Eytea brought up in the middle of her practice, "Didn't Father say he was going on a business trip last week?"

"Yes, what about it?"

"The past few he's been on, there just happened to be sizable developments in ArcNos at the same time," Eytea explained, "Brigadier General Elite HarEin's death, the only Negotiator in the outfit suddenly losing his job, and now CreSam's rise to power."

"What are you getting at?" Elemeno cautiously asked.

"Do you think Father has something to do with it? Like, maybe he's been working with CreSam all this time?"

Elemeno's mind traced back over the years, hoping to find a way to disprove the theory. Though she loathed Kabehl immensely, she didn't want to think of him as being so terrible as to participate in the corruption of a respectable republic such as ArcNos or any other nation in Ouristihra, for that matter. All she found, though, was more evidence of her daughter's suspicion.

"Actually I think you're right," she reluctantly agreed, "and it's been going on for longer than that. Fourteen years ago, a waterlogged corpse in an Infantryman uniform washed ashore from the north. Your father was gone that day, too. All he said was that he was going north. I… I think he may have killed that man."

The gate opened, abruptly interrupting their conversation. Two booted footsteps followed the sound of the gate closing. They both turned to look as Eytea lowered her halberd.

"You think who may have killed whom?" Kabehl asked.

"Oh, nothing, we were just talking about a novel we've been reading," Elemeno fibbed.

"No Mother, there's no reason to lie," Eytea insisted, stepping toward her father, "She thinks you killed the man that washed ashore from the north when I was a toddler, and I think you've done worse."

Kabehl folded his arms and laughed.

"Oh really? And what do you suppose I've done?"

"Well, I think you killed HarEin. You fired the Negotiator. And you pulled some strings to put CreSam in office."

"Heh, there's proof enough that you don't know as much as you think. HarEin's death was not my doing, although I do know the man who slew him. I did not fire Phylus. CreSam did so voluntarily to bolster our plan. But yes, I did play a part in putting him in his position. It's what I do, you see," Kabehl explained, "After all, that's why they call me The Scout at work."

"Proof enough?" Eytea scoffed, "Sounds to me like proof enough that facing you is part of my role as a destined hero."

"Facing me? Well then, let's see exactly what you know of destiny," Kabehl barked, drawing a metal cylinder from a holster on his belt, "Halberd, is it? Show me what you've got, then."

He held a button with his thumb and slid a switch with his index finger. A gray tubular grid extended from the end of the pipe, stretching to a total length of about two meters. Two blades formed at the end, one of an axe, the other of a spear. It was a wire frame halberd. Color filled the grid, which vanished upon completion. Now a hologram, it was still translucent. It acquired opacity, and with it solidity. Kabehl twirled it dexterously around his wrist, snatched it in his hand, and snapped back into a warrior's stance.

"Part of being The Scout for the most powerful guild in Ouristihra is knowing my way around a considerable variety of armaments, largely for training purposes," Kabehl explained, "Now let's have this hero business you're so worked up on."

Eytea lunged and leapt forth, thrusting her wings back for momentum. She swung with explosive force, only to have the blow deflected by the axe blade of her father's solidified hologram. Despite its electronic origins, it was nothing short of the authentic issue. Kabehl countered, only to find his attack knocked off course. This continued for several minutes, both building momentum in their strikes and recoveries. Soon, there was no discerning between attacks and counters as the two dodged swings and crossed blades repeatedly.

In a fleeting blink of clumsiness, Kabehl's tenacity faded. As she deflected yet another thrust, Eytea swatted his halberd from his grip. As it skipped along the dirt, the device shut down, and the hologram faded to nothing. She lunged forth and thrust the spear at his throat, stopping just short of the flesh.

"Part of being a destined hero of calling by the Chieftain Sage is adapting to any situation and learning quickly what I must know for my role," Eytea hissed.

"Destiny? What do you know of your destiny when you barely know who you truly are?" Kabehl jeered, "By the way, your wings no longer disturb me. My employer explained the situation to me, and now I know exactly who you are. He was quite pleased, in fact, that I knew you. You see, you were right about one thing in your destiny. You and I are on opposite sides."

"I've heard enough!"

Kabehl sidestepped as Eytea lunged, dodging the thrust of her blade. She turned quickly and placed the other blade to the side of his neck.

"But how pitifully amateur of you to strike now," he continued, "The queen advancing on the rook out of position? Please, you have no idea of the game you're in, much less of your role."

Eytea eased her tension involuntarily, confused by his statement. Kabehl lunged and barked at her. She jumped a bit, but what happened to her halberd was entirely more startling. The blade glowed for a split second, and a bolt of lightning ripped from the tip and struck the ground several meters behind him. Smoke rose into the wind from the freshly blackened patch of soil.

"Just as I thought. Despite what you may already have learned, you cannot fathom who you really are."

She pulled the blade back and aimed the tip at his neck. Instinctively, she recreated the effect and fired another bolt at his throat. Despite being at pointblank range, she missed. The bolt split in two and forked off along either side of his neck.

"Oh, I should also tell you that part of my job is coming equipped with the necessary protections, especially against threats that sit right under my nose," Kabehl taunted.

Eytea thrust the spearhead against his throat. Blood trickled down his neck, pooling on his clavicle before running down the front of his shirt. She stopped suddenly, overcome with last minute grief. Despite their alignments, he was still her biological father. Even after all that had happened, she couldn't bring herself to drive the spear into his neck, no matter how many times she had wished she could end the pain.

"Heh, so weak," he muttered, "After all I've done to you and all that you now know, you still don't have the guts to strike down your enemy. You've created the perfect opportunity to make the best of a terrible move, and now you're going to ruin this as well, all because you're too weak to kill me."

"You're right. I can't do it," Eytea admitted, retracting her weapon, "but I know someone who can."

Eytea's nodded toward Kabehl's right shoulder. He glanced back nervously and was met by a hand gripping a length of rope. Startled, he looked over his left and found another hand and Elemeno's face.

"Hello dear," Elemeno said, wrapping the rope around his neck, "How amateur for the rook to assume checkmate when a pawn is sitting ready to take him out. Wouldn't you agree?"

She jerked the ends of the rope, tightening her grip on his neck. His face reddened as his expression quickly faded from anger to excruciating pain. He tried to call out in anguish, but his voice was trapped in his constricted throat. The blood stopped dripping from his neck, the rope acting as a tourniquet.

"I hope your employer has a good human resources department," Elemeno mocked, "because he's about to need a new scout."

Eytea raised her halberd to her shoulder. Kabehl found an iota of strength and reached back to clutch at the fabric of Elemeno's pants. She stumbled slightly, her grip loosening for a brief second.

"Eytea, now!" she shouted, hastily restoring her hold.

Eytea delivered a backhand swing with the greatest force she could muster, the axe blade turned away from its target. The butt of the blade struck his face with a resonating crack and forced its way across. His head jerked while the sound of bones cracking reverberated through his flesh and down the pole of her halberd. Snapped fragments of upper spine stabbed through his skin. Blood trickled down his shoulders. She withdrew her halberd, and his head fell limp. Elemeno loosened her grip, and he collapsed with blood pouring from his wounds.

Elemeno and Eytea stood over him, watching the life wash from his body while catching their breath. Both had learned things that cannot be forgotten and seen what cannot be unseen. And through it, they had done what could never be undone. For years, they had longed to be free from his abuse, but now both had the blood of murder staining their hands. By his claims of employment, it was undoubtedly one that

would hurl them both into a future of endless conflict.
Eytea had just dived headlong into her destiny.

72

Chapter 7

White waves sloshed against the shore in a constant line of churning foam. Beyond these, the sea rolled in a steady motion. That is, aside from the occasional bubble popping silently upon the shimmering surface.

Some score of meters below the smooth waves, Galo sat in silence. With weights strapped to his shins and forearms for ballast, he meditated upon the ocean floor. His gills pulsated in a rhythm synchronized with the waves above. Each inhalation was deeply drawn, extracting both oxygen and energy from the surrounding water as though he was cherry picking the most nourishing molecules. His hair billowed around him, suspended in the water.

Across his lap sat his glaive, the sword of the sea as Gijin had called it. The salt water had inflicted no adverse effect upon the handle or the head. The wood had not weakened, and the metal shimmered just as brightly as it had the day he received it. In fact, the water seemed to enhance its gleam.

His torso shuddered with the steady draw of energy and transcendental levels of concentration. A strangely warm chill tingled and vibrated up his spine from deep within, and the surrounding water trembled with him. As his body relaxed, the water continued to churn.

His eyelids flickered like candle flames as he succumbed to rapid eye movement in his state of heightened consciousness. In his mind's eye, he could see his body at the bottom of the ocean. The water diverged from his body as he exhaled and magnetized to him as he inhaled. With each draw of oxygen and energy, his movements became more synchronous with his environs. No longer did he sit at the bottom of the sea, but now he was becoming a part of it.

The shuddering ceased entirely. His eyelids fell calm. His breathing held its rhythm, and the water around him continued to shudder.

He opened his eyes to find he could see far more clearly than usual through the salty seawater. Blurry though his surroundings still were, the improvement was beyond notable. He rose to his feet, held fast to the sea floor by the weights and resisting the ocean's will by virtue of his own strength and balance. Gracefully, he shifted his body into a warrior stance, his hand tenaciously gripping his glaive.

He thrust his palm heel forth. At full extension, a ripple of water rushed forth from his hand. He smirked, removed the weights, and dropped to a crouch. With a powerful leap, he launched himself toward the surface. A series of ripples streamed behind him as though they were propelling his body, carrying it to the surface at a steadily accelerating pace.

His body ripped abruptly through the waves, much to the startle of the shoreline onlookers. Aided by a jet of water, he pushed himself about a meter above the surface. He spun sideways in the air, executing a high arcing kick followed by a similar hook kick. Arcs of water shot from his feet, but they stayed intact rather than spraying apart. In midair, he thrust his palm heel toward the water. A sheet of water burst from his hand and froze just before meeting with the surface. Galo landed upon the sheet of ice on his hands and knees

He rose to his feet, glaive in hand and standing proudly. His breath was heavy as his gills closed and his lungs reclaimed control. The waves carried him toward the Masnethegean shore as he looked onward to his people gathered upon the beach and in knee deep breakers. In the middle of the crowd stood Gijin, watching his grandson with great admiration. He met him at the shore as he jumped off of the sheet of ice.

"My child, you've done it," Gijin congratulated, "and with such a breakthrough of control."

"Thank you, Grandpa. I surprised myself as well with that sudden display of power," Galo gasped, still catching his breath.

"Ah ah, be wary of where you place your faith. Power means nothing without appropriate maintenance. Be not one who seeks strength without first finding wisdom and thus knowing control," Gijin warned.

"I understand," Galo complied, "So can you tell me anything more about your talk of destined heroes? I would like to know exactly what I am."

"You are not a what, my boy; you are a who, regardless of your gills and hydromancy," Gijin clarified, "And I will tell you more later today. Now is not the time."

"Now is not the time? Can I ask why not?"

"Because, Sinkua isn't here yet. He should be arriving any minute now."

Galo looked back to the watery horizon. There was no sign of a boat in the distance. He looked over his grandfather, studying his demeanor carefully. He contemplated the possibilities.

"Did Sinkua… send you a letter earlier?"

"No, my boy. Just as you did now, your brother had a breakthrough last night, as well. As we both know him, he most likely set sail to visit us shortly thereafter."

"Grandpa, how do you know of his accomplishment?"

"Call it clairvoyance."

The two of them began walking up the beach and toward their hut. Galo had so many questions racing through his mind that it was difficult to determine which to ask first and which not to ask at all.

"Clairvoyance? So you can see ether and spirits?" Galo asked, "I never knew that of you."

"No, not exactly. My clairvoyance involves a different type of energy. You're thinking of common spiritual energy call tsora, possessed by all living things. The energies which I can sense are carried only by Hybrids such as yourself."

"I suppose these energies are what fuel my hydromancy."

"Exactly right. It's an energy which was once known the world over as milystis."

His eyes shot open with a sudden start, faintly illuminating his face for a fleeting moment. The blankets atop his body rose and fell with his deep heavy breathing. He was wide awake now, but outside, the sky was still pitch black.

Dense nimbostratus clouds conquered the sky, swallowing the light of the moons and stars. It was a rather perfect backdrop for the nightmare, and with every passing eve, he feared that nightmare was becoming a reality.

Sinkua sat himself up, his body heavy with fear and anxiety from his nocturnal terrors. Sweat coated his torso, despite being in the midst of The Frigid. He reached over the side of the bed and fumbled for something in particular.

His thick hair moist with sweat, he tied a red bandana around his head and wrapped it over the top, leaving two tails hanging down his neck in the back. Thick locks of hair ending in dull points hung from it on all sides, his bangs shrouding his eyes. He scratched at the facial hair around his lips and exhaled heavily, trying to calm his body of the aftershock of the night terror.

"That same dream again," he mumbled, "but this time, so much more vivid."

His nightmares were abundant, but one in particular occurred the most often by far. It was the one he had the night before he embarked on his journey away from CreSam, away from ArcNos, and away from enlistment. This one had returned to haunt him numerous times, often multiple times in a week. On nights when his sleep was interrupted, it would sometimes invade his subconscience twice.

Stranger still was the fact that this particular dream aged. Unlike the one of his mother's death, which was a clipping of memory immortalized in dreams, this one developed with time. His self in this nightmare now carried the morningstar and the dagger. On the day he received his red bandana in a trade with a Berininite, that night he wore it in the nightmare.

The people of the city didn't age so much as decompose. Those already dead when he arrived looked as though their corpses had already begun to rot. The ones who died in his presence met more gruesome ends, as though their bodies had become increasingly fragile.

The firepower of the ArcNosian military grew to the point that buildings and vehicles crumbled seemingly at their will. Their strength was becoming decreasingly combatable and nigh immeasurable. The voice in the war machine was becoming more distinguishable, as well as more prominent and foreboding. It sounded undeniably like CreSam, but lately it no longer referred to him as MeiLom nor as the son of a soldier. Oddly enough though, it still offered a chance to surrender, albeit at the ends of innumerable blades, gun barrels, and missile bays.

This time though, it was too real. Sinkua could no longer shake the suspicion of remnants of truth in his nightmare. It wasn't necessarily an exact truth but more of an implication. Perhaps, they were a reflection of the developments in ArcNos, the shift of military power, and his role in it all, as well as CreSam's.

His own strength had also developed considerably. He stood over a hundred ninety centimeters tall with broad sturdy shoulders. The morningstar was no longer a tool but rather an extension of either arm, more so his right than his left. The dagger, on the other hand, had remained unused since he was still contemplating its purpose.

That was not to say that it remained in its holster at all times. He had withdrawn it on several occasions to examine and admire the intricate craftwork. It appeared ancient in design, but felt like it defied the very concept of aging, as though it had transcended the passage of time. An abundance of mystery was carried in this blade, but he trusted Gijin when he assured him that the rest would come in time.

He felt a swell of heat over his chest. In his right hand, he clutched the medallion. It radiated with warmth, and when he looked down, he witnessed the last seconds of its fading glow. Indeed, the dream was becoming more of a reality. He dropped the medallion as he set his feet on the floor, and he stepped outside into the cold night's air, glancing down once more to the silent gemstone upon his chest.

"Your answers are so close to me," he muttered behind the harsh wind, "but still they escape me when I awaken."

A few centimeters of faintly trodden snow blanketed the landscape. None fell from the sky, though a storm appeared to be impending. It was one of an unusual nature, at that. The scent of the air suggested a blizzard, yet the clouds foreshadowed a thunderstorm. Sinkua looked out over the forest, the snow hugging his ankles. Clumps of icy powder fell from limbs and onto his shoulders, melting shortly after impact. He adjusted his bandana and embarked further into the forest.

He aimed for nowhere in particular, simply away from the cabin. Staying inside after those nightmares only led to anxiety and further sleeplessness. About a year ago, he had taken to walking them off. A brisk hike typically helped to clear his mind, but tonight, something about the backdrop of the weather kept it lingering in the most inevitably accessible reaches of his thoughts. Although perhaps, it may have only seemed to be a result of the weather. Such thoughts only served to confuse and frustrate him further though.

Despite going nowhere in particular, he moved with aggression. His head stayed low, as though he was avoiding eye contact with the trees. Feelings of hatred were swelling along with ones of doubt and fear. With all of these came feelings of shame.

As he stepped, he could feel the snow melting under his feet. The medallion now emanated a steady warmth. Snow fell lightly from the clouds now. Though it accumulated on the ground, it melted upon impact with his shoulders. The medallion's energy was enveloping him and protecting him from the harsh conditions of The Frigid.

On the side of a nearby tree, he spotted a pudgy chipmunk. Most of them had gone into hiding for the season, but this one in particular had fallen behind. Perhaps he was stubborn, or perhaps he failed to prepare for the change of seasons. Regardless of the history behind the chipmunk's circumstances, his misfortune was Sinkua's boon.

Having traded many of his crops to the Berininites, his surplus had been depleted. He had left himself enough for the dead months, but most of it fell victim to the weather, regardless of his best preventative efforts. The meat had all been eaten as well. Now, with his food supplies so low that he neared the point of desperation, a potential meal was perched upon the side of a trunk.

There also sat an opportunity for crafts and trade. He had taken to using other parts of the animals he slew, such as bones for tools and the hides to make various cloth goods. A chipmunk of this size would make for a nice hat or a pair of gloves if he could stretch the hide enough. Either could be swapped with a Berininite for something of more use to him, like another meal.

He reached into the snow and fished out a rock about the size of the chipmunk's head. The rodent appeared oblivious, resting on the side of the tree the same as it had when Sinkua first eyed it. He swiftly pitched the stone at the chipmunk and struck the back of its head. It dropped from the tree and plopped onto the snowy cushion below, dead before landing. Sinkua approached the victim, but he stopped short when a heavy rustling caught his ear.

Nearby browned foliage shook about, and the sound of clawed footsteps in the snow could be heard. He slowly continued his approach, but he kept his eyes on the bush. His pulse quickened. As he reached down to fetch his victim, a rapid flash of teeth and claws burst from the dying thicket.

He dropped the chipmunk and jumped back to dodge the pounce. An adult hyena stood before him, prowling menacingly from side to side. It had been eying the chipmunk and waited for someone else to do the work of hunting it. The hyena snarled and snapped. Sinkua took a defensive stance, mirroring the movements of the hyena. Any closer, he knew, and it would attack. Any further, and it would pilfer his kill.

The hyena stopped, still watching Sinkua, and stepped toward the chipmunk. It snagged it in its mouth nonchalantly. Not wanting to risk losing a meal, Sinkua lunged at it, hoping to at least frighten it.

"Think you can steal my dinner?" he snapped.

At Sinkua's show of aggression, the hyena dropped the chipmunk. He reared back and snarled, his coarse hair standing on end. His eyes filling with bitter rage, he snapped and spat at Sinkua. When Sinkua bent down to take the chipmunk, he struck.

Sinkua found himself now at eye level with what he first saw burst from the brush. Teeth and claws lunged forth with an aggression driven by hunger and now anger as well. He stood up hastily and stumbled back.

"Son of a bitch!"

He raised his forearms to block his face as the teeth closed in, ready to bear down upon his flesh. The medallion swelled with warmth. His forearms shuddered; he felt a strange sort of spiritual adrenaline surge through him. Teeth struck his forearm and punctured the skin. As the blood began to trickle, with a sudden flash of heat and light, his hands and wrists were alight with flames and scorching the hyena's fur.

The hyena fell to the ground, whimpering and rolling in the snow to douse its head. It eyed Sinkua cautiously and fearfully. Sinkua looked at his hands, bewildered by what had just happened. He felt frightened initially, but that quickly passed and was replaced with awe.

As he thought more about it, he found thrill in what had happened. This was the true power of the medallion, and he was the one it had chosen at its bearer. He gained a greater understanding of what being an Hybrid meant. That aside, it answered his questions about his role regarding the events in ArcNos. If anyone were to stand against a military force anywhere near as strong as the one in his nightmare, a power such as his would prove indispensable. It seemed all too perfect when he recalled CreSam's pyrophobia.

He chuckled menacingly. Meanwhile, the hyena had backed away, beginning what it hoped to be a tactical retreat. Sinkua spotted it and his grimace became a sneer. The hyena made eye contact and turned to run.

"You're not going anywhere!"

He gave chase in full sprint. The two of them tore across the snowy landscape, kicking up powder and forest debris. They shredded through withering foliage and snapped low twigs and branches. The snow slowed the hyena's run and, to its chagrin, Sinkua gradually closed in. Calculating that he was near enough, Sinkua instinctively reignited his fists and leapt at the scavenger.

He came down upon the hyena and pinned it to the ground, smothering it in the snow. It writhed and struggled to break free, as its fur was set afire in Sinkua's clutches. Fists ablaze, he ferociously pummeled the back of its head with devastating blows. Flames engulfed its head, and it yelped in anguish. Sinkua pulled his right arm back, swelled the flame, and came down with crushing force. The back of the hyena's skull cracked with this final strike, and it lay dead beneath him.

He let his breathing slow to a more tolerable rate. His mind raced back over what had just happened as well as the events leading up to it. His purpose, his nature, and his birthright were all becoming clearer to him. In a moment of revelation, he withdrew his dagger and held it over the hyena's head.

"This night is a landmark in my development as an Hybrid and in my survival as well. It has led me to answers I've sought for many years," he announced, "My encounter with you brought about this landmark, and I fought for it. Tonight, this is that for which I fight, to survive and to develop myself for what's to be my mission."

With those words, he buried the blade in the hyena's neck, and a light tingle ran up his spine.

Broken glass lay scattered over the sidewalks alongside shops reduced to ruin. Structural foundations had grown weak, and fragments of brick and wood were strewn about inside buildings as well as among the glass on the concrete. Garbage bins lay on their side with wiry mutts feeding upon scraps too old to be identified by sight alone. As a whole, the people scarcely looked in better shape than the dogs or the refuse.

Many of them had fallen ill from malnutrition and sleeping in the rain. In tattered clothes stained by blood and storm, they wandered the dilapidated avenues without direction but not without destination. Some looked for answers. Others looked for a way out of the situation. Others still looked for a way out at all. One year had passed since Brigadier General Elite CreSam had been inaugurated, and the outskirts of the capital of ArcNos had been eviscerated.

All formal trade existed exclusively within the military facilities, allowing this new leader to control every aspect of the economy. Although, he was more of a ruler than a leader. This removed all jobs from the city, leaving most of the populous unemployed. A few refused to join the military for the sake of employment as a show of their own pride and loathing for what it had become. Most, however, were on the streets inevitably.

Formerly established business agreements stated that, once released from a position, one could never again find employment in that particular organization. Those terminated during the federal takeovers could not return to those companies in any capacity, nor to any of the others that had been overtaken since they were all under the same ownership. New modifications denied immediate family, as well. Moreover, CreSam had acquired the right to filter all applications for enlistment, allowing only those he approved, for any reason he wished. Also, those released from military positions could never rejoin or work for any organization under federal control.

Among the victims to such circumstances was Phylus. He sat against the side of a rundown antique shop, his elbows resting on his knees with a cigarette between his thumb and forefinger. His hair was matted with rain and dirt. Beside him always was Vielle, clinging to what optimism she could scrape together.

At that moment, for her, it may have been a bit easier than for others. While her hair was also matted, her skin dirty and riddled with flakes, she sat not upon a filthy sidewalk. Rather, her seat happened to double as a basket of apples. She and her father were each enjoying a piece of fruit as best they could despite the conditions of everything else.

Regardless of the state of things, few people had succumbed to a life of figurative cannibalism. In fact, what was once a city of strangers was becoming more of a community. Everybody had next to nothing, but they generally looked out for each other. People who walked by often nodded or waved as though they were friends with the two of them. They had met most of them no more than once though, if at all. Nonetheless, they had become extended family. One particular citizen, a withering middle aged man, stopped when he saw them eating apples with many more to spare.

"Excuse me, miss," he greeted, "but where did you get those fine looking apples, eh?"

Vielle swallowed the bite and cleared her throat, thrown off by the syntax of the question. She chuckled to herself, embarrassed by her own thoughts.

"We found an apple tree," she answered, tossing one of the fruits to him, "You know that bridge about a kilometer east of here? Go there, and head down the hill to the creek. Turn left and head upstream and into the forest. A couple of kilometers back, there's an abandoned arboretum."

"Things have been growing awfully well down there ever since we first visited, too," Phylus added, "Makes you think maybe someone is on our side."

All the man could manage was a smile. He nodded his gratitude and rushed off to the east to find the orchard. From the looks of him, it seemed weeks had passed since he last ate anything of notable sustenance. After he was out of earshot, Phylus turned to Vielle.

"You know, Vielle, you put a smile on a lot of people's faces out here," he told her.

"Yeah yeah, I know, Dad. Men are perverts," she agreed, "But I can't help it. These shorts and this old shirt of yours are the only clothes I have."

"What? No. Well, yes they are, but that's not what I meant," he clarified, trying to hide his embarrassment, "I mean your optimism is contagious."

"Oh no, don't get the wrong idea, Dad, I'm not optimistic at all. I lost optimism a few months ago. What I have is hope, a lot like optimism but far more realistic. Optimism is believing that things will get better. Hope is knowing that things can get better, even if there's barely a chance."

"How'd you get so articulate, huh?"

"Well, look who raised me," she said with a smile, "Best Negotiator around, of course I'm going to pick up a few things."

Phylus snickered through his teeth as he took another bite of his apple.

"Well either way, you've got charisma going for you," he complimented, "and at a time like this, the people could use someone like you."

"It's hard to hold on to, you know," she admitted, "what with Uncle Spril being gone."

Phylus sighed and closed his eyes. He shuddered as his mind took him back to that evening when Spril was assassinated. To be accurate, murdered was a better word for what happened. A year later, the images were still as vivid as when he witnessed the atrocity.

Vielle placed her hand gently upon his shoulder. She closed her eyes and sighed with him, consoling herself as much as she was him. Many nights, horrific flashbacks of that evening returned to her in dreams. The bullet ripped through the air in slow motion, literally choking the breath from people's mouths as it passed. As Spril collapsed to the floor, so too did many of the spectators in the stands. It had become surreal and metaphorical, but these traits only served to drive the pain deeper within, burying it nigh irrevocably.

They both opened their eyes and looked up again. Phylus took a long drag from his cigarette, reducing it to near its butt. Vielle got to her feet and stood out on the edge of the sidewalk, leaning one hand against a lamp post.

"You know, some mornings, I wake up expecting to see him here with us," she confessed, "That's what makes it so hard to cling to hope, so often thinking we'll see him again, only to be disappointed every time."

"I know how you feel, Vielle. Try to hold on though," Phylus assured her, "We're fast approaching the days when hope may be the only thing left to hold the people together."

Vielle gazed long and deep down the street in each direction, first to the east, then to the west. To the east was the bridge, the first landmark on the way to the orchard. To the west were the outskirts of the flourishing and rapidly expanding military establishment. Something closer, however, caught her attention. A flight of stairs led under the sidewalk. Epiphany struck.

"The Subtransit, of course!" she remarked with a smile in her voice.

"Hm? What about it?"

"Dad, we're going home."

"What? Oh no, we can't go home, remember?" Phylus reminded her, "Even if we can take a Subtransit train into our old neighborhood to get past the guards, they'd spot us as soon as we surface. Besides, soldiers live in our house now, and we can't fight them off."

"That's not what I meant, Dad. I mean we're about to have a home. We all are," she corrected, "How are you at rallying a mob?"

"Never tried it," Phylus shrugged, "You're the one with the charisma though. You give it a try."

With his blessing, she ran off into the streets, hoping to unite the people under the common cause of reclamation and reformation.

His eyelids slowly flickered open, the light of a dim lamp greeting him. He was groggy and dizzy, felt like he had slept for weeks. The room was unfamiliar, but that was not the foremost of his concerns. Every joint in his body had grown stiff in his sleep. He sat up slowly, his elbows and spine popping along the way.

"You're finally awake," a female voice greeted softly, "I was worried that you'd never come out of your coma."

"Yeah. Good morning," he returned, "Where am I?"

"You're safe. That's all that matters."

He looked at her, his neck cracking as he turned his head, and smiled at the familiar face.

"You brought me here, huh? That was nice of you."

"Even after all this time, you still recognize me? I'm flattered."

He turned to place his feet on the floor and gradually stood up. He rubbed the back of his head, which was throbbing with pain.

"Do you have anything for a headache?" he asked, "My skull is killing me."

"No sorry," she said, "I don't think any sort of drugs would be a good idea right now."

"Okay, you're the doctor."

"Are you ready to start your physical rehabilitation?"

"Can it wait?"

"Of course it can. I understand if you need a few days to recuperate mentally first."

"No, I don't need a few days, just a few hours. I'm starving. I could really go for some breakfast, and a lot of it."

"What? Oh, of course. I'll cook something up for you."

"Really?" he asked, surprised by the continued charity, "Thank you for everything, Yrlis."

Chapter 8

A man in his early forties stood out on the northern edge of the peninsula with a telescope in his hands. Behind him stood another man, a couple of years younger, straining to see beyond the watery horizon.

"What do you see out there, Nenbard?" the younger man asked.

The elder of the two stared hard into the telescope, trying to discern the blurred vision just beyond the horizon. As moments passed, it gradually became clearer. A fleet of ships approached. As the nearest row came more clearly into view, another emerged behind it. Aside from waiting out the fleet, there was no way to ascertain the number of ships. He had seen quite enough as it was though.

"They're coming, Ocronn," Nenbard warned, "They will arrive by evening."

"An ArcNosian aquatic fleet approaches?" Ocronn asked, "Very well. What would you have me do, sir?"

"Undoubtedly, they come for the Sacred City," Nenbard postulated, lowering his telescope, "Head south to Masnethege. Warn the Chieftain Sage of the impending attack."

"Are you certain they intend to attack?"

"Absolutely. A fleet such as that comes not to discuss politics, my friend, especially not from what ArcNos has become in the past year."

"Very well, sir. Shall we send reinforcements, as well?"

"No. Just warn him. We will hold them off as best we can from here. I am confident that they can manage against the rest or at least flee to safety in the meantime."

With Nenbard's orders, Ocronn left on foot for the capitol of Berinin.

The curled blade sliced gracefully through the breaking tide, arcs of mist fanning from it with every swipe. Galo stood in nearly waist deep waters, carving the sea with his glaive. Just as the morningstar had with Sinkua, it was fast becoming an extension of his being rather than a separately existing tool. His hydromancy allowed him agile movement in rough waters, almost as unhindered as in open air. Now and again, he would freeze the spray of water from his blade, or create a larger fan of water much like a liquid blade.

He trained in his robe, its mass resisting his motion in waters of that depth. Enveloping his forearm was a copper bracer, its surface greened by the salty mist. Its shape was that of a mighty serpent, coiled around his forearm with the head resting atop his wrist and looking down the back of his hand as though it was keeping guard.

This Serpent Bracer was a gift from Gijin, presented to him on his sixteenth birthday. It was yet another relic of unspoken origins, and Galo suspected that it also served some greater purpose, one that would reveal itself in time. As these relics accumulated, Galo began to offer credence to foreign rumors that his grandfather was some sort of oracle. Regardless of his true nature, he was family nonetheless, and they both had been born as something remarkable. Galo was an Hybrid, and he felt quite fortunate to have been born into a family with some knowledge of such things.

A man tore through the foliage to the north, his body sticky with sweat and bloody with fresh thorn scratches. Galo ceased his training and walked inland. The visitor approached his and Gijin's hut and reached for the flap.

"Stop there, my friend," Galo called.

"I'm sorry, but I've come with a message for the Chieftain Sage," the man beckoned.

"He meditates at the moment. Please, do not interrupt him," Galo insisted as he approached the visitor.

"Oh, pardon my intrusion then," he apologized, "I was asked to deliver the message to the Chieftain Sage himself though."

"You may give it to me as an intermediary. I am his grandson, Chieftain Heir Galo," Galo offered, "So, what is your message?"

"Chieftain Heir Galo? I see. Excuse my indiscretion."

"Water under the bridge, my friend."

"Thank you, sir. My name is Ocronn; I'm from the northeastern peninsula of Berinin," Ocronn introduced

"You ran here all the way from the northernmost point of the island?" Galo interrupted, his eyebrows raised.

"I walked some of the way, but yes sir. Endurance is far from lacking in me," Ocronn explained, "As I was saying, a few hours ago, my friend Nenbard spotted a fleet of ArcNosian ships approaching from the north."

"Oh, you're an associate of Judge Nenbard?" Galo asked.

"I'm his brother-in-law, actually. So yes."

"I see. Now about this fleet?"

"Right then. We believe they come for your village, perhaps the Chieftain Sage himself. You have until nightfall to either fortify or flee. Those back in town will hold them off for as long as they can, but their efforts will not be enough to stop them."

"How many ships in this fleet, Ocronn?" Galo asked.

"Countless, sir."

"I see," Galo sighed, losing himself in thought for a moment, "Ocronn, return to your town. I request that you and Judge Nenbard remove yourselves from their line of travel and prepare a small boat, kept discreet. Return here at midnight."

"Very well, sir. In the interim, what will you do?"

Galo looked over the sea toward the southeast. His lips curled into a confident smirk.

"I will head southeast," Galo answered, "Worry not about me. All I ask is that you look out for yourself and your friend."

"You would flee, sir? Hardly the course of action I was expecting from one of your ilk."

"Flee? Hardly. I go to fortify, Ocronn," Galo explained, "We have something of a secret weapon out there."

"I see," Ocronn answered, dubious of such a claim, "Best of luck, my friend."

Galo watched as Ocronn turned and ran back into the thick foliage. As he disappeared in the brush, Galo nodded, silently bidding both thank you and farewell. He glanced over his shoulder to his and Gijin's hut. Gijin's breathing was heavy enough to be heard outside.

He pulled the edge of the flap aside and peeked inside. Gijin's hair billowed in the windless room, his body faintly trembling. Something was stirring within him, but all Galo could do was wait, no matter the pain of watching his grandfather struggle. Part of him felt it unkind to leave with him in such a state, but a greater part knew it unwise to stay with the ArcNosian fleet just hours away.

"Destiny approaches, Grandfather," he whispered breathlessly, "It's time I prepared a welcoming committee."

Perhaps it was his imagination, but Galo could see Gijin's trembling eased by those words. He raised an eyebrow, watching a moment longer. Indeed, it had lightened notably. It was as though he heard his inaudible farewell. Galo smiled and backed out of the doorway.

He approached the breakers with his eyes fixed on the horizon, looking toward Sinkua's haven island. Along the shore was a line of canoes and dinghies, each fastened to a different post by a length of rope. He began to untie one of the ropes, struggling with the tangled fibers.

Frustrated, he stood up, rubbing the back of his neck. He looked toward the north, trying to envision the approaching fleet. After a moment of thought, he pulled his glaive from the holster on his back and he chopped through the rope in a single swipe, leaving an eyesore of woven fibers hanging off the post.

In the canoe, he sat in a meditative pose with his glaive lying across his lap. His hands were folded over it, and he closed his eyes. He meditated both to align his thoughts for the impending attack as well as to focus his hydromancy. Simultaneously, he hoped for the strength to save the people who could not save themselves.

Though he did not paddle, he still moved the boat. Rather, he used his influence over water to push a steady stream back from behind the canoe, propelling it in the desired direction. This passive employment of his power helped him to maintain control and build endurance.

His eyes opened suddenly. He looked first toward Berinin, then toward Sinkua's island. Neither was in sight. Silencing his aquatic influence, he allowed the boat to come to a gradual stop. Glaive in hand, he leapt from the edge of the canoe, diving gracefully into the sea and slipping through the water with scarcely a ripple.

Below the surface and beneath the canoe, he breathed deeply of the oxygen in the water. His hands were turned upward at his sides, water churning around them. He closed his eyes for a moment, building the orbs of white rapids in his hands. With each one the size of a coconut, he opened his eyes and thrust his arms upward. The two spherical swirls crashed into one and shot upward, freezing as it churned and twisted. This frenetically gyrating sleet ripped through the bottom of the canoe. Galo pushed himself aside and watched as the boat descended past him, swallowed by the sea. He then surfaced once more.

A pair of bare feet slid across the sand in deliberate motions, tracing combat techniques along the beach. Sinkua trained by the shore, honing his skills with the morningstar. Now and again, he would hurl an orb of fire, which died upon the sand, from either his free hand or the head of his weapon. With each, he could feel a slight warmth from his medallion. It was as though it communed with him, almost like it had a life of its own.

A sound from the water, one of attempted stealth, caught his ear. Pretending to ignore it, he continued his training. His back to the shore, he heard something streaking through the air toward him. Deftly, he stepped forward and spun, leaning back as he approached the half turn. With a powerful swipe, he swung his morningstar in front of him, the spiked head colliding with the projectile in mid flight. Water and shards of ice spewed radially as the ice encasing the liquid orb was shattered by the spiked ball. He lowered his weapon and relaxed with a grin on his face.

"Nice try, Galo," he complimented, "You almost got me that time."

"Glad to see your reflexes are as good as ever, Sinkua," Galo returned, walking up the beach, "I fear we will soon need to put them to use."

Sinkua set down his weapon and sat upon the sand, breathing heavily. Galo joined him.

"It's ArcNos, isn't it?"

"Yes, brother. A fleet of ships is approaching Berinin as we speak. The northerners and our Judge believe they're coming for the capitol."

"I would think so, as well, and this attack can only mean CreSam has taken command. If that's true, then I doubt he'll spare any city along the way."

"Perhaps not. The messenger mentioned no sign of attacks on Ivaria. Their mission might only be to strike the Sacred City."

"Sacred City? I've never heard you call it that."

"We don't often, but it's a fine reminder of all it stands for when peril impends," Galo explained, getting to his feet, "Have you ever wondered why we are so technologically undeveloped."

"At times, I suppose," Sinkua admitted, joining him in standing, "but I assumed it was a matter of cultural preference."

"It is, but it goes deeper than that. Grandfather taught me of it not long ago. In the current epoch of humanity, Masnethege is the oldest formally established community. Since then, the land area has expanded along with the population, but technology has remained intentionally stagnant. The first members of the Chieftain Bloodline had nothing against the practice of technology carried by others who followed. They simply wished to remain static in the practice as a sign of permanence. We have been as such for thousands of years and we will continue to be for thousands more."

Sinkua nodded in understanding. "I see. So history hangs in the balance here, is what you're saying."

"Yes, and as Hybrids, I believe it's up to us to do something about it."

"Of course," Sinkua agreed, "Then we'd better get to work and start building."

Without another word, Sinkua began walking toward the forest. The ball of his morningstar dragged in the dirt behind him until he hoisted it into his back holster and clipped the end of the chain to the handle. Galo, admittedly puzzled, followed close behind, trying to understand that last remark.

Through the years, they had learned to read each other rather well, nearly to the point of telepathy. Galo knew Sinkua would not behave so surely without a plan, but it took him a moment to ascertain what it was.

"Wait, you're thinking of building a ship to get the Berininites out to sea, aren't you?"

"Yes, I am. We need to get them out of harm's way," Sinkua answered, still looking forward.

"Sinkua, we have to fight back and defend the city itself. It's not just the people but the presence of the city. If it falls, it will be an omen of ill fortune for the rest of Ouristihra, as well," Galo argued.

"We'll fight back better with them out of the way," Sinkua insisted, "Besides, if there's any truth to my nightmares, we'll be lucky to leave there alive."

"You really think so?" Galo fearfully pried.

"I know so. We can worry about the rest of the continent if we survive, but for now we need to focus on keeping your people and ourselves alive."

"I see. We'll get the people out of the way, then do what we can to hold off the attack while my people make their escape," Galo reluctantly agreed, "What will we use for building materials? We don't have time to chop down any trees."

Sinkua was silent for a few minutes. Pushing aside a tangle of brush, he revealed his cabin. He turned to Galo and smirked.

"Something tells me I won't be returning here any time soon."

"Going to scrap it to build the ship, huh?"

"It's finally coming around from a ship to a cabin and back to a ship again."

"It's like the circle of life but with carpentry."

The two of them began ripping and pulling sheets of plywood, along with lengths of woven branches, from the walls of the cabin. As they tore it apart, unsupported sections collapsed upon the hide flooring within and the grassy dirt without. There was no discernable order to the disassembly, what with speed being the only real focus.

"Sinkua, I have a question," Galo piped up after several minutes of silence.

Sinkua looked him over for a moment, studying his expression and body language.

"Yes, they can, Galo," he answered without hearing the question, "I had the same thing in mind."

Galo smiled and nodded. Not only did he understand, but he had been willing to offer voluntarily. Truly, Sinkua felt himself to be a part of Galo's community, far more so than of his birthplace and homeland.

After about an hour of weaving branches and tying sheets of plywood together with vines, the ship was complete. It was an ugly yet functional patchwork design. Mostly, it was a buoyant wooden platform with a large sail made from stretched hides and sheets of fabric, but it could get the Berininites out of the path of the advancing ArcNosians.

The two Hybrid brethren boarded the raft, each with their weapon in hand. They sailed onward with their eyes awaiting the shores of Berinin. A moment of judgment was upon them.

A starless sky loomed over the Sacred City that night. A feeling of ill omen was thick in the air, almost palpable. Though they had not been told of the oncoming fleet, many of the townspeople were overcome with anxiety. Galo had disappeared without mention and quite hastily judging from the chopped tie rope. Gijin's continued meditation was the subject of a great deal of curious speculation, but no one dared to disturb him.

To the north, mechanical clanking and a mass of footsteps faintly penetrated the woodland sounds. Many a Masnethegean began walking toward the north end of the village, naively curious of the noises. Others turned their attention to the east as a raft, formed of scrap lumber and mud with a sail of stripped animal hides, bounced along the rolling waves. Galo and Sinkua stood at either side of the mast, both clutching it tenaciously, as the tide carried them to shore.

The Chieftain Heir had returned safely, but obviously not in the boat he took from the shore. Worse still, Sinkua had come carrying only his morningstar. Such an unusual arrival in the dead of night could do naught but cement the overwhelming feelings of dread that hung with the clouds. His past was catching up with him, and they were in the way.

"Everybody onto the boat," Galo commanded as the mechanical clanking grew more distinct, "Masnethege will not remain safe for much longer."

Masses of his people scrambled to the makeshift craft. Sinkua guided them, encouraging the weary along, all the while keeping his glimmering eyes toward the trees. A loud burst resounded from the forest, calling the collective attention to the north. A massive iron orb shot from the canopy, roaring with its momentum as it bludgeoned the air. It loomed high above, appearing to suspend in the air as it slowed in the zenith of its arc.

"Run!" Galo shouted, "Come on, faster!"

"Stay low!" Sinkua added.

He placed himself between the falling projectile and the villagers boarding the raft. He watched and calculated as it came streaking toward the freshly turned sand. Its path clear, he took a few steps toward the shore and turned his back to the cannonball. He thrust his arms out, forming a barrier of flame between himself and the metallic meteorite.

The aerial munition exploded violently against the sand, hurling smoldering shards of metal across the land in a wide ring of choking smog and fire. Sinkua was knocked to the ground by the shockwave, but his wall of fire remained to absorb the flames of the blast. Bits of smoldering shrapnel rained upon him, embedding themselves in his back.

Galo looked back, giving Sinkua a concerned look. The flames subsided and died as Sinkua rose to his feet, gritting his teeth. Being able to command fire, the heat of the shards was scarcely a problem so much as the feeling of a handful of small knives embedded in his flesh. Still, he endured the pain and nodded to Galo, who returned the same.

"I'm going to check on Gijin," Sinkua announced, "Stay here and keep loading up the boat."

As he spoke, another burst resounded from near the source of the first. Another bomb arced above, heading for the path between Sinkua and Gijin's hut. Galo stared up in horror. Sinkua hastily backed away toward the shore.

"Cover yourself," Galo shouted, "I've got this one."

He drew back his arm, a spire of water coursing around the Serpent Bracer. It quickly solidified into a spiraled icicle. With a powerful war cry, he punched at the sky and launched the icy drill with a trail of water spraying behind it. Still several meters overhead, the ice missile punctured the falling bomb, detonating it in flight and dulling the blast. Chilled shrapnel rained down, lying strewn across the sand.

The clashing metal grew increasingly louder, now joined by electrical humming and the sounds of motors churning. Indistinguishable voices accompanied the footsteps, increasing in number the closer they came. Galo joined Sinkua on the dry sand as huts continued to empty before them.

The two stared intently at the southern edge of the forest. No more bombs were launched, but the fleet still approached. Galo and Sinkua clutched their weapons.

"You ready, brother?" Sinkua asked.

"Destiny is upon us," Galo gasped through heavy breath, "and we are the welcoming committee."

The air grew eerily thick with smog from the approaching unseen mechanized soldiers. Shattering the tension, dozens of shots rang out simultaneously, the sounds piling atop each other. Galo ran toward the shore and Sinkua inland.

As the bombs rained down, Galo urged his people toward the sea, indiscriminately sending them onto the raft or into the rollers. Blast after blast resonated behind him, launching smoldering shrapnel all across the landscape. Those near the shore were safe from the shockwave, but only those who had reached the water were spared from the shrapnel. Strips of brown flesh were ripped from their bodies by the searing shards. A layer of ice over his back protected Galo's body, which protected those fortuitously positioned. Many still on dry sand were tossed and battered by the shock of the blast, their bodied shredded and bloodied by dense sprays of accelerated shrapnel. Galo swallowed the swelling lump in his throat as his people were ripped asunder by the falling bombs. Another set followed as nearby trees collapsed before the coming surge.

Sinkua dashed to Gijin's hut. As he passed people, he grabbed them and shoved them toward the shore. He ducked and dodged the first few blasts, suffering a few injuries, but adrenaline carried him onward. As he neared the door to the hut though, a sudden cluster of shadows captivated his attention. He looked up to find the next set of bombs following before the previous blasts had even subsided.

"Galo!" he shouted, "Let's bring 'em down!"

"I'm with you, brother!" Galo called back.

Each stood with their hands turned up at their sides, fire swirling around Sinkua's and a compressed torrent of water around Galo's. The bombs neared the top of their arc, decelerating rapidly in their ascent. Those who had found safety held their breath as they watched.

All at once, the bombs peaked and plummeted toward the ground. With a pair of powerful war bellows, the two Hybrids launched their attacks into the air. First, Galo hurled his upward toward each other. As they crossed paths, the crashed and sprayed into a fan of watery spears. He pulled his arms back to his sides and clenched his fists. The spears froze in flight, piercing several of the bombs. Just behind this, Sinkua launched the orbs of fire from his hands in similar fashion. When they collided, he pulled his arms apart, manipulating an aerial wall of fire. As the bombs detonated in midair, this barricade inferno absorbed the raining flames. The rapid cooling and heating rendered the shrapnel brittle, and much of it cracked upon impact with hard surfaces.

As great as their display of power and control may have been though, nearly half the wave of explosives still remained. Galo and Sinkua covered who they could as the lightened load of bombs crashed into the ground, tearing still more land and people asunder. Berininite corpses lay strewn all about the sands.

"Sinkua, go check on Gijin," Galo urged, "I'll take care of the survivors."

Sinkua ran once again for Gijin's hut, taking advantage of the few seconds between waves of bombs. Galo checked the least damaged bodies for wounded survivors, but he found minimal fortune in his pursuit. Trees collapsed progressively further to the south. As Sinkua neared the hut, he was interrupted once more.

A war machine similar to, but smaller than, the one from his recurring nightmare bludgeoned through the towering trees. He stumbled back in horror. It mounted itself to the sand directly behind Gijin's home. Three metallic prongs drilled into the ground around it and resurfaced further outward, now pointing upward. The sand between was strewn about violently.

Sinkua composed himself and hastily hurled a ball of fire at the center of the war machine. As his attack passed between the foremost metal prongs however, a sudden webbing of electrical current snagged it. The triangular formation was generating an absurd but effective barricade around the mechanical colossus.

A pair of large guns unfolded from the peak of the machine. The intimidating barrels pointed down at the village. Sinkua ran for one of the prongs, morningstar drawn and swaying in the wind of his sprint. He reared back and swung from overhead. The strike was stopped short ricocheting off of the intangible barrier. These obelisks shielded themselves as well.

A rapid stream of bullets rained down like angry hail, exploding on impact with homes, bodies, and sand alike. Scores of minute blasts lit up the decaying village, bullets and fresh blood glistening in the ominous illumination. Galo sprinted to avoid the strafe of bullets, nary able to protect anyone but himself, partly because of the scarcity of survivors on land.

Sinkua tore aside the flap to the hut. Inside, Gijin continued to meditate. Sinkua called out his name but received no answer. Gijin's chest heaved steadily with his breathing. Calm and under control, he was a contradiction to the chaos beyond his hut.

Several tanks and other instruments of siege and demolition plowed through the foliage, rolling and climbing over the felled trees. Heavily armored foot troops gathered around the central machine, safely within the confines of the barricade. Bullets and bombs delivered by the abominable mechanizations shredded and collapsed homes and people. Chunks of wood were ripped away from the escape raft. Those on it panicked and fled into the water for relative safety.

The foot troops drew their weapons and aimed at anyone left by the machines. Their bullets were able to pass through the barrier without even a glint of light. Somehow, they were calibrated to only intercept incoming projectiles.

Sinkua and Galo both chased the machines, desperately trying to end their coordinated rampages, but the spray of bullets from above kept them from getting near enough. Also the handful of survivors left on land gave them both a sense of restraint.

"Galo! We've got to take out that one behind your home," Sinkua exclaimed.

"We can't get past those barricades though," Galo called back, "Besides, we still need to gather survivors."

"There won't be any survivors if we let this go on," Sinkua snapped, "It's time to fight back! Cover me!"

Sinkua burst into an adrenaline-fueled sprint toward the foremost barricade tower. A spray of bullets from the infantry within raced toward him. At the sound of gunfire, Galo intercepted the bullets with rapid sheets of sleet. As much as it pained him, he ignored the wounded and dying to focus on helping Sinkua.

A nagging feeling inside had him wondering how Sinkua could be so heartless while another part argued that such was hardly the case. He knew that Sinkua understood the urgency of the situation. The difference between them was that Sinkua could tune out the cries of despair to pursue what caused them. While he would endure the assault to aid those in need, Sinkua would charge headlong into it to hold it back.

Sinkua pulled his fist back, fire swirling violently around it. Still in full sprint, he charged his fist at the prong with the release of a long winded war call. The ball of fire dissipated into the barrier. He pushed his fist into it, the shock surging up his arm. Despite its appearance of raw energy, somehow the barrier felt semisolid. His face contorting with pain and rage, he pressed his fist harder against the barrier. He steadied his arm with his other hand as it began to shake violently. The flesh on his knuckles curled and wilted in a smoky bleeding mess. Sweat rolled down his face.

Through excruciating strain, his hand penetrated the barricade. He grabbed the obelisk, clutching as tightly as he could. The wall of energy clenched his forearm tenaciously, trying to eject the intruder. Though it shocked and surged through his blood, he held fast to the metallic obelisk. His ruby emitting a strong glow, he forced a powerful surge of pyromantic milystis up his forearm and through his hand. A section of the pillar softened in his grip and slowly began to bend. Unfortunately, before he could damage it beyond a slight droop, the overwhelming pain and the will of the barrier forced him away. He jerked his hand back, knuckles and forearms covered with electrical burns, and retreated southward away from the towering monolith and its triplet guardians

"You okay, Sinkua?" Galo asked.

"Yeah, but we need a new approach for this thing," Sinkua insisted as he joined him.

No survivors remained on land. Bullets continued to rain down upon the remaining structures. The escape raft was all but abandoned as it had been shredded by sprays of explosive ammunition. Little more than enough room for one person remained around the cracked mast, and the sail was ruined.

"Perhaps if we both charge the barricade," Galo suggested, "we can push through and get in the middle with the infantry."

"We run a high risk with all those gunmen," Sinkua warned, "but we have an advantage in close quarters. I'm with you."

They charged toward the machine, covering both self and each other with quick blasts of fire and ice. Sinkua took the lead, having longer strides in his sprint. Before they came near though, the flap to his hut abruptly opened, and Gijin stepped out in the midst of the chaos. The two ceased in their tracks along with the mayhem.

"Leave the old man unharmed," boomed a voice from atop the war machine, "We have direct orders from Lord CreSam to leave him alive."

The rain of bullets ceased.

"Galo, the bracer!" Gijin called out.

"Grandfather!" Galo shouted, still surprised by his sudden presence.

"Quickly, my boy, throw me the Serpent Bracer."

Galo twisted and pulled the Serpent Bracer from his forearm and tossed it to Gijin, baffled but compliant. Gijin caught it and slipped it over his wiry forearm. He clenched his fist in front of his face, gripping his forearm with his other hand. As he muttered to himself, it began to emit a swelling cool blue glow. Under his breath, he spoke as the onslaught remained at a standstill.

"I fear not death, for it is not a curse. One final breath; one final burst. I have lived well, and I have stood tall. One final swell, and with this I fall."

He raised his fist high, then quickly slammed it into the sand with surprising force. His fist pushed through the moistened sand, burying his forearm. The blue glow shot out of the bracer, spreading across the ground in a luminous web, water churning in the sands behind them. As they converged beneath each of the metallic obelisks, an armored sniper climbed out of the top of the war machine and took aim.

Three stalagmites of ice, larger than the metallic ones, thrust upward from the sand. The barricade pillars shattered against Gijin's subterranean crystalline assault. The sniper cocked his gun. Sinkua turned to Galo.

"Galo! Now!" he shouted.

Galo swiped his glaive out in front of himself, forming an arc of ice in midair. He reared back and thrust the head of his weapon at it. It shot forth, a large curved blade of ice with a thick frozen spearhead at the center. As he launched his attack, the sniper fired a single bullet. Sinkua sprinted toward Gijin, who remained kneeling on the wet sand. Desperately clinging to a shred of hope, he launched a stream of fire at the bullet as a final ditch effort.

The spear of ice punctured the machine, starting a wound which the blade rapidly widened. A massive gash ripped across the belly of the beast. Succumbing to its weakened structure, the monolith collapsed. The infantrymen frantically scattered along with several more soldiers abandoning the war machine as it collapsed onto Gijin's hut. The sniper leapt away and vanished into the forest canopy.

The stream of fire intercepted the bullet. Gijin withdrew his fist from the sand. Galo and Sinkua froze in anxious anticipation. Unfortunately, the scorched bullet passed through the stream of fire and streaked toward Gijin nonetheless.

It bored into his gut, shredding flesh and spraying blood. Gijin remained stoic while physical pain overwhelmed him within. Sinkua stared on in horror, but Galo turned away and covered his face. Now inside his abdomen, the bullet exploded, tearing and spraying shreds of organs and sinew with radial splatters of blood. His back hit the ground, sand grinding into his exposed organs.

Spattered lines of blood stained Sinkua's pants. Finding his courage, Galo dropped the glaive and raced to his grandfather's side. Sinkua simply stared at the forest, watching as the insurgents fled. Galo put his forearm under Gijin's head.

"Grandfather," he gasped hoarsely, "stay with me."

"Galo, my boy," Gijin forced breathlessly, "You've done so well."

"Thank you, Grandfather," Galo managed through tears, "I will always keep you in my thoughts and actions."

"Thank you, Galo," Gijin smiled, his voice weakening, "I wished to tell you so much more, but I cannot. Go forth into the world, find the others like yourself."

"Other… Other Hybrids?" Galo asked.

"Yes," Gijin gasped nigh inaudibly, "Don't let this go any further than it must. History is in your hands now, grandson."

With that, his final breaths escaped him. Galo laid him over the sand and got to his feet. Despite the wretched condition of his torso, Gijin's face appeared remarkably peaceful. In his final moments, he witnessed a coming of age for both his grandsons, genetic and surrogate. He perished knowing they would carry his guidance into the world and the conflict ahead.

Chapter 9

Galo staggered back from the peaceful corpse as a drastic contrast to his grandfather's restful state. His hands trembled, fingers twitching uncontrollably. His breath grew heavy and irregular as his face became flushed. He held his head in his hands, fingers digging through his hair as though sanctuary lay upon his scalp. His hands violently shook his head with tremors of a panicked collision of remorse and rage. His fingertips pressed hard against his skull, as though they were trying to bore into his brain and expel the images of horror before they became haunting memories. Tears streamed down his face. The lump in his throat became an audible gurgle. His head thrashed about in his hands, hair tossing about wildly. All at once, he pulled his arms down to his sides, fists clenched nearly to the point of bleeding his palms, threw his head back and shouted painful opposition to the sky in a bellow raspy with phlegm.

"Chieftain Heir Galo! What in the world?" a female voice interjected.

He whipped around, startled and poised to strike in his panicked state. The woman stepped back cautiously. Galo paused for a moment to regain what he could of his composure. The look of anger slowly left his face.

"Chieftain Sage," he began, "No, my grandfather, Gijin, fell in the thick of the attack. He died defending us."

"Oh my goodness," she gasped with tears gathering in her eyes, "What will you do, Galo?"

"I… I don't know, Nalygen. Is anyone else alive down there?"

Roughly a score of people emerged from the coastal shadows. Galo managed a sigh of relief, knowing that a vague sign of life still remained.

"We are still here, Galo," one man said, "The Sacred City will not fall."

"Thank you, Borret. You're confidence is an inspiration."

"When you are ready to rebuild, so too are we," Borret offered, "We await your order."

"My… My order?" Galo asked, stumbling back in a stupor.

"Yes, sir. We understand it's quite sudden, but the situation is equally dire," Nalygen urged, "You, Galo, are now Chieftain Sage of The Sacred City of Masnethege."

All his life had been spent preparing for this moment, but never had he imagined it would come in a nature at all like this. He broke eye contact, turning his attention introspectively in a desperate attempt to gather his thoughts. He sighed and shook his head, heavy with scrambled thoughts and mixed emotions.

"No," he resisted, "No, I'm not. I cannot claim my birthright at this time."

"Galo, are you sure of this?" Borret asked.

"Yes, I think so," Galo persisted with uncertainty, "If I stay here, I would be letting those responsible for this go unpunished. But if I pursue them, I would be leaving The Sacred City in shambles. Either way, I would hardly be much of a leader. I can't stay, and for that matter, neither can any of you."

The small crowd of Berininites was in a clamor. First their city was razed and their leader assassinated. Now the heir to the title was denying his position. Rumors and theories wove swiftly through the small crowd.

"Listen!" Galo shouted, breaking the clamor, "It's not safe here. If they have an inkling of a suspicion that some of us survived, they will come back to finish the job. Of that, you can all be certain. I want you all to head out to sea in the direction from which Sinkua and I arrived before the attack. Take shelter on the small island you find out there. Seek out the remains of a cabin in the woods, and there you will find a cache of food and possibly some seeds to expand the existing garden."

"The raft was destroyed, as were all of our canoes," Borret protested.

"Then build new ones!" Galo snapped in frustration, "I'm not the savior you want to think I am, so you'd best learn to save yourselves."

"Galo, what will become of our city?" Nalygen asked.

"If I have any control over our fate, we'll stand together again someday. When that day comes, the Sacred City will be reborn from its own ruins."

"Thank you," Nalygen said, "Your words are an inspiration to us all. By the way, what would you like me to do with the Chieftain Sage Robe."

This detail had not even occurred to him until now. What he donned was an adult sized Chieftain Heir Robe, the difference being the number of sleeves. His grandfather's robe now had a large hole in the back, the edges singed and lined with blood. He looked back to Gijin's corpse and swallowed the lump in his throat.

"Take it with you and keep it safe," Galo ordered, turning to face Nalygen, "I leave for war tonight. I will not shed the blood of hatred upon so sacred a garment. Nor upon this one."

He removed his robe, folded it in half and handed it to her with his head down. This left him in only a pair of shorts which hung a few centimeters past his kneecaps. Kneeling beside Gijin, he sat him up carefully. The body was already growing cold and frail. First, he removed the Serpent Bracer and returned it to his own forearm. He then removed the robe and laid him back on the sand again. After kissing his grandfather's forehead, he got to his feet once more. This robe he also folded in half and handed to Nalygen.

"I understand, Galo," she accepted, "Thank you for entrusting this task to me."

"Thank you. Now, I have one last request for the lot of you. I would like to ask that you give Gijin a proper memorial and a burial at sea. It is as he would wish."

His heart was heavy as he spoke these words. Despite all that his grandfather had done for him, raising him alone for as long as he could remember, he would not stay for the memorial. It was not so much that he could not, but he knew that if he did, he would become overwhelmed with dismay and anxiety. As Gijin told him, history was in his hands. Through painful prioritization, he was forced to put greater issues before his personal affairs.

"We will do just that," Borret complied, "but I have one question."

"Thank you," Galo said solemnly, "What is it now?"

"Excuse my prying sir, but where has Sinkua gone? It seems rather unlike him to not be at your side for this."

"What the…?"

He turned and looked in all directions. All this time, he had been so wrapped up in issues of family and home that he had failed to notice Sinkua's absence. He looked to the ground where he last saw Sinkua stand. A windblown trail of prints in the sand led north from that spot.

"Oh no…"

He glanced back over his shoulder and nodded his respects to the Masnethegean survivors. The crowd split down the middle. Galo paused and turned the rest of his body to face them. A child no older than ten years stepped to the front.

"You'll need this, sir," the child insisted.

The young boy handed Galo his glaive with as steady an arm as he could manage with so awkward a construct. Galo took it from him, smiled, and nodded.

"Thank you. Now, I must go quickly. Farewell to the lot of you."

With those parting words trailing off his lips, he pursued Sinkua in full sprint.

The last of the ArcNosian infantry vanished into the forest, the vehicles before them long since swallowed in the thick of the trees. The air was heavy with the stench of death and grease. Sinkua stood with his arms hanging like deadweights, staring off into the forest as the assailants slipped away into it. His torso rocked involuntarily as a fading sliver of his subconscience persistently tried to calm him in the most humanly basic of manners. Behind him, Galo stammered on, but even this was reduced to white noise by the torrent within. His focus remained on the departing soldiers.

So smugly they walked away, heartless and methodical. They had laid an historical landmark to waste with nary a hint of guilt, and now they took leave of that killing field as though it were an ordinary day on the job. The centerpiece of their disaster had collapsed upon them, yet still they were unmoved.

Attempts to comprehend it only led to frustration, and this frustration only amplified the anger inherent in Sinkua's grief. A vein pulsated in the side of his neck and his left eye and temple twitched uncontrollably. He clutched his medallion, looking down to find it emitting that familiar warm glow. He looked up once more, back to the forest, and his eyes flared with a similar glow. It subsided into a faint shimmer, the light guising his pupils from view. A malicious grin spread across his face as he began to walk toward the forest, his body piloted by a unified amalgamation of subconscious urges more than by any conscious will.

The tire tracks in the forest made their trail laughably easy to follow. He looked up to the branches and studied their intricate patterns. With a firm grip and a strong pull, he hoisted himself onto the lowest overhead branch of the nearest tree. He climbed up another and another, quickly placing himself a few meters above the ground. From this vantage point, he could see the back of the infantry line a short distance onward.

"Well well, leaving so soon?" he muttered under his breath, "Apparently you've forgotten the basis of Berinin's criminal law system. Time for the lot of you to pay your dues."

Staying low to keep his center of gravity as such, he sidled along the branches. As he neared the edge of one, he stepped cautiously to another on the next tree. In this manner, he progressed along the trail, undetected by the soldiers below. Time and again, the gap between trees was wide enough to necessitate that he jumped. In these cases, he landed on all fours, clutching the branch with his hands for extra balance. Soon, he was directly above the back of the infantry line.

He got to his feet, balanced precariously upon the branch but unmoved by the wind and elevation. With a cold sneer, he stared down upon the soldiers below. They had judged the value of the Masnethegeans' lives, so now too would he judge theirs. He withdrew his morningstar from its holster, the chain still clasped. Just after the last soldier in line passed under him, he hopped from his branch, streaming smoothly to the ground below.

His feet struck the ground with a crunch of twigs and leaves, the sound blending with a multitude of others. He dropped to a crouch, absorbing the impact with his knees. As he erected his body, he glared into the back of the last soldier as though to stare through him. With a flick of the thumb, he unclipped the chain, letting it unravel and drop at his side.

The metallic clank caught the attention of the trailing infantryman. Sinkua pulled back, arcing the chain back and upward. The soldier turned his head slowly as the metallic spiked ball neared the top of its ascent. Rage and adrenaline flooded Sinkua's body. Though the vein still pulsated, the twitching stopped as the soldier made eye contact. The soldier's face morphed from confusion to fear. He looked up to see the ball and chain of the morningstar. They reached the peak of their ascent, the ball hanging at its zenith for a split second.

Sinkua jerked the handle of the morningstar downward, and the chain snapped down like a whip, the ball plummeting with fatal force. The spikes raped the infantryman's skull through holes of their own design. Several plasmatic fountains spewed outward with the impact. The skull collapsed under the force of the blow, bits of brain splattering on the trees and fragments of bone puncturing the weakened flesh from within. The body was jerked down with the spiked ball jammed forcibly into the head and thus dropped and discarded upon the bloodied soil.

Sinkua's breath was deep and ragged as he stared down remorselessly at the aftermath of his rage. In judging the living worth of others, so too had they relinquished their own. No longer were they his people, regardless of an inevitably shared nationality. To think of them as ethnic kin had become blasphemous. Furthermore, for the atrocities they had committed, to let them live was an insult to all others in Ouristihra. All humans had a right to life, and in infringing on that of others, they had forsaken their own. This, it seemed, was his purpose as an Hybrid, to punish those who could not otherwise be punished.

The crunch of bones and splatter of brain mass halted nearby soldiers. Together, they turned about slowly to find what had caused such a macabre sound. Despite their numbers, anxiety was growing in each individual, and Sinkua could feel it hanging sweetly in the air. He was their feared unknown, and he reveled in it.

"Put down your pistols and pick up your swords," he remarked, eyes flaring a poison green hue, "It's time to see how strong you truly are."

The lot of them stood silently, each one sizing him up individually. Many flinched as though they had intentions of heroism, but it appeared none were willing to act upon them. Their explosive rounds could easily set the forest ablaze before they could escape, but they also knew that Sinkua was forced to forgo his pyromancy for the same reason. However, his talent and aggression with the morningstar had proven deadly, and too few of them had trained with their melee arms lately.

One was bold enough to step forth and quite hurriedly at that. From the midst of the crowd he dashed forth, those nearby parting a path for the potential hero. He charged with clear intent of a reckless offensive, a war hammer drawn back over his shoulder. A deep and lengthy battle cry exploded from the depths of his lungs.

Sinkua perked up, listening intently to his immediate environs as he watched the oncoming soldier. As his assailant drew near, he relaxed once more, staring coldly into his impending death. The hammer rose before him, his eyes following it, as the soldier decelerated his charge. The head roared toward him, and he closed his eyes and exhaled.

Split seconds before impact, Sinkua ducked and pivoted out of the way. To the shock of the soldiers, Galo burst forth like a bullet of flesh. The hammer slammed into the soil, shattering discarded bark and scattering dust into the wind. Galo leapt over the crouching assailant, his legs tucked in. As he passed over, he turned and delivered a hard kick square to the small of his back. Galo landed behind him and pinned the soldier face down on the forest floor with one foot. With a cold sneer, he drove his glaive through the man's spine, a fan of blood spraying upward upon impact. The bone split and cracked with the most horrific of sounds. His entrails could be heard sloshing about as the blade was abruptly forced through them. He was dead before the tip touched the back of his sternum.

"Come now!" Galo called as he whipped the warm blood from his blade, "Who among you wishes to join their fellow soldiers in the tsoran ether?"

In a scattered frenzy, scores of soldiers charged forth. Their pistols and rifles remained in the holsters as they withdrew various blades and cudgels, some for the first time in years. A mess of battle cries resounded through the forest.

One charged Sinkua headlong, a long sword drawn back at his side. Sinkua stepped aside to dodge the thrust and followed with a solid kick to the kidney. Hearing footsteps approaching rapidly from behind, he spun about and arced his morningstar across the air. It met sickeningly with the face of a failed sneak assailant. Nonchalantly, he returned his attention to the first. His hand ablaze, he mercilessly squeezed the soldier's neck, melting the flesh and scorching the trachea.

Galo leapt and spun with great agility to dodge falling and thrusting blades. He abandoned awareness of his senses and allowed instinct to take over. Parrying a thrusting sword, he dropped to a squat. Supporting his weight on his hands, he spun on the ground, his legs sweeping across the soldier's and dropping him on his back. As he erected himself, he stood the glaive on end, planting the blade in the soil with one hand on the middle of the handle and the other on the butt. With impressive agility, he lifted himself off the ground, balancing on the glaive, and thrust his body backwards. Both feet met forcibly with the chest of another approaching from behind, a battleaxe held high overhead.

The soldier stumbled back, disgruntled but not discouraged. He charged once more, as Galo had returned his attention to the tripped soldier beside him. This otherwise faceless pawn would soon become a hero among the ArcNosians, yet his jubilation was quickly shattered when he felt a tug against the handle of his axe. He looked up to find the chain of a morningstar wrapped tightly around it, the spikes wedged into the wooden fibers.

With a strong jerk, Sinkua pulled the soldier onto his back. Galo slammed his glaive down into the chest cavity of the first felled soldier. Glaive still buried in flesh, he turned to face the other, sweeping his arm outward. A blade of ice shot from his forearm and sliced into the neck of the soldier at Sinkua's feet.

Over and over, necks and torsos were met with the blade of Galo's glaive and the spikes of Sinkua's morningstar. The sounds of ripping flesh and shattering bone resonated throughout the forest. Blade-wielding soldiers were consistently disarmed by the morningstar while those carrying cudgels found their handles bisected by a swift swipe of the glaive. Time and again, each of them were met with successful attacks, but only ever enough to leave a scar.

The troops were in a panic. A mess of horrifying corpses lying around them, most of those remaining turned to flee. Sinkua and Galo looked to each other as the fleet retreated, and both nodded and smirked.

Like twin bulls, they charged the escaping troops. Spinal cords were severed clean as Galo sliced through the back of necks. Skulls were crushed messily as Sinkua swung his morningstar about, the chain in constant motion. Bodies were flash scorched, the metallic parts of their uniforms welded onto their burnt carcasses. Torsos were sliced open by icy blades, spilling blood and organs down the legs. Few turned to face these mad assailants, but all who did were met with swift slaughter.

Galo caught up to one of the small gunnery vehicles, as they had been slowed down by panicked infantry scurrying past them. Maintaining his stride, he slammed the blade through the tinted window. Glass and sparks sprayed out in a cloud of smoke. As it cleared, he was surprised to discover the vehicles were unmanned. Though a bit taken aback, he pulled the glaive from the aesthetic cabin and swept it through the tires nearest to him. He slowed to let it pass, sending it careening into a crowd of pedestrian soldiers.

Those remaining of the fleeing foot troops had all passed the line of automated gunnery vehicles, so Sinkua and Galo turned their aggression toward the machines. Galo used his glaive to slash tires while Sinkua smashed body panels with his morningstar and melted tires with carefully aimed blasts of fire. The dilapidated vehicles careened through the retreating faction. Many with exposed electrical working were met with a torrent of water from Galo, adding yet another hazard to the uncontrollable death vehicles. Before long, the gunnery trucks had all been either destroyed or sent as weapons into the diminishing fleet.

Only a handful of troops remained ahead of them. One by one, they dropped in a horrid mess of blood and sinew. The edge of the forest was quickly approaching, and for the first time they noticed the most absurd detail of all. The war machine that loomed over the Sacred City was nowhere in sight.

As it appeared the battle was won, each turned to face one another. Their bodies covered in fresh cuts, bruises and blood, though most of it not their own, they clenched their fists and bumped knuckles, nodding to each other. No words were needed. Each knew what the other was trying to say, thanking and commending for their help and efforts.

"Fuck the consequences!" came a voice from up ahead, "I'll take you out even if I have to lay the entire forest to ash!"

Sinkua looked to the edge of the forest just ahead of them. There at the end of the trail stood one last infantryman. As his hand reached over his shoulder for the butt of a shotgun, Sinkua took off in full sprint. The soldier's arms trembled as he tried to steady his gun and get either of them in the crosshairs, a task made all the more difficult by Sinkua's erratic weaving.

Still running, Sinkua raised his hand and manifested a whirling ball of flame. Dumbstruck, the soldier dropped the shotgun from his shaking hands, gazing fearfully at the swelling fiery orb. Abruptly, Sinkua stopped and let his arm fall to his side, the milystic fire doused in a cloud of smoke. Galo's glaive ripped through the night air, the blade reinforced with a crystalline coating, and plunged into the chest of the last assassin.

"Looks like that's the last of them," Sinkua observed, "You okay, Galo? I'm not sure you noticed, but you took something of a beating in the midst of that madness."

"You amaze me sometimes, brother," Galo chuckled, "Look at yourself, and you're asking me if I'm okay. I'm surprised you're still standing."

Sinkua looked down to discover his shirt was shredded. Its tattered remainder was caked with blood from a grisly collection of scratches, scrapes and slices. Only now did the wounds begin to sting. He winced at the sight of himself.

"I got caught up in the moment," he dismissed with a shrug.

"You took most of those disarming or distracting soldiers that tried to attack me from behind," Galo clarified as they continued toward the edge of the forest, "It's like you lose sight of your own wellbeing when I'm in danger."

"Sorry," Sinkua halfheartedly apologized, "I guess I have a tendency to throw caution to the wind and forgo my own safety when yours is jeopardized."

"Well, it's honorable nonetheless, but too much of such a practice will be the death of you, as much as I hate to think of it."

"Death is a very real thought after what we've seen and done."

"Speaking of which, did you ever see that bastard who sniped Grandpa?"

"Do I hear a little Hybrid talking about me down there?" a third voice interjected.

A ways ahead, two decorated soldiers stood on the deck of a ship just off shore, surrounded by smaller abandoned vessels. Galo immediately recognized the one who had spoken so condescendingly.

"You son of a bitch! You killed Gijin!"

"Yes, I know what I did, boy," he snidely boasted, "He posed a direct threat to the operation."

"We had direct orders not to harm him," the other scolded judgingly.

"Oh? And what do you intend to do about it, Admiral SenRas?" the assassin asked.

"Lord CreSam will deal with you upon our return," the Admiral reminded, "but I would just as soon throw you to these wolves and watch them rip you to pieces."

Sinkua studied what he could see of the assailant's arms. On one, he saw what appeared to be the bottom half of a familiar tattoo. He furrowed his brow at the sight of it.

"Oh, that's a good one. You think I'd fall by their hands? I'm The Hunter, you stupid son of a bitch. It'll take more than these two to take me down" the assassin hubristically remarked, "So what do you say, you two? Does your hunger for vengeance outweigh your desire to live?"

Galo stepped forth only to be stopped by Sinkua's outstretched forearm.

"Not now, brother," Sinkua insisted, still staring at the assassin and the Admiral, "Let them go."

"So there is a limit to your drive," the assassin noted.

"You're wiser than I gave you credit for," Admiral SenRas complimented, "Pity I'll have to kill you in the near future."

Sinkua scoffed and smirked at the remark. The two remaining assailants, those who had led the assault, returned to the cabin of the mostly submerged war machine. Sinkua lowered his forearm as the ship carved through the water toward the horizon.

"What was that about?" Galo asked, "My trust in you remains intact, but tell me what the hell you're thinking, letting them go like that."

"Let me explain," Sinkua calmly began, still watching the sea, "If they sent that large a fleet to level your village, there's no telling the strength of what we're up against. With those two alive to tell the story of two renegades who slew an entire fleet, they'll send out more fleets to hunt us down. As we make our way toward ArcNos, we'll whittle away at its forces. When we arrive, the borders will be weakened, and we'll be left to face a depleted military. Not to mention, you get to take pleasure in hunting down The Hunter."

"I see," Galo complied, calming with understanding, "But what of SenRas?"

"Well," Sinkua continued with a smirk, "I can't let you have all the fun."

Chapter 10

A series of sea blue sconces lined the walls at regular intervals, shining a flickering glow against the wooden paneling. Four men of various ages sat in armchairs arranged about the room, their bare feet resting on therapeutically designed carpet. In the corner sat two pairs of sandals and pair of black combat boots. A young woman entered, holding a pitcher.

"More tea, sirs?" she asked politely.

The eldest among them looked about, surveying expressions and nods.

"No thank you, Sanus," Nenbard dismissed, "We're alright."

"Right, save for the wounds these two endured, eh?" Ocronn interjected.

"Well, we're better off than most of that fleet," Sinkua added, rubbing at his shoulder, "I'd almost feel sorry for some of them had they not gone after the Sacred City."

Shortly after their exchange with The Hunter and Admiral SenRas, Ocronn had come for Sinkua and Galo in the boat Galo requested. That dinghy was welcome refuge after the macabre storm. However, upon noticing the wounds the two of them bore, Ocronn offered them a place to recuperate before they continued northward.

"By the way, Ocronn told me what became of your grandfather," Nenbard relayed, looking sympathetically to Galo, "I'm sorry for your loss."

Galo closed his eyes and nodded as he sipped the warm tea, his cup nearing its bottom. He had not been much for words since arriving, nor had he spoken more than sparingly on the boat. Ocronn asked what had become of the city and of Gijin specifically. Galo's answers were brief, and the longer he talked of it, the shakier his voice became.

Sanus reentered the room with empty hands. Ignoring the arm chair against the wall, she opted instead to sit upon the ottoman. She leaned back on her hands and turned to acknowledge Galo.

"You know, my husband here knew Gijin personally for a while," she boasted, "Well by near proxy at least. His son tutored him in herbal medicines."

"Mmhmm," Nenbard confirmed, sipping at his tea, "That was back when I was not much older than Sinkua here, actually."

Galo's eyebrows shot up with curiosity. He had been told that both his parents perished before his first birthday, leaving him to be raised by his aging grandfather. Sinkua, having been so young at the time, could never offer any more details beyond the stories Gijin told. Yet now, by the grace of coincidence, sat a man who knew his father personally.

"You knew my father, did you?" Galo asked, trying to retain his composure, "I never even knew his name. I was told he passed away before my first birthday, a bit more than fifteen years ago."

"Fifteen years, you say?" Nenbard asked with one eyebrow arched, "I . . ."

Sinkua coughed loudly to interrupt him. Nenbard glanced over in his direction. Sinkua discreetly nodded dissent, and Nenbard vaguely nodded in agreement.

"I guess it has been only fifteen," Nenbard admitted, appearing to be resorting his memories, "It just seems like so much longer. I thought it was nearing seventeen, to be honest."

"You never have been good with dates," Ocronn added, supporting the charade.

Sinkua quietly sighed with relief. He knew Galo must someday learn the truth of his origin and his parents, but tonight was not the time. He had just lost his last known predecessor; this was not the time for him to learn he technically never had parents. It was bad enough for him believing an illness overwhelmed them both only months after his birth.

Despite the tragic memories he carried through his childhood, the irrefutable highlight of which was his mother's death, he would sooner endure both their memories than let Galo know the true burden of his childhood just yet. The boy was to be a leader; he needed not be anchored by the guilt of tragedy.

"Well, as it were, what can you tell me of my father?" Galo asked.

"When last I saw him, it was about two years before his death was reported," Nenbard admitted, "so the memories are vague. But Gabdur was a remarkably well-educated man. As Sanus said, he tutored me in herbal medicine. I can't say he taught me all that I know, but rather, all that I was able to commit to memory was because of him. Just as my brother-in-law told me of you, he was as comfortable at sea as any marine life. He was built quite like you, in fact."

Galo closed his eyes, trying to picture a man of such a nature, digging to imagine his father. The outcome was fairly generic in appearance, but through the personality poured into this artificial recollection, he still felt an attachment to it. This was the closest he had, and perhaps ever would have, to a vision of his father.

"How did he pass away?" Galo pried, braving territory he knew he may well regret treading upon.

"Disease, just like you were told," Nenbard said bluntly, "He was stricken ill shortly after your birth. His wife Zheal followed shortly thereafter. Nalygen did all she could to treat them, but alas it ate away at her sister and her brother-in-law and claimed them both within five months of a diagnosis."

"I see," Galo nodded, letting it all sink in, "Wait, did you say my mother was treated by her sister Nalygen just now?"

"Mmhmm."

"Strange, I never knew she was my aunt," Galo pondered, "Shortly before we left, I charged Nalygen with safeguarding the Chieftain robes. Lucky coincidence that I happened to keep them in the family."

"I wonder why she never mentioned her relation," Sinkua interjected.

Of course, he knew why no one related to Galo had ever come forth. The charade needed to be carried out by as few people as possible, lest it may become convoluted with excessive participation. Believing them all to merely be fellow townspeople, he would not pry for stories about his late parents.

"Do I have any other aunts or uncles that you know of? Cousins perhaps?" Galo asked of whomever might have an answer.

"Zheal also had a brother named Ebralgi," Nenbard confirmed, "If either of them had children, I was never aware of it."

"Ebralgi, huh? I think I vaguely remember that name. Haven't heard it in a long time though."

"I remember Grandpa Gijin mentioning his leaving for Ferya a while back," Sinkua confirmed, able to recall memories from those days with more clarity, "I didn't know he was your uncle either, but I heard he took a refugee with him."

"That much I remember, as well," Galo agreed, "Grandpa told us that a Midlander woman brought him her newborn daughter and asked that he protect her, because she feared what was becoming of ArcNos. He and Ebralgi must have felt that she would not have been safe in Berinin either. Looks like they were right."

Sinkua swirled the last of his tea, getting lost in contemplation. He was recounting the days leading up to his departure from ArcNos and what he could recall of his time on the island. Though he never met her, he felt he could somehow relate to this young refugee. He chuckled under his breath.

"And now here you are, leaving Berinin with a refugee of your own," Sinkua added, "What is it about you Berininites that has the rest of us investing so much trust in you?"

Galo chuckled a bit and grinned. For at that moment, a similar thought had crossed his mind. Perhaps it was some draw of his family, but it did seem a peculiar coincidence that both he and his uncle ended up abetting foreign refugees without really knowing each other. However, he knew nothing of the whereabouts of Ebralgi and his runaway, but he doubted that he was trekking into battle alongside a little girl. Therein laid the difference. They were traveling with ArcNos as their destination, carrying plans of retaliation upon arrival. Ebralgi and his travel companion were likely just waiting out the storm.

"By the way, when did you want to leave?" he asked.

"You guys can stay the night if you need to," Nenbard offered.

"Thanks," Sinkua said and paused for a moment of thought, "I think we will. We'll leave in the morning, head for the southern Ivarian ports and find out if anybody knows anything of use to us."

"Morning? Are you sure it's a good idea to travel in the daylight?" Galo doubted.

"Of course. Only Admiral SenRas and The Hunter know what we look like," Sinkua explained, "If we travel inconspicuously by day, we won't draw as much suspicion as if we moved by night. It's called hiding in plain sight. Besides, they have search lights and we don't. Their crafts are more easily spotted at night than we are, but we'd have to spend all night dodging those lights and navigating by moonlight."

"Daylight will level the field on account of visibility," Galo agreed and accepted, "Now there's just the matter of evening the odds."

"As much of a strategist as I am," Sinkua admitted, "even I know we'll mostly have to improvise in that respect."

The following morning, the two of them left on the boat given to them by the brothers-in-law Judge Nenbard and Ocronn. It had been generously equipped with nonperishable foods, a first aid kit, a cache of money, and a new robe for Galo among other clothing. The sun hung halfway up the sky upon their departure, just far enough to the east to serve as an approximate compass. The boat was fairly small, only big enough to carry the two of them and the luggage with little space to spare. Given the lengthy travels they knew laid ahead of them, they would need to upgrade their transportation to something with living quarters as quickly as possible.

Sinkua sat at one end of the boat, picking dried blood and sinew from the spikes of his morningstar. Meanwhile, Galo monitored the wind and occasionally tweaked the sails. So far, the wind had been favorable enough that they found no need to paddle except to avoid large fish now and then.

It was Sinkua's intent to take their time on his return home. The longer they stalled and wandered, the more troops would be sent after them, thus weakening the ArcNosian border defenses once they did arrive. He could only hope that the civilian populous had not given in to the hostile takeover. That was when epiphany struck.

"Call me crazy," he piped, "but somehow I don't think ArcNos is behind what happened last night."

"Sinkua, I'm sorry to say it, but we both know those soldiers wore ArcNosian uniforms and piloted ArcNosian crafts," Galo replied with a sigh, "Regardless of your heritage, don't hold yourself to blame. Your lineage is not yours to choose."

"How eloquent of you," Sinkua sneered, "but that's not what I meant. I think an outside force may be behind this, um, revolution so to speak. ArcNos always had a strong military but I've never seen anything from there even faintly comparable to what we witnessed last night."

"Hmm, so you think some foreign organization is empowering them, huh?"

"Exactly that," Sinkua verified, "And I'm nigh on certain that Amirione and the man who wrecked my ship are part of it."

"They know each other, you think?"

"I know so. They have the same tattoo in the same place. That can't be a coincidence. I'd bet my only iola it's there insignia."

"That explains why you were eyeing Amirione so intently," Galo realized, "So then who are we after, ArcNos or the foreign organization?"

"We need to find out who the organization is first," Sinkua noted as he clipped his morningstar and slid it under the seat.

"Maybe we can figure something out on the way there," Galo suggested with a touch of optimism, "Hopefully we can conjure up an hypothesis at the very least."

Admiral SenRas rapped firmly upon the double doors standing before him. After receiving a baritone response from within, he entered, slipping in and closing the door behind himself. His breath and pulse were still heavy from the stress of the previous night's events.

"I've returned from Berinin, Brigadier General Elite," he panted, "I have much to report, sir."

"Admiral, you needn't bother with such formalities with me in private," CreSam insisted with a smirk, "I've yet to forget the days when you were my commanding officer. I'd not be half the soldier I am today without you."

"Thank you, sir," SenRas replied, still quite shaken in spite of CreSam's efforts to the contrary.

"So," CreSam continued, leaning back in his chair, "What of Masnethege? Did they subjugate willingly?"

"No," SenRas sighed heavily, "No, in fact they did quite the opposite. They fought back, much to our surprise."

"This is no good," CreSam muttered, "Damned beachfront fools."

"Do you wish to hear the casualty report?" SenRas asked, swallowing nervously.

"Not exactly, but for formality's sake, I know I ought to anyway."

"Well, we departed with three units in our fleet. They countered with two. When they reduced our forces to two and collapsed the Triad Titan before we could inflict a single casualty upon their defenses, we resorted to a tactical retreat."

"They felled a hundred of our soldiers before you could fell a single one of theirs?" CreSam asked in disbelief, "It seems we underestimated them."

"Sir, you still do. As we retreated, they gave chase, and the death toll continued to rise until we were left with only two soldiers," SenRas choked, "Amirione and I were the only survivors."

CreSam muttered under his breath, "Even with those odds, that cocky bastard is still alive."

"CreSam?" SenRas asked, "Are you well? I hope I wasn't too blunt."

"What? No, not at all. Just lost in thought," CreSam answered, "It's just amazing that a nation with no formal military and a rather peaceable history would counter with a force of two thirds our fleet and reduce ours nigh to eradication with scarcely a casualty of their own. It seems those beachfront fools may have been hiding something from us this entire time."

SenRas's pulse accelerated, throbbing in his neck. He knew CreSam well enough to know he wasn't taking to the news as well as he let on. What's worse, his interpretation thereof was not entirely accurate. The truth was far more unsettling.

"No sir, they boasted far less than two thirds our fleet," SenRas corrected.

"You said a moment prior that they countered with two to our three units."

"Yes sir. We came with three units of soldiers. They countered," SenRas began, pausing to clear his throat, "with two soldiers."

CreSam stared at him for nearly a full minute, his gaze feeling as though it pierced his very flesh. SenRas stepped back cautiously, fearing the anger may be taken out upon him. In those eyes, he could see CreSam's mind racing faster than a common mind could follow. After a minute or so, however, CreSam's eyes relaxed and he leaned back in his chair once again.

"Well, this certainly calls for a few changes in our agenda," he insisted, "Don't you agree, SenRas?"

Early in the evening, Sinkua and Galo arrived at an empty dock in the southern ports of Ivaria. The air was thick with the odiferous scents of sea salt, dead fish, and commerce. The wooden piers were riddled with wet footprints along with the occasional drippings of blood, undoubtedly from broken blisters. Portsmen were renowned for their nigh unwavering work ethic, particularly in Ivaria, second only to those in Poravit.

For anonymity's sake, Sinkua slipped on a pair of sunglasses offered to him by Nenbard. They no longer fit him, and Sinkua had more use for them anyhow. The two sought information and wares, not combat. Thus, he wished to keep his identity to himself, and his eyes were the one distinguishing feature that could end any uncertainty for those who had only heard a description.

The two wandered up and down the piers for some time, seeking a portsman who looked to be able to spare a moment for a pair of strangers. Several dozen portsmen were on the job that evening, but with most of the docks occupied with various manner of cargo vessel, all they spotted were deeply immersed in their labor. A callused hand set upon Galo's shoulder. Startled, he jumped and turned cautiously.

"Careful there, boy," spoke a middle aged male voice, "Elsewise, you'll jump right outta your skin, you know."

"Sorry, sir. It's just that, well," Galo apologized, catching his breath, "I've seen some horrid things of late. We both have. Pardon if you find either of us a might on edge."

With concern in his eyes, the portsman looked them over, scrutinizing their disposition and their faces. Of course, he recognized neither of them but could easily discern Galo's nationality. Sinkua, on the other hand, had tanned to the point that gleaning his origin was a touch more difficult. The man had yet to hear him speak, but since he had integrated Berininite into his natural ArcNosian accent, it would have done little to clarify.

"You two boys must be from Masnethege, judging from what I'd been told upon this morn," the portsman proposed, "Heard me a bit of news spoke of a military fleet what wiped 'em out nigh to extinction."

"How do you already know of this?" Sinkua snapped back, stepping between Galo and the portsman.

"Are you pullin' my leg, boy? News travels a might faster than you young scrappers realize, you know," the portsman countered, continuing with his odd dialect, "Know this well, those carrier pigeons fly swiftly plumb regardless the weather, unlike boats and such. Fact is, could we human folk move about such as they, my job would be a might different from what it is now. Cleaning bird scrap from rotors rather than fish and such. Course, we'd have no need for those bobbers what hang from our fishing lines. Less you was to go fishing in a cloud field. Or rather, birding I would suppose. But would there really be any need to . . ."

Midway through the old portsman's ramblings, Sinkua had heard all he needed to take from the meandering monologue. He turned to Galo to discuss what may have transpired while the talkative stranger continued about flying boats and fishing for birds. The best they could determine was that the survivors had sent pigeons with news of the attack in a northerly direction, hoping word of the assault might fall upon other ears before Sinkua and Galo set out on their mission. To have met someone whom the news had already reached was quite fortunate, and though he spoke oddly and quite much at that, he seemed to be a well-informed stranger. As it were, the two knew he would likely be of use, so long as they could endure his quirk.

"Alright, so anyway, we're in need of a boat," Sinkua interrupted, "and it's urgent."

"What? Well, you boys got yourselves a perfectly good dinghy settin' right there in the docks, you know. Or didja get yourself bit by some suckerfish and forget?"

"No. No. No! We need a bigger and sturdier boat," Sinkua snarled back with his forehead in his hand, "Get us something we can travel in for days at a time."

"From now on, I'm in charge of diplomacy," Galo mumbled.

"Eh? You boys want to, um…" the portsman began, studying the two more intently now, "Oh, oh, oh. I see what you're talking about."

Sinkua and Galo each raised a single eyebrow, in an almost telepathic unison. Now, Galo found himself clutching his own forehead just the same, his frustration growing as well.

"Look, get your mind out of the gutter. We're survivors of the attack on the Sacred City, and we need a boat that will get to ArcNos in one piece," Galo snapped, "Now, either find us one, build us one, or take us to someone who can, or so help me, I'll abuse my diplomatic immunity in skinning you and using your flesh for sails. Are we clear?"

The portsman took a couple of steps back, shocked at this abrupt display of anger from the young Berininite. Obviously, he had struck a nerve, but he knew not how.

"Alright, alright, calm down. Nobody's judging you boys or nothing. What a man does is his own business, I always say, even what he and another man do in closed quarters," he retracted, cautious with his words, "But what's this you say about diplomatic immunity?"

"I suppose introductions are in order," Galo said with a smirk, "The name is Galo, Chieftain Sage Galo, what with the recent death of Gijin. And this is my brother in arms and cousin in blood, Sinkua."

Sinkua darted a glance at Galo. He couldn't ascertain why he lied about his origins for him, but he appreciated it all the same. The fact was he wished to deny his ArcNosian heritage, or at least the purity thereof. He had come to terms with it long ago but knew it would be best for strangers not to know of it, lest they lump him in with the soldiers.

"I, um, I see," the portsman said, curbing his excitement, "Well, you see, we been finding ourselves in a might of a fix as of late. The northern ports were working on an engine what runs on combustion, but the ArcNosian military stole the rights to it. Now as much as I'd like to give you one of them engines, they stole the blueprints as well, and it would take a few days to recreate the design. Besides, that was up north some scores of kilometers away."

"Do you have anything close to that power, but a bit less dangerous?" Sinkua asked, "I'm none too comfortable with the idea of a wooden ship being moved about by contained explosions. I don't know, call me crazy, but that doesn't seem a safe way to travel."

"You don't sound much like a Berininite, you know. In fact, you sound a bit . . ."

"ArcNosian. Yes, I know," Sinkua interrupted, "My mother was ArcNosian, and I spent my childhood there. Anyway, the engine?"

"What? Oh right, yes," the portsman continued, leading them into a building at the head of the docks, "Combustion engines are safer than you might think, but I suppose that's beside the point, now ain't it. We got this prototype steam engine, but those hippie bastards what infest Haprian got a bit of a qualm with the thing. Without their approval, we can't get clearance from the Ouristihran Union to even test 'em outside of local waters, and I'd hate for you boys to get cut short for something as paltry as an arrest for an unlicensed vessel."

Sinkua and Galo turned to discuss the situation between themselves once more. Here they found their two best options out of reach. One was missing and stolen, and the other currently illegal, thanks to some hydrologist environmentalists.

"What problem do they have with the engine?" Galo asked.

"I hoped you'd ask, because the design is really quite clever. You see, the engine is partially self powering, like an upgrade on the clockwork machination engine, you know. A propeller sucks water into a tank, and the flow of water keeps it spinning. That propeller powers a heater, the water is boiled, and the outputted steam powers the motor. Ain't exactly perpetual motion, but once you get it started, it takes nigh all day for the propeller to stop on its own. Trouble first came from Haprian when fish started getting sucked into the propellers. We installed a wire mesh filter, but more protests came with the radiant heat cooking fish and plants alive."

"Hmm, so you've got a steam motor that can run all day, but it boils nearby fish," Galo said, "Is that what you're saying?"

"Did freon not work?" Sinkua asked, "I assume that's the first thing you'd try, but I can't imagine why it couldn't work."

Galo and the portsman both looked to Sinkua with eyebrows raised.

"That was one of our first ideas. It didn't work at first, so we moved to other substances. I always got the feeling it could with a few adjustments though. I'll bring that up with the development crew tonight, but we still have a bit of a problem on our hands," the portsman reminded, "It might take days to perfect the design, and weeks more to get satisfy Haprian and get the approval of the Ouristihran Union. Looks like you boys will have to go a different route or stay in port a spell."

The two brethren lost themselves in thought for a moment. Though neither spoke a word, they communicated volumes to one another through body language and breathless mutterings. Slowly, a sly expression slipped over Sinkua's face.

"Wait, what of an onboard steam engine? Have you been denied use of that?" he asked.

"Well, no I suppose not. But even if it's not denied yet, it's got to be approved for use outside of local waters."

"We'll keep the sails and oars as a façade," Sinkua assured, "and if anybody asks, we'll say it's a prototype in the testing stages. Tell 'em we can't run proper tests without leaving local waters."

"Better still, tell them we're on our way to Haprian to demonstrate the new design," Galo added.

"Heh, alright, I can do that," the portsman agreed with a smirk, "I'll just extend the intake with a length of pipe, grease up the propeller, and it'll be all set. My shift is just about to start, so I should be done by morning."

"Thank you," Galo said, extending his arm for a handshake, "We'll find a place to sleep for the night and return here on the morn."

"For this excitement, the pleasure is all mine," the portsman countered with excitement in his voice, "I feel like some kind of pirate."

The morning after a night spent at a nearby lodge, Galo and Sinkua left aboard the modified steam ship. They spoke little to the portsman, only exchanging a few light pleasantries, but Sinkua did make a point to acquire a vial of his tracking scent before they left port.

This behavior raised Galo's curiosity, as he had done the same with the desk clerk at the lodge as well as a handful of other strangers. Suddenly, his brother was becoming oddly personable. In all their time together, he had never known Sinkua to have much of any desire for socialization. The fact is, that was why he did so well living alone on an island.

Sinkua spoke little else to any of them though. He simply stated that it was in case he needed to contact anybody in the area in the future. They bought it, of course, though his intentions were far different from what any of them likely figured. Galo could see it in his eyes, that look that told he was plotting something, and with each vial, it came a bit closer to its eventual fruition.

The seas were remarkably kind to them over the following days. Much of their time was spent on deck, sparring with all combinations of their weapons and milystic powers while the boat drifted in a general eastwardly direction. Aside from lagging in reaching ArcNos, they only wished to make port every now and again. While they lacked a general route, there were a couple of nations they particularly wished to hit. The latter of the two would be Haprian.

After a bit of discussion, they had thought it to be odd that the Haprianites would deny usage of a steam engine to Ivaria but approve that of a combustion engine to ArcNos. Aside from the obvious hypocrisy, Ivaria had only narrowly been granted permission to release combustion engine land vehicles to the general public, and even then it was strictly regulated. Yet, ArcNos had the combustion engine approved for use in sea crafts even after pilfering the technology from its creators. The whole mess of it stunk of scandal, and Sinkua felt an investigation was in order, given his suspicions of foreign influence behind the new ArcNosian order.

However, just south of the path between Ivaria and Haprian sat the relatively small nation of Eprilen. Here was the seat of the Historical Guild. Their libraries and museums were lined with historical annals, pages ripped from old school books and forgotten manuscripts, and artifacts of cultures long since otherwise vanished from existence.

Through many sleepless nights, Sinkua found himself recollecting key moments from his childhood. Looking back, he could almost see where he began to lose his father to whatever toxicity overcame and became him. Yet, he failed to comprehend what may have caused it. Regardless, because of this, he realized the ripple effect of seemingly inconsequential events. The idea of small occurrences yielding great changes in the future was not lost on him, and for this reason, he felt the truth behind ArcNos may lie in its history.

Galo often found himself kept awake by Sinkua's nocturnal tossing. He took to developing his hydromancy to pass the time. The fact was, days on the sea were idle. Both knew they were biding their time, but Galo grew increasingly anxious with each passing day. The pain of losing his grandfather was still hanging at the surface, and he feared it would be for quite some time.

After several days, in the still of the night, Sinkua ascertained a particular peculiarity he had noticed long ago but only recently assured himself to be true. There was an unmistakable repetition in the scenery surrounding them, and not just the fact that they were on open sea. Off on the horizon, from the starboard rail, he could see land through his binoculars. Explicable enough, but the land continued on for days and was only ever visible from that side of the ship.

"Galo, were you aware of a strip of land in Ouristihra several days long?" he called toward the cabin, rubbing at his goatee, "Or did we mistakenly sail beyond of the continent?"

"What? No, we're still in Ouristihra," Galo assured as he emerged from the cabin, putting his robe on his shirtless body, "We've just been circling Eprilen for a week and half. Are you just now noticing this?"

"No, I just now confirmed my suspicion. And why are we circling?"

"Biding our time," Galo casually answered, leaning on the rail, "That and I'm hoping we'll draw attention and perhaps another strike from ArcNos."

Sinkua paused to reflect on what he was just told. It was apparent that Galo's thoughts were more on vengeance than tactics, what with their being in a wooden ship entirely devoid of armaments, save for the two of them, and in the open sea. If they capsized, Galo would be able to make land with little trouble, but Sinkua would have significantly worse fortune. Regardless of all that, Sinkua knew it best not to contest the issue in such a way. He could sense that Galo was only speaking through his anger.

"We'll make port in the morning," Sinkua ordered, "Until then, what would you say to a bit of night sparring?"

Sinkua raised his fist to chin level and ignited it, illuminating his smirk. The light shone upon his face with a wicked glow, shimmering against the vague glow of his green eyes and refracting through the ruby.

Galo removed his robe and discarded it upon the deck. He lifted his fist to level with Sinkua's, encased in ice through which the flames shimmered. Looking Sinkua square in the eyes, he raised his eyebrows quickly and a mess of spikes burst from the crystalline block.

"Name the game," Galo ordered, accepting the challenge.

"Hand to hand combat," Sinkua proposed, surprising Galo since he usually opted for weapons, "Powers allowed."

Galo opened with a sweeping arc kick, nearly swift enough to cleave a solid tree trunk. Sinkua dropped to his side and tilted his head to evade the careening foot. He caught himself on his hand and, with the other, delivered a quick hard punch to the top of Galo's thigh. Galo stumbled but swung his kicking leg around behind him and swiftly dropped to all fours, perched to pounce.

Sinkua pushed himself upright again and flashed a wisp of flame before Galo's face. Before it could meet flesh, Galo pushed off the deck and flung his body upright. Sinkua took a solid and stationary stance. Galo took one with his arms swinging at his sides and his feet shuffling, a signature of the Tide Dancers.

Sinkua thrust forward abruptly, fiery fist clenched. Just short of collision, he deftly pivoted around and behind Galo. Galo nimbly arched his back, planting his hands on the floor behind him, pulled up into a handstand, and ensnared Sinkua's torso in the grip of his legs. Sinkua pulled back for a strike to the inner thigh, knowing it best to leave his feet on the ground. Anticipating such a counter attack, Galo flung a thin sheet of sleet at Sinkua's bare foot, momentarily supporting himself on one hand.

With Sinkua distracted for a blink, Galo flung his legs forward and Sinkua with them. However, Sinkua clutched his ankles tenaciously. When he landed, Galo was slammed down onto the dock with him. Sinkua rolled to sit upright and jerked Galo toward him. Galo rolled aside agilely to dodge the fiery fist barreling at his spine a split second after. Each pushed himself onto his feet once more with notable celerity.

Sinkua advanced viciously with a fiery spinning hook kick. Seeing an opening, albeit brief, Galo countered with a swift inside arc kick, foot coated in ice, aimed at the side of his ribcage. Having anticipated this gambit, Sinkua accelerated, revealing that he had baited Galo with a purposely slow spin.

Both decelerated to a near halt almost in unison. Galo's foot set lightly against the side of Sinkua's ribcage just as Sinkua's did the same to Galo's neck. They held their poses like statues, each smirking at his proven opponent. Slowly, they lowered the legs and relaxed their bodies.

In their sparring matches, the standard ruling was that it would end when either of them was able to land a single blow on the other. Throws, shoves and powers were not included, nor was striking with anything not permitted in the match. This was because, as they found in their first match aboard their new ship, they spent several minutes countering each other's counters and so forth before either could even make contact, short of a quick grab and throw or the occasional grapple. Neither was out to prove himself to be better than the other, only to have improved since their previous match.They stepped back from each other, panting from the rush. Galo slumped forward and rested his hands on his slightly bent knees, while Sinkua wiped sweat from his forehead and his sweaty hand on his shirt.

"Tell me one thing, Galo," Sinkua beckoned, "How in the hell did you pull that off, bending back and grabbing me with your legs?"

"Well," Galo began, wringing out trickles of sweat that had pooled in his ponytail, "It's one part agility, three parts confidence. That's one of the first things they taught me as a Tide Dancer. Everything is three quarters. . ."

In the middle of his Tide Dancer credo, he was cut short by the blare of a fog horn from off the port rail. Both jumped with a start, having assumed they were alone since no other ship lights punctured the darkness. Sinkua rushed to the port rail and snagged the binoculars he had hung from it.

Near the skyline sat a large ship heading in their general direction. Large pipes adorned the deck and periodically vomited black smoke into the starry sky. This was undoubtedly a combustion ship and therefore another ArcNosian vessel.

"It doesn't look to be armed, so far as I can tell," Sinkua observed, "Don't do anything to draw attention to us, and it ought to pass."

"Provided SenRas and Amirione aren't on board."

"Especially Amirione," Sinkua emphasized, "but I'd presume they're not anyhow."

Over the next several minutes, they continued on their eastwardly heading as the ArcNosian ship carved a perpendicular path to south. Eventually, the ArcNosian ship faded into the horizon, having passed behind them with no interference or acknowledgement otherwise. As Sinkua had suspected, they were making for Eprilen. Their purpose, however, he could not ascertain.

The walls were adorned with massive paintings within frames intricately carved from the finest known metals in all of Ouristihra. Each image was of a bygone ArcNosian leader, the last being the late Brigadier General Elite HarEin. Still beyond it were several meters of empty frames. Some thought the number of frames to be prophetic. Those of sounder mind knew it was nothing more than a matter of finite space.

"It truly is an inspiration. Wouldn't you agree, Admiral SenRas?" CreSam asked as the two traversed the timeline of leadership, dressed in painstakingly pressed black suits, "I feel a spark shoot up my spine every time I'm here."

"This is my first time visiting the Ouristihran Union Parliament," SenRas admitted, "But I'll agree, the artwork is quite good is this hall."

"Quite good? You're a fine soldier, but your vocabulary is sorely lacking," CreSam scoffed, "This hall radiates with power, the same power of revolution that I feel has become ArcNos. Yes, a coming of age is upon us. The world is evolving around us, and we will be the ones to carry Ouristihra into the future."

At the end of the ArcNosian Hall stood a pair of towering double doors. The surface was intricately engraved with the coat of arms which adorned the ArcNosian flag. One such flag hung from the ceiling, with the end a meter above CreSam's head. He gripped the gold plated door handle and pushed it open with a grunt.

They entered a sparsely lit circular room with sconces at regular intervals. Twelve sets of doors, one for each nation, were arranged along a semicircle. Their being listed alphabetically, eleven doors stood to SenRas and CreSam's left. Along the other half of the wall sat a semicircular table lined with thirteen seats, all facing the doors. This was the assembly house of the Ouristihran Union Parliament.

Twelve of the seats held an elected official from each nation. The position was one of democratic representation and regulation, the twelve of them holding the collective power to execute the will of the people when their leaders acted against their best interest. As for the thirteenth seat, this was for the Eprilenese Prime Duchess, leader of the Eprilenese government and member of the Ouristihran Union. Every five years, the newly elected members of the Ouristihran Union Parliament appointed one federal leader to oversee their operations and mediate on internal disputes.

"Prime Duchess Olsa," CreSam remarked as they entered the room, "We always seem to meet under these circumstances."

"Brigadier General Elite CreSam," the Prime Duchess replied dryly, "No surprise seeing you back here again."

"What can I say? I'm a sucker for a pretty. . ."

"Cut the bullshit, CreSam. In the past three weeks, you've been accused of two international crimes. Now I understand that you say you did not issue orders to gun down Chieftain Sage Gijin. . ."

"I say I didn't because I didn't!" CreSam snapped, "Do you intend to punish me for someone else's insubordination?"

"Sir, if you cannot keep your own men in order, you are not fit to lead!" Olsa barked, "but even I understand there will always be at least one rotten apple in the basket. Once the rebel is disposed of, we can move past this issue. Until then, your seat in the Ouristihran Union is under restriction for one year. You will only be permitted to vote on select issues, and you may not raise any issue to be put to a vote. Every instance in which you fail to cooperate will extend your restriction by one month."

"Understood, Prime Duchess Olsa," CreSam agreed begrudgingly.

"Now then, on to more recent events," Olsa continued, "I understand your nation recently acquired the exclusive right to mass produce combustion engines for use in aquatic transportation."

"Actually, after recent investigations, we feel the information given was inadequate," interrupted the Judge from Haprian, "After this, I would like to put the licensing to a second vote with the newly acquired information in mind."

"We'll address that shortly," Olsa noted, "It's recently been brought to my attention that the blueprints and equipment for the prototype were stolen from an Ivarian development center. That makes them government property. Foremost, the blueprints are to be returned to the lab."

"That won't be a problem, madam. I'll have them returned when I arrive home."

"Did you really think that was your only punishment? You are going to be operating under surveillance from now on. Admiral SenRas is your right hand man, and I will assign you your left hand woman. The Eprilenese Judge will be my eyes and ears, reporting back any actions she feels need to be brought to my attention. Your sentence begins today and continues either until you no longer hold office or three quarters of the Parliament elects to end it, votes to be held annually. Do you have any questions?"

A middle aged woman, a couple of years CreSam's junior, with lightly tanned skin stood up from the Eprilenese chair and walked around to the front of the table. She carried a distant familiarity, but he could not discern if he was wrong, she had forgotten, or she was merely feigning an introduction when she extended her hand. As she did, CreSam eyed the bottom half of a tattoo on her arm, the same as Kabehl's and Amirione's.

"Glad to meet you, sir," she greeted, "You can call me Malia."

Chapter 11

That night, after the ArcNosian ship passed, Galo lowered the sails and Sinkua deactivated the steam pump. They had decided to let the boat sit idle until the ArcNosians returned northward. Still restless after their sparring session, Sinkua spent much of the night watching the southern horizon.

Leaning against the railing, he held a pomegranate in one hand and his dagger in the other. He had used it first to slice the fruit in half and was scooping out the morsels and pouring them into his mouth with it. Despite Gijin's urgings, he had come to use it for everyday tasks such as that. Though Galo didn't fully comprehend the purpose of the dagger, he feared Sinkua may have been desecrating it in some way. Still, though he kept his intentions to himself, Sinkua remained confident in his approach to this enigmatic blade bestowed upon him. So Galo kept his speculative anxiety silent.

Conversely, he lacked confidence in his understanding of CreSam's goals for ArcNos. After the attack on the Sacred City, he had been certain of his theory of martial dominance. However, after discovering that Ivaria was bypassed and instead the target of a crippling economic strike, he began restructuring his analysis. It was becoming obvious that two of his worst mistakes were assuming he understood CreSam and, furthermore, underestimating his tactical malice.

Continental dominance still appeared to be his goal, but the approach to each nation was to be subjective. Aside from that, the matter of reason was still a mystery. He couldn't postulate what CreSam hoped to gain from overpowering and crippling the rest of Ouristihra, only that it couldn't have been simply for its own sake. Regardless of the reason, knowing his methods thus far was enough to stand firm in defiance.

"They're probably down there now," he muttered to himself as he spat seeds into the ocean, "Threatening the locals or some such. I'm surprised I can't hear the gun shots from here. Bastards."

With that he pitched an enflamed piece of rind into the ocean with a grunt. The fire was doused with a flash of smoke and steam upon impact. He turned around and propped himself up on the railing and shook his head as he dug fruit from the other half of the rind.

"What is it you're after, old man?" he mumbled, "Are you really so blinded by power that you crave more just for the sake of having it? What good is being king of the mountain when you're the only one who lives there?"

"I'm curious as to what business he has in Eprilen," Galo added, emerging from the cabin yet again, "Maybe some interest in dusting over history's tracks before we find them?"

"That's the best I can figure, as well," Sinkua agreed, "but the thought that he would just now have decided to do so, right after we decide we're going to research the matter, feels a touch too coincidental. By the way, shouldn't you be asleep? It's still two hours until sunrise."

"I was coming out here to ask you the same thing, brother."

"I can't sleep. You know I've had trouble with that ever since, well, that afternoon."

"Yes, I know. With CreSam and your mother in the living room," Galo reiterated with a hint of empathy, "but I'll not have you collapsing in the middle of the day. At least lie down and let your body rest."

Sinkua lowered his head and sighed.

"Fine then," he agreed, following Galo back to the cabin, "You're pretty maternal for a guy, you know."

"Well, somebody has to look out for your health," Galo insisted with a smirk.

After he awoke for the day, Galo started up the steam pumps and set a course for the northern ports of Eprilen. They arrived early in the afternoon, greeted by a small group of portsmen. Galo stood at the bow of the ship where one of them tossed a rope to him. He tied it to the bowsprit, and the lot of them guided the ship into the port.

"Thank you for your help, sirs," Galo announced as he leapt agilely from the railing to the dock, "Sorry I have little else to present in the way of gratitude, but know that you have the thanks of the Sacred City."

"What do you speak of, boy?" a grizzled portsman asked, "Masnethege was wiped nigh clean off the map some two fortnights ago. Little good it does having the gratitude of a dead man, eh."

"Sad state of affairs, isn't it? One month, and foreigners are already assuming the Sacred City was eradicated in its entirety," Sinkua mused, standing atop the railing of the ship, "Imagine the theories that manifest when you're cut off from society for four years."

"Always one for an entrance, eh brother?" Galo shouted back to him.

Sinkua leapt from the railing and landed next to him.

"This young man here beside me has recently inherited the title of Chieftain Sage of Berinin. If that's not proof enough for you that the nation still exists, take a trip there yourself," he informed the portsmen, "You'll find that everything west of the capitol is quite intact. Masnethege itself was almost entirely destroyed, but enough of its people survived to rebuild it. Now, if you don't believe the two gentlemen who resisted the onslaught, well I don't know who you would believe. So, either you can take your chances in traveling to a wasteland that may still be a target, or you can aid us in our mission and direct us to the nearest historical museum."

"What? You speak nonsense, boy," the grizzled portsman insisted, "We heard in the newspaper that it had been destroyed. And ain't no way two young scrappers could hold off an entire fleet."

"Hmm? How did my hand get wet?" Galo asked with water dripping from his hand.

The lot of them cocked their heads in his general direction. He raised his hand, water now spilling over from atop it. Their collective attention in his grasp, he slowly eased nearer to them, now watching their faces instead of his hand. With a flick of the wrist, he froze the spiral of water into a mess of frozen spikes. The portsmen stumbled over each other jumping back with surprise.

"Two ordinary young scrappers, no," Sinkua initially agreed with his hand ablaze, "Two young scrappers who can do something like this, yes perhaps."

"Now," Galo continued, "The museum."

"Head directly south, some two kilometers as the crow flies," one of them instructed after nervously clearing his throat.

"Thank you much," Galo accepted, "Again, you have the gratitude of Berinin."

"Y-you're welcome."

After Sinkua had collected a vial of tracking scent from each of the portsmen, the two of them took their leave of the crowd and headed south on foot. When they reached the end of the docks, however, they were interrupted once again.

"Wait! Wait, sirs!" a panting portsman called to them, "There's something you should know."

Sinkua stopped first, then Galo. Sinkua cocked his head to glance back over his shoulder.

"Oh? Something about a man setting his own hand on fire really gets you to open up."

"Last night," began the portsman, still catching his breath, "Brigadier General Elite CreSam showed up here. He had an older man, another soldier I think, with him. Called him Admiral SenRas or some such."

"CreSam and SenRas came here?" Sinkua asked, turning the rest of the way around.

"Yes, yes. They left this morning before the sun came up, had another person with them."

"Who was it? Can you give me a name?"

"Any Eprilenese who saw them could give you a name, boy. It was Judge Malia of the Ouristihran Union Parliament. Means they had business at the Parliament Hall, and judging by how quick they left, it must have been their only business here."

Sinkua shoved his hands in his pockets and tapped his foot introspectively before speaking, "Thank you. We'll keep that in mind."

Sinkua and Galo turned to resume their southward hike, reflecting on this new information. The first bit of news worked quite perfectly into their plan. Despite not being his second in command, it seemed SenRas may have been CreSam's assistant, perhaps his confidant in some sense. As SenRas was not known to hold a seat in the Union Parliament, there would be little other reason for him to accompany CreSam in his visit to the Parliament Hall. Thus, he had undoubtedly heard about their exploits in Berinin as early as the following morning.

The latter part of the news, however, troubled them both. Sinkua kept his hands shoved in his pockets while he walked, and Galo only watched the ground a couple of meters before him. Both were locked in thought, and through their body language they seemed to silently communicate with one another.

CreSam's escorting the Eprilenese Judge back to ArcNos suggested that an alliance between the two nations may have been under development. While Eprilen would have little to offer in the way of direct military or technological advancement, it still put them a step closer to dominion. Having Prime Duchess Olsa at the helm of the Union Parliament could certainly prove advantageous. Furthermore, having unhindered access to the historical annals would allow CreSam to essentially rewrite history and purge anything leading to the theoretical foreign influence. Had they waited much longer to visit Eprilen and look into the records, they feared they may have stumbled into false information.

Roughly an hour or so later, they arrived at the nearest historical museum, just as the portsman had promised. A young female curator, no older than Sinkua, greeted them at the door.

"Welcome," she said delightedly, "What brings you guys here today? Interest in your lineage perhaps? Or just brushing up a bit?"

"A little of both, I suppose," Sinkua replied, "We need to know all we can about the history of ArcNos, particularly any conflicts before now."

"I think you'll find what you're looking for here. Follow me to the ArcNosian Division."

With that, she turned and walked back into the building, vaguely swiveling her hips as she walked to ensure she didn't lose her guests. Sinkua gave it a quick glance, nodded in approval, and resumed watching directly ahead. Near the back of the long corridor, they reached the ArcNosian Division of the building. The curator opened the door for them and waved them inside.

"The displays date further back as you head to the right," she told them, "I'll leave you two to your research."

"Well, she was something of a flirt," Galo commented after she had closed the door.

"Yeah, she was. Not bad to look at though."

"Oh, I'm not complaining, just pointing it out."

Beginning in the far left corner, they studied each display, working their way to the right. The first few held familiar imagery. Samples of uniforms adorned some of them, denoting significant changes throughout history. Copies of vehicle blueprints were a common site as well, along with weapons both new and antiquated. All of the latter were under thick glass of course, which was undoubtedly connected to a security mechanism as well.

Some two centuries back, something worthwhile finally caught their attention. It served not only as a possible explanation for recent events in ArcNos but as a definitive explanation for the current condition of Kirts. The display was titled The ArcNosian Kirtsian Trade Conflict.

Up until two hundred years in the past, Kirts was the Ouristihran leader in ore refinery and metallurgy. Their Blacksmithing Guild was the largest and most prosperous known, renowned for the impeccable quality of their finished goods and seemingly endless cache of raw materials. They were the primary source of metals for all of Ouristihra, but ArcNos was by far their best client. The two worked symbiotically, Kirts supporting the stability of ArcNos's military and ArcNos supporting Kirts's economy almost single-handedly.

However, a time eventually came when ArcNos decided it would be more cost effective to produce their wares domestically. Retired military personnel took up blacksmithing first as a hobby, then later as their own trade. In their old age, they passed this to younger recruits, particularly ones who were physically sound but either could not or would not serve in combat positions. As this trend became more culturally ingrained, the economy of Kirts began to crumble.

At the current time, only a couple thousand citizens remained in Kirts, most of them descendants of the families who either refused to leave their home or simply could not. However, while nothing of recent conflict had been reported, those who stayed behind had harbored feelings of animosity, as was shown in rebellious demonstrations.

"So, Kirts is behind all this?" Galo asked, a bit dumbfounded, "I never would've thought."

"Neither would I, but I don't think they're behind all of it," Sinkua agreed, "But this does suggest that they're a significant catalyst. Descendants of the Kirtsian squatters and rebels are now working to empower ArcNos, probably with the ulterior motive of ruining their integrity."

"Perhaps to later crush them politically," Galo suggested, "or maybe to turn the rest of Ouristihra against them, maybe drive them to be forced out of the Ouristihran Union."

"It's a brilliantly laid plan, regardless of the exact ultimate goal of it all," Sinkua admitted, "It takes great minds to plot vengeance such as this. I would venture to say this conspiracy dates back to the days of the original squatters, simply biding their time over generations until this information was stricken from school texts and the conflict faded into obscurity."

"So then, are we off to Kirts next?"

"No, not yet," Sinkua clarified as they exited the ArcNosian Division, "There are too many nations between here and there. I'd like to head a bit further east before we turn northward."

"Looking into Haprian and their silence about the ArcNosian combustion ships?"

"Precisely that."

When they returned to the docks, one of the portsman helped them untie their boat and launch to the east, apologizing for his and his colleagues' behavior that morning. They left port with the sun creeping toward the western horizon, casting a long shadow off the bow of the ship. This shadow stretched to the eastern horizon, guiding their trip to the coast of Haprian. Once dusk neared, Sinkua could spot the docks through his binoculars.

"We've almost reached Haprian," he told Galo while still watching the horizon, "We should be there tonight. We'll find a place to sleep and . . ."

"Hold that thought," Galo called back, "We've got company. Come take a look."

Sinkua urgently jogged over to the port rail, binoculars hanging from his wrist. When he arrived at Galo's side, Galo pointed out a ship near the northern horizon. It appeared to be heading southeast and was of ArcNosian design. Sinkua watched it through the binoculars for a moment and sighed with disdain.

"It's an ArcNosian war ship," he cautioned, "Similar to the model they deployed to Berinin on that night."

"So it's a comparable assault," Galo added, "but why are they poised to attack Haprian?"

"Not necessarily."

"Not necessarily comparable or not necessarily attacking Haprian?"

"This ship is alone, but it's considerably larger than the flagship that led the fleet into Berinin. It alone may hold more troops than the lot of them," Sinkua explained, "but like you said, there's still the matter of why they're attacking Haprian."

"Well, the attack on Berinin was unprovoked as far as I know."

"That's true enough, but recall that Haprian has been aiding ArcNos."

"Perhaps they changed their minds."

"Or perhaps they've outlived their usefulness. Either way, it appears we're set to collide near the coast."

"So are we to attack them from the side as they deploy upon the harbor?"

"No, we'll cut them off before they reach land. Turn us fifteen degrees to the north."

As the hours passed, and the sun fell upon the western horizon, the skewed shadow of their ship stretching toward the docks. The ArcNosians seemed to be unaware of their approach. Sinkua could not see any soldiers or crew members on deck. Either this was an automated unit, such as the vehicles in the forest in Berinin, or all were below deck awaiting the signal to emerge.

During the remaining hours until collision, Galo immersed himself in deep meditation. His right forearm trembled as hydromantic milystis surged through the Serpent Bracer, amplified by its greened copper scales. When he heard a clamor just beyond the rails, he reclaimed his consciousness.

Sinkua was out by the bow, watching the colossus of a warship as they closed in. Galo joined him, each with their respective weapon in hand. The coast of Haprian was still a kilometer or so away, not the distance they had hoped for but enough to eliminate collateral damage nonetheless. The clamor within the ferocious vessel rumbled on the fringes of audibility, though the words were indistinguishable.

"Have you prepared yourself, brother?" Sinkua asked.

Galo closed his eyes and breathed deeply of the salty ocean air mixed with the scent of exhaust fumes spewed forth by the warship. Memories of his last night in the Sacred City of Masnethege flashed through his mind, twisted images of carnage and remorse. A shudder ran down his back at the recollection of it all. He opened his eyes and exhaled slowly as he nodded.

Galo quickly clenched his fist and popped it open, manifesting a ball of ice the size of an orange. He took a few steps back and charged forth, hurling the ice ball at the cabin wall of the mighty warship. It cracked on impact, sending a crashing echo resonating through the wall.

Soldiers emerged by the fistful, many of them appearing to be Northlanders but not ArcNosian. By the time they noticed the ship beside them, Sinkua was already upon the bow. Galo was further back, making for the railing just to the right of the bow. Sinkua drew his morningstar and let the chain fall as he sprinted skillfully up the bowsprit, the enflamed spiked ball flailing behind him. Those soldiers not stupefied by the seemingly unprovoked assault drew their weapons, an assortment of blades and pistols. Sinkua leapt from the tip of the bowsprit, his free arm blocking his face and trembling with milystis.

Startled by the display, the Infantrymen found themselves unable to take steady aim. Presumably, neither SenRas nor Amirione had told them of these unidentified renegades. As Sinkua barreled toward the deck of the warship, one brave Infantryman managed to position himself directly in his path, trembling as he aimed the pistol at this plummeting stranger. He dropped his gun and stumbled back when Sinkua's boots slammed against the deck and his forearm burst into flames. Sinkua swung his fiery forearm, striking the Infantryman across the face and searing his flesh. The side of the soldier's neck exposed, Sinkua fluidly followed with an overhead swing of his morningstar. The spray of hot blood gave the illusion of an explosion triggered by the trauma.

As quickly as this soldier had been stricken down, Sinkua ripped the morningstar from his neck, spinning with the withdrawal to swing at a soldier thinking to strike from behind. Flames and blood spewed about as he ripped flesh in spite of armor plates, all the while ducking and dodging swinging blades. One bloodied soldier managed to sneak through the clamor, grabbing Sinkua's neck from behind, a pistol pointed at his head.

"Nice try, boy," he muttered, "but you'll not bar our mission any longer."

"I should say the same to you," Sinkua said coldly, glancing back toward his ship, "Do you know how to swim?"

With that last question, Sinkua dropped his morningstar and clutched the man's forearm, digging into the flesh with red hot fingers. The soldier trembled in anguish, his gun arm wavering and grip loosening. With his opponent of the moment startled, Sinkua thrust the side of his pelvic bone into the soldier's gut. He crouched and flung the damaged Infantryman over the railing. With his other hand, he struck the wooden deck and ignited his immediate surroundings. The flames spread rapidly, catalyzed by the mess of blood, sinew, and armor oils. Sinkua's eyes flared as he turned to face the remaining defensive unit.

"Who else among you would die in fealty to a faceless tyrant?" he boomed through the crackling flames, "I offer you this one chance to surrender to me and stop this cannibalistic plague."

Galo leapt from the railing just as the wounded soldier passed, careening toward him with his glaive drawn back. The soldier slammed into the surface of the sea, his spine cracking on contact. Galo set upon him immediately thereafter, driving his glaive through his torso for good measure as well as to dampen his own impact with the sea. He dismissively removed the blade and swam below the ship.

He turned to face upward, crawling along the underside of the rumbling hull. He ran his hand over the surface in search of a brace between metal plates. Eventually, he found one near the middle of the hull. Two plates overlapped by a few centimeters, held fast by a series of mechanically tightened nuts and bolts. Galo pressed his free hand against the surface, steadying himself and holding his position as the ship continued to move forward.

Carefully, he wedged the tip of the blade between the plates. He grasped the handle with both hands, letting the water guide his body to its end. He dangled for a moment before bringing his feet up to the hull and freezing them to the surface for leverage. Over and over, he thrust and lunged, driving the glaive further into the joint. Finally, when he could push no further against the bolts, he ripped the blade from the crack. Water rushed into the hull, the onslaught of pressure forcing the bolts from their holes. Galo held fast to the plates, using his own hydromancy to protect himself from the torrent. When a large enough rip had formed in the hull, he released himself from the metal plate and let the gushing water carry him inside.

The entirety of the deck was in flames now, contrasting against the deep purple hues of the dusk sky. Sinkua's eyes emitted a steady green glow, masking the angle of his pupils and allowing him to see more clearly than usual through the smoke and flames. Sinew hung from the spikes of his morningstar, and blood and frayed fabric, both from soldiers and himself, decorated his clothing.

"All this time, the lot of you have been here on this deck, running through fire and struggling to retain what's left of your worthless lives," he shouted through the flames, "yet the true threat lies several meters below your feet and draws ever closer."

The skyline appeared to be rising somehow. Over the railing, the sea could be seen rising up the walls of the ship. Survivors ran frantically to jump overboard.

Ignoring them, Sinkua leapt and stomped firmly, crashing through the weakened deck and into the hatch below. Nearby, he spotted a floor panel with a lever. He opened it and dropped into the engine room. He looked about, tuning out the clamor of soldiers and fire in the cabins above. Galo was nowhere to be seen, and the torrent could still be heard below. Sinkua stomped the floor twice, sending an echo resonating into the hull, and stepped back. Moments later, an icy blade pierced the floor. It withdrew for a moment only to return more forcibly. After a few of these, Galo had cut himself a sufficient hole and climbed up from the hull, followed by a gush of water.

"How are the soldiers on deck?" he asked.

"Half burnt and half drowning," Sinkua answered dryly, "Now let's do away with the remains."

Galo nodded and gathered a frigid mist around the Serpent Bracer. All at once, he drew back and punched the air with brutal force, launching the torrent of frozen mist at the central combustion unit. The mist coated the metallic shell, cooling it rapidly upon contact. Against the flames within, it wasn't enough to freeze it, though it was more than sufficient to frost the surface.

After a few moments, he stopped and the two of them waited in silence. Within, the fires of combustion reheated the shell, the process significantly weakening the surface. Sinkua raised his arms and formed a barricade of fire between Galo and the unit.

"Any time you're ready, brother," he urged.

The blade lined with ice, Galo gripped his glaive like a javelin. He ran forth and lunged it at the combustion unit, the blade screaming past Sinkua's shoulder. Both of them dropped to a crouch, and the blade shattering a gaping hole in the shell. The combustible fluids spewed violently from the lifeless wound. Smoldering chunks of brittle metal coated in enflamed oils streaked overhead. The fires on the floor behind them were consumed as Sinkua maintained the barrier of flames. When the chunks of metal began falling near them, they erected their bodies.

Up on the deck, the flames had all but died. Seared corpses were strewn about, the twisted fruits of Sinkua's initial labor. The ropes holding the life boats had been burned away as well, and those life boats were overturned in the sea below. The clamor was nearly silenced now. What few survivors remained would soon be consumed by the sea.

The railing of the warship was now lower than that of their own vessel. Galo sprinted across the deck, leapt from the railing and grabbed the bowsprit. He shuffled down it a ways before pulling himself atop the narrow plank. Sinkua followed shortly behind, though he climbed atop it where he grasped it. Safely back on the deck of their own ship with heavy breath and rapid pulses, they brushed a myriad of smoldering substances from their clothing while they watched the sea consume the smoking ship.

"Haprian is safe for now," Galo complimented with a relieved sigh.

"For now, yes," Sinkua agreed, "In the morning, we'll look into what could have provoked such an attack."

"We're not to make port tonight as you said earlier?"

"No, after what just happened, I'd rather stay with what lodgings we have than seek out new ones in foreign territory."

As he made for the cabin, something caught his eye to the northwest. He stopped abruptly and peered toward the horizon, trying to discern the identity of this floating object. It appeared to be a small dinghy with a single sail, and the man on board looked to be watching them as well.

"Galo, hand me the binoculars!" he beckoned.

Galo snatched the binoculars from the railing and tossed them to Sinkua. Just as he suspected, the man aboard the other boat was watching them as well. This aging sailor donned an ArcNosian uniform and an unmistakable familiarity. The soldier lowered his binoculars, and Sinkua sighed and did the same.

"SenRas."

Chapter 12

Sinkua found himself restless throughout the remainder of the night, tossing about in a partially conscious state until the following dawn. The rage that had overcome him felt unlike anything he knew of himself. Such feelings first consumed him in the forests of Berinin, but last night's events had further cemented his suspicions. An intangible force was carrying him through these battles. Outside of combat, he could not replicate the speed, power or techniques that had become second nature within. The adrenaline consumed him and guided his body. His rage blinded him, but at the same time, it sharpened his senses beyond anything he could know without it. Perhaps, it was just another quirk of being an Hybrid.

However, he feared he was heading down a path to becoming CreSam. Genetically speaking, he tended to favor the old tyrant, somewhat to his regret. Now he found himself slaughtering soldiers for little more than reasonable speculation of their intentions. Granted, the evidence was substantial, but they lacked concrete proof. Regardless, he had laid waste to scores of strangers with nary a hint of remorse in the act.

Of course, given his reason for combating them, he thought he was staying on the righteous path of which Gijin had always spoken. They were working their way up the hierarchy of the new ArcNosian order to discover what caused the sudden growth and aggression. Still, he feared that his anger was on its way to overcoming him, and he knew there was no righteousness in losing oneself to rage.

As the light of the next dawn pierced through his window, he rose to his feet, too restless to fail at sleeping for any longer. He dressed himself and stepped out onto the deck, rubbing the fatigue from his eyes. The ports of Haprian were but a stone's throw away. A pair of uniformed men, uniforms not befitting of portsmen, waited at the docks.

"Well now," Sinkua muttered, "This does not bode well for us."

He knocked vigorously on Galo's cabin door.

"Galo! Wake up!" he shouted, "We've got a welcoming committee, and it's not a warm one."

Something metallic clunked against the inner side of the door and hit the floor with a deep thud. A few minutes later, Galo emerged, groggy and clothed. He knelt down to pick up the Serpent Bracer and slipped it over his forearm.

"What's going on now?" he asked.

"That," Sinkua said, pointing toward the dock, "I think they may have seen through the façade."

"Perhaps," Galo halfheartedly agreed, "Or perhaps they witnessed our actions last night and wish to commend us for protecting them."

"I'd like to believe that, too, but they don't look terribly grateful."

"You there!" one of the uniformed men shouted through a megaphone, "Identify yourselves!"

"My name is Galo," Galo announced, placing his hands upon the railing, "This fellow's name is Sinkua. We're from Berinin, sirs."

"Galo and Sinkua?" the man confirmed, "We're going to launch a tow rope to guide you into the port. We ask that you do not resist lest you make this difficult for everybody including yourselves. If you are armed, we implore you to disarm yourselves immediately."

"We come ashore with only the clothes on our backs," Sinkua shouted back, also placing his hands on the railing.

From a holster on his back, the other man withdrew a loaded spear gun with a rope tied behind the head of the spear. He took steady aim and fired the spear into the bow of the ship. After giving it a tug to check the hold, he mounted the gun atop a post on the edge of the dock. Clearly, the two had been designed around one another. He flipped a release switch on the gun, and it began recoiling and guiding the boat into the port.

"That was quite a show you boys put on last night," the apparent spokesman of the two commended while his associate escorted them, "sinking an ArcNosian freighter with just the two of you to accredit to the act."

"It's a talent. Some people can paint. Some people can dance. We sink ships," Sinkua shrugged, "Oh, and he can dance, too."

"How you did it is of little consequence to us," the second officer interjected, "Your reasons are our concern, rather, and that is notwithstanding your piloting an unlicensed watercraft."

"We can explain that," Galo insisted.

"I'm sure you can," the first one countered, pulling Galo's forearms behind his back, "Otherwise, this will be a disappointingly boring day."

Galo turned to Sinkua with a look of desperation as his wrists were cuffed. Sinkua sighed and shook his head, signaling not to resist as he was cuffed by the other officer. The two of them were led shamefully down the docks.

About a quarter of a kilometer inland, they came to a station. Within, Sinkua and Galo were led down a series of hallways with plain white walls and gray carpets, undoubtedly designed to befuddle guests hoping to make a break for the exit. They stopped in front of an unmarked door beside a large window. Through the vast pane, they could see a plain wooden table and a few folding chairs. Inside the room, they found the other side of the pane was a mirror. They were shown to their seats, facing the two-way mirror.

"Where should we begin?" one of the officers pondered, drumming his fingers on the table.

"You could start by taking these cuffs off," Sinkua requested, "Or do you think too little of your building's design?"

"We pose no threat to you, we promise," Galo added, "Your uniforms are not ArcNosian."

"We're to decide how much of a threat you pose," the first argued.

"Then introduce yourselves to us," Sinkua insisted, "You want information out of us, we need to know who we're giving it to."

"Of course," the same officer complied, "I am Alucan, and this is my partner Doriman, of the Northern Haprianite Coastal Patrol."

"Very well then, Alucan and Doriman, what brings you to bring us here this morn?" Sinkua asked.

"Foremost, we ran the serial number engraved on the underside of your bowsprit and found no records matching that number. You care to explain why you're piloting an unlicensed craft?" Doriman asked.

"It's only illegal until we get it licensed," Galo contested, "Which must be done in Haprian, must it not?"

"And we were on our way to Haprian, were we not?"

"That you were, but the serial number did not match the syntax of those on record," Alucan added, "We found that odd enough in and of itself, until we noticed your ship moving on a windless night. Your craft is not only unlicensed but uncertified as well."

"You speak of the engine on board, undoubtedly," Sinkua confirmed, "We learned on a visit to Ivaria that your government had denied them the certification to mass produce ships with outboard steam powered engines. But they had recently finished work on a prototype with an onboard engine, a more ecologically friendly design."

"Rather than have them call one of yours out there again after such a short time, we instead offered to bring the ship out here for you to see," Galo added, "Now you can witness it in action rather than settle with but words."

"So you would have us believe that you're piloting an illegal ship for the convenience of our government?" Doriman scoffed.

"Exactly that," Sinkua answered calmly, "You saw our actions last night, so you could tell even then that we were bound for Haprian well before you spoke to us this morn. Our coming here was no mistake."

"Very well, I see your point," Doriman conceded with a sigh, "but you would have done well to send word of your approach ahead of time."

"Slipped our minds," Galo confessed with a shrug, "The excitement of innovation can be overwhelming, I suppose."

"Now that that's out of the way, on to more pressing matters," Alucan dismissed, "The two of you blindsided and sank an ArcNosian freighter last night."

"You're welcome," Sinkua boasted.

"That was no freighter," Galo argued, "It was a military carrier vessel and not the first we've encountered."

"You lie like dogs!" Doriman roared, "Innocent lives were lost to your hands!"

"Innocent lives?" Sinkua snapped, "Those people were coming to kill you, you ungrateful jackass!"

"What proof do you have of this?" Alucan inquired.

"A similar model of ship came to Berinin a few weeks ago. I'm sure you caught wind of what transpired, though it cannot compare to witnessing it yourself," Galo recollected.

"You have an alibi for everything, don't you boy?" Doriman hissed, "Are we to just take your word that you walked away from that slaughter unscathed?"

"That slaughter is the reason we treated with ArcNos," Alucan admitted, "That shipped came to deliver the goods of our treaty and finalize the terms thereof."

"What?!" Sinkua blurted, "You can't be serious!"

"Oh but we are. Don't get us wrong, we'd rather not think well of killing on that scale or any other for that matter, but ArcNos showed a sense of aquatically friendly innovation unseen in other foreign developments."

"You speak of the combustion ships they stole from Ivaria," Galo confirmed.

"They stole nothing, because the production rights had not yet been granted to Ivarian manufacturers," Doriman insisted, "They simply finished what Ivaria started and improved on it."

"So dead fish are more of a concern than tainted air?" Sinkua asked, "Good to know where your priorities sit, you shitheads."

"Our concerns are hydrology and aquatic ecosystems," Alucan insisted, "If there's an issue with threats to the air quality, the Ierodhesan Judge can take it up at the Parliament Hall. Aeronautics are more their concern."

"That aside, why would you treat with a nation who laid waste to longest standing city in the continent?" Galo asked.

"The ArcNosians put it to us quite clearly," Doriman recalled, "Those third world fools were against innovation, plain and simple. They tried to stand in the way of advancement, and so were bowled over."

"You heard wrong! We had no voice in the matter before we were stricken down!" Galo shouted, "Continue speaking such lies of my homeland, and I swear I will lay waste to the both of you with my hands cuffed."

Doriman jumped to his feet and aimed a swiftly drawn pistol at Galo's head.

"Galo, calm the hell down!" Sinkua snapped, "I'll not walk out of here carrying you on my shoulders."

"You gentlemen heard wrong about what happened in Berinin," Galo hissed through heavy breath, "You have no reason to believe me, but if we let the next ship of that design enter your ports, you will find your reason. They lied to you."

The debate was interrupted by a rapping upon the door. Alucan excused himself to answer it. A female officer stood in the doorway, her body language weighed down with remorse.

"I have some news to report," she began through shaky breath, "After Judge Mikalan's extended absence following his business at the Ouristihran Union Parliament Hall, an investigative squad was sent to search for him. Last night, he was found dead just off the northeastern coast."

"Did they say how long he appeared to have been deceased?" Alucan asked, deceptively calloused.

"No more than a day. Those two in there may be killers, but they laid not a hand on our own, sir."

"Thank you," he said as he closed the door.

Alucan turned to face Sinkua and Galo once again. He lowered his head and sighed heavily.

"It's dreadful when an icon falls, is it not?" Galo sympathetically offered

"I knew Mikalan personally," Alucan confided, forgetting of the interrogation for a moment.

"And I knew Gijin personally, as did Sinkua," Galo related, "Along with many more Berininites."

"You have to understand," Sinkua implored, "what we did last night, we did with memories of carnage. Carnage that would undoubtedly have found its way to your shores had we not intervened. Hopefully you can see that, now that you've lost one of your own."

"You speak much of loss for someone who killed numerous unsuspecting soldiers just last night," Doriman interjected, "Do you not think them to have families as well?"

"We do," Galo admitted, "but they are, themselves, part of an organization that we have sworn to combat and hinder. They undoubtedly know of what transpired in Berinin, and yet still they chose to side with ArcNos."

"They're victims of their own conscious decisions," Sinkua added, "Now those decisions have taken Judge Mikalan from you just as they have taken so many others from the Southlands."

"Judge Mikalan was a good man, a man of distinction," Alucan hissed, "So do not try to lump him in as just another victim of the conflict amongst ArcNos, Berinin and Ivaria. My guess would be that one of the latter two was more directly involved in his death."

"Speculate all you want," Sinkua dismissed, "but do nothing in the way of countermeasures until you know the truth of his passing. That's all we ask of you."

CreSam leaned back against the wall, reexamining his personal notes. Malia and Amirione stood opposite to him with their arms folded. An earpiece adorned the side of Malia's head. Amirione watched CreSam intently as he gathered his thoughts. Meanwhile, Malia avoided eye contact, speaking under her breath with her finger against the earpiece.

"Yes ma'am. The platoon was thirty-five percent ArcNosian blood," she muttered, inaudible to CreSam, "You may think little of it, but I find it disconcerting. Forward the report as you see fit."

"What did she say of it?" Amirione asked under his breath.

"She spoke little on the matter, except to trust him to stay in line lest our liege speaks otherwise, but she'll let him know of this regardless."

Beyond a nearby door, a clamor was building into an uproar, nigh drowning the voice of Brigadier EshCal. From where they stood, the acoustics of the amphitheater were not favorable. Vaguely hearing mention of his name and title, CreSam stepped out onto the stage. Amirione followed while Malia remained backstage. EshCal smirked at the two of them and clapped with the audience. She set a hand upon CreSam's shoulder and showed him to the podium.

"They're all yours, sir," she offered, barely audible over the roaring crowd.

CreSam centered himself behind the podium and laid his hands atop it. He lowered his head and sighed, his breath upon the microphone echoing throughout the amphitheater. The crowd fell silent. He raised his head once again and lifted his hands from the podium.

"People of ArcNos!" he boomed, "Our neighbors continue still to doubt our dominance. They stand in the way of innovation and furthermore in the way of unification. Of whom do I speak this morn, you ask? I speak of Haprian. They who once stood beside us in innovation have decided rather to stand against us. The certification to mass produce combustion engine ships was stripped from ArcNosian hands. Now, I stand before you as witness that it began with doubts from Judge Mikalan of Haprian. Haprian who just days prior had endorsed the certification. Haprian with whom we were to treat two days ago.

"However, given the recent turn of events, we decided to take other actions. Yesterday at this time, a full scale attack was launched on Haprian, set to arrive by nightfall. We erred greatly in Berinin, but we would not with Haprian. We sent a faster ship, a stronger ship, and furthermore, a more fortified ship. This more populous brigade has undoubtedly laid waste to their northwestern shores, and we expect to hear their stories of heroism with the next dawn.

"Beyond that, we await news of developments in Ivaria. We are under suspicion that the certification may instead be returned to them with blueprints perfected by ArcNosian developers. Be that the case, they too will fall victim to our might, just as Berinin did and just as Haprian has.

"The future is near, and those who deny it will be consumed by the continuing flow of time, left in the past, and forgotten. That future lies in our power, the power of unification of all Ouristihra under the rule of one nation. Our nation! A nation strong enough to stand alone! We showed it first with Kirts two centuries ago and again with Ivaria two weeks ago. Progress has been slow until now, but know that a long overdue age is soon to be upon us."

He courteously lowered the microphone and stepped away from the podium. The crowd burst into an uproar of applause. CreSam raised a hand to the crowd, the applause swelling into a standing ovation. He turned to Amirione and smirked.

"They're all yours, Negotiator," he offered, patting him on the shoulder.

"You seem to have them rather warmed up," Amirione complimented, "Who knew you were so eloquent?"

CreSam stood a couple of meters to the left of the podium with his wrists crossed behind his back. He stood rigid as Amirione approached the podium and adjusted the microphone to his suiting. Amirione cleared his throat, and the crowd quieted again, though far more gradually than they had for CreSam.

"For those of you not already familiar with my face, I am Negotiator Amirione. Though my name lacks ArcNosian syntax, I assure you I was born upon ArcNosian soil. My name, however, is of Kirtsian origin. You see, I am descended from ore miners who nearly fell victim to the economic collapse two centuries ago. That is, had ArcNos not intervened. I understand that ArcNos also stood as they who would cause that collapse, but know that they did so with an assimilation plan already in mind. Those who chose to stay behind out of pride perished of their own consequence.

"You may be asking yourselves, at this point, why I choose to speak so loosely of my heritage or why I even speak of it at all. Well, I do so to make a point, and I wish to make it loud and clear. At that moment in history, my heritage was split between those who would continue into the future and those who would live in denial in the past. Furthermore, I've heard an increasing amount of disconcerting talk of pity for the victims of Berinin. So hear this, and know it well.

"All men control their own destiny. Thus the only true victims are that of their own consequence. Though we are the Avatars of Fate, none are to blame for the results of one's actions aside from oneself. This is the principle of The Epimetheus Trial, and it shall not be contested."

Admiral SenRas sailed into port at dusk, alone in his dinghy. His mind was heavy with the events of last night. Flashbacks to the massacre raced through his mind, twisted visions of the two renegades sinking ArcNos's newly developed warship. These two Hybrids, a name by which Amirione had referred to them, were proving themselves more than formidable.

He made for home that night, despite the length of the drive. The old soldier was too restless to check into a motel. Ierodhesan classical music filled his car, washing over him and relaxing him even if only slightly. Still, his mind kept returning to the massacre. He worried how he would break the news to CreSam and furthermore how Amirione might take to it. Odd as it was, CreSam seemed more ready to make sport of the situation, while Amirione held a more personal grudge after the events in Berinin. CreSam had always been the assertive type, even when the roles were reversed and he was his commanding officer. Lately though, it had become a more quiet and brooding sort of confidence. CreSam was plotting, day by day.

By the time he arrived home, only a small handful of hours remained until daybreak. CreSam would be in his office shortly thereafter. SenRas sat in his living room under the light of four corner lamps, mentally replaying the events and trying to find a clear way to explain it. The Ierodhesan disc from his car now played in his home stereo. He sipped warm tea in an arm chair, hoping to relax himself before dawn.

His walls were decorated with a vast array of framed certificates, marks of achievements in his decades with the ArcNosian military. While his rank was not as indicative of his time in service as that of the average veteran soldier, his accomplishments were extraordinarily numerous. Slightly less vast was his array of weaponry. Long blades in sheathes adorned the wall along upon perches with chain weapons hanging from hooks. They had not been used in years, not since CreSam appointed him as a fleet commander.

His teacup empty, SenRas found himself needing to keep his hands occupied by other means. Thus, he found himself doing what he had not since his appointment to fleet commander, reaching for one of his old weapons. Despite the more apparent power of all the others available to him, he drew the smallest and perhaps simplest one of all. It was a length of chain with the end links notably more weighted than the rest, called a manriki.

He leaned back in his chair with one end link hooked over his index finger. He practiced snapping the chain like a short metallic whip, beginning with it running down his sleeve and concealed almost entirely. With an index finger through either end, he mimed catching a blade with it. With a quick twist of the wrists, he practiced the motions of entangling that same blade and disarming his opponent.

Aside from two more cups of warm tea, he continued as such until sunrise. At that point, he straightened his uniform and left for the office. Not since he picked up the manriki had he actively thought about the events near Haprian. He thought he had mulled over it long enough that, so long as he remained calm, he would be able to report the events as such.

The streets were cluttered with garbage strewn about, apparently unattended for quite some time now. It had been worsening for a while, but lately it was starting to get under his skin. A civilian walking the streets had become a rare sight as of late, which eliminated anyone of public janitorial duty. The only regions with any upkeep to speak of were the gated communities in which the soldiers now dwelled and the military community at the center of the capitol. The contrast between them and the open roads was becoming impossible to ignore.

The garbage aside though, SenRas itched to know what had become of the civilians. However, he knew it best not to ask, especially not in Amirione's presence. Despite his relative lack of authority, he seemed like the type to take excessive countermeasures against anyone who misspoke or showed suspicion, and SenRas suspected he might know something of the civilians' whereabouts.

When he entered the building, Malia was standing in the lobby. She had a finger to her ear and was mumbling under her breath. SenRas disregarded her disposition, knowing that she was only reporting back to Olsa on CreSam's actions over the past days. As he was waiting for the elevator though, she removed her finger from her ear to wait for a response. It was vague and indiscernible, but SenRas was certain that the voice he heard was male. Olsa's voice wasn't particularly effeminate, but he didn't recall it being as masculine as the voice he overheard. Still, it wasn't enough to raise any suspicion over, so he opted to keep it to himself for the time being.

"Personally, I'd like to do something about those insufferable fools in Eprilen, what with their sending in a reporter to shadow me nigh indefinitely," CreSam threatened with his back turned as he gazed upon the city below.

"I'm sure you would," Amirione agreed, twirling a pistol around his index finger, "but given the crimes you've committed, they were being lenient with your punishment. Leave Olsa out of this."

CreSam was surreptitiously watching Amirione's reflection in the window. When he heard Amirione pushing for civility between himself and another world leader, his suspicion and a single eyebrow were raised. His attempts to discern a reason were interrupted by a knock at the door.

Admiral SenRas entered in full uniform dress and looking of death for his lack of sleep over the past two days. In spite of his face, his body moved forward with the pride and posture of an experienced ArcNosian soldier. He nodded to Amirione and saluted CreSam.

"Good morning, soldier," CreSam greeted, returning the salute, "You look like shit."

"I feel like it, too," SenRas admitted, "After I make my report on Haprian, I'd like to take a day of leave, seeing as how I haven't slept since the night before we left for their ports."

Amirione turned in his chair to face the two of them, now curious as to what may have transpired on the mission. For the first time, he almost looked a bit concerned, worried even.

"Very well then, you look as if you need it," CreSam agreed, "So, what of Haprian? Did our enhanced warship yield a greater result than our shortcomings in Berinin?"

"Not exactly, sir. Quite the opposite, in fact."

"What the hell happened this time?"

"Well, the short of it is that the resisting forces suffered no casualties, and I was the only one to survive from this fleet. We never even made it into port."

"What's this, the Haprianites are using land to sea ballistics now?" Amirione asked.

"No, not at all. As far as I could tell, no Haprianite played a direct role in the counterassault, though one of the two did have the complexion of a Midlander."

"Wait, one of the two?" CreSam interjected, "Were these the same two who pushed back the assault on Berinin?"

"Precisely them," SenRas confirmed, "This time they attacked by sea, taking the initiative while the troops were inside the cabins. The one who looks to be a Midlander took to the deck, felling soldiers by the fistful, while the Berininite took to the waters and carved a hole in the hull. Those who survived the Midlander drowned because he scorched the lifeboats."

"Wait, then how did you get back alive?" Amirione asked.

"I was in a separate boat a few kilometers back. My order was to not directly involve myself in the combat, but rather to issue orders remotely but still close enough to see the action."

"That it was," CreSam verified, "Calm yourself, Amirione."

"How do you expect me to be calm when these damn Hybrids keep tearing our troops asunder?" Amirione roared.

"Wait, what did you call them?" CreSam asked.

"Damn Hybrids, that's what."

"You called them the same thing in Berinin," SenRas added, "and I know this isn't just some Kirtsian lingo because you've never called anyone else that."

"They throw those balls of fire and ice about. They're Hybrids," Amirione remarked, "They used to be more common, but now those boys are two of the only ones left. Bloody fools oft think themselves gods in their own right. This world would be better off had they not reappeared."

Before any questions could be raised in regards to his odd lexicon, there came another knock at the door. SenRas had neglected to close the door behind him, so this was more to draw attention than to beckon permission for entry. EshCal entered as three heads turned to see her.

"Pardon the intrusion, but I couldn't help but overhear you speak of the counterassault and these two Hybrids," she began.

"Yes, what of it?" CreSam asked.

"Might I make a suggestion as to our next course of action in this regard?"

"Of course, but know that I reserve the right to ignore it, regardless of your rank."

"Understood," EshCal complied with a harsh glare, "It seems that these two have been keeping us from accomplishing any of our goals ever since they reared their ugly heads. It's only a matter of time until more start to emerge from the woodworks, Hybrids with other talents, perhaps even political influence and technological skills. I say we directly target these Hybrids rather than risk running into them on our next mission."

CreSam paused to reflect on the idea. He looked first to SenRas, then to Amirione. Both merely nodded. CreSam grinned and faced EshCal.

"SenRas, excuse yourself to go home and rest. I'll see you tomorrow morning," CreSam dismissed, "As for you, EshCal, come in and have a seat. The three of us will lay flesh to this proposition of yours."

Chapter 13

Sinkua stood with his back against the cold steel bars, wiping the dust from his sunglasses with his shirt. The dank stench of mildew wafted from three cinderblock walls. Galo sat on the bottom bunk bed, watching cockroaches skitter about outside the gate.

"How many days has it been now?" Galo spat, "I agreed to this under the impression that ours would be a short stay."

"It will be, I assure you," Sinkua reminded, "We'll be out either when they learn who killed Judge Mikalan or they learn the truth about ArcNos."

"We don't even know the truth about ArcNos. For all we know, they may actually have treated with them," Galo countered, "Be that the case, the best we can expect is to be exchanged as prisoners of war for some bounty."

"Sure, we have no evidence that they weren't coming to finalize the terms of treaty," Sinkua admitted, hanging his sunglasses from his shirt collar, "That is, if you ignore the scores of armed troops on that ship."

"Perchance they came to offer protection."

"From whom? Themselves? Don't lose sight of reality, Galo. ArcNos is out to lay ruin to its neighbors. They razed Berinin. They wounded Ivaria's economy, and now they're trying to scam Haprian into submission."

"I'm sorry, I just can't help but feel we're getting in over our heads," Galo worried, "How long can we fight on speculation alone?"

"This is the first instance of speculation, and the evidence is solid enough to treat theories as truths. So, I expect you to fight as such. This is just as much your war as it is mine."

Galo simply nodded and laid on his back, staring at the upper bunk and lost in thought. The sum of it all baffled him more each day. Every day, a new piece was found to be missing from the puzzle. First Berinin, then Ivaria was spiraled toward ruin. Now Haprian was allegedly to be stricken after treating with ArcNos, along with Judge Mikalan's death occurring around the same time. Each new clue seemed to require another to make sense of it all.

Sinkua sat on the floor, indifferent to the puddle beneath his buttocks, lost in similar comprehension. It didn't make sense for ArcNos to attack Haprian after they approved their mass production of combustion engine ships. The High Magistrate issued the license with the approval of the Union Parliament, and if he were to fall as Gijin had, the license would be revoked.

Then there was Judge Mikalan's death.

"Wait a minute," Sinkua piped, "CreSam and SenRas were recently in Eprilen. They left with the Eprilenese Judge, meaning they had business at the Hall."

"And Judge Mikalan was recently assassinated."

"He must have said something to upset CreSam, maybe something to offset the treaty, and unwittingly marked himself."

"And he was picked off before he could send a report back home."

"So CreSam knew the treaty was endangered," Sinkua continued.

"But the people of Haprian didn't," Galo remarked, "Son of a bitch!"

"They set us up! They knew we'd attack that ship, and somebody on shore would assume we were interfering and arrest us."

"They used Haprian to get us out of the way."

For ArcNos, the situation had actually been painfully serendipitous since the ship had left port before CreSam heard Mikalan raise doubts over their license. Regardless, it did work out to turn Haprian against the Hybrids for the time being. Further aggression against Haprian would surely break that opposition though, a mistake they would soon make with their ignorance of the events following the destruction of their ship. Off in the northward distance, gunshots could be heard echoing through the air. Galo sat up to listen.

"Well, it sounds like our hosts are about to learn the truth of the matter," Sinkua mused, "Shame they have to learn it as they do."

Out on the northwestern shores, massive artillery munitions rained down on the docks. The wood shattered, and the following explosions radially vomited shrapnel and ash. Portsmen scrambled for safety only to find themselves charred and lacerated by the shrieking shrapnel. Once stable piers collapsed under footfalls, sending strong men and women falling to their deaths upon broken posts and a rocky shore.

The wave of artillery ceased for a moment, and a ship penetrated its own smoke. It appeared similar in model to the ship from a few nights earlier though it was significantly smaller.

"Those two vagabonds felled a ship easily thrice this one's size," Doriman remarked, "Surely the lot of us can do the same to this."

"I certainly hope so," Alucan agreed, "and I feel I may owe an apology to our guests, as well."

"You don't think this is because of their sinking that ship a few nights ago?"

"No. I have proof that it was a battleship that came for our shores that night."

"Very well," Doriman complied, "Let's make for safety until that ship draws close enough to board or strike."

Quite to their chagrin, easily a dozen more ships of similar size broke through the smoke behind the first. From unseen cannons upon their afts, another wave of artillery ripped through the sky.

"You had to open your mouth, didn't you?" Alucan spat as they both turned to flee the monsoon of artillery.

Alas though, a munition crashed down upon Doriman. His spine and ribs were crushed under the impact and his body incinerated in the following explosion. Alucan watched in horror as his comrade was obliterated.

Another came streaking down toward him. Knowing flight was futile, he drew his communicator from his belt, pounded a couple of buttons and pitched it away. As it landed, so too did the bomb. The flames scorched his flesh while large fragments of shrapnel lacerated his burnt skin. His ruined carcass collapsed among portsmen and other officers who had suffered similar consequences.

A mess of bodies lay strewn along the shorelines, accompanied by splinters of wood and patches of burning grass. Just beyond them, buildings laid in ruin, smoke streaming into the night sky from the smoldering wreckage. Shattered glass had been scattered around them. And still, the artillery rained down as the ships continued to advance. Soldiers emerged onto the decks both on foot and in vehicles, making ready to go ashore.

"Just to warn you," Amirione told EshCal, both of whom stood at the fore of the rearmost ship, "I call dibs on the Berininite."

"Just so long as I can stake a personal claim in the matter," EshCal agreed.

"I like your attitude, Miss. Our Honorable Guild may have a place for you, if you play your cards right."

From their holding cell, Sinkua and Galo could hear the gunshots and explosions drawing closer. No longer were they accompanied by the faint sounds of splashing water. The troops had come ashore and were working their way inland.

"So I suppose now we just wait for them to realize they need us and come to let us out?" Galo asked.

"Only if Doriman or Alucan survived."

"Or if somebody on the night shift is still here," a voice added from down the hall, "We caught word of a ship with an ArcNosian insignia approaching. They had sent no word of visiting, as they had before, so several of our officers left for the shore."

"And they left you here to watch the place?" Sinkua asked.

"I among others, yes," the officer confirmed, fiddling with a collection of keys, "but more importantly, Alucan asked that you be released if the approaching ship proved your innocence."

"I assume it did, then," Galo supposed.

"Exactly that. He said if it did, he would transmit a Type-2 signal," the officer verified as he opened the cell, "We also received an horrific transmission of the wreckage, up until his communicator was destroyed, probably along with himself."

"Now is the time to decide," Sinkua implored, "Will you fight or flee? Neither will guarantee your safety, but know that you mustn't take them lightly should you choose to fight."

"We will fight," the officer proudly insisted, "The lot of us here at the station will bring up the rear, provided the two of you are willing to spearhead the counterattack."

"We'd have it no other way," Sinkua accepted, flaring his eyes with a smirk.

Out in the parking lot, roving bands of ArcNosian soldiers could be seen approaching from the horizon. The flames of ruination grew brighter as they drew closer. The stench of burning flesh and seared mortar hung chokingly in the air. Sinkua and Galo stood in the middle of the parking lot, their weapons having been returned to them from the station's confiscatory room. Behind them, some score or so of armed Haprianite officers lined the front of the building. Galo turned to face the lot of them.

"Stay back and hold this line," he ordered, "and you might live. We'll not let them past this station; I swear it on my grandfather's grave."

"Galo!" Sinkua shouted, "They come!"

What had appeared to be merely a small band of soldiers was now revealed to be one of many. The one anticipated ship had evidently been joined by several more. Many of the officers shuddered nervously, yet still, they held to their duty, readying their rifles and spear guns. All together, they took aim at the converging swarms of soldiers.

Trees collapsed atop vehicles as artillery and mechanized soldiers ripped their trunks asunder. Sinkua stood statuesque with one arm raised to the sky and his other hanging at his side, clutching his morningstar and surging with milystis. The first bomb crashed near the entrance to the parking lot, leaving an asphalt crater. Sinkua dropped his arm swiftly.

"Fire!" he bellowed.

All at once, bullets and spears came screaming past them, ripping through the air at the approaching plague. One by one, they met their mark, rending flesh and bone, plunging through torsos, shattering windshields, and puncturing armor plating. A handful of soldiers collapsed to their deaths and a couple of vehicles were rendered inoperable and careened to their mechanical demise. The spear gunmen reloaded while those holding rifles took aim and fired once more. The artillery shots continued to close in.

In unison, Galo and Sinkua charged forth into the assault, bullets continuing to streak by from behind, occasionally joined by dashing spears. They swerved about to avoid the last of the artillery as the troops neared the parking lot. Sinkua began twirling his morningstar, building momentum as the milystis continued to surge.

All at once, he halted and lunged his weapon forth. A massive ball of fire shot from the head of his morningstar, setting scattered oil patches ablaze amongst the soldiers. Galo followed with a powerful swipe of his glaive, sending a torrent of water barreling through the platoon. Soldiers and vehicles were seared and crushed by the counterassault, and more continued to fall to the bullets of the Haprianite officers, unable to advance any faster due to the sheer density of their platoon. Masked by the wreckage, Sinkua and Galo advanced as the officers entered the parking lot.

What was thought to be an easy hunt by many an ArcNosian soldier, what with the reinforcements over the strike on Berinin, was proving to be a nightmare realized. They were relegated to graves by the dozen as their two marks carved through the crowd with destructive force.

Galo spun and dashed deftly, his heels never touching the ground as he ripped gracefully through the troops. He was integrating techniques of the Tide Dancers into his combat, swiftly dodging and countering blades. With their guards dropped, he delivered quick blows to knock them off balance, followed by a plunge of his icy glaive.

Sinkua, meanwhile, barreled through the crowd, setting soldiers ablaze and smashing windshields with his morningstar. The swinging blades were not so easily dodged for him, but what he did manage reduced evisceration to tolerable flesh wounds. He stormed onward in spite of them, bludgeoning bodies and setting the remains ablaze.

The bullets and spears continued to rip through the mob from behind them, though their numbers were diminishing. Odd shots here and there had taken out a handful of officers along with the front windows. Fortunately, the end of the mob of soldiers could also be seen, though it was a ways in the distance.

"Cease fire!" an amplified voice echoed from the rear.

From the rear to the front, the soldiers halted in a wave of bitter compliance. A soldier who had engaged Sinkua stopped abruptly, much to Sinkua's confusion. The soldier lowered his weapon and stepped back along with the rest. Sinkua glanced over his shoulder to find Galo looking back at him in similar manner. They looked back to their respective sides of the mob, baffled by the command.

The one who had issued the command stepped forth through the divided mob. She was a highly decorated ArcNosian soldier, a Brigadier in her mid-thirties. At her side was The Hunter, Amirione.

"Amirione," Galo muttered, "A bit of scandal followed by a bit of mayhem. I figured you would have a role in this port."

"Mayhem is something of my forte," Amirione boasted, "but that's not why they call me The Hunter. We've come for you and your friend."

"Anyone who falls in our path is inconsequential collateral," the Brigadier Elite added, "You may call me EshCal, arbiter of the end of your rebellion."

"Perhaps you've failed to notice, but we've not been the only ones fighting back all this time," Sinkua informed, after which he paused before muttering, "Fire."

Only a handful of officers remained, but their bullets and spears tore abruptly through the divide. Through the smog and wreckage, most of them missed their mark but still took Amirione and EshCal by surprise. In the midst of it all, two met their mark and a third brushed past. A bullet plunged into Amirione's shoulder, his arm trembling in immobilizing pain as his gun fell to the ground. A metallic headed spear wedged itself between pads of armor and pierced EshCal's right thigh, collapsing her. A bullet grazed her side, spilling blood down her legs.

"We'll not fall to some petty officers," Amirione yelled defiantly, reaching for a pistol with his good hand.

"No, fall back!" EshCal called out, "That's an order!"

"What?! Are you fucking daft?!"

"The order was for you and I specifically to eliminate the two Hybrids, and we cannot in our state," EshCal conceded, "We will attempt once more at a later date."

Sinkua extended his arm to bar Galo's approach to the wounded soldiers.

"No, let those two go," Sinkua insisted, "Their deaths will serve us better on their home turf."

Throughout the remainder of the night, Sinkua and Galo assisted in cleaning the station and its parking lot. Dead bodies were hauled out to sea in trailers and set adrift, sure to arouse the sharks a handful of kilometers out into a frenzy. The parking lot was hosed down and cleaned of oil and sinew, though that did little to dissipate the lingering stench of death. Broken windows were boarded up with scraps of wood gathered during trips to the shore.

"We owe you an apology," the officer who had released them admitted, "and our thanks, moreover."

"Not so much an apology. It's not your fault you were misled," Sinkua corrected, "But your thanks, yes you do owe us that. And as I told Alucan, you're welcome."

"Alucan and Doriman were both found dead near the docks, by the way."

"That's a real shame," Sinkua sympathized, shaving splintered edges from the patching boards with his dagger, "Had to die in learning the truth."

"Sorry to change the subject," Galo interrupted, "but what's become of our boat?"

"The confiscatory docks are a kilometer or so east of the docks where you arrived. Your ship is safe. We received word from one of our boys in the field that they didn't pass through there."

"At least we have that good news."

"But, what about permission to pilot it?" Sinkua asked.

"We'll send for blueprints to be delivered to our High Magistrate for his review. If he approves, our next Judge will be urged to bring it up at the Ouristihran Union Parliament Hall," the officer assured them, "In the meantime, you can use yours as a demonstrative prototype, and we'll cover for you."

"We appreciate it," Sinkua thanked, still shaving edges, "but I ask that you not take action at the Union Parliament Hall until you receive word from us to do so. We suspect foul play from ArcNos with Judge Mikalan's death, and there's no point in sending another of yours to die over a boat."

"Sounds reasonable. Very well then, we'll wait for your clearance."

Rather than spend another night at the station, they opted to set sail that night. From memories of his early childhood, Galo could vaguely recall his grandfather speaking of a trip to Ferya, which sat directly north of Haprian. With Gijin being the only person either of them knew with both knowledge and a positive opinion of Hybrids, he gleaned that something or someone of importance was likely to be found there. Although Sinkua had grown accustomed to navigating, he agreed that it would be worth a visit. At the very least, it could perhaps serve as a pleasant diversion from analyzing the advancements of ArcNos.

Sinkua laid atop the sheets, staring at the ceiling. His body was exhausted, but his mind jolted throughout the night. A third nation had fallen victim to ArcNos, and two victims were almost turned against each other. Furthermore, their methods were becoming increasingly underhanded and complex. What began with a simple military siege had now grown into political scandal and economic sabotage.

He snatched his belt from the bedside table and withdrew the dagger. The moonlight shining through the window behind his bed glimmered against it and illuminated it with a pale white glow. His mind awash with anxiety, he touched the tip to his neck. He didn't break the skin, nor did he try to, but he let it sit there for a moment. For a moment, he found it somehow calming, but this only served to worry him further.

His arms began to tremble, and soon the rest of his body followed. His hand tightened its clutch on the handle and his arm trembled involuntarily. Pensively, he stared down at the blade, heaving unevenly as sweat dampened his face. Over and over, he swallowed lumps in his throat, struggling to speak but incapable of even breathing.

The tension abruptly escaped his body. He gasped for air loudly and snapped his arm out to the side, flinging the dagger at the wall. It hit sideways and landed on the floor. He lay clutching the bed, fingers tangled in the sheets.

"Why can't I?" he panted, "Why can't I make sense of anything? Why can't I keep up? Why can't I sleep? Why the fuck can't I do anything to stop it!?"

A knock came at the wall adjoining the two cabins. Apparently, his panic had awoken Galo, who wanted only to sleep after the previous night's events. Sinkua's uneven heaving slowed to a steady but heavy breath. In a diminishing fit, he pitched the sheets and the pillow, leaving them strewn across the floor. So he lay, sprawled out on his back, in the middle of a bare bed. There, from sheer exhaustion, he passed into slumber.

Chapter 14

Sinkua sat on the starboard railing, watching the western waters off the port side of the ship. In one hand, he held half a pomegranate, in the other his dagger. He was scooping out the crimson pellets with the tip to keep from breaking them in his hands. Blood he didn't mind, but sweet juices he took precautions to keep off his fingers.

The skies were awash with tracking pigeons that morning, many of them suspected to be spreading gossip of the developments with ArcNos. Most of those likely involved Haprian, and perhaps a few traced as far back as Berinin, assuming the chattering masses were still swapping conspiracy theories about it.

"Something occurred to me last night, brother," Galo announced as he emerged from his cabin, fully dressed, "Once ArcNos catches word that Haprian knows of Mikalan's intentions to return the license to Ivaria, won't they just strike again, possibly both nations? They might even go after Eprilen, simply on principle of the Union Parliament being powerless to stop the revocation of their license, guilt by association if you will."

"No, that won't happen," Sinkua insisted, picking a seed from his teeth with his tongue, "I'm certain of that much. We were the catalyst in bringing the truth to Haprian, and we made the push to get the license transferred to Ivaria. They're specifically coming after us now. EshCal said that she and Amirione had direct orders to kill us."

"That's a fine mess to find ourselves in, marked by a decorated soldier and a bounty hunter," Galo spat as he sat on the railing next to Sinkua, who offered him a handful of pomegranate pellets.

"I'll say," Sinkua empathized, obviously less bothered by the thought of it, "I wonder what the prices on our heads are. Actions such as ours must add up to a rather sizable stack of iolas."

"Oh but, what about Eprilen?"

"Eprilen is in even less danger. Their Judge is shadowing CreSam, and I suspect he would have trouble slipping that past her."

"Still, I can't help but feel we're aiding in what could prove to be the undoing of this entire continent. We're getting in over our heads."

"We're taking part in it, but at the very least, we're delaying it. You and I are giving back to these other nations, even if only in small portions. All nations eventually fall, but we're giving them a chance to stand up to ArcNos and thrive in the aftermath."

"That's what I mean, it's overwhelming. How long can we keep playing at international diplomacy when we know so little?"

"You only think we do, but the evidence is plain as day," Sinkua dismissed.

The wing flaps and throaty whistles of tracker pigeons steadily amplified, more mail having been dispatched from windows and lawns as the morning progressed. The sun was almost directly overhead now, casting bird shaped shadows upon the deck. Sinkua watched them move about, shadows weaving around each other. He tried to track the movement of several at once with a reasonable amount of success, sometimes predicting paths based on past motions. Though one of them, he noticed, hovered over the middle of the deck.

He looked up to find this bird looking down at the deck, waiting for a chance to land. The skies were so thick with them that it was proving difficult to find a path downward. Sinkua walked to the middle of the deck and swiped his arm up at the flock above, grunting at them for emphasis. He came nowhere near touching them, but it startled them enough that many of them dispersed briefly. The one who had been watching the ship quickly swooped down through the opening and over to Galo. Galo put out his hand, letting the bird settle on it.

The letter seemed to be an obscure riddle encrypted in a code he had never learned. He read it over and over again, so consumed by it that he continued to hold out his free hand long after the pigeon had flown away. Sinkua was watching him, somewhat concerned but more curious. Galo handed him the letter in a huff of frustration. Sinkua snatched it and read over it a couple of times, raising his eyebrow at the obscurity of it.

"A Marked man Single-handedly plunged into the Depths," he read aloud, "and the Chair has since gone cold. J. N."

"Well, unless J. N. is an acronym for another clue, the J would stand for some title. My guess is Judge Nenbard, unless there's another Judge N."

"I was thinking the same," Sinkua agreed, analyzing each word, "So this probably pertains to Judge Mikalan's death. See, he capitalized Depths and Chair. Depths for Haprian's involvement in hydrology and Chair for Judge Mikalan's seat in the Union Parliament."

"How did I not notice that?" Galo asked, rereading the letter over Sinkua's shoulder, "I didn't even think there was a pattern to the capitalized words. So Marked and Single-handedly are also clues."

"We're marked men, but he can't think we did it. Unless this is to warn us that we're being framed for Mikalan's death."

"He doesn't know we were recently marked though."

"No, he doesn't know of our encounter with EshCal, but he knows we bested the assault on Berinin and could reasonably assume that we marked ourselves that night."

"Wait a minute, Amirione has that tattoo on his arm. He could mean that by Marked."

"Yes, he could, but how could Amirione have killed Judge Mikalan, then been in that fleet from ArcNos last night? Even their ships aren't that fast yet."

"So it's somebody else, either another man with a price on his head or another man with that tattoo."

"Single-handedly!" Sinkua exclaimed, "Remember when you chopped off that man's hand after he tried to loot my boat? He had that same tattoo."

"Of course!" Galo remarked in shared epiphany, "Nenbard needed to tell us who was responsible for Mikalan's death, but he had to keep it discrete enough to not get himself killed as well."

"Exactly that," Sinkua confirmed as he rolled up the letter and handed it to Galo, "but we can endure the fire drawn from our spreading the news. When we port in

Ferya, we'll gather tracking pigeons."

"Do we really have that many people to inform?"

Sinkua grinned and signaled for Galo to wait a moment. He returned to his cabin and dug about beneath the bed. A couple of minutes later, he returned with a wooden box, the same one in which he had kept his medallion as a child. He opened it before Galo, revealing dozens upon dozens of scent vials. Galo's eyes widened greatly.

"You've gotten this many already?" he asked in astonishment, "Is this why you've been collecting scent vials, in case something like this happened?"

"Well, I considered it as a possibility," Sinkua admitted, "but I have bigger reasons, ones which I can't yet bring to fruition, not until we reach ArcNos and get settled in."

"Dare I ask?"

"You dare not, but suffice it to say that the people of Ouristihra will be their own cavalry."

Two mornings later, the southern coast of Ferya was within unaided view. From morning through early afternoon, Sinkua and Galo prepared to go ashore for a few days. Galo reminded him of the expectations he had gleaned from knowing Gijin visited Ferya on a personal trip.

In the middle of the afternoon, they reached the coast. No ports had been built in that area, so they were able to eschew the formalities of docking and signing in with the portsmen. They simply tied the boat to a large tree and dropped anchor as an additional security measure. With a week's worth of supplies on their backs, they hiked northward.

"What is it you suppose we'll find here?" Sinkua pondered.

"I don't know. Maybe some history, maybe some clue to our origins," Galo said with a shrug, "We might gain a better understanding of our ilk, or perhaps it will just give us a couple of days to breathe and observe the turmoil from the outside."

"Assuming they don't track us here. Let's hope they haven't found a way to tail us remotely."

"Thank you, I was running low on paranoia."

Sinkua snickered under his breath. He knew that their doing so, if they could, would ultimately only lead more soldiers to their demise as they deployed fleet after fleet to try to assassinate the two of them. He almost wanted to be tracked, as it could easily be turned to their advantage.

The flora in southern Ferya was rich and lush, vibrant foliage casting bushy shadows across thick green grass under the late afternoon sun. The bushes and many of the trees were beginning to flower, colorful buds both bold and pastel speckled along the boughs. It reminded Sinkua of the refugee island as it was the day he arrived. He felt subdued.

Galo found it calming, but moreover relieving. Despite the brewing international conflict in the outside world, this place was abundant with life. What others may have dismissed as just another scenic view, he considered an oasis in a world otherwise headed for perdition. While the rest of the world tore itself apart, Ferya was alive and thriving.

That evening, they settled under a riverside tree with a broad canopy. Each of them had brought a bed sheet for cover, but the unseasonably warm weather deemed them unnecessary. Galo crouched on the riverbed, watching the fish and holding his glaive behind its head. Meanwhile, Sinkua gathered fallen branches into a pile and set them ablaze with his open palm.

In one quick motion, Galo plunged his glaive into the water and withdrew it with a largemouth bass hanging from the blade. Sinkua held out a tin plate when he saw the bass, and Galo flung it over his shoulder. Sinkua caught the fish on the plate and set it upon the fire.

"Damn, we're good," Galo boasted with a chuckle.

"Me and you, we've got synergy," Sinkua complimented as he sat at the base of the tree.

"That's the truth."

The following morning, the smell of cooked fish was still lingering, despite their having discarded the bones and entrails in the river before they settled down for the night. Sinkua managed to sleep a bit more than usual, though it still felt insufficient. Enduring it as he always had though, he rolled up his bed sheet and packed the tin plate, and they continued northward.

By the middle of the day, they had hiked three kilometers or so without rest. At that point, Sinkua suddenly stopped. He put his arm out to signal for Galo to do the same.

"Do you hear that?" he asked, listening to a nearby rustling, "Somebody's watching us."

"Amirione, perhaps?"

"No, he's too garish in his manhunting. Nowhere near this discreet, ironically enough."

A female figure leapt from a tree, donning a duster and clutching an halberd. Sinkua swiftly drew his morningstar and released the chain's binding. She pointed the blade at his face as she landed, only to have it caught by the chain coiling around it.

"Well played," Sinkua acknowledged, "but on whose behalf did you try to jump me? Where do your allegiances lie?"

"A case of mistaken identity, I'm afraid," she confessed, removing one hand from the entangled halberd and relaxing the other, "I apologize."

"Apology accepted, I suppose. Nobody got hurt," Sinkua accepted as he unwound the chain, "but can I ask who you thought we were?"

"You're going to laugh, but I thought the two of you were a man and a woman who came through here last night," she admitted, nodding to Galo when she mentioned the woman.

"What? You thought I was a woman?" Galo asked in disbelief.

"Only from a distance," she assured with a mischievous grin, "Besides, they said she was a tad masculine, and you do have that flowing hair."

"So, what did they do to put you on countryside guard duty?" Sinkua pried, keeping the conversation on track.

"This is going to sound absurd," she began, continuing to study Sinkua's face, "but they overturned several acres of land in my village a few kilometers north of here."

"Why in the world would they do that?" Galo asked.

"My father's body was exhumed, but I'm not certain what they hoped to gain or if that was all they were after."

"Are you thinking the same as I?" Sinkua asked, turning to Galo.

"Do you know them?" she asked.

"I would be, but she's quite a bit paler than I am," Galo reminded, physically ignoring her.

"They said nothing of her skin tone, actually," she interjected.

"What of her gait though?" Sinkua asked.

"I was told that she favors her left leg, and so does he, what with his pack hanging from his right shoulder."

"So it is them, then," Galo verified, surreptitiously adjusting his pack.

"Most likely, yes," Sinkua agreed, "I'm not sure what to make of the body snatching, but it sounds for all the world like Amirione and EshCal."

"So you do know them?" she asked with surprise, now studying Sinkua's face far less discreetly.

"You could say that," Galo confirmed, "They're out to kill us, is all."

"It's a love hate relationship, really," Sinkua flippantly explained, "They love to think they can kill us and hate it when we stop them."

"Hey let me see your eyes," she insisted, abruptly derailing the conversation.

"What? I, um, I can't sorry," Sinkua refused, holding one arm of his sunglasses, "My retinas are extremely sensitive to the sun."

"Only for a moment. Please?"

"Just a minute of exposure when it's this bright out, and I could go blind."

"Oh you are so full of it," she laughed, "It'll be okay. I'm just curious. You remind me of a boy I knew as a child. I want to see if you have the same eyes as him, too."

"Maybe later, but right now, it's really not a good idea."

"I'll show you what's under my trench coat," she offered with a flirtatious smirk.

Sinkua went silent and raised an eyebrow, while Galo raised both.

"I fail to see how that's a fair trade, and I wouldn't ask you to expose yourself like that just to see my eyes," Sinkua declined, beginning to pull his sunglasses off slowly.

"No, it's okay."

Her coat fell to the ground. She stood before them with a pastel purple long sleeved shirt clinging to her body. Three ponytails were draped over her shoulders. Two massive dark purple wings spread from her back. Sinkua pulled off his sunglasses, and he and Galo looked her over in amazement. She looked into his shimmering green eyes and smiled, gasping with awe.

"We shouldn't have to hide who we are," she mused, spreading her wings to their full span.

"Sinkua, she's…" Galo gasped, unable to finish his sentence.

"She's one of us."

"I knew it was you," she exclaimed, "Once I saw your face that is. I've dreamt about you."

"Well, this certainly is bordering between creepy and cheesy," Galo interjected.

"Not like that," she corrected, "The dreams were far from romantic."

"Tragic, perhaps?" Sinkua asked with a look of suspicion.

"I've drawn pictures of them. Follow me back home, and I'll show you them."

"You've piqued my curiosity. Lead the way," Sinkua accepted, "By the way, my name is Sinkua. My friend here is Galo."

"I'm Eytea," she introduced as she began to walk north, "So where are you two from? I know from the dreams that you're from ArcNos, Sinkua. You're probably not a native though, since your name has three syllables. But what about you, Galo?"

"We're both from Berinin," Galo confirmed, "but he spent a few years in

ArcNos."

"That I did," Sinkua confirmed, "My mother was ArcNosian and my father a Berininite."

"Oh, so do either of you guys know Gijin?"

"Knew him, yes," Galo specified, "He was my grandfather."

"Knew him?" she asked with a look of concern, then turned to look up at Sinkua, "Did he...?"

Sinkua simply nodded, and Eytea lowered her head with a frown.

"I met him as a toddler," she recollected, "I only vaguely recall it, but I've wanted to see him again ever since my wings sprouted."

"Grandpa Gijin would have been pleased to see that, I'm sure," Galo comforted, "So you must have been the reason for his trip back then. I was too young to remember it at the time, but he mentioned it later in my childhood, as well."

Sinkua wasn't entirely sure what to think of this specimen. She was an Hybrid like he and Galo, but her dreaming about him seemed a touch suspicious. He pondered the notion that an Hybrid's milystic powers were not strictly limited to the physical, but could possibly branch out into the mental as well. Where he was gifted with pyromancy and Galo with hydromancy, she may have been born telepathic. On the other hand, he considered that she would likely have settled his internal argument were she privy to it, as telepathy would allow.

Also, for someone who had lost her father before adulthood, she seemed unusually chipper, almost sickeningly so as far as Sinkua was concerned. People took to tragedy in all manner of ways, he knew, but her behavior was simply bizarre. It was difficult to discern so soon if she was simply optimistic or a psychological masochist. Moreover, it seemed odd that she had been having tragic dreams about him but was now happy to see him.

She whistled sharply, interrupting his thoughts. Promptly on command, two adult horses rose to their feet, looking out from behind a nearby thicket. They emerged together and stood before her, patiently awaiting her next move.

"Seschnel, Sestak, this is Sinkua and Galo," she told the horses as she petted their noses, "They're going to ride you home, okay?"

"Wait, did you know we were going to be out here?" Sinkua pried.

"Not at all. These two just like to follow me and stand watch when I travel alone this far from home. Sestak likes to think he's my bodyguard. Anyway, saddle up, boys."

Since neither of them had any experience with horseback riding, she explained the basics to them, emphasizing how best to avoid injury during a gallop. As the two horses began to trot off with their new riders, she rose to eye level with Sinkua with a firm flap of her wings.

"Wanna race?" she asked.

"Seeing as how I have to follow you to get where we're going," Sinkua answered flatly, "no, not particularly."

She furrowed her brow and flew away, gliding a touch more than a meter above the thick grass. She kept one forearm guarding her face from dust and debris kicked up by Sestak and Seschnel. One leg remained straight, serving as a rudder. The other was bent with the foot propped on the other knee, helping to guide it.

After a short trip, a wooden fence came into view. Eytea stopped and dropped to the ground. On signal, Sestak and Seschnel stopped as well.

"This is my village," Eytea informed, "Wait a moment, and I'll open the gate.

My house is just up the road from here."

The three of them proceeded through the village on foot with Eytea's two horses walking alongside them. Once smooth dirt roads were now covered in loose soil kicked up from lawns. Likewise, what looked to have once been rich green lawns had been reduced to heaps of caked dirt and shredded grass. Shrubberies were shredded and left strewn upon the desecrated soil.

Whoever was responsible for this disruption had thoroughly eviscerated the landscape, and Sinkua and Galo shared a strong notion as to who was behind it. On the other hand, what they sought from the dead father of a flying farm girl was a distant mystery. Sinkua considered the possibility that the fathers of Hybrids were of value to those tattooed people, but he discarded it when he recalled that CreSam seemed unaware of his being an Hybrid when he started working with them.

"Mom? Hey, Mom!" Eytea called out as she headed across a ruined lawn, "Come on, guys, she's around back."

"Oh hello, dear," Elemeno welcomed as she hoisted a bag of grain from a cart and set it atop a pile of others, "Did you find anything on your walk?"

"You could say that," she answered with a quiet giggle.

"Oh really now? Well, let's…" Elemeno said, turning to see Galo and Sinkua standing with her daughter.

"Madam," Galo greeted, nodding to her.

"Eytea, I shouldn't have to tell you that bigamy is frowned upon here," Elemeno scolded.

"What? No, Mom, they're…"

"I don't care who they are," Elemeno lectured, "I'm fine with your bringing boys home to meet me. But honestly dear, two at a time? Show a little class."

Sinkua lowered his head and covered his mouth to try to contain his laughter.

"And what's so funny? Is this some kind of a joke?" Elemeno asked him.

"No, no not at all," Sinkua guffawed, "It's just that you and your daughter certainly have a knack for misperception. When she met us, she tried to attack us because she thought we were the ones that tore up your village."

"She thought I was a woman!" Galo remarked, "A masculine woman, but a woman nonetheless."

"And now, you think we're courting your daughter," Sinkua continued, "Not just one of us, but both of us."

"Well, what do you expect me to think when she brings home two young men such as yourselves? She's eighteen years old. You can't really think I'm simply going to…"

"Has she seen the drawings?" Sinkua surreptitiously asked Eytea.

She nodded in confirmation.

"Madam, look at me please," Sinkua beckoned to Elemeno.

She complied, though she found his sudden assertion a tad absurd. He snatched the sunglasses from his face to reveal his deep green eyes shimmering in the sunlight. Elemeno gasped and recoiled with a look half of fear and half of intrigue.

"Perhaps, you might think we have some answers for her, or maybe that we're of common ilk."

"You can't honestly have thought there was no one else in the world as unique as your daughter," Galo added, "I was raised by my grandfather. I know he would not have led you to believe such falsehoods."

"Your grandfather?" Elemeno asked.

"Chieftain Sage Gijin. You met him some fifteen or sixteen years ago. Eytea told us."

"So you two are, um, actually, he never told me what you're called."

"Hybrids," Sinkua interjected, "All three of us are Hybrids."

"Fascinating," Elemeno remarked, "Honestly, I never thought that the other heroes would be as different as her. I always imagined that her wings and electromancy would have her spearheading the revolution."

"Electromancy?" Galo asked, "You mean she can…"

Answering in the most succinct way possible, Eytea shot a bolt of lightning skyward.

"Oh, she's gonna be fun to have around," Sinkua said with a smirk.

"So what can you two do, anyway?" Eytea asked.

Sinkua held out an open hand, looking Eytea straight in her eyes. She looked back into his, enthralled and losing herself in their depth. Sinkua shot a glance upward. Following his eyes, Eytea looked up to find a spiraling orb of fire floating overhead and gasped with surprise.

"Oh, that is amazing!" she remarked, "Galo, what's your power?"

Galo raised his cupped hands, separated by the width of his shoulders. Two hemispheres of water materialized on either side of the orb of fire. He clapped his hands together, and they slammed into the flames, dousing them. He raised an open hand toward the cloud of mist and steam, and slowly curled his fingers inward. The mist froze, minute ice crystals falling to the ground.

Elemeno was awestruck and speechless. Here with little warning, she learned of people similar to her daughter and with such impressive control of their powers. Though more than jealousy or animosity, she felt relief. Her daughter wouldn't have to lead alone. She had common people, and they could stand beside her along the way.

"I must know," Elemeno asked, "How did you survive that mechanical beast in ArcNos?"

"That what?" Sinkua asked, befuddled by the question.

"Mom, I haven't told him exactly what happens in my dreams, yet," Eytea butted in.

"Oh, oh I'm sorry," Elemeno apologized, "Hold here a moment. I'll go get one of the sketches."

"Any idea what she's talking about?" Eytea asked as her mother walked toward the back door of the cottage.

"A touch of one, yes," Sinkua assured, "I have my suspicions."

Elemeno promptly returned with a sheet of paper and handed it to Sinkua with the drawing turned upright from his perspective. As he suspected, here was a still frame from his recurring nightmare, the one he had the night before he left ArcNos and again the night that he discovered his pyromancy. A key difference though, the drawing was from a third person perspective. Here, he was looking at his own back as he faced the mechanical colossus with his morningstar drawn and ready to charge.

"How did you survive that?" Elemeno asked, "It must be an amazing story."

"You really want to know my secret?" Sinkua asked, handing the drawing to Galo, "I woke up. My pendant here glowed blindingly bright as I charged the beast, and I woke up. The whole thing is a dream."

"You mean my Eytea is dreaming your dreams?"

"She's seeing the events in my dreams from her own perspective. We're in the same dream, as best I can tell."

"Oh this is just too much to take in at once," Elemeno excused, sitting upon a wooden crate as she caught her breath.

"By the way, Mom, these guys have an idea of who dug up Kabehl's grave," Eytea interjected.

"Oh really now?" Elemeno asked, looking up to them, "You have a lead on my late husband's body snatching?"

"More of a strong suspicion than a lead, but it would be worth looking into. But I'd like to know, do you have any idea why they would exhume his body?" Sinkua specified and pried.

"None whatsoever, but that's not what concerns me, really."

"Well, I can understand your being upset about your lawn, what with your having horses to feed and raise."

"No, it's just that I feel they've hurt Eytea and myself by digging him up. It took a lot of effort to get him in the ground."

"I see," Sinkua empathized, "You couldn't afford a proper burial and a grave plot, so you had to do it yourselves."

"No, we could afford those things, but we couldn't afford to risk it," Eytea corrected, "Plus we really didn't want to."

"And now our secret is threatened with exposure," Elemeno added.

"Wait, what secret? Is there a Feryan law about unregistered human graves?" Galo asked.

"No, not that," Elemeno nervously answered.

"We put him in his grave," Eytea added with a sigh, "in every sense of the phrase."

"What in the hell?" Sinkua roared, "You killed your father, and you seriously think I'm going to help you? No. Fuck this. I'm out of here."

"Sinkua, wait! I can explain," Eytea beckoned.

"Oh, really now? You think you're going to justify yourself to me, of all people? Or is that drawing the only one of my recurring nightmares you've seen?"

"You mean the one of you as a child, standing in a foyer?" Eytea asked, "Oh my goodness, that was your…?"

"Yes, the woman in the picture is my mother. I came home to find my father executing my mother in the living room. And now you expect me to help keep you and your mother from being exposed for a similar act? No, forget it!" Sinkua snapped, "Galo, come on. Looks like we've only got two mouths to feed after all."

Galo sighed and joined Sinkua as he walked away.

"He used to beat me, you know," Elemeno spat in an effort to save her daughter from losing her new companions.

"It's true, and he neglected me the whole time I was growing up," Eytea added, "You have to understand, he was a horrible person."

"So then you leave him," Sinkua hissed as he stopped and turned to face them, "Pack up and skip town, rid yourself of him."

"We couldn't afford to," Elemeno confessed, her eyes welling up, "I couldn't raise my Eytea without the money that his work brought in. But now I regret taking such ill-gotten gains."

"What did he do for a living?" Galo asked, now curious.

"I don't know," she admitted, "but he claims he helped put CreSam in office."

"He called himself The Scout. Something about working for an Honorable Guild," Eytea added.

"So he's one of the people behind ArcNos. Not a Kirtsian though, so that hurts that theory," Galo relayed to Sinkua under his breath.

Elemeno sketched something on the back of Eytea's drawing. Cautiously, she approached Sinkua and handed it to him.

"He had this tattooed on his arm," she told him as he took the paper from her hand.

"All those things I said about misperceptions earlier," Sinkua recalled, looking over the drawing, "I suppose I'm a might prone to them, as well."

"Come inside," Eytea beckoned, "It seems we have much more to talk about."

Chapter 15

The living room was rather bland in contrast to Eytea's personality. A locally made area rug lay in the middle of a dusty wooden floor. Two chairs sat in the corners of one wall and a couch against the wall opposite of them. A coffee table with books underneath was positioned before the couch.

"Honestly, I hope you two don't think ill of us for what we've done," Elemeno pleaded as she handed Sinkua a cup of coffee, "I will admit I feel a touch guilty about it."

"Quite the opposite, actually," Sinkua assured, sipping the coffee, "That tattoo is an insignia. There are at least two more people with those tattoos that I'd like to rid the world of."

"What is it, then? You're hunting some cult?" Eytea asked

"I don't think I'd call them that," Galo said.

"They're too intelligent to be a cult," Sinkua added.

"Too intelligent to be a cult?" Eytea asked, "So, what would you say if I said I was in a cult?"

"I'd say you're dumber than you look, and then I'd leave again."

"Hm, backhanded flattery. Lovely. Then, what's up with the tattoo?"

"Your guess is as good as ours," Galo admitted, "All we know is that they have something to do with the recent developments in ArcNos. We don't know how deep their involvement is, what they call themselves, or how many of them there are."

"I think they might be somehow, um…" Eytea began, "well, like us."

"You mean they're Hybrids?" Galo asked.

"Maybe, I don't know. But when I shot a bolt of lightning at Kabehl's neck from point blank range, it missed. The lightning forked around his neck, and he didn't even flinch."

Sinkua leaned back in his chair and shot Eytea a grin. In a matter of minutes, he had come to find her a kindred spirit rather than feel animosity toward her. She was so detached from and calloused toward her father that she called him by name, just like he did with CreSam. Here was someone who could understand his plight if only he was comfortable enough to confide in her. Still, he took solace in knowing he was in relatable company.

"This could be what Gijin was referring to when he asked me to keep you on a righteous path," Elemeno added, "Good Hybrids and Evil Hybrids, you know."

"I suppose that's possible," Sinkua agreed, "In fact, from what we've seen, their being a different nature of Hybrids makes a lot of sense."

"Are you referring to when Amirione leapt from atop that colossus in Masnethege?" Galo asked, "This guy jumped from above the trees and appeared unhurt when we saw him a few minutes later. I suspect he has an inhumanly sturdy bone structure."

"Exactly that," Sinkua agreed, "Then there's the one that wrecked my ship. He was unarmed, but there were large holes in the hull. Normally, a man his size would only be able to take out small pieces at a time with his bare hands, but it sounded like he was knocking it apart in sheets."

"So we have superhuman strength, reinforced bone structure and immunity to electrocution," Eytea reiterated, "That's a bizarre spread."

"You're one to talk," Sinkua countered with a sly grin masked by his mug.

"That still doesn't tell us what the symbol means though," Galo reminded.

"He told me it was a diagram for an excavation project at his work," Elemeno interjected

"Naturally, he was full of shit, I'm sure," Sinkua presumed.

"Of course," Elemeno agreed, "I traveled to Lenguardia and visited one of their research centers. They said they were working on new methods of excavation, but the symbol had no relevance whatsoever to any ongoing developments."

Eytea collected the empty coffee mugs and took them to the kitchen. Sinkua scanned her body when she had her back turned.

"Well, we know what we don't know, and we know what the two of us have been told," Eytea called from the kitchen, "but what do you two know?"

"What news have you heard?" Galo called back.

"We heard about the attack on Berinin, though there was no mention of Gijin, and also about Judge Mikalan's death," Eytea answered as she returned to the living room.

"Well, they stole the blueprints from Ivaria for a product that would bolster their economy. Having completed the first working prototype, they were able to claim exclusive rights to their production. Haprian treated with them, agreeing to ignore the ecological threat in exchange for their own safety. But, we suspect that Judge Mikalan had second thoughts on the issue, and it led to his murder and cancellation of the treaty. But the people weren't informed of the development, so they imprisoned us when they witnessed us sinking an ArcNosian war ship, thinking it had come to finalize the terms of treaty," Sinkua recollected, "Then there's the fact that one of them killed a federal authority figure, and neither he nor CreSam has been stripped of their position. They're manipulative and frighteningly cunning."

"There's also the ArcNosian Kirtsian Trade Conflict," Galo added, "Two hundred years ago, ArcNos began producing its metal goods domestically. This crippled the economy of Kirts. Most of the people left the nation, which is why it's so sparsely populated now. Those who refused to leave often harbored feelings of animosity, holding riots and rallies."

"We think these people may be working primarily out of Kirts, and that their leaders are native Kirtsians," Sinkua continued, "As far as we can tell, their aim seems to be to turn the rest of Ouristihra against an empowered ArcNos. They either want to cripple ArcNos for what they did to them, or destroy the rest of the continent as vengeance for ignoring their plight. Either one is a believable motive, and I wouldn't be surprised if they would settle for whichever happens first."

"Then who do we attack, ArcNos or Kirts?" Eytea asked.

"These people are ghosts. Very few people are aware of them. They simply manipulate from behind shadows and closed doors. One lived under your roof for several years without your knowing. Even if we're right, we'd probably find nothing of significance in Kirts. We have to flush them out of hiding," Sinkua explained.

"And that means fighting the empowerment in ArcNos," Galo added, "When the new nation has been collapsed and their influence removed, it will be rebuilt as its former self, and more of them will be drawn out into the open. Or rather, so we hope."

Eytea sat silent for a moment, mulling over the facts and letting them sink in. She knew Kabehl was part of a group with access to technology and capabilities otherwise unheard of, yet still this news was a lot to consume at once. It was all so simple yet so ingenious, the way they were manipulating multiple nations. Their influence and power ran deeper than she ever imagined, and then there was the notion that this had been developing for two centuries.

"It's sad knowing that ArcNos is the victim but having to attack them anyway," Eytea sympathized, breaking the silence.

"No, believe me, they would still be corrupt with CreSam in office without the outside influence," Sinkua argued, "These people just enhance his capabilities and enable his tendencies toward international ruin and power hunger."

"Although SenRas did say that he had given direct orders not to harm Gijin," Galo reminded.

"Only because he would be of more use to him alive, I'm certain."

"That's, well… That will make this a bit easier, I think," Eytea assured with a sigh, "So do we go to Kirts first, or what?"

"No, like I said, we'd be wasting our time there," Sinkua reminded, "We continue westward. We'll make for the coast and take a ship to Quarun. From there, it's on to ArcNos."

"I always knew this day would come, and yet still I'm not ready for it," Elemeno confessed, "I know you must be in a hurry, but could you wait until tomorrow to leave?"

"Of course," Galo agreed, "I think we all wish we could have one more day."

The sound of rubber feet clapping against marble tiles echoed throughout the corridor. It was accompanied by the sound of combat boots in similar rhythm. They turned a corner with a sharp squeak to head down a hallway with a massive set of double doors at the end.

"The Geneticist and The Engineer are really something when they collaborate," Amirione boasted.

"Oh sure, but I wish the chip had finished the job with my ankle," Kabehl halfheartedly agreed, "Do you realize how difficult it is to fuck with people's heads when you're walking on crutches?"

"Mind games aren't my concern, Scout," Amirione answered, "but I'd imagine it's difficult to hold a shotgun with those things. By the way, do you still have the product?"

"I was buried with it," Kabehl reminded, withdrawing a syringe with the tip covered, "Did he tell you what this is going to do?"

"Yes, he did," Amirione succinctly answered as he reached for an elaborated decorated door handle.

CreSam sat behind a huge oak desk, stained with a deep burnt red lacquer. His walls were adorned with plaques marking various achievements on his rise to power and notoriety. The air smelled of leather, the binding material of nearly every book upon his shelves. Atop the center of the wall behind his desk, his broadsword was mounted to a mahogany plaque.

He leaned back in his chair with a stack of papers in his hands, casually thumbing through them. When the door opened, he cocked his head nonchalantly to glance toward it without taking his eyes off his reading.

"Good afternoon, Amirione," CreSam dismissively greeted, "I received word that there was trouble in Haprian."

"A minor setback, CreSam," Amirione argued.

"One of several. You call yourself The Hunter, yet you can't even rid me two vagabond marks, now can you? And what's worse, one of my best soldiers is incapacitated because your incompetence put a bullet in her thigh," CreSam replied bitterly, still reading the papers, "I'm beginning to question what you people can actually offer me beyond empty promises and ego storms."

"Do you recall talk of The Scout's death?" Amirione asked.

"Yes, I do. His daughter and his wife snapped his neck," CreSam recalled, "Pity he couldn't fight as well as you. Oh wait, my mistake."

"Hello, sir," Kabehl interjected, "I'm home."

CreSam set his papers down on his lap and turned to face the two of them, baffled by this development. Here before him stood a man whose death had been confirmed, yet now his worst injury was a broken ankle.

"I'm implanted with a self-repair mechanism in my blood stream," Kabehl explained, "It takes a while to work, but when I die, it repairs all fatal damage, keeping my body in hibernation the entire time. Once the job is done, it jump starts my vital organs, and I'm alive again."

"That is incredible," CreSam remarked, "If everybody in your organization were half as competent as the ones who developed that, we would already have met our objectives."

"Perhaps. Now then, The Geneticist has asked that I give you a sample product. Roll up your sleeve for me," Kabehl ordered

"So what's it going to be? A dose of self-resurrection?" CreSam asked, "Or perhaps superhuman strength to match my existing stature?"

"My guess would be no," Kabehl hypothesized, pushing the air bubbles out of the syringe, "The former would require a nanochip, not a liquid injection, and the latter is unnecessary."

"We're going to compensate for your weakness. This will increase the elasticity and durability of your cartilage and sinew, thus making you far more limber," Amirione informed

"Now hold still," Kabehl implored.

Kabehl prodded CreSam's upper arm with his fingertips, searching for a healthy vein. It was apparent enough that phlebotomy was not his expertise, though he had seen enough of it to know the basics. He set the tip against the skin at a sharp angle and shoved it firmly into the vein. CreSam's arm shuddered as the fluid invaded his blood stream.

"Stings a bit, doesn't it?" Amirione asked with his arms folded, watching callously.

"No," CreSam spat bitterly, "It burns."

"Don't worry about the burning," Kabehl assured, removing the syringe and chucking it in the garbage can, "That just means it's working."

Eytea awoke shortly after dawn the following morning. She had sat up late talking with Sinkua and Galo long after her mother retired for the night. Yet in spite of this, she was too anxious to sleep for long. From her bed, she could see light from one of the living room lamps. Apparently, the same was also true of at least one of them. She put on her slippers and a robe and crept down the hall.

"Morning," Sinkua greeted in a throaty tone, not looking up from his work.

A wooden box sat atop one end of the coffee table. To his left was a stack of blank paper, and to his right a pile of used ones. Before him on the table was his current page in progress.

"You couldn't sleep any longer either, huh?" Eytea asked, sitting beside him on the couch.

"Any longer? No, I wouldn't say that," Sinkua corrected, turning to glance in her direction, "Has your dreaming my dreams become increasingly infrequent?"

"Actually, yes, but I never really thought anything of it."

"Then I would imagine that if you don't see my dreams, I probably didn't sleep that night," Sinkua explained, continuing to write, "at least not long enough to dream."

"You have insomnia, huh?" she asked sympathetically.

"Something like that, but don't worry about it. It's my problem, not yours."

The stack that once sat to the left had been exhausted and moved to his right. He tapped and shifted them into an even stack and thumbed through it, recounting the pages. After this, he opened the box and counted the vials of tracking scent.

"Oh are you sending letters to your extended family?" Eytea asked optimistically.

"No, I have no remaining family to speak of, at least not in terms of blood or legality," Sinkua insisted as he closed the box, satisfied with the count, "I'm getting ready to spread knowledge. Galo and I were given word of who killed Judge Mikalan, and we're sending the information to everybody from whom I've collected these on our travels."

"That's quite bold of you," Eytea complimented, "Fighting manipulation with truth. I can definitely get behind this."

"That's good to hear, Eytea. In that case, can you get me some binding ribbon? I don't want to dig through your drawers without permission."

Eytea slid into the gap between the couch and the table. There, she pulled out the drawer near Sinkua's feet. After a bit of shuffling, she withdrew a spool of blue ribbon, set it atop the table, and snaked back up onto the couch.

"Do you need scissors, too?" she asked.

"No, I've got it covered," he assured, pulling his dagger from his belt, "By the way, why were you hiding your wings yesterday if you think we shouldn't have to hide ourselves?"

"Oh that? That wasn't exactly hypocrisy, despite how it seems," she explained, "It was nippy outside, and I like that coat too much to cut wing holes in it."

"Does it hurt your wings to confine them like that?"

"A bit, yes. It's troublesome to keep them from spreading against the fabric, but it's either that or freeze."

"Wait here; I have something for you then."

Sinkua stood up and walked to the coat rack by the door. At the foot sat his and Galo's travel packs. He opened his and dug through it for a moment, eventually withdrawing something he had kept with him since the day he made it, a hyena fur coat.

"Here, I made this, but it's too small for me," Sinkua offered, "I kept it anyway as a memento."

"Oh, hyena fur, huh?" she asked, trying not to appear taken aback, "Where did you get hyena fur?"

"From an hyena, of course. My encounter with it was how I discovered my pyromancy. It's a keepsake of a milestone in my life."

"Oh, so this is something special," Eytea accepted, "Why were you hunting hyenas anyway?"

"I wasn't. I was hunting a chipmunk because it was the middle of the Frigid, and my food stores were running dangerously low," Sinkua explained as he carefully sliced two holes in the back of the coat with the tip of his dagger, "And the son of a bitch tried to steal my dinner."

"Oh, that's awful. I'm happy to know you made it through that though. It's comforting knowing that I'm going into this with someone who can work through dire circumstances," Eytea sighed as she squeezed her wings through the holes, "So did you eat the hyena, too?"

"Are you kidding?" Sinkua asked, "I take it you've never tried it. It's akin to chewing on a rain-soaked tire."

"Sorry, haven't done that either. But you have, huh?"

"As far as you know, I may very well have at some point," Sinkua answered with a smirk, "But at least I don't look like a flying hyena."

Eytea giggled a bit, running her fingers through the coarse hairs of the hyena hide coat. Typically, she would have thought it hideous, but given the circumstances, she rather liked the way she looked in it. Since the day they emerged, more so since Kabehl's death, she had embraced the uniquity that came with massive purple wings. This just made her all the more so.

"You two are up a might early," Elemeno noted as she emerged into the living room, still brushing remnants of fatigue from her eyes.

"Early. Late," Eytea clarified, pointing to herself and Sinkua respectively.

"Got yourself a spot of insomnia, do you? A sad thing, that," Elemeno sympathized, "Your friend seems to be sleeping rather well."

"I don't know how well he's actually sleeping, but he does seem to get quite a bit more of it than I do."

"Which just means he sleeps at least an hour every night, huh?" Eytea added.

"We just take to tragedy differently. Maybe I've dealt with so much that I've grown numb to the pain of coping," Sinkua spat, "I barely sleep, yet I don't feel tired. Galo, on the other hand, once he's in bed he'll stay there for several hours, even if he's wide awake. He's been that way since the day we left Berinin."

"That's the day that Gijin passed away, was it not?" Elemeno asked.

"Murdered, is more like it," Sinkua clarified, "Gunned down in a final blaze of glory, even. I tried to save him, but obviously to no avail. I still recall it so clearly."

Sinkua proceeded to recount those events as though they had occurred last night. Eytea and Elemeno listened intently as he wove intricate details of that evening's onslaught and the heroic uprising that followed.

Meanwhile, Galo lay in bed, staring at the ceiling. His eyes scarcely moved, and he blinked only every couple of minutes. The sheets had been cast off his torso and were tangled around his calves. In a fit of claustrophobia, his entire body convulsed as he kicked his legs about, throwing the sheets to the floor. His breathing was heavy, his chest heaving up and down.

From the living room, he could faintly hear the events of that night being vividly retold, though not enough so to be consciously aware of it. So, as it often did when he was alone, his waking mind replayed those moments, now even more clearly than usual. Yet while the loss of his grandfather was painful, that was not the worst aspect of his recollection, as heartless as that may have seemed.

Rather, he was frightened for the rest of the village and ashamed of himself. Sinkua had always spoken of feeling as though he was abandoning somebody when he ran away from home. It took years, but he was finally beginning to empathize. His shortcomings had left his village cast asunder with more survivors than it could accommodate in its state. But rather than stay behind to guide the restoration, as one of his ilk would be expected to do, he turned and ran. He appointed an interim leader with no rational basis, and he ran.

He knew he was chasing the cause of the destruction, rather than running away from the problems it created, but still he couldn't help but feel he had abandoned his people when they needed him the most. They were vulnerable and in need of guidance, but he thought it more urgent to give chase to their assailants. The more he replayed that night, the less he could help but feel he should have stayed to rebuild first.

Worse still were his thoughts that he should not have intervened at all. Perhaps, he pondered, that night was to be the end of The Sacred City. No kingdom was eternal. He sometimes wondered if he had offset the order of the world and made matters worse, leaving his people to wither rather than letting everyone fall with their village, himself included.

The replay of the night slowed abruptly. In his mind's eye, he could see Amirione atop the war mechanism, one of his many guns aimed and ready to shoot. In excruciatingly painful slow motion, the bullet burst from the barrel and streaked toward his grandfather, just as a stream of fire shot forth, carrying hopes of heroism. A moment of lucidity interrupted his waking nightmare.

This was the night as Sinkua recounted it, his critical shortcoming played slowly to torment him, as his subconscious mind was wont to do. His mind wasn't simply recounting the events. He sat up and listened closely to his surroundings. It was faint, but he could hear Sinkua putting the finishing touches on his retelling of that night. He now realized that this was why his subconscious mind was replaying them as well, at least this time. Still, sleep had become a farfetched option by then.

"Morning, brother," Sinkua welcomed as Galo came into the living room, straightening his borrowed robe atop his shoulders, "We were just talking about…"

"Yes, I know," Galo interrupted, "Our last night in Berinin. When are we leaving?"

"In a hurry, are you?" Elemeno asked as she stood up from her seat and walked to the kitchen, tussling Galo's mussed hair as she passed, "Well, wait just a bit, could you?"

"I'm sorry; I don't mean to rude, madam," Galo apologized, "Recalling the fall of my city fills me with an overwhelming sense of urgency."

"Imagine having to wait four years to make your next move," Sinkua added.

"I couldn't do it, I know," Galo agreed, "and I'm still not certain how you pulled it off."

"Wait, you spent four years on that island? The one where you got the hyena fur?" Eytea exclaimed, "How did you survive?"

"Very carefully," Sinkua nonchalantly answered, "Built a cabin, planted a garden, hunted, and fished. After the first couple of months, it wasn't all that bad. And I was close enough to Berinin to sail there periodically to trade furs and crops for whatever else I may need, this head scarf included."

"You needed the head scarf? I thought it was just an accessory."

"Well, I don't technically need it; I could do without it," Sinkua admitted, untying the knot in the back.

For the first time in the company of others, he whipped the scarf off of his head. His hair, sweaty and bunched, rolled down his head as it was set loose. The peripheral spikes hung to his neck, while his bangs tickled his mustache, giving him the hilarious appearance of a wet puli from the neck up. Eytea's eyes grew wide. Elemeno glanced back over her shoulder and began to look away, only to do a double take with one eyebrow climbing her forehead. Galo folded his arms and smirked with his head down, his chest bouncing with a contained chuckle.

"But it's not exactly a pretty sight when I don't wear it," Sinkua added.

All at once, the entire room burst into a hearty laughter. Eytea's eyes watered, she was laughing so hard. Sinkua looked at her with a smirk and chuckled. She tried to return the glance but failed every time. It wasn't so much for the hair covering most of their surface, but more because she couldn't even look in his general direction without laughing to the point of pain. Sinkua shook the stray hairs out of the head scarf and wrapped his hair in it once again. The laughter in the room tapered off and slowly came to a stop.

Elemeno turned from her task in the kitchen, having completed it through the tears and laughter. Into the living room, she carried a platter covered with various meats and crops as well as eggs, all wrapped in plastic. Galo followed her and took a seat on the couch next to Eytea, putting her between himself and Sinkua. Sinkua's eyebrows shot up when he saw the platter of food.

"Throwing a going away party for your daughter?" he asked.

"Oh, how I wish I could, but no, I understand time is essential," she answered, "This is for you guys to take on your trip."

"Are you sure you can afford to spare all of this?" Sinkua asked, "It looks like you must have spent a lot on it."

"Not too well read on the history of this area, are you?" Eytea asked, "This town abolished the currency system some five years ago. The only use for it is when traveling abroad, which neither of us do any longer."

"We work off of a direct trade system now. One good or service for another," Elemeno added, "We use Sestak and Seschnel for everything from hauling goods to horseback dates, and in return we get whatever we need around the house."

"I haven't been outside of the area, but I'll bet this stuff is the best of its kind you're going to find anywhere," Eytea bragged, "Each and every one of these came from breeders whose specialty you'll find on this plate. Eggs from a chicken breeder, potatoes from a tuber breeder, and bacon from a pig breeder."

"Wow," Galo gaped, sifting through the pile of wrapped foods, "Sinkua, there are even a dozen or so pomegranates in here."

"Well that's great news. I'd been meaning to seek out a few of those," Sinkua remembered, "How long did it take you to save up all this?"

"Save up?" Elemeno asked, "This is what we normally have on hand. Takes less than a month's work to get this much food though. And there's plenty enough in the refrigerator that I'll be quite fine sparing this to you kids."

"Thank you, we could definitely use it," Galo accepted.

"Indeed. Thanks a bunch," Sinkua agreed, "It's been too long since I ate something that I didn't plant or kill. By the way, did I just hear you mention bacon?"

"Heh, yes you did," Eytea answered, "Mother, where did you put the bacon?"

"It's underneath the hard-boiled eggs," Elemeno directed, "behind the chopped celery."

Eytea pulled aside a sack of easily two score eggs. Beneath it was a bundle of celery. She rolled it back, revealing a clump of bacon strips wrapped into a log shape. As she withdrew it with one hand, she carefully set the celery and eggs back into place with the other. She handed Sinkua the bacon log.

"There's about a kilogram of it there," Elemeno informed as Sinkua unwrapped the end of it.

He pulled out a single strip and looked it over, marveling at the size and purity of it. There was barely a trace of fat on the whole thing. He sank his teeth in and tore off a piece. It had just the right crunch to it, thick and moist, just a touch peppery. It was, as bacon went, perfect.

"Galo, you gotta try this," he insisted as he ripped the remainder of the strip in half, "This is what bacon is supposed to taste like."

Galo bit into it, pausing abruptly as it hit his tongue. His eyes widened and a grin spread across his face as he resumed chewing once again.

"Oh man, you're right," he agreed, "This is far better than the stuff you brought us."

"I know. Eating this makes me wonder how I put up with my homemade crap for so long."

"I'm glad you like it so much," Eytea boasted with a knowing smile as she rewrapped the remaining bacon and returned it to its place on the platter.

"Well, of course we… Wait. You made this, didn't you?" Sinkua gleaned, "Oh, I am gonna like having you along for the ride."

"That's my little protégé," Elemeno boasted with a wink, "Raises horses and cooks almost as well as I do. She'll surpass me if I'm not careful."

"You've definitely taught her well," Galo agreed.

"Thank you. Here, I'll pack these into your bags."

"Thanks," Sinkua accepted, "We'll leave shortly thereafter, head for the west coast."

"Shouldn't we go back for our ship first?" Galo asked.

"It's been found by now, I'm sure of it. Probably crawling with ArcNosians if it's even still afloat," Sinkua countered, "Besides, now that SenRas has seen that boat, we can't sail anywhere near ArcNos on it."

"We'll need to head northwest then," Eytea insisted.

"Is that the way to the nearest west coast port?" Sinkua asked.

"Not exactly. It's about another dream I've had. Assuming my recurring dreams are ones from memories of other Hybrids," Eytea admitted nervously, "I think there's another one in Ferya being held against her will. I'll show you the sketch of the building on the way there."

"Northwest it is, then."

Chapter 16

Quite to their relief, the trip was remarkably uneventful. Sinkua and Galo felt they had seen quite enough action for a while, and Sinkua was growing especially tired of the interruptions. They served as little more than a distraction anymore, the soldiers seeming more set on getting in the way than actually stopping them. Still, the combat was good exercise, and laying waste to the troops felt rather gratifying in the moment.

Sinkua traveled atop Sestak, Galo on Seschnel. Eytea flew between and behind them, hovering some half a meter above the ground. Elemeno had insisted that she could manage without the horses to provide services for trade, but Eytea worried for her mother nonetheless. She tried to restrain that anxiety to the back of her mind though, focusing on the task at hand. Nonetheless, she found her mind wont to fearful wandering, causing several near misses with the horses.

The events of the dream replayed in her mind, freshening her memory of another's nightmare. Brief flashes of a two story building, cut out from the rest of civilization, had gradually accumulated into a composite sketch. Inside, conditions were nigh survivable at best. The stone floor was slick with water and blood, mildew growing in every corner. Rats scurried about, sick from the mold. And that man. He stood over the girl as she cowered in the shadows of the corner. His face was indistinguishable, a dust mask covering his nose and mouth, a visor shadowing his eyes. He donned a suspiciously immaculate white coat, reaching to his ankles, and held an empty syringe.

Her arms were riddled with puncture wounds, giving her the appearance of a heroin addict. Dismally few of them had healed properly, leaving her with patchy bruises and dirty scabs. Off in the distance, young men could be heard groaning and screaming in agonizing pain, though she knew not from what. She seemed to envy them somewhat. Their screams either stopped abruptly or were followed by heavy breathing, which ended in similar fashion. They had been granted a welcome reprieve, one her captors dared not let come to her. And she knew not why.

A bundle of horse hairs swept across Eytea's face, jerking her attention back to her own surroundings. In the midst of her daydreaming, the horses had stopped, and she had flown into Sestak's tail. She brushed the stray hairs from her face and dropped to the ground. Sprawled out before the five of them was a community a touch more developed than her own, mostly suburban with subtle hints of industrialization.

"Is this the place?" Sinkua asked.

"No, no this can't be it," Eytea refuted, "It was a building in the middle of nowhere, not in a community."

"Were there any landmarks in your dream?" Galo asked, "Perhaps, this other Hybrid's subconscience filtered out everything but the building and a landmark."

"Well, nothing too distinct, but these trees feel familiar."

"Have you had the dream lately, aside from recollecting just a minute ago?" Sinkua added.

"It's been a few years, maybe six. Why?"

"With a handful of construction crews, that would be more than enough time to build this town as a cover up. Let's start searching."

"You two go ahead. I'm going to hitch up the horses. They don't do too well in the city," Eytea insisted.

"I wouldn't exactly call this the city, but do as you wish."

The streets were made of coarse gravel mechanically fashioned into uniform pieces. The buildings were mostly one story tall, built primarily of brick and concrete, some with wooden or vinyl siding. Those painted were done so primarily in earthen tones. Here and there, buildings donned brighter hues, but muted tones dominated the landscape.

"Maybe we're in the wrong place, after all," Sinkua admitted, "I don't see a building like the one you described, and I'm quite certain we've checked every two story building in the area."

"Eytea, could you fly up and see if there's any more that we haven't checked?" Galo requested.

"I think that may draw unwanted attention," Sinkua insisted.

"She's already got purple wings hanging out of an hyena hide coat," Galo argued, "I doubt it will make much of a difference if she starts flying, too."

"No, no it's okay," Eytea insisted, "I've got it."

"You'll do it? Great."

"No, I mean I've got it. Right over there," she corrected, pointing to a nearby house.

She held up the drawing for the two of them to see alongside the house. At first glance, they appeared dissimilar, especially since this house was one story tall, but the shape of the building's first floor coincided with the shape of the house, as did the arrangement of the windows and the position of the door.

"If you're right about the town being built as a cover up," Eytea told Sinkua, "then maybe they altered the building as an added measure. The basements would have to have been sealed off, but I'm sure we could find a way through."

"Ingenious," Sinkua said, speaking both of the cover up and Eytea's deduction, "Now how do we go about getting inside to find said passage? Somebody probably lives here, and I'd rather not cause any unnecessary damage to their home."

"Galo, why don't you look around for a hidden key to the front door?" Eytea suggested, "Sinkua and I will go to the back and see if any windows were left unlocked."

While Galo examined the front, Sinkua and Eytea made their way to the back of the house. They crouched under a window, hiding as they tried to open it. The patch of dirt beneath it was rather barren and a bit moist, wetting the bases of the few blades of grass. Either it had rained in that region that morning, or the owner watered the lawn too frequently, so Sinkua assumed. Eytea, on the other hand, found it peculiar.

More to the point, it didn't open. In fact, what few windows lined the back of the house were all locked, and after rechecking the first window, they crouched beneath it and waited to hear from Galo. In his boredom with the awkward silence, Sinkua singed grass blade tips with his index finger. Eytea watched him and smiled, having missed out on such opportunities to, for lack of better terms, see boys be boys.

"So, how long have you and Galo known each other?" Eytea whispered, softly breaking the silence.

"All our lives," Sinkua answered, still watching the back door over his shoulder, "All his at least."

"You two are pretty close, huh?"

"Yeah, you could say that. I can't think of anyone I've been closer to since my childhood."

"Oh?" Eytea remarked, sounding awkwardly timid, "Are you two, well, you know...?"

"Are we homosexuals?" Sinkua nonchalantly asked, "No, we're not. Even if I was, he's too much like a brother to me anyway."

"Oh, that's good to know."

"Uh-huh. So you're a homophobe?"

"What? No no no, nothing like that," Eytea snapped back hastily, "It's just that, well, I wouldn't want to assume anything and embarrass all three of us later."

"Take my hand," Sinkua ordered as he saw the doorknob twitch and wiggle.

"Hm? Well, okay," Eytea agreed, lightly gripping his hand.

It felt warm against hers, but she couldn't distinguish if it was the fire within or genuine human warmth that she felt. He was capable of emotion, she could tell, but mostly he was cold and calculating. It seemed so inhuman that she knew something must have snuffed that spark of humanity.

Interrupting her split second daydream, she was jerked to her feet. She stumbled to keep up as Sinkua ran them both across the back of the house. Up ahead, she could see the door opening. Apparently, Sinkua had grown impatient and intended to rush the occupant to gain entry. As suddenly as it had begun though, the rush came to a halt. Carried by their momentum, she crashed into his back. Regaining her balance and composure she peered over his shoulder to see a familiar face looking back from the door.

"The lights are out, and nobody's home," Galo called from the doorway.

"Did you put the key back and lock the front door behind yourself?" Sinkua asked.

"No need to. It was unlocked already. I just decided to take a look around for myself first."

"Hey, that spot we were sitting on felt pretty wet for such a barren patch of land," Eytea reminded before they entered the house, "and the path from here to there is dry."

"Right over there?" Galo asked, pointing toward the patch, "I don't know much about indoor plumbing, but I'd say something probably leaks. That's right by the bathroom."

"I didn't see any water spots on the wall," Eytea corrected, "and the water seemed like it was coming from below the surface."

Without another word, Sinkua walked back to the spot with Eytea and Galo in tow. He crouched and ran his palm over the tips of the scattered blades, this time making note of their condition rather than simply burning them as he had done with the peripheral blades. They were a tad moist but quite a bit less so than toward the base. Indeed, it seemed unlikely that this water came from above, and it was too late for lingering dew.

"Pry down along the wall and feel around," Sinkua instructed Galo.

Galo shoved the tip of the blade into the moderately loose soil. He stared down at it for a moment, and the dirt began to churn with water flowing from the blade. Deeper he drove it as the soil loosened, until he buried half the handle. He pulled back, pushing the blade toward the wall. A muffled clink sounded. He repeated a couple of times, studying the sound.

"Sounds like stone," he said, still tapping, "Probably concrete."

"That could just be the foundation. Let's not get too excited," Sinkua reminded.

Galo pushed down further and repeated his pull and listen method. This time, he had to pull a bit more to strike the surface, and it felt as though he was hitting further up the blade. He pressed it against the surface and slid it from side to side.

"Feels like it's under a lip now," he explained, "I think Eytea was right."

Maintaining the angle, he thrust the glaive further downward with a firm push. The subterranean surface resisted initially but gave way abruptly, causing him to stumble into the thrust. He knocked his head against the wall and dropped to the ground.

"I think I broke something," he groaned, rubbing his head.

"Let me take a look," Eytea beckoned, peering over his head.

"No, not there," he corrected, bracing himself on the handle of his glaive as he stood himself, "I think I broke a window down there."

"Sounds like you were right, Eytea," Sinkua admitted, "Let's start digging."

With the soil having been significantly loosened by Galo's efforts, digging barehanded was a viable option. Thirty digits bore into the mud, tossing it aside as quickly as it was withdrawn. They dug along a slope, running down the wall and working slowly outward. The intent was to dig a path along which they could slide down to the broken window.

After a few minutes, and now up to their armpits in muck, they had dug a deep enough passage for Eytea to slip in through the window. Aside from the fact that she was the most slender among them, so long as she tucked her wings, her ability to fly made her an ideal candidate for dropping blindly into the building.

"Okay boys, brace me please," she beckoned as she stood at the edge of the hole.

Sinkua and Galo each took an outstretched hand as she stepped lightly into the pit. She shuffled her feet and tightened her grip as the mud shifted, overly cautious not to slip. They lowered her slowly, until she was up past her waist and could get her legs in through the broken window. As she hung from their hands, she kicked at the glass, knocking away lingering fragments.

She let go, sitting back on the slope of the pit, and slid down into the open window bay. Aside from the angle, the internal structure felt ominously familiar. It was far more barren than she recalled, but her foremost concern was with the thirty meters between her feet and the floor.

"I'm going to have to go in alone," she insisted, "There's a big drop from here to the floor. I'll look around for a ladder or some such before I go any further though."

With that, she scooted off the window sill, wings spread, and drifted down to the moldy concrete floor below. As she descended, watching the dilapidated scenery pass, she found herself immersed in involuntary thoughts, surrounded by this incarnation of what she had hoped was only her imagination. An amalgamation of disturbing smells strangled the air, creating an almost palpable pollution. Blood and other bodily fluids were among the most apparent, as was death, of course. Even a bit of fecal matter seemed to linger within the stench, though the methane could have come from any number of sources, given the nature of her nightmare.

The pipes running up the walls were cursed with rust, many of them worn straight through. Several bolts were either stripped or absent entirely. The occasional hopeless spewing of steam, along with cracks in the concrete walls, explained the subterranean leak so high on the wall. The electricity struggled to stay on. Most of the light was what shone through the shattered window above, making her thankful that the sun hung at a favorable angle for the time being. Aside from that, a few fluorescent bulbs still flickered, proudly refusing to die in such substandard conditions.

Several metallic catwalks lined three of the walls, all connected by a series of stairways, the fourth being the one by which she entered. The guard rails were covered with rust. Eytea could only imagine that the same was true of the walkways and stairs. The concrete floor was cracked and crumbling, chunks of it rolling under her feet as she walked.

Dilapidated machinery laid about, all of it familiar but only in appearance rather than function. Much of it appeared to have been stripped for parts, what with control panels sitting open, wires frayed about, and miscellaneous scrap spilled out from undercarriages. From the looks of it, she concluded that the place couldn't have been operational for long after those nightmares began, if at all. As far as she knew, they could have been flashbacks to a distant past, and the more she saw, the more likely that seemed. The more pressing matter, however, was that a ladder was nowhere in sight.

With a bit of ingenuity and a couple of tools, she probably could have fashioned something resembling a ladder from all the scraps, but she felt it best not to put Sinkua and Galo at risk on so rusted a contraption. She spread her wings and wrapped them around herself, opening and closing them a couple of times before returning them to their resting position once again.

"On to Plan B," she whispered to herself, "I hate Plan B."

She flew back up through the stream of sunlight to the broken window. Sinkua and Galo were sitting by the pit sharing in conversation so mild that she couldn't distinguish a word. She whistled to them.

"Since I hear whistling, I'm guessing you didn't find a ladder," Sinkua said.

"What? Well, maybe I did, and I'm just here to tell you," she argued.

"A ladder would clank," Galo countered, "They don't whistle."

"Okay, fine. No, I couldn't find a ladder," Eytea confessed, "So, now we go to Plan B."

"I hope your Plan B is better than his Plan A," Sinkua said, "Thinking to break into the facility from inside the house, like whoever lives here has an inkling of what their house is built atop."

"And what were you planning to do when you were charging the door?"

"Rush whoever was on the other side and let you in at the front," Sinkua argued, "If I didn't care about damaging this house, I could have burned it down twice over by now."

"Oh, well why didn't we just do that?" Galo snapped, "That's always your answer, kill them all and leave the bodies to rot."

"Hey, calm down," Sinkua retorted, "And while you're at it, give me a break. Back in Berinin, you were stacking bodies almost as fast as I was, and you only picked up speed after Gijin died."

"That's only because…"

"I'm going to fly you guys down," Eytea interrupted, growing weary of the toxicity of the conversation.

"Can you do that?" Galo asked.

"I have no idea," Eytea admitted, "I mean, I doubt I can lift either of you, especially not for any length of time. I have a strong back from working in the stable, but it's not that strong."

"Well, I would think it's more a matter of how strong your wings are," Sinkua assured, "I'll admit that I'm none too familiar with the structure of animals with independent wings and arms, but I suppose it makes sense. So, how strong are your wings?"

"Strong enough that I don't struggle to float here."

"In other words, they're not underdeveloped," Sinkua summarized, "I guess that's the best we can hope for with what we know."

Eytea drifted aside as he put his legs in the pit and slid down to the window, bracing himself as he went.

"Are you sure you want to try this?" Galo asked.

"We don't have any other choice," Sinkua insisted, "Besides, the fall won't kill me."

"I'm not worried about it killing you," Galo said, "I'm, well…"

"What is it, Galo?" Eytea asked softly.

"Nothing, I'm just worried about him getting hurt, but he always gives me reason to worry about that."

"You're a sweet guy," Eytea complimented with a smile, "but I promise I'll take care of him on the way down."

He looked away as Sinkua set his hands upon her shoulders. Eytea slid her fingers along his shoulders and locked them behind his neck. She looked in his eyes, nearly opaque twin abysses, and took a deep breath, feeding off of his borderline hubristic confidence.

"Are you ready?" she asked as she wrapped her legs around his waist, pulling herself to him.

"As ready as I can be," he accepted, almost beginning to lose himself in her stare.

Galo had turned his back to the pit, wholly tuning out the conversation below. Interactions with Sinkua had become toxic as of late, ever since they met Eytea. Since the night of Gijin's death, he had feared such a wedge was inevitable. His secrecy about his intentions with the scent vials was uncharacteristic as well. Sinkua had always been open with him. Still, he wasn't often wont to sharing a plan until it was about to be set into action, hence why he heard nothing about his fleeing ArcNos until he was already on the water.

But then there was Eytea. Neither of the two had much of any social experience with the opposite sex, Sinkua even less so. He heard how she spoke to him though, and saw how she looked at him. Although Sinkua tried to hide his reaction, he had known him long enough to see past the façade. Yet that same sweet demeanor was sent his way as well. What truly worried him was that he wasn't sure who he felt bitter toward. Where Eytea was involved, he couldn't tell if he was jealous of Sinkua, worried for him, or despised Eytea for coming between them.

"Okay, slide toward me," Eytea beckoned as she slowly flapped her wings, "and I'll glide us down to the floor."

Sinkua nodded in agreement as he advanced into the clutches of her legs, his hands now on her hips. The air of silent confidence between them quickly turned to panic though, as he plummeted from the window. The weight yanked them both down,

Eytea fluttering her wings in a flustered struggle to keep them afloat.

"Not good. Not good. Not good!" she cried out as she strained to slow their fall.

Having never carried much of any extra weight, her wings could do little to counter gravity's pull on them, the two accelerating almost as fast as they normally would. Still, in spite of her panic, Sinkua still looked straight ahead, waiting for her to return her eyes to his.

"I'm so sorry," she whispered as they hesitantly did so.

"You can do this, Eytea," Sinkua urged, "I know you can do better."

"No, no I can't," she insisted, "It's too much."

Sinkua looked down, then back to her eyes and simply stated, "Fine."

With no further acknowledgement, he pushed out of her grasp. He seemed to hang in the air for a split second before plummeting the remaining five meters to the ground, the efforts of Eytea's wings abruptly becoming more apparent. She called to him and reached out a hand as he dropped. He collapsed to one knee and rolled across the floor as he landed.

He sat up and laid his right foot over his left leg. He rolled it a couple of times, popping his ankle. It was sore but not broken or even sprained. Eytea was still floating up there, looking down at him.

"I'm fine," he called up, "Galo's still waiting though."

"Are you crazy?" she called back.

"What? No reason for both of us to take the fall."

"I know why you did it. I'm talking about Galo. If I can't fly you down, I can't fly him down."

"Then go up there and tell him we need a Plan C," he ordered, "or at least a Plan B2."

She flew back to the window to find Galo sitting with his feet in the pit. The screaming he just heard had piqued his concern.

"Hey, so that didn't go too well," she admitted to him.

"I could tell," he said dryly, "You didn't let him get hurt did you?"

"Well, I wouldn't say I let him," she weaseled, "I mean, he says he's fine, but I couldn't do anything about his actions."

"That's just the way he is. You might get used to it. So, what now?"

"Plan C or B2 as Sinkua put it."

"And that is?"

"I don't know, he just said to tell you we need one."

"That's strange. Usually he's the one with the plan and insists that we follow it," Galo pondered, "Well, how far is the drop?"

"Thirty meters maybe."

"Sounds too far for me to make an ice slope, at least without exhausting myself."

"The same thing occurred to me on the way up here."

"Are there any large cracks in the wall near this window?"

"Not big enough to hang from, no. But there are a couple of pipes running most of the way down, about as big around as my upper arm."

"That might work. Give one a good strong jerk."

She checked them both with her finger tips. One was a steam pipe for the heating system, the other a mere plumbing pipe. She grasped the latter with both hands, planting her feet firmly on the wall as she pulled back repeatedly. It shook a bit, but it didn't feel like it would break.

"If you're quick, you should be able to make it."

"That looks like it could work," Galo agreed, having watched the demonstration, "Ask Sinkua what he thinks."

"Are you sure?"

"Go ahead."

"Sinkua!" she called down, turning away from the wall, "He wants to climb down on this water pipe."

"Is he sure he feels safe doing it?" Sinkua yelled.

"Yes, I'm sure," Galo shouted back.

"Okay, sounds good, then."

Galo slid down into the window, sending loose soil raining down into the building. He stretched toward the pipe only to find it just beyond his reach. Recalling his initial thought of an ice slope, he placed his hand on the wall and pulled back slowly, creating a single jutting of ice. He held it as firmly as he could, took a deep breath, and swung out from the window. Eytea floated nearby, poised to grab him if he slipped, even though she knew she could do little to help.

Fortunately, her assistance was unneeded. He hung from the horizontal icicle for a moment, pausing with relief, before he reached for the pipe. It felt unstable, but not nearly as much so as he had expected. He shuffled down it hurriedly but carefully, not wanting to put his weight on it for too long but also fearing what might happen if he pulled too hard. The pipe bent at a right angle about three or four meters above the ground, much of the distance offset by his height when he hung from the corner. He dropped to the floor, crouching into his landing. Eytea was close behind.

"Damn," he gasped, taking in his surroundings as he got to his feet, "If I lived on top of this place, I'd want it barricaded, too."

"Yeah, so would I," Sinkua agreed as he went to join them with a slight limp, "but I doubt whoever lives here knows about this place."

"How's your ankle?"

"It's fine, just stiff."

"When we get near the coast, I'll make some pain killers if I can find the right plants," Galo offered, "Gijin taught me about some Northland roots that are good for exactly that."

"It's really not necessary, but thanks."

"I need the practice, anyway," Galo insisted, "Now then, do you know where we're going, Eytea?'

"Down," she answered, looking about for signs of a passage.

The various cracks aside, the stone floor appeared to be as solid as any other of its sort. The only doors in sight were along the upper catwalks. Flickering lights illuminated evidence that these had largely been offices and observation centers. Finding a path to the lower levels through any of those rooms sounded too unlikely to be worth pursuing the notion.

"Unless they've been paved over, I don't think there are any stairs on this level," Sinkua observed, "But why would they take that much of a precaution, only to leave all these other machines behind?"

"It wasn't a staircase. It was an elevator," Eytea corrected, "but I don't know what part of the room it's in. I remember this room. Then, everything is a blur until she's exiting the elevator."

"They sedated her so she couldn't remember," Galo explained, "Since she has no memory of it, you see nothing of it in your dream."

"Sure, if your idea of a sedative is a lead ball wrapped in leather," Eytea spat as she began to roam the floor.

"Wait a moment!" Sinkua urged, "They struck her upside the head before taking her below?"

"Quite hard, at that. Why?"

"The elevator is hidden, has been since they built this room. They built the town over this factory to hide it from scavengers."

"But they built the interior to hide certain passageways from their hostages," Galo added.

"So we're not going to find an elevator door anywhere," Eytea concluded, "I'm going to pace for a bit, see if I can catch a spark of recognition. You two see if you can find a hollow pillar."

As peeved as they were by the chore of tapping every column in the room, Sinkua and Galo calmly complied. Eytea headed off in the opposite direction, but she had not walked far before an epiphany struck. When she glanced back at them, that spark of recognition set her memories alight. She refocused her eyes, perceiving the three dimensional room as a two dimensional drawing. What caught her attention was the way two of the pillars and the stairs behind them stood in comparison to each other. This was her guiding point.

"Guys, come here!" she called, "I think I found it."

Eager to escape their assigned task, Galo and Sinkua swiftly returned to her side. She pointed out the pillars and the staircases, urging them to try to view them as though they were upon a flat surface.

"It almost looks like their insignia," Sinkua observed.

"Except the middle stroke is missing," Galo added, "Is that what we're trying to see?"

"That's exactly it," Eytea beamed, "And if you lean just a little to the left, the height of that corner makes the final leg."

"Are we sure this is one of their outposts?" Sinkua asked.

"Kabehl made it apparent that some part of his organization had a special interest in Hybrids," Eytea explained, "He seemed to think us subhuman, but I gathered that we're of some importance to his superiors. They spoke of my wings to him."

"Perhaps some sort of superiority complex is at play here," Galo suggested.

"Exactly that, I think," Eytea agreed, "I hate to think what their intentions are for us, but from what I recall of the nightmare, some among them have blood experiments in mind."

"So what was Kabehl's position in the company?" Sinkua asked.

"He called himself The Scout. I suppose that means he was in charge of recruiting," Eytea recounted, "He said he knows who killed HarEin and admitted to having a connection to the body that washed ashore from Kirts when I was a child. In fact, he even claimed…"

"If your suspicions are correct, this was most likely one of their outposts," Sinkua interrupted, "Let's check that corner for a passageway."

Memories of his childhood rushed to the forefront of his thoughts, forcibly retelling what he had been told of CreSam's deployments. He remembered the time when he returned early, interrupting a surprise visit from Gijin and Galo, and how bitterly irritable he was. News of the disappearance of another soldier, also on a mission

162

across the Northlands, reached the public a short time later. The pieces fit. Something changed in CreSam during that trip, and Kabehl was the one to set it all into motion.

Mixed feelings about Kabehl's death wrestled for dominance. On the one hand, the life he now wished to be ended already had been. On the other hand, he missed out on participating in the death of the man responsible for urging his father toward madness. Of course, this made the exhumation of his body all the more curious.

"It sounds hollow," Galo confirmed, knocking on the wall with his ear against it.

The corner, along with the others in the room, was formed of two forty-five degree angles rather than a single right angle.

"So how do we get in?" Sinkua asked, snapping out of his introspection.

"Well there aren't any cracks, and I don't see any buttons or switches either," Eytea noted with disappointment in her voice, "The access panel must be hidden."

"Or there isn't one, and they used remote controls to open the passage," Sinkua considered, "Whichever the case, it'll be faster to just break through the wall."

He withdrew his morningstar and permitted the chain to unravel. Eytea and Galo cautiously stepped back as he twirled it, building momentum with each rotation. He lunged forth, bludgeoning the wall. The spikes penetrated the surface, making a handful of small spider web cracks.

"We need something more direct, like a battering ram," Sinkua insisted.

"I've an idea," Galo offered, pacing backwards from the corner, "I just need you two to be ready to catch me."

"What is he doing?" Eytea asked.

"Sorry, we've never looked for hidden elevators together," Sinkua facetiously replied, "but I suppose he's going to dropkick the wall."

Galo barreled toward them, chest heaving with short rapid breaths. A short distance before the wall, he leapt forth, coating the bottoms of his feet with a thick layer of ice. With a twist of his body and a unified thrust of his bottom half, he pounded the wall with both feet. One made a flat impact, while the other was slightly off point. His left foot twisted under the pressure for a split second before he dropped. Sinkua and Eytea extended their arms to catch him and slowly lowered him to the ground.

He withdrew the ice on his feet and checked his ankle. It was swollen and bruised, but when he didn't feel a crack in the bone, he supposed that it was likely only sprained. The wall, however, did crack. Two large spider webs had formed, deep enough that the pieces could be pulled away with bare fingers. Eytea began tearing them away with furious curiosity as Sinkua offered to assist Galo.

"Hey, my plan worked," Galo grunted through gritted teeth.

"Aside from spraining your ankle, yes," Sinkua somewhat agreed, "Can you walk?"

"Not well, but I can use my glaive as a walking stick until I find those roots."

"Sounds good. How's that passage coming, Eytea?"

"Just about to open the door," she proudly announced.

She had torn away enough to reveal a set of metallic double doors behind the wall. Whether Sinkua's brain storm about the motives behind the design were correct, her visions and his postulations had led them to the right path. She forced the axe head of her halberd between the doors. They budged slightly as she lifted the handle to wedge the spearhead in as well.

Sinkua accompanied her, the two of them clutching the handle with all four hands. Together, they lunged forth, forcing the halberd deeper between the doors.

When they stopped, Sinkua gave it a firm tug to check for stability. Pleased with the penetration, they pulled back on the handle, leaning the whole of their combined weight against the lever. Unfortunately, the effort proved fruitless as the doors moved little. Galo dropped his glaive and braced himself upon the halberd in offering.

"Are you sure about this?" Sinkua asked.

"I don't see any other way," Galo insisted.

He positioned himself nearest to the door and crouched to put the handle at shoulder level, balancing on one foot with his bum leg extended forward. Eytea and Sinkua crouched with him. In unison, the three leaned back with the handle. The doors steadily parted, soon opening enough for any one of them to slip in sideways. The bonds loosened, Sinkua grabbed the two doors and forced them apart just a bit more than the breadth of his shoulders. The three stepped inside.

The control panel had been ripped open. A mess of frayed wires hung out where it would have been. Eytea leaned in to look it over.

"I've only ever seen a couple of elevators in my life, but I think this little piece right here was the button to take us to the bottom floor," she guessed, running her finger over a single pressure point among a grid of several.

"Are you sure we're looking for the bottom floor?" Galo asked.

"Considering how moldy it was in her cell, I'd say it was a long ways underground," Eytea reasoned.

"Best to start at the bottom and work our way up then," Sinkua agreed, "But what of powering this thing?"

"I have an idea," Eytea offered.

She bent and repositioned the wires, bringing the frayed ends within a few millimeters of each other. She was careful to keep them out of contact with each other though, since she didn't know which ones had originally been connected. Content with her efforts, she set the spearhead of her halberd in the middle of the mess, using it to fill the gap.

"Are you sure about this?" Sinkua asked, "I don't know much about electricity, but I'm almost certain that overcharging this panel will get ugly fast."

"I'll be careful, don't worry," Eytea whispered, focusing on her task.

The blade began to crackle and whir, feeding a minute current into the wires. A couple of the bulbs, backlights for the missing buttons, flickered briefly. Steadily, she increased the strength of the current flowing through her blade. Eventually, the tiny bulbs held a steady glow, and the lights in the ceiling kicked on. Painstakingly, she held the current steady.

"Okay, one of you guys hit that pressure point," she urged.

Sinkua complied and pressed what had once been a button. Still a bit surprisingly, the doors closed and the elevator began to drop with a loud whir.

"At least something went right today," Sinkua sighed as he leaned back against the wall, closing his eyes.

After a couple of minutes, the elevator stopped and the doors opened. Eytea removed her halberd and exhaled loudly, a hint of relief permeating her tensed chest. The three of them exited into what could only be described as a nightmare incarnate. The stenches of blood, death, and excrement hung far heavier in here. Eytea shuddered quite visibly as her eyes panned the room.

Several gurneys were scattered about, few of them still standing and whole. The sheets were strewn over the floor, most of them stained with blood and other bodily fluids. Glass shards and shattered syringes lay among them, some so old that what fluid remained had congealed and the needles had rusted. Various machines lined the walls, many emitting a weak pale blue glow, with cords running out to where gurneys once stood or, in a few scattered cases, still did.

Sinkua crouched beside one of the gurneys and plucked a broken syringe from the carnage. A bit of congealed red fluid lined the edges. He poked it with his pinky finger and smelled the sample.

"It's blood," he said plainly as he wiped it on his pants, "Do you recognize this room from your nightmare?"

"Only vaguely. She was just starting to come to as they got off the elevator," Eytea admitted, "but if this is her blood, then it's just as I feared."

"Which is?"

"They were using her blood for experiments, probably on the unwilling or at least unwitting," Eytea explained, "but I have no idea what they were after."

"Just testing the interactions between human and Hybrid blood, maybe," Galo suggested, "and hoping something useful came out of it."

"Perhaps, but they had a specific idea of what they wanted that something useful to be," Sinkua insisted, "We've seen their technology; they don't take aimless shots."

"No, they definitely don't. I knew we were up against something powerful and calculating the day I confronted Kabehl, but even through my nightmares, I never imagined we'd be up against something so overwhelmingly macabre."

"We can't let it scare us away though. We just have to keep whittling away at them to move forward," Sinkua urged, "and calculate our every move to counter theirs."

"You're absolutely right," Eytea accepted with a half smile, "So I suppose we should see if she's still alive."

"Perish any thought to the contrary," Sinkua insisted, "but I think we've all feared the worst since we found this shithole."

Guided by flickering memories, Eytea led the small entourage to a narrow corridor masked by shadows. A ways down at the end was a small cell, no more than four square meters in floor space, with a coat hanging on the gate. Threads of fabric were scattered about, embalmed in dried puddles of blood. In one corner sat a plate of what once was food. The glass of water beside it was coated with dust throughout. Two pairs of chains hung from the wall with open shackles at their ends.

"She's gone," Eytea gasped with a mix of worry and relief, "They took her with them."

"Maybe she's still alive somewhere," Sinkua hoped.

"Or maybe she's still here," Galo suggested, reaching for the glass of water.

He stood over the drain and poured a bit of it down. He waited, listened, and poured a bit more. There was nothing, no sound aside from that of trickling water. He poured the remainder of the water, hoping to hear something else, anything at all. Still, there was nothing.

"Damn, I guess she was moved with the operation," Galo finally agreed.

"As long as she's useful to them, they'll keep her around," Sinkua insisted.

Sinkua examined the white coat that hung from the gate. In one breast pocket, he found a folded sheet of paper. Scrawled upon it was an obscure diagram beyond both his recognition and his deciphering. He suspected it may have been a crude design for a machine or a representation of their experiments.

"Does this mean anything to you?" he asked as he handed it to Eytea.

"Not that I can think of," she admitted, "but let's go ahead and keep it. If we can find someone who can makes sense of it, whatever information is on there will probably be useful."

"I hate to ruin the party, but what's that red light pointing at us?" Galo interjected.

The three walked toward the source until they were standing under it. Sinkua held up an ignited hand.

"Oh crap," Eytea muttered, "It looks like a security camera, and apparently it's still operational."

"We'll just take out the film, then," Sinkua suggested, "I doubt they were going to come back for it anyway."

He swatted the camera with the handle of his weapon, dislodging it from its mount. It bounced down the hall a short distance, leaving a trail of plastic shards. Lacking the tools and patience to open it properly, he stomped the camera until it lay open and battered.

"This is strange," he observed as he crouched to examine the remains, "There's no film in this camera. I don't even see a place for it."

"What does that mean?" Galo asked.

"I've never seen anything like it, but I think the video is being sent straight to a receiver elsewhere," Eytea theorized, "They know we're here."

Chapter 17

A slender young woman stood before a circuit breaker embedded in a concrete wall with the panel hanging from a single screw. Having just finished her work, she flipped the panel upright and tightened each screw, beginning with the hanging point and moving across to the one opposite it. Upon completion of the task, she closed the cover and returned the screwdriver to her tool belt.

"MalVek! I'm done with Breaker Box F," she called out, "Do you mind if I go on my lunch break now?"

"No, go right ahead, kid," MalVek called back, walking toward her, "Hey, thanks for giving me a hand with these here boxes, Yrlis."

"No problem. Thanks for the work," Yrlis countered as she took off her tool belt and started to walk, "You have no idea how badly I needed to get out of medicine after my last patient."

"What happened with him anyway?" he asked, walking alongside her, "You mention him all the time, but you've never told me who he was."

"My oath keeps me from being able to talk about it," she insisted, "The operation went smoothly, but the story behind it was so tragic. It just took so much out of me. You know what I mean?"

"Yeah," MalVek agreed, nodding his head, "Actually no, but I think I understand."

"After everything that transpired in that case, I knew I'd eventually end up trying to link every patient to it," Yrlis continued, "I had to get out of the medical profession before that obsession could manifest."

"Hey, well I know it ain't as glamorous or profitable, but you're a natural at this stuff," MalVek complimented.

"Well, machines are just bodies without emotions," Yrlis mused, "Anyway, I'm off to the sandwich shoppe. I'll see you in an hour."

With that, they parted ways. MalVek moved on to Breaker Box I, continuing down his own list.

The shoppe was built in what had once been a filing clerk's office, back in the corner of a station. The name of the business was painted on the window by hand. Upon close examination, outlines of the station name and the title of the last occupant were vaguely visible where the vinyl stickers had been scraped away.

"Hey, AlsRim," Yrlis announced as she walked through the door, "How's business?"

"Good as ever," AlsRim boasted, emerging from the back of her shoppe, "Let me guess, a Reuben with extra pickles, a sack of potato chips, and a Diet Popken?"

"You know me well, babe," Yrlis accepted with a smirk.

She paid for her meal in advance and went to her usual table. There she sat and waited for a moment before pulling her portable phone from her pocket and making a call.

"Hey, hon, it's me…" she surreptitiously opened, "Yeah, I just finished Box F… Right, two hours for a full charge… You sure you'll be okay on that thing?… Okay. Love you, too. We'll see you tonight… No, I'm still going to let you surprise them…. Okay, bye."

A few minutes later, AlsRim brought out Yrlis's order and set it on her table. A contented smile spread across her face as she took the first bite.

"What do you suppose we should do with this thing, then?" Eytea asked, holding the largest part of the busted surveillance camera.

"Bag it up," Sinkua said.

"What use do we have for it?"

"None right now, but just like that diagram, it could be useful later if we find somebody who can make sense out of it."

Eytea shrugged, willing enough to accept the reasoning, even though she doubted anything would come of it. She gathered up the pieces, scattered across the moldy hall, and crammed them into her travel pack.

Galo leaned in the doorway to the cell, and staring at the shackles. His attention periodically turned to the coat, but only briefly. He tried to imagine the sort of person who could put another through the horrors that must have occurred here, but more what it would mean to endure them. Having spent his entire life in an agora community, the claustrophobia was already choking him.

"What's on your mind, Galo?" Eytea asked, calling from up the corridor.

"What? Oh, nothing," Galo lied, "Just waiting for you guys to be done talking technology."

"Well, we're going up. You joining us?" Sinkua asked.

"Yeah," Galo blankly answered, still staring at the coat, "I'll be right there."

On the way back to the elevator, Sinkua paused for a moment as his eyes scanned the room. He signaled for Galo and Eytea to wait as he braved the cemetery of gurneys. Vague recollections of a nightmare, indistinguishable whether they were imagination or otherwise, flashed rapidly as his fingers ran over the railing of a busted gurney. A rough patch urged him to lean in for a closer look. They were teeth marks, and they appeared human. He cringed at the thought, running his tongue over his teeth.

Nearby lay a metal arm broken off of another gurney. The edges were rough and jagged, indicating that it had been broken off rather than mechanically detached or cut off. Rotten sinew covered one end, with a trail of blood caking three quarters of the length behind it. He picked at the sinew to find tiny fragments of bone. More visions flickered, the shock causing him to drop the bar as he staggered back.

"Are you okay?" Galo called.

"I… I don't know," Sinkua gasped, "but I know why they kidnapped her. What they were trying to do here. They succeeded. But to varying degrees. And not with everybody."

He picked up the broken arm and wheeled the bitten gurney closer to Eytea and Galo, pointing out the bite marks to them.

"I'd like to see anybody with natural jaw strength do that. Human or Hybrid," he insisted, "Have a look at this, too."

"Did somebody break that off?" Eytea asked, a look of fear in her eyes.

"It looks like it," Sinkua confirmed as he showed her the sinewy end, "And this, it looks like somebody was stabbed with this end of it."

"Looks like it was plunged straight through," Galo morbidly observed, his lips curling with disgust, "even through some bones."

"So, this is some kind of…" Eytea began "… some super human test lab?"

"Something like it," Sinkua agreed, "I think they were harvesting Hybrid blood and injecting into people to try to create their own. I don't know if they were ever successful, but somebody reacted to it, quite violently at that."

"They're turning humans into monsters," Galo interjected, "Amirione and his ilk are likely among them, the ones with more fortunate results."

"If they inoculated themselves with Hybrid blood, it was only after they perfected the mix. They obviously wouldn't put their own lives at risk on a crap shoot," Sinkua qualified, "The cocktail certainly changed something in this one, but it was only a step on the way to what they were after. That is, unless they fudged an operation after they found a suitable mix. Either way, he took at least one life before they could put him down."

"All I know is that I want out of here," Eytea urged, "This place gives me the creeps."

"Yeah, it's pretty eerie in here," Sinkua agreed.

With Eytea now more confident in her control over her electromancy, the returning elevator ride was far less stressful. Though now they each had their own reasons to be swamped in introspection. Eytea had found the aftermath of her nightmare incarnate and came to wonder how much time had passed since those memories were current. Sinkua found himself contemplating what sort of horrors must have happened there, as well as why his imagination of them was so inescapably vivid. Galo's thoughts were dominated by shame, knowing that the study of medicine was being used for such inhumane purposes, and couldn't shake the feeling that he was somehow connected to this wretched place.

Back on the entry floor, a large pile of dirt sat under the window. A vague rattling could be heard, resonating through the rafters high above. Bits of paint flakes rained down periodically, followed soon by tiny stripped screws and bolts.

"Is that an earthquake?" Galo asked.

"We're nowhere near a fault line," Eytea refuted, "So I wonder what's shaking the house."

"They know we're here," Galo reminded, "Either of you think they could have found us already?"

"If they did, I think I know who we'll find up there," Sinkua postulated, "Let's go. Eytea, fly out and take cover until we get there. Galo and I will take the pipe."

"Wait, how do you know who it is?" Eytea asked.

"I think I know, but there's no time to explain," Sinkua corrected, "Now, go! We're right behind you."

With his encouragement, Eytea hit full sprint toward the window. The ceiling continued to shake, raining more paint chips and metallic chaff. Near the dirt pile, she leapt and spread her wings, swooping upward along the wall. She glanced back over her shoulder to find Sinkua and Galo nearing the wall, close behind as Sinkua said they would be.

"You go first," Galo urged.

"Are you sure?"

"Yeah, it needs to be you. She's nervous, but she'll be calmed when you reach her."

Sinkua nodded and backed up a bit. With a short running start, he took a few quick steps up the wall and grabbed the pipe. Up at the top, Eytea was climbing through the window with her head low to keep the falling dirt out of her eyes. The pipe shook as he climbed, swaying a little more with each pull. Soon, it was starting to rattle. He stopped to listen.

With each shake of the ceiling, the sound of metallic rattling resonated down the pipe. He glanced down to the floor, then back up to the window, to find that he had only made about half the climb. He swallowed the lump in his throat and called back to Galo.

"You have a backup plan?" he shouted.

"No. Why? Do I need one?" Galo called back.

"I don't know if this pipe will hold up."

"Well quit shouting and hurry up! I'll think of something."

The echoing rattle grew louder.

"Son of a bitch," Sinkua muttered.

He planted his feet against the wall, trying to take some weight off of the pipe. His fists climbing over each other on the pipe, he walked his way up the wall, inevitably shaking the pipe with each grasp. A bolt dropped from the joint above, falling past him surreptitiously and hitting the floor near Galo.

Galo crouched to examine the source of the small clink. He looked up to the window; Eytea was nowhere in sight. Turning his attention to the pipe, he could just see the top joint shaking itself loose.

"Oh shit," he murmured.

Fearing that something was soon to go awry, Sinkua began climbing more hastily. The pipe jostled increasingly as he ascended. Galo frantically sprinted toward the wall and leapt at it. At the peak of his jump, he planted his hand against the wall, adhering it with an enveloping sheet of ice. He pulled upward, repeating with his other hand. Over and over, one hand after the other, he climbed the wall in this fashion. The more the pipe jolted, the more momentum he gained.

"Not this," he grunted.

Sinkua was growing more frantic with each passing second, the pipe quaking loudly as debris rained down over him.

"Not here," Galo continued.

Residual water dripped from the fracturing joint at the top of the pipe. With a rush of adrenaline, Galo kicked up the pace, hurling himself up the wall with each pull and thrust.

"Not now," he muttered, gritting his teeth.

The pipe now shook uncontrollably, even when Sinkua sat still. He was still a good ten meters from the top but more importantly, twenty meters from the floor.

"And not!" Galo growled.

Cautiously, Sinkua continued climbing. Another bolt dropped from the joint. "On!"

More residue trickled down, wetting Sinkua's strained knuckles.

"My!"

Galo angled his body toward the pipe. The last of the bolts broke free, the long pipe anchored only by the bottom joint. Even as Sinkua stopped and planted his feet firmly against the wall, it continued to sway, being awkwardly top heavy with minimal support at the base. Placing his trust in his compatriot, he leaned toward Galo as Galo swung to him.

"Watch!" he shouted.

Sinkua wrapped his limbs around the pipe as it dragged across the wall. Galo stretched his leg and hooked his foot under the pipe. His ankle, the same one he had sprained, popped loudly upon impact. He gritted his teeth and froze his foot against the wall. He then froze his free hand to the wall and brought his other appendages closer before freezing them to the wall as well. He looked up with hopeful worry. Sinkua was still hanging from the pipe.

"Are you okay?" he shouted up.

"Shouldn't I be asking that?" Sinkua shouted back, "That was incredible."

"I know. Now hurry up and climb. This thing is killing my ankle."

Sinkua grinned and nodded. He swung his legs out, hooking his right foot over the pipe, and pulled himself atop it. Perched on all fours, he scurried to the top of the pipe and reached for the window sill above.

Once Sinkua was on his way through the window, Galo resumed his climb. As he climbed over it, the pipe went crashing to the floor below, cracking both itself and the concrete on impact. Through the ceiling, Sinkua could hear a crashing noise, as though something was banging against the wall above. He looked up from the hole, checking for Eytea.

She was sitting with her back against the wall, her eyes wide with fear, as it banged and rumbled. Sinkua reached his hand up from the pit and patted the ground to get her attention. Her eyes darted to his hand.

"Could you give me a hand here?" he beckoned.

She took his hand, clutching it as tightly as she could, though more for her comfort than his assistance. Sinkua pulled himself onto steady ground and looked upon the house with more of an analytical eye than a fearful one.

"Can you see if there's anything in front of the house?" he asked.

"I… I haven't checked," Eytea admitted.

"You're scared, aren't you?"

"Um, well, a little bit, yeah."

"Whatever it is that's doing this, we can take it. Trust me on this," Sinkua promised.

"How are the three of us supposed to take on something that can shake an entire house and that laboratory?" Eytea doubted.

"If I knew what it was, I could tell you. When Galo gets up here, I need you to fly up to the roof and check for us."

She swallowed the lump in her throat and nodded in nervous agreement. A short moment later, Galo emerged into the pit. Sinkua offered his hand to pull him up.

"How's your ankle?"

"Unbelievably sore," Galo admitted, "but I've got ice on it."

Eytea compliantly flew to the roof, landing on the back slope. On all fours, she crawled up to the apex and peaked over. No machine was to be found at the front of the house. Instead, there were two men, a guest with something sheathed upon his back, and the house's occupant, returned from whatever errand had created an opportune absence.

With one hand, the visitor had pinned the resident to the wall by the throat. With the other, he repeated struck the wall within centimeters of his head. Between each strike, he shouted something indistinguishable at her distance. Somehow, this was shaking the entire house. She gasped in horror as the strikes moved incrementally closer to the home owner's head.

Hearing the gasp, the visitor turned his attention upward. He took a few steps back to get a better view of the roof. Her wings peaking over the apex, she had been spotted.

"Peekaboo," he shouted.

From the side of the road, he got a running start, still dragging the resident by the neck. A couple of meters from the wall, he sprang up to the gutters, perching on the edge of the roof. The man in his hand was barely conscious.

"I see you, little Hybrid," he continued.

With wide fearful eyes, Sinkua shouted, "Eytea! Get down from there, quick!"

She was imprisoned by this strange man's stare, unable to blink. He was breathing heavily. His glare felt of anger. Breaking the stalemate, he charged up the roof, dragging the barely conscious man. Eytea screamed in shock, desperately scrambling down the roof. Barely on balance, she leapt back and spread her wings. With a bellow of hellacious rage, the bizarre intruder hurled the now unconscious body of his last victim at her.

The wheels of the mail cart rattled and clanked over the tile floor, one wheel stubbornly pivoting on its mount as it always had. Atop it was a basket nigh overflowing with thick letters and small packages too large for the pigeons, posted to various departments and individuals within the ArcNos Military Executive Committee.

The Main Hall was bustling that morning as rumors of an underground resistance organization, perhaps a splinter group of past military corps, rapidly permeated both conversation and operation. Aside from hearsay though, no confirmation or refutation could be found otherwise. Naturally, this encouraged more rumors and further speculation, which grew into a conspiracy theorists' buffet. Though many were discounted as ridiculous, any that couldn't be expressly disproven necessitated several days' worth of examination and investigation, even for thoughts as farfetched as soldiers returning from the dead.

Malia entered the crowds from the sparsely populated Platinum Hall with urgency in her gait. She halted the mail cart worker before she could pass through the double doors.

"Sorry, Miss, we've got a lot going on right now," Malia urged, "Here, I'll take Lord CreSam his parcels and let you be on your way."

"Oh, well, thank you, sir," she replied awkwardly, seemingly unaware of her gaffe.

Malia snagged a fistful of envelopes from atop the basket, each one addressed either to Brigadier General Elite CreSam or Lord CreSam, as some had come to abbreviate his title. She slipped back into the Platinum Hall and let the doors fall closed behind herself. Leaning against the wall, she flipped through the stack of envelopes. One in particular stood out from the rest, one with a logo reading OMPC in the return address slot. She pocketed this envelope and headed for CreSam's office at the other end of the hall.

Through the window in his door, SenRas watched her pass. He had been pacing and sipping coffee all morning, unsettled by the rumors flying about as well as by what truth he knew. If his suspicions about Malia's intentions were correct, his suspicions about the Avatars of Fate likely were as well.

Malia knocked on CreSam's office door, waiting for permission to enter. Upon receipt of such, she walked through the open doorway with confidence in her stride.

She held up the stack of envelopes, minus the one from OMPC, and fanned them out between her fingers.

"Mail call, sir," she announced.

"Why are you delivering my mail?" he asked flatly.

"Mail cart lady's swamped, what with the crowded halls," she explained, "So I thought I'd save her the trip."

"Mm. I see," CreSam accepted, still not looking up from his desk, "Let's have it then."

"Here you go," she offered, handing off the stack of envelopes, "By the way, what happened to your pictures?"

"My what?" he asked, flipping through the envelopes.

"Didn't you used to have pictures of your family on your desk?" she asked, sounding as though she was doubting her own memory.

"Malia, I'd have to have had a family to have pictures of them," CreSam explained, finally making eye contact, "Where did you get such a notion?"

"I'm sorry, sir. I must be thinking of someone else."

"I suppose so," CreSam said nonchalantly, breaking eye contact again, "but enough of your oddity. Away with you now."

Malia chuckled at her deliberate gaffe as she turned to exit the room, internally satisfied with the exchange that had just occurred. As she headed toward the other end of the hall, she withdrew her portable phone from her pocket and started dialing, holding it to her ear as she slipped into her office.

"Hello, sir," she opened, "The side effects of CreSam's treatment have come to fruition."

Without another word, she closed the device and returned it to her pocket. From the opposite pocket, she withdrew the folded envelope. She sat at her desk and dug through the drawers. Pinching the envelope at the corner marked with the return address, she suspended the piece of mail above a lighter she found and flicked it on. With a grin of contentment, she watched the unopened letter burn beneath her fingers, the ashes falling atop a stack of papers on her desk. When about half of it had been torched, she was alarmingly interrupted as SenRas burst into the room.

"Don't you know how to knock?" she snapped, whipping the envelope to the floor, snuffing the flame.

"Malia, someone just broke into your car!" SenRas exclaimed, "I saw it from my window just a moment ago."

"What? Thanks for telling me, old man."

Without question, she bolted past him and ran to the Main Hall. SenRas stepped aside to let her pass, urging her to hurry. She had taken his bait. He peered back over his shoulder before entering her office and closing the door behind himself.

Behind her desk, he found the half burnt envelope. The return address was just as he feared, the OMPC logo. He pulled out the remainder of the paper, scattering ashes on the floor, and unfolded it. What text was still legible read as follows:

"To the Estate of Briga…
 The following case:
Name: MeiLom
 Age (at the date of filin…
Age (current): 20
 Case Number: MP3974…
 has officially been close…

-ation, and with our lack…
continue our search, the…
-ly dead. In 14 days, Me…
will be purged.
 We apologize for our…
 Ouristihran Missing Per…"

He sighed and returned the paper and envelope to where he found them, disillusioned by the news he found and the news he feared. The information was sparse, but enough to draw an indubitable conclusion. CreSam's missing son had been declared dead. The search was over.

SenRas departed for his office across the hall, this newfound knowledge weighing down on his very being. When he was halfway across, a door to the Main Hall swung open forcefully. Malia stormed in and grabbed him by the shoulder.

"Hey, old man, nobody was breaking into my car," she snapped.

"Oh? I guess they gave up," SenRas muttered and continued walking.

"What are you trying to pull?" she asked, turning him back around again.

"Set your hand upon me once more, young lady, and I'm going to keep it for myself," he calmly promised, holding her by the wrist.

"Let go of me, you dirty coot," she hissed.

"I smell something rotten in your baited breath. You think yourself untouchable, but I've lived through enough to know better. Whatever your game is, I will end it, you wretched little girl," SenRas continued, clutching her wrist more tightly, his glare freezing her expression, "Do not fuck with me."

He released her wrist, and she quickly pulled it back, rubbing it as she countered with a seething glare. Unmoved by her anger, he simply turned his back and continued to his office.

Once inside, he immediately went for the coffee maker. The pot was empty, the last bit of coffee swimming in itself in a cup on his desk. Still holding the empty pot, he opened a drawer with his free hand. Plenty of filters left. He opened the other drawer and found it empty. He was out of grounds. He stood over the drawer, staring at it for a moment. His breath grew heavier, and his grip on the coffee pot tightened.

"Son of a bitch!" he burst, hurling the pot at a wall.

The pot shattered, scattering glass shrapnel over the carpet. SenRas's heart jackhammered against his ribcage. He stormed over to his desk, jerked the chair out and dropped into it. He sat for a minute, clutching the arms of the chair and trying to calm his breath.

In a moment of desperate revelation, he opened the bottom drawer. He frantically dug through old files and envelopes, most of them antiquated and thus yellowed around the edges from disuse. Toward the back, he found a sealed envelope with a faded red OMPC logo. He had initially expressed an interest in MeiLom's search case, although he never let it be known to CreSam. Three years ago, it came to trouble him too greatly, and he asked to no longer be updated. He reached into the envelope and pulled out two pictures he had never previously dared to look upon

One was a pencil sketch of how the committee's analysts believed MeiLom looked at that point. The other was a copy of the photograph CreSam had submitted upon filing the report; the child appeared to be about eight or nine. The sketch was remarkably detailed and lifelike, but the photograph was what truly grabbed him.

"MeiLom…" he gasped, "This child… Is that young man… Sinkua?"

His eyes never moving from the photograph, he reached for his intercom. He buzzed CreSam's office and waited for a response, his foot drumming rapidly against the carpet. A beep sounded from the speaker, followed by CreSam's greeting.

"Admiral SenRas," he opened, "What brings you on the line?"

"Brigadier General Elite CreSam?" SenRas greeted, trying to steady himself, "I know where your son is."

"My what?"

"Your son."

"I don't have a son."

"I know, sir. He went missing, but I know where he is."

"You misunderstand me, SenRas," CreSam said flatly, "I never had a son."

"Sir? It's MeiLom. Your son, MeiLom, is still alive," SenRas insisted, desperately grasping at a better reaction.

"Sorry, SenRas. The name doesn't even ring a bell. What is it with you people thinking I have a family?"

"You people?"

"Just a moment ago, Malia was in here asking about family portraits."

"Malia?"

CreSam cut the line, leaving SenRas with one more clue and another handful of questions.

The body crashed into Eytea, knocking both wind and blood from her lungs. Her wings flapped frantically, panicked to keep herself aloft as she pushed the body away. Unsteadily, she landed in the back lawn once again. The assailant was close behind, leaping from the roof and landing behind her.

"So they sent you again," Sinkua greeted bitterly.

"Don't think I like seeing you, boy. I just happened to be in the area when the call went out."

"Lucky for you, nobody competent was nearby," Galo goaded, "Now you have the chance to make a name for yourself. Not much of one, but a chance nonetheless. By the way, how's that prosthetic hand?"

"A name? I have a name, child," the assailant growled, "You will know me as The Criminal."

He charged forth, effortlessly knocking Eytea aside on his path to Galo. Galo backed up to the wall and locked his stare on The Criminal's. The Criminal drew back his prosthetic fist, Galo remaining stoic. As he came down upon him, Galo deftly spun to parry. The enhanced appendage slammed into the wall, shattering the siding and shaking the house on its foundation.

"It was you, wasn't it?" Sinkua interjected, "You're the biter from down in the lab."

"That guy? No, not me," The Criminal hissed, "He was a failure, had to dispose of him. One of many on the trail of bodies leading to me."

"You're a sick, sick man."

"Heh heh, you're not much different, little Hybrid."

He approached Sinkua slowly, locking eyes with him. The two circled each other, keeping a distance of a handful of meters.

"Galo, check on Eytea. Get her out of here," Sinkua urged.

Eytea was stubbornly clinging to consciousness, lying nearby. Galo quickly slipped away from the stalemate and pulled her upright, slumping her arm over his shoulder. With an emphasized gait, he dragged her out of the back yard. She muttered incoherently, trying to keep from blacking out.

"That's why you're here, isn't it? You didn't just happen to be in the area," Sinkua pried, "You're an end result of this place, and you can't stand that we found out about the process behind it."

"You know nothing!" The Criminal bellowed.

"We know enough. Enough that you've lost your luster. You're not special anymore," Sinkua continued, letting the chain of his morningstar unravel, "Instead you're just an adolescent, too pathetic to accept his human shortcomings like the man he thinks he is."

"I never wanted to be a freak like you. Shut your filthy mouth, boy."

"I suppose that's why you had yourself injected with Hybrid blood, isn't it? Or maybe it's not the uniquity, but the principle. We stole from The Criminal, and you can't stand that we beat you at your own game."

"I'm here on principle beyond your understanding," The Criminal snarled, "to uphold The Epimetheus Trial."

"Epimetheus?" Sinkua asked, pausing in their circling.

"All men control their fate, thus the only victims are those of their own consequence. None are to blame for the results of one's actions aside from oneself. This is the principle of The Epimetheus Trial, and it shall not be contested," he explained, "As an Avatar of Fate, it is my duty to see that this consequence comes to fruition."

"In other words, we invaded your operation, and just like last time, you're here to try to dispose of us. But now you have self-righteous justification," Sinkua summarized, "What of him though? How does he fit into your principle?"

"He got in the way of reaching you."

"I'll see to it that it doesn't happen again."

Sinkua lunged toward him, swinging his morningstar overhead. The Criminal stepped into it, pivoting to dodge the falling ball, and delivered a swift kick to Sinkua's rib cage. Sinkua stumbled to the side, the ball of the morningstar swinging clumsily toward his leg. With the flick of his wrist, he brought it to rest.

"Good, you've improved," he bitterly complimented.

"I was toying with you."

Sinkua lunged again, this time veering to the right. The Criminal did the same, moving to Sinkua's open left side. Sinkua swiped his left arm out to the side, a trail of fire streaking in front of his opponent's eyes, blinding him momentarily. Sinkua pivoted beyond his reach and swung the morningstar from the outside. Hearing the motion, The Criminal ducked to avoid the careening spiked ball.

Hunched over, he pulled a scimitar from the sheath upon his back as the chained ball passed over his back. Sinkua yanked back on the handle, swinging the weapon back toward him. The Criminal jerked himself upright, thrusting his blade through the chain and snagging it.

"As I told you, such a clumsy weapon," he taunted.

"Hmph, I expected something more interesting from the likes of you."

The Criminal pressed two fingers into the handle and twisted his hand. A series of metallic thorns jutted out of the blade, hooking into the chain links. With Sinkua now trapped in the standoff, he tugged on the sword. Sinkua tightened his grip and dug his heels into the soil. Gritting his teeth, he pulled back on his morningstar, each of them trying to disarm the other.

"So much for superhuman strength," Sinkua taunted, "Not much of a match for raw obstinacy."

"You know far less than you think, boy."

The Criminal pulled the handle up to his shoulder, pointing the blade at Sinkua. Sinkua pulled back, trying to dislodge his morningstar, with no success. The Criminal slammed his organic hand against the butt of the hilt.. Attached by a chain, the blade shot off the hilt. Sinkua released his grip and fell to the side, catching himself on his hand. His weapon dangling from it, the blade shot past his shoulder and slammed into the wall behind him, breaking through the siding and penetrating the masonry. He clutched the chain with the other hand and pulled himself upright.

His hold on it tightened. The Criminal pulled back on his hilt, but the chain barely moved. Sinkua's fingers dug into the chain. Again, he pulled, but neither the chain nor the blade would move. Smoke seeped from between Sinkua's fingers. One last pull and the chain split, the links melted in Sinkua's searing grasp.

Sinkua grabbed the remainder of the chain with both hands. The Criminal looked up from the broken chain to be caught by a stare of ferocity with jaws clenched and expression unwavering. With a wrathful grunt and bellow, Sinkua jerked the blade out of the wall, swinging both it and his morningstar by the broken chain. The Criminal ducked to dodge the flying weapons, narrowly avoiding an undoubtedly fatal impact. Sinkua recoiled and caught the chain behind the blade. He melted the joining link and discarded the chain. Not how he anticipated arming himself at the start of the fight, but he now found himself wielding a morningstar with a spiked blade hanging from the middle of the chain.

"Have you got it in you? Have you sunk into such dishonor as to execute an unarmed man?" The Criminal goaded.

"Honor? Tell me what you know of honor," Sinkua spat, walking toward him.

"This rage becomes you, little Hybrid."

"Tell me what the fuck you know of honor!"

"I know you're losing your sense of it."

"And I know you can't tell me," Sinkua hissed, tossing the weapon aside as he came within arm's reach, "why you deserve to die with any."

At close range, he pounded his fist into The Criminal's sternum. He felt the bone crack and split upon impact, a trail of blood running out of The Criminal's mouth as he coughed. Again and again he bludgeoned, the split running longer and wider with each smashing blow.

"We let you get away in Berinin," Sinkua snarled, "but I swore to myself that the next time we met would be the last."

"And the last time we met," The Criminal gurgled through the blood in his throat, "was not the first."

"I suppose you expect me to ask for an explanation."

The Criminal began to speak, but Sinkua slammed his hand against his face, shattering his nose. Palming The Criminal's face, he bored into the flesh with smoldering fingers. The Criminal writhed and thrashed violently but ineffectually. He clung to Sinkua's forearm with both hands, desperately trying to pull him away. He raked at the flesh, leaving trails of both their blood. Sinkua's hand came alight, and his fingertips worked through the melting flesh like fresh clay.

"I'd rather figure it out for myself."

Holding the back of The Criminal's head with one hand, he removed the other from his face, revealing his grotesque visage. His features were gnarled and smeared, what remained of his flesh covered in boils. The exposed bone matter was scorched and brittle. Sinkua clenched his fist, popping each knuckle. Jerking The Criminal toward him to amplify the impact, he slammed his fist into that decrepit face. Tiny shards of bone flew about, melted flesh and sinew trailing over his wrist. Blood gurgled up from the broken Avatar's throat as his breathing ceased. Sinkua loosened his grip, discarding the lifeless body to collapse upon the warm bloodied grass.

He forcefully untangled his morningstar from the thorny scimitar blade. Without any further acknowledgement to his victim or the resident, he simply staggered away. His breathing ragged and raspy, he braced himself against the side of the house, leaving a trail of blood along the siding. Galo came running with Eytea in close tow.

"Are you alright?" Eytea shouted.

Sinkua stopped, falling against the wall. He turned his head quickly, gasping for air as his eyes grew wider. Galo slowed as they came near him, putting his arm out to halt Eytea as well.

"Sinkua?" Galo asked, still a couple of meters away.

"Does he get like this often?" Eytea whispered.

"Never that I've seen," Galo whispered back.

Sinkua hacked loudly, his throat gurgling with each painful bark. Blood pooled behind his lips, dripping to the ground. He paused to clear his throat before releasing a short series of notably louder coughs, spewing blood onto the grass and along the wall. His hand slid further down the wall, desperately clinging for balance as he gasped for air.

"Sinkua? Are you okay?" Eytea asked, setting her hand upon his shoulder.

In a moment of blind instinct, he jerked away violently, throwing her hand from his shoulder and knocking her off balance. Clutching his head with enraged digits, he vomited a bellow of pain and rage, punctuated by a sudden collapse.

Chapter 18

Yrlis hung her tool belt in the office she shared with MalVek. Her day's work finally done, she snatched her purse and recorded in her hours on a roster sheet pinned to the cork board. On the way out, she locked the door behind herself. As she walked home alongside the tracks, she took a glance up one of the staircases. The triad of moons hung high, resembling three grains of rice. She had expected to work late that evening, but not quite so late as to miss dusk. Her portable phone rang from her pocket.

"Hey, babe…" she greeted as she opened it, "Yeah, I just got off… Uh-huh, I'll be there in a few minutes… Okay, see you then. Bye."

Her pulse quickened with excitement. Her friends and roommates would soon meet the man in her life. When she reached the front door, the telltale hum of an approaching electric motorcycle had just found its way into the range of audibility. She opened the door and whistled delightedly.

"Phylus! Vielle! I'm home!" she announced.

"Hey, kiddo," Phylus called back from the couch, "Long day on the job?"

"Yeah, but you know, the pay is good, so what the hell."

"Hey, Aunt Yrlis," Vielle called from the kitchen, "Supper will be ready in a few minutes."

"Ooh, sounds good. Did you make enough for four?"

Vielle peeked in the pot and glanced in the oven. She looked back at Yrlis, who was looking at the meal over her shoulder, struggling to maintain a straight face.

"Um, I wasn't trying to, but I guess there's enough for an extra person," Vielle answered, "Or, you know, leftovers. Whatever."

"You expecting company?" Phylus asked, getting up from the couch.

"Maybe. You know, just my boyfriend dropping by," Yrlis said as nonchalantly as she could manage.

Vielle's eyes sparked with anticipation. She examined the meal once more to assure herself beyond doubt that she had made enough for four, now taking Yrlis's question considerably more seriously. The electric hum of the approaching motorcycle permeated the sounds of household, even through a closed front door.

"So we finally get to meet that man of yours, huh?" Phylus remarked, "Well, that sounds great. Here I was starting to think you'd made him up."

Yrlis laughed nervously, realizing now how close she had come to ruining the surprise. Her alibi, though based on truth, was becoming flimsier with each passing day.

"Aha, no no no. He just got out of the hospital this morning," Yrlis explained, "Just recovered from his surgery."

"We know, we know," Vielle dismissed with a half smirk, slapping Yrlis's arm with her free hand, "You only told us about this 'boyfriend' and his 'surgery' a hundred times."

"Well it's all true," Yrlis insisted, pouring herself a drink, "I think you'll really like this guy, too. Just don't go trying to steal him from me, you little flirt."

The hum grew too loud to doubt. Yrlis turned her attention toward the door.

"Is that a motorcycle?" Phylus asked.

"Sounds like it," Yrlis verified, walking back to the door, "That should be him."

Vielle turned down the temperature on the stove. Phylus followed Yrlis to the door, and Vielle was close behind. From the open doorway, they could see a motorcycle approaching from a handful of meters away.

The driver accelerated when he saw the three of them waiting for him. Under the track lighting, the overlapping shadows of himself and his bike whipped back and forth, rapidly weaving in and out of each other. As he came near enough to discern their expressions, he noticed that two of them were straining to see his face through his visor. He grinned widely as he realized the surprise held strong even in its final seconds.

He hit the brakes and whipped the back end into a fishtail skid. He cut the power to the motor and pulled off his helmet.

"Hey guys," he casually greeted, "I'm home."

Phylus's eyes grew wide with shock and disbelief, neither appearing to wane in the slightest with each passing second confirming the reality that his sensibilities refused. His mouth quivered, trying to form words, but only strained breath could escape. Vielle gasped loudly, her eyes transfixed on their dinner guest. Yrlis calmly sipped her drink, smiling at their reaction and laughing under her breath.

"What? Not even an 'hello?'" the guest asked.

Vielle burst forth from behind Yrlis and Phylus and leapt at him.

"Uncle Spril!" she cried out.

Galo crouched to help the barely conscious Sinkua to his feet. He signaled to Eytea for her to take Sinkua's other arm. His head slumped and bobbing, the two stood him upright. His feet dragged as they walked with him, proving the task ahead to be a test of both patience and willpower.

"Is there anything you can do for him?" Eytea asked.

"If I knew what was wrong with him, maybe," Galo regretfully admitted, "but this could be any number of things."

"Well, let's see if we can find a hospital then."

Sinkua drifted in and out of consciousness, though most of his time was spent out of it, as his two friends carried him down the road. Even with the ice on it, Galo's wounded ankle was proving to be a burden on their travel. Eytea used the strength of her wings to help hold the lot of them upright, as far as they could manage to do so.

After an excruciating kilometer, a road sign directed them to a hospital up ahead on the right. The top of its rooftop sign could be seen peeking over buildings nearer to them. Atop the horizon, the sun punctuated the fuchsia sky. Sinkua groaned as he incrementally regained consciousness.

"What's this?" he mumbled.

"You killed one of those marked men," Galo recounted, "When we approached you, you yelled out in pain, spewed blood and collapsed. Now we're going to a hospital."

"Avatar."

"What?"

"Said Avatar of Fate."

"So that's what this 'Honorable Guild' is called," Eytea chimed in, "Can you stand?"

"I think," Sinkua said, stepping away from them and bracing himself, "Need hospital?"

"Did you suffer any serious injuries?" Galo asked.

"Don't think."

"Then we don't know why you're spewing blood or what made you scream. So yes."

Their travel was hindered by Sinkua's staggering, though not nearly as much as by carrying him. Light conversation distracted them from the strain and distance and also served to restore Sinkua's speech patterns to something closer to normal. In spite of the hindrances, their feet hit the hospital parking lot before dusk, even if only by minutes. A fleet of ambulances was parked nearby. A young medical technician spotted them heading for the door. Noticing Sinkua's unfortunate state, he rushed to help.

"What happened to you, man? You nigh look of death," he empathized, setting his hand upon Sinkua's shoulder.

"I coughed up blood and fell," Sinkua mumbled, lifting his head to acknowledge him.

"What's with your eyes? Some strange ocular condition?"

"Yes, that's why I'm here," Sinkua muttered, "I'm spewing blood! Get me to a doctor, you idiot."

"Right, right, just come on in. I'll find a doctor right away," the technician stuttered nervously as he walked backwards into the building.

The three of them followed into a sparsely populated waiting room. A nervous security guard held out his night stick, halting them in the foyer. He nodded to acknowledge the armaments strapped to their backs.

"Those will have to be locked up while you're here," he ordered as sternly as he could manage at the sight of them.

After readily complying with the order, Sinkua and Galo went to find seats, but Eytea was stopped by the guard yet again.

"And your costume, madam," the guard continued, pointing to Eytea's wings.

"These are a part of me, sir," she argued.

"Look, I know you kids like to find your own little quirk or whathaveyou, and I'm sure you wear those everywhere you go. I've got a daughter your age."

"No, I mean they're growing out of my back. See?"

She turned her back to him and hooked her index finger in one of the slits in her top, exposing her skin.

"See, look in there," she invited, looking back over her shoulder.

He leaned in for a closer look. When he ran his finger over the joint of wing and flesh, she instinctively jerked away.

"What are you people?" he asked.

"Just a patient and his friends. Now, if you'll excuse me."

Shortly after she found a seat near Galo and Sinkua, the aforementioned technician returned to the waiting room with a middle aged doctor close behind.

"This is the guy I told you about," the technician indicated, leading him to Sinkua.

"Oh my, solid green, just like you said," the doctor observed, crouching in front of a clearly agitated Sinkua.

"Did this idiot tell you I'm here about my eyes?" Sinkua snapped.

"Have you had this condition all your life?" the doctor asked.

Sinkua hung his head to avoid eye contact and gritted his teeth. His breathing grew ragged, much in the same way as earlier. The technician stepped between them.

"Hey buddy, he asked you a question. Are you alright?" he urged, setting his hand upon Sinkua's shoulder.

Sinkua jerked his head upright and socked the technician in the eye.

"Is this temper normal for him?" the doctor asked Eytea and Galo.

"I've never seen it this bad," Galo promised, "So I'd say it's not."

Sinkua began coughing, blood gurgling up from this throat and eventually dripping on the tile floor.

"Neither is that," Eytea added, "but he got in a fight with an old rival earlier and the same thing happened afterwards."

"Did you suffer any injuries, young man?"

"Not the first time."

"What about this time?"

"No, he didn't get hurt," Galo interjected, "We asked on the way here."

"The last time wasn't the first time," Sinkua mumbled, "but there won't be a next time."

"Any idea what he's talking about?"

Both of them shook their heads.

"Well, if you two think it's safe, walk him back to my office. I have a couple of ideas, but I need to run some tests first."

Galo and Eytea helped Sinkua to his feet and followed the doctor. Sinkua struggled to walk, his feet dragging between steps as they headed down the hallway. Near the end, the doctor led them into a room. Inside was a white bed in front of an array of machines unfamiliar to Galo, despite his niche lying in medicine. Upon a countertop running along the opposite wall was a myriad of paperwork and charts.

"Put him up on the bed, and we can get started," the doctor ordered as he filled out a bit of paperwork, "By the way, my name is Ophalin. And you folks are?"

"I'm Galo," Galo introduced as he propped Sinkua up on the bed, "This young lady is Eytea, and your patient there is Sinkua."

"Galo, Eytea, and Sinkua, names I won't soon forget. Now if you'll excuse me, I need some privacy with Sinkua."

"Do you have any idea how long it will take?" Eytea asked.

"Running the initial blood tests, x-rays and possibly a CT scan will take a couple of hours," Ophalin warned, "If you're hungry, the directory in the lobby will point you to the cafeteria. Patient family members get two free meals a day with these cards."

He produced two visitor cards from a drawer in the counter. The two of them kept quiet about not being family, just in case Ophalin was wrongfully assuming rather than being charitable.

"Thanks, Doctor," Eytea accepted, "We'll be down there if you have any questions for us."

Down in the cafeteria, Galo ordered a chef salad and a bass fillet. Eytea opted for grilled chicken with a side of steamed broccoli and a baked potato. They found a two seat table near a wall and settled in for a long night.

"What do you think happened?" Eytea asked as she cut into her chicken.

"I don't know, but it seems like something inside that place set him off," Galo suggested, "I've never seen him that angry."

"That may be," Eytea agreed between bites, "but it doesn't explain his coughing blood and fainting."

Galo nodded in agreement. The two of them ate in verbal silence for a few minutes. The bass was a bit overcooked for Galo's tastes, but he wasn't one to complain about a free meal. After a while, Eytea broke the silence.

"So, he hasn't lost control like that before?" she reassured, "You know, in the lobby."

"No, that was the first time I've seen him do such a thing. Why?"

"I don't know, it just worries me."

Galo looked up from his plate to meet her eyes and find a look of concern deeper than just worry.

"You really care about him, don't you?"

"What? Well, I don't know, it's just…" Eytea began, "Something about him intrigues me. He's so direct and unbiased in his principles."

"This is true. He was ready to leave when he heard you killed your father."

"Kabehl was nary a father," Eytea countered, "but let's not dwell on him."

Shortly thereafter, they finished their meals. The two of them returned to light conversation, speaking of their upbringings as well as of Galo and Sinkua's travels. After an indeterminate length of time, Ophalin entered the cafeteria and approached their table.

"Do either of you know a man named Doriman?" he asked, "Sinkua keeps mentioning him."

"What is he saying?" Galo asked.

"He says he forgot to send a copy of the letter to him. Does that sound like it means anything?"

"It means he's losing his memory," Galo sighed, turning away from Ophalin, "Doriman is dead, and he knew that."

"Oh my, that is unfortunate for both of them," Ophalin sympathized, "Did he die before or after Sinkua distributed the letters?"

"Well before."

"Then memory of such must still be seated primarily in the hippocampus," Ophalin mumbled to himself, "Okay, thank you."

"Son of a bitch," Galo snapped after Ophalin had left the cafeteria.

"This is horrible," Eytea agreed, "What if it gets worse? He could forget who we are."

"I'm not sure about that. He remembers Doriman, but not his death," Galo reiterated, "But if he starts losing memories too quickly, he could slip into a case of amnesia."

"And if he loses his past, he'll lose sight of his objectives."

"He'd likely lose his knack for strategizing as well," Galo added, nodding in agreement as he took a sip of his drink, "but more importantly, all the progress we've made in deciphering the Avatars of Fate."

"You and I can remember those things though."

"But if he doesn't understand or remember, it will be difficult to keep him involved."

"Maybe that's good for him," Eytea suggested, taking a sip of her drink.

"No, not as much as you would think," Galo insisted, glancing out the window and across the night sky, "He needs to finish what was started, even if just for principle."

"Do you speak of your grandfather?"

"For one, yes," Galo solemnly agreed, "but it goes deeper than that. Sinkua has been a vagabond for several years, and my village was one of the only places he could call home. He blames them for his mother's death, and they tried to stop him from relocating."

"What of his father?"

"He never knew him all that well, only that he disappeared sometime shortly after murdering his mother," Galo fibbed

Despite knowing it best to uphold Sinkua's wishes, Galo still felt guilty about fabricating partial truths to a new friend. For his own principles, he was keeping Eytea uninformed about his past, and so Galo had implicitly sworn to follow along. It was something of a chore, but hardly too troublesome a façade to maintain. Eytea already knew that Sinkua was from ArcNos, but the depth of his ties remained beyond her knowledge.

The conversation was slowly forced into more casual topics, eventually turning to an exchange of simple pleasantries and observations. It was calming cafeteria conversation, distracting them from worrying about their friend. Minutes turned to hours, and drinks were refilled numerous times as they combated fatigue. Eventually, the sun peeked over the horizon, casting long shadows across the cafeteria.

Ophalin entered the cafeteria, a cup of steaming hot coffee in his hand.

"Have you two been here all night?" he asked.

"Yeah. Looks like you have, too," Galo replied.

"It's that obvious, is it?" Ophalin admitted, "Your friend's case is quite bizarre. I wouldn't let myself go home until I made sense of it or collapsed of exhaustion. It took all night, but I finally get to leave."

"I'm hoping your reason is the former, for everybody's sake," Eytea empathized.

"I'm proud to say that it is," Ophalin boasted between yawns, "I've figured out what's behind his symptoms, but I'm not sure how he became afflicted with such an amalgamation of conditions. It's as though he was poisoned with a chemical cocktail, and without on the exact composition, all I can offer is a suppressant."

"What about a blood transfusion?" Eytea asked.

"That would do no good," Ophalin insisted, "Allow me to explain. One chemical, which has affixed itself to his bone marrow, has enhanced his body's ability to process proteins as well as muscle reflex and tension. This has resulted in a sort of superhuman strength, but nothing overly extraordinary as of yet, as far as I can tell."

"That doesn't sound too bad," Galo shrugged, "Strange, but not bad."

"It's worse than it sounds," Ophalin disagreed, "Stimulation of the amygdala, such as anger, is triggering the formation of benign microtumors in the frontal cortex of his brain along with blood clots under his brain stem. The first are interfering with his distant memory as well as his judgment, though more recent long term memories are maintained in the hippocampus. As for the others, they induce severe headaches, maintaining the anger, which is also seated in the hippocampus. The cycle stresses his body until he coughs up blood and collapses. I believe this stress is what's interfering with his recollection of recent long term memories after he has an episode."

"What does that have to do with the first chemical?" Eytea pried.

"The chemical causing this condition has bonded with the proteins in his blood stream, hence the futility of a blood transfusion. Even a full hemodialysis did no good," Ophalin explained, "For now, make sure he takes his medicine on a daily basis and limit his protein intake."

"Can't you do a bone marrow transplant?" Galo asked.

"That would work, but he said he has no living relatives. Is that true?"

Eytea and Galo glanced at each other, both knowing to different extents that Sinkua and his father were on horrible terms with one another.

"Unfortunately, yes," Galo corroborated, technically being honest.

"Well, we match transplants based on six indicators, and the best way to match all six is with a nuclear blood relative. The risk of a failed transplant is significant even with only one mismatch," Ophalin explained.

"So then I suppose all you can do is medicate him," Eytea accepted, "and suppress his symptoms, as you put it."

"I'm afraid so."

"If he stayed here, would that help you find a cure?" Galo asked.

"That won't be necessary. I've kept several samples of his blood and marrow. If I can isolate the foreign compounds, I should be able to start working on a cure, but even that initial process could take months. I also took the liberty of removing his microtumors, so he may regain some clarity in his memory, but they'll form anew as soon as he's angered again. The more frequently it happens, the more wont he may be to a loss of upper level rationale," Ophalin warned, "In short, your friend has become a time bomb."

The anesthetic from multiple exploratory surgeries was still being filtered out of Sinkua's blood, limiting his coordination for some time. It took a couple of hours, but he gradually regained his ability to walk without assistance. By late morning, they had returned the southern edge of town. Sestak and Seschnel were still tied up nearby, laying down for a rest in the shade near a large patch of freshly chewed grass. Eytea hurried to loose them.

"Here, Doctor Ophalin said you need to take one of these capsules a day," Galo relayed, producing a bottle of pills from his pocket.

"What are they?" Sinkua asked.

"Protein suppressant and mood stabilizer," Galo explained as he opened the bottle and handed off a tablet., "It was the best he could come up with to control your condition."

"Makes sense, I suppose," Sinkua agreed.

Galo pointed at Sinkua's face and shot a stream of water into his open mouth. Sinkua smirked and swallowed the pill.

"By my recollection, there should be a port about ten kilometers west of here. We can make it by early afternoon," Eytea assured, leading the horses to them.

"Great. Any idea how we'll acquire a boat?" Galo asked, turning to Sinkua.

"Not offhand, no. What about you?"

"That shouldn't be necessary. Ferries leave from there every couple of hours," Eytea explained.

"Don't those cost money?" Sinkua asked, "I'm not certain we can afford that."

"Normally, yes," Eytea began.

"Are the ports in a no currency jurisdiction?" Galo asked.

"No, not at all," Eytea continued, "Thousands of coastal Feryans work at the docks in Quarun. They'll go out for a few days at a time, then come back to see their friends and families. The taxes on their paychecks go to the Quarunite government. In exchange for the stimulation to their economy, they run a free ferry service between Ferya and Quarun."

"So we're in the clear for once. Excellent," Sinkua remarked.

Sinkua hooked his hands under Galo's foot, hoisting him up onto Seschnel's back. Galo's ankle, in spite of the suppressed swelling, still proved to be a hindrance toward doing such tasks unaided. Sinkua only felt it appropriate to assist him since it was on his behalf that the existing injury had been further aggravated. Soon thereafter, the three of them were making for the west coast. Sestak and Seschnel drummed out an eight beat rhythm as their hooves clomped against the dirt in steady succession. Eytea flew between them, the backwind of her flight blowing against the dust they kicked up and forming a wake of particulate and dirt.

The town fading behind them had left something of a mark on them just as they had upon it. Of all that they had learned about the Avatars thus far, this was easily the most alarming. Perhaps it was because it was recent history or maybe the fact that it was explicit enough to know that something was horribly amiss. Or perhaps, and most likely, it was due to the macabre remnants of the unrelenting carnage that took place there.

Eytea found herself lost in her thoughts again as the trees blurred past. Fortunately, the docks were nearly a straight shot to the west. She replayed that fall from the window, her memory consumed with implacable regret. In part, it was for giving up so easily, but to some extent, it was for even bothering to try. She hated Sinkua's callous attitude when he pushed himself away, but that paled before the hatred for herself for putting him in such a predicament.

Memories of home surfaced intermittently. In a matter of days, she had experienced more than she typically would in a matter of months, save for certain landmark moments with Kabehl. With the bond between them as strong as it was, she couldn't help but worry about her mother, especially knowing how concerned she must have been about her. Still, there was no time for turning back. She promised herself she would send a letter from the ferry.

Galo was developing a swelling sense of doubt in his identity as a medicinal apprentice. For one, he knew nothing of how to treat or even identify Sinkua's condition, but more importantly, it was through similar studies that he had been stricken so ill at all. Also, whatever had transpired in the bowels of that subterranean tower was the result of some bastard black sheep of the medicinal studies. The slightest association was shameful.

Perhaps though, it was just a presentation of the shame he had been suppressing since he left home. Despite telling himself otherwise, part of him still wasn't entirely convinced that he had taken the right path or that he could even make good on his promise. He had yet to avenge his grandfather, and every step toward the Avatars of Fate showed him two things. He knew even less about them than he thought, and the influences and reaches of their organization ran deeper than he ever imagined. It was apparent enough that Masnethege could not be safely rebuilt where it once stood as long as they existed. As of lately, he had come to doubt he could see his people through such a time.

Sinkua remained as headstrong as he could manage, especially on the surface. He knew that ArcNos was not their final target but rather their first on their path to the Avatars. Yet part of him couldn't help but worry that he was walking the wrong lines. It had been this way since he first made the Southlands his home, evading his impending birthday draft in ArcNos. Now he had pulled another like himself, a rare specimen to say the least, away from her only living relative for what felt like his own gain. Compared to Galo and himself, she had relatively little connection to the conflict, but still she followed. He knew it to be her place to contest the Avatars alongside them, as he trusted Gijin's advice, but still he felt he had wronged both her and her mother by pulling them apart as he had. As such, he had come to take it as his duty, not so much to protect her, but rather to guide her into protecting herself.

A wave of indecipherable voices washed up from the approaching horizon. A foghorn let out its bass bellow. As they came into the clearing at the edge of the forest, the western docks could be seen bustling with industry. Eytea dropped to her feet, Sestak and Seschnel obeying her signal to halt.

"Why are we stopping?" Galo asked.

"I'm trying to find the ferry dock," Eytea answered, scanning the docks.

"Ah. No need to wander around down there in that mess of workers," Sinkua agreed.

The stretch of boats was impressively expansive. From a handful, several large cages brimming with fish and crustaceans were lowered onto the salty wooden docks. Others were producing larger game, marlins and sharks and such, tied up and laid flat on the planks. Most of them delivered stacks of crates of miscellaneous goods from afar, passed through Poravit for examination and distribution. Easily as many as those making port were preparing to depart, signaled by foghorns while those arriving were signaled by bells. Passenger ships appeared to be sparse but not entirely absent.

"Over there," Eytea indicated, pointing to the northwest, "There's one loading up."

"What of the horses?" Sinkua asked, "You said they don't do well in the city."

"They can come. It's the large buildings that bother them, but they're quite comfortable with people."

"Will they need proof that we're citizens?" Galo asked.

"Nope," Eytea promised, already walking toward the ferry, "They just frisk you and let you on. Means our weapons will be confiscated again, but they'll give them back."

Down by the ferries, the lines eased along as passengers were fed into the boats. Sinkua and Galo both dismounted to walk alongside the horses. As they neared the front of the line, all three of them withdrew their armaments. Eytea was the first among them to reach the security checkpoint. She offered her halberd with the blades pointed downward.

"I assume you'll want this, sir," she offered

"Good on you, miss," the guard replied as he took the halberd.

He handed it off to his assistant who set it on a nearby table. Galo approached next, along with Seschnel, and did the same with his glaive, nodding to the guard at the handoff. Finally came Sinkua and Sestak, expressionlessly handing off his morningstar with the chain safely fastened. With a bit more reluctance, he withdrew his dagger and handed it off as well.

"I apologize," began a guard, "but we've no space in the stables. Your horses will have to stay at the docks until you return."

Eytea looked away awkwardly, afraid to divulge the fact that this was a one way trip. She cleared her throat and began to speak but was preemptively interrupted.

"These boys aren't exactly comfortable in boarding stables," Sinkua explained, "We'll just send them home. Eytea?"

"Oh, um, that's right," Eytea agreed, "They get a might unruly if they're holed up away from home overnight."

Eytea pulled Sestak and Seschnel to the side, speaking to them softly and almost inaudibly. After a moment, she patted them each on the neck, and they turned and trotted away, both a bit reluctant to do so. Eytea then rejoined Sinkua and Galo, and the three of them boarded the ship.

"How did you know they could find their way home?" Eytea asked surreptitiously.

"You seem to think highly of their intelligence," Sinkua explained, "and I trust your confidence in them."

Being a tool of international commerce, this passenger ferry was far larger than even the ArcNosian warships that Sinkua and Galo had seen. The lower deck expanded several meters in all direction, with directories posted about, stairs at each corner, and elevators along the side. Small business kiosks speckled the floor, strategically positioned at scarcely avoidable spots among a captive audience. Crowds of people pushed and wove through one another.

A young man with a clipboard locked eyes with Sinkua and pushed his way through the crowd to reach him. He tapped him on the shoulder to get his attention, fortunate that Sinkua had not been previously irked. Sinkua turned to acknowledge him.

"Good afternoon, sir. First time on board?" he asked.

"Yes, it is, but I'm not in the mood for a survey. Sorry," Sinkua declined.

"Oh no, I'm just making small talk," the young man clarified, "but I noticed you folks were carrying weapons when you came on board. Any chance you'd be interested in participating in this year's event at the Radial Axiom Arena?"

"This year's event?" Galo asked, placing himself in the conversation, "Is there some kind of festival? I do love a good festival."

"I can sign you up right now. A complimentary shuttle bus for registrants will be leaving from the docks in Quarun shortly after we arrive."

"What's the event?" Sinkua reiterated.

"You don't know? It's the twentieth annual Tournament of Duelers! The prize pool this year is up to nearly a million iolas with eight positions paying," he exclaimed, "The spoils come from ticket sales and merchandising, so registration is free."

Sinkua turned to check Galo's and Eytea's reactions. They appeared to like the idea.

"Sure, sign all of us up," Sinkua insisted, taking the clipboard and pen.

"I must warn you, women rarely enter and are given no preferential treatment," the young man noted to Eytea as Sinkua was signing.

"You needn't worry about me when my turn comes," Eytea assured with a wry smirk.

After they had all signed the registration, the young man thanked them profusely and went on with his search. They continued pushing their way toward the stairs, weaving around passengers and kiosks.

"Ferya's economy looks to be rather healthy," Sinkua commented.

"For the time being, yes," Eytea agreed, "but I suppose it's only a matter of time until we're taken in by the Avatars."

"It's ArcNos you have to worry about first," Sinkua corrected as they reached the stairs to the main deck, "ArcNos seems to be under the control of the Avatars, but I'd say they've embraced their rule. But if any of those laboratories remain operational, you're safe from a militant strike."

"That's a rather big if, though," Galo countered as they emerged into daylight at the top of the stairs, "Their having discovered Kabehl's corpse will do little to help the situation either."

"Do you mean to say we doomed the nation when we killed him?" Eytea asked.

"I wouldn't say that," Sinkua disagreed, "I'd say you did them a favor."

"But you would have been wise to dispose of the body more thoroughly," Galo added, to which Sinkua nodded in consent.

Despite how casually brash their conversation was, nobody in their immediate environs appeared bothered by it. Clusters of people were all wrapped up in their own exchanges. A few simply relaxed in preparation for whatever was to come at their westward destination, leaning on the rails and watching the sea ripple past. Galo decided to join them and was soon followed by Sinkua and Eytea.

Just as the ship was overflowing with activity, so too was the sea. Several schools of fish swam alongside the boat, keeping pace with it. Further off, larger fish and aquatic mammals swam back and forth, most of them traveling alone but a few remaining in schools. Galo admired the display set out before them.

Gradually, more people began gathering along the railing. They were chattering amongst themselves, pointing off into the distance. Galo, having been watching near the boat, looked out further. Several crates were bobbing in the sea, some with holes in them.

"Looks like there was a ship wreck earlier today," Galo sighed, "Such a tragedy."

"The weather's been calm, and I don't see any icebergs or rocks," Sinkua observed, "Foul play may be the case."

"I hope you're just paranoid this time," Eytea pleaded, "but if you'd like, I can fly out there and check the cargo."

"Go right ahead," Sinkua agreed.

Strangers gasped in awe as Eytea took flight from atop the rail. She looked over her shoulder and waved to Sinkua and Galo. Galo waved back while Sinkua merely nodded. As she neared the mess of crates, she observed that the busted ones were empty. She perched atop one of them, its buoyancy enough to hold her afloat. Looking down the side, she made a mental note of the serial number. She paddled over to the next crate, noting its serial number as well. She wasn't so much memorizing them as looking for commonalities. The next was a crate which appeared to be intact. However, when she turned it upright, she found that the lid had been pried open, and that it too was empty. Again, she observed the serial number. She didn't bother to check every crate, only a handful of them. In all of them, she found two common features in addition to their being empty. Feeling she had gathered enough information, she flew back to the boat. Again, the other passengers were in awe as they watched her return to the ship. Sinkua and Galo stepped back to give her room to land.

"They're all empty," she relayed, "which means you were probably right about foul play. Many of them had been pried open and unloaded. I'd say the only other possibility is that another ship came through to recover the cargo for delivery."

"In that case, leaving the original crates wouldn't make any sense, unless whoever did recover it wanted to load it into their own crates to take payment for the goods," Sinkua refuted.

"Well the serial numbers all had two things in common," Eytea added, "They started with the letters ARC and ended with KTS."

"I think those are abbreviations for ArcNos and Kirts," Galo explained, "which means somebody wrecked and pillaged a cargo ship going from one to the other."

"The first letters denote the exporter, and the last are for the destination," a nearby stranger piped in.

"Somebody is keeping ArcNosian exports from reaching Kirts," Sinkua concluded, "and probably the same people are recovering the goods."

"What do you suppose it means?" Galo asked.

"It means we're wrong about Kirts."

Spril stood near the top of the staircase, peering out upon the dilapidated urban landscape under the night sky. Off in the distance, large metallic footsteps could be heard. A layer of smog hung above the rooftops, shrouding the view of the moons and stars above.

"Any luck finding an opening?" Yrlis asked from behind him.

"I'm still timing them," he insisted, holding up his index finger.

He listened more intently now, trying to judge distances and directions of each set of footsteps. For at least an hour now, he had stood near the top of this staircase, ears level with the surface, trying to time the patterns of the mechanical sentries.

Shortly after the discarded and downtrodden had overtaken the Subtransit system, the people of the surface had dispatched inhuman guards to walk the streets. They were assigned to watch for subterranean dissenters who would think to resurface for any reason, be it animosity or restored association. Formidable though they were, they were not impassible. Under the cover of night, passage was more probable since the worry of crossing paths with human guards as well was nearly nonexistent.

"Are you sure you want to risk this?" Phylus asked, standing further down the stairs.

"Absolutely. This is important to me," Vielle insisted, "I won't get to join you for the last stage of the plan, so I at least want to see this through."

"Okay, I think I've got it," Spril announced, "Wait for my signal."

"If anything goes amiss, I've got your back," MalVek promised, a sledgehammer in his hands.

The seconds crawled by as the five of them waited in silence. Spril listened a bit longer, his timing confirmed with each footstep. He pointed to Vielle and Phylus and signaled for them to come up the stairs.

"You two and Yrlis go first. MalVek and I will be right behind you," Spril ordered.

"Shouldn't you two go first since you're armed?" Yrlis asked.

"You three are unarmed, so we need to be able to keep an eye on you," Spril explained, "Now go. We'll follow as soon as you hit the asphalt."

Spril and MalVek stepped aside to let Vielle, Phylus, and Yrlis pass. Just as Spril had promised, the moment the three of them were on the surface, he and MalVek followed up the remaining steps. Heading eastward, they ran along the sidewalk, more out of habit than necessity. Aside from the sentries no less than a couple of blocks away, the streets were empty that night. Because of the machines' heightened alert parameters at night, even the citizens and soldiers of the surface made themselves scarce in that region after dusk.

As Vielle passed under a streetlamp, she heard a vague humming. She thought nothing of it until she noticed it was growing louder with each lamp she passed. Listening more intently, she could hear a faint click interrupting the hum as the others behind her passed under the lights as well. She pivoted around one, standing behind it and out of the spot light. There she stood as Phylus came into the light, halting to see why she had done so. From within the lamppost came a faint click followed by a continuation of a similarly dull humming. The sound wasn't so much amplifying as stacking upon itself.

"The streetlamps are making noise when we pass through the light," Vielle pointed out as the others joined her, "What do you think it means?"

They all stood in painfully awkward silence, each afraid to say what they all were thinking. Spril cocked an ear to the north. A couple of smaller sentries had changed course.

"It means I made an oversight," Spril confessed, "Phylus, Vielle, Yrlis?"

"Yeah?" Phylus answered, Vielle and Yrlis listening as well.

"Run."

One of the two sentries appeared from the nearest intersection to the north. A warning siren wailed as it came storming down the road. As ordered, the three of them sprinted onward to the east, now behind the streetlamps, Since Vielle's diminutive stature gave her a rather short stride, Phylus grabbed her by the arm in a fit of adrenaline and flung her onto his back, keeping in full sprint. Spril and MalVek jogged to stay a good distance behind, watching the sentry over their shoulders. A couple of blocks ahead, another joined the first as it passed. A stream of bullets strafed across the asphalt behind them, narrowly missing. Another followed in front of them, abruptly halting their escape.

"Remember when you said you've got my back if something goes amiss?" Spril asked, "I hope you meant it."

One of the sentries launched a long chain, still attached at the barrel, with a large spike at the end. Spril and MalVek leapt away from each other, the spike driving into the asphalt between them. The other followed suit, launching at MalVek.

"MalVek!" Spril shouted to alert him.

MalVek pivoted away, raising his sledgehammer over his head. As the chain passed, he brought the hammer down upon it with devastating force. The spike still found its way into the ground, but the chain was far less taut than it would otherwise have been. With another blow, MalVek pushed the slack to the ground and cracked one of the links. The two sentries withdrew their chains together, the second one leaving its spike in the ground as its chain snapped.

"I'll take this one," MalVek spoke of the partially disarmed sentry, "You take the other."

Having turned that sentry's attention primarily on himself, MalVek resumed his escape, watching over his shoulder. Spril, complying with MalVek's order, jogged backwards to bait the first sentry. He studied its motions carefully, learning the patterns and signals.

With a sizable lead, MalVek stopped for a moment and pounded the ground with his hammer, leaving a spider web crack. He took a few more steps and made another. Over and over he followed this pattern, making a trail of cracked spots in the asphalt.

Spril stopped and stared up at the barrel mounted upon the sentry's shoulder. He could vaguely see movement from within, denoting that it was ready to fire. A loud whir and a click echoing from within the chamber confirmed his suspicion a split second before it came to fruition. As the chain zipped toward him, he quickly spun out of its path. Once the spike was planted firmly in the asphalt once again, he drove his quarterstaff through one of the links. He grasped the ends of it tightly as the sentry withdrew the chained spike.

The one chasing MalVek set foot upon the freshly damaged asphalt. The ground cracked further under the impact of its metallic footsteps. At the end of the trail, MalVek continued to pound, loosening the asphalt further. With each step, the sentry damaged the pavement further, but it still continued forward. A three pronged spike emerged from within the barrel, replacing the single prong one that it had lost a few minutes prior.

Spril held firmly to his quarterstaff as the sentry rewound the chain, riding it up to the mechanical beast's shoulder. On the way up, he pivoted and twisted, tangling the chain. Near the barrel, he swung himself atop it, still holding the quarterstaff. He continued to twist the chain, straining to keep it from recoiling entirely. The spike turned entirely sideways, he yanked his quarterstaff from the chain. The spike lodged itself across the barrel.

The other took one more step and stopped as it stumbled. His sledgehammer slung over his shoulder, MalVek stared down the automatonous beast. It fired off the chain, the spike landing several meters past him. MalVek raised the hammer over his head.

Even with Spril perched on its shoulder and the barrel jammed, the sentry continued its march. Fortunately, its peripheral vision was limited, and Spril was just outside of it. He reached behind its head and grabbed a large bolt. He swung out and hung from it, making his way to the other shoulder.

MalVek watched statuesquely as the chain was withdrawn, but rather than the spike returning to the barrel, the sentry launched itself forth. MalVek smirked knowingly. He leapt aside before the sentry came crashing down upon him, the asphalt shattering on impact. He spun the sledgehammer, raising it high overhead. With a loud bellow, he slammed the head into the asphalt, near the sentry's foot. The unstable beast fell completely off balance with that final blow, crashing to the ground. A cloud of smoke and asphalt particulate shot up around it. After a moment of struggling against the inevitable, the sounds of its mechanisms came to a halt.

Spril sat on the back of the shoulder, patiently waiting. The sentry continued its march but didn't attempt to fire its chain. After a moment, Spril realized it had thought him dispatched and was returning to patrolling functions. He looked down the arm, watching it sway back and forth. As it began to come forward, he hurriedly sidled down the slope. Making it well past the elbow before it became too vertical, Spril leapt to the ground, rolling as he landed. He sprang upright and continued running, the sentry following once again.

It fired off a stream of bullets behind him, followed by another ahead of him. He stopped and turned about, staring defiantly up at the sentry. Confident in his actions, he held his quarterstaff behind his back. The sentry attempted to fire the chain, but the spike jammed the barrel. It attempted again but still to no avail. Smoke flooded out of the barrel and seeped from between the panels. With each repeated attempt, a loud pop echoed from inside the barrel. Soon, the pop was replaced with a blast, flames and black smoke spewing from the remains of the barrel as it shattered. The impact knocked the smoldering beast off balance, collapsing it over the sidewalk. A handful of streetlamps were crushed under its impact as it came crashing down upon the pavement. The internal motors strained for a moment longer, then fell silent.

Spril turned and walked away. MalVek waited for him just ahead, beside the sentry he had felled nigh simultaneously. Spril jogged to catch up.

"We should hurry," Spril insisted, "No doubt they've begun to worry."

MalVek nodded in agreement and began running with him.

"Impressive strategy you took back there," MalVek commented, "You've got balls of steel to ride the chain and climb that thing like you did."

"I could say the same of you, baiting it into stomping on you like that," Spril complimented, "How did you know it would launch itself at you though?"

"I didn't," MalVek shrugged, "Just got lucky."

A few blocks ahead, three people came up the crossroad from the south. They stopped in the middle of the intersection, one of them waving to Spril and MalVek. Being as worried as Spril had predicted, Phylus, Vielle, and Yrlis had paused to wait for them.

"Are you two okay?" Yrlis asked as they caught up.

"Yeah, we're fine," Spril assured, giving her a hug and a kiss on the cheek.

"Looks like the city limits aren't too far off," Vielle observed as the five of them continued to walk down the middle of the road.

"So we're almost safe. Good," Phylus sighed, "Let's just hope our boat is still afloat when we find it."

Chapter 19

"Dear Mom,

"I've not been gone long, but my life has already changed in so many ways. I'm learning new things about myself, but I'm not so certain I like it. I fear I may be outclassed here and out of my element. The details, I feel, should remain unspoken for the time, but I almost got Sinkua killed. He suffered little more than a twisted ankle and frustration with me, but I still feel horrible. And with his being so calloused, I find it troublesome to apologize and gauge whether it was accepted or even necessary.

"A short time later, I was knocked from a rooftop and left barely conscious, all for my inability to react against fear. Galo shielded me while Sinkua disposed of the one who had done such. In spite of my incompetence, both of them take great care of me, even if I cannot do the same for them.

"Though lately, the two have grown hostile toward each other, and I fear I have something to do with it. I don't so much think they're fighting over me but rather that my relative ineptitude has them both a might ornery. I know I worry overmuch sometimes, but this is getting overwhelming. I intend to tough it out and hope I grow to overcome it, but I needed to get these things off my chest.

"We're on a commuter ferry to Quarun now. Upon arrival, we'll be taking a shuttle bus to the Radial Axiom Arena where the lot of us have entered the Tournament of Duelers. Perhaps a decent performance will do the trick for my self-esteem.

Love,

Eytea

"P.S.: I sent Sestak and Seschnel home because there was no room for them on the ferry. To be honest, it was Sinkua's idea. Anyway, don't be alarmed when you see them."

Eytea rolled the letter up, binding it with a length of ribbon from her travel pack. From a small vial, she dripped a bit of her mother's scent. She leaned on the rail, salty mist weaving through her hair, and looked about for a tracking pigeon. Out of the corner of her eye, she spotted Sinkua munching on a fistful of bacon.

"Are you eating that cold?" she asked, puzzled.

"Of course not," Sinkua countered, switching hands to show that his other palm was glowing red with heat.

"Well stop eating so much bacon," Eytea insisted, "Somebody has to look out for us."

"Oh right, don't want to burn through it all too quickly. Not sure we'll find a wild pig running around in Quarun, much less be able to afford to buy more with our winnings. Good looking out," Sinkua flippantly dismissed with a smirk and continued eating.

"No. No. No," Eytea argued, snatching the bacon from his hand, "I mean protein is detrimental to your condition. Ophalin likened you to a time bomb. Who's going to look out for us if you detonate?"

Sinkua sneered and shrugged, looking away. He chewed on a bite of salty bacon, rolling it around in his mouth and savoring the flavor as it faded. A ways up the railing, he spied a tracking pigeon.

"Eytea," he beckoned, "There's a pigeon for your letter."

Eytea turned to look and Sinkua swiftly snatched a strip of bacon from her hand. Before she could react, he had stuffed the whole of it in his mouth. She turned back, mouth agape though smiling a bit. She reached in to slap him on the stomach.

Sinkua pulled back and grabbed her wrist. He pulled her in by her own momentum and poked at her sides. She squirmed and laughed, blocking her sides with her upper arms as she blindly tried to deflect his jabs. After a few tries, she finally succeeded, leaving his sides open now. Seizing the opportunity, she reached in to reciprocate the treatment. Instead, Sinkua put an arm around her waist and flipped her up, laying her body across his shoulders.

"Ahh! What? What are you doing?" she asked, frantically slapping his arm.

"You asked for this, Eytea!" Sinkua remarked, "Never stand between a man and his bacon."

With that, he started spinning in place. One of Eytea's ponytails curled around and flailed across her face. With one hand, she held on tenaciously, while the other continued to slap his arm.

"Put me down! You're insane!" she exclaimed through gasps and laughs.

A nearby door opened and out came Galo, rejoining them by the railing after a search for herbal painkillers from the crowd of vendors. Eytea greeted him incrementally each time she passed through his line of sight.

"Oh!.... Hey!... Galo!.... Find it!... Alright?!" she remarked.

"Galo!" Sinkua chimed in, stopping abruptly, "She stole my bacon. Had to do it."

"Heh, you mean our bacon?" Galo corrected.

Without another word, he walked past them. Eytea still lying on his shoulders, Sinkua turned to watch him. The tracking pigeon was still sitting nearby, and Galo coaxed it onto his finger. He returned with it and held it up to Eytea.

"My guess is you were looking for this," Galo deduced, "and Sinkua took the opportunity to put you in this position."

"That's about the sum of it. Stole back a strip of bacon, too," Eytea confirmed, still laughing as she presented the scent and tied the letter to the pigeon's leg.

The pigeon took off, heading back toward Ferya. Eytea relaxed her body, still lying across Sinkua's shoulders. Sinkua didn't seem too bothered by the load.

"So, can you tell how much further we have to go?" Eytea asked Galo.

"Hm? I thought you'd know," Galo answered.

"What? Oh you mean because of what I know of these commuter ferries," Eytea supposed, "Sorry, I misled you, didn't I? I've never ridden on one before this. I've just heard how they operate."

"Oh, I see. For a moment, I thought you were patronizing me," Galo said quite flatly, "From the look of the sea, I'd say we're no more than an hour from the coast."

"Great," Sinkua remarked, "Now to kick back and wait for the shore to appear on the horizon."

He leaned back against the wall with his arms folded and his head down. Eytea still on his shoulders and held in place by the wall, he closed his eyes and pretended to nap on his feet as though he had forgotten she was there. Eytea stretched in arm down and poked him in the navel, raspberrying in his ear. He awoke, so to speak, with a start. When he saw her, he appeared alarmed though far from authentically so.

"Oh, you're still up there, aren't you?" he asked, "Well that simply won't do." He crouched down and flipped her back onto her feet.

"He seems livelier than usual," Eytea surreptitiously commented to Galo.

"I suppose that means the medication is working," Galo whispered back, "Though he doesn't seem quite like himself."

"No, he really doesn't. I'd already grown accustomed to his brand of cynicism," Eytea agreed, "Though it does explain why he was gorging himself on bacon."

"Because of the protein inhibitors, you suppose?"

"Exactly that."

All the while, Sinkua continued to watch the sea drift past, squinting a bit as the sunlight managed to angle its way to his eyes. He caught bits and pieces of their conversation, enough at least to know they spoke of his condition. He didn't allow it to bother him though. Everyone had their secrets, and he was far from any different.

A bit less than an hour later, Quarun's eastern docks appeared on the horizon, verifying Galo's prediction. The three of them made their way through the crowds, each on their two feet. Eytea resisted the urge to fly atop the lot of them and cut to the front. As they departed, their armaments were returned to them. Sinkua examined his dagger to check that it had not been used out of his possession. To his relief, it had not.

All around them, dozens of steel toed boots clomped against the wooden planks. Though not quite the most abundant, this was certainly the loudest sound of the arriving migrant workers. Many still had some distance to travel until they reached their job sites, as was evidenced by the fleet of shuttle buses. Everything from folders and briefcases to sacks of grain and crates of machine parts were taken aboard the buses, along with boxes of knick knacks, clothing, and such. Some, it seemed, were here for little more than to relay parcels.

A ways toward the north end, one bus bared the name Radial Axiom. Spotting it first, Galo pointed it out to Sinkua and Eytea. When they reached the bus, they found a line filing aboard from the opposite side. A young woman with a clipboard was checking each of them in as they boarded, ascertaining the presence of all registrants coming from east of the arena. They positioned themselves at the back of the line and waited.

There were easily a couple of scores of people in line, ages ranging from the mid-teens to middle aged. Few of them carried their own weapons, and most of those who did seemed to carry them more as keepsakes than with any intent of use. Only melee weapons could be found though, no ranged armaments whatsoever. The only female among the registrants was Eytea, so that and her wings attracted many stares. Of the three of them, Eytea reached the front of the line first. As she expected, there was much ado over her wings. After a brief exchange at the door, and proving they were attached, the woman by the door turned and leaned her head into the bus.

"Hey!" she called in and waited for response, "Call the arena and tell them to get out a climbing harness. Thanks."

"Got it under control?" Eytea asked.

"Yes, I think so," she answered, "It's a bit unorthodox, but well…"

"So is a person with wings. I understand. So am I all clear to board?"

"Go right ahead."

Galo had no trouble boarding. For Sinkua, there was a bit of confusion about his eyes, but eventually it tapered off from suspicion into curiosity. Despite finding the hubbub wholly unnecessary, he tolerated it quite a bit better than he had in the hospital waiting room.

The bus nearly filled to capacity, the lady from the door and a young male coworker stood at the front looking over the checklist. They appeared bewildered.

"Have any of you folks seen Masfaru?" he called out, "Any word from Masfaru?"

A dull roar of quiet conversation washed over the bus. Apparently, there was something of a fuss over this Masfaru. Eytea leaned over the seat and tapped on someone's shoulder.

"Who's Masfaru?" she asked, "You guys seem to be making a pretty big deal about him."

"You don't keep up with these tournaments much, do you?" he commented, "Guy's the reigning champion, four years running. Started when he was only nineteen and took the gold his second year."

"Wow, he sounds pretty tough," she agreed, "Too bad it looks like he won't get to face my friends."

"Hey, well I wouldn't go feeling disappointed about that one."

All the while, the young man had been on the phone with the staff at the arena, frantically trying to track down the champion. A moment after Eytea's conversation ended, he returned the phone to his pocket with a look of empty disillusion.

"Masfaru, the reigning champion of the Tournament of Duelers, will not be participating this year," he announced solemnly, "He was found dead last night, seemingly mauled by a wild animal, in Ferya."

He shuffled into his seat and slumped down. Before joining him, the young lady turned to the bus driver.

"Take us to the arena," she ordered.

While in transit, the details of what was to come were explained to the rookies and reiterated to those making return appearances. The tournament was to start the following afternoon with lodging available in the basement of the arena. Only melee weapons were allowed, explaining the absence of ranged weapons in line. Armaments were to be provided by the arena; some combatants brought their own merely as souvenirs and good fortune and such. As this was a no kill tournament, the weapons were to be made of wood. Spikes were filed to studs and blades were dulled to the point of being painful without being fatal.

As for the tournament itself, the top sixteen registrants were to participate in single elimination head to head combat, determined by a complex algorithm of performances and demonstrated capabilities. These sixteen were to consist of the last four standing in each of four preliminary battles royale, the population of each determined primarily by random chance. There were projected to be about a score to two dozen people in each preliminary.

This year's prize pool was up to nine hundred fifty thousand iolas. The top eight positions paid, meaning that those who made it past the first bracket would go home richer than they came. The payment doubled at each level. Fifth, sixth, seventh and eighth paid five percent apiece. Ending at the semifinals granted a prize of ten percent each. Second place paid one hundred ninety thousand iolas, and the champion would take home a cool three hundred eight thousand iolas, forty percent of the prize pool. Sinkua, Galo, and Eytea all felt confident that at least one of them could eke their way into the money.

The trip was slow since the bus still operated via clockwork mechanisms. ArcNosian interference in Ivaria had continued to stifle the spread of transportation technologies, as an increased effort in recovering the rights to the combustion and aquatic intake steam engines had been siphoned out of other pursuits. Still, the slow pace gave rise to relaxation and time to admire the scenery.

Much of Quarun had been industrialized and thus urbanized by the influx of migrant Feryan workers, which had been caused by overpopulation in Ferya. Short wide buildings, constructs of either brick or concrete and steel, lined the roadsides along with the usual shops and restaurants found in any town. A few of the concrete and steel buildings were adorned with large pipes, jutting upward from the four corners of their rooftops. The occasional office building zipped past, becoming gradually more frequent as they made their way inland.

The sun was fading behind the horizon and two of the three moons were visible as they arrived at the arena. The Radial Axiom Arena was a vast construct, built to house all manner of events as it was among Quarun's chief sources of foreign income. Its design appeared archaic in display though advanced in intricacy, an elliptical monolith formed of stone and metal with a frame of arches and woven trellises left bare.

One by one, the passengers filed off the bus. The others had arrived nigh simultaneously and were in the process of unloading as well. Two decades of practice had made the directors adept at timing the departures to synchronize the returns. As Sinkua, Galo, and Eytea stepped off the bus and into the open, still more began to arrive, adorned with the name Radial Axiom Arena and the subtitle Spectator Charter.

"See anybody you think might pose a threat?" Sinkua asked.

"Hard to say, really," Galo answered, "I've no knowledge of what weapons they might choose. What about you?"

"Anybody notably taller than me might prove to be troublesome, what with their reach advantage," Sinkua explained, "No spikes on the morningstar, so they may be able to grab the chain and strike from beyond my reach."

"We just arrived, and you're already sizing up the competition?" Eytea asked, somewhat surprised, "I wouldn't even know where to begin."

"Well, you want to make some money from this, don't you?" Sinkua asked, "Care for a few pointers?"

"From you, always," Eytea answered with a smile.

"You're light on your feet, even without your wings, though lacking in physical strength. The muscle-bound can be your easiest victory or your quickest loss. Keep moving and evade their advances until you see an opening. Act too hastily, and you'll put yourself in danger. If you stumble, use the likely reach advantage of your halberd to keep them at bay until you regain your composure," Sinkua explained as Eytea listened intently, "As for the more nimble, strike swiftly the moment you secure an opening. Once again, don't get hasty and use your reach advantage. If you find your attacks frequently parried, draw their advances until they take a swing at you. Again, with your halberd, you ought to be able to step beyond their reaches and still deliver a solid blow as they leave themselves open."

"I see. So, move quickly but act with forethought. Stay beyond the reaches of the physically foreboding, and draw the offense of the agile to create an opening," Eytea recapped for confirmation, "I think I can do something with that."

"Also, during the battle royale," Galo added, "watch with your eyes as well as with your ears. In other words, take heed to what sounds approach from beyond your line of sight."

During the conversation, they had been given a room key and a map of the quarters area. They had reached the last straightaway leading to their room, a corridor of solid colored walls lined with sconces and carpeted floor. Galo unlocked the door as they reached the one matching the number on their key. In these lodgings, they were to await the coming morning and the Tournament of Duelers.

The following afternoon, they were summoned to the hall by a loud banging on the door. There they rejoined the other combatants who had arrived from the east. The lodgings were divided based on shuttle bus attendance, with a fourth section for those who had traveled independently. Near the center, the halls started to merge. The East Hall and West Hall lines meshed together in one hall, as did the South Hall and the Independent Hall in another.

As East and West merged, a shoulder mistakenly nudged Eytea's. She glanced aside to catch a glimpse of a stranger, apparently in his late thirties, with an odd air of familiarity. He was a bit taller than Galo and light in complexion with close cut hair, broad shoulders, and a goatee tuft upon his chin. She looked him over for a moment, sifting through her memories to ascertain the reason for his distant familiarity.

"Namias," he offered, extending his hand while still facing forward.

"Hm, what?" Eytea answered, unaware that he had caught her staring.

"Namias," he repeated, "The name's Namias. And you are?"

"Oh, I'm sorry. Eytea. And these fellows with me are Galo and Sinkua," Eytea greeted, "I didn't mean to stare, it's just I feel like I recognize you."

"Quite alright, Eytea. I get that a lot," Namias accepted with a smile, "Sinkua and Galo, huh? The same who pushed back invasions in Berinin and Haprian?"

"They sure are," Eytea boasted.

"Such luck to meet them here. Their exploits have come to be quite far known. Anyway, I thought to wish you luck, but if you've trained with them, I may need to keep those well wishes for myself."

"Hah, I'm far from their league," Eytea admitted with a nervous smile, "but good luck to you."

"Likewise, madam."

Interrupted strips of sunlight illuminated the end of the hall, casting an elongated shadow of the wrought iron gate at the end. As they drew nearer, the dull roar of the crowd reached the outskirts of audibility. The first of many anticipated moments was fast approaching, and the onlookers were growing restless. From one gate emerged the interwoven East and West lines, while from the other came competitors from the South and Independent Halls. The dull roar grew more voluminous as some ninety potential champions filed onto the sand strewn field, expanding along the perimeter as ordered.

Still facing forward to avoid drawing further attention to herself, Eytea scanned the competition with her eyes. She was one of only three women, verifying claims of the rarity of female registrants. From across the field, she found herself eyeing Namias, digging through her memories in an attempt to place his face. Next to him stood a more elderly man, perhaps in his fifties, with a rugged jaw line and broad shoulders. His age was something of an anomaly, as he appeared to be the oldest competitor by a good ten years or so.

Announcements had been coming from a series of loudspeakers, delivered from a window walled room perched high above the top rafter. Eytea had barely heard a word of it, as she was wrapped up in her own thoughts. Sinkua cocked his head a bit to look up to the announcer's booth. He squinted his eyes a bit for the distance, but he saw clearly through the glare on the window. He could just make out a figure standing behind the announcer, arms folded and adorned in dark clothing. Rather odd about him though, he appeared to be wearing a metallic mask.

Within the booth, the Commissioner looked over the competitors from behind the announcer's table. A grin spread across his face, hidden by his mask. When the announcer turned off the microphone, the Commissioner brought a narrow whistle to his lips through a small hole and blew into it. A brief moment later, a young woman appeared in the doorway, dressed in a long black skirt and a scoopneck top.

"Yes, Commissioner?"

"It's finally happened," he announced in a mildly raspy baritone voice.

"I apologize, sir, I don't follow," she confessed, coming around into his view.

"The vagabonds have come," he clarified, loosening the phlegm from his throat, "I've waited for this day for most of this event's existence."

"Do they know you?"

"No, but if all goes well, they will."

"I mean no disrespect, sir, but it seems a bit odd for a man of your caliber to dedicate such a large portion of his life to the possibility of meeting such relatively ordinary people," she buttered, placing her hand gingerly upon his shoulder, "Even if they do appear quite, well, unique."

"You're something of a paradox, young lady," he countered, still facing forward, "Flattery will get you everywhere, but ignorance will take you nowhere."

Mouth agape, she withdrew her hand.

"I do apologize for my rudeness. I've grown relentlessly honest with age, but you oft know not what you say," he continued, digging through his coat pocket, "Regardless, see to it that these three are in separate preliminary bouts. I'd hate for any of them to eliminate each other."

"Yes sir," she agreed as she regained her composure, "Anything else?"

"Place the old man with the Berininite prince," the Commissioner ordered, "Consider it a test of mettle."

Situated at ground level sat a room which circumvented the battlefield. The announcements over, the lot of them dispersed to the multitude of doorways connecting the two areas. For a swarm of folks soon to literally be upon each other's throats for a pocket full of iolas, most were refreshingly polite as they pushed their way into the round room.

Therein, the walls were lined with wooden weaponry sorted by function. Sinkua split off by himself while Galo and Eytea stayed together, and the three chose their expected weapons in oaken form. All the while, a slender young woman in a low cut top and a black skirt had been handing cards to combatants as they stepped away freshly girded. Some simply pocketed them. Others, mostly curious newcomers, read their cards the moment they received them. Sinkua glanced at his as it was handed to him.

"Alpha?" he asked.

"That's your preliminary bout," the young woman explained before walking away.

Galo and Eytea rejoined with Sinkua, cards in hand.

"Which preliminary did you get?" she asked excitedly, "I'm in Gamma, and Galo is in Beta."

"They put me in Alpha," Sinkua said, flashing his card.

"Just my luck. I'm in Delta," a voice familiar only to Eytea interjected.

"Sorry if I sound like an ass, but what bearing do our placements have on your luck?" Sinkua asked the approaching stranger.

"Oh, that's right, I never introduced myself to you. I'm Namias," Namias greeted, "When I saw that you two had entered, I hoped I would get to face one of you. Now they've gone and separated the four of us."

"Hm, how dreadful for you," Sinkua said flatly, turning his back to Namias.

"Just as well though. Means I'll only have to topple one of you to reach the finals," Namias added before walking away.

"Well, that one's certainly a character," Galo observed with one eyebrow raised.

"He's certainly cocky," Sinkua added, "Of course, if he can't back it up, I'll have to teach him a touch of humility."

"I don't think he means any offense by it. I spoke to him on the way up to the field. Seems like a decent man," Eytea assured, "but I can't help but feel like I recognize him."

"How does he know who we are though?" Sinkua asked.

"He said your exploits have become far known," Eytea explained.

"I never mentioned our names in the newsletter about Mikalan," Sinkua recalled, "Someone else must be spreading news of our actions."

"So, we can expect to meet with significant resistance on the last leg of our trip," Galo deduced, "Well, it's what we wanted, isn't it?"

"I was hoping it would be more gradual, but we'll just have to take it as it comes," Sinkua agreed, "A fortified coast will mean an unfortified inland all the same."

Over the speaker system came a summons of the Alpha Preliminary participants. Sinkua rolled his neck and gave the wooden chain a firm tug, testing its durability one last time. Of course, it paled in comparison to his usual armament, but this would need to suffice. He turned to face Galo and Eytea. Galo nodded and grinned, wishing him luck. Anxiously brushing her inhibitions slightly aside, Eytea reached out to him for a one armed hug. She wrapped her right arm around his shoulders, clutching firmly. As he set his hand on the small of her back, she whispered well wishes and a bid of good fortune in his ear. After she pulled back, he smirked and walked away.

"You're a bit nervous, aren't you?" Galo asked.

"Of course," Eytea admitted, her voice somewhat shaky, "I've never seen combat beyond dealing with Kabehl, and now I'm within an hour of a battle royale among two dozen people."

"Heh. Here I thought you were worried about Sinkua."

"What? Why would you think that?"

"I don't know. Let's just go watch his preliminary."

The remaining combatants gathered at a row of seats at the edge of the room, providing a ground level view of the fray just beyond. Across the sandy field stood some two dozen potential champions, adorned with an array of weapons ranging from quarterstaffs and chains to swords and spears. Sinkua, to little surprise, was the only one to wield a morningstar.

"You got a lot of balls, picking one of those things," an opponent told Sinkua with a cocky chuckle.

"Just two," Sinkua flatly answered, waiting for the signal to start the fight, "but you'll have a nice view of them just before you pass out."

"Hah! You really think you could handle one of those things, kid? I spent two years trying to…"

He was interrupted by the abrupt blaring of a horn, signaling the commencement of the Alpha Preliminary. Ever vigilant in keeping a promise, Sinkua pivoted and pulled back his morningstar, spying this loudmouth for the first time. With a bellow and a jerk of his arm, he brought the wooden studded ball down upon his head. The unsuspecting opponent dropped with a loud thud, a trickle of blood matting his hair. Sinkua assumed a defensive stance straddling the felled man's head, watching for his next opening.

"The view from here is great!" Eytea remarked, "Man, he doesn't waste any time, does he?"

"No, usually not," Galo agreed, "That guy must have said something to get under his skin. Or, well, anything at all."

Eytea watched in fascination as Sinkua and a handful of other combatants quickly set themselves apart from the remainder of the crowd. Sinkua was none too graceful, but he struck with such force and precision that the cries of pain could almost be heard over the roar of the crowd. His tolerance for pain in combat was comparably impeccable, as he often used his forearms to deflect blows from cudgels and staves.

One by one, wannabe champions fell to the blows of his morningstar, the remainder falling to each other. Soon, and perhaps surprisingly so, only five men were left standing. They were down to the bubble. The five of them stood roughly equidistant from one another, sizing each other up. One man's eyes darted to the side, looking to his friend.

"I say we take out Morningstar, here," he barked, "None of us will get anywhere with him in the tournament."

As though on a remarkably unexpected cue, the man to whom he spoke turned to face him and thrust the head of his oaken spear against his abdomen. The wind knocked out of him, he hunched over and clutched his stomach, only to receive a second blow to the back of the head.

"Pussy," the assailant muttered as he spat upon the barely conscious bubble, "We don't take conspirators in the Tournament of Duelers."

An announcement came blasting over the intercom.

"Ladies and gentlemen, in a record time of 9 minutes 47 seconds, we have our four Tournament combatants from the Alpha Preliminary. Akrulan from Haprian! VanSen from ArcNos! Quarun's own Lial! And Sinkua from Berinin! Great match, boys! Great match! The Beta Preliminary will begin shortly."

Sinkua had already returned to the perimeter room to rejoin Galo and Eytea, rather than stay and make idle small talk with the other three winners. He plopped down in a chair next to Galo and rolled his neck, popping it repeatedly.

"Great work out there, brother!" Galo remarked.

"You were unbelievable," Eytea added, "How can you not get hurt, taking hits like that?"

"I've learned to block it out," Sinkua grunted, twisting his back in his chair, "but it doesn't always last."

The participants in the Beta Preliminary were summoned onto the field. Sinkua and Eytea both wished Galo luck, and he left for the open sand, oaken glaive in hand.

"If you'd like, I could help you with that," Eytea offered, "Not blocking the pain, but well, your back."

"Are you offering to give me a back rub?" Sinkua asked with a wry smirk.

"Yes, I am," Eytea confirmed, "What? Too forward?"

"Not at all," Sinkua comforted, "Feel free to start any time you like."

Eytea hopped over her chair and positioned herself behind Sinkua. She set her hands firmly upon his shoulders, pressing her fingertips against the meaty flesh. Slowly, she worked her way inwards toward his neck as he watched Galo in the Beta Preliminary.

Though he lacked his capacity for pain, Galo moved with impeccable grace, rendering him a particularly troublesome target. He deftly spun and ducked around and under blades, staves, and cudgels alike, often delivering whipping blows in return as their guards were left down. Similarly, what he lacked in aggression, he made up for in raw physical strength, putting his melee strikes on par with Sinkua's.

"I feel I should warn you," Sinkua began as Eytea worked down his spine, "I harbor no intentions of going easy on you just because you're doing this favor for me."

"Is that so?" Eytea asked as she pressed her knuckles into his vertebrae.

"Okay, okay!" Sinkua remarked, his back becoming rigid, "Perhaps just a bit."

"Heh, it's okay. If you were, people might get a touch suspicious," Eytea accepted as she continued the massage, "I don't want you to be soft with me."

"Hey, Galo's down to the bubble," Sinkua announced, abruptly changing the subject.

Once again, the five of them stood in a ring, a behavior that seemed to be an implied tradition of the preliminary bouts. Galo watched their eyes, noticing that they all but one pair seemed to dart back and forth between him and any one of the other combatants. He deduced that they were sizing him up with the intent to focus their aggression solely on him. It was a bit flattering, but actually more of a nuisance that none of them were willing to risk facing elimination on their own conviction.

He scanned the spread, though it was little more than a deterrent. His primary foci were on the men adjacent to him, gauging his distance from each of them. With no warning, he snapped the glaive out to his right. The flat of the blade met forcibly with the nearest opponent's unguarded face. Caught by surprise, the bubble collapsed to the ground.

"You likely feel yourselves lucky that he stood closest to me," Galo announced, "but know that for conspiring against me, only one of you will be lucky. The others, dreadfully far from it."

He turned to exit the sand field before the announcements on the intercom ended.

"Ladies and Gentlemen, in 14 minutes 9 seconds, we have our last four standing from the Beta Preliminary. MalVek from ArcNos! Setura from Eprilen! Galo from Berinin! And Emoran from Ferya! We're going to break for a fifteen minute intermission, so feel free to use the facilities or get a drink, and we will commence the Gamma Preliminary shortly thereafter."

"Can you believe those guys were trying to plot against me?" Galo asked as he rejoined his friends in the perimeter room.

"To be honest, yes," Sinkua empathized, "The bubble in my match suggested they focus on me since I was the biggest threat. Apparently, they all felt the same way about you."

"Not all of them," Galo corrected, "At least, I don't think so. The old man from ArcNos held eye contact with me that entire time. It was as though he was sizing me up for his own agenda, rather than joining some childish pact."

"Galo!" a vaguely familiar voice called out.

Galo glanced over his shoulder to find Namias beckoning for his attention from behind the seats. As usual, he was alone and strangely nosy.

"Namias," Galo acknowledged, "What brings you here?"

"Came to congratulate you," Namias complimented, "Care to join me for a drink?"

"Sure, why not?" Galo agreed with a shrug.

Out in the periphery of the competitors' area was a bar and diner. The tables and chairs sat high, placing the sitting patrons at eye level with those standing. Overhead lights shone through covers patterned with the Radial Axiom logo and reflected off the freshly polished hardwood floor. Behind the bar, the wall was strewn with shapely glass bottles and brewery signage.

"Hey, can I get a Schauzen's Deluxe beer?" Namias beckoned as he propped himself up on a bar stool, "What's your preference, Galo?"

"What? Oh, I don't drink alcohol," Galo insisted, "Do you have any fruit juice?"

"Sorry, that's reserved for the vodka," the bartender replied.

"He'll just have a cola then," Namias suggested, "Or is that all for the rum?"

"One Schaudie and a cola? Eight iolas, please."

Namias produced ten iolas and slid them across the bar. His attention then turned back to Galo, who was occupied scanning the wall of brewery signs.

"I hadn't the faintest notion we had so many kinds of beer," Galo commented, "How many do you suppose there are?"

"Easily hundreds," Namias remarked, sipping the beer that had just been handed to him, "Does nobody in your family drink, or do you just not travel much?"

"Both," Galo answered before taking a swig of his cola.

"The abstinence from alcohol comes as no surprise, given your standing, but for the same reason, your being homebound is a bit odd."

"You're aware of my identity then," Galo acknowledged, "World travels were to begin when I reached adulthood. Up until such point, I was to be versed in fine detail on the history and nature of my people."

"So, what brings you to Quarun? Surely, you didn't come all this way just for the tournament."

"Why are you so interested in the decisions I make?"

"Call it a fascination with celebrity."

"Celebrity? I'm a runaway leader, hardly a celebrity by any stretch of the term."

"You're a federal leader who abandoned his post and disappeared after combating an attack on his people," Namias explained, finishing his beer, "People are going to bother you when they recognize you. It comes with the territory."

"Are you implying that I should simply put up with people like you pestering me for morsels of gossip for little more reason than my standing in the world?" Galo asked, firmly setting his empty bottle on the bar, "I think not. Pester me no more."

Galo hopped down from his seat and walked away. Namias lowered his head and sighed, clutching the empty beer bottle. As Galo neared the door, Namias lifted his head and cleared his throat, pausing Galo in the doorway.

"It isn't like that," Namias insisted, "I need to know if my suspicions are true."

"What might your suspicions be?" Galo asked without turning around.

"You intend to dock at ArcNos after the tournament, do you not? Seek revenge, set things right for your people?"

Galo sighed, memories of that night flashing through his mind, as he confirmed, "Yes, exactly that. Again I ask, why are you so interested? Obviously, this goes beyond a fascination with celebrity."

"You and I are quite the same," Namias assured, "I simply wished to know if we were on the same track."

"How do you suppose we're the same?" Galo answered, glancing back over his shoulder.

"I can't say yet," Namias answered, "See me after the tournament."

Galo returned to his seat alone, the sweet taste of cola still fresh on his breath. The carbonation gurgled in his stomach as he surreptitiously belched in his throat. Soda had been a scarce part of his childhood.

"How did you fare?" Galo asked Eytea, "I apologize for having missed it."

"It's alright, Galo. No worries," Eytea assured him, "As for my match, I placed."

"Oh, that's great! Did you have any trouble?" Galo congratulated.

"A touch, but nowhere nigh as much as I thought I would," Eytea bragged, beckoning Galo to sit with her and Sinkua.

"She was great, took out the bubble before they even had time to circle each other," Sinkua added.

"I didn't even realize there were but five of us standing. His guard was down, so I took a shot," Eytea admitted, "Actually, it took a few strikes to take him down, but he was so dazed after the first, that he gave me no trouble to speak of."

They sat proudly, all three basking in their collective accomplishments. The sunlight angled into the room, shining over their feet. Out on the field, clouds of dust were kicked airborne as the Delta Preliminary got underway. Galo focused his attention on Namias, recounting their conversation as he watched.

On the surface, his proclamation of their similarity seemed presumptuous, perhaps even conceited. He had heard nothing of other potential world leaders abandoning their people, despite the fact that other nations had been stricken by ArcNos. Still, it occurred to him that assuming no stranger could relate to him was comparably pompous. Regardless, he found it exceedingly difficult to shake the comment, trying to discern to what he could be referring.

"I have to admit, this Namias guy is as good as he implies," Sinkua observed, studying his motions through the mess of dust, "What did he want, by the way? I assumed he wished to have a word with you in particular."

"What?" Galo asked, just realizing Sinkua was speaking to him, "He wanted to know what brought me all the way up here to Quarun. Then he insisted that we're quite similar, but he refused to divulge his reasoning until after the tournament."

"He thinks you're similar? How does he figure he can relate to your situation?"

"It's strange to me, as well."

"Maybe there's more to him," Eytea insisted, "He seems oddly familiar, and I think I draw near to discerning who he is."

"Namias is an alias, you suppose?" Sinkua asked.

Eytea nodded. The Delta Preliminary came to an end. Aside from Namias, the other finalists were a Tanelenese woman, a Haprianite man, and another man from Ivaria. Namias's claiming to be an Ivarian served to draw Eytea closer to a conclusion regarding his identity.

Chapter 20

The crowd burst into an uproar as the combatants for the first fight were announced vivaciously over the intercom. From opposite ends of the circle of sand, they emerged under the midday autumn sky: Akrulan from one end, Sinkua from the other. Sinkua eyed the crowd, but mostly he focused his attention on his opponent, with a wooden morningstar laid across his shoulders. Conversely, Akrulan waved to the crowd, feeding from their applause, his other hand gripping a large sickle.

"It would seem the crowd has taken a liking to you," Sinkua complimented with a smirk, "Return appearance?"

"I suspect it will be brief though," Akrulan confirmed with a nervous chuckle, "You and your friend defended that police station in Haprian a while back, right?"

"Galo and I, yes."

"Good to know. Come what may, I'll feel no shame in the outcome," Akrulan declared, assuming a defensive position, "Let's tangle."

Sinkua took an offensive stance. They faced each other, waiting until a blare resounded from the intercom. Akrulan abruptly lunged with a bellow and a swing of his sickle, hoping to catch Sinkua off guard. Instead, Sinkua spun out of the way, pivoting himself partially behind his opponent. As he did, he whipped the morningstar, swinging wide at the opposite side of Akrulan's head. Akrulan leaned away from it and swung his sickle upward, snagging the chain, and spun around to face Sinkua.

"You're quick," Sinkua complimented.

"Same to you."

Sinkua jerked back on the morningstar, intending to disarm Akrulan. Akrulan held fast to his sickle and instead went barreling toward Sinkua. In the split second before impact, both drew back a fist and laid into each other nigh simultaneously. Sinkua delivered his to Akrulan's shoulder, causing him to drop his sickle, and Akrulan's fist met hard with the right side of Sinkua's lips, bloodying his gums.

Akrulan stepped back, rubbing his shoulder. Sinkua was rubbing his jaw, and Akrulan hoped to exploit the opening. Before he could take more than a step though, Sinkua spat blood in his eyes, blinding him for a moment. Disoriented, he tried to clean his face while backing away. Too slow to act, his vision cleared just in time to see the morningstar extended toward him, arcing with impressive velocity.

"Good match," he complimented with a strangely calm demeanor.

Akrulan spun around halfway and collapsed on the sand as the studded ball crashed into the side of his head. He tried to push himself up, but because of the pain in his shoulder, he could not. He patted the ground three times, signaling that he could not go on.

The excited announcement came booming over the intercom, announcing the official time as well as the winner of the bout. As the announcer was going through his obviously scripted monologue, Sinkua rolled Akrulan over onto his back and helped him to his feet. They stood side by side, holding up each other's hand, bathing in the uproar of applause.

"You did great, Akrulan," Sinkua complimented.

"It was a pleasure facing you," Akrulan returned, "Good luck in the next round."

Galo and Eytea had watched the fight closely. His performance aside, namely his improvised tactic of essentially weaponizing his own blood, Eytea was most impressed by Sinkua's demeanor throughout the battle. She knew that pain and anger were triggers for his condition. So, while his friendliness toward his opponent was relieving, it didn't add up. She supposed that he may have kept himself calm because the tournament was little more than a game, meaning he had no reason to be angry with his opponents. Galo sensed her confusion.

"I doubled his dosage this morning, opened one capsule, and packed its contents inside a second one," Galo explained as they applauded Sinkua's victory, "That's probably why he's being so uncharacteristically friendly."

On his way to rejoin his friends and watch the second fight in the Alpha quartet, Sinkua was stopped abruptly by an arena employee. This man handed Sinkua a ticket and informed him that the winner of each fight was entitled to a free drink, compliments of the Commissioner. The card was embossed with the official seal and logo of the Radial Axiom Arena and read "To the victor goes the beverage." Sinkua was pointed toward the bar and diner, thanked the man, and headed on his way.

When he arrived there, a familiar presence sat at the bar, holding his second bottle of Schauzen's Deluxe. Namias turned to greet him as the door opened, the initial look on his face suggesting that he had looked back several times already only to be met with somebody else. He grinned when he saw Sinkua and even more so when he noticed the card between his fingers.

"So, you won your first round, huh? Congratulations," Namias welcomed, "Have a seat."

"You didn't watch the fight?" Sinkua asked as he propped himself up on a stool, "I must say, I find that surprising. Shouldn't you observe your opponents' techniques?"

"I've heard that's one way to go about it," Namias agreed somewhat, "but I'm taking a different approach. By staying in here, I get to talk to each of you after your bouts, learn more about you and size you up based on what kind of people you are."

Sinkua nodded and signaled for Namias to wait a moment when the barkeep approached.

"Do you have Cherry Popken?" Sinkua asked.

"Cherry Popken?" Namias interrupted, "Don't tell me you don't drink either."

"Okay," Sinkua flippantly complied as he took a sip of his cherry cola.

"I understand Galo, but why don't you drink? Are you underage?" Namias continued, swigging his beer.

"I'm twenty, so not since my last birthday," Sinkua denied, taking another swig of his drink.

"Then what's the big deal?"

"I just don't like the stuff, is all."

"I bet you've never tried a Schaudie. Here, take a sip," Namias urged,

208

extending the bottle toward him.

Sinkua shot him a glare and took another swig of his cherry cola.

"Come on, one sip," Namias pressed, lunging the bottle at him.

"You want me to take some? Fine!" Sinkua snapped, gritting his teeth.

He snatched the bottle out of Namias's hand and flung it at the wall. The bottle shattered, spraying a fan of beer across the wall. Ignoring both Namias and the barkeep, Sinkua turned to walk away, taking his soda with him.

"What was all that about?" the barkeep pried.

"Nothing, just a little psychological test," Namias explained.

"Well, since you pushed him on purpose, you're cleaning that up."

"Yeah. I know."

Upon the field of sand, Galo emerged from the gate, Setura from the one opposite. As they neared one another, Galo spun his wooden glaive menacingly, his glare never faltering. Setura walked rigidly, enraptured by Galo's stare, dragging his spatha behind him.

"I suspect this will be quick," Galo flatly stated, "what without your little confidante to abet you."

"Don't be so sure of yourself, boy," Setura countered, "Your presumption about our conspiracy is just that. Presumption."

"Is that what it is?" Galo asked, assuming a dynamic offensive stance "Well, you and Emoran can iron out the kinks in your lack of a conspiracy while you watch MalVek and me in the next round."

When the horn blared, Setura slashed at Galo's chest. Galo leaned back and to the side, catching himself on his hand. Balancing on that hand and the ball of one foot, he slapped Setura's face with his other foot. As he pushed himself upright, Setura reared back and lunged his spatha. Seeing the approaching blade, Galo dropped his glaive and bent backward, falling onto both hands. He flung his legs back and kicked the sword from Setura's hand at the base. Reversing his momentum, he sprang forward, planting both feet forcibly against Setura's chest. Setura collapsed onto his back, and Galo set his foot firmly upon his sternum.

"I suggest you tap out now, lest you feel the need to be humiliated further."

Setura glared stoically, despite his every attempt to sit up being swiftly thwarted. Galo lifted his foot, ready to stomp Setura's sternum. As his foot came barreling down, Setura desperately clutched Galo's ankle with both hands. Not one to be so easily deterred, Galo swept his other foot out and collapsed himself onto Setura, his elbow crashed down against Setura's eye socket.

"Son of a bitch," Setura screamed as he tapped the sand thrice.

"Put some ice on that," Galo suggested, "before the swelling takes your vision."

Without acknowledgment to his victory, Galo exited the sand field. Setura laid upon the sand, clutching his eye socket and gasping for air, blood seeping between his fingers. A pair of field attendants rushed to escort him out. Back in the perimeter, Galo was handed a free drink card. He interrupted the employee to inform him that he had been to the bar earlier that day.

Namias sat with his third beer, though technically it was his second after what had happened to the previous one. As he had anticipated, Galo entered with a free drink card between his fingers.

"Going for a drunken combat style, are we?" Galo asked as he approached the bar.

"I have an abnormally high tolerance. Comes with the metabolism," Namias explained, "Back for another Popken, I take it."

"Well, they don't have mango juice here," Galo excused as he was handed a bottle of Popken.

"So what's the deal with Sinkua, anyway?"

"Depends," Galo dismissed, "What did you say, and what day of the week is it?"

"I offered him a beer and he went apeshit."

Galo snickered between sips of his cola.

"What's so funny?" Namias pried as he sipped his beer.

"The obviously implied ellipsis in your story. Let me guess. You offered, and he refused. You pressed the issue, and the beer ended up somewhere around that splatter on the wall back there."

"You're astute," Namias complimented with a smile, "and faithful to your friends. I can respect that."

"You lied just to test me?" Galo asked, confirming his suspicions.

"Pretty much, yeah," Namias agreed, "Hey, when you see Sinkua, do me a favor. Let him know I respect his decision to abstain from alcohol."

"Then why'd you push the issue?"

"Testing his conviction."

Eytea made her way across the field of sand, using her wooden halberd much like a walking stick. Her wings were bound via a climbing harness. From across the way came her opponent, an Ierodhesan man in his thirties. At his side, he carried flanged mace polearm. He grimaced and sneered as they approached one another.

"You got lucky in the Prelims," he insulted, glaring down at her disdainfully.

"Call it what you like," Eytea brushed off with a smirk, "and keep calling it that when you're watching me in the next round."

"Hey, I'm not like those other guys!" her opponent snapped, "I'm not gonna go easy on you just because you're a woman."

Eytea smirked and looked away, chuckling quietly to herself. Thanks to the advice that Sinkua and Galo had given her, she had already sized up her opponent for a quick clean victory. Moreover, she finally understood their cockiness and found it surfacing in herself. It must have come with grasping the nuances of one's weapon, she concluded. The horn blared.

From the corner of her eye, she saw his foot come forth. She leaned back to dodge the arcing mace, the head whisking past her face so close that the wind from it tussled her hair. She swung wide and from the outside, striking him in the left kidney. His back went rigid as he called out in pain and clutched his side. With his free hand, he took another swing. Before he could, she jabbed him in the lower abdomen with the head of the halberd. As he hunched over, she bludgeoned the right side of his head with a swift backhand swing. Humiliated and disoriented, he collapsed on the sand, tapping thrice almost immediately. Eytea crouched beside him and smiled.

"Well, aren't you just the cutest little misogynist!" she remarked.

Despite having not heard her comment, the crowd burst into an uproar of applause. By a significant margin, hers had been the quickest victory by a female contender in a handful of years. Many of the women in the crowd, along with quite a few infatuated men, offered a standing ovation. She stood and waved to them, pumping her fists as her victory was exuberantly announced over the intercom. Before she left the field though, she used her halberd to help her opponent to his feet.

As she stepped off the field, an associate stopped her to give her a free drink card.

"You know I'm not of age, don't you?" she asked, "I'm only eighteen."

"I know better than to guess a lady's age," he answered with a sly grin, "but they have virgin drinks available over there. Just head that way, and you can't miss it."

As she entered the bar, she was greeted by Namias, who looked to be on his fourth Schauzen's Deluxe. The stain that Sinkua had left upon the wall had been cleaned and the glass swept from the floor.

"Congratulations, Eytea," Namias offered with an affirming nod, "I wasn't sure if I should expect to see you here."

"Virgin strawberry daiquiri, please," Eytea ordered before turning to Namias, "Now, what's that supposed to mean?"

"Just what it sounds like, no subtext. I've heard no rumors of your combat abilities. Galo and Sinkua, on the other hand, I'd be surprised if I didn't run into them at least once back here."

Eytea nodded as she took a sip of her drink.

"You'll probably see them back here after the next round, as well," she boastfully added, "and so on up until the finals. They may be the only two here who can eliminate one another."

"I wouldn't go so far as to say that," Namias refused with a confident smirk, "Galo will have to face MalVek next. That fight's too close to call."

"We'll see," Eytea accepted, noting the possibility of his affiliation with MalVek.

The two of them sat in silence for a few minutes, each sipping their drinks until Namias broke the silence.

"So, do you not care about my outlook on your next match?"

"Not particularly, no."

"You don't care at all that I had far lower expectations of you than I did of Galo and Sinkua?"

"Am I supposed to?" Eytea bit, "Look, I don't know what sort of reputation you may have at this event, but even if I did, I wouldn't be here to prove myself to you. I'm just here to see how far I can take it."

"Good to know," Namias accepted before he took the last swig of his beer.

An announcement came on the intercom, signaling that the first fight of the Delta quartet was soon to begin. Namias bid Eytea farewell, and she wished him good fortune.

Eytea rejoined Sinkua and Galo at the perimeter as Namias's first tournament match began. None spoke a word for well over a minute as they all followed Namias around the field with their eyes. His combat abilities spoke significantly greater volumes in a one on one match than they did in a group melee. However, they were more trying to size him up as a person in general. Though none of them had mentioned their individual encounters beyond Galo's first meeting, each suspected they all had unconventionally probing conversations with him.

"You know," Sinkua began, breaking the long silence, "He told me that he chose to get to know us as people in lieu of observing our fights."

"That's how he gauges us, by pushing our buttons with amateur psychological evaluations?" Galo asked.

"Apparently. He pestered me about abstaining from alcohol."

"He did mention that to me. He told me he was doing it to test your conviction. Of course, this only came after I used the stain on the wall to refute his accusation that you lost your temper without cause."

"So yours was a test of gullibility?" Eytea guessed.

"I'm not sure, but when he admitted his lie, he told me I was astute and faithful to my friends. What about you?"

"He spoke of his surprise that I won my first match," Eytea explained, "Apparently, he wanted to know if I felt like I had something to prove by being here."

"Well, do you?" Sinkua asked.

"Why would I?" she shot back with a shrug.

"Doesn't really seem like he's gauging our combat abilities with his little evaluations, does it?" Galo asked, "Sounds to me like he's sizing us up as people."

"I don't doubt that he has his reasons," Eytea assured him.

"Nor do I, but I sincerely doubt they relate to his placement in the tournament. That man obviously has his own agenda."

A while later, the last fight of the Alpha Preliminary was quickly approaching. The others would follow in usual order, but the semifinals would bring about a necessary change. The winners of Alpha and Gamma would face one another in one match with Beta and Delta facing off in the other. Realizing what another victory would most likely bring, Eytea jested about hiding in their room during the semifinals. After seeing his performance in his first bout, Galo suspected he would face Namias in the semifinals, assuming he was able to eke out of a victory against MalVek.

Sinkua entered the field for his second match, his morningstar sitting on his shoulder. From the other end, VanSen approached, rubbing the handle of his cat-o'-nine-tails. They locked eyes with one another, each carrying their own preconceived notions.

"You changed weapons. Was the spear not working for you?" Sinkua asked flatly.

"I felt this piece from my collection more appropriate for the likes of you. Understand that I only sided with you in the Preliminary for my own personal agenda," VanSen bitterly spat, "Killing you here would make me an international fugitive, but the least I can do is humiliate you at nine whip ends."

"I should've known," Sinkua muttered, gritting his teeth, "Very well then."

As the horn note struck, Sinkua plunged his booted foot into VanSen's abdomen. VanSen stumbled back as the horn still resonated through the air. Sinkua stepped closer to bludgeon him across the back of his head only to have VanSen jerk himself upright and snap his whip upward. Sinkua squinted as all nine tails lashed across his face with nine wisps of blood trailing off the ends. When he opened his eyes, he could see the tails snapping once again. Being that he was still shaken from the first strike, these laid into his neck scarcely defended. VanSen drew back for a third strike. His face dripping blood, Sinkua plowed his fist through the barrage of lashings, delivering a devastating blow to the bridge of VanSen's nose. VanSen staggered back a few steps, holding his nose. Blood caked in his mustache as it poured from his nostrils. The bridge of his nose was dark purple and swelling quickly.

Sinkua's breathing was growing heavy and ragged. He raised his morningstar for a backhand swing. VanSen reflexively whipped his nine tails. With a snap and flick of the wrist, Sinkua diverted the chain's path downward and snapped it forward, bludgeoning VanSen in the sternum, and followed with a backhand punch to the chin. He swung again, and VanSen ducked to evade the strike, slinking back to put himself out of the reach of any possible redirection. VanSen countered with a sharp crack of his torturous whip. Sinkua leaned back, almost losing his balance in doing so, and the tails snapped within centimeters of his face. This exchange of narrowly parried attacks continued through a handful of iterations, each holding the audience's unwavering attention.

Weary of their game, Sinkua immediately followed a failed offensive swing with a successful defensive one, catching VanSen's counterattack and ensnaring their weapons. Unfortunately, VanSen proved himself to be of greater physical strength, at least when Sinkua's condition was suppressed. When Sinkua tried to draw him closer, he instead found himself yanked forward and whipped around. VanSen jerked his arm up into a hammer lock. Sinkua dropped his weapon and ground his teeth, grunting in pain. Blood trickling down his face and neck, he tried with little success to steady his ragged breathing. The taste of blood drifted into his mouth from the depths of this throat. His medication was wearing off.

"All men control their own fate," he muttered.

"What did you say, whipping boy?" VanSen bellowed in his ear, "Unless you're surrendering, shut your mouth."

"All men control their own fate!" Sinkua repeated.

"I said shut your mouth!"

"Is this not your credo?"

"Shut your fucking mouth!"

"All men control their own fate, thus the only victims are those of their own consequence," Sinkua grunted, "Is this or is this not the credo on which you base your coups?"

"Yes! What of it!?"

"Then live by it!"

Sinkua snapped his head back, slamming it against the bridge of VanSen's nose. VanSen released Sinkua's wrist and piercingly cried out in agony. Disoriented beyond recovery, he collapsed and, despite his dizzied stupor, managed to find the ground thrice with his palm. Sinkua snatched the whip as a trophy and walked away in the midst of the victory announcement.

When he entered the bar with a new coupon in his hand, he was once again greeted by Namias, who sat conversing with the barkeep. The barkeep threw a wet dish towel to Sinkua.

"Just saw your fight on the monitor, kid. Looked like you could stand to get cleaned up," the barkeep explained.

"Thanks," Sinkua gasped, his breath slowly steadying, "I'll be alright once the blood is out of my eyes."

"Cherry Popken, right?"

Sinkua glanced to Namias, expecting more commentary.

"I'm not here to pry this time," Namias explained as the barkeep handed Sinkua his drink, "From here on, we're just two people having a drink between bouts."

As he pulled the bloodstained towel from his face, Sinkua nodded in approval.

Galo walked across the field, using his oaken glaive as a walking stick. As MalVek approached with his sledgehammer in his grip, the two of them locked eyes. MalVek abruptly stopped some ten meters away. Though he found it a bit odd, Galo stopped as well, implicitly agreeing to play along with whatever this strange elder may have had planned.

At the second the horn blared, MalVek crouched and hurled his sledgehammer with astonishing force. It spun parallel to the ground, seeming to smash the air. Galo leaned to the left, bracing himself on his hand, and raised his glaive. When the two handles collided, the hammer pulled his arm back, jerking against his shoulder. He resisted and stopped the hammer, the heads of the weapons snagged on one another. He shoved himself upright and bounced the hammer from his glaive to his free hand.

When he caught the sledgehammer, he threw his glaive like a javelin. As that left his hand, he hurled the hammer in the same manner that MalVek had. MalVek leaned to dodge the glaive and ducked to parry the hammer. His focus having been on those, he failed to notice the third strike approaching just behind the hammer.

Galo set forth in full sprint just after releasing the hammer from his grip. A split second after the hammer passed over his head, MalVek looked up to find Galo too near to parry or counter. Galo leapt and struck with a crushing drop kick, both feet crashing into MalVek's unguarded face. MalVek was knocked back and off his feet. Galo rose to his feet only to find MalVek still lying on the sand, motionless aside from the heaving of his chest. Apprehensively, he awaited his opponent's next move. After a moment, he opted to cautiously approach.

MalVek lay on the sand, staring up at him with two black eyes and blood seeping from his nose and lips. His grey chinstrap beard was caked with blood. Despite Galo's expecting him to tap out, he abruptly kicked Galo upon his shin. Galo stumbled back as MalVek sprang to his feet. MalVek grabbed up the nearby sledgehammer and tossed it aside, far from either of their reaches.

"No weapons!" he barked, "Just you and me, straight fisticuffs!"

"As much as I wish to win, I'd rather lose than be forced to break you for your obstinacy," Galo refused.

"No pity!"

MalVek swiftly thrust his foot forth, slamming it squarely into Galo's abdomen. Galo staggered back, stunned by the sudden blow. MalVek lunged forth to deliver a fist to his chest. Galo pivoted to parry only to be punched in the small of the back instead. He called out in pain, his back arching. Having created an opening, MalVek took a swing at Galo's head. Galo leaned to the side to dodge it, then back to parry the kick that the punch was meant to direct him toward. As he righted himself, his fist plowed through the dusty air, barreling toward MalVek's throat. MalVek punched his fist off course and clutched his wrist.

"You're faster, I'll give you that," MalVek grunted, "but I'm stronger."

MalVek tightened his grip on Galo's wrist. Galo's fingers gnarled and stiffened as he clenched his teeth. A large portion of the crowd cheered through it all, apparently for MalVek. Galo managed to grasp his composure for one defining moment.

"I've got one more advantage," he hissed through clenched teeth, "Periphery."

He whipped his free hand up to clutch MalVek's ear and press his palm heel against his temple. MalVek's grip weakened as he tried to resist disorientation. Galo twisted his wrist, popping free of MalVek's loosening grip, and slammed his fist against his other temple. MalVek's eyelids flickered, and his body wobbled. When Galo released his grip, he collapsed into a heap of himself. After a moment of reluctance, MalVek tapped out.

"That MalVek guy is pretty good," Sinkua commented to Eytea, "Too bad he's an ArcNosian."

"Namias warned me about him, said this match would be hard to call," Eytea relayed.

"Looks like he was right. Do you think maybe they know each other?"

"Perhaps, but I've yet to see them converse."

"Suddenly, Namias seems quite a bit more suspicious," Sinkua disdainfully sighed, "I sincerely hope I'm wrong about him."

Galo hobbled into the bar where he was greeted by the barkeep and Namias, who appeared rather disillusioned. Galo settled in next to him and handed the barkeep his card. The barkeep confirmed his repeat order for a Popken.

"You look like you lost something important to you," Galo empathized, "Or is that just part of your probing this time?"

"I had a lot riding on MalVek beating you," Namias replied, "Do you know why they cheered at that moment when he had you at his mercy?"

"I fear to say it, but is it because he's an ArcNosian?"

"It's because you're the heel at this event."

"I'm the heel? Why?"

"Political reasons, mainly. People have mixed feelings about you, but the general consensus is that you suck," Namias explained, "Most of us up here have a limited scope of the events in the Southlands. There are those who believe your inadequate resistance brought unnecessary harm to your people, that your obstinacy sent them to their graves. Others believe your decision to leave them to their own devices was an act of cowardice. And then there are others still who believe your resistance to have been an impedance to the advancement of ArcNos and Ouristihra as a whole"

Galo listened in disbelief, swigging his cola as Namias rattled off this list of unpleasant reputations. When he finished, Galo let it sink in, trying to regain his composure. All at once, he realized what his grandfather never explained to him about being a world leader. People will draw assumptions no matter how little information they've acquired.

"Are there any who hold me in a positive light?" Galo nervously asked.

"There are those, though they are few, who believe we don't know the full truth," Namias assured, "They believe that your inaction would have had more dire consequences than what occurred. They also feel that your departure was necessary for some reason or another."

"My people will grow stronger if they rebuild in my absence," Galo insisted, "and I believe that getting rid of me is more of a priority for ArcNos than destroying the remainder of Masnethege. They're safer if I separate myself, and I don't have to concern myself with protecting them."

"So you hope," Namias qualified between sips of beer, "but there's really no need to explain yourself to me."

"There's not? To what school of thought do you subscribe."

"I think you made the right choice in taking action, but that your choice to leave was rash but not wholly unreasonable," Namias explained, "Though now, I'd say you're impeding the progress you sought."

Eytea entered the sand field for her second match, her halberd lying over her shoulder. While her eyes were fixed on her opponent, a man of comparable age to her, her mind was elsewhere. Her anxiety became visibly apparent as she contemplated what might come of a victory in this bout. She repeated a mantra in her head, assuring herself that her fears were nothing over which to throw the fight.

"You're cute," her opponent complimented with a wry grin, "For a dyke, that is."

"Excuse me?"

"Yeah, you know the only birds that enter this game are all dykes," he clarified, "but you look to be worth saving. Maybe I'll take you for a drink later to show there's no hard feelings, try to bring you back around."

"I don't date women, and I'm already with someone," Eytea deflected.

"Who? One of those Southland blokes you been sitting with?"

"Perhaps."

"Or is it both of 'em? Yeah, I'll bet you're with both of 'em. You closet dykes are all the same. Buncha man hungry whores, trying to convince everybody you ain't a lezzy."

"Oh that's it!" Eytea snapped.

She uppercutted him with the handle of her halberd, exposing his throat for a sharp jab with the butt of her weapon. In his moment of disoriented stupor, she clapped the broad side of the blade against his temple. Out of either tactical sacrifice or sheer oblivion, he tapped out of the match. About a second later, the initial horn blared.

"Well," Namias commented to Galo as they watched on the monitor, "looks like Sinkua is going to the finals."

Chapter 21

"What was that all about?" Sinkua pried.

"Oh, you know how kids bicker," Eytea snidely remarked, "He called me a dyke and tried to hit on me. I told him I have a boyfriend. He called me a man hungry whore. So, I knocked his ass out."

"He thought that calling you a lezzy was a good way to get at your knickers? He can't have suffered much of a loss from that blow to the head, then."

Eytea giggled, finally cracking a smile about the whole situation, then added, "I hope you don't mind about the boyfriend thing."

"It's fine that you never told me. It hasn't been an issue as of yet. But since you told me, I guess it's only fair that I tell you that I'm single. You know, just to get us on the same page."

"What? No, not that. I don't have a boyfriend," Eytea clarified, "I was using you as a decoy. Or well, I was going to before he interrupted me."

"You told him I was your boyfriend?"

"Uh huh. You don't mind, do you?"

"I didn't know I was your boyfriend. Shouldn't I know that sort of thing before strangers do?"

"You're not, Sinkua," she clarified with a coy grin, "I was just going to say you were to ward off his advances."

"Oh… Oh, I see what you're getting at. Sure, if you want to say that to get rid of guys like him, I'll play along."

A few minutes later, an announcement summoned Eytea and her last opponent to the judge's booth. As an attendant led them both to the booth, standing between them all the while, he explained that they were to receive word of their winnings and final standings in private.

The booth was a long narrow room with sound dampening panels and no windows. Some twenty judges with headsets sat at monitors, each viewing the arena from a different perspective. The three of them entered the booth from behind the row of judges. On the other side stood a man clad in black and donning a metallic mask.

"Hello to you both," he greeted, "and congratulations on your achievements. My name is Mortvill, Commissioner of these events and owner of the Radial Axiom Arena. Please, do not be alarmed by the mask. It is simply because of my leprosy and abnormally sensitive flesh that I wear this."

"Pleasure to meet you, Mortvill," Eytea returned with a polite nod.

"The same," the other added humbly.

"We've reviewed the fight and have concluded that neither of you can be deemed victorious. Listening to your altercation from the on-field microphones, some of us believe that Eytea was justified in her actions. However, that is not what we are here to judge," Mortvill explained.

"Justified? The bloody lezzy went batshit on me," the young man interjected.

"Do you mind!?" Mortvill snapped, quickly silencing him, before continuing, "The short and long of it is that we have no alternate option but to consider the fight a draw. Eytea proved herself capable of winning were she to deliver the first blow, but she did so only by acting prematurely. Therefore, this places both of you in the fourth prize tier. Come forth to receive your rewards."

The two of them rounded the table at opposite ends, meeting before Mortvill on the other side. His face obstructed, he expressed his pride for them in his posture. In each hand, he held a plastic card embossed with the arena's insignia.

"Once again, congratulations on reaching the top eight. Your achievements warrant boasting, and I am certain your friends and families will be proud to know of them. Therefore, it is with great pleasure that I present to each of you your fourth tier spoils of forty-seven thousand five hundred iolas," he boasted as handed them their cards, "You may use those like any other bank card."

The young man thanked him and immediately shuffled out of the booth.

"Thank you, Mortvill," Eytea accepted, "I had a wonderful time competing this year."

"It was a pleasure having you, Eytea, and we hope to see you again soon. We had been hoping to see an Hybrid here ever since what happened in Berinin, curious to know how one of your ilk would fare on a level playing field."

"Perhaps, I'll come back next year. Time will tell," Eytea considered, "By the way, is there a branch of this bank on site?"

"A branch, no, but there is a teller machine outside of the diner."

"Fantastic. Thank you."

Back in the perimeter room, Eytea walked surreptitiously behind Sinkua's seat. As she passed, she waved the card in front of his face. She withdrew it as he turned around, holding it between her fingers with a smirk on her face. She nodded toward the diner, pocketed the card, and walked away. Excited for what he anticipated, Sinkua promptly followed.

On the way, she explained the payment decision. He found it reasonable enough, though the fact that they were nearly fifty thousand iolas richer certainly swayed his opinion. She withdrew one hundred iolas from the teller machine next to the diner. Inside, Namias and Galo sat at the bar discussing politics over Schauzen's Deluxe and Popken. Eytea cleared her throat, and they turned to see her waving her withdrawal.

"The semifinals start in an hour. Who's up for supper beforehand?" Eytea offered.

"Oh, are you buying?" Namias asked.

"What? No, this is just to assure you that I can foot my own bill," she facetiously corrected, "because I'm that damn famished."

The four of them laughed for a moment until Galo cleared his throat and answered, "Supper sounds like a wonderful idea. Thank you, Eytea."

Namias asked the bartender for four menus, and they all took seats around a table in the middle of the dining area. When it came time to order drinks, Sinkua took his usual Cherry Popken and Eytea her virgin strawberry daiquiri. Before Galo could order, though, Namias ordered a vodka mango tonic and insisted that he preferred to mix them himself. He flashed Galo an assuring wink, and Galo insisted that he wasn't thirsty. When the drinks came, Namias passed the mango juice to Galo and kept the vodka for himself. Galo thanked him for his efforts and smiled almost childishly as he took his first swig.

"Are we ready to order now?" the waiter asked.

"Could I get the balsamic glazed pork tenderloin with extra grilled onions?" Eytea asked.

"I'll have the t-bone, medium well, with a baked potato and corn on the cob," Namias requested.

"Steamed Northwater crab with rice pilaf for me, please," Galo ordered.

"I'll take the crispy chicken citrus salad with extra egg crumbles, if that's alright," Sinkua beckoned.

As they waited for their orders to be filled, they conversed about the events of the day. Though he had asked them to deliver messages to one another, Namias confessed the intentions behind his somewhat intrusive prying. He explained that his ArcNosian friends, such as MalVek, suspected that they were heading to ArcNos to challenge the new administration. Being that he had studied behavioral psychology for two years and was fit enough to compete in the tournament, he had been asked to attend and evaluate them. His mission had originally been for general scouting purposes. However, upon receiving word of their attendance, his focus was narrowed.

"What's your verdict then?" Sinkua asked anxiously.

"I believe you all to be fit to aid in the reclamation. You are of sound enough mind to act rationally and adhere to our principles and sound enough body to protect the weak should civil protests turn violent," Namias assured him, "I'll not attempt to stop you from reaching ArcNos."

"Just curious, how do you suppose you would have stopped us?" Galo asked.

"Not physically, I can assure you of that much," Namias admitted outright, "I would have thrown out a red herring, come up with a way to convince you that you're needed more urgently elsewhere. Perhaps, keep you warding off militant advances in the Northlands."

A brief time later, the waiter returned with a large platter. Each meal's unique aroma was blended under the ceiling fan, creating a bizarre yet appetizing amalgamation of smells, indescribable except as the sum of its parts. The waiter set each plate before its recipient, confirming the orders as he rounded the table.

"Do you plan on staying for dessert as well?"

"No thank you," Eytea answered for them all, since she was paying.

"Very well, I'll be back shortly with your ticket."

They ate mostly in verbal silence. Brief exchanges were made, though never on matters even remotely serious. They commented on their meals, asked about each other's, and quipped like old friends. When the waiter came with the ticket, Eytea snatched it before any of the boys could see it. Their meals and drinks cost roughly eighty iolas, so she offered the hundred in her pocket to cover the balance and a modest tip. The waiter thanked her sincerely and took his leave of them.

"Oh Namias, you've got a spot of sour cream on your cheek," Eytea indicated, pointing to his left cheek.

"Did I get it?" he asked after a quick swipe of his napkin.

"No, it's still there. Here, let me."

She leaned in and swiped the dairy stain from his cheek, grazing his flesh with her fingernail. He thanked her with a smile, and she wiped her finger against her napkin.

After their plates were empty and their bellies full, the waiter returned to clear the table. For the next several minutes, they sat together, contentedly engaged in idle chatter. They spoke of neighbors, pets, good fishing spots, and how much the seasons change with latitude. Anyone who knew no better would nary have suspected that three of them were soon to be in fierce competition for the biggest share of iolas. Inevitably, that time came as Galo and Namias were summoned to the field.

"Thank you so much for supper," Namias said to Eytea, "I had a great time with you three. We should all get together again sometime."

"Sounds great. Next time it's your turn to buy," Eytea insisted, "Good luck to both of you, and congratulations no matter what happens."

After they left the room, Sinkua turned to ask Eytea, "Be honest now, did you get yourself disqualified from the semifinals because you were nervous about competing against me?"

"I'd be lying if I said I wasn't nervous, but I had no intention of throwing the fight to avoid you," Eytea assured him, "My own temper disqualified me."

"Fair enough," Sinkua accepted just before he swigged the last of his Cherry Popken.

On the field, Galo and Namias entered from the same side, an unprecedented entrance that day, bumping fists as they emerged from the shadow. Given their contradictory reputation, seeing them behaving amicably toward one another on the field created something of a stir. Namias stopped near the center of the field, and Galo took a few more steps before turning to face him.

"That supper isn't weighing you down, is it?" Namias asked.

"Not in the slightest. I feel fantastic," Galo boasted, bouncing on the balls of his feet, "What about yourself?"

"The same and glad to hear it," Namias assured, "I want to face you at your best."

"Still intending to avenge MalVek?"

"Naturally, but with no hard feelings any longer," Namias explained, "Now my concern is my own combat abilities. You seem more than suitable for a test of such."

Namias positioned himself in a mixed stance, leaned forth and poised to strike but with his quarterstaff defensively positioned before his torso. Galo stood a couple of meters away, his glaive held above his head like a scorpion's tail, vigorously shuffling his feet as he bobbed. Their eyes remained fixed on one another's, Namias being rather too disciplined to be befuddled by Galo's animated display.

"Sinkua," Eytea beckoned, "I've figured it out. I know who Namias is."

"Oh? Anybody important?" Sinkua asked, not yet taking his eyes from the field.

"I would say so, but I'm not sure you'll believe it," Eytea warned, "He's the late Brigadier Elite Spril."

"The one that was assassinated when he competed with CreSam for rule over ArcNos?" Sinkua asked, not as shocked as Eytea had expected.

"The one and only. Seems he's not as dead as they hoped."

"I thought Spril was in his twenties. This guy looks like he could be pushing forty."

"That threw me a bit, as well," Eytea admitted, "Remember when I swiped a bit of sour cream from his cheek at supper? I used that opportunity to test a theory. Look at this."

She held out her index finger, and under the nail was a deposit of pinkish powder.

"It's makeup," Eytea explained, "Foundation makeup, to be particular. Most women use it to look younger; he used it to look older as part of his disguise."

Sinkua leaned in and smelled her finger with a look of suspicion on his face.

"Are you wearing a scent?" he asked.

"No, aside from soap, I go natural. Why?"

"The makeup smells like cherries."

She sniffed her finger and replied with a nod, "That's a tad odd."

Upon the field, the fight had just begun. Namias lunged into a rapid double swing of each end of his quarterstaff. Galo leaned back on the ball of one foot, evading both strikes, and thrust his glaive over the staff, striking Namias in the torso. Namias responded by whipping his staff around with one hand and striking Galo's rib cage before he could retract.

Galo hook kicked the staff away as he regained his balance, pulling Namias's arm with it. As that foot came down, he agilely followed with the other, aimed for Namias's head. His entire body twisted with the momentum, and he clutched the end of the staff with his free hand, forbidding Namias from retracting or striking. Namias bent backward, narrowly dodging the powerfully arcing appendage. Galo landed and jerked the staff, sending Namias barreling toward him. Anticipating he would be matched in speed and strength if he used his momentum in a counterattack, Namias instead grasped Galo's glaive just behind the head and engaged him in an improvised tug of war.

Namias was first to take the offensive, thrust kicking at Galo's torso only to fall a few centimeters short. Galo followed in similar manner, only to fail similarly. Namias raised both feet, supporting his weight on the staff and glaive for a blink of a moment, and thrust at Galo with the length of most his body. Galo released both weapons and struck Namias's soles with his palms, halting his advance. Rather than collapse though, Namias withdrew his legs and fell into a crouch, now holding both weapons. He erected himself and promptly tossed the oaken glaive to Galo with an approving nod.

This was immediately followed with an aggressive dash, staff poised and ready to strike. Galo caught the glaive and planted the wooden blade firmly into the sand. Using it as a balancing point, he hoisted his body and thrust both feet at the charging Namias. Finally breaking the stalemate of reach advantages, he met Namias with two feet to his chest. As Galo landed, he dragged his glaive along the sand and uppercutted Namias with the broad side of the blade. Just after impact, Namias snatched the glaive from Galo's unsuspecting hand and pitched it aside.

"Nothing personal, but I'm here to win," Namias reminded, "Admittedly, good sportsmanship puts me at a disadvantage here."

"Bad sportsmanship all the more so," Galo replied with a cocky smirk.

Galo bobbed and shuffled more aggressively now, unburdened by the oaken glaive. Namias advanced to strike, and Galo ducked agilely beneath the staff, countering with a quick jab to the chest. Namias attempted an upward swing which Galo deftly parried by leaning back and falling onto one hand. With an arcing kick, he deflected the staff yet again, and as he pushed himself upright, he followed with a thrust kick to Namias's sternum. Namias staggered and gasped loudly.

Landing in close proximity, Galo rapidly pummeled the same spot with the heels of his palms. Namias stumbled back, and Galo followed with a spinning hook kick. Namias regained his composure and ducked to parry the careening foot. As Galo landed, Namias countered with a backhand swing. In an astounding display of acrobatics, Galo brought his foot down upon the staff and used it as a spring board, striking Namias with an upward kick leading into a back flip. When Galo's back was to him, Namias seized the opportunity by thrusting his staff against Galo's spine. His revolution abruptly interrupted, Galo hit the ground with atypical clumsiness, tumbling across the sand. After he halted himself, he spat a mouthful of reddened sand and looked up to see the end of the fight.

Immediately following his opportunistic jab, Namias charged with staff drawn back and clutched firmly in both hands. As he neared he swung upward, never slowing his gait. Galo looked up only in time to see the end of the staff carving the air with astonishing velocity in unavoidable proximity. It met the underside of his jaw with impressive force, knocking him onto his back. Dazed and sore, he laid on his back, hacking as blood pooled in his cheeks. Namias stomped firmly upon Galo's sternum. Galo gasped hoarsely, spewing blood over his own face. Too pained to continue, Galo patted the sand thrice.

Namias stood over him, presenting his quarterstaff held in both hands. Galo suspiciously scrutinized the offering. Namias assured him with a respecting nod. Galo grabbed the staff, and Namias helped him to his feet. Galo swished the fluid in his cheeks and spat a stream of diluted blood onto the sand.

"You should have told me you were anemic," Namias insisted.

"I'm not anemic," Galo assured, shouting over the exuberant announcement of Namias's victory and advancement to the finals, "I'll explain later."

"I'll insist upon it. Fantastic match, by the way."

"The same to you," Galo agreed.

They firmly shook hands, patting each other's shoulder with their free hand, and departed the field side by side while waving to the excited audience. The moment they stepped off the field, Galo was snagged by the arm as Sinkua abruptly pulled him aside.

"Oh hey, Sinkua," Namias casually greeted, "Looks like it's me and you in the finals, huh? You wanna grab a drink first?"

"No thanks. I need a word with Galo," Sinkua anxiously declined.

"Suit yourself, then," Namias dismissed with a shrug, "See you in an hour."

"What was that all about?" Galo asked after Namias walked away to claim his free drink.

"He isn't who he claims to be. Eytea figured him out," Sinkua explained as they headed back to their seats.

"I assume by your tone that his true identity is of some concern to us," Galo gleaned.

"He's Brigadier Elite Spril," Sinkua answered, "He would have been the leader of ArcNos had it not been for his supposed assassination."

Galo sat silently, staring blankly out onto the empty field. The news was proving difficult to swallow, learning that the threshold between peace and war had been claimed broken under false pretenses. His traveling incognito seemed rational enough, but maintaining the guise before them seemed a might unreasonable. His continued opossum behavior was all the more suspicious, as well.

"Do you mean to tell me that the man whose death marked the birth of the warmongering ArcNos we know today has been alive all along?" Galo asked, a look of disdain on his face.

"It would seem so," Eytea agreed, "which means the only truth to his story is that he's here on a scouting mission."

"The man has been playing dead while the continent falls apart," Galo insisted, "How can we be certain of anything he's said to us?"

"I imagine he's been biding his time," Sinkua explained, "Thousands of people saw him take a bullet to the head. Such a wound can't have been quick to heal, and his death was likely made official. So, he can't simply sail to Eprilen, announce to the Union Parliament that he's still alive, and attempt to once again claim rule of ArcNos. We've seen the juggernaut that spawned in his absence."

"Maybe you're right," Galo reluctantly agreed, scratching the side of his chair as he continued to stare at the field, "but I can't shake the notion that it was his negligence that brought this all to fruition."

"You can't expect one man alone to stand up to the Avatars," Eytea insisted, "As Sinkua said, he's likely been biding his time."

"Do you suppose he's attempting to set things right?" Galo asked, turning to face them, "Reclaim his place and restore ArcNos to its former glory?"

"I can think of no other reason for his scouting mission," Sinkua assured, "Though I'm not certain how much truth there was to his talk of civil protests. He may have come in search of guards, as he said, but I suspect he's come more in search of soldiers."

"So, you're of the mind that he's preparing for war?" Eytea asked, "What would you say of it were it to come to such?"

"I am indeed," Sinkua confirmed, "and I'll aid in any necessary means to collapse the current administration, be it war or civil protest."

"As will I," Galo added, "My people deserve that much."

"Then I will, as well," Eytea agreed.

"What's your reason to join the fight, anyway?" Sinkua asked, "I have my familial ties, what with my maternal lineage tracing through ArcNos. Galo has vengeance for his people and capitol. Are you joining us only because you're a fellow Hybrid?"

Eytea pondered the question. Mostly in vain, she searched her mind for a clear explanation of her motives. In her heart, she knew there must be a reason, but for all her efforts, she could not find a clear thought to put to this feeling, much less words to explain it. She tried anyway, though it was apparent she wasn't entirely satisfied with herself.

"Kabehl is an Avatar, or he was rather, and I've caught a glimpse of their capabilities through him. From the news I've heard of their exploits, they should not be allowed to progress their operations," Eytea explained, "Perhaps, it is little more than a sense of duty as an Hybrid, but I prefer to think of it as a sense of morality and insisting on being a part of the solution rather than sitting idly by and hoping it passes."

"So it's because you're merely opposed to the Avatars and wish to be an active part of the counter operations?" Sinkua asked, "Fair enough, though I would have thought you'd have something to say about the pain he brought upon you and your mother."

"That would be a bit of a selfish reason, wouldn't you say?"

Sinkua shrugged, somewhat offended by the comment, though he suspected she may have been right. Admittedly, a similar vengeance had been a great part of his own driving force. Of course, he held similar sentiments regarding the Avatars of Fate and also felt something of a sense of dutiful morality encouraging his active rebellion. Being that he was the son of the federal leader of the ArcNosian administration, along with his gift of pyromancy, did give him something of a sense of responsibility.

On the first hand, a part of him felt that he should have been able to deter CreSam. On the latter, his being an Hybrid gave him a rather inhuman advantage, one that he knew should not be used for wicked ends. But behind it all was petty vengeance. CreSam killed his mother, and the Avatars drove him to do it. Such crimes warranted punishment, and with their apparent immunity from judicial means of such, he would take it upon himself to see it through, even if the means grew so vast as to make his purpose seem petty.

What had once been a proud nation, respected by Ouristihra as its great protector, was now feared as its bane. He had vague memories of this place and had witnessed the downward spiral from his bedroom window. He could not forgive the death of his mother. Still, he began to think that perhaps reviving the ArcNos he briefly knew and loved, the nation so many generations of Ouristihrans had respected and revered, was a better reason for such drastic measures. As impersonal as Eytea's reasoning had been, his had been comparably too personal and thus rather selfish given the scale of it all.

"Not entirely," he insisted, still a bit lost in thought, "I mean, if it's your only reason, then sure, that would be selfish."

"But you can never forget those closest to you whose lives were claimed by the ravages of war," Galo added, giving Sinkua a knowing look.

"You have a point," Eytea agreed, wandering through childhood memories, "What will you do until your bout?"

"As much as I'd like to say I'm going to take a nap, the chances of that happening are about as good as your last opponent taking you on a date," Sinkua said wryly, "So I'm just going to rest."

"I'm going to join Spril at the bar," Eytea told, "I could go for another daiquiri."

"Could you do me a favor though?" Sinkua beckoned, "Don't out him, please. I may be able to use that to my advantage on the field."

"Fair enough."

As she neared the diner, Eytea could see Namias sitting at the bar with his free beer, hopefully his last where she was concerned. Next to him was MalVek, and they looked to be engaged in rather animated conversation. She saw this as a prime opportunity to gain some insight on his true intentions, but only if she could enter undetected. She bided her time until another competitor stopped by for a drink. As he entered the bar, she slipped in behind him and made for a corner and eavesdropped from beyond their sight.

"I know it goes against our plan, but I think it's time I was more forward with them," Namias insisted.

"I don't care if you think they have figured you out. It's all hearsay until you confirm it," MalVek argued, "and until we know what they're after, we can't have you doing such things."

"What they're after? MalVek, do you even know who they are? They're coming to liberate ArcNos with us."

"By what means? And how can you be so sure they'll take well to working for or even with you?"

"They're people of solid merit, MalVek. If I ask them to line up behind me for our common cause, they'll do it. But if I keep lying to them, I'm going to lose their trust permanently."

"Sure, they'll line up behind the means, but will they line up behind the person? Or have you forgotten why we gave you your name?" MalVek asked, "Within the Subtransit, you're a hero because we know the full story. But on the outside, you're either an enemy or a coward. The outside world hates you."

"Thanks for the reminder, asshole," Namias muttered.

As he walked away from the bar, Namias spotted Eytea out of the corner of his eye. Improvising an alibi, she noticed a bathroom door nearby. Namias turned to approach her, looking rather quizzical.

"Eytea, I didn't even hear you come in," he observed, "What's going on? You come for a drink?"

"What? Oh, yeah I did," Eytea lied, "but I had to use the restroom first."

"You came to spy, didn't you?" Namias gleaned, "I can't honestly say I'm offended, nor do I blame you. I haven't been terribly forward with you."

"You have been a might suspicious."

"How much did you hear?"

"Just that some folks who share your cause are of solid merit and that the world hates you, whoever you are," Eytea lied, "Oh, and that you've been lying to us."

"Namias!" MalVek called from the bar, "Watch what you say!"

"You're right, I have been lying to you," Namias admitted, "I'm not from Ivaria, nor have I studied psychology."

"Go on," Eytea urged, her arms folded over her breasts.

"I'm a former Negotiator for the ArcNosian military," he lied, "Around the time that HarEin went into hiding and the Avatars began exerting their influence over our administration, they began cutting many of the diplomatic and labor positions. I was among the first Negotiators to go."

"How tragic. Why did you keep this from us for so long?"

"From the outside, ArcNos in general is the enemy. I knew you wouldn't take well to working alongside a former ArcNosian operative, but you might cooperate with an outsider who has connections to an internal rebellion," Namias explained, "It's a classic negotiation tactic. Give the impression that you're close to their side while still having the necessary ties to get what they want out of your side."

"I suppose that makes sense," Eytea agreed, "but why would you come here in search of support for a civil protest?"

"Civil protests are bound to turn violent, and we need people strong enough to protect the crowds."

"If that's your only method, I'm afraid you'll be fighting an uphill battle for the remainder of your days."

"Of course not, those are partly a decoy and partly to draw attention to our cause," Namias continued, "We intend to bring people together from all corners of Ouristihra and push to have the ArcNosian administration declared criminal and stripped of its authority. At such time, we will rebuild what was once our nation from the ground up. I need you, Galo, and Sinkua to help us reach out to those people."

"And to serve as guards during the protests?"

"I assumed that was a given."

"Fair enough. I'll speak to the boys about it," Eytea accepted, "Thank you for eventually being forward with me."

She exited the bar, knowing quite well that she had been lied to yet again. However, she only knew that his identity and origins were lies. His claiming to be a former ArcNosian military operative was honest even if his position was not, and she could assume some truth to his being part of a resistance force and his needing them as guards. Naturally, this left her uncertain as to the truth of his intended means, much less what he expected of them. The answers, it seemed, wouldn't come until he learned that they knew his true identity and, more importantly, that not the entire outside world hated him.

Namias exited shortly thereafter, keeping his distance. While he knew he had followed the protocol he had assisted in setting forth, he couldn't help but wonder if a loophole should have been put into place for a situation such as this. He was covering lies with more lies, even going so far as to lie in his confessions and admissions, continuously deceiving the people with whom he might entrust several thousand lives.

The sun descended upon the western horizon, setting the sky ablaze with illuminated cirrus clouds. This sunset marked the beginning of the final bout in the Tournament of Duelers. The two contenders were summoned, interrupting Sinkua's idle chatting with Galo and Eytea, and Namias's introspective pacing throughout the halls. With every passing minute, the sky grew darker as dusk approached. Spotlights, yet to be switched on, dotted the perimeter of the field. Sinkua and Namias entered the field from opposite ends. Both were greeted with an uproar of applause, Namias ironically more so.

"I assume Eytea told you of my confession," Namias said plainly.

"She did, indeed," Sinkua confirmed, knowing as well that it was mostly a lie, "If it's guards you seek, you've found them."

"So you will return to ArcNos with us? Thank you. That's all I wanted to know."

"We were heading there to collapse the administration anyway. You just happened to have a team for us to join."

"How serendipitous," Namias mused, "Now, let's get down to business."

Each of them assumed a warrior's stance, indicating to the judges that they were ready to begin. As darkness began to creep over the arena, the spotlights were dimly lit, faintly illuminating the sand field. Sinkua's eyes shimmered, obstructing Namias's view of his pupils. The horn blasted, echoing across the sand.

Sinkua whipped the wooden head of his morningstar at Namias's neck. Namias dipped and pivoted away from the recoil and snapped a counterattack. With a flick of the wrist, Sinkua diverted the recoil to block Namias's counter. In one fluid motion, Namias followed the momentum of the redirection, twirling his quarterstaff around to strike at the studded head. Sinkua ducked and lunged under the collision, pounding Namias in the abdomen with incredible force. Namias doubled back, swinging his staff down and around from the outside and bludgeoning the side of Sinkua's rib cage. This exception aside, they continued parrying and dodging one another's attacks for several minutes, their attempted attacks often coinciding and colliding in midair.

When their weapons entangled, Namias spun to place himself behind Sinkua at the length of his quarterstaff. He jerked the staff free of the constraints of Sinkua's morningstar and thrust it forcibly. At that same moment, Sinkua leapt and pivoted, kicking the end of the staff and pushing off of it before jogging several steps backward.

Namias was knocked off balance, and Sinkua charged opportunistically.

Namias responded with a charge of his own, tracing his path with the tip of his staff. When they were a couple of meters apart, he brought the staff forth with an underhand swing. Sinkua pounced and sprang off the staff as it rose toward him, careening toward Namias with a powerful thrust kick. Namias fell back onto his hand, allowing Sinkua to narrowly clear him. Sinkua spun about with an aggressive swing of his morningstar, hoping to strike Namias down before he could right himself.

The ball crashed across Namias head, but undaunted, he snagging the chain with his polearm yet again. This time he jerked back, ripping Sinkua's morningstar from his grasp. He nonchalantly flung it over his shoulder and whipped his quarterstaff around for a strike he assumed would not be blocked by an unarmed opponent. Despite the momentum, Sinkua grabbed the end of the staff, halting its careening arc. He yanked the staff, sending Namias stumbling toward him. As his foot crashed into Namias's chest, so too did Namias's fist into his eye. Namias desperately gasped for air as Sinkua winced and doubled back, both still holding the staff but with diminished grip. Namias stubbornly pulled the staff from Sinkua's grasp and tightly clutched it in both fists, implicitly admitting a disadvantage as his was now a more defensive stance.

Sinkua responded with an abrupt palm heel thrust through the center of the quarterstaff, snapping it into three pieces. The middle bounced off Namias's chest, and Sinkua caught it. The other two remained in each of Namias's hands. Where they had started with a quarterstaff and a morningstar, now one had two wooden daggers and the other a single two-headed one.

Namias stabbed with one piece, an attack which Sinkua knocked away with his empty hand, and slashed at the opening with the other. Sinkua leaned to dodge this other strike and slashed at Namias's exposed side as well. The two narrowly dodged each other's attacks, the jagged ends of their wooden daggers ripping at the threads of one another's clothes. Sinkua pivoted to Namias's other side, ducking under his daggers, and slashed again. Namias turned to face him, stepping beyond his reach.

Sinkua lunged and thrust his dagger at Namias's stomach. Namias stepped into it and clapped his daggers together. Both stopped a split second before the moment of collision. Jagged oaken ends lay against Namias's stomach and either side of Sinkua's neck, all faintly piercing the skin and demonstrating that contenders of lesser reflexes would have found the scenario to be fatal. Silence washed over the recently roaring crowd under the purpled sky.

"You stopped," Namias observed, "How could you have been so sure I would as well, after the things I've said to you?"

"You won't kill me, not in a time and place such as this," Sinkua perceived, the two of them still locked in a stalemate.

"Don't be so certain you can't die here, even if by accident. Great people have made their final stand in a place such as this."

Sinkua smirked. His opportunity had finally come. How serendipitous, indeed.

"And sometimes, great people get to avenge their own death," he countered with a piercingly knowing stare.

Startled by the shattering of his illusion, Spril reared back, failing to notice that he had pulled the wooden daggers away from Sinkua's neck. Sinkua raised his foot and thrust it with seemingly impossible force into Spril's stomach. Knocked back, he gasped and hacked up traces of blood. As he doubled over, Sinkua watched stoically and from a safe distance. Spril collapsed onto the sand, still choking and gasping, and Sinkua watched as he patted the sand once, twice, and thrice. The fight was over, and Sinkua was the champion of the tournament.

He dropped the dagger and approached Spril to offer him a hand getting to his feet. Spril reached for the offered hand, eyes glazed and blood trailing from the corner of his mouth. He righted himself slowly, but as he regained his balance, a look of lucidity returned to his eyes, followed immediately by a look of cunning. With Sinkua unsuspecting, he delivered a powerful backhand punch, followed immediately by another with his other hand. His opponent disoriented, Spril finished with a direct blow to the bridge of the nose. Sinkua collapsed to his knees.

Enraged and pained, Sinkua began hacking uncontrollably, blood pooling in his throat. Unaware of the full scope of the situation, Spril simply watched the spectacle unfold before him. Blood streaming from his mouth, Sinkua glared up at Spril with a look of nothing less than unrelenting rage. He fell to his hands and knees, coughing and spewing blood across the sand.

"Get back!" a voice shouted from the sidelines, "Namias! Get away from him, now!"

Spril looked up to see Galo coming through the gate and running toward them. From the other side came Yrlis, first aid kit in hand. Their being at the sidelines, both had responded before the in-house emergency staff could do so.

"You have to get away from him," Galo ordered as he came near and to a halt.

"He's just coughing up blood," Yrlis argued, "That's not contagious through blood to skin contact."

"That's not what concerns me," Galo countered, "It's his mental state. He's in a blind rage."

"How can you be so sure of such a thing, simply because he looks wicked in this state?"

As though to prove Galo's point, Sinkua attempted to erect himself, slashing at Yrlis's femoral artery. Galo socked him across the temple, knocking him to the ground. Sinkua lay on the sand, barely conscious but still coughing blood.

"Fair enough," Yrlis admitted, "but he's starting to choke. We need to clear his airways."

"Already on it," Galo announced, presenting a green pulp in his open hand, and knelt next to Sinkua.

"That won't do," she argued, also kneeling beside Sinkua and producing a pocket knife, "We need real medicine."

"And what do you call this?"

"Look, your sticks and grass may work for people who believe in them, but the real medicine lies in science," Yrlis insultingly insisted, "They're not going to save him now."

Yrlis pressed the tip of the blade to Sinkua's throat.

"If you cut him, I swear to every spirit in the sea I will gut you from groin to chin," Galo snarled in objection.

"I'm not cutting him. I'm doing a tracheotomy," Yrlis argued, "but if you knew a thing about medicine, you would know that."

"I know enough to know the risk of staph infection if you do it without disinfecting your little pocket knife," Galo countered.

"So, you do know something. I'll admit there's a risk, but it's far less than his risk of drowning in his own blood if I don't do it."

"Your way puts him at risk whether it works or not. Mine doesn't. I do things my way, and if they don't work, you can intervene."

"You ignorant jungle whelp! We don't have time for your little leaves and roots!" she snapped, pressing the blade into Sinkua's flesh.

Galo snatched the blade from her hand and whipped it across the field.

"Go fetch, bitch," he barked.

Appalled and insulted, she stormed off to retrieve her discarded knife. Galo rubbed his index finger in the green pulp, made from wet mashed leaves of a particular sort. Spril crouched beside him to observe the treatment.

"That's my girlfriend, you know," he informed Galo.

"Really?" Galo asked, sensing that he expected an apology, "Well, your girlfriend is a bitch."

"She's just opinionated, especially when it comes to medicine," Spril explained, holding his tongue, "I'll explain to her who you are, and I'd like you two to make an effort to get along since we'll all be working together."

"If we can avoid mentioning medicine, that could be possible," Galo accepted as he pried Sinkua's mouth open, "Hey, hold his jaw."

Spril complied, taking a firm grip on Sinkua's lower jaw. Galo shoved his finger in Sinkua's mouth and swabbed the pulp on the roof. He quickly retracted, and Spril released Sinkua's jaw. Both of them stepped back to watch. As they did, Yrlis returned, pocket knife on the ready. Spril held out his arm to stop her, signaling for her to give them a moment.

Inside Sinkua's mouth, the pulp mingled with his saliva. The resulting vapors caused his airways to expand, allowing some air into his lungs, and the moisture resulting from the stimulation of his salivary glands thinned the blood. Galo cautiously took his hand and sat him up. As he came upright, his mouth fell open and diluted blood poured out. His throat cleared for the moment, he gasped for air, filling his lungs via temporarily expanded airways. He coughed a few times, blood spraying from his mouth, but quickly caught his breath again. He slowly regained his composure, and eventually the hacking of blood stopped.

"Why?" he raggedly asked, looking up at Spril, "Fight was over."

"I faked my surrender, stopped just short of the ground on the third pat," Spril explained, "but I'm sorry I did this to you."

"Spril," Sinkua throatily gasped, "You bastard."

Chapter 22

The train station was roaring with commerce that late Harvest morning. Competitors and spectators from the Tournament of Duelers had effected a significant influx in business. Spril approached the ticket counter, his newly expanded entourage in tow.

"Morning," he greeted, "Is there any chance we could get a private cabin for the, ah let's see, eight of us on the next train to the west coast docks?"

"Let me just check the records, but I believe we still have an opening," the woman excused, scanning the schedule that was laid out before her, "Yes sir, we have a cabin for you on a train leaving in thirty minutes. It'll be fifteen hundred iolas. Cash or charge today?"

"Thanks so much. It'll be charge."

The lot of them spent the next half hour pacing about, mostly keeping to themselves. They had much to discuss, but it was best done beyond the reaches of searching ears and prying eyes, hence the private cabin. Among the eight of them, they had a similar goal but varying intents, means, and knowledge. Before they could move any further, they would need to get up to speed with one another and come to an agreement on their methodology.

For such a rustic exterior design, the interior of the private cabin was lavishly decorated. In the corner sat a darkly stained hickory liquor cabinet, atop which sat a sleek stereo system. A handful of armchairs formed a semicircle around it all with a coffee table in the middle. Lining one wall was a series of bench seats, more like loveseats given how padded they were, with long tables set out before them. All of the seats were made from hickory, similar to the cabinet though less darkly stained, and lined with padded velour. The walls were lined with wood paneling, stained a burnt red hue, with faux gold weavings trimming the top. It looked more like the living room in a luxury hotel suite than a train car.

Spril took a seat next to Phylus shortly after they entered. Yrlis sat next to Spril, Vielle across from Phylus, and Galo next to her. Sinkua and Eytea sat together at a smaller table, and MalVek sat in an armchair with a drink. Spril and Phylus mumbled under their breath for a moment or two, eventually nodding in agreement at the end of what appeared to be a befuddled misunderstanding. As the train began to leave the station, Spril turned to face the other attendants and cleared his throat for their attention.

"Alright, here's where we sit. Between our current funds, my winnings and MalVek's winnings, we now have enough capital for two hundred forty citizens," he announced with nary an explanation for the newcomers, "That puts us short by ten citizens, or fifty thousand iolas."

"I think I see now why it was so important for MalVek to make the semifinals," Galo deduced, nodding his head, "but now I don't see what you're talking about."

"An explanation would be nice," Sinkua agreed, "Would have been better before you started rambling on about capital and citizens."

"We're declaring ourselves our own nation," Spril proudly announced, "Those of us living in the Subtransit away from the overbearing eye of the Autonomous Empire of ArcNos will be declaring ourselves the Parliamentary Republic of ArcNos and breaking away from their federal bonds."

"Our only obstacle is money. We've set up an economic system as well as a political one," Phylus explained, a wisp of cigarette smoke swirling from his lips, "but we need enough federal capital or highly liquid assets to equal five thousand iolas per citizen with a minimum citizenship of two hundred fifty people. After this tournament, we have one million two hundred thousand, enough for two hundred forty."

"You know, this would go a lot faster if you would simply say what you want," Eytea impatiently interjected, "You need our winnings in order to go forth with your plans, right?"

"That's exactly right," Spril verified, almost embarrassed to be asking for such a large sum.

"The three of you totaled three hundred thirty-two thousand five hundred iolas," Yrlis calculated, "That's enough for another sixty-six citizens."

"What do you say?" Spril urged.

"Put us in the Parliament," Sinkua bargained, "and the money is yours."

"Sorry, no can do," MalVek countered from his armchair, a bottle of malt liquor in his hand, "You know those bastards with the Avatars would dig it up as a scandal, you folks buying your seats. That's how they got the original Parliament disbanded and discontinued."

"I have political experience, so bring me on as a Foreign Representative," Galo insisted, "and Sinkua and Eytea as Advisors. We won't actually hold Parliamentary Seats, but we will have influence over your decisions."

"MalVek?" Spril asked, "Sound too risky to you?"

"Might be risky, but I think we can pull it off. I say go for it."

"Fantastic, that puts us at three hundred six citizens, now," Phylus boasted, taking the final drag from his cigarette.

"To be quite honest, I'm pleased to hear you've already made such progress," Sinkua added, "Before we met you, I had intended to incite a rebellion upon our arrival in ArcNos. We would take refuge somewhere beyond federal grasp, form our own community and declare ourselves an independent nation. What luck to hear you've done so much of that already."

"Is this why you've collected scent vials from so many people in our travels?" Galo asked, "As outside support for the secession?"

"You have outside contacts as well?" Phylus asked, "That may prove useful for our further intentions. Just as the Avatars destroyed the old Parliamentary Republic, we intend to collapse the foundation of the Autonomous Empire."

"As do we," Sinkua agreed with a grin.

"I don't see a restroom anywhere in this place," Galo noted, changing the subject quite abruptly though out of necessity.

"Private cabins don't have 'em. Too much of a stench to be considered a luxury amenity," MalVek explained, his back still turned, "You'll have to go into one of the regular cabins back behind us."

Galo thanked him properly and exited the cabin, entering one occupied by those not traveling in secluded luxury. The furniture was significantly more crowded, but the passengers largely seemed to be enjoying themselves. They spoke amongst themselves, joking and carrying on. Children admired the scenery zipping past, much of it coniferous forest. Galo found the facility with little ado, did his business, and exited once again.

"Got a minute," a vaguely familiar voice asked as he passed.

Galo looked down to see SenRas sitting alone and reading a newspaper. The man had not even bothered to stop reading his paper long enough to wait for an answer. He cocked his head to glance at Galo but quickly returned his eyes to the newspaper.

"I suppose I could spare a moment," Galo bitterly agreed, sitting next to him, "What did you want to talk about, Admiral SenRas?"

"Oh, it's Colonel now; CreSam promoted me recently," SenRas explained, "The responsibilities are nigh overwhelming, but the authority is nice. But I'm sure you know all about that, Chieftain Sage Galo."

"It's just Chieftain Heir."

"Whether you wear the robe or not, you're still Chieftain Sage," SenRas flatly argued, "which brings me to my first point. A couple of folks named Nalygen and Borret have been sending us threatening letters claiming to be writing on your behalf. Amirione is pushing for CreSam to declare war. I recommend you tell your citizen rebels to stand down."

"I will do that, thank you. I put them in charge of the capitol restoration effort, but apparently they took it upon themselves to speak on diplomatic matters in the meantime, since I chose not to ascend to my inherited title."

"You failed to make it official though. Had you done so, through the Ouristihran Union and its Parliament, Judge Nenbard would have been declared Interim Chieftain Sage in your absence. In other words, you still rule Berinin. I suggest you take a pilgrimage to Eprilen at your earliest leisure."

"Thank you again, Colonel SenRas," Galo accepted, nodding respectfully, "but I cannot help but wonder about your end game. You take part in destroying my nation's capital only to seek me out for an unofficial meeting to advise me on such matters that would surely counter your operations."

"I suspected you were not as connected to those threats and Nalygen and Borret let on, so I felt it was only fair you knew of their exploits. But to be honest, I was at the tournament for personal reasons; suspecting I might find you merely gave me a new reason."

"Oh, did you have a friend competing?" Galo asked, turning the conversation a bit more personal.

"I did, but he didn't show," SenRas somberly clarified, "That's the larger issue I wished to discuss with you. Masfaru was my step grandson. I have always watched him compete, so imagine my chagrin when I learned of his death."

"That was rather tragic," Galo agreed, "From what I heard of him, he would have been a fantastic competitor."

"One of you already knew that to be true," SenRas added flatly, "Though I suspect you did not know him by name when you slew him, perhaps by an alias."

"The only person any of us killed in Ferya was…"

"… a one-handed Avatar of Fate who calls himself The Criminal," SenRas interrupted.

232

"Exactly," Galo nervously confirmed, "Sinkua killed him just before he choked on his own blood and collapsed unconscious. I suppose you think that makes us even, wish to pay off your blood debt with the blood on his hands?"

"By no stretch of the imagination," SenRas argued, "I come not to seek vengeance for Masfaru nor to pay blood with blood. In fact, I wish to thank you, or rather Sinkua, and seek your forgiveness."

"You've lost me," Galo admitted, baffled by the request.

"Masfaru had been losing sight of himself ever since he fell in with the Avatars of Fate. I have been trying for years to find an escape for him, but it seemed death was the only way out. Thanks to you, his family can be at peace."

"Don't you work with the Avatars?"

"We do, but I'm not particularly fond of them, especially how they treat their younger and newer recruits. His business with them was more like a terminal illness than a career."

"Well, this certainly is a strange and interesting turn of events," Galo observed, "Does CreSam know you're speaking with me on such matters?"

"He does not. Their influence over him is too strong now," SenRas explained, "It is for this reason that I seek your forgiveness, so that I might know you understand my plight. I have committed a great atrocity against you and your people, but if you could understand my remorse, I would be most grateful."

"What are your plight and your remorse?" Galo asked sternly.

"I wish to remove the influence of the Avatars of Fate from ArcNos," SenRas clarified, "but I am largely unaided in this effort, due primarily to fear and psychological manipulation. I regret having not spoken with you on this matter sooner, preferably before I let the Triad Titan wreck your capitol and Amirione murder your Chieftain Sage."

Galo leaned forward, resting his elbows on the table and absorbing the weight of the news. He always suspected that SenRas's heart wasn't entirely in the operation, but to learn that he alone was plotting against the Avatars of Fate came as something of a shock. Just as surprising was to find him seeking forgiveness for the act even after Sinkua had brutally slain one of his relatives. Offering him forgiveness would not absolve the others involved of any of their crimes, though he knew they would likely be dismissed before the Ouristihran Union Parliament. Still, it was comforting to know that somebody on the inside wanted what they wanted, to restore ArcNos to its former standing. Besides, the more he thought about it, the more he realized he never particularly held SenRas responsible for the events of that horrible night.

"I cannot forgive you," Galo somberly insisted, "because I never blamed you. Amirione pulled that trigger against your orders. It was obvious he had usurped control of the operation. Your only fault was that you failed to secure your grips upon the reins, but for that I can forgive you."

"You have no idea how much this means to me," SenRas sighed with relief, "I hope you understand that the atrocities committed have been largely due to the influence of the Avatars. Though the more they get into his head, the more that becomes a moot point."

"We suspected as much and thus never sought to destroy ArcNos," Galo assured, "only to collapse the current administration and reinstate the previous one."

"Speaking of your counter militant efforts, expect to find a war brig waiting for you about half a kilometer from ArcNos," SenRas advised, "They learned of the departure of the Subtransit dwellers and suspected foul play."

"Thank you. It's truly relieving to know we have a man on the inside."

"Mention that to nobody."

With that, Colonel SenRas dismissed Galo to return to his private cabin. Spril was wiping his face with a white rag from a drawer beneath the liquor cabinet. His hairpiece sat on top of the stereo, his bald scalp gleaming with sweat. As he pulled the rag away, he revealed his unmasked face, far more youthful than the false visage he presented at the tournament.

"One thing still confuses me though," Eytea posed, "Why did you smell like cherries?"

"You picked up on that, did you?" Spril asked with a laugh.

"Sinkua did, but yes, we noticed that from the sample I picked from your cheek at supper," Eytea clarified, much to Spril's surprise.

Vielle scooted nearer to her, craning her neck and easing her cheek toward her. She brushed the hair back from her slender neck with a smile. Feeling her breath, Eytea turned her head, nearly grazing Vielle's cheek with her lips. Galo stood in the doorway and stared.

"Smell my cheek," Vielle insisted as Eytea inhaled the essence of her aroma, "I did his makeup, but all I had was my usual cherry scented foundation."

"Galo, you're back. Everything go smoothly?" Spril asked.

"A bit too smoothly," Galo jested with a sneer, creating an alibi for his prolonged absence.

"No details, please," Spril insisted with a chuckle, "Anyway, before that interruption about my costume choice, we were discussing our methods for collapsing the Autonomous Empire."

"We've compiled a list of domestic and international criminal offenses committed by this empire," Phylus explained, "We're going to present our case in Eprilen to have their government disbanded and ours reinstated."

"The more support we have, the better," Vielle added, smiling at Galo, "especially if we have international support."

"We need protection though. Spril and I can't do it on our own," MalVek admitted, "When they learn of the trial, they're sure to take offensive measures, silence the opposition."

"We have several thousand resistance members in the Subtransit though, so it may be too large a task still for the five of us," Spril insisted.

"I think we can handle it, honestly," Sinkua countered.

"We all fared quite well in the tournament, I know, but that's small game compared to what we're…"

Spril was cut short not by interrupting words but rather by an act most stunning. Before him laid Sinkua's open and upturned hand, a large flame set upon the palm with no visible ignition source or fuel. Stranger still, his hand was unscathed.

"We were holding back at the tournament. Figured we'd be disqualified if we used our, ah, talents. We can handle guard duties quite well enough."

"And the others of you?" Spril asked, both mesmerized and frightened.

"Hydromancy," Galo answered, presenting his hand encased in ice.

"Electromancy," Eytea added, a jolt of electricity passing from one hand into the other.

"We had no idea you Hybrids were capable of such things," Spril gasped, "We assumed it was because of your inhuman physical traits."

"There is that, as well," Galo clarified, "Eytea can fly, obviously, I can breathe underwater for several hours, and Sinkua can see clearly through smog and such."

"How fortunate that you're on our side, then," Phylus thanked.

"This may prove easier than we once thought," MalVek added.

Sinkua's discomfort with the situation was visible only to Galo and Eytea, those who knew him the most intimately. His presenting their capabilities as combative advantages, thus dismissing the need for further aid, suggested that his means were more aggressive despite serving the same ends. Both had their suspicions, but both knew better than to oust him or pry. He would speak his mind when he felt it to be appropriate, and he apparently did not feel this moment to be as such.

Given their current approach, Sinkua suspected that his methods would not be well received. Thus, he thought it best to wait until a separate nation had been established and his position as an Advisor had been secured. That way, were they to reject his proposition, he would still have influence over future decisions and operations. Furthermore, if he waited until they acted on their means, their potential failure would necessitate a secondary plan, something on which none among them had yet to speak.

About an hour later, after ample conversation both business and personal, drinks all around both alcoholic and otherwise, and several rousing card games, the train reached the station. The Northland Sea was clearly visible from the window, a breathtaking spectacle. As the doors opened, the sound of squawking seagulls echoed off the walls of the cabin. A salty aroma filled the air, mingling with the musk within. One by one, the eight of them departed onto the platform.

Vielle clutched Galo's hand and tugged on his arm, beckoning him to follow her to the shore. They had spoken of his nautical wisdom, and she yearned for a demonstration of his talents. As soon as he complied, she released his hand and hit full sprint. He jogged a short distance behind, chuckling and shaking his head at the situation. Despite her usually being a bit precocious, excitement over the new and fascinating still surfaced her inner child.

"We've nigh reached your mother's homeland," Eytea reminded Sinkua softly, "You must be a might nervous"

"Far more than you might readily believe," Sinkua confessed, rubbing the back of his neck anxiously.

"Looks like Vielle has taken to the jungle whelp," Spril noted, nudging Yrlis with his elbow.

"Looks like I have no choice but to pretend I like him," she wryly accepted.

"I know you two had your disagreement in the arena, but you can't honestly be holding a grudge over it."

"He's an icon for holistic medicine," Yrlis spat, "and there's no science behind it. Witch doctors like him have killed people, coaxing them out of empirically proven treatments with their pseudomedical hokum."

"Well, until he starts killing off our own, I need you to regard him on his other qualities. Anything aside from his involvement in herbal medicine."

Following Phylus's lead with MalVek trailing behind, they headed for the boat at the end of the docks. Galo and Vielle joined them shortly thereafter, approaching from the south. Once he was certain of which boat was theirs, Sinkua was rather taken aback.

"We intend to travel on an ArcNosian infantry transport?" he asked.

"I would nary be surprised to find a welcoming committee awaiting our arrival," Galo added opportunistically.

"We salvaged it from a junk heap," MalVek explained, "My older brother NalSet fixed it up for us, made it seaworthy again."

"But why would you not paint over the markings?" Sinkua pried.

"ArcNos invested in the Tournament of Duelers in exchange for a share of the profits," Phylus explained, "So, the two nations have something of a treaty with one another, for the time being."

"And you came under the guise of ArcNosian officers and their families to ensure your safety," Sinkua deduced.

"Exactly that," Phylus confirmed, "We couldn't have them suspecting our true intentions, so we came appearing that we were here to collect payment for ArcNos after the tournament."

"Unfortunately," Spril added as he boarded, "we can count on that disguise failing if we're met with resistance upon our return. This model was discontinued six months ago."

The ship appeared to be edging on inoperability. Most of the wooden surfaces were riddled with termite damage and rotting from unyielded exposure to the sea air. Metallic surfaces were largely lined with rust, and the dank sails were stained with odiferous mildew. Unfortunately, their use was necessary as the offboard combustion motor had rusted to the point of uselessness. Six months in the junkyard had proven unkind to the old vessel. Apparently, NalSet had elected not to bother so much with the ship's aesthetic shortcomings as with the mechanical ones, save for the condition of the motor.

Since this particular model of ship had been used primarily for daytrips, onboard sleeping quarters were glaringly absent. This meant that they would need to sleep any place they could find to lay down. Fortunately, it was barely more than an overnight trip. Most of them had slept in far worse conditions, so this was nary an inconvenience.

That evening, they all immersed themselves in various tasks. Phylus examined and modified papers, finalizing his case for the secession of the underground community. He also sorted and resorted the Autonomous Empire's crimes by such measures as chronology, severity, and victim groups, determining the best arrangement for their presentation. He leaned toward severity, starting with the relatively petty crimes to get their attention and moving on to more heinous ones to secure their votes. The razing of Masnethege and their abetting the assassination of Chieftain Sage Gijin would be at the end of a long list.

From behind, he heard a faint coughing. He ignored it at first, too occupied to be concerned. It repeated, this time more loudly and obviously forced. Realizing someone was trying to get his attention, he turned around.

"Do you have a moment, Phylus?" Galo asked.

"Finally got my daughter to give you a moment's peace, I see," Phylus answered with a smirk, "Sorry about her. Her curiosity and enthusiasm sometimes turn into nosiness and meddling."

"I enjoy her company, actually," Galo admitted, "Anyway, I wanted to ask if I could join you on your trip to Eprilen."

"Why would you assume I'm the one going?" Phylus asked, "You're right, but I'm just curious."

"You were once a Negotiator, making you the top diplomat in this group. As far as I can tell, you're the only parent here, making you a conscientious leader. And you have this air of wisdom about you," Galo explained, "Besides, MalVek comes off as too cynical to resurrect a fallen nation. Yrlis seems more a supporter than a leader. And Spril is technically a zombie."

"Come again?"

"He's legally dead," Galo clarified, "So, can I join you? It's occurred to me that I never officially designated an interim replacement in my absence."

"Sure thing, Galo. It'll be good having some company on the trip," Phylus agreed, "In the meantime, I'd like to ask that you watch yourself around my daughter. She's just a child."

"She's only a year my junior, but I understand."

"And you are but a child yourself."

Those parting words stuck in Galo's mind as he left Phylus to his work. He found himself immersed in introspection, doubting if he should reclaim his inherited title and role immediately upon returning home. He was only seventeen now, sixteen when his grandfather perished, making him a might younger than preceding heirs dating back at least a few centuries. Gijin scarcely had time to prepare him for the responsibilities without accounting for the possibility of wartime. This decision was not one to be made without much further deliberation, but he took comfort in knowing his official interim replacement would be trustworthy.

Sinkua leaned against the starboard rail near a cannon, watching the northern waters ripple past. Off in the distance, he could faintly discern the southern coast of Tanelen as a dark ripple on the horizon. He remembered that CreSam was leaving for Tanelen the last time they saw each other. This memory triggered an epiphany, as he recalled that Tanelen was the home of the Technological Guild. The advanced technology used by the Avatars of Fate implied a connection between the two, but it was as of yet impossible to distinguish whether the relationship was parasitic or symbiotic. Were it symbiotic, CreSam could have been traveling to Tanelen to iron out the terms of his impending enlistment.

"Hey you," Eytea cooed, nudging his arm with hers as she settled next to him, "What are you watching?"

"Do you see that line on the horizon?" he pointed out, "That's Tanelen. It's bringing back some rather uncomfortable memories.'

Eytea studied him before replying, "I'll not pry. You'd volunteer the memories if you wished them shared, wouldn't you?"

Sinkua nodded, still watching the faint southern coast drift past and knowing that ArcNos was now less than half a day away.

"Did you find it odd that Galo mentioned a welcoming committee?" Eytea asked, changing the subject from what manner of unpleasant thoughts consumed Sinkua.

"Why would that be odd? We're returning on a stolen ship," Sinkua dismissed, turning away from the railing.

"True, but it was salvaged from a junkyard. Do you suppose they monitor rubbish heaps for theft?"

"Ones with military grade equipment, I would think so. Even if they don't, they might know we're coming and be on the prowl for suspicious vessels."

"Wait, wait, wait," Eytea urged, "How would anybody of consequence to the ArcNosian military know that we were…"

She was cut short by a bellowing foghorn to the west. Everyone perked up, turning to face the front of the ship. Recognizing the tone of the horn, Phylus approached the bow with his hands exposed. MalVek sidestepped to the coffers, and from the mist came a domineering ArcNosian war brig. Here was the welcoming committee of which Galo spoke.

"VanSen," Sinkua muttered behind gritting teeth.

"Hoy there!" Phylus blindly called, unable to see the deck of the towering ship as it neared, "I was hoping perhaps we could reach some sort of agreement as to our safe passage. I understand we're traveling on stolen goods, but this ship had been sent to the junkyard. It would be like punishing the dog for partaking of the fat trimmings, a pointless bother and a might unjustifiable, don't you think? Besides, it's been reconditioned, so perhaps we could trade you the restored components when we make port."

The bow of the war brig yawned, and a massive cannon emerged from its throat. The diplomatic approach, though noble in its intent, appeared to be floundering.

"No interest in the junkyard ship?" Phylus asked, clinging to his composure, "What about the Tournament then? MalVek's participation surely spiked ticket sales, what with all the political controversy. Perhaps the fact that he bolstered your profits should buy us safe passage."

The cannon lowered to take aim directly at the middle of the deck.

"Not that either?" Phylus called back, running low on ideas, "Well then, perhaps we could…"

"Drop!" MalVek bellowed.

Shocked by the outburst, everybody immediately complied and fell to the deck. MalVek barreled forth from the stern of the ship, his sledgehammer held behind. The cannon fired and he hurled the hammer with an animalistic roar that could rattle the foundation of the most stoic people. The hammer collided with the cannonball, detonating it into large chunks of shrapnel. A couple of pieces stuck in the mast, the cannon's apparent target. As the smoke cleared, everyone rose to their feet.

"They take roughly a minute to reload," MalVek announced, "We need to strike swiftly or make a strategic escape."

"We can't possibly strike back against it. I vote we flee, as much as I hate to admit defeat," Spril urged.

"The cannons don't need to work, so long as we have ammunition," Galo interjected after a moment of silent deliberation, "How much does a cannonball weigh?"

"Eighty kilograms, perhaps," Spril answered, "Why?"

"What about a cannon?"

"Some eight hundred kilograms or so," MalVek answered.

"Perfect!" Galo announced, backing up toward the stern, "As many of you as it takes, grab a cannon and push it overboard at the bow."

Everyone looked at him in baffled silence, dumbfounded by his order. A wry smirk slowly spread over Sinkua's face. He had a suspicion, and, were it correct, Galo's success would prove a remarkable feat.

"You heard the man!" Sinkua shouted, "To a cannon!"

Joined by MalVek, Spril and Yrlis, he made for the foremost starboard cannon. Phylus stomped the bowsprit loose before stepping aside. From the stern of the ship, Galo called for them to signal when it was about to drop. The war brig's cannon took aim again. Sinkua gave Galo the signal, and Galo hit full sprint toward the bow.

They shoved the cannon overboard when Galo was halfway between the mast and the bow, his chest heaving as adrenaline coursed through his body like blood. Certain of his suspicion, Sinkua crouched and interlocked his fingers. Galo stepped into his hands and was launched in cooperation with the strength of his own legs. From within the brig, the sound of a striking match could be heard. From the sea erupted a mighty pillar of water as the discarded cannon shattered the surface. Galo froze the water beneath his feet, from the top down, and sprang through the cannon bay.

He entered to find the wick freshly lit. In an improvised panic, he grabbed the barrel and shoved the cannon back, slamming it against the operator. Unbeknownst to him, his good fortune lay in the fact that the wheels had not been properly locked. In an adrenalized fury, he spun the cannon on its mount, aiming it downward and toward the rear of the ship as the wick burnt out.

Galo jumped back as the cannon recoiled upon firing. Despite his acrobatic talents, he stumbled back through the cannon bay and into the sea in front of his bobbing ice pillar. Aboard the brig, the shot from within blasted through each layer of lower deck, spraying wooden shrapnel with each pass, and finally exploded through the hull. Galo could see the damage of the explosion especially well from his watery vantage point.

When Galo emerged from the water, Sinkua was crouched atop his teetering column of ice, extending his morningstar downward and holding the bow with his other hand. Galo grabbed the chain was pulled atop the ice. Once that was accomplished, Sinkua pulled himself back aboard the ship, and Galo followed shortly behind.

Everyone was bewildered by the stunt, though Sinkua stood out from them all, what with his odd propensity to laugh at such a situation. MalVek was first to break the stunned silence.

"How was that even possible?" he asked in belief, bordering on anger, "How the fuck did you pull that off!?"

"That's what I'd like to know," Sinkua added, still laughing as the brig sunk before them, "That was incredible!"

"My plan only went as far as getting through the bay," Galo admitted, "What happened next was spur of the moment and probably just lucky."

"Of course it was," MalVek accepted, trying to calm himself.

Galo and Sinkua both brushed it off as enraged envy. He who thought himself to be the alpha male had just been upstaged by a new dog in the pack. It made sense for him to be so animatedly perturbed. Eytea found it rather more suspicious than that, though it may have had to do with her lack of experience with team dynamics and especially alpha males. That inexperience could have hidden a sensible truth from her, or it may have allowed her to notice a deeper subtext to his outrage.

"Provided we have no other interruptions, we should reach ArcNos in the late morning. We should all get some sleep until then," Phylus suggested, ending the silence that had laid thick since MalVek's last remark, "Sinkua, can you steer us around the wreckage and set it straight west again before you settle in for the night?"

"I'm on it."

As the rest of them dispersed, Eytea halted Galo. Sinkua watched apprehensively from the wheel as she clutched his bicep. Eytea peered back to ascertain that MalVek was out of earshot before turning to face Galo again.

"Are you alright?" she pried, "You seem shaken."

"By what? By the cannon and that war brig?" Galo asked, "It was rather overwhelming, but my pulse feels to be calming."

"No, I mean by MalVek," she corrected, drawing herself closer so as to shroud her words from distant ears, "what with how he nigh threatened you for that feat.'

"Don't worry about it,' Galo assured her, stepping back, "He likely feels threatened as the physically dominant one in the group."

Fatigued, he departed to find a heap of discarded burlap to lie upon. Eytea stood alone at the middle of the ship, finding no comfort in Galo's words. A small hand set upon her shoulder, and she turned to find Vielle had surreptitiously approached from behind. Vielle looked up at her concernedly.

"Are you alright?" she asked, "You look a bit frightened."

"It's not myself I'm frightened for."

Toward the back of the ship, Spril grabbed MalVek by the shoulder and spun him about to face him.

"You care to explain that little outburst back there?" Spril barked.

"It's of no concern to you, kid," MalVek spat.

"It's of great concern to me," Spril corrected, "We can't afford to push any of the Hybrids away, and in case you haven't figured it out, those three are a package deal."

"Did you notice that ship used outdated cannons?" MalVek asked, changing the subject, "Why do you suppose that is?"

Chapter 23

The eastern skyline was raked with orange cirrus claws as the sun climbed over the horizon. Through blurred eyes, it appeared as though the horizon had been set ablaze. Land approached a few hours ahead of schedule, thanks to a nocturnal tailwind for which Phylus had not accounted. Just as he did have the foresight to intend though, they struck land a few kilometers from the nearest operational port. Three or so kilometers of dense forest lie ahead, but it was a better greeting than they may have received otherwise, especially if the war brig transmitted an alert before its nautical demise. All but Phylus and Galo climbed down to the sand, and Phylus retracted the ladder.

"Galo!" Sinkua shouted up to the deck, "I need to ask you something before you go!"

Galo fished in his pack and withdrew a pouch of the herbal mixture he had used to open Sinkua's throat in the arena. He held it up to show and pitched it down to him.

"If you have an episode, have Eytea mix that with water to make a pulp!" Galo called back, "She also has your backup pills!"

"Thanks! Have a safe trip!"

"How did he know what you wanted?" Eytea asked in astonishment.

"We've known each other his entire life," Sinkua explained, "After a few years, you start picking up on things."

A dismally minimal amount of light punctured the dense canopy to fall upon the forest floor. The trees themselves were especially thick, this area having been protected by environmentalist agencies for several generations. Handfuls of rare and endangered species, particularly of bugs and plants, were indigenous to that area.

A rotting root snapped under Yrlis's step, but Spril swiftly snatched her by the arm before she took a fall. She clutched his hand as she regained her balance and warded off a moment of vertigo.

"You have to be careful around Glaucus Firs like that one," Vielle warned, "The mature ones have weak roots."

"Don't larger trees need stronger roots?" Yrlis asked as they continued hiking.

"That's what's so interesting about the Glaucus Fir," Vielle explained, "You can tell a tree's age by its rings, and you can tell how many times a Glaucus has tried to reproduce by the strength of its roots. When fertile cones fall from it, they feed on the roots until they grow into saplings."

"Wait, so the tree is basically getting eaten by its children?"

"Pretty macabre, isn't it? It's a close relative of the Sisyphus Fir, basically the end result of an attempt to breed them here."

"Sounds as if you know quite a lot about trees," Sinkua noted, "I can see why you latched to Galo as quickly as you did."

"Herbal medicine does make me curious," Vielle admitted, "It can't just be a coincidence that it worked for the Berininites for so long, can it?"

"It can if you consider the placebo effect," Yrlis interjected.

"You can't honestly think that everybody who's been cured by an herbal remedy was only healed because they believed it would work," Vielle contested, standing akimbo.

"I know it to be true," Yrlis countered, "and if disbelief in something invalidates it, it isn't science. Science is truth whether you believe it or not, and real medicine works whether you believe in it or not. Unlike what those jungle whelps have been…"

"I just got a brilliant idea," Eytea announced, "Let's all try to go one day without talking shit about our allies, shall we? Especially allies who have left their own people behind to travel across the continent and save our sorry asses instead."

A distant thunder resonated throughout the trees, suggesting in impending noonday downpour, but the sky indicated otherwise. Save for small handful of clouds, the sky was oddly clear for ArcNos that close to the Frigid. Avoiding a thunderstorm in such cold conditions would undoubtedly be a boon, but few alternative explanations for that thunder would have been better than getting caught in the rain.

"Does anybody else hear that?" Vielle asked, bracing herself against a tree as she stepped over its jutting roots.

"If you mean the thunder, I think we all hear it," Sinkua answered, "We just kept quiet until now."

"No, not that; I know we can all hear that," Vielle clarified, "I keep hearing voices, only vaguely. I can't tell what they're saying, just that they're coming from up ahead."

Nobody gave any vocal regard to Vielle's claims, but the silence among them grew increasingly uncomfortable as they neared the city limits. The thunder grew louder, and eventually a rhythm could be heard in it. It was methodical. Deliberate. Mechanical. When the city was in sight, the voices became audible to all, but what they said was of little consequence.

A smoky reddish glow loomed over the city, obstructed from within the forest. Baritone sirens blared and pulsated, the sound puncturing through numerous holes in the streets. Citizens fled, all diverging from a single point, as buildings toppled around them. A small car engulfed in flames came careening their way and smashed into the asphalt a few meters shy of the entourage.

Eytea motioned for everyone else to stop as she turned her attention to Sinkua, gazing apprehensively into his eyes. Sinkua stared blankly at the smoldering rubble that was once a vehicle, absorbing the carnage in his peripheral vision. Bodies were crushed under collapsing buildings. Others fell carelessly through the holes in the street, either to their death or crippled agony. Fiery vehicles crashed through third story windows, and those left standing choked on the blood-laced smog and waves of smoldering ash. His eyes grew wide, his teeth ground against each other, and his breathing became ragged. Before he collapsed, he managed to utter a single expletive through his gritting teeth.

He fell to his knees, hacking blood over the already crimson stained asphalt. His spilt would nary be noticeable among the others, a death here being nothing short of inconsequential. Eytea pulled a pinch of herbs from her pocket, spat upon them furiously, and rubbed the mixture into a pulp.

"Yrlis!" she shouted, since Yrlis was closest, "Hold his head back!"

Yrlis's hands trembled uncontrollably. Anxiously, she staggered back a couple of steps. Blood pooled in Sinkua's throat more quickly than he could expel it. A gurgle echoed from the depths of his esophagus with every choking cough. Somehow appearing to be the only other one who didn't fear him during his episodes, Vielle shoved Yrlis out of her way as she rushed to Sinkua's side. She knelt beside him and tilted his head back, whispering softly.

"Vielle, don't!" Spril urged, "He's dangerous. He doesn't know what's going on."

"He's not a monster, Uncle Spril," Vielle insisted, "He knows me. He won't hurt me."

She continued to whisper to him as Eytea spat upon the pulp once more. Sinkua gasped repeatedly, almost seeming deliberate. He coughed forcibly a few times, spraying blood farther than it had gone yet. Vielle ran her fingers through his hanging locks and kept whispering to him comfortingly. Through the gasps and between the hacks came a sound that left nearly all of them awestruck.

"Help," he muttered hoarsely, straining to crane his neck and face Eytea.

Eytea fell to her knees, disregarding the pain of her joints smacking against the asphalt. She swabbed a copious helping of the pulp over her index finger. When he started coughing again, she shoved her digit in his mouth and swiped the pulp on the roof. He faintly nodded as she withdrew her finger, and the blood trickling forth slowly thinned. Soon, his throat was clear, but the episode seemed not to have waned. His breathing was still ragged, and he continued to grind his teeth. As he got to his feet, he coughed and spat blood once more, but his hacking was contained and controlled. Vielle steadied him, still calming him with her whispers.

"Sinkua?" Eytea asked, "Do you know where you are?"

"Home," he muttered, "Living nightmare."

"How do you feel?" Vielle asked.

"Agony. Rage," he mumbled, pausing for a moment, "Control."

As far as any of them could tell, Vielle had saved Sinkua from blacking out but had not stopped the episode. Obviously, the drug cocktail was still hard at work, perpetuating his anger into excruciating pain. Her soft familiar voice had served as a counteracting stimulus, anchoring him to reality and consciousness. Eytea offered him one of his pills. He held up his hand and politely declined, still staring forward into the spreading wreckage.

"Need this," he uttered as he staggered deeper into the city.

"Yrlis, can you and Vielle get someplace safe?" Eytea asked.

"I, I don't know if there's even…" Yrlis stammered.

"I'll find one. Come on!" MalVek urged as he snatched her by the arm, his other hand already being clutched by Vielle.

"Eytea, keep whispering to him!" Vielle ordered as she was led away.

Eytea and Spril remained, following Sinkua's lead. All about, missiles struck concrete, exploding on impact and radially spewing fiery wreckage. Of those who died, the ones caught in such blasts were the most fortunate to be ended so quickly. The sight of it was no less horrendous, smoldering fragments of corpses strewn over asphalt and brick in a chokingly macabre display of humanity's fragility before its own creations.

Their surroundings became increasingly morbid, and the thunder grew louder. Through the bloody smog, an outline of a figure could be discerned, one that dwarfed the sentries Spril had faced with MalVek and even the amphibious colossus

Sinkua had faced with Galo. Sinkua had been deliberately following the noise. This was his nightmare, and he intended to see it through.

As the wind parted the smog, a towering mechanical monolith came into clear view, quadrupedal by structural necessity. Its prehensile plated tail repeatedly whipped the asphalt, turning it asunder. Upward from the center, where the four legs converged, sat the torso of the armored beast, stained with bloody sinew and riddled with armaments. The scattered burns upon its surface could undoubtedly be attributed only to damage that it had caused, for it was otherwise structurally immaculate. From bays within its shoulders, a slew of missiles zipped through the air like blow darts and raped the avenue. When it came near enough that craning his neck to see the titan's head became painful, which still put it several meters away, Sinkua stopped and signaled for Eytea and Spril to do likewise.

"Got leaves?" Sinkua asked, the swelling rage of his macabre ailment hindering his speech.

"Yes, Galo gave me quite a bit, why?" Eytea asked.

"Gimme some," he ordered, "Spril ahead. Eytea follow."

"Should we trust him like this?" Spril asked.

"If it looks like he's going to get himself or either of us killed, we can stray from the plan," Eytea assured, "but the best thing for now is to follow along."

Spril and Eytea continued a few meters further until Sinkua called for them to halt. Eytea turned back to await further instruction, while Spril stared up at the colossus apprehensively.

"This thing is getting dangerously close," Spril announced anxiously, "We need to either fight back or haul ass."

"Spril! Staff! Eytea!" Sinkua shouted through gurgles of blood.

"I think he wants you to hand me your quarterstaff," Eytea clarified.

Spril shrugged and complied, to which Sinkua bellowed, "No! Spril! Eytea! Staff!"

Spril looked at him with an eyebrow arched, then to Eytea for a translation. Eytea shrugged and shook her head in dissent. Spril looked back at the approaching monolith and noticed a split in the knees when its legs bent.

"Hand me one end of my quarterstaff," Spril ordered, "He needs leverage."

"Finally decided to trust him?" Eytea asked, offering and end of the staff.

"Might as well see what this guy can do," Spril agreed as he tenaciously clutched the staff.

Sinkua grinned and nodded, poising himself for a dash. A mechanical foot set down behind Spril, who tightened his grip on the polearm. His pulse accelerated, fearing that either of them would soon be crushed, slain for trusting a man barely in control of his own mentality. Sinkua placed the mixture of leaves in his mouth, soaking it on his tongue, and burst forth in a sprint, leaving a small tower of flames where he stood. As he neared the horizontal quarterstaff, he leapt and sprang off of it, the impact pulling both Eytea and Spril down in spite of their rigidity. The moment he was airborne again, Spril took the staff, and they scattered.

Sinkua flailed his arms upward and grasped the split in the bent knee of the giant, deftly pulling himself up into it. The knee began to close as the leg came down. He jumped onto the thigh, scrambled up the ever steepening incline, and bounded onto a narrow ledge surrounding the torso. As he stared up it, he turned to spit a mouthful of blood upon one of the legs. His own saliva mixed with the leaves was assuaging the swell of blood in his throat, allowing him to breathe, but he knew it would only serve as a stopgap solution.

"I assume you can't carry him in flight," Spril pondered.

"No, I can't," Eytea regretfully confirmed, "Otherwise he would have a much easier time of this, wouldn't he?"

"Can you at least slow him if he falls?"

"That much, I can do."

"Be ready to do that," Spril ordered, "Just in case."

His breathing growing ragged and a stream of thinned blood trickling from his mouth, Sinkua agilely scaled the torso of the monstrosity. For all the destruction it caused at such close range, the structure of it was remarkably sound. Fueled by adrenalized rage and a sort of borderline superhuman strength, Sinkua barreled upward, hurling his body from one handhold to the next. Soon, he sat upon its shoulder.

He could hear odd noises next to him, clicks and beeps. He put an ear to the side of the monolith's head, and they not only became clearer but were now accompanied by vague mutterings. Just as in his nightmare, this sentinel was piloted, and unlike the one he had encountered in Berinin, it sounded as though it was piloted by an individual soldier. He clung to the side of its head with one hand and sidled out onto the chin, crouching under the windshield. In his other hand, he held his morningstar, the head glowing red with intense heat.

A massive burst of flames exploded from the head of the morningstar. Sinkua flung it upward with incredible force and jerked downward with equally impressive momentum as it lay over the windshield. The glass cracked in a growing spider web pattern, and he could hear the expletive outburst from the pilot within. He shuffled back to the shoulder while the pilot leaned toward the windshield in useless hopes of a better view.

After fastening the chain of his weapon, Sinkua moved around to the back of the head and frantically scaled it. Soon, he stood atop the zenith of the beast. He double checked the bindings on the chain and purged the blood from his mouth. He braced himself, took two steps forward, and leapt from atop the colossus.

From the ground, it appeared to have all been an elaborate and garish suicide. When the pilot looked up and saw that body looming above, he knew otherwise. Sinkua landed with both clenched fists and both booted feet striking simultaneously. For the weakened structure of the glass, he crashed straight through and landed between the pilot and the control console. His body covered in glass shards and the blood stains on his clothes growing, he looked at the control panel with befuddlement. He looked back over his shoulder to see a familiar face, though that man's previous hubris toward him was replaced with fear and dismay.

"VanSen!" Sinkua shouted, "Turn off!"

"Piss off, freak," VanSen stuttered halfheartedly.

Sinkua spat a mouthful of saliva-laced blood at VanSen's face, grabbed him by the shirt collar, and slammed his head against the console in one swift motion.

"Turn off!" he bellowed again.

VanSen elbowed him in the stomach, hoping to bring him to his knees. Instead, quite to his chagrin, Sinkua simply gritted his teeth, squeezing moisture from the remainder of the herbal mixture. Again, VanSen found his head slammed against the console.

"Off!" Sinkua commanded for a third time.

VanSen finally complied, pounding his hand against a button on the side of the console. The cockpit jostled as the mechanical beast came to an abrupt halt. Outside, the creaking of snapped metal and the crumbling of severely compromised structures became abundantly loud over the sudden silence of the monolith.

"Now what?" VanSen asked bitterly.

Sinkua erected himself, jerking VanSen's body upright. He turned his back to the open windshield and stared at VanSen, his glare burning through him as a fiery hand burned into his chest. Despite the pain of his flesh being boiled, VanSen was paralyzed by fear. He wanted desperately to look away, but he was transfixed on the luminescent malachite stare that consumed him.

Sinkua swallowed repeatedly, trying with little avail to clear his throat long enough to inhale more than a small gasp. His teeth clenched as his jaw became painfully rigid. As he clutched VanSen's shirt, choking him with fear, his anger swelled unrelentingly. In a fleeting glimpse of control, Sinkua's jaw popped loose and his arms relaxed slightly. With this opportunity, he shouted a single word.

"Out!"

He twisted and hurled VanSen over the console and out the front of the halted monstrosity's head. He collapsed to his knees, hacking blood across the floor as VanSen screamed toward the asphalt. He pounded his fist repeatedly, desperately grasping for a shred of control that was not to be had. A distant crashing sound, followed by a rumbling, echoed through the floor. It was accompanied first by another, then by several more. These were the last sounds he heard as he blacked out and collapsed on the floor of the cockpit, blood pouring from his mouth.

In his descent, VanSen withdrew a remote control and engaged the detonation of the monolith, his final attempt to rid the ArcNosian Empire of the fiery Hybrid. From the feet up, segments of the titan swelled and shattered, soon leaving only the head which, because the speed of the destruction, still hung scores of meters in the air.

"Eytea! Quickly!" Spril urged.

Though they had fallen back to stay clear, Eytea was perilously near the beast and already in flight when the self-destruction began. Where she had last stood was a spray of ash from the blast of electricity that burst from her body as she launched herself upward through the fires. With forceful beats of her amaranthine wings, she streaked toward the plummeting head. Because of its imbalance, it tipped forward, and out fell Sinkua's unconscious body. Eytea could hear a distant scream of opposition, but chose to ignore it and angled herself toward Sinkua's falling body, hoping to intersect their paths.

Her heroism was interrupted by leafy vines rapidly surrounding her. They grew all about at an unnatural rate, initially to her dismay, but soon to her relief as they enveloped Sinkua's body and eased him to a halt. Confused but calmed, Eytea flew over to join him, perching on a nearby tangle of vines. Her panic quickly waned at the sight of him, unconscious and battered but safe and alive, she found a sense of tranquility in spite of the dilapidation of their environs.

"Does your father know about this?" Spril asked, kneeling.

Barely awake with her head resting on his hand, Vielle whispered, "It's a secret."

Galo stood at the center of a semicircular room, the arc lined with twelve seats. Two of them were empty, the gold plates set before them indicating that they were otherwise reserved for CreSam and himself. Along the wall behind him, every nation's flag was draped, one over each of twelve doors. Just as in the Union Parliament Hall, those bringing business before the Union were only permitted in the passageway allocated to their nation of current citizenship.

"What business do you bring before us today, Chieftain Sage Galo?" the Noble Doyen of Tanelen asked.

"It is regarding my title, sir," Galo replied nervously but respectfully.

"You do not care for the label of Chieftain Sage?" Prime Duchess Olsa pried, eyeing the young leader and seeming to size him up.

"No madam, I do not care for my inheritance of it," Galo corrected, "Great leadership comes not from one's lineage but rather from proper training and experience, as well as an ability to understand the people. I only have one of those traits, and in my eyes, that does not qualify me to be entrusted with maintaining the growth and stability effected by my grandfather."

"You wish to step down from your post, then?" the Grand Sultan of Ferya posed, "Do you understand the tradition you are breaking? The men of your lineage have led Berinin for several centuries. Have you thought this through thoroughly?"

"Since the end of this past Swelter, I have dwelled on this decision. And for what reason have the men in my family always led? Beyond tradition, what qualifies us to do so?" Galo argued, "However, I only intend to step down temporarily. If, after two years, I still feel inadequately prepared, I will decide how to proceed. My eschewing of the title may or may not become permanent."

"According to protocol, Judge Nenbard would replace you, and an interim Judge will be elected to fill his seat in the Union Parliament," the High Magistrate of Haprian explained, "I have just one more question for you, though."

Galo stared at the floor for a moment before he looked up and answered the anticipated question as firmly as he could manage, "Yes, the freedom to pursue Masnethege's assailants is my ulterior motive for this decision, but it is not my primary reason."

"Fair enough, Galo," the Haprianite leader accepted, "We will round up the paperwork, and once you sign it tomorrow morning, you will be relieved of your duties as Chieftain Sage of Berinin until two years from today."

Across the street, Phylus anxiously treaded the ArcNosian corridor in the Union Parliament Hall. Beyond the double doors, he was met with a room strikingly similar to the one in which Galo had stood, except it donned thirteen chairs, the central chair elevated significantly. The chair for the ArcNosian Judge remained empty, as did the central seat. He stood before them, awkward and apprehensive, with a stack of papers clutched in his hand.

Occasionally, he and the Eprilenese Judge caught each other's eyes, seemingly making and breaking eye contact in unison. Her shirt had short sleeves, and when she leaned forth to rest her breasts atop her forearms, she revealed the bottom of a tattoo on her upper arm. Phylus wanted a better look to verify his suspicion, but instead he looked away for fear that she might think he was staring at her full chest. Still, he was at least certain of her familiarity, but it was mostly because of disbelief that he was not convinced of his notion.

Prime Duchess Olsa entered from his right, waving to him and excusing herself for her tardiness. She shuffled around the end of the table and made her way to the central seat.

"So then," she began, "what brings you before the Union Parliament today, Phylus?"

"Secession," he firmly announced, instigating a clamor among the small crowd.

"You wish to secede from the ArcNosian government?" Olsa asked nervously, "Do you understand the undertaking you will be attempting?"

"This is not an attempt, nor is it a simple protest," Phylus argued, "We have secured a locale for our sovereign nation, raised the necessary capital, and developed an economic structure including a taxation system. The only thing we lack is approval."

"How many citizens can your capital accommodate by current standards?" Olsa asked.

"Three hundred, twenty percent above the necessary quota."

"And where will your nation be located?"

"In ArcNos's Subtransit for the time being," Phylus answered, losing the edge in his voice for fear that the location may ruin their plan.

"So, you intend to develop a sovereign community on ArcNosian property?"

"We already have developed a community of our own, because their political and economic overhauls drove the working class into the streets," Phylus countered, "Furthermore, the Subtransit is privately owned, because Brigadier General Elite CreSam could not force or buy IlcBei out. She's one of our three hundred citizens."

"I stand corrected. Consider my previous argument null," Olsa humbly accepted, "However, there still remains the issue of geographical coordinates. Your cities would possess the same latitudinal and longitudinal measurements as the cities above them. No two geopolitical landmarks are permitted to possess identical coordinates."

"Actually, madam, they can in this instance," the Lenguardian Judge interjected, creating another clamor, "The Lenguardian Geographical Survey Committee recognizes depth or elevation as a third coordinate to distinguish landmarks. This change was brought about when the commonality of basement apartments necessitated allowing their occupants to register a different street address than their ground level landlords."

"Do you mean to tell me that the Subtransit of an ArcNosian city can be considered a different city in and of itself, provided they have the necessary capital and political and economic structures?" Olsa asked, apparently perturbed by the development.

"Certainly sounds that way," Phylus remarked with a cocky smirk, sensing her inexplicable annoyance at his success thus far, "but I understand such a matter must be put to a vote. I will return tomorrow at this time, and I expect to find my approval signed and notarized."

He turned around to exit but stopped to give the Eprilenese Judge one more glance. Indeed it was her. He spun about for an addendum with the ulterior motive of a longer look. She sickened him, but for some bizarre reason, he found it worse to try to divert his attention.

"In the event that my proposal is rejected," he continued confidently, "I will still be moving forward with my plan."

Without another word or pause for a response, he exited the Hall.

Their business through for the time being, he and Galo reunited for supper at a seafood restaurant a few kilometers from the two international establishments. Rather than hop a trolley or hail a cab, they chose to walk. The weather was a tad brisk for the southern Midlands but still unseasonably warm. Galo clutched his robe around his body, while Phylus left his clothes as they were.

During the walk, they conversed quite sparingly about the political revolution they were effecting and instead kept it to home life and such. Phylus mentioned having been a baseball pitcher during college, which led to an in-depth explanation of baseball, given Galo's absolute absence of prior exposure to the game. Soon thereafter, the conversation shifted to Phylus's daughter.

"I think I understand why your daughter has attached herself to me," Galo awkwardly supposed.

"Keep in mind, you're speaking to her father," Phylus countered, trying to appear undaunted by Galo's stature, "So wield your words cautiously."

"She grew up without a mother, too," Galo postulated, "didn't she?"

"Yrlis is the closest she's ever had to a maternal influence," Phylus confirmed, calming significantly as he took a long drag from his cigarette, "and that girl ain't much of one."

"Everybody who knows my name knows my story. Parents died before my first birthday, and I was raised in their stead by my widower grandfather."

"You were born into much greater expectations than she was," Phylus added, understanding and agreeing with Galo's reasoning, "She might believe that if she can discover how you've held together under so much pressure, she can learn how to thrive without a mother figure, too."

They stopped before a large dark green awning extending from a brick building. Scrawled across the front in painted white cursive was the name of the establishment, The Half Shell Pearl. Judging by the name, most people would have rightfully assumed the place specialized in all manner of oysters.

To ease the trouble of deciding, they both opted for a sampler platter. Those consisted of oysters prepared in nearly every way offered along with a choice of four dipping sauces. They collaborated their efforts to ensure they received no duplicate sauces. To anybody who didn't recognize them, they appeared to be nothing more than a couple of excited seafood aficionados. That was exactly what they wanted, but the experience was culinarily tantalizing enough that acting was unnecessary.

After their meal, they headed to a hotel for the night. It was a midtown place, not particularly upscale, but decent enough that they needed not worry about their temporary neighbors bringing in hookers and drug dealers and whatnot. At the last minute, Galo insisted on footing the bill for a room of his own across the hall from Phylus's. He explained that he felt awkward being one of only two people sleeping in a room, a discomfort that Phylus found odd but one with which he complied anyway.

Upon entering his room, Galo plopped down in a large armchair. Nearby, atop a small bureau sat a fresh daily newspaper. Judging by the fact that it was still in its bindings, he assumed it had been delivered that morning after the previous guest had checked out. He unfolded it to read the front page, but an article on the back page captivated his attention. The headline claimed that a letter suggesting a conspiracy to shroud the nature of Judge Mikalan's death had been a hoax.

In spite of his bitterness, he read on about how it was part of a plot by a militant regime to undermine international coordination. The only mention of the Avatars of Fate was to dispel them as a rumor, also created and perpetuated by this antiestablishment militia, designed to instill fear and deflect both attention and blame. It came as no surprise that they would hide their own existence, but the fact that underground ArcNosians knew their name suggested that they were speaking it in public fora. This brought him to ponder how they could expect this truth to not leave ArcNosian borders and spread onto foreign soil.

His ponderings were interrupted by a rapping at the door, one to which he quickly turned his attention.

"Galo," Colonel SenRas greeted as the door was opened, "Mind if I come in?"

"Go right ahead," Galo invited, stepping aside, "I nary expected to see you again so soon, much less for you to come looking for me here."

"It is for your own good, Galo," SenRas reminded, sitting at the foot of the bed, "I needed to see to it that you followed through successfully."

"Do you fear you cannot trust me?" Galo asked, returning to the armchair.

"I fear I cannot trust others," SenRas corrected, "Due to crimes committed, we no longer have a seat in the Union or the Union Parliament. That means we've no messenger to relay news that you have stepped down and dissociated yourself from any threats sent by Nalygen and Borret."

"What of the threats already transmitted? Do you really think your people to be the sort to simply stand down when they hear the man they think threatened them has done the same?"

"A copy of the paperwork will prove those letters to be forgeries, thanks to the handwriting sample you will have provided."

Galo glanced at the newspaper on the arm of the chair, a conflict of calm and rage rolling in his mind. On the one hand, he was eased by the knowledge that the purported threats were soon to be disregarded and that his people would be in more capable hands. Three quarters of the voting population had elected Nenbard to represent them in the Union Parliament, so it stood to reason that they saw him fit to lead. However, he found it difficult to distract himself from accusations of spreading an anarchist hoax.

"Why did you come here to my room?" Galo asked, pulling himself away from that back page headline, "Certainly, you have more reason than to simply ease my mind."

"That I do. You are wise for your youth to read me so well," SenRas admitted, "I came here to confess something, something I must confess if I am ever to believe that you trust me."

"Before you confess, keep in mind that a single word can make you my enemy again," Galo cautioned as he folded the newspaper and laid it atop the bureau.

"I ordered the attack on Masnethege," SenRas announced shakily.

Galo sprang from the chair and rushed to SenRas's side, his arm extended with a blade of ice jutting from his tightly clenched fist.

"You were warned, and yet still you spoke," Galo snarled, "Either you're running from something and would rather die at my hands, or something you need to show me looms behind that wall of guilt. There's a third possibility, but I'm willing to give you the benefit of the doubt for the time being."

"What's the third…?"

"That you're just plain stupid. Now keep talking, and we'll figure out which it is."

"The scale of it was greater than I had intended, likely Amirione's doing, or so I thought," SenRas continued, "CreSam had fortified the platoon from a small troop to the onslaught which you witnessed."

"So, you meant only to scare us?" Galo concluded, relaxing his arm slightly, "What of the order regarding my grandfather?"

"CreSam said no such thing; he never spoke of Gijin," SenRas elucidated, "That order was mine only and part of the initial mission briefing as I had penned it. The Avatars nary take orders from me, so I thought it might be more effective if he believed the order came from the top. Obviously, I was wrong about that."

"You put your own life at risk to save his," Galo commended, lowering his arm and retracting the frigid blade, "and now you've risked it again to let it be known. I've no need to kill you today."

"Thank you, I feel a greatly relieved. Do you feel you can trust me?"

"I need to know more first. What was it you were after, you personally, in Berinin?"

"Revolution. The Avatars have infected ArcNos with immeasurable militant aggression against which no single nation can stand. However, were we to strike Masnethege and let Gijin live under the given pretense of forcing subjugation, the respect he commanded would have been enough to turn the majority of Ouristihra against ArcNos and crush the new order."

"But because of my inexperience, I do not command that same respect," Galo agreed, "One more thing, you sounded as though you were surprised to learn that CreSam had ordered a larger fleet to attack Berinin. Why is that?"

"Because I was surprised. Initially, he had his own agenda with the Avatars. He never shared it with me, but I've always suspected he had a particular disdain for them. He seemed to be following their agenda only as much as he needed to get to the top while harboring secret ulterior motives. So his order is a might puzzling to me. Was I wrong about him, or was he only doing what he thought necessary to keep his plans from being interrupted?"

"I suspect you were wrong about him, but I have a limited scope through which to judge CreSam's character," Galo admitted, "If you were right, do you suspect his motives to have been worse than those of the Avatars?"

"I do not know the Avatars' motives," SenRas confessed, "Nobody seems to know. However, the idea of accepting CreSam's over theirs is moot. They've cut off many of his memories, possibly because they anticipated he might rebel. I've got a hunch that they haven't erased them but have simply blocked conscious access. I've been trying to reach my ex-wife on the matter. She's a neuropsychiatrist, so she ought to be able to help, although I'll probably have to do it behind his back."

"How much of his memory have they tampered with?" Galo asked, a discernable hint of worry in his voice.

"He would not recognize his own son."

Across the hall, Phylus found his attention bitterly absorbed by the same article. He didn't know of the letter's origins, but he had his suspicions. Unaware of the coincidence, he wondered as he read it if Galo had done the same. Since he knew firsthand of the Avatars of Fate, he knew that the article was a hoax itself. This confirmed that their influence had reached Eprilen, engendering compliance either willingly or out of fear.

Just like Galo, he too was interrupted by a knocking at the door. Not expecting company and thus being in no hurry to answer, he carefully folded the newspaper and set it neatly upon the center of the bureau. The knocking repeated as he heaved himself onto his feet. He casually shuffled barefoot across the carpet as the person at the door knocked for a third time. When he opened it, he was understandably taken aback.

"Hi, Phylus," she sheepishly greeted, "Do you remember me?"

"Malia," he gasped, losing himself in her eyes, "Of course I remember you. Come in."

"How long has it been now? Seventeen years, I believe. I hope you've been well."

"You know how I've been doing."

"Oh come now, don't give me that lost puppy act," Malia argued, easing closer to him, "We all know you're stronger than that."

Phylus set his hands upon her shoulders and bunched her sleeves to reveal her biceps. Adorning one of them was the indisputable marking of the Avatars of Fate.

"Why have you come here?" he asked bitterly.

"To remind myself what I gave up for this life, Phylus."

"You gave up a safe working class life with a husband and a family to be an empowered enemy of the state," Phylus iterated, "But now you want to know if it was the right choice?"

The moment he stopped speaking, she showed no hesitation in countering. She argued with her mouth but not with words. She thrust herself at him, wrapped her slender arms around his torso, and planted a firm kiss on his lips.

"I left you for my own reasons," she insisted, "The Avatars of Fate came later, and it was an opportunity I couldn't afford to pass up."

"Just as this is one you can't afford to miss, I assume," Phylus postulated, still embracing her and reminding himself of the warmth they shared in their youth, "Obviously, you aim to seduce me into leaking information."

"Obviously, I'm succeeding in seducing you," Malia wryly boasted, glancing downward, "but we both know I'd never succeed in making you turn on your people. You never were one to be bribed with sexual favors, at least not by me."

"Then you aim to use this as a scandal," Phylus argued, trying to reason against his physiological reaction to being in such tight quarters with her hourglass figure.

"Phylus honey, let me explain something to you," Malia began, pressing into him, "If I reveal that you, the leader of the underground nation, had sex with me, an Avatar of Fate, I'd be putting myself in far more danger than I would you. I'm not here for them. I'm here for my own agenda, one of curious lust. Nothing more."

"You say that, but how can I...?"

She kissed him again, this time with relentless use of her tongue. He forgot his argument. In fact, he forgot any reasons he had formulated as to why this was a bad idea. After all, she was the mother of his child. Even if she had no knowledge of that daughter, it didn't change the fact that bedding her mother was completely normal and acceptable.

What transpired was something of curious lust, exactly as Malia had promised. There were no allegiances, no alliances, and no scandals. They were merely two former lovers, separated for most of their adult lives and reunited for one opportune night. And they seized that night with tenacity comparable only to that with which they seized one another.

"Wow," Malia gasped as they finished, her body relaxing atop his.

"You're better than I remembered," Phylus added.

"I've had my share of practice," Malia boasted, "and I would dare say the same of you. Again, wow."

"Actually no, you were the last woman I had."

Malia rolled off and lay beside him, visibly surprised.

"You haven't had sex since the last time we were together? Did you turn homosexual or something?"

"No, I still prefer women, obviously."

"You weren't, y'know, waiting for me, were you?"

"You broke my heart, so that may have been the case for a while," Phylus admitted, "but don't flatter yourself. I decided to focus on my career instead of chasing tail all night."

"Well, whatever happened to you, it was definitely for the better. You'll make some woman very happy as soon as you let yourself. I almost regret that it wasn't me."

"So was I worth giving up for a life with the Avatars of Fate?" Phylus confidently asked.

"If I knew where my life was going to end up when I left you, I wouldn't have done it. The empowerment outweighs what you've shown me, but that greatly outweighs the risks," Malia explained.

"Then why not defect and join us against them?"

"I hope you're not always so quick to expect scandalous women to throw down their allegiances for a chance to throw themselves on your bed sheets," Malia laughed, "You're damn good, amazing even, but what I need from them, and would lose if I strayed, I can't get from returning to a life with you."

"Don't be so sure. I've got an amazing amount of resources at my disposal," Phylus bragged as he buckled his belt, "What is it you need from them?"

"That much, I can't say," Malia insisted as she fastened her bra.

"I suspected as much."

"But I can tell you this. You've improved incredibly, and while maybe you weren't quite the best I've ever had," she continued as she put on her shirt and got to her feet, "you were way better than CreSam."

Leaving him silently dumbfounded, she gave him a peck on the cheek and exited his hotel room.

Chapter 24

Following their encounter with the colossus, they headed inland roughly one hundred kilometers to the capitol of ArcNos. This was to be the site of their capitol, as well. Spril went ahead on his electric motorcycle to announce the arrival of newcomers, while the rest took a Subtransit train. Sinkua remained asleep for the duration.

"So, Vielle," Yrlis began awkwardly, "You're an Hybrid just like them."

"I guess so," Vielle nonchalantly accepted, avoiding eye contact.

"You don't guess so; you've known all along," MalVek corrected curiously, "That's why you ran off when you saw what Sinkua was doing, wasn't it?"

"Why did you keep this from us?" Yrlis asked accusingly, "This is the sort of thing that we deserve to know."

"We? The only connection you have to me is through Spril, and you went nearly a decade without speaking a word to him until you heard someone tried to kill him," Vielle snapped, "So, don't act like I'm selfish for not sharing intimate details of my life with you."

"Listen, I will not be spoken to in such a manner, certainly not by an immature child such as…"

"And exactly who are you?" Eytea interrupted, "You have no idea what she's gone through, coming to grips with her identity. Did you even think for a moment that she was keeping quiet to protect everyone else? If word got out that she was an Hybrid, they would come for her and kill anybody who interfered, and that includes her father and your bald-headed mantoy."

"What's your problem with me?" Yrlis barked "This is the second time you've snapped at me since we got to ArcNos."

"It's also the second time you've given me cause to do so. First it was trashing Galo's culture behind his back, and now you've lashed out at your boyfriend's surrogate niece when you find out she's an Hybrid," Eytea argued, "So here's what I'd like to know. What is it about us that makes you such an insufferably heinous bitch?"

"Need I remind you that you are our guest?" Yrlis bluntly countered, "If you cannot work with any one of us, you'll have no choice but to find some other resistance to join, and I can assure you that none will be as adequately prepared."

"Keep in mind that she's of more value to the cause than you are," MalVek added, keeping his attention out the window.

"That, too. So watch what you say," Yrlis agreed, glaring at an undaunted Eytea.

"Actually, I was speaking to you," MalVek corrected, much to Yrlis's humiliation, "Compared to Hybrids, electrician apprentices and medical practitioners are about as common as snow in Tanelen. Whatever vendetta you have against any of them, you need to get over it or keep it to yourself, lest you find yourself left by the wayside."

"If you reject me, you reject Spril as well," Yrlis argued, "and I know you cannot afford such a sacrifice."

"I wouldn't be so sure," Eytea countered, "He spoke much of the cause and his goals here, but he never mentioned his girlfriend until you and Galo argued over how to treat Sinkua."

"His community comes before you," Vielle added, "It comes before all of us. If any of us turn against the Subtransit resistance, we turn against him. You're no different."

Yrlis looked back and forth anxiously between Eytea and Vielle. Their common bond had been discovered mere minutes ago, and they were already uniting against her. She was beginning to understand why they were upset, but something about the idea of an Hybrid secretly living in such close quarters with her carved away at her sense of security. She found it bothersome somehow, but she couldn't discern if the trouble was with her having kept such a hefty secret or with her having been an Hybrid at all. Were it the latter, that brought about the question of her reasons. She had never been the racist sort, nor did she judge others on their looks any more than was considered normal. After all, she had developed an interest in Spril before puberty, back when he was just an awkward bald kid.

The train pulled into the station, the jostle of the brakes awakening Sinkua. Throughout being lowered to the ground, the conversation with Spril, awaiting the train, boarding slumped across MalVek's shoulders, and the one hundred kilometer ride, he had remained asleep. It may have been the longest continuous sleep he had managed in at least a year. He sat up, steadying himself, and examined his surroundings with obvious confusion.

"You fell out of the sentinel, but we managed to save you," Eytea explained, "Then we took a Subtransit train, and now we're below the capitol of ArcNos."

"This is where they're staging their rebellion," Sinkua confirmed groggily, "They're making themselves their own nation."

"Good, you remember. You had a pretty bad episode. Do you remember it?"

"I remember throwing somebody through a window. Did that really happen?"

"It did, but then you fell out the window, too."

"Oh, good, that means I really did rid myself of VanSen. That prick."

Sinkua tried to stand, but his legs were still rather unsteady. It wasn't so much a matter of fatigue as a result of irregular blood flow caused by his earlier episode. Eytea stood next to him and crouched down, offering her shoulder. He looked up at her and grinned slightly.

"Come on, hon, I'll help you up," Eytea insisted.

He began to rise again, but much to her disappointment, she stumbled under his weight. Quite abruptly though, the burden was diminished. She looked across him to see Vielle supporting him on his other side.

"I remember hearing somebody scream 'No' when I fell," Sinkua recounted, turning to Vielle, "It sounded like you. Did that really happen, or was I just dreaming?"

"That really happened," Vielle answered as they stepped off the train, "Right before I caught you, that is."

Sinkua stepped away, bracing himself. He was fully conscious now, and his blood flow seemed to have normalized. From his pack, he pulled the cat-o'-nine-tails that he had stolen from VanSen and offered it to Vielle.

"I took this from VanSen as a trophy, after I eliminated him in the tournament," he recalled, "Since you saved my life after I dealt with him again, I want you to have it."

"Thank you, Sinkua," Vielle graciously accepted, examining the weapon with curious wonder.

"Surely, you do not intend to lead her into battle, do you?" MalVek asked.

"She saved me from an inopportune death. I only intend to thank her properly."

The underground city was impressively active, much to the surprise of Sinkua and Eytea. Both had anticipated a small gathering narrowly passable as a community. Yet, people roamed and biked through the stations as though they were sidewalks in any other city. Electric motorcycles and scooters were speckled about, but no cars were in sight. After all, they did seem a might unnecessary given free access to the train. Track lighting ran along the ceiling, compensating for the absence of sunlight. Station offices had been converted into a multitude of businesses. Blocks of concrete had been removed to plant short trees.

"From the looks of it, I'd say you've been down here for a few years," Sinkua supposed.

"Actually, only about a year," Spril corrected as he joined them with his helmet under his arm, "Recall how I said we needed enough capital to cover two hundred fifty citizens to qualify as our own nation? Well, that's only a small sliver of our actual population."

"Are there more cities like this?" Eytea asked, studying her surroundings to get a feel for her new home.

"Just this one, but we're working on branching out. People have been coming in from all over. Got between fifty and sixty thousand at last count, and there are still more to retrieve from upstairs."

"That's how you built so much in just a year," Sinkua presumed, "Everybody must contribute to earn their spot down here. Am I right?"

"Exactly right," Spril confirmed, "So if you have any ideas to add to our community, or if you find someone who needs help executing their plans, go ahead and get to it."

"I'll be looking out, then."

"Good to hear. By the way, if you happen by a little place called NieRie's Bakery, pay her a visit and say I sent you."

Sinkua nodded before he departed to learn his way around the city. Eytea followed, never leaving his side. The population was far more impressive than either of them had ever anticipated, and the knowledge that this community was spreading to other districts gave them a bit of hope. Hope was always a fleeting feeling, though. Sinkua recalled that when he left ArcNos five years prior, their population was nearing a million. By his reckoning, the underground community's population was maybe five percent of that of the surface. Granted, those were better odds than he and Galo often had in their past skirmishes, but not everybody in the community was suited for battle.

Sinkua sized up a potential combat force as he walked the underground streets with Eytea. He and Galo would undoubtedly be on the front lines. Eytea had more than proven herself worthy of fighting alongside them, and her recent assertion made her all the more welcome. He knew Spril would be able to hold his own against long odds, what with his having bested both Galo and himself in the tournament. Sure, they were implicitly restricted from using their elemental talents, but he had demonstrated fierce prowess and clearly had no qualms with fighting dirty. MalVek had his own unique skills to contribute, but Galo showed that he was wont to be overcome by his own machismo. His rage was more of a hindrance than Sinkua's, up until he fainted, that is. Despite what he said about Vielle, he sensed that she carried an untapped potential. At the very least, she could trail behind and support them remotely.

Obviously, the first obstacle was her lack of control over her arbormancy. Perhaps in her panic, she had intentionally exhausted herself so rapidly, but Sinkua suspected she was not yet capable of much else. Granted, it had saved his life, a fortune for which he was grateful, but her capabilities needed to be refined if they were to be of any reliable use. He made a mental note to ask Galo to train her since he had worked most directly with Gijin. Of course, the first priority was to ensure that Vielle was comfortable with his knowing the secret she had been keeping.

Above a windowsill flowerbed, hot glued to the wall was a wooden plank with rounded corners. Painted upon it was the name NieRie's Bakery. Just as Spril had urged, Sinkua stopped for a visit. He held the door, inviting Eytea to enter before him.

"Hello there. The name's NieRie," called a petite woman in her late thirties from behind the counter, "What might I get for you folks?"

"We're really not sure, to be honest," Eytea admitted.

"Ah, thought I didn't recognize you folks. New to the bakery or new to the city?"

"New to the city," Sinkua answered as Eytea scanned the menu board mounted upon the wall.

"Oh, more new blood from upstairs. Good to see you made it," NieRie welcomed, "I've got scones on special, if you're interested in treating yourselves to celebrate."

"Actually, we're from beyond the border," Sinkua explained, "Spril told me I should stop in here for a visit. I suppose he's a fan of your scones."

NieRie gave him a puzzled look, trying to comprehend why anybody would willingly immigrate there from outside of ArcNos until she recalled her conversation with Spril.

"Ah right, you must be Sinkua. Spril told me you were coming. Wait here just a moment," she beckoned as she walked toward an oven in the corner, "Spril is a might fond of my scones, but that isn't why he sent you here. He asked me to whip up something special for you. His way of apologizing, he said. Wouldn't say what for, but I should assume you know."

"I could guess," Sinkua verified, "but if I'm right, he has no need to apologize. I don't blame him for what he did."

"Then I suppose you have no interest in these," NieRie played as she presented a basket of muffins.

"Muffins?" Sinkua indicated with an arched eyebrow, "Instead of just apologizing to me, he sent me to you for a complimentary basket of muffins. That's more than a tad odd."

"Take a bite of one."

Sinkua shrugged and snatched a muffin. He looked it over for a moment. The shape, color and texture were all clear marks of her expertise. He bit into it, rolled the piece over his tongue, and smiled as he began to chew.

"Pomegranate muffins? I thought there was no such a thing," he remarked.

"There wasn't, at least not on my menu," NieRie confirmed, "That is, until Spril came along and asked if I could make some for you. Said he heard somewhere that you were quite fond of pomegranates. I told him all the seeds might be a problem, but he made it worth my while."

"If you keep these on your menu," Sinkua began between bites, "I just might become your favorite customer."

"I would say so," NieRie beamed, "Go ahead and have a seat with those, and I'll bring a couple of glasses of orange juice for you and your girlfriend."

Sinkua paused awkwardly, mouth agape and poised for another bite. Eytea had already chosen a seat, and she looked up abruptly when she heard what NieRie had said. Granted, they were friends of opposite genders, and she had admitted to herself long ago that she was attracted to him and hoped it was mutual. But now she wondered if NieRie had only assumed they were a couple because they had come together and alone, or if her attraction had visibly gone beyond physical.

Quite to her surprise, Sinkua didn't bother to correct her. Instead, he just thanked her and walked to the table with the remaining eleven muffins. After a brief exchange though, Eytea learned that he thought it simpler to let NieRie have her harmless assumption, rather than endure rambling relationship advice from a stranger. She found it somewhat disheartening but not terribly surprising. She reminded herself, as she bit into a muffin, that no mention of any relations beyond friendship had ever arisen between them before. So, rather than let herself be bothered, she chose to simply enjoy the meal with him, silently hoping that perhaps his decision stemmed from a reciprocated attraction.

"I think I know what I want to do to help out here," Sinkua announced between sips of orange juice, "and I could use some help if you or Galo don't have any other ideas."

"I was thinking of doing something artistic, but I might pitch in. What did you have in mind?" Eytea asked, half a muffin resting gingerly on her fingertips.

"My plan is to take the train back out to where we came here from," Sinkua explained, "I'm going to clear out some of the rubble so people can build out there, too. Maybe they could start another city like this one."

"They would need to work their way out there. Quite a bit of unpopulated space in that hundred kilometer stretch."

"Others can concern themselves with that. I need to give back to those survivors out there if I'm going to make right with myself," Sinkua explained, "It's a personal burden."

Galo awoke with a severe headache, his mind still reeling from the previous night's conversation with SenRas. They all had marked CreSam as their initial target, the willing instrument of the Avatars of Fate sharing in a wanton symbiosis. Now, he was considerably less certain of CreSam's compliance with the whole operation and pondered what motives the Avatars had hated so much that they would cut off his memories. Furthermore was the confusion of whether they were truly combating him or some neurologically shuffled reincarnation. It didn't seem fair to destroy the body of one man with the mind of another trapped inside. Galo attempted to assuage his guilt by reminding himself that CreSam had fortified the fleet bound for Berinin while mentally sound. The only death he truly needed to prevent among ArcNos's militant operatives was SenRas's, and that burden was tricky enough without complicating it with presumptuous guilt trips.

Phylus similarly awoke to a reeling mind and feelings of bitterness. Of course, his body was having no part in this tension and was contrastingly relaxed thanks to having been truly relieved for the first time in almost two decades. Regardless of how pleasurable it was though, almost worth the seventeen years waited, the fact remained that CreSam had bedded her in the meantime. Their relationship was probably long since over at that point, but that was still his sworn enemy, the man who had destroyed his livelihood, his home, and his community. This bitterness led to other obscure suspicions and accusations, including the notion that Malia seduced him to give him a venereal disease or more realistically, that it was all a head game to distract him from his operations.

Their encounter in the hall was brief and awkward, as though each sensed that the other was somehow privy to last night's occurrences. Both muttered incoherent greetings and nodded, avoiding eye contact. Together, they walked to the front desk, but each kept changing his pace to avoid walking alongside each another. After they had checked out of their rooms, they made for their respective meeting houses.

Galo's visit was brief and concise. The paperwork was awaiting his signature, and a few sheets awaited additional signing by Nenbard, who would be available after an assembly regarding Phylus's proposition. Due to that same meeting, Olsa was noticeably absent, but her presence was not needed to inform him that his leave of absence had been predictably approved. A few of the other leaders expressed their disappointment that such a long tradition was being interrupted and that the successor of one of the lineage's greats would not be joining their ranks at due time. As nice as it was to know that he would be missed and treated respectfully in spite of his youth, avoiding their disappointment could not be a concern of his. His duties laid in an urban battlefield clear across the continent from his home, not with political guidance, a topic on which he had sparse education and significantly less experience. He signed the paperwork, mentally noting to let a page of his copies fall into SenRas's hands, bade farewell to the other leaders, and took his leave of them.

Meanwhile, Phylus stood before the Ouristihran Union Parliament, minus the necessarily absent ArcNosian Judge. Malia immersed herself in reviewing paperwork, though Phylus knew that she was avoiding eye contact. Frankly, he found it impossible to blame her, since he knew he would do the same were she not. Nenbard glanced repeatedly at the clock on the wall, obviously in a hurry to leave.

"Well Phylus, we've reviewed your proposition," Olsa opened, "and after a rather heated exchange, we have decided that it would be more of a benefit than a hindrance to your fellow communities if you were granted sovereignty."

"Thank you, all of you," Phylus called, trying to curb his elation as his eyes panned the panel of Judges.

"There will, however, be certain restrictions."

"As is to be expected," he interrupted, "Go on."

"Because you occupy the same surface coordinates, your nation will be also known as ArcNos. To avoid confusion, the surface nation will be Imperial ArcNos while yours will be Parliamentary ArcNos. Any crimes committed by a citizen of one ArcNos against a citizen of the other will be regarded as international crimes of the state. An elevated frequency of such by Parliamentary ArcNosians will result in your sovereignty being brought under further scrutiny and possibly revoked."

"Hypothetically, how could we go about changing our name?"

"A case for the forced disbandment of the Imperial ArcNosian government must be brought forth, either by a federal leader or a Judge, to both the Ouristihran Union as well as the Union Parliament. In both, the proposition must be favored unanimously, less the votes of both sides of ArcNos and the nation making said proposition."

"In that case, we intend to start the process of changing our name today," Phylus proudly announced, "I have brought with me a list of international crimes committed by Imperial ArcNos, proving their inefficacy in service as a pillar of our international community. In fact, they have served as little more than a hindrance to international growth with neither regard nor respect for historical culture."

"That's all well and good, Phylus, but it won't happen," Olsa argued, unmoved by his energetic monologue.

"Because you would not vote for such a proposal?" Phylus asked, gleaning that the Eprilenese Prime Duchess held something of an inexplicable disdain toward him.

"No, because you don't qualify to make such a proposal. Your seat in the Ouristihran Union does not take effect until one year from today, and the privilege of presenting cases to reshape international political infrastructure is forbidden until five years from today," Olsa explained, "Besides, you haven't even proven the efficacy of your parliamentary government, and it would replace the current imperial one."

"So that's it, then? We're stuck living under Imperial ArcNos for five years, plus however long it takes for our proposition to be approved?" Phylus asked, audibly disgusted.

"I'm afraid so," Olsa flatly confirmed, "Meeting dismissed."

Judge Nenbard launched himself over the table and fled to the Berinin corridor, offering a quick apology and a pat on the shoulder as he passed. The other Judges filed out more neatly, chatting amongst themselves as they headed to their respective exits. Malia paused next to Phylus.

"I'm terribly sorry," she sympathized, "How are you feeling?"

"Disillusioned and guilty," he muttered, "I want to tell myself that you had a part in this, but I cannot."

"Even if I wanted to, I couldn't have. You never spoke of such plans."

"I know, but you could easily have assumed such," Phylus countered, "I know you didn't though. Thinking you did is just my way of trying to excuse my lack of foresight."

"It might not be as bad as you think, though," Malia optimistically suggested.

"That's easy for you to say. You live on the surface."

"No, I mean the wait," she clarified, "It's been several centuries since anyone has made such a weighty proposition, and restrictions on such have not been reviewed since before the last occurrence. That law is severely outdated, so others might take it as more of a formality at this point."

"What exactly are you getting at? Do you think I might be able to present my case sooner than five years from now?"

"I do, but you should try in warmer weather when moods are easier. Return with your case in the middle of next year's Swelter."

Aside from a nameplate, CreSam's desk was wholly devoid of personal effects. Where once had sat a framed portrait of the wife he executed and the son who briefly knew, a bitter reminder of what he sacrificed for aspirations now left by the wayside, sat a cup of fountain pens. His broadsword, a relic of bygone days of glory, hung on the wall collecting dust, relegated to an existence as antique decor. Behind his high backed leather chair, visible through the continuous window wall was a towering military-centric community, his office building at the center and apex. Beyond that, a cloud of smog hovered above the horizon, choking the life out of the unfortunate to be exhaled into the empowered. Yet for all of it, he could feel naught but stoicism.

He apathetically dragged his fingertip along a thinly engraved line atop his desk. When he reached the end, a luminous video display appeared a few centimeters above the line. The video played for the fourth time that day, and once again he watched as a single Hybrid, someone the Avatars of Fate had been hunting for weeks, scaled one of their piloted colossi and felled the beast. On his first viewing, he was in a bit of disbelief. The second time around, he found himself perplexed. The third viewing engendered curiosity. This time, he only snickered.

About when the video ended, Kabehl barged in, visibly infuriated. Having grown indifferent to such loud and aggressive entrances, CreSam glanced to him with a rather nonchalant expression.

"Speak your piece, boy," he muttered, "I'm busy."

"Where is Malia?" Kabehl impatiently demanded.

"She was called to a Union Parliament meeting."

"What about…?"

"SenRas went as well but not with her," CreSam cut off, harboring no desire to suffer Kabehl's ranting, "He said he wants to appeal the terms of my restrictions. Both will return tomorrow."

"Then, I suppose I have no choice but to…"

"Take your leave of me, boy."

"… take up my case with you," Kabehl defiantly continued, "I assume you know about the sentinel we lost on the southeast coast this morning. Enlighten me as to why you allowed an inexperienced pilot to operate such an expensive piece of equipment."

"VanSen expressed a personal vendetta against one of the Hybrids you so deeply loathe and aimed to eliminate any new recruits to the underground resistance he heard tell of in Quarun. Any idiot can commit acts of mass destruction in such a monstrosity, just as I suspected and proved."

"You did it to prove a point?" Kabehl spat, "You wasted sixty million iolas to prove a goddamn point?!"

"Actually, VanSen wasted sixty million iolas on his temperamental vengeance," CreSam corrected, "and it was one of your people who implemented the self-destruct option on the sentinel. So leave me out of it and Malia as well. She could have done naught to stop me. My reach is beyond her and both the Union and the Union Parliament."

"You seem quite sure of yourself," Kabehl snickered, "and cocksure of the inefficacies of our designs. Then what, pray tell, do you say of what became of the guard ship that you allowed SenRas to arm?"

"It was sunk by a single Hybrid, because…"

"Because it was equipped with antiquated cannons, a defect in one of which proved opportune to our enemy!" Kabehl interrupted, "I'm beginning to wonder which of you is the lap dog in your relationship. Did he even verify the inspections record with you?"

CreSam gritted his teeth and grunted, punching a button beneath his desk. The massive double doors behind Kabehl slammed shut and locked. A black shade unraveled from the ceiling and covered the window.

"Inspections were to be overseen by Amirione's new bitch. Or did you conveniently omit that detail from the report to your authority?" CreSam bellowed, "As for SenRas, keep in mind that were it not for him, you would not have ArcNos as your plaything and testing grounds. He was my last commanding officer before I was placed in charge of my own platoon, and you will respect him as such, lest you find yourself shipped back to your master in six wooden crates."

"Even without him, we would have found a way to reach you, and since we've done so, you're inoperably weak without us. Without our aid, a soldier such as yourself would nary have achieved such status, much less so meteorically as you did," Kabehl argued, "As for SenRas, I hold no respect for those who aim to hinder our progress. That was why your order to spare that fossil in Berinin was stricken from the mission agenda."

Chapter 25

Sinkua crouched and wrapped his arms around a large chunk of concrete. Bracing his legs, he slowly rose to his feet, the muscles in his upper back tightening. Broken beams of sunlight lay upon his shoulders, illuminating beads of sweat. Eytea watched in perplexed awe as he hoisted yet another fragment of debris perhaps thrice her weight. He had been performing as such for the better part of the morning. She had tagged along to help, but her role had become more that of a spectator than a participant. It wasn't so much that nearly every piece of wreckage was too heavy for her as it was that she felt her lesser contributions would be inadequate.

She reminded herself that it was unnatural, not to downplay him but rather to remember the cost of his strength. She tried to imagine how he may have been without the affliction, but the conjured incarnation was still a pillar of a man, sturdy and infallible. Her thoughts and his work were interrupted by a loud knocking from above.

Dust and pebbles rained from the ceiling. Sinkua and Eytea backed away from that particular area. The knocking repeated, sending down more dust. Sinkua stood atop a pile of rubble, grabbed a crack in the ceiling, and hoisted his body up to look through. Galo dropped through a nearby hole, the surprise dropping Sinkua and sending him tumbling down the pile. Eytea's vision of him as unshakable was cracked.

"Well, I've done it," Galo announced, "Berinin is no longer my burden to bear."

"You denounced your position as Chieftain Sage?" Sinkua asked in disbelief, "You told us you were accompanying Phylus in case of complications along the way."

"I kept my intentions to myself because I knew you would try to stop me," Galo explained, "but what was to be done was my decision alone."

"You're damn right I would try to stop you," Sinkua agreed, "We can't go forth with you acting like you'll never return home."

"I know I will see the shores of Berinin again. That was not my reason," Galo clarified, "On the train in Quarun, I overheard talk of threats being issued from Berinin to ArcNos, apparently on my behalf. It seems Nalygen and Borret have taken it upon themselves to perpetuate a conflict in my name but not to my knowledge. I stepped down to invalidate any further messages and forwarded proof that I neither penned nor signed past messages."

"You broke a family tradition and gave up your birthright in order to save your people," Eytea interjected.

"That, I did. Besides, leadership should not be the exclusive realm of those who inherit it."

Sinkua nodded in understanding, calmed by Galo's justification. Still, he wished he could have been privy to this information before Galo carried out his plan. Of course, he would have argued against it, but Galo was not so easily dissuaded from his principles and agenda. Perhaps it was a bit selfish and even more hypocritical, given the secrets Sinkua was keeping.

Eytea and Sinkua proceeded to tell Galo about what was ahead, beneath the capitol of ArcNos. They explained the need for tangible contributions from all inhabitants, the regulation which had engendered the rapid development of the community. They were joined by Phylus, who decided to enter via the remainder of the nearest staircase.

Sinkua recounted the story of what had become of the city block above, at the beckoning of both Galo and Phylus. Naturally, Phylus's primary concern was with Vielle. While Galo's concern may have been partially with Vielle, though in a decidedly different sentiment, his was more with what display of prowess he had failed to witness. Eytea chimed in periodically with details from her sideline account. After all, between the two of them, she was stably conscious for more of the duration.

While they headed back toward the train, Sinkua chose to explain his comment to Eytea from a few days earlier. In NieRie's Bakery, he had told her that his clearing this area was to relieve a personal burden. Though she entertained the notion, she had decided not to insist on an explanation. As he scratched away at the shroud over his past, she wondered if he knew that she had been contemplating his reasons since he made that nonchalant remark. The landscape upon which the city above had twice exploded was once the site of his childhood home. He had returned to ArcNos to find his hometown by birth decorated with the blood of a city he never knew. She understood, and suddenly his chosen contribution wasn't quite so absurd.

"Where have you two been staying?" Phylus asked as they took their seats on the train.

"Spril invited us to sleep in your living room. I've been on the recliner, Eytea on the couch," Sinkua detailed, "I hope you don't mind."

"Nary a bit. I'm just glad you kids have shelter," Phylus welcomed, sounding quite relieved, "Galo told me about the vagabond lifestyle you've taken up for the past few years."

"I grew accustomed to it, but your recliner is remarkably comfortable. I'd hate to give it up."

"I'm not about to ask you to, buddy. Don't worry about it."

"I know, but you see…"

"Sinkua thinks it's a bad idea for us all to take up quarters together," Eytea interrupted snidely, "He says it'll make us all one target."

"Actually, he has a good point," Galo reluctantly agreed, "It might sound like a good idea since we'll be able to watch over one another, but considering their firepower, that won't matter if they launch an attack on us."

"They won't attack us down here because of their firepower," Sinkua corrected, "The risk to their own infrastructure would be impossible to ignore. Whatever damage they inflict below would be amplified above."

"You've thought this through, haven't you? So then, what's your motivation for splitting us up?" Phylus asked curiously.

"Offensive purposes."

The intentions he had harbored were all soon to come to light. There still remained the factor of Phylus's initial plan, but his body language spoke of disillusion. Recalling Phylus's career as a Negotiator, Sinkua encouraged stories about his foreign dealings during CreSam's rise to power. Aside from fulfilling a particular ulterior motive, this also served to ward off unwanted prying and kept his mind occupied while his subconscience ordered his thoughts.

As relieved as he was by the thought of ridding himself of one of his secrets, the stress was replaced by anxiety. He suspected Galo may have deduced his intentions, and he could trust him to support his cause. He hadn't known Eytea or Phylus long enough to predict how they might take to his approach, much less how the other members of Parliament would react to a disagreement. Perhaps it was because his image of ArcNos had been stained by his childhood and the imperial regime, but in the back of his mind, he was preparing an argument against threats of exile.

Spril and Vielle were waiting at the station when they arrived in the capitol. Vielle greeted her father with a hug and Galo with a warm smile, while Spril offered both an encouraging pat on the shoulder.

"Oh hey, I just remembered. I need to talk to you about something," Vielle told Galo, "It's pretty important."

"Can it wait a couple of hours?" Phylus asked, "We need to assemble a Parliament meeting, and Galo is a Foreign Representative."

"Mind if I sit in, then?" Vielle asked.

"I think you probably should," Sinkua insisted before Phylus could entertain the notion of refusing her presence.

Before leaving for Quarun, Spril and Phylus had designated a meeting hall for their Parliament. Naturally, Phylus would head the committee, which was populated by Spril, Yrlis, MalVek, NalSet, and a few others that the newcomers had not yet met. NalSet was of particular interest to Sinkua, if nothing else out of morbid curiosity. MalVek had told stories of his older brother, a cynical genius inventor illusively on the verge of senility, but Sinkua's numerous requests to meet him had been summarily refused. Along the way, they stopped to gather each member. Rather than allowing the lot of them to interrupt his brother's work, MalVek insisted upon fetching NalSet himself and catching up at the hall.

The meeting hall was a renovated station house located near the Epsilon boarding dock. Torch lamps were positioned in each corner, and draped upon the back wall was the former flag of ArcNos. The new flag was similar to the old but incorporated characteristics of the Avatars' insignia. The conference table was an old dining room table, polished and refinished to appear newer than it actually was. It was surrounded by more chairs than there were members of Parliament, few of them matching. A couple of them clearly belonged with the table, but most had been orphaned from other dining room sets. A few folding chairs were also waiting in the corner. Galo dug his bare toes into the thick carpet as he stepped upon it, nostalgic for the sand of Masnethege.

Phylus took a seat below the flag in a chair with a somewhat higher back than the rest. The other members filed in behind him, seating themselves in no particular order.

"Very well then, since we have a few newcomers from beyond the coast, I suppose this calls for introductions," Phylus began, "They possess information on the Avatars of Fate as well as other talents."

On cue, Eytea laid her upturned hand on the table, electricity surging across her fingertips. Galo followed suit with an icy hand, and Sinkua joined in with his own set ablaze. Vielle smiled nervously.

"You must be the vagabond Hybrids all the rumors have been about," a gruff middle aged man postulated.

"I would imagine so," Sinkua confirmed, "I'm Sinkua, a native ArcNosian who immigrated to Berinin. This is Galo, former Chieftain Heir of Berinin. And she's Eytea, a citizen of Ferya."

"Heard you kids have collapsed quite a few of their machines and dropped some ships in your travels," the old man added, "I must say I'm impressed."

"Well thank you, sir," Galo answered, "We can only hope…"

"What I meant is I'm impressed at their achievements in spite of such overwhelming mechanical incompetence."

"You must be NalSet," Sinkua guessed with a smirk, "Pleasure to meet you."

NalSet looked at Sinkua's outstretched hand, then to his face. He disapprovingly shook his head, and Sinkua awkwardly withdrew his hand.

"I'll decide if the feeling is mutual after I size you up. Then you can have your handshake," NalSet insisted, leaning back in his chair, "Maybe."

"Over here we have Farim, a forensics analyst from Poravit," Phylus continued, pointing out a blond woman a little older than Spril, "Uulan, a Quarunite historian. And IlcBei, owner of the ArcNosian Subtransit."

Uulan was an elderly gentleman, appearing to be roughly a decade NalSet's senior. His eyes were marked with sharp crow's feet, likely from restless nights spent examining the fractured annals of Ouristihra's history. IlcBei was a middle aged woman, perhaps in her late forties, with auburn hair and calloused fingers.

"So what news do you have of your trip to Eprilen?" Spril asked eagerly.

Sinkua's stomach turned as Phylus recounted his experience before the Ouristihran Union Parliament. Naturally, his night with Malia was deliberately omitted. Looks of optimism upon learning of their sovereignty waned into disappointment when he explained the hindrances to advancing their plan. A clamor broke out amongst them, arguing over who was to blame for such a setback and less frequently what should be done about it. Their certainty was so great that they had neglected to develop a contingency plan. Sinkua cleared his throat loudly to turn all heads in his direction. A few among them appeared annoyed by his interruption, but still they listened.

"There's one more way we can reclaim the surface," he announced, "and save the rest of Ouristihra from Imperial ArcNos. Now that we're a sovereign community, it only requires approval from the people in this room."

"What would you have us do?" Spril asked.

"We issue a declaration of war," Sinkua firmly ordered, effecting another heated clamor, "They can't attack us down here. Their firepower would collapse the streets above."

"But for that same reason, we can't effectively attack them up there," Spril argued, "Don't get me wrong, you ultimately fared well against that one piloted sentinel, but we can't expect that to always be the case."

"Yes, the assault will be slow at first, but by declaring war, we guarantee safe passage to foreign aid," Sinkua reminded, "In case you've forgotten, I spent my travels gathering the tracking scents of numerous citizens, all of them worried about what to expect if Imperial ArcNos is left unreined."

"I'm sorry, politics was never my best subject," Farim piped in, "but how does declaring war guarantee that we'll get their help? Won't they help us even if we don't declare war?"

"Of course they will, but a declaration of war ensures that they and any aid they forward will reach us safely."

"Care to elucidate?"

"The Wartime Passage Act," Phylus remarked with an epiphanous grin.

"Ah, of course," Uulan interjected, "It was passed following a brief conflict between Eprilen and Haprian. War was never officially declared, though both parties did aggress militantly. Unwary visitors to Eprilen were mistaken for reinforcements, and their ships were sunk by Haprianite operatives."

"After the dust settled, it was agreed that during an official war, all incoming vessels bearing a mark of invitation from a federal agent will be granted safe passage into the shores of all nations involved, thus protecting passers-by," Phylus completed, "I vote we declare war, then. How many vials do you have?"

"Several score, each with friends and family who would be willing to assist us, as well," Sinkua proudly claimed.

"Can we be sure that Imperial ArcNos will fall in line with this law, though?" Eytea asked, nervous about offending Sinkua as well as the argument that she was undoubtedly instigating.

"The punishment is absolute surrender to the strongest directly opposing nation, under terms penned by said nation and approved by the remainder of the Ouristihran Union," Phylus smirked.

Uulan and Spril both smiled and nodded confidently. Uulan knew the details of the Wartime Passage Act already and thus was proud to see his new colleagues employing historical wisdom so well. Spril was simply pleased to hear that, within a week of the Hybrids' arrival, one of them had issued a proposal that would ensnare the imperial regime.

"So do we have agreement?" Sinkua asked, leaning forth with his hands locked over the tabletop, "Because once we do, Imperial ArcNos is politically fucked."

"I would imagine we do, but there's still one problem," IlcBei announced, "Pardon my pessimistic foresight, but it's safe to say that the Avatars of Fate operate from beyond our borders. How are we to keep them from striking back when Imperial ArcNos is forced to surrender to us?"

"We will decide that during the war," Phylus calmingly promised, "We would first need to determine their base of origin, an effort yet to come to fruition."

"Actually, I recently had a breakthrough," Farim corrected, "I was just waiting until we were past this order of business."

"I've come to my own conclusion as well, but probably not the same way you did," Sinkua interjected, then signaled for Farim to continue.

"No, go ahead," she curiously urged, "I want to see if we came up with the same answer and how you got there."

"Fair enough," he complied, "Consider the points on the map that have been hit. ArcNos has obviously become their current base of operations, despite their not being of ArcNosian origin. They destroyed the capitol of Berinin. Nautical combustion engine blueprints and development rights were stolen from Ivaria. Haprian was suckered into a treaty and later attacked when they voted to terminate those development rights. Phylus told me that the Eprilenese press denies the existence of the Avatars of Fate and discredits any association with Judge Mikalan's death. ArcNos collects a share of the profits from the Radial Axiom Arena in Quarun. Kirts had the trade conflict, and we suspected they might be behind this. But shipments of goods from ArcNos to Kirts have been pillaged, so that was most likely a cover up. Poravit has continued to forward them despite never receiving confirmation of safe shipment. We found an abandoned Avatars of Fate laboratory in Ferya. I heard recently that they're trying revolutionary excavation techniques in regions untouched by the Subtransit, the forte of Lenguardia. And finally, Spril spoke just days ago of witnessing test flights of aerial vehicles, and Ierodhes specializes in aeronautics and air safety. This leaves just one nation suspiciously silent."

"You're good, and you're right," Farim complimented with an intrigued grin, "But while you've got the deductions to give us probable cause, I've got the science to prove it."

"So what have you discovered?" Phylus asked.

"Back when Brigadier General Elite HarEin was still alive, my supervisor spent the end of his career trying to track the Avatars of Fate, during my internship. He had received an unmarked gun believed to have been their property given the events surrounding its discovery. He started where anyone would by dusting for fingerprints. Nothing came up at all. DNA technology was in its infancy, too unstable to give reliable results," Farim explained, "Since then, they've developed more effective fingerprint dust, a compound that prints can't be hidden from so easily, but their prints are blank, like they've been sanded flat. Even if they weren't, the most complete prints were on the grip, and the texture created too many voids. DNA testing has come a long way, but the results came out as invalid.

"So I started looking deeper into the materials. All of them appeared to be very common, originating from no fewer than three nations each. That is, until I went beyond the conventional methods of disassembling a firearm. I noticed the grip was fastened by an adhesive instead of screws. I pried it off, ran a few tests, and determined that it was derived from tree sap. So I consulted a tree surgeon to find out exactly what kind of tree it came, and that's where I found our answer."

"What kind of tree did it come from, then?" Vielle asked with intrigue.

"The Sisyphus Fir."

"Oh right, father of sorts to the Glaucus Fir."

"The tree surgeon told me about that," Farim confirmed, "He also told me that they only grow at high latitudes. So high, in fact, that only one nation in Ouristihra has any land that far north, and it's the same one that Sinkua found to be suspiciously silent."

She looked to Sinkua and smiled a tad flirtatiously. Sinkua smirked and cocked his head in a crooked nod. Eytea swallowed nervously and scooted her chair a bit nearer to him. Galo grimaced proudly at what his surrogate brother had done, playing a gambit to politically ensnare the empire and now deducing where to strike at the heart of the Avatars of Fate.

"Tanelen," Sinkua and Farim declared with eyes locked.

"Isn't this mostly speculative though?" NalSet interjected.

"I had the same feeling," Farim admitted, "So I did some digging and found there aren't any companies that export Sisyphus sap in its raw form or as an adhesive. That means that gun had to be manufactured in Tanelen. Either that or it was done completely off the books. I could see that happening, but this is the best lead we've got."

"So I suppose that settles it, then" Phylus announced, "We declare war against Imperial ArcNos. Once they've been forced into submission, we redouble our efforts and move on to Tanelen where we will seek out the Avatars of Fate. Are there any other issues that need to be discussed?"

"We found a couple of items in that laboratory that might be of interest," Galo mentioned, "but I would scarcely imagine they need to be brought before the entire committee."

"Well if you have them with you, let's see them," Phylus insisted, "Now that you've mentioned it, I'd say most of us are curious as to what you've brought."

Indeed, Galo had said items in his possession. They had remained in his travel pack, which he carried with him to the conference room despite offers to leave it at Phylus's house when they fetched Yrlis. He withdrew the broken security camera and the folded note and set them at the center of the table. NalSet snatched the camera and examined it.

"Oh this is a nice model," he complimented, "Found it in a research lab, huh? They must have wanted to guard their work pretty closely. What did you want to know about it?"

"I'd like to know how something like that works. I've been told that security cameras have film to be reviewed later."

"Sure, usually they do, but in high security situations, they use a direct link model like this, called closed circuit surveillance. The data is transferred directly to a security station, where it can be viewed live and stored for later. Protects video evidence from intruders who might try to cover their tracks."

"Hey, do you think that might be how those security lights work?" Vielle asked.

"There is probably a connection," NalSet agreed, "If I study this piece, I should be able to derive the machinations of their input devices. I'm going to hold on to this."

"I harbor no intentions of stopping you," Galo permitted, "Now this note, we found folded up in the pocket of a lab coat. Yrlis, you might be able to make sense of it. Nothing like this diagram ever arose in my studies."

"Sure, let me have a look," Yrlis sheepishly accepted, choking on her words as she withheld the insult she so desperately wished to deliver.

She immediately recognized its layout, much to her pride. More to her surprise though, she found that all previous unknowns had been filled, ending a medical and scientific struggle decades in the making. But that elation turned to chagrin when she realized it was written in a script she had no hope of deciphering. Aside from that, yet another bizarre feature caught her attention.

"It's a map of the human genome," she answered with bewilderment, "but it's complete. Last I looked into it was about three years ago, but at that point, it was only three quarters complete after forty years of research."

"What exactly is a genome?" Galo asked.

"Basically, it's the layout of DNA, determining what genes and chromosomes are linked to what features and conditions," Yrlis explained, "It covers everything from blue eyes to brain cancer, as well as the switches that activate the genes and the genes that control the switches. But what I'm finding especially strange is that there's one more pair of chromosomes than humans are known to have."

"Any idea what that could mean?"

"Not offhand, but I also can't read whatever language this is written in."

"I thought Ouristihra only had one language," Eytea interjected, "Maybe it's a code."

"I doubt it. I'm no codebreaker, but it doesn't feel like a code."

"I have a colleague in Quarun who's an etymologist," Uulan offered, "If we invite him here, he will be able to give us a definitive answer."

"Would he be able to translate it?"

"I make no promises, but your knowledge of the genome should help him."

"Okay is that everything now?" Phylus asked after a long and eventually awkward silence, "Very well then. We will declare war on Imperial ArcNos and move on to Tanelen once it's over. In the meantime, NalSet will study the direct link camera as research on the street lamp security system. And, once Uulan's colleague arrives, he'll be assigned to work with Yrlis on translating the genome map. I declare this assembly adjourned."

Colonel SenRas walked along the center of the Platinum Hall, his stare fixed on the massive double doors at the end. They towered three stories in height, making it an incredible task to open them single-handedly. Kabehl stood in the doorway to his office, sending SenRas a dissenting glare and snicker as he passed. SenRas didn't waiver, as he was occupied by the fear that he marched toward the demise of his military career.

After a momentary struggle with the door, he slipped through the opening which promptly slammed shut behind him. CreSam sat behind his desk, appearing quite disconcerted. They stared at one another for a moment, all of the authority that SenRas once had over him being reduced to submissive fear. CreSam sighed and shook his head, initiating the conversation.

"It has come to my attention that certain oversights on your part have been the cause of depleted enforcements," CreSam began.

"I assume you speak of quality control responsibilities on the recently sunken guard ship," SenRas replied after a small pause, "Not to undermine your authority, sir, but I was not responsible for such. You should not overlook that EshCal disappointed."

"I thought the same until I learned that you never delivered the inspection notice to her. That places the blame on your shoulders alone, SenRas," CreSam scowled, "For that, I have no other choice but to severely punish you."

"If you intend to suspend me, I will be visiting my relatives at their home out west," SenRas nonchalantly accepted, seeming to have anticipated such disciplinary measures.

"Well, pack for a long trip, because you'll be off the payroll for eight weeks, effective tomorrow. For a start, that seems a reasonable enough punishment."

"I accept the punishment for my negligence"

"Afterward, you may or may not return to the same post of duty. You'll likely be stripped of your rank, demoted back to Admiral or possibly further. When you return, we will discuss your official rank then."

"I certainly hope I'll stay equally employed, sir."

SenRas took leave of CreSam and returned to the Platinum Hall. He watched Kabehl from the corner of his eye as he approached. His gait remained rigid and his face stoic, too shamed by his punishment to acknowledge this enemy within. After exiting the hall though, he paused for a moment and chuckled under his breath, congratulating himself on a personal victory.

A feminine hand set softly upon Kabehl's shoulder. Though he didn't see it coming, the surprise caused nary a flinch. He glanced at the long slender fingertips, then returned his attention to CreSam's towering double doors.

"What is it, Investigator?" he asked.

"So, the old man is out of the way, as per our plan?" Malia asked.

"Not entirely, no."

"Was he at least suspended?"

"For two months, plus a possible stripping of rank," Kabehl confirmed, "but he may still be an interference during that time."

"I'm sure you're just paranoid," she assured him, rubbing his shoulder.

"No, they exchanged encrypted messages," Kabehl argued, "I am certain of that much."

Chapter 26

Sinkua sat in NieRie's Bakery, enjoying his usual breakfast of pomegranate muffins, bacon, and orange juice. As he munched on the meticulously crafted baked good, he pondered the discussions from the Parliamentary meeting. Undoubtedly, the good news was the sweepingly welcome reception of his proposal to declare war, the statement for which he was to issue later that day. But that diagram was nothing short of revolutionary, to state the scale of its importance in the weakest of terms.

Talk of etymology and indecipherable codes conjured up some of the more pleasant memories of his childhood, nigh invariably days when CreSam was away on business. In the early days of his youth, he had discovered a cache of deteriorating tomes under his mother's bureau. Their spines were too brittle for any of them to be opened by conventional means without causing irreparable harm. So he had suppressed his curiosity out of respect. The covers and spines were fascinating enough without viewing the text within, as they were adorned with unfamiliar symbols, some resembling letters of the modern alphabet. Now, he had confirmed that his mother was in possession of textual relics from a thus far unknowable era. Furthermore, if those symbols and the ones on the diagram originated from a common language, historians and etymologists could begin deciphering the surviving annals of that era.

The concept of it was overwhelming, imagining that a scrap sheet of paper could start a chain reaction to unlock centuries of lost history. He gazed out the window, consumed by his own contemplation. So consumed was he, in fact, that he bit his fingers with the last bite of his muffin. He promptly shook himself from his contemplative daze, finished his last strip of bacon, and downed the remainder of his orange juice, washing down his medication with it.

Eytea worked diligently with a brush between her fingers. Several buckets of paint lined the walls, and even more colors adorned her once white apron. A red bandana much like Sinkua's rested over her hair, protecting it somewhat from stray paint droplets. She had decided to translate her talent with pencils into brushes by painting a mural on the walls of the Epsilon boarding dock.

This was also where they slept. It had been decided that members and affiliates of Parliament would pair off. This would prevent the entirety of them from being eliminated by a single tactical militant strike, were Imperial ArcNos and the Avatars to ignore the unavoidable aftermath, while still placing two pairs of eyes on each residence. Of course, Phylus and Vielle stayed together. Spril and Yrlis took up common quarters in an annex to MalVek's shop. MalVek, who had been staying there, moved in with NalSet. IlcBei invited Farim to move in with her under a few personal conditions. Uulan stayed alone, but he intended to invite his colleague to stay with him. That left Sinkua, Galo, and Eytea. Rather than leave one of them to live alone, they set up hammocks in the corners of the Epsilon boarding dock.

Sinkua had woven the hammocks from vines and flexible branches gathered from a nearby abandoned arboretum. Vielle's arbormancy was thus far too volatile to be a source for such materials. Their positions put them within shouting and viewing distance of one another but separated them enough that incendiaries such as those seen in Masnethege could only take out one of them at a time. It was a macabre notion but one that needed to be rationally addressed.

Regarding her arbormancy, Vielle had yet to find the opportunity to speak with Galo. Phylus was still unaware of her unique ability, and she wished to keep it that way until she had learned better control of such. Of course, she had intended to keep her secret, which she discovered when she awoke from a vivid nightmare to find strips of bark peeling from the backs of her hands, entirely to herself until such time, but saving Sinkua's life took undebatable precedence.

Phylus sat alone in the meeting hall, occasionally glancing up from his work to observe Eytea's artwork. He smiled at the sight of children playing games on the boarding dock, adapting to subterranean life with impressive understanding. Still, he persisted in keeping his attention on the papers at hand, for he scrawled upon them the official declaration of war against Imperial ArcNos. The spark on the cigarette between the forefinger and thumb of his off hand neared the filter. It was sent to join two others in an ashtray.

As he neared the end of the document, a knock on the door attempted to interrupt him yet again. This had happened several times before, only for him to learn that it was a stray ball from one of the children's games. After a moment, it repeated in rapid succession. He promptly rose to his feet to answer it.

"How much longer do you suppose you'll be?" Sinkua asked.

"I was just finishing, but I still need to proofread it," Phylus promised as he fumbled with a malnourished lighter, "You don't need to deliver this statement, you know, at least not alone."

"Yes, I do," Sinkua flatly insisted, lighting Phylus's cigarette with his fingertip, "I need to look for someone on the other side, and it's my own burden to bear."

"You're a real enigma, you know that?" Phylus noted, eyeing him suspiciously and waggling his cigarette, "Always seems like you're hiding something."

"Everyone has their secrets," Sinkua shrugged.

After the door closed, Phylus returned to his work, rereading the last few sentence. Meanwhile, Sinkua took a seat against the wall, just past the window. There he watched the children play, attempting in vain to ignore his anxiety.

His intention, as farfetched as it may have been, was to deliver the statement of war to CreSam in person. It would be their first meeting in over five years, so he scarcely had a notion as to what to expect. He had no reason to suspect that CreSam had ever issued a missing person search, but he had ordered soldiers to hunt him down. Of course, those threats were against Sinkua, while CreSam only ever knew him as MeiLom. It was particularly unreasonable to think he could have forgotten about any mention of the name Sinkua from several years prior. Regardless of how painful it might have been to look into his own past, it was a pursuit he accepted as both necessary and inevitable. Delivering the message was his top priority. His ulterior motive was to learn if CreSam knew he had issued a death warrant to his own son.

A stray ball bounded toward him with a child close behind. It bounced off his knee, and the child caught it with both hands. Sinkua blinked several times, taking momentary stock of his surroundings. The child looked him over, appearing concerned.

"Hey, you're that guy, aren't you?" the child asked, "The guy that's gonna save us?"

"I am?"

"Yeah! I heard you're gonna save us from all the monsters," the child remarked, "So why do you look so scared?"

"I'm not scared," Sinkua lied, "I'm just nervous."

"How come?" the child asked, sitting next to him.

"You wouldn't understand. You're too young to relate," Sinkua excused, "At least, I hope you are."

"You could explain it to me. My teacher says I'm real smart for my age. She says I'm precocious."

"Well, let me rephrase that. You're too young for me to want you to understand," Sinkua insisted as he rose to his feet, "You'll just end up like me."

Sinkua walked away from the conversation, staring ahead to avoid eye contact with any of the children. The conversation had grabbed the attention of many of them, and they were moving their game to keep him and the curious child in view. Gossip spread through the crowd as they realized who he was, one of the superhuman vagabond heroes of whom they had heard several tales. That gossip evolved into an uproar as they vied for his attention, albeit almost entirely in vain.

Hundreds of words melded into an indecipherable white noise as he tried to tune them out. Occasionally, a word or two would slip through with some remnants of clarity. They spoke of his being a hero or a legend, and of saving them, fixing things, and making everything right. In all his travels, these were exactly the things he set out to do, to help save the people of ArcNos, and the rest of Ouristihra by extension, from its own government. But being back within its borders rekindled childhood fears of inadequacy and guilt by association. He stopped abruptly and turned to face the mob, glaring down at a crowd of adoring children.

"I am not your savior!" he snapped, "I've killed hundreds of people, possibly thousands, for doing their job. Then I get here, and the first thing I do is propose to declare war so that I can march thousands of innocent people into their graves all in hopes of saving a nation that's probably beyond saving. Sure, maybe it will make your lives better, but it comes at the cost of several others. I'm irrational, unreasonable, and uncaring. Up until this moment, I've been an apathetic utilitarian with no capacity for human empathy. I'm no better than him, and it scares the shit out of me that it took me this long to acknowledge the monster I've become."

The children stared up at him in stunned silence while he stared back in an introspective rage. Just moments ago, he had spoken of preserving one child's innocence and saving him from knowing the ugly reality that he had learned far too early. Yet now he had stripped away the innocence of dozens more, unable to remain rigid against their incessant prying. His inner rage became anguish, and his anguish became remorse. Unable to face them any longer, he shuffled away, leaving only himself to face.

He made for his hammock to sit and collect his thoughts. He hoped to take a few minutes alone to regain his composure before he hit the streets. As he emerged from the crowd, he learned that was not to be. Eytea was sitting on his hammock, waiting for him.

"So, we're really going through with this, huh?" she commented, "Are you nervous?"

"What? Of course not," he blatantly lied, "I've been preparing for this day for years."

"Do you want me to come with you?"

"No, you should stay here," he insisted as he fetched his morningstar.

"Don't be chivalrous with me, Sinkua," Eytea argued, "You're putting your life in danger, and holding me back will do nothing to ensure your safety."

"Phylus offered to accompany me, and I refused him, too. I'm not chivalrous. I'm just stubborn."

"So, even if Galo asked to join you, you'd turn him down?"

"I'd be a liar if I didn't. Where is he, by the way?"

"Vielle took him to the arboretum," Eytea answered, lowering her voice, "I think she's finally going to talk to him about her being an Hybrid."

"Well, it's about time she did. If any of us can guide her, he's the best one for the job," Sinkua reiterated, "Anyway, I'll be back in time for supper."

"Just don't do anything stupid, okay?" she pleaded.

"The things I do aren't stupid," he argued, "They're calculated and retrospectively irrational."

Eytea laughed and shook her head as he walked away, fastening the chain of his morningstar as he went. He paced the dock for several minutes, never stopping for more than a few seconds so as to avoid conversations. His mind was too occupied with what most people would call an internal monologue. For him, it was more a matter of internal altercation, perhaps even a riot.

By pushing those children away as he did, he was becoming the monster he struggled to avoid. However, giving in to their prying would ruin their innocence all the same and uncover the secret of his past. If he accepted their praise, he feared he would be setting them up for crushing disappointment.

As necessary as it was to declare war, he was putting everyone involved in mortal danger. His point that Imperial ArcNos could not launch an attack against the Subtransit was little more than speculation, but it was a notion he believed he had no choice but to follow. By declaring war, he was granting them legal clearance to take any offensive action, essentially giving them exactly what they discernibly wanted. Worse still, he was taking up arms against his father, thus destroying what remained of his family, just as he had wished CreSam not to do.

After what could have either been minutes or hours, Phylus caught up with him. He came from behind but had the presence of mind to veer to his front and make his presence known. No words were spoken, as they weren't particularly necessary. He simply nodded as Sinkua took the twine-bound document and walked away to the nearest staircase.

The capitol was in markedly better condition than Sinkua's hometown had come to be, but that was not to say it had not been reduced to an uninhabitable slum. Shattered glass and splinters coated the streets, lining ashy potholes. To the north stood an icon of prosperity, contrasting garishly with the urban ruins through which he hiked.

Towers of glass and steel alloy loomed above the slums, taunting whosoever may have clung to a life on the surface. Sinkua's lips curled as he felt them call to him, beckoning him to stand among them as a living conflagration of retribution. He was not so much offended by the prosperity as he was by their methods of gaining such. The new ArcNosian empire had been economically raping their foreign traders and their own people, meanwhile hunting anyone who they even suspected stood to hinder them.

As he neared the inner city, Sinkua began to suspect that he may have mislabeled himself a monster for wanting to tear asunder anyone actively participating in such heinous crimes. Another part of him persistently insisted that the soldiers he slew were only human, while the utilitarian portion of his conscience argued that he saved more lives than he ended. Ultimately, he reminded himself that they willingly opposed his efforts to stem the spread of the imperial plague. They knew what they were fighting for, and they knew they could quit and seek shelter in the Subtransit. Yet they chose to kill in scores just to save their own lives. At least, that's what he told himself.

The towering community was enclosed by a tall wrought iron fence. Sinkua stood in the middle of the street before a massive gate, easily triple his height. His eyes darted back and forth as they scanned the gate from top to bottom, examining its design. He removed the morningstar from its holster and hurled it over the top of the gate. It landed with a loud crash, the ball scratching the asphalt as it rolled. He then slid the document through the gap beneath the gate.

Sinkua stepped back a few steps, reexamined the gate, and charged at it. Still a couple of meters shy, he leapt and grasped at the gate with his right hand. He caught it and found a foothold with his right foot. From there, he bounded upward and grabbed another pair of holds with his left limbs. After a few iterations, he flung his body over the top of the fence and dropped the entire six meters to the pavement, absorbing the impact with his legs.

As he retrieved his morningstar and the document, one particular flaw in his plan dawned on him. It became so obvious in fact, that he felt downright foolish for lacking the foresight. He had no way to discern from which building CreSam worked or even where to find him in that building.

"Sinkua?" a vaguely familiar voice called out.

He clutched his morningstar behind his shoulder, bracing for an attempt on his life. The voice called again, and Sinkua loosened his grip. Whoever it was, they didn't sound threatening, more curious in fact. He turned his head to find a face he had longed to see for some time.

"SenRas!" he called back, walking toward him, "There's something I've been meaning to tell you."

"It's a bad idea for you to be…" SenRas cautioned, only to be cut off.

When he came within arm's reach, Sinkua grabbed him by the shoulders and angrily headbutted him between the eyes. The bridge of his nose swelled, and blood dripped from his flaring nostrils as he spat a chain of expletives.

"I suppose I deserved that," SenRas admitted with a sigh, diverting the blood from his lips with his index finger.

"No, you deserve worse," Sinkua bellowed, drawing back an enflamed fist.

"You wouldn't kick a man when he's down, would you?" SenRas pleaded, gazing fearfully at those fiery knuckles poised to strike.

"Normally, I wouldn't, but I'll make an exception in your case."

"I was just sentenced to two month's suspension and a demotion!" SenRas spouted so rapidly that it sounded like a single word.

"What? Why?" Sinkua asked, lowering his fist but still clutching SenRas's shoulder.

"For undermining the Avatars of Fate"

"Go on," he insisted, releasing his shoulder.

"I sabotaged the ship that Galo sank just beyond the coast, equipped it with old cannons with faulty locks and pinned the blame on EshCal for neglecting the inspections."

"EshCal? She's the one who took a bullet to the leg in Haprian, right?" Sinkua recalled, feeling strangely confident in the man he had vowed to hunt down, "Is she an Avatar, as well?"

"No, but they seem to have an agenda in mind for her, and she seems to aspire for it."

"In that case, I suppose I'll let you live at least until you're off your suspension," Sinkua offered, feigning callousness, "Just tell me where I can find CreSam. I need to speak with him in person."

SenRas gave detailed directions to CreSam's building and how to reach his office. He also explained why CreSam's office was two floors down from the top. Sinkua thanked him stoically and went on his way, a long walk ahead with ample time to reflect on his new discovery.

Vielle stepped lightly upon the dirt trail, freshly fallen leaves bowing and crumbling delicately under her bare feet. The grass alongside swayed with the motion of each step as she passed. She breathed deeply of the scent of the trees as she reflected upon the day of her discovery. It was one of overwhelming grief, and that grief drove her to this place for sanctuary. She had invariably returned to the arboretum every day since. Now, she had found a kindred spirit with whom to share it. Galo followed close behind, his admiration drifting between the abundance of trees and Vielle's gait.

"So, I suppose Sinkua told you why I brought you here," Vielle assumed, stopping abruptly beneath an apple tree.

"Actually, no, and I'm not too keen on surprises lately, so whatever you have to say or show to me, I would appreciate your being forward," Galo apprehensively insisted.

"It's nothing bad, I promise," she assured, turning to face him, "A few years ago, I took a job in a factory to help my father. After I was fired, I came here."

"Why did they fire you?" Galo interrupted.

"That's not important," Vielle hastily diverted, her eye contact waning, "The following morning, I awoke to a pretty disconcerting discovery, but I wasn't sure what to make of it. I came here to pick flowers to try and cheer myself up. I spotted a lone ripe apple on this tree next to us, and that's where I found my answer. Now, if you could, lock your fingers and hold your hands out for me."

"Like this?" Galo asked, complying with her request.

Vielle nodded affirmatively. She placed one foot in his hands and set her hands upon his shoulders, smiling and visibly impressed by the firmness of his shoulder muscles. With one quick thrust, Galo hefted her upward. As she clutched a branch, she lifted her foot from his hands.

"So, I climbed up to pick it, and this happened."

She reached up to pluck a ripe apple from the clutches of the branch. When her hand was a few centimeters away, the twig began to grow, urging the apple toward her fingertips. She pulled her hand away, and the twig retracted. She repeated this process twice more, while Galo watched in exuberant amazement, before finally plucking the apple and dropping it to him.

"You're one of us!" he exclaimed

Trusting him implicitly, she dropped from the branch with her arms extended. Galo opened his arms and caught her as gracefully as anyone could have managed.

"Sinkua would be dead if I wasn't," she boasted, looking up at him proudly.

"But how?"

"He was unconscious, and…"

"No, how is it that you're an Hybrid? You look so human. I have these scars on my neck that open as gills underwater. Sinkua has his solid green eyes that allow him to see through smoke and such, and Eytea's wings have an obvious function. What are you hiding?"

Vielle brushed her hair behind her ears to reveal her other secret, what she had once thought to be a birth defect. That was, of course, until she learned about the Hybrids and the two renegades who defended Masnethege. Since then, it had become her symbol of introspective pride. There they sat in plain view, normal in size and color, bizarre in shape. Galo ran his finger along the edge of one of her crescent moon ears, admiring the symmetry of each one.

"What can you do with them?" he asked, "Aside from hearing, of course."

"Trees speak to me," she answered enigmatically, "Well, they relay sound, and I can hear it. They don't say anything themselves, at least not that I'm aware of."

"We could have used you in Masnethege."

"I've had the same thought," she agreed, "Sinkua asked me to bring you here so that you could teach me to understand and control my arbormancy better. Do you think you can help?"

"What problems are you having?"

"Moderation, mostly. I can grow vines out of my body, but I can never control how much. When Sinkua was free falling, I panicked and released a huge tangle of vines. It caught him, but I passed out from exhaustion. I'm happy he's alive, but I'm also not fond of fainting."

"Is this typical, only being able to use them up to the point of exhaustion?"

"No, that was a worst case scenario. Usually, I'll try to wrap a vine around something, but I end up thrusting it straight through instead."

"Sounds like you need to meditate then," Galo suggested, taking a seat upon grass, "and this is an ideal place for you to meditate upon your arbormancy. Come sit with me."

She sat in front of him, mirroring the positioning of his legs with their knees nearly touching. Galo laid his hands open in the same manner as the offering hands of the statue from his childhood home. He beckoned her to place her palms upon his, an urging with which she eagerly complied. He breathed deeply, concentrating as he sent a torrent of milystis coursing through his arms. It was enough to send a tingling warmth into his palms but insufficient to manifest water upon them.

"Feel that warmth," he beckoned, "Feel it. Know it. Become it. That warmth is milystis. Just as tsora flows through all living things, so too does milystis flow through us. It is what drives our elemental manipulation and manifests at our will, conscious or otherwise."

"This is incredible," she gasped, her eyes still shut.

"Search deep within yourself. Focus your thoughts on your spirit. Search for that definitive glimmer that makes it feel so different from the tsoran ether which surrounds us," he urged softly, "So different, yet one could not be without the other. Grasp it in your thoughts. Move it through your body at your will."

Her hands trembled at the sensation. She felt as though his milystis was flowing into her and calling to her own. That same tingling warmth surged down her arms, the energy of her Hybrid spirit moving with her thoughts. The flesh of her hands parted painlessly as small vines pressed through and delicately encircled Galo's hands.

He smiled and opened his eyes.

"See?" he indicated, "You just needed to understand the source. Now that you're in tune with your milystis, the rest will come naturally."

She retracted the vines with an ease previously lost on her. As she removed her palms from his, she grew and retracted intricate patterns of foliage from her hands and forearms, marveling at her newfound control of such a unique talent. She looked to Galo again, beaming with astonishment. Grateful beyond words, she lunged herself at him and wrapped her arms around his neck. He set his hand upon the small of her back, rubbing it lightly.

"Thank you so much," she whispered, "You'll keep helping me, right? At least until I'm sure I've got the hang of it?"

"Of course," he promised as she pulled her head away from his shoulder to face him.

Galo sensed something of a spark between them, a sign that his attraction to her was undoubtedly reciprocated. Being two people with capabilities no one else alive could experience, here he was presented with a moment of similar uniqueness. He seized the passion of it, leaning in to kiss her. Instead of the response he anticipated, she placed her hand over his mouth and looked away nervously.

"I, I don't think that's a good idea," she insisted, her voice trembling.

"Oh gosh, I'm sorry," Galo profusely apologized, backing away nervously, "It just seemed the right thing to do."

"Don't worry about it," Vielle anxiously assured, "You can't have known, um, well, uh…"

"Right! I had to try to find out, didn't I?"

"Of course!" Vielle agreed, still avoiding eye contact, "Maybe we should head back home now. What do you think?"

"That sounds like a great idea."

Eytea sat upon a bench in front of NieRie's Bakery, an orange scone in her hand and a citrus soda beside her. Spril had recommended the scones but couldn't decide on a personal favorite. Citrus fruits were not particularly common in Eytea's hometown, thus making oranges something of a delicacy. Speckles of dried paint coated her wrists, fading in abundance as they ran up her bare forearms. A once white apron, now spattered with an array of colors, laid over her hyena fur coat.

The bell on the door rang for the second time in about five minutes. She looked up to see a familiar young blond woman looking back at her. Farim took a seat beside her, a cinnamon almond bagel in one hand and a mocha in the other.

"Oh, hi Eytea. Taking a lunch break?"

"Mm-hmm," Eytea mumbled as she swallowed a mouthful of scone, "Either that, or I'm done for the day. We'll see how I feel about it when I'm done eating."

They sat in silence for a moment, each sipping at their drinks. Farim popped open the lid and blew on her mocha, her lips pursed softly. Eytea's eyes wandered toward her, and her mind wandered back to the Parliament meeting. The scene of Farim and Sinkua making eyes at each other replayed in her thoughts, reminding her yet again that she had done nothing about it.

"I'm really worried about Sinkua," Eytea sighed, cracking the silence, "He hasn't been himself since we got here."

"He seems alright to me," Farim disagreed with a shrug, unknowingly assuring Eytea that she was out of tune with him, "but then again, we just met not long ago."

"You don't know Sinkua like I do," Eytea reminded, "He's usually more confident and at least makes you believe he feels like everything is going to be fine. He always has a plan, even the moment one fails. Then we get here, and it's like he's losing touch with himself."

"You really care about him, don't you?" Farim noted between bites of her bagel, "I can tell he feels the same way even if he won't admit it."

"I don't think he does," Eytea disdainfully refuted, "I wish he did, but he's so disconnected that I honestly don't think my feelings toward him will ever be reciprocated. Besides, he's seemed more interested in you ever since you two met."

"What? Eytea, that's insane. I've watched you two, and he gives you more eye contact than anybody else. He's got you on a pedestal even if he doesn't realize it," Farim argued, "Besides, he's not my type. I don't find him that attractive."

"You don't?" Eytea gaped, now inexplicably offended, "You're telling me that you don't find him even the least bit attractive?"

"I find him, well, intriguing at least."

"No, I mean physically attractive."

"Well, he does have those eyes."

"The eyes don't count; they get everybody."

"Then no, I guess I don't. Good news for you, I suppose."

"What, so you don't like tall guys with broad shoulders?" Eytea teased.

"It's more his face that puts me off," Farim clarified with a laugh, "He reminds me too much of my ex-husband. It's nigh impossible for me to have naughty thoughts about anyone that looks like him."

"Too many painful memories?" Eytea asked empathetically.

"Emotionally stressful, is more like it. I'm sure they're plenty painful for him, though. He rented himself a hooker on our anniversary, so I took a wrench and gave his nuts and bolt the old lefty-loosey righty-tighty."

Eytea spewed soda across the floor. Her face reddened with laughter, partially at the image of this somewhat petite woman taking such vicious vengeance and partially at her whimsical retelling of it. Her laughter being contagious, Farim joined her as she thought back on her style of revenge and his reaction to it.

"Okay, I have to ask," she panted between laughs, "Where did you get that hideous coat, and why would you wear hyena fur in the first place?"

"It's not ugly!" Eytea shot back, running her fingers over the fur, "It has sentimental value. Sinkua gave it to me."

"Oh, so he's the fashion-deficient one. That makes more sense."

"He wasn't trying to be fashionable. In fact, he didn't even plan on making it until he wound up with a dead hyena."

"Okay, now I'm intrigued," Farim admitted, "What could he have possibly been doing to end up with a dead hyena?"

"Has he told you about his time on the island?" Eytea asked, to which Farim shook her head, "He spent a few years in self-exile, living on an otherwise unsettled island in the south. One winter, he was running dangerously low on food and went out hunting. He happened upon a chipmunk and killed it, but an hyena came along and tried to make off with it. So, he chased it down, killed it, and reclaimed his prize, discovering his pyromancy in the process. He says hyena meat tastes horrible, akin to chewing on a wet tire, so he skinned it and made a coat. Turned out to be too small for him though, so he gave it to me as a gift."

"That's, well, strangely sweet," Farim complimented with a crooked smile, "He must have been in a pretty bad spot to go to all that trouble over a chipmunk. There can't be much more than a kilogram of meat on one of those."

"If even that much, but there's also his pride and the principle of the matter. As he put it, son of a bitch tried to steal his dinner."

The strangely immaculate streets of the inner city were suspiciously empty, save for an occasional vehicle. Nearly every driver and passenger rubbernecked as they passed. Sinkua met their glares, focusing especially on the drivers out of hopes that the distraction would send them veering into a utility pole. His disgust for these people grew with each step toward the heart of the capitol, but he quelled the urge to set fire to anything, largely out of fear of legislative repercussions. Pyromania would have to wait until his return trip.

His internal argument was coming to an end, and it seemed the violent retribution for which he planned was coming into favor. As much as his more humane and forgiving side screamed for his attention, another voice he had until recently yet to consider was drowning it out. Such sharp contrast between the lifestyles of the military and government employees and those of the civilians could not have come abruptly. Even if they didn't actively perpetuate it, these people watched it happen and chose to let it. However the events transpired, none of them took a stand and instead chose to trample others for their own prosperity.

At the end of a long trek, Sinkua found himself staring up the polished south face of the capitol office building. This was the center of federal regulation in ArcNos, had been since time immemorial. Only recently had it become such an eyesore of a beacon and an insult to civilian lifestyles.

Sinkua's luminescent eyes scanned the side of the building, counting the windows. A drain pipe ran the height, but while it would make for a speedy escape, climbing up it seemed a might too risky. Either way, a direct entrance was unadvisable, given the likelihood that someone had relayed a photograph or at least a detailed description of him. After the damage he had inflicted upon their ranks, he thought they would be foolish not to take such measures. Instead, he would have to enter through a window, and the higher the better.

He made note of which windows were darkened. It was a bit presumptuous, but he took it to mean that those rooms were currently empty, making it safe to climb on those windowsills and to enter through one of those windows. He lost count of the floors well before reaching the top. A nearby mail truck gave him the idea to hide in a mail cart once he was inside, but he took the laundry cart into consideration as a contingency plan.

With his path to the twentieth floor plotted, he double checked the fastening on his morningstar. He tightened the binding around the document and tucked it in his pocket. He stepped back and braced himself, breathing deeply to calm his rapidly pounding heart. After one last look over the pattern of darkened window, he charged forth.

Recalling his days spent scaling rock walls and awkward arrangements of branches upon that humanly desolate island, he agilely sprang from the first windowsill to grip the next one and hoist himself upward, the muscles in his shoulders and arms tightening. The safe spot on the third floor was one room over. He leaned out from the edge of his perch and grasped the next corner. Putting faith in two fingers and a thumb, he clenched his teeth and swung away from the relative safety of the second story windowsill. He thrust his other hand upward to accompany the first and pulled himself up.

This pattern continued for several minutes, periodically interrupted as he caught his breath. For fear of vertigo, he never turned his eyes from the wall. The map of his ascent had been committed to memory, and he opted to trust it. Ophalin had said nothing of his medical condition affecting his short-term memory, and even if he were to err, he was confident that he could improvise an exit strategy.

Fortunately, that wasn't necessary. After a mental recount, he concluded that he had reached the twentieth floor. A darkened window on the twenty-first floor was directly overhead, but considering he was already easily seventy-five meters above the ground, he thought it wise not to press his luck. He ignited his fingertip and pressed it against the window.

After a moment, his finger passed through the pane. He eased his finger along, carving through the glass nearly in silence. The method was painstaking, as necessitated by clandestinity. Several gruelingly slow minutes later, he had cut three sides of a large rectangle. For the fourth side, he applied only enough heat to soften the glass. When he finished that line, he folded the carved sheet of glass inward and climbed through.

As he had anticipated, the office was empty. A note on the desk told that the occupant was out to lunch until fourteen o'clock. The clock on the wall read half past thirteen. Knowing he was safe for a while, Sinkua poured himself a cup of coffee to sip on while he recuperated from his hazardously ambitious climb. He wasn't too keen on vanilla roast, being more a classic black roast man, but at that point, he wasn't going to be picky.

He paced the room with the lights off while he sipped stolen coffee from a paper cup. Upon the wall was a diagram of the building, outlining emergency escape routes. From it, he gleaned that he was nearly halfway to the top of this fifty story insult. That put his destination on the forty-eighth floor.

From beyond the door, he heard the rattling of solid wheels against tile floor. Surreptitiously, he peered through a small window in the door. Much to his good fortune, he had arrived only ten minutes before the laundry service came through, delivering freshly cleaned uniforms. He crouched in the corner next to the door and waited.

Quietly, he squeezed back against the wall as the door opened. He flinched and squinted when the attendant turned the lights on. The attendant fumbled with the hangers as she arranged clean uniforms in the tiny closet. Staying low, Sinkua slipped out into the hall. Rubbernecking considerably, he gazed down the hall to count the doors between there and the elevator. He then climbed into the laundry cart and took cover in a lemony hiding place.

Thanks to four adequately oiled axles, the attendant failed to notice the additional weight on her cart. Sinkua waited patiently, counting stops on his fingers in case he lost count in his head. He had made a hole through the pile, wide enough through which to breathe without being seen. When the attendant entered the last office before the elevators, he climbed out with a uniform shirt.

Crouching below the office windows, he made for the elevators. Nobody was around. After hitting the up button, he anxiously waited for perhaps a full minute before an elevator opened. He boarded and pressed the button for the forty-eighth floor. Shortly after the elevator began to rattle and climb, he was stricken by the foresight to push the express button.

During the ride, he threw the uniform shirt on over his own shirt. Suspecting that the bandana would be an identifying trait, he removed that and used it to tie his hair back in a spiky ponytail. He fished through his pockets and found his sunglasses. The arms were severely bent, but the length of the ride gave him ample time to fix those. When the elevator door opened, he looked more like a new soldier in need of grooming and discipline than the vagabond Hybrid surely featured in their cautionary war stories.

The halls on the forty-eighth floor were loud and bustling. Sinkua shuffled along, avoiding eye contact as part of his improvisation of a lackadaisical soldier reporting to his commander for disciplinary action. He checked the name on each pair of double doors as he passed, eventually stopping to enter the Platinum Hall.

Malia was pacing in her office as he passed her door. She leaned out for a look at this stranger who had defiantly invaded her territory. He paused and cocked his head to listen, presenting his profile. She gasped and slipped back to her desk, shuddering anxiously. Not only had the Hybrids reached ArcNos and joined the resistance forces in the Subtransit, but now one of them had walked straight into the Platinum Hall. She feared what carnage she might find outside, but worse, she feared what may have been on the verge of transpiring in CreSam's office. She reached under her desk and fiddled with a dial until she heard a loud creaking from a bud lodged in her ear.

Sinkua looked up the double doors, stretching three stories high exactly as SenRas had told him. They doors appeared to be constructed from dense wood, stained a deep reddish brown reminiscent of bloodied topsoil. Their elaborately crafted gold-plated handles looked to have been polished several times daily. He clutched the handle with one hand and pulled the door open.

CreSam jumped slightly, looking up from his desk with a puzzled expression. Too many questions raced through his mind to decide which to ask first. Some disheveled soldier had entered his office without summons or invitation to his recollection. Even beyond his identity and such was the matter of how he opened the door so easily.

"Hello, CreSam," Sinkua bitterly greeted, tying the bandana over his head and removing his sunglasses, "I have a message for you."

Chapter 27

"I've heard of you," CreSam epiphanously remarked, "You're one of those Hybrids. Aren't you?"

Sinkua continued forward, clutching the twine-bound document. He stared straight into CreSam's eyes, awaiting a response behind a facade of stoicism. His heart pounded viciously, distraught as no sign of familial recognition was offered.

"You're the one who destroyed that sentinel I gave to Sergeant VanSen. How did you do that?"

Sinkua sighed and shook his head.

"How did you get in here unscathed?"

Sinkua stood over CreSam's desk, glaring down with disdain for both of them.

"Exactly what are you people?"

That still wasn't the question Sinkua sought to hear. He looked down at the document in his hands, emotionally bracing himself for the burden.

"What is it you're after?" CreSam bellowed, "Answer me, boy."

"I said I'm here to deliver a message," Sinkua muttered, dropping the document before his hopelessly distant father, "Not to answer your questions."

Still bewildered, CreSam glanced at the stack of papers this strange Hybrid had laid before him. The cover denoted that it was from Parliamentary ArcNos. He had not been informed of such a nation, and now an established enemy was delivering messages from them. Before he could contemplate it much further, a soft static hum followed by a click sounded from the front of his desk. He looked up to Sinkua, who had just opened the door.

"That's why you kept quiet," he assumed, "You knew the room was bugged."

Sinkua nodded and exited to the Platinum Hall. Not a second later, CreSam spoke over the intercom.

"Attention all officers and personnel, this is Lord CreSam speaking. One of the Hybrids has been spotted in the building, nearly two meters tall, black hair in limp spikes, red bandana, and solid green eyes. He may be wearing sunglasses when you see him. Be warned, he has the ability to create and manipulate fire. Your orders are to kill on sight. I repeat, your orders are to kill on sight."

Knowing he had lost his chances at a clandestine exit, Sinkua took off in full sprint, leaving a pillar of flame where he once stood and a wake of fire in his path. When he was halfway to the end of the hall, CreSam appended an incentive.

"Double promotion and three weeks paid vacation to whoever lands the killing blow."

A clamor erupted beyond the Platinum Hall. Several meters back, Sinkua heard a door open, followed by the clomping of combat boots on floor tiles.

"Oh great, now you'll think I'm doing this for the benefits," Amirione mocked,

"Just so you know, I would've killed you for free."

Sinkua swept his arm as he spun to face him, the ruby in his necklace shimmering as a torrent of fire erupted from his forearm. Amirione aimed his pistol at Sinkua's heart. The flames spiraled forth, roaring with ferocity. The sound of metal pounding against metal echoed within the chamber as Amirione fired his pistol. Sinkua charged forth as the bullet ripped through the barreling inferno. Unable to withstand the heat, the bullet exploded in flight.

Assuming success, Amirione returned the pistol to its holster. Green eyes shimmered through the smoke and dying flames that outlined that dreadfully familiar face. With only that brief glimmer of a warning, Sinkua burst from the black smoke and slammed his fist across Amirione's jaw. Blood and tooth chips spewed from his mouth as he collapsed in his doorway. Other doors began to open, which Sinkua took as his cue to endure the ravenous masses beyond the Platinum Hall

Through narrow windows, he caught glimpses of all manner of personnel eagerly awaiting their opportunity to collect the bounty on his head. Those not in combative duties were easy to spot, marked by their wielding of office equipment in lieu of traditional weapons. Sinkua held his morningstar back and kicked the door open. They closed in as the door flew ajar and slammed against the wall. His foot still raised, he arced the chain upward.

Sinkua stomped and dropped to one knee, jerking his morningstar down as a thunderous bellow burst from the depths of his lungs. The blood-rusted spiked ball shattered the tiles, and flames erupted from the cracks. The mob cleared back in a shock. He rose to his feet, whipping his weapon in a full circle with a backhand swing, leaving a wake of fire in its path. With his face covered, one soldier penetrated the barrier inferno.

His morningstar tucked under his arm, Sinkua spun to welcome the assailant with a palm heel to the nose. Simultaneously, the ominously hovering flames fanned outward like some bizarre and deadly flower. Sinkua charged forth, testing the limits of his Hybrid eyes.

His gusto got the best of him though, as he soon found himself running beyond the shroud of the flames. Up ahead a ways, he spotted the elevators. The mob had thinned significantly, but the remainder persisted as fervently as ever. He pivoted to face them, his morningstar swinging feverishly and colliding with heads, torsos, and weapons indiscriminately. Neither he nor they had more than a moment to prepare, but it seemed a defensively frantic offense was serving him well enough. Throughout the assault, he shuffled backward toward the elevators. He glanced over his shoulder to see an elderly woman waiting to board. The doors opened.

Sinkua snatched a freshly disarmed soldier by the arm, holding him back against his body with his arm over his neck. His assailants took pause, deliberating over how they might get to their target without sacrificing his human shield. Sinkua glared through them and slowly withdrew his dagger. As a couple of them advanced, he shoved the soldier back into the midst of them and sprinted toward the elevators. The old woman had just stepped into the open elevator alone.

Swallowing for fear of the eventuality of his failure, he pitched the dagger at the open car. It stuck in the wall at a sharp angle behind the woman. Mortally frightened, she frantically pounded the door close button. The doors began to close when he was still a good ten meters shy. He gritted his teeth, the bloodthirsty personnel closing in behind him. With his heart pummeling his rib cage, he pounded out a few long strides and slipped through the narrow gap, scraping his chest and back as the doors tried to close on him.

Fearing a regretfully unanticipated episode, he breathed deeply to calm his anger. The elderly lady cowered in the corner, eyeing him fearfully. Sinkua turned to face her and sympathetically smiled.

"Sorry to have frightened you," he apologized as he recovered his dagger, "I needed the elevator to close as soon as I boarded."

"Y-you mean you're not going to kill me?" she asked as she apprehensively emerged from the corner.

"Why would I do that?"

"Because that's what your people do, isn't it? You kill people like us."

"Nobody decides who I kill but me," Sinkua shrugged, "You weren't trying to kill me, so I intend to return the favor. What were you doing up there, anyway?"

"Biroe asked me to report that his window had been damaged so he could file an expense report for the repairs. I assume that was your doing. Burned open on the twentieth floor. Ring any bells?"

"Clearly," he confirmed, "I take it you work in accounting then. That explains why you didn't attack me. Not much for combat?"

"You're right about accounting, but I neglected to attack you out of fear for my own life," she defended, "Some of the accountants are notorious for thinking CreSam is full of crap, but they stick around for the paycheck. They've all pieced together conspiracy theories about economic scandals and such, but as for me, I've kept my head down."

"So, I suppose using an accountant as a human shield wouldn't do me any good," Sinkua mused as the elevator slowed.

"I'm afraid not, young man."

"Well, when the door opens, be ready to run."

As they stepped off of the elevator, they could hear the humming of another car close behind. Sinkua looked up to find that it had just reached the twenty-second floor. He took the old lady by the hand and bolted for the hall. As she had suggested, no one there seemed to be interested in attacking him. Perhaps some shared her philosophy of self-preservation, but he assured himself that some among them withheld an assault out of a combination of contempt for their employer and sympathy for the resistance.

He released her hand and decelerated to give her the lead. A cacophony of footsteps echoed through the hall. As the old woman opened her office door, Sinkua glanced back to see a troop of soldiers approaching. She urged him in as she slipped inside. He promptly followed, and she slammed and locked the door behind them.

"Now what?" she asked, "You can't stay here."

"Open the window," he urged, "I'll go out the same way I came in."

"You're going to climb down from here?!"

"I climbed up to here!"

"Oh right. Sorry, I'm a little discombobulated," she confessed as she complied with his request.

"In case one of us doesn't make it, or I don't see you again, it was nice meeting you," Sinkua offered, the sound of soldiers growing louder, "Thank you for your help, um…"

"RoeZal," she introduced.

"Sinkua," he returned as he climbed through the open window and clutched the drain pipe.

RoeZal waved farewell as he swung his legs out over the ledge. He braced himself along the pipe with his feet, tightened his grip with his hands, and began a steady descent. Trying to ignore the height to which he had climbed in his earlier hubris, he reflected on what had just transpired.

CreSam no longer recognized him and could no longer be considered his father. That man was a hollow shell of the father Sinkua once knew, back when he still allowed others to call him MeiLom. The transformation was complete. Worse still, he had ordered him killed and bribed the hungry masses with a promise of scraps from the king's table.

From five floors above, he heard a loud smashing sound. Instinctively, he looked up despite knowing he would not be able to see what had caused it. He halted pensively, fearing for RoeZal and feeling helpless to stop it. To his shock and dismay, a fan of blood and flesh ripped through her window, meshing with a nearly simultaneous spray of shattered glass.

While he was transfixed by the trauma, a gunman emerged from the bloodied window and took aim at him. Frantically, he quickened his descent. Before a second shot could be fired though, another person leaned out the window through which he had entered. Providing a diversion most absurd, he hurled what looked like a human leg. Regardless of what it was, Sinkua told himself, it disarmed the gunman and gave him a fighting chance to escape.

Biroe pushed his chair back away from the window. His combative co-worker was undoubtedly vexed and would have no qualms with reassigning his next bullet. He wheeled his seat to the door and tucked himself behind the hinges. The door swung open, and he rammed against it. The door ricocheted and slammed into the unsuspecting soldier, knocking him to the ground. Biroe emerged from behind the door and snatched the fallen soldier's gun, aiming it defiantly at the other five soldiers.

"Tell ya folks what," he sneered, "You get me clear passage outta here, and I won't report your horizontal comrade for performing an execution without a trial. Try to stop me, and I'll make RoeZal's murder look like euthanasia."

Calling his bluff, one of them reached for the pilfered firearm. As promised, he was met with a frenetic barrage of bullets, ripping horrifically through his groin and erupting from the back with a wake of brackish blood. The remaining four soldiers recoiled with shock and disgust.

"Don't test me," Biroe flatly barked.

Sinkua dropped to the ground, his arms and legs throbbing. Among that, the murder of his new acquaintance, and trying to comprehend how CreSam couldn't find him even vaguely familiar, he ached through and through. Still, returning to the Subtransit was imperative. He limped along, his right leg too cramped to maintain a normal gait.

The roads were slightly more crowded now, but it seemed most people were still at their jobs. This boded well since it meant he was unlikely to be run over were he to stumble into the street during his excruciating journey home. Behind him, he heard a car slow as it approached. He cocked his head to see it stop next to him with the engine still running. The window came down, and out peered a raven-haired gentleman perhaps thirty years old.

"Followed me for the bounty?" Sinkua asked hoarsely, "You people don't let up, do you?"

"Get in the car, kid," the gentleman ordered.

"Kid?"

"Just get in the car, will ya? You look a wreck, and I'm offering you a ride home."

"Why should I trust you?"

"Any attempt I take at your life in here would jeopardize mine, as well," he explained, "That bounty won't do me much good if I'm dead, now will it?"

"Good enough," Sinkua accepted, though admittedly he was seeking to silence his doubts.

"So, where do your people live?" the driver asked as Sinkua closed the door behind himself, "Some place out in the ghetto?"

"We live in the Subtransit system. I'm staying at the Epsilon boarding dock."

"The Subtransit? You live in those run down abandoned tunnels?"

"They do a fine job of keeping you folks misinformed," Sinkua muttered, shaking his head in disbelief.

"What do you mean?" the driver asked curiously.

"I'll show you when we get there. What's your name, anyway?"

"Biroe. What's yours?"

"Sinkua," he introduced, suddenly feeling awkward in this coincidental encounter, "Sorry about your window, by the way."

"Water under the bridge," Biroe assured him.

"So, that was you who threw a leg at RoeZal's killer before he could pick me off. I'm not sure which to do first, thank you or ask why you had a leg to throw."

Biroe grabbed the right side of his pants and lifted his stump for Sinkua to see. Having somehow not anticipated this, perhaps because his life had brought him to expect something more bizarre, his eyes widened with surprise. It made sense though, as much sense as any explanation for an accountant throwing a leg from his office window could have made.

"Why the fake leg and the wheelchair?" Sinkua pried.

"The leg is just for balance, keeps the chair from tipping," Biroe clarified.

"In that case, I'll see if Yrlis can dig up a replacement for you," Sinkua offered.

"I don't know who that is, but thank you."

"Oh, and I'm sorry about RoeZal."

"Barely knew her," Biroe shrugged, "but it wasn't your fault."

Uulan shuffled along the walkways of the Subtransit system, peeking through the windows of open businesses as he passed them. His head tilted and turned constantly, his eyes never fixing upon one spot for more than a moment. He nervously avoided eye contact with anyone who offered it, suggesting that he was looking for something while hiding something. At NieRie's Bakery he found what he sought. His shoulders relaxed, and he exhaled with relief as he entered.

Farim leaned across a booth against the farthest wall, a damp rag in her hand. A bottle of generic cleaning spray hung from her belt loop, drooping her jeans on one side and exposing the top of her hip. She hummed along with the music on the intercom, classical Poravitian music performed on modern Lenguardian instruments.

"Farim, might I have a word with you?" Uulan asked as he approached.

"What the shit!" Farim flailed, "Geez, don't sneak up on a girl like that."

"Oh, I'm sorry. What are you doing here, anyway?"

"It's okay," she assured, "I was looking for something to pass the time, and NieRie said she could use a hand here. Anyway, what do you need?"

"If you're working, it can wait. When do you take your break?"

288

"Whenever I want," she shrugged, "I'm just here as a favor."

"That's awfully kind of you," Uulan paternalistically complimented, "Now then, do you recall why we cannot challenge Imperial ArcNos's status as a legal nation?"

"Yes. Why?"

"That law was repealed because nobody could agree on an objective method for determining what was too weighty a proposal," Uulan explained, "but apparently, the Union Parliament forgot about this often overlooked detail."

"Are you certain?" Farim asked, taking a seat in the newly cleaned booth.

"Ninety-five percent certain," Uulan admitted, acknowledging that his memory may have been fading at his age, "This is where you come in. Do you have any friends in Eprilen?"

"I have business contacts, but no friends."

"That will suffice."

"Do you need me to have them look into it for you?"

"No, no, that part is under control," he insisted, "I've written one of my former graduate students to request a copy of that page from a text."

"I don't see where you're going with this, Uulan. What do you need a contact in Eprilen for, then?"

"To look into my suspicion," he finally revealed, "I'm wondering if this was an honest mistake on their part, or if somebody in the Union Parliament is working against us."

"Do you think they may have been infiltrated by the Avatars?" she asked, leaning over the table and whispering.

"I fear the worst, yes," he confirmed with a pensive nod, "Ask your business contacts what rumors they may have heard on such. In the meantime, keep this between us. This is only a hunch, so I don't want to create an undue disruption."

CreSam tapped the surface of his desk, anxiously waiting for someone to claim the bounty. Smoke from the hall continued to drift under the door, much to his growing chagrin. The hubris of that Hybrid was insufferable enough, but the notion that all available personnel failed to dispatch him was downright intolerable. The door finally opened, but who followed was not at all who he expected to see.

"You of all people?" CreSam barked, somewhat surprised but more bitter.

"No, I never came near him. I couldn't find my weapon," Kabehl admitted, "I'm here to report the aftermath of your orders."

"I'm not going to like the sound of this, am I?"

"The target escaped through a window on the twentieth floor after leaving just over a dozen casualties. He was abetted by an accountant named RoeZal."

"Have her executed," CreSam interrupted.

"An officer in pursuit took care of that," Kabehl assured in brief tangent, "Biroe escaped with him, and the two are now on the road together, likely heading for the gates."

"Who is this Biroe? Another accountant?"

"Yes, sir."

"How much does he know?" CreSam asked, contemplating the risk of allowing a financial insider to travel with an infamous dissenter.

"He was involved with our acquisition of the nautical combustion engine and everything that followed."

"Hunt them down."

"Shall I deploy troops into the city?"

"No, let the failures stay behind and lick their wounds. We needn't stain the pavement with more of their blood," CreSam sneered, "Deactivate the locks. Manually override the surveillance units beyond and nearest all gates. Deploy the nearest sentinels when you see Biroe's vehicle pass. That boy may be able to handle one, but he'll not be so fortunate against a swarm."

"Anything else?" Kabehl asked with a wickedly satiated grin.

"Tell The Hunter to stand by for coordinates," CreSam ordered, "He'll appreciate the sound of that, I'm certain."

"If you don't mind my asking," Biroe began, breaking a long silence, "how did you get through the gate?"

"I climbed over it," Sinkua answered, "Why?"

"Well, that's no good," Biroe muttered.

He drummed his fingertips on the steering wheel, contemplating how he could get his car beyond the gates. Were he a high-ranking officer, this would not have been so much of a problem. They were given permanently functional cards which allowed them to open and close the gates at will. Everybody else had conditionally functional ones, operational when duty called for it and plastic junk the remainder of the time. Biroe's last trip out of the city had been several months prior, so there was no bother in hoping his card's deactivation had somehow been overlooked.

He briefly considered asking Sinkua if he could carry him over on his back. That idea was dismissed for several reasons, the most pressing being the fact that Sinkua would then need to push him the remainder of the trip. This strange young man in his passenger's seat was undoubtedly cut from sturdy stock, but such a task would be quite too much to ask.

"What kind of lock is on the gate?" Sinkua asked.

"It's an electromagnetic system, requires an active passage card to disengage it," Biroe explained, worrying the explanation would go over his head.

"In other words, the console turns the lock off if you swipe a working card and turns it back on after you pass through," Sinkua reiterated for confirmation, "It sounds like the console powers the lock, then. What if we just destroy it?"

"I sincerely doubt that would work, but I won't stop you from trying."

Soon thereafter, they reached the gates. Biroe rolled to a stop, nodding to Sinkua to execute his markedly flimsy plan. Of course, even if it were to fail, Sinkua would get the pleasure of destroying imperial property, and Biroe would have the privilege of watching it happen.

Sinkua reared back and bashed the console with his morningstar, puncturing the shell and producing a cacophonous resonance. He repeated a couple of times until frayed wires dangled from the holes. Quite serendipitously, they heard the telltale whir of the locks disengaging. The gate remained shut though, but after Sinkua reentered the car, Biroe nudged it open with the nose. Given the circumstances, the fact that Sinkua's idea had worked was not so lucky as they assumed. In fact, it was more a show of his unwittingly impeccable timing than of any inherent electromechanical knowledge.

"I should have you know, they'll probably decide to pursue us somehow," Biroe warned, shattering the illusion of good fortune, "I played a part in obtaining the manufacturing rights to Ivaria's aquatic combustion engine and in the false treaty with Haprian."

"Then you're probably right. You know too much for them to let you flee," Sinkua agreed, "Get us to the Epsilon boarding dock, and I'll take care of anyone in pursuit."

From the corner of his eye, Sinkua noticed the head of a streetlight pivoting as they passed it. The next one did likewise, along with two more beyond that. He assumed only one possibility, and were it right, he knew it could not bode well. A fleet of troops, he could handle, but disposing of a sentinel while preserving Biroe's intactness would be a rather troublesome undertaking, especially considering he nearly died destroying the last one he faced.

Quite to his disappointment but none to his surprise, the sound of metal striking asphalt in a steady rhythm echoed throughout the city blocks, growing louder with each iteration. He lowered the window and leaned his head out, rubbernecking in hopes of catching sight of the sentinel in pursuit. While he could not yet see the sentry, his ears caught another set of mechanical footsteps joining in. It was either that, or the first had quickened and staggered its gait for some inexplicable reason.

One emerged a few blocks away on a cross street. The sound of its footsteps amplified as it hastened its pursuit. Still hearing another set of footsteps, Sinkua was certain that a second sentinel was approaching as well. Gradually, the sounds of a third and fourth became audible.

"They must really hate us," Sinkua muttered.

"What makes you say that?" Biroe asked, unaware of the impending assault.

"Can you not hear that?"

"I lost half my hearing in my right ear, so I suppose not. Is someone after us?"

As though on cue, the first sentinel burst onto the street, its presence overflowing the rearview mirror. Biroe whipped his head around to look over his shoulder, hoping that what he saw in the mirror was an hallucination somehow rendered by apprehension

"Oh, fuck me sideways!" he shouted.

He stomped the accelerator as the sentry barreled toward the car, guns aimed and ready to launch. Both he and Sinkua were forced back in their seats by the sudden jerk and held there as their speed persisted. A second came into view a couple of blocks ahead. Biroe whipped around a corner with the right tires only grazing the asphalt. Sentinel number three burst onto the scene soon thereafter, necessitating a hard right at the next intersection.

Biroe wove through ruined city blocks, guided by his intricate knowledge of the city from before the imperial uprising. Despite his hopes to slow their pursuit, the sentinels plowed through the corners of buildings to narrow the gap. Every corner he turned was punctuated with a spray of brick fragments and dust. From the west, a fourth sentinel came sprinting to join the hunt. Their only solace was that they had reached the street from which Sinkua had begun his travels, albeit still a few kilometers from the Epsilon boarding dock.

Sinkua turned backward in his seat to study each sentinel's movement. Though all four were bipedal, each had a uniquely structured torso. He analyzed their designs, anticipating what armaments and capabilities each one might possess. Squinting to peer through the airborne debris, he could faintly see an outline of a chain coiled within a chamber upon one's shoulder.

"Get that one with the barrel on its shoulder in the lead," he ordered, "Then, get back on this road."

The target was at the back of the line. Biroe immediately took the next right turn, and the first three followed. He moved up three blocks, took another right turn, then a third. Less than two blocks shy of coming full circle, the chain-wielding sentry caught sight of them and ripped through the corner for a frontal assault. It followed as Biroe pulled hard to the left, cutting in front of the other three pursuing from behind. After two more right turns, they were back on the street where they had started.

"Now what?" Biroe asked, looking back nervously.

"Turn us around and kick it into reverse," Sinkua commanded as he opened the door and rose to his feet.

"Are you insane?!"

"We'll debate that later. Just do it!"

Fraught with doubt, Biroe skillfully whipped the car around. Once it was facing the sentinels, a position he thought to be suicidally vulnerable, he threw the car into reverse and stomped the accelerator. Sinkua was nearly knocked off balance but held fast to the open door. He set a foot in the open window and another atop the car. Bracing himself, he brought his first foot to the top of the door. He stared up at the charging sentinel as it narrowed their lead, feeling those lifeless eyes glaring through him. Two instruments of revolution, one forged of steel and the other of flesh, they met gazes as they analyzed one another's motions to anticipate what gambits may be played.

The sentinel closed in, and the remaining three followed close behind. It launched a flurry of bullets just past the back of the car. Biroe ignored the threat and pressed through, putting a constellation of bullet holes in the trunk. Another storm of bullets followed, puncturing the hood. Oil poured into the street. Sinkua stood as erect as he could without releasing his grip on the top of the door. Biroe's eyes anxiously darted between Sinkua and the sentinels, fearing both for the death he may face or further beatings his already damaged body might suffer should they survive.

The chain stirred, and a steel spike emerged from the darkness of the barrel. Biroe's eyes widened with fright. His leg tightened as he jammed the accelerator against the floorboard, eliminating the need for all but one final order. The entrance to the Epsilon boarding dock was five blocks away. Tipped with a steel spike half the size of a man, the chain roared from the barrel. Sinkua leapt from his perch as two words thundered forth from his chest.

"Find Galo!"

292

Chapter 28

Because of the momentum, Sinkua's body soared backward when he sprang from atop the car. As he had anticipated though, the sentinel accounted for its target's persisting velocity and aimed well beyond. Biroe managed to clear the chain, and Sinkua dropped onto it exactly as planned.

He staggered and stumbled, fumbling to grasp the links before he collapsed onto the cratered pavement. With an agility born from years in the wilderness, he quickly gained his balance. Gripping his enflamed morningstar, he bounded up the chain and bludgeoned the side of the chamber. Mechanisms within rattled, and he pounded again and again, piercing and denting the barrel. The chain rumbled as the sentinel failed to extract it from the asphalt and recoil it. Sinkua ran down half the length of the chain and leapt to the ground, charging at the other three the moment his feet struck pavement.

Next in line was one comparable to the beast from his nightmare, although it was significantly smaller in stature. He stood in a pool of discarded oil from the engine of Biroe's car. Biting with hopes of a feast of insolent flesh, the second sentinel bored its two tripod spikes into the ground by Sinkua's sides and launched itself forth. The moment it left the ground, Sinkua leapt back and continued backpedaling. With a swipe of his hand, he sparked the pool of oil into an angry inferno. The sentinel slammed down upon it, an eruption of fiery rubble and scorched asphalt blooming skyward around it as it staggered.

Sinkua cocked an ear to hear the sound of Biroe's dying car approaching once again. He veered to the sidewalk to offer Galo a battlefield free of collateral lives.

"Galo!" Biroe shouted from atop the stairs, bound by his wheelchair.

No one called back. He shouted again, still to no avail. Leaning to one side, he could see children playing on the loading dock. Just as Sinkua had told him, it had become a subterranean community. Given the scandals he had been forced to perpetuate, it came as no surprise that the imperialists would hide such a thing, but the knowledge that the Subtransit system had been converted into an underground metropolis on such a small budget of time and resources was nothing short of astounding. Inspired by their will, he clung to the banister and cautiously scooted out of his wheelchair. He stretched his body down the staircase and set his foot down on the farthest step within his reach. Using the banister for leverage, he hoisted himself upright. Flirting with unstableness, he hopped down the stairs with both hands clutching the banister.

"Excuse me!" he called into the mess of children, "Do any of you know Galo?"

Diverting from their play for only a moment, one of them pointed toward Galo's hammock. The game resumed as though nothing remotely strange had just occurred.

Galo laid upon his hammock, immersing himself in an old Kirtsian epic novel, a gift from Uulan. He had been trying to distract himself from embarrassing memories of his morning with Vielle, but he was bound too tightly in the intriguing confines of the narrative to hear his own name being called. Biroe lightly tapped his shoulder, and Galo jumped with a startle.

"Why is a one-legged imperialist down here interrupting me?" Galo asked with a cold piercing glare.

"I've defected, and Sinkua needs your help," Biroe succinctly answered.

"He must be at the center of that racket above," Galo deduced as the noise breached the newly shattered barrier of narrative intrigue, "Take me to him."

Vielle had heard the noise above and had come running from other tasks. Seeing Galo rise from his hammock with his glaive, her memories flashed with vivid recollections of Sinkua's near brush with a grisly demise.

"Take me with you!" she called to him, still sprinting.

"You're not ready yet," Galo called back, failing to understand her worries, "Stay back and spread a warning."

Galo hoisted Biroe onto his back and hurried up the stairs, his legs braced under the additional weight. At the top, he deposited his grateful passenger first into his wheelchair then both into the driver's side of the car, bypassing its lift mechanism. Galo agilely slid over the hood and entered on the passenger's side.

"I know what he wants me to do," Galo asserted, looking onward into the crowd of sentinels as Sinkua jumped from one paralyzed by its own mechanism.

Inspired by memories of his grandfather's final moments, he clenched his fist and meditated upon the Serpent Bracer, gripping that forearm with his other hand. A familiar blue glow radiated from the bracer, creating a dry moisture that coursed over his flesh. The bracer still alight, he opened his eyes. Up ahead, he saw Sinkua standing defiantly in the path of a sentinel.

"We'll need to bail out," he commanded with his glaive poised.

"Are all of you this crazy?!" Biroe shouted.

"We can take a vote on that later," Galo insisted, eerily similar to Sinkua's response to essentially the same question, "Take my hand."

Finding himself trapped in trusting him, as doing otherwise would definitely kill him whereas complying only might end his life, Biroe held Galo's outstretched hand. Galo pulled Biroe's body against his, simultaneously wedging his glaive between the wheelchair and the accelerator. As he did so, Biroe reached across his body and pulled the door handle. Galo rammed the door open with his shoulder. With Biroe clinging Galo's side and shuddering with dreadful anticipation, the two rolled out of the speeding car and met painfully with the asphalt.

They rolled several times, wincing and calling out in pain with each strike of body to pavement. Galo pushed Biroe away and left him lying on the asphalt as he rolled into a crouching kneel. The abandoned car screamed forth, pissing a trail of oil. Galo raised his fist, the Serpent Bracer radiating a brilliant blue glow, and with courage born from the memory of salvation brought forth at the hand of his grandfather, pounded the pavement.

Biroe rose to his hands and knee and watched in amazement as three blue streaks zigzagged along the ground. As both Galo and Sinkua hoped and intended, they passed the car in spite of its roaring velocity. Sinkua slipped back into an alley and watched with great pride. Galo looked back over his shoulder and pointed his hand at

Biroe, creating a protective shell of ice over his body with a small air hole. Biroe began to call out in puzzled protest, but his request was muffled and thus ignored.

Exhausted, Galo stayed hopelessly on his knees and watched the streams of highly concentrated milystis scream into the midst of the sentinels. Each of them formed a large pool beneath its own target. The abandoned car was a stone's throw from the one bound by its own chain. Three massive crystalline obelisks exploded from the asphalt, crushing through the armor of the three metallic colossi.

Those soulless beasts could do naught but watch as the car they once hunted carved through flames freshly quenched by oncoming streams of oil. The car slammed into the leg of the stomping monolith and burst open in a fantastic display of gnarled chrome and scorched glass and steel. Hot shrapnel ripped into the other two frigidly bound guardians of imperialism. The one at the center of it all was annihilated from the waist down. Between the icy impalement and the fiery shredding, the other two were forced to cease function.

Unfortunately, Galo had failed to notice the fourth sentinel trailing in their shadows. It barreled forth through the wreckage, one arm aimed incessantly at him while he remained helplessly on his knees. Sinkua sprinted alongside it on the sidewalk, adrenaline coursing through his body as he strove to match its massive mechanical stride. The sentinel stopped a few meters from Galo, and its fist spiraled open into a gaping barrel.

In the typical dead silence of the streets, a distant metallic click may have been heard, but buried in the cacophony of destruction, it was rendered inaudible. A cannonball bellowed from the sentinel's fist cannon. Sinkua ran into the street and sprang high, swinging his morningstar with a straining outstretched arm. The highest spikes knocked against the cannonball. That was far from enough to knock it off course, but it did stall for a blink of a moment.

Much to their fortune, the effort proved sufficient though in a remarkably bizarre way. From origins unknown and aimed for Galo, a bullet shrieked through the smoky air and instead pierced the delayed cannonball. The bullet exploded within the surface of the dwarfing projectile, and the cannonball plummeted. What appeared for a fleeting moment to be another psychologically debilitating near miss on Sinkua's part had become fantastically serendipitous salvation.

Sinkua landed and turned to charge the final sentinel. Instead, he was surrounded by a flash of shimmering warmth. A surge of electricity enveloped the jaded sentry, jolting it violently. As the shock waned, the monstrosity slumped over.

"I thought you two might need me to finish things," Eytea confidently called out as she descended.

A loud metallic creaking caught Sinkua's attention as he turned to face her. Anxiously, he glanced over his shoulder to see that last sentry tipping forth. Mind reeling, he quickly looked from the dead beast to Galo, then to Biroe, then to Eytea. Frenetically scraping a plan together, he sprinted toward a fading Galo, hurling a ball of fire at Biroe's crystalline enclosure along the way.

"Eytea, grab him!" he shouted.

Sinkua deftly swerved, dodging the fallen sentinel. Its compromised structure shattered on impact, spraying debris and sheets of shrapnel. The head snapped loose and rolled down the street. Sinkua coughed a few times and spat blood rather passively as he lengthened his stride, pounding out meter after meter and trying to outpace the runaway head.

Biroe hoisted himself up on his arms, gasping for air as though he had just emerged from a deep dive. His eyes widened with fear as he was greeting by a careening sheet of smoldering metal, spewed forth by a felled pursuant. From behind him, Eytea swooped low, her breasts nearly grazing the battered asphalt, and scooped her arm under his torso. He jumped with surprise as she scooped his body and agilely veered to evade the oversized shrapnel.

Desperately, Sinkua rammed the head with his shoulder as he caught up to it. This was minimally effective, but it wobbled nonetheless. Again and again, he butted his shoulder against it, veering it from its course and, more importantly, decelerating its roll. He swerved several steps away from it as they neared Galo. Gritting his teeth in preparation for the impact, Sinkua charged the runaway metallic boulder one last time. At the moment of collision, he reached just beyond and snatched Galo out of its path, his shoulder loudly popping. Adrenaline surging to help him endure the pain, he hoisted Galo onto his shoulders and began walking the remaining distance bowlegged.

"Are we flying?" Biroe asked as he emerged from his stupor.

"Yep," Eytea replied casually, "It's something of a specialty of mine."

"With actual wings?" he followed, trying to see around to her back.

"As natural as the fibers in my coat," she said.

Biroe looked back to the wreckage. Sinkua had just saved Galo and was struggling to walk with his unconscious comrade and brother. Their walk was to be a long and undeniably arduous one. Empathizing with the struggle for mobility, he beckoned Eytea to help them. She explained sorrowfully that she could not, because even Sinkua by himself was too heavy for her to carry in flight. His request was noted however, as she had already been considering how she might aid them.

When they reached the top of the stairs, Sinkua and Galo were still several scores of meters behind. The barreling head of the last sentry rolled past them. Eytea set Biroe next to the railing, which he used to hold himself erect, and flew down the stairs with a growing sense of urgency. Biroe listened intently but could not catch any clarity in her conversations as she dashed about the loading dock. The first two Hybrids' tactics had worked well enough to get them this far though, so he was willing to trust in her plan even if it meant further bruising.

Moments later, she emerged with a pair of longboards, borrowed from a couple of adolescents. She ran past him, signaling for him to wait by the railing. Granted, he couldn't do much else. As she took flight, she shouted to catch Sinkua's attention. When he looked up and saw her approaching with longboards, he laid Galo upon the pavement and sat next to him to catch his breath.

"How did I live through days like this before you came along?" he asked as Eytea landed in front of him.

"Maybe you weren't so reckless before," Eytea suggested with a flirtatious smirk.

Sinkua chuckled, wincing from the pain in his chest, as he set Galo atop one of the boards with Eytea holding it steady. He bent Galo's knees, setting his feet flat upon the surface, and curled his fingers over the edges. He then placed himself on the other board in similar fashion, except that he also held Galo's board in one hand, anchoring them to one another. Eytea released the board as Sinkua lifted his feet from the pavement, and he and his unconscious brethren rolled down the road on a makeshift tandem street luge.

Galo regained consciousness as they rolled along, instinctively clutching the longboard when he realized he was moving inexplicably. Glancing to the side and seeing that Sinkua was reasonably calm in the same situation, he assured himself that no trouble was afoot. Before he could ask, Sinkua confirmed what he hoped, telling him their plan succeeded. Unfortunately, that left them with the task of apologizing to Biroe for destroying his car and his wheelchair in the process, a burden for which Galo felt himself responsible.

Near the top of the staircase, they both dismounted and snatched the boards before they could ramp down into Epsilon. Insisting on demonstrating some independence, Biroe refused assistance and hopped down the stairs. His use of that leg was notably diminished, but he had retained enough strength to gradually perform such a task. Sinkua and Galo both waited for him at the bottom of the stairs with Eytea only a few steps behind, anticipating how Sinkua might handle this situation.

Sinkua set his hand on Biroe's shoulder when he successfully completed his awkward journey. With his other hand, he dug around in his pocket and eventually fished out the bank card with his Tournament of Duelers winnings. Most of it had been allocated to the treasury, but he had been allowed to keep a considerable sum for himself.

"Do you drink?" Sinkua asked.

"Not often, but I think this would be a good time for a cold one or two," Biroe answered, trying to appear calm about the whole mess.

"You helped save my life on more than one occasion today," Sinkua complimented, holding the card between his fingers, "and I destroyed your every transport returning the favor. Take this card and buy yourself a drink. When you finish, buy another one. Keep going until you're too drunk to care that your car is scattered all over the highway."

"Thanks, but where do…?"

"I'm going to bed," Sinkua interrupted, "Ask someone else."

"If he feels like he can sleep, it's best to just let him," Galo explained.

"Oh, you have no idea what sort of day he's had," Biroe agreed, "but where's the bar?"

"I can help you out with that," Eytea offered as she took his hand.

"You? Aren't you a little young to drink?"

"Two years shy, but MalVek can lead you to a bar," she clarified, "I don't know where he is though, but I can show you where Phylus is."

Walking as though they were in a three-legged race, Eytea led him to the meeting hall where Phylus continued to work on a multitude of federal affairs.

"And Phylus will lead me to MalVek?" Biroe assumed.

"Not directly. Phylus will lead you to Spril. Spril will lead you to Yrlis. Yrlis will lead you to MalVek. MalVek will take you to the bar."

"Oh boy, it's like a scavenger hunt for beer!" Biroe joked.

Biroe braced himself on the wall while Eytea knocked on the door and opened it. Phylus looked up from the pile of papers to see Eytea leading a former now one-legged colleague into the assembly hall. Eytea dismissed herself for unexplained personal reasons.

"Biroe?" he asked, "What in the world happened to you?"

"Too much to discuss standing here. Care to talk about it over a round?" Biroe offered, recognizing his old co-worker.

"I'm going cross-eyed looking at these figures," Phylus confessed, "Let's hit the bar. We can talk about your role in the community before we get too sloshed."

Biroe explained in short detail that he recently lost his wheelchair in a fire. So, they improvised with an office chair. One dirty wheel made it wobble and sometimes veer off course, but Phylus was able to keep it rolling reasonably straight.

The wreckage of four sentries fading in his rearview mirror, SenRas continued driving toward the eastern seaboard. Yet again, the Hybrids had proven to be masters of prevailing against ridiculous odds. More importantly, Sinkua's propensity for combative tactics was shown to be rivaled by only one person he knew. Indeed, he was Lord CreSam's son.

His lips bitten by the chilled air of the Frigid, he applied chap stick, but the surface was dry. He tried a second time, once again unsuccessfully. Puzzled, he rubbed his fingernail over the top and could not scratch it.

"Be careful with that," a voice from inside warned, startling him quite comically.

"CreSam?" he asked the chap stick, "Did you bug my chap stick?"

"Of course not, all that moisture would be hazardous," CreSam argued, "I gave you a decoy so you could report to me surreptitiously."

"These are the sort of things you should tell me, sir," SenRas insisted.

"I did tell you," CreSam countered, "I told you when I briefed you for this assignment."

"I'm not on an assignment. You suspended me and told me to use this time to observe and report."

"I suspended you? When?"

"This morning, just a few hours ago."

"What reasoning did I give for this punishment?"

"Do you remember that boat that the Hybrids sank near the east bank?"

"I remember hearing about it, yes. Kabehl mentioned it today."

"I was accused of sabotaging that ship."

"Did you do it?"

"According to the records, yes."

"Why don't I remember any of this?"

Throughout the conversation, SenRas had been digging through his remaining pockets as well as the glove compartment and the center console in search of functional chap stick, preferably one that had not been technologically altered. A moment after CreSam asked that question, his theory to which could rattle the foundation of the empire, he found one wedged between his seat and the console.

"That's what I'm going to find out," SenRas asserted before chucking the decoy out the window, sending it to crack against the asphalt.

Vielle tiptoed to Sinkua's hammock and knelt behind him. Careful not to startle him, she set her hand upon his shoulder and shook him lightly. He didn't budge. She shook harder, and still he didn't budge. Fearfully, she set two fingers on the side of his neck. He still had a pulse. He was just in an atypically deep sleep.

"Sinkua?" she whispered in his ear.

He stirred partially awake and turned to see her. He mumbled incoherently, but the puzzled expression on his face asked quite clearly why she was awakening him.

"I need to talk to you about Galo," Vielle insisted.

"Something wrong training?"

"No, the training is great," Vielle assured him, "but he tried to kiss me."

"Good for him," Sinkua murmured.

"I pushed him away, and I think he thinks I hate him now."

"Do you?"

"No, of course not," Vielle insisted.

"Why talk me? Talk him."

"You're not trying to get at my knickers," Vielle explained, "He'd play every card in the deck to assure me I don't need to be scared."

"Scared what?" Sinkua asked, his grasp of language still lacking in his diminished state of consciousness.

"Of intimacy," she clarified, "or the male body in general. I'll explain when you're awake."

"Maybe you lesbian," he suggested.

"Maybe I am," she agreed, not realizing it was a joke, "I never thought about it, but Eytea is pretty cute."

"Of course cute. She not count."

"Well, if I am, it sounds like I've got competition," Vielle teased as she patted his shoulder.

"Hmm, maybe," Sinkua grumbled, "Back sleep now."

Galo walked through the charred wreckage under a red evening sky, a long metal pole balanced on his shoulder. A crowd of citizens stayed behind, waiting at the entrance to the Epsilon boarding dock. The myriad stenches of burnt materials had grown thick as flammable wreckage continued to burn, and now hung heavily in the cold air. When he reached the remains of the sentry Sinkua had used to detonate the oil fire trap, he jammed the pole into the ground.

"That's where we'll start our search," Eytea ordered from within the crowd, "We'll work our way out from there. Bring back anything large or that looks important."

After escorting Biroe to the meeting hall, Eytea had gone off in search of NalSet. He was not to be interrupted though, so she settled for MalVek instead. She explained the situation to him as best she could, and MalVek insisted that he and his brother could build a new car and wheelchair for Biroe out of the wreckage. He also supposed NalSet may be able to use some of the scraps in his shop. So, at her behest, Galo agreed to assemble a recovery team. This left Vielle to practice her arbormancy on her own, though most of that time was spent either consulting with a barely conscious Sinkua or helping Spril in his personal endeavor to construct a combat training hall for the coming foreign aid.

Dozens of flashlight rays swept over the asphalt. One after another, findings were reported, but most were to state that certain parts had been charred nearly beyond recognition. Most of the engine components had little more use than for smelting. Anything that could be positively identified was returned to the Epsilon entrance though, in case the brothers' talent for restoration was far beyond what any of them assumed. Pieces of the sentries were returned as well, mostly electronic components. Fragment of outer casings were too large for anyone to carry.

"I've got what looks to be a backrest over here," one of the searchers called out, "Doesn't look like a car seat though. More like a movie director chair, or maybe a wheelchair."

"That's a wheelchair," Galo confirmed, "The driver was disabled."

"There's a wooden stick jammed through it," the searcher called back, "Should I try to retrieve it?"

"Don't bother, it's just a stick," another worker insisted.

"Wait there, I'll get it out," Galo announced as he ran to the worker's side.

When he arrived, he found a wooden pole impaling the singed leather backrest, just as the worker had promised. He traced it into the gnarled ruins, discarding chaff as he moved down its length. It was damaged but still whole. He uncovered the head of his glaive and withdrew it from the wreckage, pushing the backrest off the butt of the handle. Delightedly puzzled, he held it up to the moonlight, the blade glistening as though it had suffered nary a spark.

"I would scarcely say this is just a stick."

Chapter 29

A pair of empty shot glasses slammed against the bar simultaneously, joining six other pairs. Phylus and Biroe winced and gritted their teeth as they pounded their fists on the bar like a couple of college roommates. Phylus whistled to the barkeep and ordered yet another pair of shots.

"So they try to tell me there's a memo," Biroe recounted through slurred speech, "about some demolition crew blowing out a wing so they can rebuild the interior."

"They did what? Are you serious?!" Phylus shouted over the noise, mostly in his head.

"Serious as your haircut, bitch!" Biroe retorted in a stupor, "Got my leg blasted off, spine broken and a punctured ear drum, and all I got was that I should've known better. They gave me a crappy leg and a crappy wheelchair and put me back in the same crappy job for the same crappy pay under the same crappy monitoring. So y'know what I say?"

"Too crappy much!" Phylus slurred, impatiently holding his next shot with a shaky hand.

"I say, fuck the empire!" Biroe shouted, warranting hurrahs from throughout the bar, "Now where can a drunken cripple get a piece of tail in this bar?"

"Sir, I'm going to have to ask you to leave," the barkeep ordered, losing patience with Biroe's disruptive conduct.

"You can't kick me out," Biroe argued, "I have temple manic community!"

"You mean diplomatical mutiny," Phylus incorrectly corrected, "and no you don't. We should go. My daughter is gonna be pissed. Whoa!"

Biroe scooted off the bar stool and landed facedown across the office chair. Too drunk to register pain, he laughed uncontrollably as Phylus recklessly rolled him out of the bar. Unconscious derelicts were scattered around the entrance, passed out in puddles of their own urine and pungent with the stench of alcohol.

During the train ride home, they both partook of the free coffee offered during the late night and early morning hours, though most of it ended up sloshed on their shirts. As they slowly sobered, the rattling of the rails became unbearably irritating. Over and over they clashed and banged, resonating through their ear drums and seeming to shake their brains with barbed wire hands. The reality of what Phylus had done slowly sank in, weighing heavily on his alcohol laden stomach.

"If the empire finds out I tried to take them to court," he muttered, "This could be really bad for me."

"Bad for you?" Biroe asked, "Bad for you how? You got drunk, big deal."

"No, no, you don't get it. I'm sort of in charge around here."

"Get out! You? Why would you go and get wasted in public, then?"

"Wasn't in the plan, genius. I don't suppose you took up public relations after I got fired, did you?"

"No, I'm still just an accountant."

"Well, if I still have sovereignty tomorrow morning, how would you feel about managing the books for this operation?"

"It seems like you have everything pretty well under control," Biroe complimented, his sobriety notably restored, "so it shouldn't be any challenge for me to keep it that way."

"We expect a huge influx of immigrants in the coming weeks, I think," Phylus added between painful gulps of coffee, "and I have no idea how to finance the population spike. You still want on board?"

"All the more so."

When they exited the train, the track lighting had been dimmed to a dull brown hue, simulating the darkness of night. Phylus looked up at it as though it was the sky itself and sighed with disdain for his recklessness. Before facing what was surely an inevitable smear campaign in the morning, he dreaded facing his daughter through bloodshot eyes and rancid breath. He placed a shred of hope in the idea that she might see some decency in his taking in a stranded and disabled houseguest, but Biroe's own inebriation would likely prove detrimental to that angle.

He slowly opened the front door, hoping not to awaken anyone as he entered. As he reached for the light switch though, he spotted a single lamp alight in the corner. Vielle sat in an arm chair, reading a magazine.

"Dinner is on the stove, Dad," she stated, not looking up from the glossy pages.

"Were you waiting up for me?" he asked, aiming for a sympathetic angle.

"No, not for you," Vielle answered, "Eytea took a late dinner on the go, so I was keeping it warm for her."

"Well, I suppose that works out well for me," Phylus mumbled, feeling dejected as he opened the pot, "Biroe is going to stay with us for a few nights, by the way."

"Evening," Biroe greeted, waving uncomfortably from a dining room chair.

"I heard about you. You and Sinkua saved each other's lives. As far as I'm concerned, you can stay as long as you want," Vielle welcomed as she rose from her seat, "But now that you and Dad are home, I'm going to sleep."

Phylus avoided eye contact as she passed. Under her breath, she assured him that he could talk with her in the morning as his hangover subsided. In recent years, she had become a source of confidence and assurance for him, thus putting her natural charisma to further use. Once she had shut her bedroom door, Phylus served a bowl first to Biroe, then one to himself.

Sinkua stirred awake somewhat bewildered by his surroundings. He recognized the environs themselves well enough, but awakening to such dim lighting felt unusual while his short term memory was still foggy. Bit by bit, he reconstructed the day's events, distinguishing reality from dreams as consciousness accumulated. Eventually, he recalled his treacherous return trip with a one-legged accountant, leading to a battle with four raging sentinels, followed by his passing out in his hammock in the middle of the afternoon. Though he had no perception of exactly how late he slept, this made waking up fully rested in the middle of the night less strange.

The reality of his conversation with Vielle was still up for introspective debate though, and the thought of it having truly occurred was all too embarrassing. On the surface, it was his opinion that he could not appear a solid and objective leader with affections toward any of the combatants. As though to prod at his internal turmoil, Eytea appeared from the shadows, carrying a tray.

"Did I wake you?" she asked in that impossibly silken tone.

"No, I've been up for a bit," he replied with forced nonchalance, "What have you got there?"

"I asked Vielle to keep it warm for us until you awoke," she offered, kneeling beside his hammock, "It's roasted lamb stew. I also got my hands on some Cherry Popken for you."

"You did all this for me after you saved me twice?" he asked, feeling painfully unworthy of the offerings.

"I've lost count of everything you've done for me, Sinkua," she assured him, gazing into his luminescent eyes, "Besides, you saved all of our lives, the three of you together."

"I never thought of it that way," he shrugged, sampling the stew, "On that note, what became of Biroe's car?"

"Galo and I gathered a crew to bring back whatever parts could be carried. MalVek and NalSet are going to see what they can make of the scraps."

"I feel horrible about destroying it like that. I mean, I didn't do it directly, but it was obviously part of my plan," he apologized between meaty spoonfuls, "Don't tell anybody I said that though. It would completely ruin my image."

"Your secret is safe with me," Eytea laughed, knowing his calculatingly cold image needed only be preserved before his adversaries.

Since the hammock was too unsteady for both of them to sit upon it with bowls of hot stew sloshing about, he dropped from it to sit beside her on the floor. Within an arm's reach to each of them sat a single mug of Cherry Popken, shared between. As they ate the peppery stew, basking in its warmth along with that of each other's silent presence, she laid her head upon his shoulder.

"Did Phylus start on those letters?" Sinkua asked nervously.

"What letters? The ones to your friends from your travels?" Eytea asked, not moving her head from his shoulder.

"Yes, those ones. He was going to start them this evening so I could sign and mark them and send out the first wave tomorrow."

"You haven't spoken to Phylus since before you left this morning," Eytea reminded him in a concerned tone, "Are you sure you remember talking to him?"

"Quite sure," Sinkua lied, doubting his recollection.

"You came down the stairs and went straight to your hammock, been here ever since. You probably dreamt it," she assured him, though it was just as much to assuage her own fears.

"Perhaps," he agreed half-heartedly, staring worriedly into his nearly empty bowl.

After their meal, Eytea excused herself to her hammock for the night. Sinkua watched blankly as she faded into the darkness, marinating in the unsettling confirmation of his failing memory. CreSam's failure to recognize him seemed attributable to a fault in his memory, but Sinkua's memories were becoming so indistinguishable from his imagination that he considered that it may have been a failure on his part. Perhaps, he thought, he and CreSam had never crossed paths before, and the identity of MeiLom was nothing more than a daydream flowered into an elaborate false memory. It sounded bizarre and unreasonable, but such observations did nothing to assuage his fear that his childhood was a lie. He wondered what upbringing he may actually have had but stopped short of devising scenarios for fear they would become entangled with the alleged memories already in place.

Naturally, this led to his questioning the sense of responsibility that drove him to restore the Subtransit system in his supposed hometown to an occupiable state. Even if his childhood memories were imagined to suppress an even more painful truth, he still might have grown up in the same city. However, this hardly felt like enough of a reason to stand by his unspoken promise to give back to the community he watched fall by the wayside and into ruin.

Walking along the wall far from the tracks, Sinkua noticed that seemingly every business had locked up for the night. Even the bars and party clubs were wrapping up their last call and sending the stragglers out into the artificial night. One door caught his attention though, as it was propped slightly ajar, and a light from within pierced the opening. He peeked inside curiously.

"Here I thought I was the only sober person awake right now," Spril mused when he saw Sinkua, "Come in, I could use the company."

"What are you doing in here?" Sinkua asked, studying the interior construction zone from within the doorframe.

"I'm building a training facility for our reinforcements. I know you have your own project, but if you can help, I'd appreciate it."

Sinkua mulled over the proposal in light of his newborn doubts. Were he to abandon his restoration efforts, he would need to find another contribution to the community. Though he certainly had a talent for it, defending the community from stampeding automatons was thankfully in too infrequent of demand to constitute a regular contribution.

He painfully recalled the carnage that washed over Masnethege the night he began his northward journey back to his homeland, followed by the lesser morbidity of the skirmish in Haprian. The key difference in the two encounters was in the combative strength of those whom he defended. The closest thing the Masnethegeans had to a domestic fighting force was the Tide Dancers, assuming any of them had adopted Galo's martial application of their techniques. In contrast, the Haprianites were equipped with firearms and the training to use them effectively. Coming to the difficult realization that proactive measures may have saved Masnethege, he silently nodded and stepped across piles of scrap lumber. Even if the memories were merely fabrications, teaching the people to defend themselves against the hand of tyranny was an effort worthy of pursuit.

Phylus laid face down on the couch, his left arm dangling off and his hand on the floor. Halitosis breath puffed from his dry gaping mouth. Vielle stood over him, shaking her head in disdain, and nudged his shoulder. His eyes flickered open, and she slowly came into focus.

"Coffee?" he muttered as he noticed the pot and mug in her hands.

"Yep. Want me to pour you some?" she whispered courteously.

"Don't bother," he mumbled as he slowly sat up.

Instead, he took the pot out of her hands and took a long scalding swig from it. A raspy gasp burst from his throat as his cheeks turned bright red and his eyes watered. He hacked and coughed a few times to clear his throat and handed the pot back to his daughter.

"Damn, I needed that."

"Are you ready to talk about what happened last night?"

"You remind me so much of your mother," Phylus sighed longingly, "She was always so critical of my staying out late, regardless of what I was doing."

"Don't compare me to the woman who abandoned us," Vielle retorted, "So long as it's legal, I'm not in any place to judge how you spend your nights, but I'm guessing you're worried you made an ass of yourself."

Phylus nodded with disappointment for himself. An old colleague had come to visit, and he couldn't help but join him for a drink, then another, and another. Even knowing the weight of the situation they were in and the responsibility resting upon his shoulders, he couldn't stop himself from drinking into public belligerence.

"Well, I gathered something that might cheer you up," Vielle comforted as she walked into the dining room.

A moment later, she returned with a stack of sheets of various sizes and materials. Phylus took the offering and sifted through them. They were all papers and advertisements from his campaign to rule the new Parliamentary Republic, but he couldn't discern her angle in giving him these.

"Those are copies of every piece of paraphernalia you used in your campaign," Vielle explained, "What do you notice about them?"

"That my real agenda has been no different from what I said it would be," Phylus guessed, "and that I too hastily promised to shut down the Autonomous Empire."

"Well, yes, but what do they all have in common?" Vielle asked, "Or rather, what do they all lack?"

"My portrait?" Phylus asked as he noticed the only pictures were of old cityscapes and the transformation of the Subtransit into a community.

"Exactly. The only people who know your face as our leader are those who know you personally," Vielle assured him, "So, you have nothing to worry about."

Shortly thereafter, a knock came at the door. Galo had come in search of Vielle. Engrossed in memories of his campaign and restoring his confidence in himself, Phylus offered no more acknowledgement than a blind wave and a greeting that scarcely qualified as a word. While Galo waited in the doorway, she fetched her cat-o'-nine-tails, and they left for the arboretum.

Rather than walk alongside him as she normally did, she stayed a couple of steps behind with her head low. After her conversation with Sinkua, she felt awkward and embarrassed in his presence, as though he was already aware of what she confessed. Still, she continued to trust that he was the best coach for her arbormancy, so she swallowed the lumps and continued on to the arboretum with him.

Eytea roamed the darkened corridor a couple of hours before the sun was due to rise. An unexplained sound had awakened her, and she felt compelled to go off in search of it. The sound repeated periodically, slowly going louder and guiding her in its direction. From around a bend, she saw a sharp flash and a fading flickering. Realizing the potential serendipity of the situation, she sprinted for a short burst and leapt with her wings spread to glide just above the ground.

Yrlis crouched beside her lantern, sifting through her toolbox in search of a smaller flathead screwdriver than the one in her grip. From off to the left, she heard footsteps followed by a quick gust of wind. As she fetched the screwdriver, she turned to see Eytea approaching with a look of urgency.

"What in the world are you doing up this early, babe?" Yrlis asked as she got to her feet with the lantern in her hand.

"I'm a pretty light sleeper," Eytea explained, "Complete opposite of Sinkua. He sleeps heavily but rarely. I sleep lightly but get plenty of it."

"Uh oh, I didn't wake you up, did I?" Yrlis apologized

"You did, but it's not your fault. Obviously, you have a job to do with this, um… What are you doing, anyway?"

"This breaker box has been finicky lately, and this is the best time to work on it. Most people are asleep, so there's no cause for alarm I accidentally kill their power for a while.

"Makes sense. Anyway, I needed to talk to you about something. I need your medical expertise."

"I'm no longer in practice, but what's wrong? Did something happen to Sinkua?"

"Yes, how did you know?"

"That boy is a walking emergency. Besides, I've seen the way you look at him."

"Right, well, um, I think he's losing track of his memories," Eytea worried, blushing at that last comment, "Even after he had been fully awake for several minutes, he couldn't clearly discern reality from dreams."

"I suppose that makes sense since his condition interferes with his amygdala and hippocampus," Yrlis suggested, losing herself in contemplation, "As his memories grow hazy, his impaired judgment could diminish his ability to distinguish them from his imagination."

"Do you have any idea what we can do for him?" Eytea asked, "You studied neurology, right?"

"Yes, some, but it's his blood and marrow that are infected. Neurosurgery would only be a temporary fix. But you knew that, didn't you?"

"I did, but I was just hoping that, well, maybe I was wrong."

"I'll tell you what we can do though," Yrlis offered with an epiphanous smile, "We can get a camera."

"What good will… Oh, right!" Eytea remarked, "Photographs will help him tell memories from dreams. That's really clever."

"What's really clever?" a male voice asked from off to the right.

Sinkua approached from the shadows, guided by the light of his enflamed hand. Yrlis smirked at the coincidence and chuckled to herself as she thought his ears must have been burning. Eytea walked past her and toward him, still worried for his mental health but relieved after the conversation she just had.

"We're going to help you keep your memory, or what's left of it," she told him hopefully.

"How do you expect to do that?" Sinkua asked with cautious optimism.

"With a camera. Any time there's a significant moment in your life, take a picture of it."

"So I can reference them in case I can't tell what actually happened from a dream about it. That conversation worried you, didn't it?"

"Can you blame me? Your first episode was triggered after you saved my life. I'd hate for you to completely lose yourself to it."

"I suppose not, then," Sinkua accepted, trying to hide his worry from her, "Anyway, I need to talk to Yrlis."

"About what?" Yrlis asked, not looking away from her work.

"Do you have any hospital contacts?" Sinkua inquired, "Maybe some old co-workers that you've kept in touch with."

"We cross paths now and then. What do you need?"

"I need a wheelchair. A defecting imperial employee brought me home, and I had his destroyed as part of our exit strategy."

"I have no idea what part destroying a wheelchair would play in an escape plan, but I suppose it's not my place to worry about that. Sure, I'll talk to somebody and get your friend a wheelchair."

"Thanks. He also only has one leg, so he needs a prosthetic one, too."

"Why does he need both?"

"He told me the fake leg was for balance. His wheelchair is prone to tip over without it."

"How cheap of a wheelchair was he in?" Yrlis exclaimed, offended by the poor medical service offered to the imperial administrative personnel, "He won't need a prosthetic leg even with the cheapest of the newer models."

"How would that work?" Sinkua asked curiously.

"It's not your place to worry about that." she assured him with a confident smile and a pat on the shoulder.

SenRas stared nervously out the window, watching the frosted conifers dash past in a green and white blur with abundant streaks of yellow. If he focused on one spot and followed it with his eyes, he could clearly see the outline of individual trees. This clarity was brief, but it sufficed in distracting him from his anxiety even if only for seconds at a time. Stricken again between focused gazes, he frantically patted his pockets for at least the tenth time since he boarded the train.

As he found at each previous check, he had nothing out of the ordinary on him. Ever since he discovered the chap stick bug, he had been overcome by the nigh constant worry that he had unknowingly been carrying a second bug. Of course, that worry stemmed from his defying CreSam's wishes by disposing of the first bug, but he suspected that another on him would more likely have been the work of the Avatars of Fate. Their awareness of his operational disdain for them was as apparent as that disdain itself, and his attempt to sully the name of their secondary protégé made it all the more so. So, the idea that they would plant their own bug before he left the capitol was something of a rational paranoia..

He stepped off the train in a town of memories from decades long past. The city had grown considerably in his absence, but pieces of the landscape still remained unscathed since his last visit some forty years ago. A few buildings were the same as he last saw them, stirring up memories from his youth. He came in search of just one in particularly though, and he packed a necessarily heavy dose of cautious optimism.

After a short cab ride, he reached a house from his younger hedonistic years. The shape remained the same, but the paint was a different color than he remembered. A decorative pond had also been installed, and the hedges were arranged differently. Steadfast in his confidence in his recollections, he knocked on the door.

"Hello?" a woman of perhaps sixty years asked when she answered a few minutes later, "Can I help you with something, sir?"

"XalRut?" SenRas asked, studying her eyes.

"How do you know my name?" she asked suspiciously, backing away from the door.

"It's me. SenRas."

Without another word, she stepped back and slammed the door, but he caught it with his hand and foot.

"I just need to talk to you, XalRut," he pleaded.

"What's to talk about? You ran out on me and our daughter, and now you want forgiveness?" XalRut asked bitterly, "Well, that isn't going to happen."

"That's not why I made the journey. As much as I wish for forgiveness, it's your place to offer it, not my place to ask for it. I'm here because I need your help."

"With what?" she asked, incapable of rejecting the man who abandoned her so many years ago.

"It's CreSam," he said, already fearing her reaction.

"No! No way, I won't do it."

"XalRut! At least hear me out," SenRas urged.

"Unless you need help killing him, count me out," XalRut snapped, "After what he did, did you honestly think I would help him?"

"That's exactly why you should help him," SenRas explained, "He has forgotten the atrocity he committed. He lives without torment."

"I would think that a relief for you, what with his being your commanding officer," she pierced, "Now he's free to focus on his agenda with the Avatars of Fate."

"Who says he and I have the same agenda? I need him to suffer now just as he did that day," SenRas insisted, "I at least owe her that much."

"For her, I'd be glad to help you. Making him suffer is icing on the cake. Come on in, and I'll put on a pot of tea. How long will you be staying?"

"As long as you'll have me. I've been suspended for eight weeks."

"Oh good," she remarked as she shut the door behind him, "It may take a while to teach you what you need to know."

Biroe reached over his shoulder and shut the door behind himself before wheeling between two occupied seats. Phylus's eyes panned the room, silently taking roll call in his head.

"Before we start, I'd like to introduce the newest addition to Parliament," Phylus began, motioning toward Biroe, "This is Biroe, our accountant and Chief Treasurer. Some of us knew him before the imperialist revolution."

"Back when I had two legs," Biroe added jokingly, "Speaking of which, thank you for the new wheelchair, Doctor Yrlis. It works fantastically."

"Oh, I'm no longer a doctor, but you're welcome," Yrlis accepted, "Let me know if you ever need the hydraulics adjusted."

Sinkua pulled a camera from his pocket and snapped a shot of Biroe in his new wheelchair, sitting in the Parliamentary assembly room.

"So then, orders of business. Who's got 'em?" Phylus asked with a strange casualness.

"Have the letters been mailed?" Sinkua asked.

Despite the tracking scents having been gathered by Sinkua, Vielle and Phylus insisted upon writing the letters in his stead. For one reason, an offer from the federal figurehead, for whom they had yet to decide upon a title, would be received with more serious consideration than one from a young man they met in passing and might have forgotten. Also, his history as a negotiator combined with Vielle's charisma and knack for sociology would enable them to convey a sense of urgency to each recipient and take a stronger hold on their empathy.

308

"My daughter and I just finished them yesterday. You should look over them first though, make sure we've not misspoken to anyone," Phylus answered.

"Galo and I will gather pigeons near the arboretum later today," Vielle reported, "and keep them in there until we're ready to send them off."

"I'd be glad to help if you'll have me," Eytea offered, knowing her ability to fly would be integral to their goal.

"Sinkua and I have nearly finished the training facility," Spril interjected, "It shouldn't take more than two or three nights to finish, but we still need weapons."

"We could raid one of their storehouses," Galo suggested, "Perhaps, they still have a few old swords lying around, collecting dust. Would nary be a problem for us to lift them. I can't imagine the security being anything even remotely impregnable."

"Once we find one, we'll need to scout the area before anybody actually breaks in," Farim urged, "I can help you cover your trail, but I'll need to know the terrain first."

"You think too little of us. We don't need our trail covered," Sinkua countered, "Anybody who tries to stop us will wind up dead."

"Sure, and how many more dead sentinels will be scattered on the street?" Farim asked, "How many more parts will fall just short of barreling down here and crushing someone? I know precautionary measures aren't your forte, but you need to trust me on this one."

"You'll need to wait a couple of weeks anyway," NalSet interrupted.

"Because it will take at least that long for reinforcements to arrive," Sinkua added.

"No, that's not why. If you're just going to guess, you might as well shut up," NalSet barked, "I understand the direct link surveillance system now, so we can intercept the signal from the street lamps."

"If they figure out we have access to their surveillance, they'll be wont to enforce security at any facility they suspect we might infiltrate. Given our affinity toward old fashioned low tech weaponry, any such storehouses will be high on the watch list," Spril added.

"Essentially yes, but you bastards need to quit finishing my thoughts," NalSet insisted, "MalVek, show them the device."

MalVek obediently reached under the table and hefted a suitcase atop it. Inside was the camera from the Avatars' laboratory, restored to full working condition, a monitor, and a remote control. MalVek uncapped the camera lens, stood the monitor upright, and turned both devices on. The screen displayed static snow. He fiddled with the receiver a bit, but the static remained.

"I thought you said you figured it out," Uulan reminded, "My knack for technology may be lacking, but it seems to me that we should see IlcBei and Vielle on the screen."

"My brother and I aren't pleased with merely knowing how something works," MalVek boasted, "We don't stop until we know how to manipulate it to our liking."

He pressed a series of buttons on the remote, and a clear video feed of the room appeared on the monitor. With one hand, he rotated the monitor for everyone to see, while he wobbled the camera with the other to prove that no trickery was at play. Knowing a barrage of questions was to come, NalSet took the initiative.

"This type of camera uses a specialized frequency transmitter. The frequency itself is available on standard receivers, but it's encoded with a unique signature, limiting access to receivers programmed to recognize that signature," he explained to hungry ears, "As long as we know the frequency, this remote will allow us to override the signature verification. Plus, it doesn't interfere with the transmission itself, meaning the intended recipients will be unaware of the interception and thus essentially incapable of learning of it after it occurs."

"In layman's terms, any monitor could potentially pick up the video off a normal camera. This one is made so that only certain ones can read the message, but this remote gets us around that," MalVek clarity, easing many a puzzled stare.

"I'll dismantle a street lamp so you can figure out its frequency," Sinkua offered.

"They're undoubtedly transmitting on multiple frequencies, so I'll need a few from different areas of the city. Also, leave the circuitry as intact as possible," NalSet insisted, "We still have one problem though. The astute among you may have caught it, but I doubt it."

"The screen flickered for a split second as it came on," IlcBei pointed out, "We're manipulating the nature of the transmission frequency, not the receiver. That means their video feed is going to scramble for a split second as well."

"Yes, how did you know?"

"My brother did a stint as a security technician in a metropolitan mall, and they had an experimental direct link surveillance system," IlcBei recalled, "They never had anybody do anything like this, but usually if one screen for a particular camera acted up, they all did."

"That's about the long and short of it," MalVek confirmed, "This means we'll need a dead transmission to create a window of opportunity, and that means shutting off the surveillance. Or rather, letting it die."

Accompanied by his brother and at times Yrlis, he went on to explain their acquisition and security of working electricity in the Subtransit. When IlcBei agreed to work with them and refused to sell the Subtransit system, they tightened their hold on the three power plants keeping it active. This was accomplished in two ways, the first being armed guards who had thus far been perfectly effective. However, their scheme to intercept street security began with allowing that perfect defense record to be broken.

As a backup, though certainly not in anticipation of an operation such as this, each one was wired to cause a random cascading failure in the event of sabotage. In other words, if power were rerouted to the empire, the plant would shut down and take four others, though never ones under their control, with it. MalVek was confident he could direct the failure to reach the plants which powered the surveillance monitors.

Two plants carried that burden, putting them in a conundrum. If security was lax in one plant, it could be written off as an accident. Foul play would be suspected though if half of the plants in the cascading failure were linked to the surveillance system. Letting two plants fall would make the direction of the failures appear more coincidental, but it would look less like a staffing error and more like a trap. On top of that, Parliamentary ArcNos would temporarily be running on one-third power. Given those conditions, it was agreed upon after considerable deliberation that they would only let one plant fall.

"NalSet and I will work out a way to guide the cascading failure," MalVek reported, "and put the method to use at our northernmost power plant the following day. The monitors may only be down for a moment so, IlcBei, be ready to intercept on a split second's notice. We'll launch a signal flare from the rooftop."

Soon thereafter, the meeting was adjourned and everybody filed out to return to their daily tasks. As Galo and Vielle split off from the crowd, Sinkua firmly grabbed

Galo's shoulder. Galo signaled for Vielle to go ahead to the arboretum.

"Is something wrong?" he asked, "You look a might distraught."

"My condition is getting worse," Sinkua muttered.

"What?" Galo reacted in disbelief.

"My condition, that thing with my brain!" Sinkua snapped, "It's getting worse. I'm taking my pills, but it's getting worse."

"That's why you've become distant in recent days, is it not? I assumed you were upset about your meeting with CreSam."

"Why would that have upset me?" Sinkua asked, baiting the hook to separate imagination from recollection.

"After five years and some-odd months, I doubt he would recognize you as his son any longer," Galo suggested, his eyes darting about to check for ears left wandering too closely.

"Well, that much has been put to rest."

"What do you mean by that?"

"Remember how I retired to my hammock once we returned from that brush with the sentinels?" Sinkua began, "I spoke with Eytea that night over Vielle's lamb stew, and I could clearly recall having asked Phylus to start the letters to send for reinforcements even though I hadn't yet. Now, when I think about the past, I can't tell if I'm remembering or imagining. My memories don't make any damn sense, because I don't know which ones are real anymore!"

"I don't know how much I can do to help you, to be honest. I know of a mixture that will help you retain clearer memories, but I can't promise that it will ease the burden of distinction," Galo offered, "After we send the letters, I'll gather the ingredients. Meanwhile, you should come to me to ease your doubts. I've been your confidant since we were children."

"Thank you, brother. Any way you can help me keep my nightmares and reality separate would be appreciated."

"Wait a moment, do you still have that old recurring nightmare, the one from Eytea's sketches?" Galo asked through a spark of epiphany.

"Not nearly as frequently, but it visits time and again."

"That means you have the nightmare in your imagination and a similar encounter with VanSen in your memories," Galo astutely observed, "I would venture to guess that to be the root of your problem."

"What would you suggest I do?"

"Find a way to stop your nightmare," Galo mused as he opened the door to the arboretum, "The rest should follow."

CreSam stood before his desk with his arms folded behind his back. The screens were pulled tightly over the window, letting nary a sliver of sunlight into the room. With a remote in his hand, he killed the lights and initiated a direct feed of the imperial capitol's surveillance system. Using a dial on the remote, he switched the display from the gated metropolis to the ghettos beyond, the weaker regions that had fallen to imperial dominance. Sentries marched systematically, retaining their monopoly over the streets. A few felled ones were strewn about, but no human activity was to be found, quite to CreSam's disappointment. One by one, he dialed through surveillance feeds of other cities. Imperial dominion varied considerably in each of them. He stopped for longer periods on those showing signs of human activity, zooming in on suspicious people and vehicles. Until recently, his search had been concentrated in the east, but lately he had begun scanning in all directions.

"Where have you gone off to, old man?" he mumbled, "Eluding my bug, or is something more vile at hand here?"

A knock came at the door, and he hastily turned off the video matrix and turned on the lights. He glanced over his shoulder, calling back for an announcement.

"Malia, sir! Have you looked out the window lately?"

"Can't you tell? Seems you should have enough probes in this room to know my every move by now."

"Just open your window, Lord CreSam. You need to see this."

Though he was frustrated with her disrespectful prodding, he begrudgingly complied and hit the button to raise the screen. Off in the distance, he saw several flocks of eastbound tracking pigeons with letters in their clutches. Upon closer examination via a pair of binoculars, he found the binding ribbons didn't originate within Imperial ArcNos. The logic behind Parliamentary ArcNos's formal declaration of war became clear.

"What do you make of it, sir?" Malia asked, still outside in the Platinum Hall.

"They're calling for reinforcements," CreSam gleaned, "Send Amirione, EshCal, and Kabehl in here. We need to stop those birds from reaching the coast."

Chapter 30

As the last flock of pigeons vanished over the southeastern horizon, a single bird approached in the opposite direction. Long anticipating correspondence from his old colleague, Uulan watched it intently until he was certain it was aiming for one of them. With reasonable presumptions, he stepped forth to separate himself, and the bird dropped the letter into his hands before veering in the direction of warmer regions.

"That's from your friend, right?" Sinkua asked, "The one who's going to translate that, um, that thing."

"Genome map," Eytea reminded him worriedly.

Uulan unrolled the two page letter. He looked at the first page only briefly before hastily stuffing it behind the second and reading that instead. His eyes had scanned only the first two lines when he shoved it in his pocket and took his leave of the crowd. On the way, he forcefully shoved the first page into Yrlis's hand.

"I wonder what that was all about," Vielle pondered, watching Uulan walk away broodingly.

Yrlis unfolded the first sheet and sighed with disappointed understanding.

"His colleague couldn't translate it," Yrlis relayed, "Too bad."

"No, I've seen that look before," Galo corrected, "He was just reminded of his mortality."

Sinkua looked down at his camera, mulling over what Galo told him about ending his nightmare. Yrlis and Eytea's idea to have him document key moments was logical, but it was only a stop-gap solution. Galo's diagnosis was reasonable and offered a permanent cure, even if he didn't yet know how to go about enacting it. Deciding to rely on the herbal mixture he had suggested instead of that thirty-five millimeter chore, he pitched the camera over his shoulder. After all, he had no recurring nightmares in any way resembling this moment

Though he heard the camera break, Uulan continued to read the letter as he shuffled along the sidewalk, fearing the news he knew was to come. It had been written by his colleague's wife, an obvious fact since his colleague's penmanship was ironically illegible and this text was quite calligraphic. At the end of the letter, he learned the nature of the truth he feared. His old friend had died of complications with a liver transplant.

For as long as she could remember, Vielle had been especially astute at reading emotions, a talent on which she staked her ego. That she had been unable to pick up on Uulan's remorse worried her, and the fact that Galo had corrected her only worsened matters. It wasn't so much that she felt upstaged but rather that she noted a hint of shame in his voice, as though he was disappointed in her. She knew that it easily could have stemmed from her fear of his hatred, but it still set her back in her efforts to look him in the eye again.

A hand abruptly grasped hers, startling her out of her self-loathing introspection. She looked to her hand to find it clasped in the grip of dark meaty fingers. She scanned up the arm, across the shoulder, and hesitantly to his face. Galo was looking at her concernedly.

"Come on, Vielle," he urged, "We're heading back."

"Oh, oh right. Sorry, I was just lost in thought," Vielle apologized as she walked with him.

"It's okay, you have a lot to think about," Galo assured her, "By the way, Sinkua told me what you said to him."

"He actually remembers? He was barely awake."

"To be quite honest, he wasn't entirely sure if it had happened or not," Galo admitted, "but for what it's worth, you should know that I don't hate you."

"That's certainly a relief. So you understand that it was just my fear of intimacy?"

"Quite clearly, Vielle. Besides, I'm not looking to get at your knickers. If I'm to reassume the title of Chieftain Sage, I'm forbidden from bedding anyone beyond wedlock."

"So, you're still considering accepting your inheritance?" she asked optimistically.

"I've yet to refuse it outright."

Though he walked a few steps ahead of them, giving their conversation no acknowledgment, Sinkua listened intently to Galo and Vielle's exchange. His concern was not with assuring himself that the turmoil between them was calmed but rather with clarifying foggy memories. In spite of his often implacable trust in Galo, a sneaking paranoia occasionally warned him that this Southlander may have been privy to the nature and origin of his deteriorating mentality. Believing that Galo was unaware of his eavesdropping, he confirmed that he had been Chieftain Heir and put his inheritance on hold. Furthermore, he learned that his conversation with Vielle had not been a dream.

Farim walked even farther ahead, dragging an old wagon loaded with bird cages. The whole mess of metal on metal rattled loudly as the wheels rolled over the rough asphalt. A loud but distant hum resonated through the air, offering a bass accompaniment to the treble cacophony. Sinkua hurried to reach Farim and grabbed her shoulder.

"What is it?" she asked, visibly startled.

"Listen to that," he beckoned, "Somebody's coming."

Everybody gradually stopped and cocked an ear. The first hum grew louder and was joined by others, accumulating into a bellow washing over them from the west. Three or four blocks up the road, a pair of infantry troopers on a single motorcycle emerged from a cross street. Another and another followed immediately thereafter, along with more sets at further intersections.

"Farim, take Yrlis and Uulan and find cover," Sinkua ordered calmly, "Galo and Vielle, weapons on the ready. Eytea, be ready to take flight."

Farim urged Yrlis and Uulan back into an alley. Still wrapped up in trying to come to grips with the news, Uulan was physically reluctant to comply but eventually followed robotically. Galo moved to the front of the group, crouching with his glaive held out from his side. At his opposite side and back a ways stood Vielle, positioned for a convergence strike. Sinkua stayed a ways behind Galo but close enough to assist on a split moment's notice, while Eytea took cover behind him, ready to take to the air and launch a surprise assault.

Dozens of motorcycles with twice as many troopers lined the avenue now, their motors sitting idle. In rolling succession, they revved their engines, creating a swelling mechanical thunder of combustion. As the first wave burst forth, Galo charged them with a wicked battle cry resonating in his throat. From the cross street of an empty intersection came the sound of primitive gunfire. One shot, one driver down with a red stain swelling from the collar of his jacket. His passenger bailed as the bike collapsed and scraped over the pavement with the driver's lifeless body still straddling it.

A nearly silent motorcycle zipped through the intersection, also with a driver and passenger. The driver identified himself with the crack of a quarterstaff against the helmeted head of the dismounted passenger. For all the momentum behind the bike and the swing, his neck snapped loudly enough to hear over the strike of wood to fiberglass. As they crossed between the charging troopers and the Hybrids, the passenger leveled a long-barreled pistol and fired a flurry of bullets into the imperial phalanx. Scarcely a bullet was wasted as visors shattered with crimson spider webs. At the edge of the intersection, the driver dropped his foot and leaned into a hard turn to join the four Hybrids.

"Dad!" Vielle shouted, "I didn't know you owned a gun."

"There's a lot you don't know about me, honey," Phylus asserted as he loaded a new clip.

"Where are the others?" Spril asked.

"Hiding in an alley," Sinkua reported, purposely keeping his answer generic.

"We need to split up," Spril ordered as he dismounted, "This is just a diversion. Eytea, go with Phylus back in the direction you came from. He'll explain on the way."

"And the rest of us will stay and fight?" Sinkua asked.

"Of course. None of us can help them, and we have friends to protect here."

The motorized cavalry drew near, veering around felled allies and unmanned motorcycles. Galo resumed his warrior's charge, and the nearest infantryman took aim with a laser-sighted pistol. From the fringes of the soldier's peripheral vision, Vielle skillfully cracked her whip, extending one of the nine tails with a well placed vine. The end snapped on the soldier's hand and gun, separating the two. Galo pivoted out of the motorcycle's path and slashed through the side of both driver and passenger.

Sinew still trailing from the blade, Galo spun his glaive and plunged the head into the asphalt. A sheet of ice crackled and crystallized over the street, covering the intersection. Spril signaled for Vielle to back up. She looked over her shoulder to find Sinkua had almost gone to the previous intersection and ran to join him. Galo jogged backward, watching with sadistic delight as the motorized cavalry decelerated out of fearful anticipation.

Sinkua closed his eyes and breathed deeply as he clutched the gemstone embedded in his necklace. A deep warmth washed over and through his hand as though it was feeding the milystis directly into his palm. With a snap of the elbow, the width of the avenue was alight with a stream of flames.

"Galo, douse it," he promptly ordered.

Galo promptly swept his arm in a similar manner and doused the flames with an arc of water. A wall of smoke rose from the street, shrouding the environs for all but one. Sinkua's bioluminescent eyes shimmered brilliantly and faded into a dim glow. The roar of the engines was upon them, joined by the desperate squeal of street tires on ice.

"Follow my hand," Sinkua commanded.

He sprinted toward the smoke, veering toward the north side of the street. He looked to his left and pointed to a particular spot, his arm moving to keep his aim precise. Galo charged with his glaive down at his side. Sinkua pointed to yet another spot, and Spril joined the action. Vielle waited apprehensively.

Sinkua charged with a low profile and bounded forth as a bike neared the edge of the smoke. When the two soldiers came into the clearing, they were each met with a black combat boot as Sinkua drop kicked them from their motorcycle, landing atop it and adding to the weight crushing their legs. He shouted to Vielle and pointed out her target, but she remained statuesque. Around the same time, Galo spun on the ball of one foot and kicked another bike out from beneath its riders. Spril crouched and pitched his quarterstaff into the spokes of a third bike, cracking the staff and collapsing the bike. He plowed one end through the driver's visor and into his throat, and the passenger took the other end to her windpipe.

A fourth pair of riders burst arrogantly through the smoke, carving along the asphalt and taking aim at Vielle while the others were occupied. Her breathing accelerated and body trembled as she clenched her eyes shut. With the bike only a couple of meters away, a mass of roots burst from the street and enveloped it. Driver and passenger barreled over the front and collapsed onto the street, their bodies helplessly bouncing.

Sinkua lifted his pained body from the fallen bike, his breathing heavy and ragged. Each time the collapsed soldiers attempted to lift the motorcycle from their shattered legs, he bellowed furiously and stomped it again, further mangling their limbs to the response of anguished cries. More riders broke through the smoke, but he no longer pointed them out, leaving Spril and Galo to take them blindly. Vielle stayed back to handle the leftovers, lacking their combative experience and the confidence inherent therein.

"They're getting overwhelmed out there," Farim worried, peering from the alley, "We need to help them out somehow."

"Just because they're outnumbered, doesn't mean they're overwhelmed," Yrlis asserted, refusing to leave Uulan's side, "Spril, Galo, and Sinkua finished the tournament in the top three and each took down multiple opponents in their prelims."

"Well, Sinkua isn't exactly helping," Farim retorted impatiently, "Come look."

Fearing what may have occurred, Yrlis scrambled to the edge of the alley, rolling from a crawl to a stroll. She leaned over Farim and peeked out to see Sinkua repeatedly stomping on a motorcycle. Two streams of blood ran from beneath it with fragments of bone and strips of flesh flaying out from the edges.

"This can't end well," Yrlis sighed.

"What's going on?"

"Never mind that for now. Grab a cage."

Yrlis took one of several empty bird cages, charged up the street, and hurled it into the melee. It came down upon a necessarily pedestrian soldier, collapsing him. While she returned to the alley for another, Farim followed suit, knocking a pair from their motorized mount. Sinkua continued stomping, consumed by his rage, but their efforts were proving effective in buying time for the others. When the wagon was empty, Yrlis ordered Farim up a parallel street with it, reasoning that she looked to be the faster runner.

Sinkua hacked a deep chesty cough, blood pooling in his throat. Gasping for air, he spat plasmatic phlegm upon the two mangled soldiers. The carbon fumes spewing from their still running motorcycle scratched at his already tormented throat. Hearing him fall to his knees, Galo looked from his task to see an imperial soldier closing in on Sinkua. He yanked his glaive from its latest victim and sprinted to intercept the assault.

An advantageous interruption dashed from the alley. Farim raised the metallic wagon over her shoulder. Approaching from behind, she bashed it against the back of the soldier's unprotected head in full sprint, knocking him to the ground and denting the wagon. Galo pitched his glaive to her, and after a moment's hesitation, she drove it into the neck of the concussed trooper.

"Eytea would kick my ass if he died on my watch," she called half-jokingly as she hurled the glaive back to Galo.

A loud pop echoed from above, and a flurry of bloodied feathers burst from an airborne tracking pigeon. More shots followed, each accompanied by a falling bird. Letters drifted to the ground behind their felled carriers, some unfurling along the way. Eytea tightened her grip on Phylus's waist as she rubbernecked to spot what she suspected to be snipers.

"Now do you see why he only sent us?" Phylus asked knowingly.

Eytea simply nodded, not speaking a word. She squinted her eyes, trying to distinguish a figure on a balcony. When she ascertained the person held a gun, she launched a bolt of lightning in its direction. Slightly missing the mark, she hit the railing instead. Jolted off balance, the sniper collapsed over the ledge. Phylus shot a quick glance in the plummeting sniper's direction. Another was on the balcony below the one Eytea had scorched. Propping his pistol on his bicep, he fired one bullet, and a second sniper fell over the guard rail.

The two of them circled a couple of blocks, sniping snipers from below their perches. Dozens of birds were lost in the process, but their death rate was diminishing significantly. Hearing more gunshots, Eytea looked back to check an area they had just cleared. With nary an acknowledgement, she sprang from the back of the motorcycle and took to the air, twisting to aim herself away from the bike. Phylus shot a glance over his shoulder and waved after stabilizing the bike.

From a higher altitude, Eytea claimed a better vantage point both for spotting the snipers and for striking them down. Bobbing and swooping sporadically, she made herself an impossible target to track as she fired bolt after bolt of electrical surges at the soldiers and their perches. Still, some tried to halt her flight with bullets zipping by in disconcertingly close proximity. Radiant heat from the near miss bullets formed streaks of fluff in her plumage.

One particular gunman caught her eye, distracting her for a moment. He wore an ArcNosian uniform all the same, but his gun appeared more technologically advanced in some way beyond her comprehension. She shot a bolt at him, but in her bewilderment, it hit the wall about a meter above him. Startled, he crouched and looked back at the crumbling bricks. He searched the sky and grimaced viciously when he found Eytea. He stood atop the balcony, waved, and leapt from eight stories up. Eytea swooped after him and shot off another bolt, intending to assure his demise, but she missed again.

Phylus felt a shockwave resonating through the asphalt. Suspecting trouble was afoot, he turned sharply to head for the source. A soldier was plummeting to the ground, presumably from the seared ledge eight floors up. Oddly, he looked to be bracing himself to land rather than freefalling. As the soldier's feet struck pavement, he dropped into a crouch, but his body didn't break as it should have. Phylus slammed the brakes, screeching to a halt in horrified anticipation. Seeing this strange spectacle, Eytea halted in flight.

The soldier looked first to Eytea, then to Phylus, both stunned with fear. Somehow unharmed by the fall, he strode to the middle of the street and aimed his rifle at Phylus. Phylus could faintly see a red glimmer in the corner of each of his own eyes. Defiantly, he quickly leveled his unaugmented pistol and took the first shot. The soldier's head snapped back, but no blood was spilled as the bullet collided against his forehead with a sharp bang. He lowered his head and received yet another failed shot to the forehead. Bewildered and horrified, Phylus lowered his pistol as the enigmatic soldier did likewise with his augmented sniper rifle.

Perhaps irrationally, Phylus charged forth on his bike, intent on running down the bulletproof sniper. Quite bizarrely, the soldier sprinted toward the electric motorcycle screaming in his direction. As he came closer, Phylus finally recognized his vicious visage. Holding the bike steady with one hand, he raised his pistol and shot a flurry of bullets in desperate vanity.

When they were a good three meters apart, The Hunter leapt and withdrew a pair of daggers from hip holsters. Phylus swerved just before he passed under him, evading the scissor slash of falling blades. From nigh pointblank range, he shot at The Hunter's temple. Though he was still inhumanly bulletproof at such close range, the force and point of impact were enough to stun him. The daggers fell from his loosened grip, and he dropped to the pavement, bouncing a couple of times before his barely conscious body settled.

Eytea swooped down and landed nearby. Phylus stopped to let her catch up, but she ran past him. As she did, he shouted for her to stop.

"He's still breathing!" she protested, itching to finish The Hunter, even though she was unaware of his identity.

"For all we know, shocking him might just bring him back around," Phylus explained, "That's one of the Avatars of Fate."

Unconscious and as vulnerable as anyone with a resilience to bullets could be, a man she could only assume to be responsible for stealing Kabehl's body laid before her. Begrudgingly and physically pained by the neglected opportunity, she walked back to the bike, never taking her eyes off of The Hunter.

"Spril will need more preparation than he's willing to admit if he's to avenge himself now."

Yrlis crouched before Uulan and set her hand upon his shoulder. He glanced up from the letter, which he had read dozens of times trying to come to grips with the tragedy. As quickly as he made eye contact, he broke it again.

"I'm not going to pretend I know how you feel," she solemnly offered, "but if you need to talk, I'm good at listening. It's part of my job."

The absurdity of her saying that part of an electrician's job was to listen to clients grieve was not lost on Uulan. He knew she meant her previous job as a doctor, but he opted to leave the verbal slip alone.

"The way you saved Spril, do you suppose that would work on a destroyed liver?" he asked after a long silence.

"Spril was alive when he was brought to me," Yrlis apologetically explained, "and your friend would need a partial donation to start anyway. The process takes too long to go without that much."

"I see. I just thought that, maybe, well..."

"I know. It's normal to reject helplessness, but that sort of medical technology doesn't exist. At least not yet," she assured him, "Now come on. Farim is probably waiting for us with the others."

Yrlis got to her feet and offered Uulan her hand. He looked to her hand, then to her face. For the first time since he opened the letter, he made and held eye contact. A step closer to acceptance, he took her hand and rose to his feet as well.

"On a side note," Yrlis began, "I had no idea Farim had such a swinging arm on her."

"That was her making that racket?" Uulan asked in disbelief, "I thought one of our boys got hold of a garbage can."

As they exited the alley, Phylus and Eytea rode in from the east. Yrlis waved them down, assuring the two that they had both survived unscathed. Phylus slowed to let them walk alongside as they continued westward. From the west, the others returned from the smoke-filled battleground. Spril carried Vielle on his back, as she was exhausted from the stress and exertion. Behind them, Sinkua staggered along with a smear of blood caking his beard and running down his neck. Galo walked with a slow gait, always keeping his shoulder available for his friend's aide. Last came Farim with an irreparably dented wagon hanging behind her shoulder and a wickedly satisfied grin adorning her face.

"There's your answer," Yrlis said, pointing out Farim to Uulan.

NalSet sat upon the concrete rooftop, surrounded by smoke stacks. To the west, the sun was falling upon the horizon. Below, the carnage escalated as the imperialists forcibly reclaimed the power plant. Tragically, the plan for the guards to surrender when they were found understaffed had met with macabre failure. Imperial ArcNos took them anyway, refusing their pleas, and they were incapable of defending themselves. NalSet remained stoic. He counted bodies in his head, supposing that most of the bloody screams were from the ill-equipped parliamentary guards. He nonchalantly sparked a cigarette and loaded his gun. The smoke stacks fell silent, and he aimed the barrel skyward.

MalVek watched through binoculars from the street level entrance to the Epsilon boarding dock. As the pipes were silenced, he signaled to IlcBei to be on the ready. She clutched the remote and reread the override code for at least the fifth time. It was six digits in all, based on the transmission frequencies of the street light cameras Sinkua had obtained on his way home from sending the letters. Although the security feeds were transmitted on multiple frequencies, the code was the same for all of them. The brothers reasoned that even the empire's receivers were only capable of having one code active at a time, thus necessitating a universal access code for ease of moving between channels.

"I still don't get entirely how this works," IlcBei confessed, "What are we intercepting if we're cutting the transmission?"

"Save it," MalVek urged.

After a few minutes had passed, the smoke stacks began to spew exhaust once again. MalVek gave IlcBei the next signal, and she placed each of her thumbs over the first two numbers, the first with a hair more pressure than the second. NalSet sparked his gun with his cigarette and fired the signal flare.

"Now!" MalVek shouted.

The operation now came down to this one crucial moment, impossible to be accurately estimated but wisely assumed a remarkably narrow window of opportunity. IlcBei mashed the six keys frantically but deliberately. Static remained on the screen.

Thirty seconds passed, far longer than the brothers had presumed, and onto the screen flickered a feed of a street just outside of the gated capitol.

"We got it!" IlcBei proudly announced, "We can only see one camera, but we got it."

"Hell yes!" MalVek called back, "We'll need to network several monitors and set each one to its own unique channel and frequency."

"We won't have to do this every time, will we?"

"No, of course not. They transmit on multiple frequencies but all with the same verification signature," he explained, "As for your question, we shut down the receivers and the cameras, but the tower was still transmitting the signal. There just wasn't any data on it, but once there was, we were already poised to catch it."

"Were you even sure this would work before we went to this trouble?" IlcBei asked worriedly.

"Theoretically, yes," he shrugged, "but experimentally, of course not."

Biroe sipped orange juice as he reviewed yet another page in what felt like an endless stack of paperwork. Laid before him was everything he needed to create a detailed profile of the Parliamentary Republic's tax revenue system. He had tax data for every business and every individual, anonymity preserved. He had also been provided a list of anticipated newcomers. They were sorted by their predicted likelihood to come with those whom Sinkua directly addressed given preference. From this information, Biroe was to glean what jobs would need to be created and filled in order to optimize tax revenue and maintain an effective community.

"I brought you something," Phylus announced, abruptly making his presence known.

"What the shit!" Biroe snapped, nearly ripping the paper in his panicked clutches.

Phylus dropped a bag from NieRie's Bakery on the table. Biroe looked at it with cautious optimism, which quickly turned to pessimism when he caught the scent drifting from it. The smell of warm cranberries flooded his olfactory, and he feared bad news was to come.

"What happened?" he asked, glaring piercingly at Phylus.

"What do you mean?" Phylus responded innocently, "You've got a heavy work load. I can't bring you some carbohydrates to help keep the motor running?"

"No, you can't bring me a cranberry bagel without looking suspicious. What happened that you feel the need to butter me up?"

"We lost some letters," Phylus spat as a single word, ripping the bandage from the wound, "about one third of them."

Biroe stared at him, his mind rushing behind his silent eyes. After a moment, he pulled the bagel from the bag and took a bite, still looking at Phylus. As he swallowed, he snatched the list of recipients and potential guests from the table.

"One third, you say?"

Phylus nodded anxiously.

"How long until they arrive, do you suppose?"

"Two weeks, maybe three."

"Okay," Biroe nodded, turning back to his work.

"Okay? That's it?"

"That's it. We can't do anything about the lost letters," Biroe accepted, taking another bite of the bagel, "So, I'm going to have to write up several potential budget plans. Two or three weeks should buy me enough time."

Phylus walked away with a gratified smile spreading across his face as he turned away from his old friend. It was a classic, perhaps even dated, maneuver to manipulate a negotiation, but it still proved to have its place. All it took was a bit of inside knowledge and a bagel, and Biroe was willing to continue running solo through the storm.

CreSam stepped away from the elevator in an impatient huff, the walls nearly shaking with each pounding of his steel-toed boots. Personnel of all ranks and positions stepped aside, cowering against the wall as their leader stormed down the corridor with tendrils of heated breath faintly visible in the cooled air. When he reached the door to the surveillance center, he kicked it below the knob, breaking it open unnecessarily.

"What is the meaning of this?" he bellowed when he found their monitors were functional.

"We're trying to figure that out, sir," a young technician stammered.

"Don't play stupid with me, boy! You have surveillance, and I don't! What are you trying to hide?"

"Sir, if you would just give me a moment to explain," the technician urged, "we lost our transmission for a moment, too."

"You lost it when you cut the transmission to my office, didn't you?" CreSam shouted as he snatched the technician by the collar, "And now you've got your eyes on the city, and I'm blind beyond my window. Isn't that right?"

Lord CreSam clutched the portly technician by the throat and raised him to eye level. He cocked his head, studying this frail intellectual specimen. He knew this seemingly hapless employee sought to conspire against him, to aid in usurping him. What treachery he wished to hide from him remained a mystery, but the theft of his omnividence was a direct threat to his authority. Such a blinding would free them to enact the remainder of their plot for his demise, both of character and of body. He tightened his hold on the technician's throat, reddening his puffy face.

"Sir, it wasn't us," he gasped desperately, "We've been sabotaged."

Frantic footsteps sounded faintly against the carpet. CreSam stared fiercely into the technician's fearful eyes, discerning if he was an honest man or a liar suitably practiced for plotting a character assassination. One last footfall set down behind him. Still gripping the technician's throat, he bent backwards at the knees and snatched another by the leg, dropping him to the floor.

CreSam righted himself and dropped the technician, who shuffled away on his buttocks as he rubbed his neck. The failed assailant was now the more pressing issue. Lord CreSam stared down at him, towering over the surveillance operator holding a flathead screwdriver. He hunched down and gave the tool a firm tug from the business end. For someone so unsuitable for combat, the operator's grip was admittedly tenacious. CreSam moved his grip to the operator's fist, his meaty hand swallowing it, and bludgeoned his forearm with his other elbow. The operator screamed in anguish, and CreSam yanked the screwdriver from his failed grip. The scream was swiftly silenced as the screwdriver was then plunged into his esophagus.

"What was that about sabotage?" CreSam asked, chucking the bloodied screwdriver on a nearby desk.

"Someone interrupted the transmission," the technician nervously explained, "It was at the same time as the blackout."

"When did that occur?"

"Shortly after a team of engineers accompanied by ground troops infiltrated one of Parliamentary ArcNos's power plants, sir."

"Son of a bitch," CreSam grumbled.

"What is it, sir? What do you suspect?"

"We've been set up. That plant was a detonator to disable our own stations and interrupt surveillance," CreSam explained, "They probably have a direct line to the system now."

"What should we do, sir?"

"About the power plants, nothing. If we take out all of theirs, we lose all of our own," CreSam accepted as he swung the broken door open.

"No, I mean about their spying, sir."

"You should be more concerned with what will happen if I still find a dead feed on my monitors."

Having heard enough to know an execution took place, people urged themselves to melt into the walls as Lord CreSam passed on his return to the elevator. He made eye contact with no one, and they dared not look at him. His mind ran frantically, straining to deduce which of them could have been in on that operator's conspiracy to destroy him and all he had become. They feared him. They envied him. They hated him.

As he returned to his office, he found that his omnividence had been restored as promised. Perhaps this was just a cover though. Regardless, these developments necessitated an impromptu meeting of the Platinum Hall. He activated the announcement system strictly for the Hall and barked the order.

"EshCal! Malia! Kabehl! SenRas! My office! Immediately!"

Almost as quickly as he cut the line, the first of them arrived. EshCal opened the door with a slight struggle, driven by a combination of fear and aspiration. Malia and Kabehl were a few steps behind. This left one straggler.

"I think you forgot Amirione," EshCal reminded as she stepped into the vast office.

"Madam Brigadier, do you understand the difference between the words forgot and neglected?" he pierced, "I have no use for that chronic failure of an officer, and therefore, he has no role in this. Now, where are the rest of you?"

"The rest of us? The only one missing is SenRas," Malia reminded.

"Yes, and where is he? I sent him on an errand, and he's been gone for days," CreSam elucidated, "I tried finding him on street level surveillance, but he's nowhere to be found."

"You suspended SenRas for two months," Kabehl explained with a contented smirk, "I suspect he fled the country in his shame."

CreSam looked the three of them over, contemplating what lies may have been shrouded by this obvious fabrication. This was a matter not to be discussed in the presence of others, and a more pressing issue was at hand. Somebody had intercepted their surveillance transmission, and innumerable untouchable reinforcements were on their way to aid Parliamentary ArcNos.

"Due to the failure to intercept primitive communications, thanks largely to a certain self-proclaimed assassin's undeserved arrogance," he began, avoiding the ludicrous idea of suspending his most trusted Colonel, "reinforcements are coming to join Parliamentary ArcNos. We have no knowledge of their numbers or their capabilities."

"And we shall crush each one as they set foot upon our land," EshCal remarked proudly.

"I prefer not to wait so long."

"Sir, the Wartime Passage Act mandates that we must grant safe passage to foreign ships bearing invitation," Malia reminded him, "If we disobey, we risk forced surrender to our enemy."

"Yes, but only in and around ArcNosian waters," CreSam insisted, having realized a geographical loophole within the regulations, "We will deploy three fleets, two smaller ones to the east and south and a larger one to the southeast. Any manned boats traveling in the opposite direction, with the scrutinized exception of certain vessels, are to be annihilated. The Wartime Passage Act overlooks such cautionary measures."

"Would you like me to staff the fleets?" Kabehl asked, offering his talents as The Scout.

"You? Of course not. The last time you staffed an assault, you trusted a soldier who was killed by a civilian with a fucking wagon. Why would I want you deploying soldiers out to sea? EshCal, you're on enlistment duty."

"Sir, permission to lead the southeast fleet?" EshCal pleaded.

"Permission granted," CreSam agreed, "Just don't put your bonehead boyfriend at the helm anywhere. In fact, he and his colleague will need to stay here to review their failure."

"At your behest, he'll remain under your watch, sir."

Chapter 31

Sinkua shuffled across the bare concrete floor with a leaf blower in his hands, urging mounds of sawdust toward the corner. Spril waited in the open doorway, drumming his fingers on the frame. Lined up along the outside wall were several armament racks, each one only sparsely populated. Behind Spril stood each of the other combatants in Parliament with coiled floor mats standing upright among them. Eytea had the end of a garbage bag tucked in her pocket with the rest draped over her hip and thigh. As Sinkua neared the door, Spril stepped aside, allowing her into position to catch the sawdust and debris.

Two by two, they entered and set the mats at the edge of the room. Phylus and Spril put themselves in position first. Farim followed with MalVek, having proven herself in the street level assault. Eytea and Vielle were next to line up. Finally, Sinkua and Galo laid the fourth mat. On Spril's count, they released in unison, and the mats unrolled across the bare surface, flooring the reinforcement training hall all at once.

Galo bounced on the balls of his feet, admiring the elasticity of the floor. In his excitement at finally having a place to further develop his agility, he bolted toward the back wall. Without the slightest deceleration, he took three strides up the wall and leapt off into a back flip.

In midair, he caught a glimpse of a purple blur behind him. That was his only warning before Eytea came screaming around and down upon him, knocking him to the mat. He sprang back to his feet as she landed, assuming his usual shuffling stance. Vielle whipped her arm to launch a coiling vine in her direction. Sinkua ran in from the side, and the vine shot forth just before he passed between Vielle and Eytea. He dropped to his knees and slid across the mat, snatching the vine as he passed under it. With a firm jerk, Vielle was dropped to her knees.

Spotting an opening, Galo readied a jagged ball of ice. Seeing the crystalline projectile manifesting in his hands, Sinkua snapped the vine from Vielle's hand and whipped Galo's arm. Galo dropped the frozen missile. In the same moment, Eytea took off toward Sinkua, careful to stay beyond his peripheral vision. As the ice hit the mat, she slammed into his side in an aerial tackle. Sinkua withstood the impact, spun with their bodies in each other's grasp, and dropped her on the mat.

"Apparently, a man can't do back flips in here without an impromptu melee breaking out. I see how it is!" Galo remarked facetiously.

"Apparently not," Sinkua laughed as he helped Eytea onto her feet.

"Well, if you kids are done goofing off," Farim teased, "I'm going to go scout some abandoned storehouses for the best point of entry."

"I'll join you," MalVek offered, "We've yet to disable the sentries, and CreSam may have deployed ground troops."

As they left, the rest behind moved the armament racks into the training facility, aligning them along the walls. The weapons ranged from basic staves to complex flails and handheld daggers to impressive spears. One rack was reserved for Parliament's combatants. Beyond the morningstar, glaive, halberd, cat-o'-nine-tails, and the quarterstaff were two empty slots. MalVek had taken his sledgehammer by presumed necessity, and hanging a banged up wagon seemed ridiculous. As for Phylus, this place hardly seemed appropriate for a pistol.

"Now that we're done, would you care for a rematch?" Spril asked Sinkua.

"As much as I'd love to knock you around for sucker punching me," Sinkua began as he withdrew his morningstar from the rack, "I have more pressing matters to attend to."

"Galo, how about you?" Spril offered cockily, "You probably want to get back at me for dropping you in the semifinals."

"Are you off to where I suspect?" Galo asked, momentarily disregarding Spril's request.

"To the Subtransit in my birth town, yes," Sinkua confirmed.

"In that case, I'll have to pass up on your offer, Spril. For his help in Masnethege, I owe Sinkua my assistance in this endeavor," Galo politely declined, "Though I certainly do owe you more than a few cracks for how you finished me in the Tournament."

"I'll stay behind and spar with you," Eytea offered, "It won't be a rematch, but I could use the training. Your staff is basically a halberd without blades, so I imagine you would be able to help there."

"Really, Galo has the closest match to your halberd, but a quarterstaff does offer a handful of similarities. Spar with me for a while, and I'll teach you what I can."

"Dad, do you need me at home for anything?" Vielle asked.

"I'm going to hone my sharp-shooting for a while," Phylus answered, eliciting a bit of visible anxiety from Spril, "Just be careful and come home in time to cook dinner. You know I'm a wreck in the kitchen."

"I wouldn't think of skipping it," she grinned, "I'm gonna join the boys out in the wreckage for a while."

"Would you mind if she joined us, brother?" Galo asked sheepishly, unable to refuse Vielle.

"We'll need to pick up a sledgehammer from a hardware store," Sinkua conditionally accepted, "She can smash up the debris we gather so it can be cleared out more easily."

"I'm not so sure I'll be of much use there. I can barely lift MalVek's hammer to my shoulder," Vielle explained nervously.

"I'll get you a smaller model. Five kilograms sound about right?"

"That should work."

Amirione and Kabehl sat begrudgingly among surveillance operators and technicians, watching those same accursed videos over and over again. Several days earlier, they had been given orders to review footage of the failed interception mission until they determined the root of their shortcomings. Although CreSam was operating under their scrutiny as a potential recruit into the Avatars of Fate, orders from on high were for their compliance with his commands.

"I swear to the gods, if I have to watch this again, I'm going to open fire in here," Amirione muttered with his head in his hands as the footage looped yet again.

"Be careful what you say in the presence of lesser lives," Kabehl reminded,

"We need to at least feign compliance, even if he's asking the impossible."

"I pride myself on my visual acuity, and I can't see a damned place where we went wrong. They just got lucky when those guys on the electric bike interrupted, and they just happened to be in the right place at the right time."

"Do you suppose they heard the assault coming?"

"You give them far too much credit, Scout," Amirione insisted, after which something finally caught his attention, "Hey, pause the playback. I see something."

"Finally found where we slipped?" Kabehl asked facetiously as he paused the video.

"Not us, someone else."

The depressing presence of a dejected old man, his lowered face hidden from view, graced the screen. In his hands was a letter which, at that distance and resolution, was hopelessly illegible. The layout of a diagram on one of the pages was somewhat clear though. Amirione barked an order for a technician to zoom in on the page, an order which was immediately followed.

"Son of a bitch, they got hold of The Diagram," Amirione snapped, "Keep your eyes on him. We need to figure out who he is."

"All I need is a face," Kabehl promised, resuming the footage.

Their eyes never wavering, they ignored everything else in the footage and instead followed this faceless old man as he passed under each camera. Eventually, he slipped into an alley and disappeared from electronic eyes. Several minutes later however, he raised his head to make eye contact with a young woman as he reemerged. Kabehl stopped the video and snapped a picture of the screen with his pocket camera.

"I'll have what we need in less than ten minutes," he confidently announced as left the room in direct defiance of his local orders.

One of the few exceptions for the order of compliance under CreSam was to mitigate any compromises to the Avatars of Fate's operations. He knew Lord CreSam would undoubtedly come down hard on him, but the fate he faced from his boss would be much worse were he to let The Diagram remain unsecured. Back in the surveillance room, Amirione also eschewed his orders and switched the monitor back to a live feed. While Kabehl traced the elderly rebel's identity, he searched street level security for any signs that he might be wandering about on the surface. Before he could find him though, another deserving target caught his attention. He dialed Kabehl on his portable phone.

"I was just about to call you," Kabehl answered softly, avoiding alerting Lord CreSam of his return, "His name is Uulan, an historian from Quarun now listed as an officer in Parliamentary ArcNos."

"Then we can't afford to let him live another day with it in his possession, and I know how we can find him. That civilian with a wagon is out on the street. We can use her to find him."

"Is she alone?"

"No, but we'll have no trouble overwhelming her chaperone."

Sinkua returned to his hammock to fetch his bank card. As he reached the Epsilon boarding dock, his arrival caught the attention of a familiar child. The children's game placed briefly on hold, the same child who said he would save them from the monsters broke away and approached him with surprising calmness.

"Are you well today, sir?" the little boy asked politely.

"I suppose I've had worse days," Sinkua answered as he rummaged through

326

his duffle bag, nary bothering to offer any physical acknowledgement.

"Last time we talked, you seemed pretty freaked out. I'm glad you feel better now."

"Don't get me wrong, that day was pretty horrible."

"Well, um, I've been wanting to apologize," the kid offered, kicking at dust on the concrete, "I think I freaked you out, and that probably didn't help."

"To be honest, I don't think the day would have been any better had we not crossed paths," Sinkua assured him as he fished the bank card from his bag, "but I appreciate the apology. I should've been more patient, so don't beat yourself up over it."

Sinkua nodded to the little boy as he rose to his feet and stuffed the card in his pocket. At the other end of the boarding dock, Galo and Vielle stood waiting. With no spoken parting words, he dismissed himself to join his compatriots.

"Hey, are you off to work? Maybe I can help you," the child offered, still feeling compelled to compensate for tempting Sinkua's temper.

"Not with this, you can't," Sinkua countered without so much as glancing over his shoulder, "but I'll let you know if I need you later. Okay?"

Their first stop was at NieRie's Bakery to purchase a few drinks and snacks for later. Lunch hour was in full swing, so they sat at a table and watched the waiting crowd slowly dwindle to something more resembling a line than a hungry horde. If the ovens weren't all lit, toasters weren't all running, and pots weren't all brewing already, it would have likely taken Eytea's body to power every appliance in the shop.

The smells of various coffees and teas mingled with those of a myriad of fresh breads and meats to create an enticing olfactory buffet. Quite admittedly, the temptation to sample and order more than they came for was nigh overwhelming, but they managed to suppress it when they reached the counter. Each of them ordered a toasted sandwich, a piece of fruit, and a drink.

Their next stop was the hardware store. Their visit was significantly briefer and considerably less tantalizing. It was a rather ordinary shop, as hardware stores went. Five kilogram sledgehammers were with all the other sledgehammers, and finding those was no difficult task.

On the train ride out to the wreckage, they outlined the general work plan. Vielle had only seen the place once before and thus was not familiar with what to expect, knowing that Sinkua had put several hours of work into it. She tried to imagine how the place looked now but found herself frequently too distracted from the conversation.

The plan, as unstructured as it may have been, was that Sinkua and Galo would gather large pieces of wreckage into a pile. Vielle would then take what pieces she could carry and break them down with her sledgehammer. At certain points, Sinkua and Galo would take turns assisting her with a larger hammer which Sinkua kept among the wreckage.

The shattered debris was then to be pushed into a corner, atop the pile Sinkua had been building since he began this undertaking. Sinkua intended to take the wood to MalVek and NalSet and send the stones to a quarry once the job was finished or the piles became unmanageably large. Shortly after the plan had been established, they were dismissed from the train at its final stop, leaving them to hike the relatively short remaining distance.

Confident in his work with his brother, MalVek and Farim walked freely under the street lamps alongside the dilapidated roads. While they had yet to disable the sentinels entirely, they had managed to sever the automation link between them and the surveillance system. Though they had inarguably accomplished such not a moment too soon, the stink of the city was a constant reminder that they had done so all too late.

A stench of death lingered even where no bodies were in immediate view. Patches of concrete were decorated in a virtually permanent crimson hue, baked in by the sun of the past Swelter. Spots of moisture formed sporadically among them, the result of leaking gutters and pipes. The frigid northern air had partially frozen those drips, causing some of the blood stains to shimmer in the daylight like morbid rubies.

MalVek pointed out a specific building among several others in comparable states of disrepair. Upon initial glance, Farim could scarcely distinguish it from any of the others of similar size, but she trusted MalVek's judgment nonetheless. Ignoring nearby sentinels, since there was no threat so long as they were unseen, they veered toward the specified warehouse.

As they neared the storehouse, MalVek stopped to cock his ear, noticing distinct pairs of mechanical footsteps beginning to cluster. The clusters grew louder as they merged into a single auditory mass. MalVek set his hand upon Farim's shoulder, the other on the end of his sledgehammer. Farim stopped and looked to him.

"What's that sound?" she asked anxiously.

"Something I didn't count on."

About seven blocks away, some dozen or so sentinels had gathered, and still more spilled in from the adjoining avenues. Rather than their standard gait, they struggled to maneuver around one another. MalVek clutched his sledgehammer.

"Take my hand," he urged.

"You're going to fight them?"

"Hell no. I just don't want you to fall behind."

Farim gripped his free hand, and he began to jog, pulling her along. The sentinels continued to stagger in their general direction, and they accelerated into a sprint. They came within visual range five blocks shy of the tangled mass, and the sentries charged, slowed by their own crowding. A couple paused occasionally, sometimes taking a few steps backward or making abrupt motions. When they came within one block, MalVek jerked Farim nearer to him.

Just a few steps separating them from the legion of sentries, MalVek veered to the left and whipped Farim off to the right. Keeping her momentum with a rush of adrenaline, she dashed through the gauntlet of massive mechanical limbs, swerving around, leaping over, and ducking under along the way. Safely out the other side, she decelerated along the next block and waited for MalVek.

MalVek took a less graceful and more forceful approach, bludgeoning anything that crossed his path as he swerved around it. The sentries seemed to panic as far as machines are capable of such things, movements halting abruptly and being replaced by ones not in their standard protocol. As he passed through to safety, he gave one last clobber before catching up with Farim.

They watched as the mob of sentinels turned in on itself, repeatedly bumping into one another. At times, they appeared ready to take swings at their mechanical brethren but stopped just short. It did allow ample time to escape though, but scouting the storehouse would need to wait.

"Do you want to look for a different spot?" Farim asked as they left the befuddled legion to its own devices.

"I'd rather not press our luck. We escaped the one horde, but the next will be larger."

"Do you really think they have that sort of artificial intelligence?"

"That wasn't artificial intelligence; their behavior was nothing like their standard operating protocol," MalVek argued, "They were being directly controlled, and judging by the clustering and awkward movements, the operator must be nearby. Operating via the surveillance system would give them scores of perspectives to work from."

"I didn't think it was possible to remote control those things."

"Any machine can potentially be remote controlled, but for one person to control so many would be a massive task. Means there's only a few people it could be, two of whom we can eliminate right off."

"You and NalSet, I suppose? Guess that just leaves one of the Avatars of Fate?"

"And he probably brought a partner to cover him while he steers the sentries."

As they headed home, sentinels well beyond five blocks away sometimes changed course. Others made awkward motions, swinging their weapons about and striking themselves occasionally. When this occurred, they would turn about and fire their guns into the asphalt, ripping even more holes through the street. This was undoubtedly the result of some interference, though perhaps not from the same source as before.

"Looks like NalSet is on to something," MalVek noted with traces of optimism, "The sentries are muddled."

"What's going on now?"

"Manual override orders are being issued from a rogue client, but automatic behavioral parameters are struggling to persist in spite of them."

"Say what now?"

"You know when you think to say one thing, but your mouth tries to say another so you just end up saying some ridiculous portmanteau like 'grood?' That's what's happening with them. Somebody is trying to hijack them, but their auto functions are still running. The conflict is making them behave ludicrously."

"So, NalSet tapped into the controls and is trying to rewrite their commands? Looks like he's having some trouble completely overtaking them."

"Trust me, he'll get there. Just give him time."

"What about the Avatars?"

"What about them?" MalVek replied callously, "Without their damn robots covering them, they won't come after us."

Working diligently in spite of cramped shoulders, Vielle hammered on yet another pile of rocks. Galo stood beside her, assisting with a considerably larger sledgehammer. Sinkua hauled another arm load of debris to them, separating wood from stone upon his arrival, and returned to the wreckage. The electricity was out in this area, so they were left to work by sunlight piercing through the holes in the street. Cold wind drifting through the cracks cooled them as they worked into an otherwise uncomfortable sweat. While Galo had the luxury of using his hydromancy to keep cool, the possibility of his clothes freezing against his body negated such a notion.

Though Vielle continued hammering, Galo stopped and stared off with a look of fascination. As Sinkua approached with another load, he noticed his brethren gazing well past him. He looked over his shoulder to see strips of crystalline powder gathering beneath the cracks. Galo laid his hammer down and curiously walked to one of them.

"What's up with him?" Vielle asked.

"He's lived his entire life in the Southlands," Sinkua explained, "I've never really thought about it, but I think this is the first time he's seen snow."

Galo mounted a heap of discarded wreckage, and with a leap and a swipe, he grabbed the edge a hole and pulled his body atop the street. He looked about in wonder as frigid particulate fell from the cloudy sky, joining a dusting upon the pavement.

The hypnosis was interrupted quite rudely by the blaring of a ship horn from the southeastern seaboard. Bells clanged loudly, the resonating cacophony piercing the otherwise calm chilled air. Another horn blared, and Galo's aggravation became anxiety. He had his suspicions as to what was afoot, but judging by the large number of bells, pursuing an answer alone was ill-advised. He laid himself on the snowy asphalt and called down for Vielle.

"Come up here. I need you to see something," he urged when she arrived below him.

"I see snow all the time, Galo. Come on, we have work to do, and Sinkua is getting impatient."

"It's not that," he countered as he held his forearms over the hole, "Take hold."

Vielle launched a pair of vines from her wrists, skillfully coiling them around Galo's forearms. He hoisted her as she slowly retracted the vines, raising her body against the resistance of Galo's rigid arms. At the top, she gripped his wrists, and he pulled her through the hole.

"This place almost looks somewhat close to pretty with the snow piling up," Vielle sighed.

"Snow, huh? I was wondering what this stuff was called. Anyway, do you hear that?"

"The bells? I wouldn't read too much into it. They still send troops out to sea sometimes."

"It sounds like a rather large fleet, bigger than the one we faced in Haprian."

"You want me to go eavesdrop?" Vielle asked, nodding to the nearby dotting of trees at the fading edge of the forest.

"It would assuage my anxiety."

Though she could hear them clearly through the first trunk to which she laid her ears, the soldiers spoke minimally at all and even less of their mission. She managed to glean that three separate fleets were being deployed, but all she heard of their purpose was talk of patrolling. When she caught word of each one's bearing, their mission became abundantly presumable.

Vielle frantically dashed back to Galo, slipping and staggering over the snow. Seeing her panic, he knew that what she learned confirmed his suspicion. He reached out to take her hand when she came near.

"You were right," she told him while she caught her breath, "Three fleets are heading east, south, and southeast."

"For what purpose?"

"Nobody said exactly, but they mentioned patrolling."

"In that case, we need to hurry back and call a meeting. Don't let Sinkua know why. He's wont to fight them, and we're at too large a disadvantage."

Galo sat at the edge of the hole and dropped back into the Subtransit, crouching to absorb the impact of landing. He held out his arms and urged Vielle to follow. With a bit of hesitance, she dropped through the street and landed in his arms.

"We should probably head home," Vielle announced as Galo set her down, "The sun will be setting soon, and I need to cook supper."

"Is it that late already?" Sinkua asked as he wiped sweat from his forehead, oblivious to the panic behind their eyes.

"Certainly seems to be getting there," Galo supported, "The sky ought to be reddened by the time we get back to Epsilon."

Sinkua downed the last of his cherry cola and stuffed the empty cup in the bag with the rest of the garbage. He was reluctant to leave after what seemed a regrettably short visit, but he had agreed to take Vielle home in time to cook dinner. If her lamb stew was any indication, depriving Phylus of her cooking would have been unforgivably rude. As they boarded the train, his regret was replaced by hopes of another of her meals.

When they stepped off the train at Epsilon, Sinkua pitched the garbage from their lunch into a nearby bin. Farim and MalVek were still near the stairs to the surface, appearing to have returned only moments earlier.

"Did you have any luck out there?" Sinkua asked in greeting.

"Some kind of luck, but not the kind we were after," Farim answered, "We couldn't get into the warehouse, but NalSet might have some good news."

"If he does, he'll soon have the opportunity to share it," Galo added, "We need to assemble Parliament immediately."

"Why? What happened?"

"I'm not comfortable discussing it in the open, but suffice it to say that pillaging the warehouse would likely have been for naught."

Sinkua struggled to calm his stress upon learning that he had been hurried home on false pretenses. Hypocritical as it may have been, being told lies for the good of holding secrets was nigh unbearably aggravating. Vielle looked to him and mouthed an apology before heading off to fetch the others.

Eytea and Spril were sitting on a bench outside of NieRie's Bakery, recuperating from an intense training session. When Vielle found them, their conversation had moved from talk of combat techniques to her mural. She isolated incomplete patches and spoke of her ideas for them. Encouraging her craft, Spril asked of her plans for areas she had not yet started.

Spril split off to find Yrlis while Eytea accompanied Vielle to retrieve her father and Biroe. Phylus was stricken with cautious pessimism upon learning that Galo and his daughter wanted to assemble Parliament after a trip near the coast. Being her roommate, Farim sought out IlcBei at home while MalVek found his brother in their laboratory. Phylus found Uulan at his home, consumed in obscure historical texts, while Vielle and Eytea took Biroe back to Epsilon.

"It's nowhere near evening, is it?" Sinkua asked, breaking a long silence.

"I'm sorry, brother. We couldn't have you knowing our purpose until we had returned to Epsilon," Galo apologized, "Your wellbeing was at stake."

As frustrated as he was, Sinkua had been lying to Galo under similar pretenses. In fact, Galo was so deeply indoctrinated in those lies that they were his reality. Acknowledging his hypocrisy, Sinkua begrudgingly let the subject fall into silence. As it should have been, his concern sat more with the reason for the impromptu assembly.

Vielle and Eytea were first to join them in the meeting hall with Biroe few short rolls behind them. MalVek and NalSet arrived shortly thereafter, soon followed by Spril and Yrlis. Farim came with IlcBei, and several minutes later, Phylus and Uulan joined them, thus completing the Parliament.

"This better be important," NalSet fumed as he took a seat between MalVek and Biroe, "You've gone and interrupted work far beyond your comprehension."

"The sentinels are well on their way to offing themselves in their confusion, NalSet. Leave them to their own devices for a bit," MalVek insisted.

"Wait, what is this about sentinels killing each other?" Galo interjected, briefly distracted from his intentions.

"I was in the process of reprogramming their operational directives, but security features implemented within the automatic processes were resisting my advances. Apparently, it's been causing them to behave rather erratically."

"All I understood was that last sentence, but if they're offing each other, that's fine by me," Galo admitted, none to NalSet's surprise, "Now then, on to more pressing matters. Apparently displeased with recent failures, the empire is currently deploying three naval fleets to patrol the waters of Ouristihra."

"They might have gleaned our plan," Spril suggested, "CreSam may be a lunatic sociopath, but surely even he is aware of the Wartime Passage Act."

"Which means their reign is soon to end, but hundreds or perhaps thousands of innocent lives are at stake in the meantime."

"And you elected to do nothing to stop them?" Sinkua snapped, "Instead, we went home and talk about it while the fucking scourge of the north runs across the ocean, pissing bullets on anyone they don't like?"

"We were too outnumbered and completely lacking any field advantage. It wasn't like in Berinin where the territory prevented the use of their guns."

"I'm afraid it gets worse," Phylus added, eyes darting nervously among anxious faces, "We overlooked a loophole in the WPA. If the attack is on international waters, they can make a case for perceived threat. They'll still be punished for an act of war against a currently uninvolved party, but the full brunt of the WPA might not come down upon them."

Sinkua's every thought was consumed by anxiety, tormented by the notion that the assault he had planned for several months was soon to backfire due to his limited knowledge of international law. As they sat in that slapdash conference hall, discussing what might come to pass, unarmed civilians were sailing into their demise at his behest. Despite his reputation for cunning strategizing and swiftly altering tactics by necessity, he came up empty handed at every attempt to conjure up a new plan. He cleared his throat as his breathing became erratic.

"So, I suppose I'm just writing a budget plan for our current population, then?" Biroe added quite callously.

"We lack the means to intervene at this point," Spril admitted, disregarding Biroe's comment, "at least directly. What we do have are the means to summon reinforcements on their behalf. Tracking pigeons travel faster than ships, even theirs."

"What's the plan?" Sinkua asked hoarsely.

"We'll send notice of the situation to all Coastal Patrols on coasts facing ArcNos's southeastern beach. They'll keep watch over any passing civilian ships and intervene as needed," Spril explained, "Phylus, I assume you still have contact information for the Coastal Patrols."

"Most of it, but we should also send a second set of letters to our reinforcements, warning them of what may be to come if they stay the course."

"I'm not sure everybody will answer our call," Galo added, "Eprilen will likely disregard the message."

"What makes you believe that?" Uulan asked, realizing the possibility of information regarding his conspiracy theory.

"Judge Mikalan died on Eprilenese soil, and the case was swept under the rug. Sinkua and I received a coded message revealing it to have been the work of an Avatar of Fate, likely unaware that he left a witness."

"I thought that was just a paranoid product of the rumor mill."

"I trust Judge Nenbard too well to assume him capable of spreading such a mistruth. Thus, we're best off not writing the Eprilenese Coastal Patrol. It would seem at least one branch of their government is in cahoots with the Avatars."

"Not to mention the Union Parliament," Phylus added, much to Uulan's cynical delight, "I have reason to believe they have an Avatar in their ranks."

Every pair of eyes in the conference hall turned to him as he collected his thoughts and ordered his next words.

Chapter 32

Phylus reflected upon his night in Eprilen, reunited all too briefly with his only lover and the oblivious mother of his teenage daughter. As right as she was that he had never been one to be swayed by carnal favors, somehow he felt compelled to protect her. Though the sex had become something of a blur, memories of the conversation retained vividness.

He recalled her mentioning needing something from them, something he could not provide for her. For a moment, he pondered the notion that she was not wholly devoted to their cause, that perhaps they were nothing more to her than a means to an end. Were that the case, her life was already in danger without his alerting his Parliament of her identity.

Having hastily presented his theory though, he was left to decide whose reputation to sully. Prime Duchess Olsa had been a heinously bitter obstructionist toward his every effort to secede from Imperial ArcNos, but given his eventual success, it seemed a bit excessive to vilify her and thus her country by extension. Rather, so it seemed until he gleaned a veiled message from Malia's advice.

She had told him to present his case again when the skies had warmed and people were in better spirits. More importantly, she had specified to return the following Swelter. Being in the southern reaches of the Midlands, nary a person in Eprilen wore long sleeves that time of year. It all finally sense, alarmingly gut-churning sense.

"Olsa," he announced flatly, "Prime Duchess Olsa is an Avatar of Fate."

"Are you certain?" Uulan stuttered after a long uncomfortable silence.

"As certain as I can be at this point. Somebody hinted that I should present my case against Imperial ArcNos again next Swelter, well before our nation would be old enough to do such a thing. Warm weather means short sleeves, and short sleeves don't consistently hide their mark. Factor in her vendetta against our contesting an empire fortified by the Avatars of Fate, and there's just one logical conclusion."

"I suppose I can call off the hunt then, Uulan?" Farim asked, noticing he was lost in bewilderment.

"What? Oh yes, of course. Write your colleagues and tell them we've no further need for their research. Frankly, I'm ashamed of myself for not seeing it sooner. Must be my age catching up to me."

"What do you mean?" Phylus asked, "About seeing it sooner, I mean, not your age."

"I'm still waiting for the text clipping, but I recall that the law preventing us from attempting to revoke Imperial ArcNos's federal status was repealed due to ambiguity. It's a lesser known piece of history since that law itself has scarcely been brought to issue since its enactment."

"The Avatars also tried to use the ArcNosian-Kirtsian Trade Conflict to appear to be operating out of Kirts," Eytea added, "as though Kirts was trying to sabotage ArcNos. They've abused limited common knowledge of history before, so there might be other instances of such a gambit in their history."

"Well shit, I guess we can forget about the Eprilenese Coastal Patrol," Spril spat, "We'd just be endangering everyone else if Olsa caught word of it."

"She might already know about the deployment," Sinkua cautioned, "which would mean she's preparing to fortify against any interference they might encounter."

"I'll be sure to include that in the letters, tell them to pack the heavy artillery," Phylus noted, "Are there any other concerns?"

"We need to leave Berinin out of this," Galo ordered with anxious haste.

"For what reason? If Eprilen is poised to aid against resistance, Berinin has the best shot at a tactical interception. We need that advantage," Spril countered.

"They can't afford the economic risk," Galo explained, "Such equipment comes with a hefty price tag, and losing it in combat would be a troubling fiscal blow. We'd be saving innocent lives now by dooming others later."

"I thought that Chieftain Sage Gijin repaired Berinin's failing economy when he assumed the title," Phylus suggested.

"He did, and all was well until five years ago. Too many alums of the Medicinal Guild were emigrating, thus diminishing Berinin's market hold on such specialized services. So, my grandfather strengthened the efforts of the herbal medicine branch with his incomparable knowledge of such. More effective medicines were developed, and we cornered the market without being consumed by greed," Galo explained, "Five years ago, somebody published an anonymous study falsely refuting the validity of herbal medicine. That being the cornerstone of our recovery and economic health, a recession soon followed and has been slowly accelerating ever since."

"Money lost can be recovered. Lives cannot," Phylus argued, "Besides, you rejected the power to withhold Berinin's aid, and you only have approximations to support your assumption."

"But…"

"I understand your concern, Galo, but you relinquished your authority. Nenbard will decide what is best for them."

"So, Eprilen is out of the question, and Berinin may or may not help us. We'll need to call upon the Ivarian Coastal Patrol at the north, east, and south coasts," Spril added.

Sinkua's eyes wandered along the grains of the table, down one leg, and onto the floor. Tiny black ants feasted upon a heap of crumbs. Sifting the crumbs with the toe of his boot, he noticed a large seed at the bottom, perhaps a pumpkin seed lost from someone's snack. It was hardened, but the ants had managed to burrow into it. Glimpses of what time he could remember on the island flickered into lucidity, replaying a specific moment which had inexplicably stuck with him.

"What of domestic security, though? Weren't we counting on those flash mob reinforcements to help us overwhelm the imperialists on their own turf?" Vielle asked.

"I might have an answer to that," Sinkua hesitantly offered, his memory too vague to be entirely certain of its reality.

"It didn't occur to you to try the plan that doesn't require reinforcements first?" Spril asked indignantly.

"This plan didn't occur to me at all until now," Sinkua countered, still staring at the ants and the seed, "Who here realizes how ironic it is that behemoth beetles are considered natural predators of the black ant?"

The lot of them remained silent, more for not seeing the point than not knowing the answer. Sinkua pinched the seed, careful not to smash any of the bugs, and set it upon the table.

"See how they've chewed through the hardened husk of this seed? When a behemoth beetle hunts at an ant hill, hundreds of them take an alternate exit and swarm the beetle from behind, chewing through its shell just like this," Sinkua elucidated, "The sentries are out of the way. It will only take a few of us to break into the capitol and secure the breach against closure. We won't need numbers to win. Just persistence."

"Break the shell, expose the flesh," Spril reiterated, "It's a risky operation, but it may be the only chance we have. We need to operate under the assumption that nobody is coming to our rescue."

"Right, once we're past their defenses, we can pour in as many troops as are willing as many times as they're capable."

"Unfortunately, very few of our citizens are former soldiers," Phylus noted, "Most were non-combative personnel or employed in the private sector before it was completely overtaken."

"That comes as no surprise," Biroe verified, "The soldiers who could not be reconditioned into the new ideals were systematically and formally executed. Those who attempted to flee met with less ceremonious ends. As for the other personnel, they spared only those of us deemed too weak of body, mind, or conviction to be a threat. Escapees were killed on the spot."

"In that case, how the hell did you get out?" MalVek asked.

"Well, would you believe that I held four soldiers at gun point and demanded my freedom in exchange for their lives?"

All but Biroe and Sinkua shared a hearty laugh, and MalVek shook his head.

"Well then," Biroe continued, leaning back in his wheelchair, "let's just say I was escorted out of the building and leave it at that."

MalVek looked him over, studying his body language. He remained nonchalant. He smirked wryly when their glances met, and MalVek chuckled.

"You son of a bitch!" he remarked, "Sounds like I need to buy you a drink."

"Trust me, that's not a good idea," Phylus interjected, "Besides, we have work to do."

"Just give the orders, and we'll go to," Spril offered, hoping to bolster Phylus's confidence in this time of turmoil.

"I'll go work on those letters. Biroe, sketch a map of the capitol to the best of your memory. Spril, use that map to find ideal points and methods of entry. NalSet and MalVek, work on designs for anything you think might help us breach the perimeter. Be ready to build on a moment's notice. Vielle, rally all willing participants and direct them to the training facility. Sinkua and Galo, combat crash course. Teach them as much as you can in whatever time we have. Yrlis, alert our hospital to schedule additional staff for the next couple of weeks. IlcBei, keep an eye on topside motion in case they launch a preemptive strike in anticipation of an assault. Everybody else, be ready to assist anywhere that you're needed on a moment's notice. This meeting is adjourned," Phylus asserted.

One by one, everybody filed out of the meeting hall. Being the least mobile, Biroe was last to leave. Sinkua stopped to hold the door for him while Galo waited nearby.

"Go ahead without me," Sinkua insisted as he let the door close, "I need to look for something back at my hammock."

Galo nodded in compliance, and they split off in opposite directions. Yrlis watched Galo pass from beside a pillar adorned with a copious number of flyers. She approached him from beyond his visual periphery. Keeping a few steps behind, she cleared her throat to announce herself, her heart bruising itself against her rib cage.

"Galo, there's something I need to tell you."

"What is it, Yrlis?" he responded as he halted, his disdain for her ilk poisoning his voice.

"I'm the one that conducted that study."

Silence. Galo remained statuesque, but within, his mind was a torrent of rage battering his last remnants of hope. Yrlis's heart tried over and over to strain itself through her ribs and out of her chest. Cautiously, she took a few steps toward him, reaching for his shoulder to offer an apology. As her fingertips grazed his shoulder, his body whipped about, and his fist cracked across her face, knocking her to the concrete floor.

"Do you have any idea how much trouble you've caused?" he bellowed down at her, "And for what? To prove your own doubts? You obviously never believed in his work anyway. So what place do you have testing it?"

"I didn't know it would do so much damage," she countered through tearful eyes, "But how can you justify duping thousands or even millions of people like that?"

"I wasn't duping anybody!"

"Fine, your grandfather, the herbal medicine industry. They thrive on false hope. It only works for people who believe it will."

"You must like getting punched in the face," Galo retorted, "Where do you get off making such ludicrous claims?"

"I ran chemical tests on samples of different diseases. None of them produced the results they claimed to effect. They're all placebos, psychosomatic."

"Where did you get the plants?"

"I didn't steal them, if that's what you're wondering. I don't agree with your work, but I'm not a thief. I grew them myself."

"In their natural habitat?"

"No, but I simulated the conditions."

"To what extent? Temperature, humidity, and soil composition?"

"That's right. Why?" Yrlis asked, growing increasingly curious of Galo's train of thought.

"I'll tell you later. Maybe," Galo countered, "But first, I'm going to prove to you that proper herbal medicine works even if you don't believe in it. Have you taken anything for your congestion?"

"No, I haven't yet. It only came about yesterday."

"I'm going to give you something for it. Don't take anything else that could aid your recovery, and tell me how you feel in two days. That's too short a time for your immune system to fend it off much alone. Do you trust me?"

"Only so far as to know you won't poison me."

Back at Epsilon, Sinkua was rummaging frantically through his duffle bag for the third time. Between the aches of the day's labor and the aggravation of all that had transpired since his work was interrupted on false pretenses, he could feel an attack viciously rising to the surface. Fearing the slightest negative stimulus might tip him off the brink, he swallowed a pill dry as soon as he found one. That only led to a greater worry though.

Only two pills remained after that. He dug through the bag repeatedly, desperately searching for spilled strays. Although he managed to find perhaps half a dozen, the count was still painfully insufficient. One per day sufficed on uneventful days, but if they were to raid the capitol, he would need two or three daily.

He could vaguely recall Galo mentioning a prescription, something about Ophalin sending a refill after a few weeks. Either the doctor underestimated how quickly the supply would be depleted, or he forgot. Still another possibility remained, that Ophalin was unable to contact him.

From a few meters back, he heard the familiar sound of bare adult feet on concrete. Knowing who approached, he beckoned Galo to his side. Noticing his brother's distress, Galo swiftly complied, crouching beside him as he arrived.

"I'm almost out of medicine," Sinkua announced, "What did the doctor tell you about getting more?"

"He said he would send a prescription when he thought you would almost be out. Have you not heard from him?"

"This wouldn't be an issue if I had. I'm worried that he either forgot or his message couldn't reach me. Do you have anything to tide me over until I can go back to Ferya?"

"Right off hand, no. I could make an anticoagulant for the blood clots, but that would only keep your anger from being accelerated," Galo admitted, "Given a little time, I might be able to come up with something to suppress the tumors, assuming there's a book store with Grandfather's texts anywhere around here. How long can you give me?"

"I suppose I could last a week, so long as I keep those throat herbs on hand. By the way, what brought you back over here? Did you forget something?"

"No, I need some ipthkys root. It's for Yrlis."

"I thought she was opposed to herbal medicine."

"That's exactly why I'm giving her ipthkys root for her congestion, to prove to her that it works even if you don't believe in it."

"Wait, but I thought that…"

"Not a word, Sinkua," Galo smirked.

As the two of them left for the training center, they passed Eytea on her way to retrieve her painting supplies. So long as no one called upon her, she intended to use this time to close the gaps in her mural as she wound down from a rigorous training session. Galo, however, stopped her to ask if she would scour the bookstore for his grandfather's books for Sinkua's sake. Bound by Phylus's orders, as well as other motivators, she eschewed her intentions and changed course.

Walking through the tunnels, they noticed strangers pausing their conversations and interrupting one another to point them out. People they'd either never met or acknowledged looked to them with expressions of familiarity. The closer they got to the training center, the more audible Vielle's voice became through the clamor, cementing what they both suspected.

The moment Vielle left the meeting hall, she had begun recruiting for the invasion. She studied each person or group from a safe distance and modified her pitch to fit her impression of them. To thrill seekers, she spoke of the risks inherent, while to narcissists, she spoke of the glory of driving a revolution. Hatred of the empire was a common appeal among the lot of them, thus designating it as her default angle when she was unable to place even a vague profile. Interest spread rapidly as recruits spoke with friends on what was to come. By the time Sinkua and Galo reached the training center, she had gathered a small army near the door and was off to the bar to exploit inebriated anger.

"I get the feeling we're going to need a formal roster and schedule," Sinkua pointed out.

The crowd parted, granting them a path to the doors. Once they were inside, Galo held the door open, inviting the waiting mob to join them. There looked to be roughly half a gross of them total, and those were only the ones waiting outside the door.

"Did anybody bring a pen, by any chance?" Galo asked the room as he locked the doors, "Paper would be useful, as well. We didn't anticipate such a large turnout on the first night."

People checked their pockets, all coming up with empty hands. Those who had satchels and purses sifted through them, some more diligently than others, yet neither a pen nor notepad was to be found among them.

"I've got lipstick," a woman in her early twenties announced, "Nothing to write on though."

"We can use the wall, I suppose," Sinkua quietly suggested.

Galo mulled it over for a moment and reluctantly announced, "Tallest person here, write the day of the week as high as you can on the wall. Under that, we need you all to make a list of your names. You will be Class One out of four classes. After this first night, you'll take three nights off and return on the fifth night at a time to be determined by the end of this session."

Given the viral success of Vielle's recruiting campaign, four groupings of this size seemed a reasonable prediction. Obviously, she could find more if left to her own devices, but he planned to request that she desist at the end of this class. Quantity was only a quality up to a certain point, and with only he and Sinkua to tutor them in the art of combat, letting her operate unfettered threatened to bypass that point and overwhelm them.

Sinkua counted the names on the wall as the last one was scrawled upon it. They numbered sixty-eight in total. He called for anyone who had not signed the wall to raise their hand. No hands came up.

"There are two fundamental rules of combat," he informed the gathered mob, "Know yourself, and know your enemy. Learn your strengths and advantages and make the most of them. If you have a strong throwing arm and a sharp eye, secure the high ground and attack from a distance. If you have a long reach, strike quickly and aim for pressure points from beyond your opponent's reach. And if you can't find a way to get the upper hand, remember that every able-bodied man has the same weak spot. A toddler can devastate a one hundred fifty kilogram bloke with a strike to the sack."

"That's right, there's no shame in fighting dirty. In fact, I'd encourage it," Galo reiterated, "We're at a considerable disadvantage both for numbers and for individual firepower. On top of knowing your own strengths and the enemies' weaknesses, you need to know how to use the terrain to exploit them. Get the drop on your opponent. Strike first and strike to stun or kill. Do not, I repeat, do not fuck around showboating or you'll get yourself killed."

"Exactly. We don't have time to train you to engage armed soldiers like we do. If your target has any sort of firearm, remain undetected until you can deliver a killing blow. If you are seen before you're ready to strike, those imperialist sheep will not hesitate to slaughter you like the cattle they think you are."

"On that note, we'll start with sneak attacks. Sinkua and I will stand facing the wall. Form two lines behind us starting as far back as you can. At irregular intervals, come forth one at a time and try to hit one of us before you're detected. He and I will not look over our shoulders unless alerted and will only communicate with each other silently."

Roughly seven or eight meters separated their backs from the foremost trainees. They counted the bricks in the wall, waiting for the moment when one of those rookies would end the silence. The first one bold enough to try his luck shattered that silence as he barreled forth with powerfully loud footfalls. As he came within arm's reach, seemingly oblivious to how loudly he heaved in his hubris, Sinkua spun about and snatched his arm in the middle of its swing.

"Feels like you could've done some serious damage had that landed," Sinkua complimented, "but you breathe and step too loudly. Think it over at the back of the line and try again later."

In pairs and alone, more of them followed, all meeting with similar results in spite of their confidence. Quite notably, all of them struck either strongly or swiftly, but disappointingly few of them did both. After a couple dozen monotonous iterations of failure, somebody broke the pattern. As Galo turned toward the wall, the smell of sweaty leather infiltrated his nostrils just in time for him to look back and take a shoe to the face.

"It's about time somebody got one of us," Sinkua remarked, signaling for all to halt as Galo cupped his icy palm over his nose, "and with a few excellent points made at that. One, shoes are loud; go barefoot. If you don't have calluses on your feet yet, you will by the time we invade. Two, if your target is not preoccupied, they're more likely to hear you. Unless you can walk silently, go for the long range attack instead. Three, don't be afraid to try unconventional methods."

"You heard the man, take off your shoes," Galo ordered as he withdrew the ice.

Scores of shoes soared across the room and bounced into a pile in the corner. Pairs were separated in flight and landed hopelessly mismatched. Once the last shoe had found its place, the lot of them faced Sinkua and Galo once again, this time in something almost resembling a deliberate formation.

"On that note, we're going to practice stepping lightly next," Galo continued, "Having a soft footfall means you need not move quickly, but it's all the better if you can do both. Some of you may already be able to do this when you actually try. The rest of you, I'll teach to be light on your feet."

Over the next couple of hours, Galo taught the sixty-eight students of Class One some basic Tide Dancing fundamentals. Sinkua taught a few places to deliver a killing or incapacitating blow and began lessons with the limited selection of weaponry. Those with shorter limbs were trained with polearms to compensate for their disadvantageous reach. The training was wholly improvised, but they made the best of it and held their pupils' interest with a promise that the two of them would spar one another at the end of the session.

In the midst of Sinkua's demonstration with MalVek's sledgehammer, a knock came at the door. He waited while Galo answered it. Vielle had come to invite them to dinner, which, to the disappointment of the class, meant the sparring would have to wait lest the meal went cold.

"By the way," Vielle began as they exited the training facility, "I posted a registration roster outside the door. It filled up while you were inside."

"You're something of an overachiever, aren't you?" Sinkua smirked, "How many do we have?"

"On top of the ones in that class, another four hundred," she casually answered, seemingly unaware of the weight of the task.

"Great, so either we hold two classes a day, or double the size of our next three classes," Galo added.

"Spril isn't doing anything until Biroe finishes that map. We'll have him take a couple hundred off our hands," Sinkua suggested.

As they neared Phylus and Vielle's home, the aroma of roasted pork hung heavily on the air, growing ever more tantalizing with each approaching step. The umami scent was accented by bold seasonings and grilled pineapple, all peppered with vague hints of conversation on the periphery of audibility. The smell latched tenaciously to hungry tongues as Vielle opened the door for them.

Eytea and Farim sat together on a sofa in the sunken living room, each halfway through a plate of pork chops and pineapples and at an indeterminate point in a markedly animated conversation. Two stacks of books lay before them on the coffee table. Phylus sat on the arm of a nearby recliner with a plate of his own, periodically interjecting and contributing what he could to the conversation. Spril sat on an ottoman, voraciously scraping together the final remnants of his meal and scarcely injecting himself into the exchange.

"Well, I hope you saved some for the rest of us," Vielle joked.

"Oh hey, Galo," Eytea called out between bites, "Your grandfather wrote way too many books for us to carry all of them. So we just got the ones that mentioned the amygdala, tumors, or bone marrow in the index."

"I might have also looked for internal bleeding or blood clots, but I suppose that's a fine place to start," Galo accepted as he prepared himself a plate, "How many texts did you fetch, then?"

"Fourteen," Farim answered, since Eytea had a mouthful of pineapple, "She found me on the way there and asked that I join her, just in case. So, how did your first class go?"

"It's slow going, but most of them show some promise," Sinkua observed with cautious optimism, "Vielle's given us a bit of a larger bite than we can chew though, so we'll need you to teach a few of the classes, Spril."

"Sure, that's not a problem," Spril accepted as he took his plate to the sink, "We'll divvy up the registrants in the morning. Biroe estimates it'll take a week to come up with a coherent map of the capitol from memory. He's back in Phylus's room with a plate and a pad of graph paper right now."

"That reminds me, I finished the letters about an hour ago," Phylus interjected, "I gave them to the children out by the boarding dock with orders to sit near the top of the stairs and send one every three to five minutes, so as to not draw attention."

"Do you really believe it wise to entrust such a task to children?" Galo asked anxiously.

"Those kids will do just fine," Sinkua insisted.

Yrlis stepped out of the bathroom, clutching her belly with one hand and a can of aerosol air freshener with the other. Mucus encrusted her nostrils, and her throaty breathing could be heard from across the apartment. She wiped away the snot with an already crusty sleeve and spoke with the voice of a chain smoking lounge singer.

"I'm sorry, hon, but you're gonna have to go visit Phylus without me," she apologized through weak gasps for air.

"Not tonight. You sound far too sick for me to leave you home alone," Spril argued, "What's come over you, anyway?"

"I think it's the flu. I've got a horrible fever, and I've been on the toilet all day."

"I've noticed. It sounds terrible," he sympathized, "Have you taken any medicine for it."

"No, but I plan on it tomorrow. For reasons I can't explain, I let that damn kid make me his guinea pig so I could apologize for writing that article."

"Given the circumstances, I'm not sure if that was bold, big, or just stupid of you to trust him. What did he give you?"

"Something called ipthkys root. He said it was for my congestion."

Spril looked her over, his expression changing from one of sympathy to one of pity, the sort offered to hapless fools. Shaking his head, he walked to the bathroom with his shirt covering his nose.

"Where are you going?" she asked hoarsely.

"To get you an antidiarrheal and a decongestant."

"But if I take anything before tomorrow, Galo will insist that I compromised the results," she argued, "and I'll have to through all this again."

"No, you won't. He's already made his point," he countered as he returned from the bathroom with two pills.

"What do you mean?"

"Ipthkys root isn't a decongestant," Spril explained from just beyond arm's reach, "It's a laxative."

MalVek and NalSet sat at opposite ends of a work bench crowded with what some may have disregarded as junk. Disheveled piles of spare parts, broken machines, and incomplete devices were strewn about, all ripe for the stripping. Remains of Biroe's car were leaning against the walls, crowding the shop and testing the limits of its floor space. In a larger room in the back was something resembling a vehicle, a gradual work in progress with salvaged components of Biroe's car at its core. The two of them silently exchanged incomplete machines and components over the table, each adding to the other's work thus far. It was something of a two man assembly line but with all the hazards of a full scale operation, as they pitched tools to one another with nary a care for safety.

"Have you come up with a way to bypass the electromagnetic security locks?" MalVek asked with cautious optimism.

"Same as I told you earlier, nothing that would work quickly enough," NalSet countered, "We'd just be guessing at the frequency, and their security panel would notice our meddling by the time we got it right."

While they lacked the means to directly breach security, they did have several potential methods for circumventing it. These ranged from simple burrowing mechanisms to travel under the fence to electromagnetic gloves and boots, which could enable even those with the weakest grip to safely scale the vertical bars. Still in the testing phase was a device they called the resonant splitter. The idea was to determine the resonant frequency of the bars and mount pistons pumping at the same frequency to two of the bars. While the pistons weakened their structural integrity, a spanner would push the bars apart. It was admittedly a long shot, but they were nothing if not ambitious.

Explosives were also considered but had been reserved largely for going under the fence. Developing a bomb that could cling to one of the bars and produced a directional blast guaranteed to split it was proving a frustrating task, one not worth pursuing given the other methods they had devised. The underground explosive would be more efficient than the burrower, but it presented a considerable hazard were the directional mechanism to fail. Additionally, it was much louder than the burrower and could thus alert someone on the inside of their approach.

"I still think it would be a much cleaner operation if we could just bypass the gate's security feature," MalVek insisted, somewhat timidly breaking the vocal silence yet again.

"As do I, but we need to know the exact frequency before we try. Sinkua could break in and strip a console, but by the time we extracted the information, they would have caught on."

"Did you ever make any further progress overriding the operational algorithms on the sentinels? Perhaps we could simply crash one into the fence and send our troops pouring in."

NalSet mulled it over for a while, making his younger brother increasingly anxious with each passing second. He had gained some control over them, but various circumstances tended to interfere, particularly when certain stimuli altered their behavioral processes. At such times, control needed to be commandeered all over again. Sooner than he could answer though, somebody knocked on the door. MalVek answered it to find IlcBei looking quite distressed.

"Come with me," she urged without greeting.

"Both of us?"

"If you're busy, one of you can stay. But I really need someone with mechanical expertise to come back to the security station with me."

"If something is broken, I can fix it. I'll be back shortly, NalSet."

Once they reached the security depot, she opened the door to reveal that everything appeared to be functioning quite normally. Every display was sharp and steady. The frame rates were up to snuff. Every light bulb in the ceiling shone brightly.

"Everything looks okay to me. What was so important that you had to pull me away from my work?"

"Take a look at this screen," IlcBei urged.

"Nothing's wrong with the video feed," MalVek insisted, failing to see past the function of the machine.

"I mean what's on the video feed."

This particular camera was situated near the perimeter fence. At the edge of the screen, the bottom few centimeters of it were visible. A handful of cameras were positioned in such areas, but the anomaly was only present on this one. A wide metallic base had been constructed at the bottom of the fence, adorned with panels of wiring, nodes, and switches.

"What the hell is that thing?" MalVek asked rhetorically.

"That's what I was hoping you could tell me."

"I must admit, I've never seen anything quite like it. I suspect it doesn't bode well for our plans though, but I have an idea as to who might be able to identify it."

"NalSet?"

"Quite ironically, no."

While those who had remained in ArcNos had witnessed and actively resisted its collapse into federal ruin, he knew they had endured less than the brunt of their combative capabilities. It was widespread knowledge that Lord CreSam and the Avatars of Fate had put considerable effort into hunting the Hybrid vagabonds. Tales of Sinkua and Galo's travels and exploits largely cemented related rumors, verifying that they had faced powers and monstrosities beyond what had been reserved for keeping the locals in check.

IlcBei went to retrieve either of them, preferably both if the circumstances allowed, while MalVek kept watch over the security depot. The alloy anomaly aside, there still remained a possibility of an assault being leveled in anticipation of their striking while the capitol was unfortified. MalVek hypothesized on what that object could have been.

Finding the two vagabonds was an easy enough task for IlcBei. In accordance with their orders from Phylus, their schedule had them at the training hall on their second day with Class Three. Upon her arrival, she found her assumption to have only been half correct.

Potential insurgents were lined up with a large bucket of fist sized stones at the head. A couple of meters shy of the opposite wall stood a large sheet of plywood with a hole the size of a cantaloupe in its center. Curiously, IlcBei paused to observe the lesson.

One at a time, students withdrew a stone from the bucket. Once they were upright, Sinkua ignited the stone with the snap of his fingers. The student would then try to hurl the stone through the hole without getting burned. It was an admittedly archaic exercise, but it served to develop a combination of speed and accuracy, even under panicked conditions.

"Sinkua!" she called out between turns.

"Something amiss topside?" he asked, signaling for the next participant to wait.

"That may be putting it lightly."

Quite to the enjoyment of those with singed palms and sore shoulders, class was dismissed early that night.

"Where's your friend, anyway?" she asked as she led him to the security station, "I thought you two taught that class together."

"We normally do, but he's busy making new medicine for me. I've almost run out of my prescription, so he offered to develop something to control my symptoms."

"That's quite the task to endure."

When they returned to the station, MalVek was still examining the bizarre object on the screen. Subconsciously, he occasionally leaned to the side as though he was trying to gain a better vantage point than what the camera offered. Of course, this meant that Sinkua needed no explanation as to why IlcBei had called upon him.

Looking at the screen that MalVek scrutinized so intently, the hairs on his right forearm raised and tingled painfully. Memories of the night in Masnethege flashed into his conscience, playing vividly in his mind's eye with every blink, as he clutched his forearm. Terrified by the recollections, he stood silently transfixed by the screen for a minute.

"Do you know what it is?" MalVek asked, finally surrendering to his ignorance on the matter.

"I do," Sinkua flatly answered, "but I'm not sure how to explain it. Suffice it to say, we're not getting in through the fence.'

"Some sort of electrical security device?"

"I guess you could call it that. We can't get in, but they can get out. Same goes for their bullets, and the obelisks protect each other, too."

"Do you know how to get past it?"

"I've seen it done before," Sinkua assured, "The best way is to go under it."

Chapter 33

Galo sat beside his hammock with three books and several bags of plant matter laid out before him. Somewhat to his surprise, the children playing on the dock kept a safe distance from his work. The different medicines were separated according to what symptoms they could treat. After reading the relevant texts, he had devised a way to clear the blood clots under Sinkua's brain stem, but it would have to be injected regularly. He also had a theory toward dissolving the microtumors, but it would only be useful during an episode. He also lacked any means to keep them from regrowing. Anger suppressants and mood stabilizers were fairly common though, and protein inhibitors were all the more so.

Those had a rather interesting selling point. For a time, popular dietitians convinced the public that prolonging the protein absorption process would allow the body to use it more efficiently and thus develop smoother muscle tone. The exact science, or lack thereof as the case may have been, was lost on Galo, but it had created a new demand for natural supplements. Though the long term promise was likely fraudulent, the initial claim was entirely honest.

"It looks like you're on to something," Sinkua commented, startling him.

"I think so, but you'll need two separate treatments," Galo agreed, catching his breath, "I can make a pill that will counteract the protein accelerator and suppress your anger, but the anticoagulant and tumor treatment will need to be administered separately."

"So, I just need to take one extra pill? Sounds like I got off easy."

"Not that easy. The other medication will need to be injected directly below your brain stem, once every three days or during an attack."

"Sounds a bit awkward, shoving a needle back there. Would you mind doing it for me?"

"Of course not. I wouldn't expect you to do it yourself," Galo agreed, "What brings you out here anyway?"

"Remember those pillars around the war machine in Masnethege?" Sinkua asked, knowing the answer perfectly well, "They've erected a series of them around the imperial capitol."

"Calling another meeting, then?"

"Actually, no. The two of us and IlcBei are to report to MalVek and NalSet's shop to discuss the best way under the capitol. Biroe and Spril will determine where to surface."

"I'll bring these with me," Galo insisted, gathering the most essential parts of his work, "They may have something I can use to process these."

During the infancy of the subterranean community, accessing the capitol underground would have been a simple matter of riding the Subtransit train. In response to IlcBei's obstinate refusal to surrender ownership of the system though, that area had been heavily barricaded with a layer of reinforced concrete too dense for the train to penetrate. This left one method of entry, though it too was fraught with the potential for hazard.

"We'll need to blast our way in," MalVek explained as they entered the shop, "NalSet and I will concern ourselves with the explosives, but we don't know how deep the barricade generator runs."

"I believe it's generated only on the surface, given how my grandfather destroyed them," Galo assured.

"Sinkua said the obelisks protect one another. How could your grandfather have done such a thing?" NalSet asked in disbelief.

"Hydromantic ice pillars deployed from beneath the towers."

"Can you do such a thing, as well?"

"Yes, but not on so massive a scale."

"In that case," MalVek interjected, "from how deep were the ice pillars launched?"

"They appeared to be just below the surface."

That much was fortunate, despite the brief flash of hope fading into disappointment. While Galo would be unable to dispatch the guard towers, their range would allow the train through the reopened passageway. It also meant they would not interfere with the explosives.

"I finished those street blasters while you were out, MalVek," NalSet announced, "but we'll need something, well, bigger. Let me show you kids."

The street blaster resembled a silver spider with a red button atop its body, like a shiny black widow. NalSet held it out on display and, to the initial alarm of all, pounded the button. Nothing happened. His confidence in the safety feature was unshakable. Continuing the demonstration, he slammed it down on the table, driving the prongs into the surface. He struck the button again, this time at arm's length, and his arm snapped back as a conic explosion blasted downward, reducing the tabletop to smoldering splinters.

"We'll work on scaling it up," NalSet assured them, "IlcBei, can you reprogram the Subtransit to run through the capitol?"

"Of course, just tell me when."

"We'll need to send a test car through first," Sinkua insisted, "just to be sure it's safe. After that, we'll deploy as many troops as we can fit onto the next train. What's the capacity?"

"Standard sized passenger train holds seven hundred comfortably."

"We have between four and five hundred troops."

"Sending in the whole staff behind the canary, then?" MalVek asked.

"We'll see."

Taking the time to reprogram the route on the Subtransit meant IlcBei would need to eschew her responsibilities in the security station. She decided she would call upon Uulan to watch the screens in her stead. Galo stayed in the shop to render the herbs into pills and intravenous fluids, and Sinkua went in search of Spril.

Just as he had every day since their duties had been assigned, Biroe wracked his memory to compile as detailed a map of the imperial capitol as he could recall. The geometric layout of the roads was easy enough to recreate, leaving the difficulty with names and order. Landmark buildings were placed somewhat quickly, as were ones on popular intersections. Trouble primarily remained with the other buildings, the criticality of each of which was not assumable, as well as municipal details. Though he was unable to assume the importance of each building to the mission, he knew he could do so with the relative positions of Subtransit entrances and manhole covers.

What he thought interesting about such a task was how details almost filled themselves in as he put knowledge to paper. He found himself reliving moments behind the wheel, some from before his accident, so vividly that he could almost sketch patches of discoloration on the asphalt. In fact, he was so consumed by the pressure he was under that he took a moment to notice when the last crucial detail had hit the page.

"I've finished!" he victoriously announced as he rolled out of the room.

"Really?" Vielle remarked, looking out from behind the open refrigerator door, "That's wonderful, Mister Biroe."

"It really is, pal," Phylus agreed as he stood up from his armchair, "I don't know anybody else who could have pulled that off. Give me the papers, and I'll take them to Spril right away."

"I'll keep dinner warm for you, Dad."

"Thank you, dear, but you two go ahead and eat while I'm out. You've both worked far too hard for me to expect you to wait."

Biroe just smiled and nodded in gratitude and agreement. He had mentally exerted himself almost to the point of physical exhaustion. At this point, he felt he had the appetite of a man twice the size he was before losing a quarter of his body, and Vielle's cooking smelled as maddeningly tempting as usual. As Phylus closed the door, Sinkua pushed through a crowd and came running with an undeniable look of distress and urgency.

"Where does Spril live?" Sinkua asked as he came within earshot, "I've never been to his apartment, and I need to find him."

"I was just on my way there with this map. Come with me," Phylus offered.

Sinkua studied the map as he joined Phylus on his walk to Yrlis and Spril's home. Using the positions of sewer lids and Subtransit entrances, he mentally compiled a general approach. Ironically, his strategy didn't involve using them as entrances or escape routes, but rather plotting those around the notion that the imperial troops would swarm those spots were they to anticipate or learn of the coming insurgence. Part of him hoped the map would have included which buildings were unoccupied and which ones had basements, but he understood that it was too high a hope to expect.

Yrlis answered the door, awkwardly avoiding eye contact with Sinkua. This was their first encounter since her humiliating ipthkys root incident, and she had been trying to avoid both him and Galo for as long as possible. With scarcely a word, she went to retrieve Spril for them.

"I have good news," Phylus announced as he came to the door.

"And I've got bad news," Sinkua added.

"Biroe finished the map, and it's impressively detailed."

"But we can't enter from the surface."

"Wait, why the hell not?"

"They've set up a bunch of electrical barricade posts. Bullets can get out, but nothing can get in."

"Can we destroy them?"

"Going around them would be faster. NalSet and MalVek are developing some explosives, and IlcBei is reprogramming the Subtransit route to take us inside."

"Well in that case, come in and we'll decide where to deploy each team," Spril offered, acknowledging Sinkua's tactical prowess, "Thanks for the map, Phylus."

Inside, they sat over the coffee table, lightly penciling deployment routes onto the map. They quickly agreed to split the troops into teams of about twenty, but disagreements persisted in deciding where and when to deploy them. Spril had worked with stubborn troops before, but few were quite as tenacious as Sinkua. Of course, it didn't help that he could usually drive a convincing argument behind his position. Had he trained under HarEin, he could have become a great leader as well as an indispensable asset on the front lines. While he was a particularly troublesome case, Spril was eventually able to coax him into something resembling a compromise. Spril's vision of the mission was largely favored in the final outline, but this was hardly the time for splitting hairs over balancing contributions.

Two days later, all four hundred plus troops packed into the training facility, most summoned by flyers. They were joined by Spril, Phylus, MalVek, Farim, and all four Hybrids. Spril drew the map on the wall with black marker, while the others panned the room, scrutinizing the spread. Once the map was transferred, Spril produced other markers from his pocket, one color for each team, and drew each deployment point and the path to be taken through the imperial capitol. He detailed which areas to target and recapped the basics from their classes.

Though they only attended two classes at that point, even he was confident that they were ready enough. The sessions had been long and rigorous, and nearly all of them showed undeniable promise or natural propensity. They also had the elements of surprise and weakened enemy defenses in their favor, and waiting through another battery of classes may have squandered at least one of those advantages.

"When do we ship out, General?" one insurgent asked at the end of Spril's monologue.

"General? Under Brigadier General Elite HarEin, I was a Brigadier Elite, the second highest command post in the nation," Spril countered, "but down here, we are stripped of our titles. Address me as Spril and nothing else. As for your question, we're waiting to receive clearance for entry."

"Our top engineers are blowing a hole in the wall, hopefully as we speak, to allow us to drive the Subtransit into the imperial capitol underground," Galo added, "At Sinkua's behest, they're first deploying a single empty car to ensure that we can safely pass under the barricade laced through the perimeter fence."

Spril scanned the crowd, observing the weapons they each chose to wield. They ranged from bags of rocks to kitchen knives, from screwdrivers to chainsaws and weed whackers. The local hardware store had clearly done some fantastic business over the past week. Unable to commit their names to memory, he acknowledged them by distinguishing features and directed them into clusters, rearranging them into groups of a score each.

The four Hybrids elected to stay together and concentrate their efforts on a single area. Aside from the fact that they were best suited to protect one another, Spril asserted that having their teachers nearby would unnerve many of the insurgents during the incursion. For that same reason, he opted to join them, as well. Phylus did likewise to stay near his daughter. MalVek stayed in the same unit because he knew the rookies might slack off if he were there to watch their backs. Farim, who had girded herself with a wide-headed canoe oar, stuck with them because she felt safer with them than with strangers.

It wasn't so much that they lacked confidence in their new troops but rather that they had considerably more of such in one another and their own capabilities. To avoid implying favoritism, the eight of them comprised an entire unit. When he had successfully split everyone else into groups of twenty and twenty-one, Spril dismissed them to pass the time by means of their choosing. The only regulations were that they remained mostly sober and stayed near the facility.

Galo leaned toward Sinkua and mumbled to him. Sinkua nodded in compliance and turned to Spril.

"Galo recommends I find someplace calmer and rest until it's time to go," he told him, "Could you fetch me from Epsilon on your way out."

"Of course, buddy, do what you need to keep your head straight."

"Mind if I keep you company?" Eytea asked, not particularly fond of the dense crowd.

"Sounds great, come on."

While they were walking back to Epsilon, Sinkua withdrew his dagger and anxiously twirled it around his fingers. Now and again, he caught the handle and stared at the blade contemplatively before resuming.

"Are you nervous?" Eytea asked after several silent iterations.

"You wouldn't believe me if I said no."

"You're right, but you have every right to be nervous."

"That doesn't help me so much as you might think."

"No, I don't mean it like that. It's just that we're going into their territory with rocks and power tools."

"I'm sure they'll do fine," Sinkua insisted as he stopped in front of the meeting hall.

"So, what has you so worked up?"

"Are you sure you want to ask that question?"

"I'll let you know if I regret it after you answer."

"I'm afraid we'll end up killing a bunch of imperialists by name only. Biroe is proof that IBNOs exist, and they're going to be stuck between execution for rebelling and murder for complying. But at the same time, anybody who knows Biroe escaped could play that card against us and try to plant themselves as spies down here," Sinkua began as he scraped the blade along the door, "On top of that, we may be so successful that we get into their federal building, find CreSam, and cut him down. Sounds great, I know, but we don't know who's going to come up behind him. His second in command could be one of the Avatars of Fate, and even if not, we can't assume that his followers will surrender the mainland to us. So we're really in a damned if we do or don't situation here. And even though some of you assume I always have a plan and a backup plan, I'm hoping Spril knows how to deal with such decisions when they come, because I am shit out of ideas."

"You really ought to give yourself more credit, Sinkua," Eytea complimented, "When the time comes, I know you'll be able to make the right choice. You did it with your plan to declare war."

"The whole point of that was to receive foreign aid, which is now under siege and still at sea," he countered as he continued to carve at the door.

"No, the point was to unite a larger mass against Imperial ArcNos, and that's exactly what you've done. You did it with this decision to launch an insurgence while a large number of troops are at sea, and you've done it with this plan to slip under the capitol and deploy anywhere but the most obvious spots. I'm sure when you saw the fence around the capitol, you were anxious as to how you might get enough of us through to invade, but once the time came, the plan just came to you. Don't deny that you have a gift, because the ability to thrive under pressure is a beautiful one."

"You're too nice to me," Sinkua solemnly replied, "but I suppose one of us needs to be."

Eytea laughed and rubbed his back.

"But then why are you so much more confident of your trainees than I am? They have two days' training, and our total count is below five hundred. We're going to be severely outnumbered, and they'll be fatally outgunned," she added, "Yet, even right before the battle, you seem so cocksure of your decision and their abilities. Why is that?"

"Imperialist firepower means nothing. What matters is what drives them to fight," Sinkua explained, "They're in it for what? An arbitrary thing like duty to some superior asshole? Or maybe a fleeting thing like money, or perhaps a promotion so they can die a Lieutenant instead of a Captain? As though that's going to matter in the annals of history. Our troops came down here because they wanted to and on a common principle of restoring ArcNos to the nation it once was, and they fight for that same reason. Those bastards on the surface may have bigger guns, but every one of us is driven by a common principle."

"Retribution?"

"No, this runs far deeper than retribution. It's a matter greater than restoration, reconstruction, revenge, or any ill-defined political affiliation," Sinkua continued, "This is a concept beyond matters of life and death."

He dusted the wood shavings from his forearm as he stepped back from the door. Returning the dagger to its holster, he checked his work and nodded approvingly before continuing to his hammock. Eytea followed but not before pausing to see what he had etched. It was a single word, simple yet powerful.

Remembrance.

Careful to keep his hand clear of the button, NalSet mounted the street blaster to the wall. His confidence in the direction of the blast and the safety features aside, he wasn't entirely sure of the amount of recoil to expect. More important still was what might spill through from the other side. Beyond the wall were the catacombs of the imperial capitol, Subtransit stations and railways untouched by people for over a year. All manner of sickly agents may have been waiting on the other side, grown in the darkness from mildew and the stench of death. As dank as it was sure to be though, paranoid speculation held no place in this moment. NalSet raised a plank and slammed it against the button.

His arms jerked back, popping his shoulder, as concrete shrapnel was spewed violently into the capitol catacombs. Smoke poured from the massive wound as the flames waned and died. Some damaged rock left standing, NalSet batted at the edges with the plank, eventually clearing a wide enough gap for the test car. He called back to IlcBei and headed toward her.

IlcBei released the brake from the vacant train car. For the first few meters, she kept pace as she walked alongside it. The car accelerated, stirring up a cacophonous racket along the tracks. The two of them met halfway as it passed through the new opening without a problem. The passageway was untouched by the barrier obelisks above.

"That certainly was anticlimactic," IlcBei noted as they walked away.

"Just as we hoped it to be," NalSet reminded, "By the way, what will happen to that car?"

"Don't worry about it. It'll stop after about half a kilometer."

"As long as it isn't going to crash at the end of the tracks. I'd hate to have accidentally alerted those imperialist swine of our coming invasion."

"Any more so than with that spider mine?"

"It's called a street blaster, and besides, that's at the border, hardly a densely populated area."

"Really? I like spider mine. It sounds, I don't know, more cunning."

A hand set upon Sinkua's shoulder, shaking his hammock and rousing him from his light slumber. His luminescent eyes flickered open, and he looked about to gauge his environs as he regained consciousness. Spril stood over him with his morningstar in one hand, Eytea's halberd in the other, and his own quarterstaff strapped to his back.

"You two lovebirds gonna come spill some blood or stay behind and repopulate the city?" he asked facetiously.

Sinkua looked down to find a slender arm and a purple wing laying over his torso. He recalled lying down with Eytea next to the hammock, and he could remember a good deal of their conversation. But he couldn't recall drifting off, and Eytea must have climbed in after he was out.

As cramped as it was in there, having her on his side was undeniably comfortable, but responsibility dictated that the moment was to be short-lived. He grabbed her shoulder and shook her. She awoke reluctantly.

"Come on, it's time to go."

"Oh no, did I fall asleep?"

"Don't pretend that wasn't your plan all along," Sinkua countered with a sly smirk.

He stood and offered Eytea his hand to help her do likewise. With his other, he took his morningstar from Spril and thanked him for bringing it. Eytea was returned her halberd, and the three of them went to the edge of the boarding dock to await the coming train.

The train was densely populated with students of the guerrilla combat crash course. Unused seats were occupied by folded ladders as well as some of the larger weapons, such as gardening equipment, lengths of chain, and even a couple of jackhammers. Barely anyone among them carried any sort of traditional weapon, but what they wielded had comparable lethal potential were the safety precautions properly disregarded.

The usual route maps on the wall had been informally redrawn to depict the new route that IlcBei had programmed. Each group had been assigned a number, and their respective stops were marked on the updated map. While the thick layer of asphalt would absorb much of the sound of the train, the same could not always be said of the intercom. For that reason, it was silenced for this trip, leaving the recruits to track stops amongst themselves.

The stops passed with the minutes, and the population of the train was slowly depleted. Groups deemed more formidable were further down the deployment list, set to be dispatched in more dangerous territory as the tracks spiraled toward the center of town. A bit more than an hour later, only eight insurgents remained, their launch point being near the federal building.

Spril checked his watch as they stepped off, leaving the empty train to return to its starting point. Two minutes remained until they were all to surface. Galo gave Vielle a boost, and she mounted a spider mine to the ceiling. He held her aloft for a moment as Spril continued to watch the time. Spril counted down with his fingers, and when he reached zero, Vielle gave the mine a firm slap.

Two dozen explosions reverberated through the catacombs in nigh simultaneity. The ground above resonated with the impact as smoldering asphalt was launched skyward in over a score of plumes of smoke and burning tar. Metallic clanks echoed throughout the chamber as ladders were unfolded, and the raiders climbed to the surface.

Boot steps clomped from a westerly direction, toward the nearest sealed entrance to the defunct Subtransit system. Knowing there was no conceivable way to make a surreptitious entry on such short notice, they had opted instead to deploy far enough from the most logical entry points in order to avoid being ambushed as they surfaced. Spril pointed to three predetermined pairs, each with one Hybrid and one human, and sent them off in different directions.

For his speed and grace along with his ability to bind foes with his hydromancy, Galo was teamed with Farim. Since he had the least personal relationship with her and would thus not be distracted by worry, MalVek was paired off with Vielle. Because of their recent training sessions together, Spril and Eytea agreed to work together. Also, it would have been wasteful to put both long range strikers together. This left Phylus and Sinkua joined by little more than process of elimination, but Phylus's marksmanship was sure to be a boon to Sinkua in his characteristically reckless moments.

Galo and Farim headed north toward a manhole cover roughly four blocks away. At the next intersection, they split off in opposite directions. As they did, Galo signaled to her by waving his hand forward twice, then holding up his index finger. She nodded in understanding.

Eytea took to the air, hovering some ten meters above Spril as they headed west toward an old Subtransit entrance. He veered a couple of blocks south as cautious footsteps drew nearer, weighed down by bulky armaments. Eytea followed his movements as closely as she could, never straying far from directly above him.

MalVek kept a low profile, creeping near the ground in a southerly direction. Vielle stayed a few steps behind him, barred by MalVek's longer stride and grip on her hand. A collection of soldiers could be heard approaching from near another manhole cover.

Sinkua and Phylus headed east along an avenue parallel to one where they anticipated guards had been positioned. Sinkua took the lead with Phylus following a couple of meters behind, shotgun loaded and extra clips on the ready. As they neared an intersection, Phylus tapped his shotgun, signaling for Sinkua to turn toward an upcoming Subtransit entrance. Whether this would allow them to flank from the side or double back and strike from behind was anybody's guess, as they had not heard anyone move from that point since their arrival.

Farim reached the designated crossroad and continued on for one more block before changing streets. Galo moved in from the other side, stalking a group of five armed guards from beyond the edge of their peripheral vision. He crept surreptitiously on bare calloused feet, his glaive in a double fisted clutch and the Serpent Bracer emitting a pale blue glow. Slowly and silently, a crystalline coating enveloped the blade.

With a swing of his glaive, the icy layer was detached and sent screaming through the air. Alerted by the sound, the guards turned only for one of them to find it lodged in his arm. Diluted blood poured from the wound as he cried out in agony and dropped his gun. The remaining four charged the Hybrid insurgent, who answered with a spiraling torrent of water rushing from his bracer. Galo dropped his fist and froze the horizontal typhoon, starting at the back to maximize the impact.

Farim rushed in from behind, oar raised back over her shoulder. With the first swing, she toppled the wounded soldier trying to get back to his feet. She stood with one foot pressed on his spine and jabbed the back of his neck repeatedly, ensuring that he had either met death or wished for it. Her next swings were aimed for the arms and shoulders of the distracted guards, disarming them one by one.

From the other side came Galo, veering around the aquatic battering ram as it froze. At the end, he leapt away from the crowd, kicked off the top of a hydrant, and bounded over the recently disarmed guards. He came down with destructive force, driving the glaive clean through a layer of woven armor to part the guard's sternum and sever his bronchial tube. Using the body's weight for support, he hoisted himself up by the glaive handle and delivered a single hook kick across two other heads. The last received a slicing blow to the neck from Farim's canoe oar. She dropped to her knees as Galo yanked the blade out of one guard and swung it in a wide arc to disembowel the two he had distracted with strikes to the head.

Eytea plucked a feather from her left wing, crumpled it, and dropped it. As it lit upon his scalp, Spril stopped and looked up. She pointed around the corner. He nodded and waited.

Eytea drifted onward surreptitiously, electrical milystis pulsating through her halberd as the blades emitted a yellowish glow. She drew back and, with a force that twisted her entire body, hurled the weapon into the oblivious crowd below. The spearhead met with the upper back of one of them, its momentum great enough to pierce the armor and drive the top of the axe blade into the soldier's spine. The others recoiled in horror before looking up to find their partner's aerial assassin.

Spril rounded the corner and immediately cracked his quarterstaff against the exposed throat of another of the soldiers. Weapons were raised, automatic rifles of various sorts, only to be knocked back with swift swings of the staff. Their grips being more tenacious than he anticipated, he found himself unable to disarm the lot of them though.

A finger curled around a trigger, and Spril bent to the side, catching himself on one hand as he swatted the soldier's kidney with his quarterstaff. As he hoisted himself upright, he circled the weapon over the soldier's arm, and with both ends in his grip, pounded his knee against the forearm. The freshly used gun hit the asphalt at the same time that the bottom of Spril's foot collided with the wounded soldier's sternum, shoving him into his comrades.

Eytea watched anxiously, her fist tightly clenched. Spril was still too close. As another soldier advanced around the newly disarmed one, he pounded the butt of his staff against his clavicle and sprang back, placing a good three meters between them. Spril bounded back a few quick steps as the guard stumbled into his partners, all of whom had been rendered oblivious to the voltaic surge emanating from the halberd wedged in their comrade's spine. Eytea unclenched her fist, and the pent up rage within her weapon burst outward, arcing to the remaining soldiers. They collapsed with flesh seared and hearts stopped.

As was his aim, MalVek and Vielle found their target from behind, a straightaway of nearly three blocks separating them. He tightened his grip on her hand as he took off in a sprint, urging her to keep stride. When they were within the same block as the wandering hunters, he released her hand and hurled his sledgehammer into the crowd. Simultaneously, she shot a tangle of vines from her palm.

The hammer felled the first soldier it met and continued along with a compromised flight pattern. The others turned about, weapons drawn and leveled. Before any triggers could be pulled, Vielle snagged the hammer with her vines. MalVek grabbed the back of her shirt and jerked her back as she retracted the milystis creeper. His hammer snapped back and dropped yet another soldier with a blow to the head, this time collapsing with its target. Vielle coiled her vines around the neck of a third, tightening them fatally as she cracked her cat-o'-nine-tails upon the arm of a fourth. MalVek caught the same from behind and snapped his neck with the swift twist of the head. The last among them had his neck sliced open with three of the nine serpentine tails.

Spotting their target as they rounded the corner, Phylus sent a bullet ripping through the skull of the nearest among them. With the swipe of his arm, Sinkua erected a pillar of conflagration beneath the feet of another as the rest scattered. Phylus took aim at the farthest one as Sinkua disappeared into an alley. For the first time though, his bullet failed to meet its mark as, recognizing a formidable marksman, the soldier dashed about erratically.

Sinkua sprinted down the alley, zigzagging to evade the oncoming flurry of bullets. In an opportune moment between clips, he manifested a barrier of flame between himself and the assailant. The sound of a single shot echoed in the alley, followed by that of an armored body hitting asphalt. Two targets remained as he circled behind the building and headed back toward the fray.

Phylus fired a second shot, dropping the penultimate soldier in their target group. With the last one distracted by boot steps approaching from a nearby alley, he dropped the empty clip and readied a fresh one. A bloodcurdling bellow echoed from the alley as the soldier fired a flurry of bullets. In a panic, he pitched the empty clip at the soldier.

Phylus slammed the new clip into place and leveled the shotgun as the last of their target group, the one who had evaded him too many times already, turned to face him. He intentionally collapsed to his side as they fired their guns nigh simultaneously. Having come to anticipate his opponent's movements, he successfully corrected for the change and placed his bullet dead in the soldier's forehead.

At the same time though, the soldier's bullet ripped along his ear, streaking blood through the air with it. Fortunately, the impact was too weak for detonation, but Phylus called out all the same as blood streamed down his neck. He clutched at the wound to find more than half his ear had been torn away. A deafening screech resonated within his ear canal.

Sinkua staggered out of the alley, his left arm caked with blood, a patch of which still emanated dissipating tendrils of smoke. In his other hand, he held a syringe of the medication Galo had concocted. He pitched it toward Phylus as he mouthed a fistful of his oral remedy and demolished the herbs between his grinding teeth.

With a short rush of adrenaline, Phylus clumsily dashed to fetch the syringe and continued to his injured friend. Sinkua dropped to his knees and spat a mouthful of diluted blood onto the street. Still holding a wound of his own, Phylus knelt beside him and drove the syringe into the back of his neck. The pressure subsiding almost immediately, Sinkua placed a fingertip upon what remained of Phylus's ear. He gritted his teeth as Sinkua employed a necessarily archaic first aid technique and seared his wound shut. The pain still throbbed, but the bleeding had stopped. The screeching persisted as well, an issue to take up with Yrlis.

"What do you hear?" Phylus asked as Sinkua hocked up another salvo of bloody mucus.

"The others have felled their marks," Sinkua confirmed after a sickly spit, "Just moments after we, if I'm not mistaken."

"Fall back!" Phylus shouted from the depths of his lungs, his voice resonating between buildings.

Chapter 34

Eight insurgents sat together on the Subtransit train, some injured but all sore and fatigued. The combined sound of their pulses was nearly audible and could almost be felt resonating in the steely walls of the car. Having been called back to the underground by Phylus's order, the survivors from the other groups were waiting at their designated stops as the train made the rounds to retrieve them.

Galo wetted the burnt blood on Sinkua's arm and wiped it away. Beneath was a fresh bullet hole. Sinkua winced as Galo parted the bloodied flesh and peered into the wound. The bullet was still lodged within.

"We need to get that out of you," he urged.

"That would be ill-advised," MalVek cautioned, "Unless they've downgraded their bullets, those explode on impact with a hard surface."

"I think he got lucky and was hit with a dud."

"He got lucky because the bullet somehow stopped before it hit his humerus. You accidentally jab it forward when you're trying to fish it out, and your curmudgeonly friend loses his arm."

"You're the engineer."

"I… You… Um, you're damn right I am."

"Could you two please quit arguing?" Phylus angrily pleaded.

"It's alright, we've settled it," Galo insisted.

"Well then quit talking at all," Phylus snapped back, "Dammit, why won't this stop?"

"What's wrong, Dad?" Vielle whispered.

"My ear canal has been screaming ever since I took that bullet."

"Let me take a look."

She urged Sinkua to her side as she scooted nearer to her father. Sinkua held a lit finger near Phylus's ear, but that light was scarcely needed, as she found the likely culprit just behind his tragus. It was a small metal disc, barely larger than a hearing aid battery, with a tiny nub of frayed copper wire jutting out from the edge.

"Oh wow, I can hear again already," Phylus remarked, "What did you do?"

"Took this out of your ear," she said, handing him the strange disc.

He held it up to his good ear and heard that same piercingly annoying screech. Indeed, the sound had come from the object rather than a side effect of having it lodged in his ear. Of course, that still left the comparably more pressing questions of its identity and how it came to be stuffed in his ear without his knowledge.

"Hand that here," MalVek beckoned.

Phylus passed it over without question. MalVek pressed his finger on the wires to muffle the squeal as he scrutinized the device. Vaguely etched on one side was an all too familiar insignia. His suspicion nearly solidified, he held it up to his ear to hear a faint static hum behind the squealing. Having no further need for it, he set it on the floor.

"It's a tap," he announced as he ground it under his boot, "Somehow, an Avatar of Fate got a bug in your ear."

"They've been spying on us? How much do you suppose they know?"

"Depends on its pick up range, whether it just transmitted what you said or what people around you said, too," MalVek explained, "Also depends on the transmission range, of course."

"That explains how they just happened to have guards patrolling where they were today," Sinkua interjected, "They knew when we were coming and that we'd come from under the street."

"So the receiver is somewhere in the capitol," MalVek continued, "I suppose that's the best news we could hope for. Judging by the size of it, I'd say you were out of range in Eprilen. Means they didn't hear your plans at least."

"Sure, if you exclude Olsa," Galo reminded, "Assuming Phylus is right about her, that is."

As relieving as that realization was, Phylus was stricken with a more painful epiphany. Shame on him, for she had fooled him twice.

Lord CreSam stared coldly across his desk, the obscenely tall windows behind him serving to emphasize his dominating frame. At the other side, a couple of meters back, sat Malia in the approximate center of the room. Her eyes met his occasionally, only to nervously dart away yet again. In the corner of the room, the minute hand on the grandfather clock groaned as it ticked another moment crawled by, echoing in the vast expanse of painful silence. He drummed his fingers atop his desk, the abrupt shattering of the long silence making her jump in her seat. She cleared her throat anxiously.

"Why have you called me here, sir?"

"Oh, I believe you know the answer to that quite well."

"Don't you suppose I would have mentioned it sooner, lest I end up wasting my time with this uncomfortable silence?"

"Unless you have something to hide. Such behavior looks suspicious on those who seek so tenaciously to know everything."

"What do you speak of?"

"The phony intelligence report you filed," CreSam snapped, his patience depleted, "You stated that the insurgents would enter through the old Subtransit access points and manholes. Your little fuck up cost us hundreds of decent soldiers, all because they were guarding the wrong spots."

"Sir, I had no idea this would…" Malia profusely apologized.

"Did they or did they not say they would emerge where you said?"

"Does it really matter what I say?" she asked defiantly, "You'll doubt me either way, and the truth is, at this point, unprovable."

"Did you even plant a bug on him," CreSam fired back "or have you simply been screwing with me all this time?"

With trembling fingers, she adjusted the receiver in the entrance to her ear canal. Her other hand snaked its way into her pocket, desperately fiddling with the controls and scanning the frequencies. All active transmissions were coming through with clarity, save for one. She plucked the receiver from her ear and approached his desk.

"I did, set to the frequency stated in my mission report," she asserted in as steady a voice as she could manage, "but the bug has been destroyed."

She laid the earpiece before him, white noise static emanating from it. Without bothering to listen to the dead transmission or check her report, he issued his ultimatum.

"Then what use are you to me?"

The train arrived at the Epsilon boarding dock with that old familiar howl of the wheels scraping the tracks. IlcBei, Uulan, Yrlis, and NalSet all eagerly waited near the doors. Yrlis fidgeted nervously. Behind them, the children had stopped their game just long enough to greet the returning insurgents from what they were confident to have been a successful operation.

"Dad, do you need me to go with you to the clinic?" Vielle asked as the train stopped.

"No, I'm okay. This will be easy to fix."

"I need to go lay down for a while," Eytea apologized, "Are you going to be alright, Sinkua?"

"I hope so. Depends who operates on me, I guess."

"I'll stay with him in case he has an attack," Galo assured her.

The rest of them were greeted with applause and accolades as they stepped onto the dock. NalSet even cracked what may have been a smile upon seeing his younger brother return from battle unscathed. Uulan was particularly relieved to see Farim come home safely, as was IlcBei. A look of frightful concern came over Yrlis when Spril and Vielle relayed what had happened to Phylus and Sinkua. She looked past them and through the window. Phylus waved to her, trying to assure her that all was as well as it could have been. Instead, she gave Spril a peck on the cheek and hopped on the train as the doors closed behind her.

"Just in case you want a second opinion," she explained as nonchalantly as she could.

"I suppose you're not avoiding me anymore," Galo pierced.

"It's that transparent, is it? I mean, I'll give either of you a second opinion if you want it, but you're right."

"So the ipthkys root worked, then?"

"Oh quite well. It did exactly what the books say it does."

"And you were too embarrassed to admit you were wrong?"

"No, I was too angry not to strangle you," Yrlis grumbled, "but Spril helped me see that I got what I deserved. I was avoiding you until I could accept that."

"I suppose that was the best approach you could have taken, then. Are you ready to admit that your experiments were wrong?"

"As much as it hurts my pride, yes I am. Will you tell me how they work now?"

"Not yet. First I need you to publish a retraction," Galo insisted, "State that the data was contaminated and that your participation in a blind study disproved your findings."

"I don't have much to go on without a scientific explanation."

"I fail to see how that's my problem. You're asking for a closely guarded trade secret after you tried to ruin the market. Most of our vendors don't even know how it works."

"Can I have a hint at least, so maybe I can try my experiment again?"

"As long as you promise not to get too specific in your papers."

"Don't worry; I won't ruin your economy twice in one life time."

"In that case, you were concentrating entirely on the flora and not at all on the fauna."

As she let that cryptic clue sink in, the train pulled up to the underground hospital. Like the rest of the community, it was something of a makeshift operation, but it distinguished itself as a beacon of stability and efficiency. Being more advocates of preserving life than ending it, the vast majority of ArcNos's medical professionals had defected to the Parliamentary uprising. Subsequently, this was also a great boon to the necessary fundraising efforts.

In addition to Sinkua with his bullet wound and Phylus with his missing ear, a few dozen others came with injuries of their own. They varied in severity from cuts in need of stitches to one who would clearly need to have his leg amputated. His pants were caked with sinew and blood dripping from a massive wound deep enough to expose the femur. Sinkua shuddered at the thought of what he might suffer were the bullet in his bicep to detonate. Others had suffered burns ranging from small patches treatable with ointment to those who would need considerable amounts of skin grafts.

Some dozen nurses greeted the crowd as they piled into the hospital lobby. The nature of each one's injury was assessed, and they were grouped based on such. Phylus was part of a group needing small prosthetics, which included such comrades as a man who, by some bizarre twist of misfortune, had lost his nose and a young lady with three missing fingers. Sinkua's group was a subset of those who needed objects removed from their bodies, particularly people who needed stitches but had not broken any bones. Galo and Yrlis stayed in the waiting room with others who had accompanied their friends.

As painful as Phylus's injury was, his was relatively easy to treat as far as replacement body parts went. There were no moving parts in it, and its primary function was performed entirely by its shape. They simply cast a mold with his right ear and reversed it to create a prosthetic left ear. In fact, it took longer for the anesthetic to wear off than it did for them to make the ear and attach it.

Sinkua's operation was significantly more meticulous, but he was conscious for the entirety of it. Undetonated bullets were not a particularly uncommon occurrence, so this surgeon had more than his share of experience with such. After administering a localized anesthetic, he pried the wound open and fished out the bullet with rubber-tipped forceps. As tense a moment as it was, the surgeon's sense of composure seemed to rub off on him. In less time than it had taken for him to be seen, he was sent back to the waiting room with a few stitches, a handful of painkillers, and the bullet

"Did they have any problems?" Yrlis asked as Sinkua returned to the waiting room, shortly behind Phylus.

"Not in the slightest. It turns out my surgeon has seen quite a few cases like mine," Sinkua boasted, "Well, at least the part about the bullet. I didn't mention the other condition."

"Did it look to you like they'd be done by day's end?" Phylus asked, "I didn't have much time to assess the situation."

"I'd say not. There was a long queue for surgery, and a handful of them will need to stay at least a couple of days," Sinkua explained apologetically, "By the way, the new ear looks great."

"I suppose that means the memorial service will have to wait, then."

"It would be better if everybody could be in attendance," Galo agreed.

"We have an hour until the train comes through again," Yrlis noted, "You guys want to get some lunch in the cafeteria? I heard AlsRim sold them her Reuben recipe."

Without any need for further coaxing, the four of them wove through the slowly diminishing crowd toward the cafeteria. The day's battle was over, and it was time to relax with friends over a fresh meal.

A score and a half each of war brigs and xebecs plowed across the Midland Sea, ripping through the water with insurmountable wake. The cumulative roar of the engines swelled and rolled well beyond the farthest horizon. Beyond the helm of the headmost was a colossal frigate, the flag of Imperial ArcNos looming high above and waving in the wind of the ship's momentum.

Another ship approached from the horizon ahead, traveling in a northwesterly direction. Its deck horn blared as they came into view of one another. Two brigs and a xebec advanced just beyond the frigate, turning about to aim starboard toward the oncoming ship. As it drew nearer, the sound of music penetrated the fringes of audibility. A lone deckhand on the frigate eschewed his duties and fled into a nearby deckhouse.

"Madam Brigadier," the radio operator urged, "It's one of the deckhands. He says there's music coming from that ship."

"Tell those three up ahead to hold their positions and not to fire unless I give the order," EshCal commanded.

At the fore of the pilot house, she peered through a telescope, scrutinizing the design and nature of the ship up ahead. Just as she had suspected, there was no cause for alarm.

"It's just a cruise liner. Order those three to fall back. No need to stain our hands with the blood of tourists."

Though the pilot relayed the order as commanded, the three ships elected to advance upon the cruise liner instead. At Brigadier EshCal's urging, the frigate also broke formation to enter the impending fray initiated by three rogue vessels. She watched in horror as the cannon bays fell open and dozens of barrels thrust forth. She assertively snatched the microphone from the pilot.

"Hold your fire!" she shouted to all ships in the fleet, "This is Brigadier EshCal speaking; hold your fire! They're bystanders!"

At the sight of the ships surrounding their nautical vacation spot, the tourists on the cruise liner were thrown into a rapid spiral of panic. Once jovial folks were suddenly tripping and climbing over one another to get clear of the railing. Others opted to commandeer lifeboats and jettisoned themselves into the open sea. Screams piled atop one another and quickly drowned the music blasted over the intercom system. Three imperial vessels closed in.

"Hold your fire! Hold your damn fire!" EshCal screamed in desperation, "Oh no, no, no, no, no, no, no!"

The sound alone of thunderous cannon fire rolling over upon itself was enough to shake the foundation of every ship in the fleet. Cannonballs pummeled the salty air, choking the very breath out of all life in the environs as they crashed through the hull of the cruise liner. Tourists collapsed in stride, many falling overboard. Fresh wounds effected bloody screams as passengers and employees below deck were ripped asunder by the assault.

"Switch me to local only," EshCal ordered as she thrust the microphone back to the pilot.

"What do you intend to do, Madam Brigadier?" he asked as he complied with the order nonetheless.

"All port side cannon operators, lock and load," she commanded into the microphone, "Starboard, stand by for orders. All infantry, be ready to board."

She handed the microphone back to the pilot with orders to have each port side deck fire upon the noncompliant vessels every two minutes successively and made for the exit. From a mount beside the door, she retrieved her epee and her pistol, suspecting more traitors may have been on board her ship.

As she traversed the maze of hallways connecting the internal chambers, she counted down the seconds with her footsteps. With only a few seconds left until the two minute mark, she stopped outside the entrance to the first port side gun deck. The remaining time ticked away, and the pilot gave the order to fire upon a rogue vessel, exactly as commanded. Cannon after cannon fired in succession while EshCal counted the shots in her head. Out of fifty-six on the first port side gun deck, sixteen had failed to fire. With her blade in her good hand and the pistol in its holster, she kicked the door in with vicious force, ready to counter the brewing mutiny.

"Ah look here big queen bitch has come to turn us soft," one of the sixteen rebels defied as she entered, "What's wrong, you wanna abandon the mission so we can all hold hands and sing?"

The other renegade gunnery soldiers joined him in a long hearty laugh. Those who had complied with the orders readied the next payload, frequently looking pensively over their shoulders. As one caught sight of Brigadier EshCal's eyes, she surreptitiously unlocked her sidearm and nodded to the nearest kindred comrade in the gunnery unit.

"Having a good laugh, are we?" EshCal asked rhetorically.

The laughter stopped. The same renegade as before opened his mouth yet again to make what his face prefaced to be another flippant remark. EshCal leveled her pistol, and as the first word left his mouth, her bullet pierced his skull and decorated the floor with his cranial sinew. As the other fifteen unlocked their side arms and advanced upon her, part of the remainder of the gunnery unit rose to their feet and pressed their pistol barrels against the mutineers' heads. EshCal smirked and returned the pistol to her holster. On the second gun deck, the next round was fired. She counted the shots in her head as she turned to exit.

"Those without hostages, follow me," she commanded from the open doorway, "The rest of you, fire."

The rest of the renegades in the first gunnery unit collapsed upon themselves as chunks of brain and skull were splattered across the deck, caking on their unused cannons. Those who had performed the executions stayed behind to resume the offensive while EshCal and the others headed for the second and third port side gun decks. EshCal was stopped on the stairs by a soldier beckoning her ear. Quite to her chagrin, the rest of the brigade was advancing on their ship from behind, and judging by their patterns, it appeared they were preparing to defend the mutinous trio. Her only option was to split the first port side gunnery unit further.

"Half of you advance to the second and third port gun decks. The rest, cover the three starboard gun decks. Mutineers are to be executed without question. Once that trio has been dispatched, have all port side cannon operators move to starboard," she commanded, "All surplus operators are to be sent back to port in case we become surrounded. I'll assemble two splinter cells, one to counter any attempt to board and another launch a direct assault should we become overwhelmed."

"What would you have me do, Madam Brigadier?" the stairwell soldier asked.

"Head for the bridge. Tell the pilot I said to employ evasive maneuvers," she confided, "And thank you for the warning."

The fray on the gun decks far behind her but growing louder with each passing moment, EshCal stood outside the first engine room. Cautiously, she peered through the window to find that half a dozen of the technicians and mechanics had overpowered the remaining workers. Armed for revolution, they stood about the room at strategic guard points, eschewing their duties as her officers. She gauged the distance to each of them and analyzed their relative positions as well as each one's apparent level of physical prowess. Weapons drawn, she stepped back and kicked the door in.

The foremost mutineer shot first, a move she anticipated as she leaned to parry the bullet before the trigger was pulled. She fired a shot into the corner to dispatch a sniper and sprinted at the one who had welcomed her with a bullet. As his finger curled around the trigger again, she sliced the air with her epee. The bullet grazed the edge of her blade and was deflected toward a wall.

With a skillful lunge, she drove her fencing blade through the guard's armor and torso. Leaving her blade in his body, she swiped his pistol as he collapsed and, with her arms crossed over her chest, eliminated two more mutineers with a simultaneous pair of gunshots. One of the last two tried a more direct approach, running at her from behind with her blade drawn, but she was stopped by an obscene donkey kick to the lower abdomen. EshCal pulled the blade from its last victim and spilled the blood and digestive fluids of the failed assailant. She threw the sword like a javelin into the corner where the last of them was posted. The blade punctured the mutineer's throat before he could take a shot and pinned him to the wall.

She returned the gun to her holster, pocketed the one she had stolen, and retrieved her blade from the wall. The hostage mechanics and technicians, disarmed by their captors, rose to their feet. Distant sounds of cannon fire echoed from the starboard gun decks.

"All of you stay here and keep things moving. I'll go check the other three engine rooms," she urged, "Your next orders will come via intercom. If they are not from me, ignore them. Understood?"

The lot of them shot back with a resounding call of compliance, their confidence wholly replenished. EshCal proudly saluted the room, for though they had fallen victim to their own comrades, they were ready to serve the moment they were able. With that, she headed for the second engine room.

Brigadier EshCal expertly navigated the labyrinth within the nautical colossus, carving through any opposition that arose to impede her. With each passing room, their numbers dwindled, leaving behind only those willing to follow her lead. Often times but only when possible, a few of them abandoned their duties to help her cover more ground. Somewhat to her surprise, all mutineers on the upper deck had already been dispatched by the time she returned to it. Their bodies were being unceremoniously jettisoned into the sea.

A fleet of Haprianite Coastal Patrol ships approached from the southeastern horizon. EshCal ordered six of the deckhands to each take a lifeboat into the cruise liner's wreckage. There, they were to search for and rescue survivors of the jingoistic assault. The others were ordered to resume their duties while she returned to the bridge.

Much to her good fortune, she found no traitors in the pilot house. They were the ones who had worked with her the most closely over the past several days at sea and had thus developed a personal sense of obligation toward serving her. Hers was a welcome arrival.

"Madam Brigadier," the pilot called out, "I can only dodge these ships for so long. I assume you have further plans."

"You're doing splendidly, sir," she congratulated, "All of you are. Now, hand me the microphone. We'll be out of this shortly."

Her flagship finally cleared of its internal rebellion, she was safe to announce her strategy to escape the remaining ships and avoid falling victim to mutiny. While a skeleton crew was to stay behind to operate the frigate, the rest were to board the nearest renegade vessel by necessary force. Once there, they were under orders to eliminate the rebellion within, sparing those who supported her order to spare the cruise liner. Every new ally was to advance toward the back of the fleet, taking what supplies they could carry. Once they reached the ship farthest northwest, they were to return to ArcNos.

"Those of us who stay on this ship will continue forth to aid the Haprianite Coastal Patrol and brief them on what occurred here," she concluded, "We will then chaperone them into the fleet and allow them to strip the abandoned vessels as they see fit. Once that is done, we will follow your wake and rejoin you in the Northland Sea."

The door to the training hall was decorated with native flora, gathered earlier that day by Galo and arranged by Eytea. Accenting the frame were speckles of paint dripped from Eytea's fingers. While Phylus stood alone at the back of the room, the survivors of the assault on the capitol, along with friends and relatives, waited to be beckoned inside. Most of those who had suffered severe injuries were well on their way to whole recovery, but there were a handful among them who had lost entire limbs. Many moved about on crutches, while those with less balance opted for wheelchairs instead

One last time, Phylus read the speech his daughter had prepared. He checked his watch again, perhaps for the tenth time in the past five minutes. It was time. As he creased the paper and stuffed it in his coat pocket, he called them into the room.

First to enter were the other Parliamentary combatants. The seven of them filed in alongside him, four to his left and three to his right. Bonded by their struggle, Sinkua stood adjacent to him with Vielle at his other side. The rest of the troops and their loved ones filled the room, courteously maneuvering around one another to optimize their use of the limited space.

Farim stepped forth and handed a bundle of black markers to an insurgent at the head of the crowd. She nodded to him respectfully, and he reciprocated in kind. Sinkua scanned the crowd and found another with stitches in his bicep. With one hand, he passed off another bundle of black markers and with the other, offered a firm handshake. Like so many others in the room, with blood had they been bonded.

The markers were dispersed among the surviving troops. One by one, they went to the wall behind the Parliamentary combatants and wrote the name, age, and occupation of someone in their cell who had fallen to the imperial defenses. It gradually became typical for individuals to have no names to write, for all the casualties in their unit had already been acknowledged. Still, most of them had someone to speak for, though not everybody in the room had received a marker. In contrast, some had to write two or three names when they noticed they were the last of their group to step forth.

Out of almost five hundred troops in their slapdash insurgence, nearly two hundred had lost their lives. As devastating as that sounded, the compilation of accounts placed the imperial casualty estimate between six and eight hundred. Granted, this was not the time for celebrating such things, but the more militant among the Parliamentary combatants felt a swell of pride in knowing that their forces had claimed three or four imperial lives for each one they lost. For the time being, that pride was contained though, brewing behind expressions of grief for the fallen and sympathy for those they had left behind.

Phylus's speech was eloquent and empathetic, though lacking in personal touch, the result of only holding impersonal connections to the victims. To compensate, he looked to the wall behind him and announced each of them individually. Based on the information given, as well as those who appeared to be each one's friends and relatives, he improvised personal platitudes. They were admittedly generic, but his efforts were undeniable.

Families and friends mingled and commiserated after the mass eulogy, though no one was under any social obligation to stay. Galo studied the crowd from the closest thing he could find to a safe distance. Seeing those people huddled around and mourning, behaving almost helplessly, resurrected memories of home and what he had left behind. Simply because a few everyday folks had fallen victim to the tides of war, they sought a savior beyond themselves, rather than looking within to find the strength to move forward. With no parting words or eye contact, he took his leave of them.

Sinkua followed shortly behind, having taken notice of his distress. Trusting Sinkua's intuition, Vielle trailed him to the door as well. Galo leaned against the wall, shaking his head in disdain.

"Looks a lot like Masnethege in there, doesn't it?" Sinkua asked.

"Besides the absence of smoldering wreckage, all too much so."

"It's the price we pay for our gifts, assuming you could even call them as such," he continued, "Everybody assumes that it translates into some kind of superhuman resolve or some other extraordinary ability."

"So, they look to people like us for help, instead of helping themselves?" Vielle asked.

"Precisely that," Galo confirmed, "We had to rally up the police force in Haprian just to get them to stand their ground, and even then, Sinkua and I still had to spearhead the defensive."

"I doubt even I could talk them into mounting another assault, not after what we faced out there," Vielle confessed.

"The only way we're going to get them to fight for themselves," MalVek interjected as he closed the door behind himself, "is if they can do so from a safe distance."

"I suppose you have a way for us to do that," Sinkua presumed.

"It's in the works, but NalSet and I have been developing various siege machines. Automatic trebuchets, spring catapults, hwachas, and that sort of thing. It's what all that scrap lumber has been used for."

"How long does it take to construct something like that?" Galo asked.

"With just the two of us, anywhere from an hour to half a day, depending on the complexity, but once we've perfected the blueprints, anybody who can swing a hammer can join the party."

"That still leaves the issue of penetrating the barricade," Sinkua reminded,

"Have you two made any headway on understanding the generators."

"As luck would have it, the shockwave from the spider mine collapsed two of the towers. We might be able to copy its design, but I can't make any promises yet. Theoretically, establishing a perpendicular barricade should create enough interference to scramble the field and create an opening."

"So, then we wheel the machines in through there and attack the capitol from the edge of the city?" Vielle asked

"I'd suggest a handful of us go in first and kill the power source for the obelisks. That way, we can surround the perimeter, rather than allow the imperialists to cut around behind us," Sinkua insisted, "The initial danger is greater, but we can't risk leaving ourselves vulnerable."

By then, the remainder of Parliament had joined them outside. Friends, relatives, and survivors began to trickle out shortly thereafter. Rather than wait for the room to empty, they returned to their homes and daily obligations. MalVek and NalSet went to their lab to resume work on the siege machines. Sinkua and Galo headed for Epsilon to discuss potential details of the next attack. Eytea continued putting the finishing touches on the mural, picking up from where she had left off to collect flowers for the funeral. Spril went home with Yrlis to relax and celebrate his survival. So it went for the lot of them, celebrating their relative success and continued existence by moving forward with life as they always had since establishing the subterranean community.

A loud rumbling thundered along the streets above, resonating through the asphalt and into the occupied tunnels. As usual, it was dismissed as sentries meeting their end at the hands of forced malfunction. Such a sound had become increasingly rare in recent days, but the notion that a handful still remained operational was not at all unreasonable.

Several weeks of work had brought Eytea back to where she started, completing the wrapping mural around the Epsilon boarding dock. She leaned in close, meticulously dabbing the finer details into the last meters of what had by far been her most grandiose work. It was a true testament both to her persistence and her creativity. What was to be the punctuation to such was interrupted rather alarmingly.

"Not often I have the honor of meeting a person with wings," a voice from atop the stairs called down, "I presume you to be the one they call Eytea."

"How do you know my name?" she called back, rising to her feet and clutching the paintbrush like a dagger, "Who are you?"

"Let's just say your father owes me his life," the woman atop the staircase muddled.

"Consider that debt paid. Kabehl died by my hand."

"So I've heard, but your need for an explanation will need to wait," she insisted, "I've come to speak with Sinkua. I see you're a bit preoccupied at the moment, but I would deeply appreciate it if you would fetch him for me."

"Um, sure, just hold on a moment."

She rubbernecked as she passed the staircase, struggling in vain to see the mysterious visitor shrouded by the late evening sky. Though he and Galo were in the middle of discussing structural weaknesses in the imperial capitol, Sinkua was willing to put the conversation on hold at Eytea's beckoning. His curiosity about who came in search of him was also too burdensome to ignore.

"Here I am," he announced from the bottom of the stairs, "What's your business here?"

"Sinkua?" the voice called down to him.

"Yes, that's me."

"What place do you have for a contrite traitor such as myself?" she asked, descending a few steps and sitting on the stairs to show her face.

"EshCal!" Sinkua snapped, "You of all people? Why should I trust you?"

"I've had a change of heart. I'm sorry it took me so long to see past my own greed and ambition, but I finally realized what had become of us," EshCal apologized, "I see now the corruption brought upon ArcNos by CreSam and the Avatars of Fate and the monsters they've made us. I refuse to stay on that side of history."

"She sounds genuine," Eytea told Sinkua.

"With the history we have, I can't trust her simply because you say I should."

"Then bargain with her."

"What do you have to offer us?" Sinkua called back, "I've witnessed your combative prowess. Impressive though it is, it's only as such for an imperial brat such as yourself."

"Your tongue is as sharp as your own prowess," EshCal noted, "but my offering lies not in my own talents. My entourage waits nearby, some twelve hundred likeminded traitors, all of whom began their training under the late Brigadier General Elite HarEin. We've come with a caravan of supplies including food, tents, tools, and an array of blades, cudgels, and firearms"

"You certainly have my attention," Sinkua admitted, impressed by the size of her following, "Are they willing to stand with us against the empire they defended such a short time ago?"

"If I say they are to serve you, they will do so without fail," EshCal confidently declared, "By the way, we also have about two hundred cannons. Just thought that might be worth mentioning."

"Come down here and we'll speak further," Sinkua invited, "But just you. Your troops are to stay up there for the time being."

Nervously, EshCal continued down the stairs to face that brutal curmudgeon she once called her enemy. Though she maintained her composure externally, her mind was rife with humility as she recalled the relatively merciful grazing she received the last time they were in such close quarters. It was much the same as when she first stood before CreSam as his inferior.

"So then, what changed your mind?"

"What? Oh right, it's all here in this report, sir," EshCal fumbled, handing him a stack of papers.

The cover page stated that the report was produced by the Haprianite Coastal Patrol. Sinkua lacked the patience to read the entirety of it, a dozen pages in all, but the bullet points on the next page summarized it well enough for his needs. According to witnesses within the fleet, a cruise liner had been attacked by three Imperial ArcNosian war ships. Shortly thereafter, the flagship opened fire on those three. After the civil battle spread throughout the fleet, the flagship broke away to assist with the rescue and recovery efforts. Brigadier EshCal of Imperial ArcNos had received a personal commendation from the Fleet Admiral of the Haprianite Coastal Patrol

"Impressive," Sinkua admitted, trying to remain stoic, "How are your troops with their old weapons, before they started getting spoiled by exploding bullets and automatic rifles?"

"Out of twenty thousand troops in the fleet, only ten percent stood in support of my command while the other ninety percent thought to stage a mutiny for my decision to eliminate the rogue ships," EshCal boasted, "None of the mutineers survived. So, we lost about eight hundred, but they lost eighteen thousand."

"I've no doubt you used cannons and guns though."

"I admit we did, but the survivors demonstrated a considerable amount of retained skill."

"Looks like your blade saw its share of action, as well," Sinkua acknowledged, noting the discoloration of her epee.

"That it did. My passion for combat has never waned."

"In any case, your troops will need a refresher course before I'm comfortable sending them into battle alongside our own. Otherwise, we're just wasting each other's time."

"I understand and agree completely. All I ask for is a place to train them."

"I wouldn't think to have you do it alone," Sinkua countered, "Aside from the fact that this might be an elaborate infiltration, leaving you to train that many troops by yourself would be stupidly inefficient."

"Are you offering to help me?" EshCal asked, presumptively grateful.

"No, I'm not much for teaching," Sinkua admitted, "We have somebody here with quite a bit of leadership experience though, but you may find working with him to be rather, well, discomforting."

"Why, what's wrong with him?"

"Nothing at all, which is exactly why he has that effect on people," Sinkua muddled, "but I suppose whether that's the case with you comes down to just one question."

Spril set his hand on her shoulder and asked, "Do you believe in ghosts?"

Chapter 35

It was that haunting old voice, the one she thought could remain forgotten. It was undeniably distinct and inarguably familiar, yet its continued existence was impossible by all sensibilities. Though as befuddling as it was, its existence was made all the more disconcerting by the history between them, supposing he knew the scope of her involvement.

"B-Brigadier Elite Spril?" EshCal stuttered, turning her head slowly to soften the shock.

"General EshCal," Spril returned, "And yes, I know."

"You're supposed to be dead!" she remarked, ignoring the fact that he overlooked her promotion.

"Like I said, I know."

"But how? I watched you die."

"No, you watched me get shot in the head, but you never saw me buried," he countered, "Somebody dragged my body to a hospital, and Yrlis spent the following year nursing me back to health. But I assume Amirione thinks I'm dead."

"He's never given any impression otherwise. But how do you know it was him? Nobody saw the shooter."

"How stupid do you think I am? Phylus gets replaced by some clown with more guns than a sporting goods store, and suddenly the contest for Brigadier General Elite begins with a fight to surrender or death. Doesn't take a genius to put that together."

"Wait, you knew you would die in that arena, but you still came?" EshCal asked, awestricken.

"No, I knew I might die if I came, but I also knew that CreSam would take over if I skipped out. And I would be stuck working under him. If I lost and survived, I could publicly forfeit my title and fall off the radar, where I could undermine him undetected. If I just disappeared before the fight, people would come looking for me," Spril explained, "Oh, and I also know you tried to be the one to do it."

"I, well, I didn't want to be the one to kill you," EshCal stuttered, "It's just that, well, I wanted to be the one to ensure CreSam's victory."

"Wouldn't have made a difference anyhow. If Amirione couldn't hit the mark, I doubt you could have either."

"Now what's that supposed to mean?"

"The man is an assassin. It's what he does. HarEin, Gijin, me, or so he thought. What makes you think you'd do any better?"

Her temper overheated, she lunged tauntingly. With a speed her eyes could scarcely follow, he grabbed her wrist and turned her back to himself, putting her in a hammer lock. By sleight of hand, his other had withdrawn her epee from its previously locked holster, and he now held the tip under her chin.

"Let's get something clear, EshCal. I know you tried for the chance to kill me, but that's all in the past now that you're willing to work with us," Spril spoke into her ear as she trembled, "But down here, I run the show when it comes to military operations. And if you flip on us and somehow manage to kill me, working for CreSam will feel like a vacation."

"W-Why? Who takes over after you die?"

"That guy," Spril said, pointing to Sinkua.

"Oh shit."

"Hey, this is great and all, catching up on old enemies, but I'm still waiting to hear what the deal is with you and Kabehl," Eytea impatiently interjected, "Why does he owe you his life if he's already dead?"

"Sweetie, your father has died dozens of times," EshCal patronizingly remarked as Spril released her, "It just doesn't make sense for Spril to have survived death even once because, well, he's not an Avatar of Fate."

"How is that even possible?" Eytea asked, "We snapped his neck and watched him die. We even buried his body."

"I don't fully grasp the science behind it, but he has this device in his blood stream. Whenever he dies of anything but old age, it repairs the fatal damage and restarts his heart," EshCal explained, "But since he was trapped beneath two meters of soil, he was revived only to die again shortly thereafter. That cycle repeated until Amirione and I dug him up."

"So you're the one who robbed his grave!" Eytea snapped, "You've got those two covered, but now why should I trust you? You're the reason he's up and alive."

"Well that's hardly a fair statement. Amirione could just as well have dug him up on his own. I merely agreed to help because I was trying to get close to him. Part of my own personal agenda," EshCal defended, "Besides, look on the bright side, this means you get to kill him again, as many times as you'd like, in fact."

"I don't want to kill him repeatedly. I want him to stay dead. That asshole spent every day since I was born verbally, emotionally, and physically abusing my mother. And do you know why? Because of me. Because I was born an Hybrid, he wouldn't claim me as his daughter, and instead of a wife, he treated my mother like a two-iola crack whore. So pardon me if I'm not delighted at the idea of killing him again just to know he'll come back."

"I, um, gosh, I never knew he was like that with you and your mother. He's even worse than I thought. You have my deepest condolences," EshCal humbly apologized, "Tell you what, if somebody down here can figure out how to disable that device, I'll make sure the last thing he sees is your face as you rip his last breath from his lungs."

"That I can live with," Eytea agreed, her temper waning, "Dying repeatedly is too good for him if it means he gets to live even a moment between."

"Well now, am I going to have to prove myself to everyone here, or have I earned my place?" EshCal asked, shifting away from the subject.

"You can stay, but I'm not quite sure where to put everyone. Space is rather limited, especially with all the supplies you brought," Spril worried.

"They could stay out in that area I've been clearing," Sinkua offered.

"Oh, did you finish out there?"

"No, but with twelve hundred of them, they could wrap it up in a matter of hours."

370

"Where is this area you speak of?" EshCal asked.

"It's east of here, last city before you reach the coastal forest. I've been clearing debris out of the Subtransit in case we have to spread out in the future," Sinkua directed, "You and your troops can set up camp and store your supplies out there, and you're welcome to visit whenever you like."

EshCal graciously accepted the offer and invited half of her entourage down to travel with her on the Subtransit. They were to haul the lighter yet more abundant fare, such as tents, nonperishable foods, and light weapons. The considerably heavier weaponry and equipment salvaged from the fleet were transported by the other half, traveling on street level.

"Oh and by the way," Sinkua continued as the troops awaited the train, "If any one of you steps out of line, I'll incinerate your ass and piss on the ashes."

"I wouldn't put it past him," EshCal warned, "He's as brutal as the stories about him suggest."

As likely as it was that EshCal was on some kind of elaborate infiltration mission, the possibility of her honesty offered a boon they could not afford to refuse. After all, even if she and her twelve hundred troops were to lash out against them, a victory over that parasitic assault would afford them a cornucopia of heavy artillery. On top of that, Spril judged the report from the Haprianite Coastal Patrol to be legitimate. So even if her change of heart was a ruse, it was at least true that Imperial ArcNos had lost sixty ships and nearly twenty thousand soldiers. It also meant their letters to the Coastal Patrols had arrived on time.

"Why didn't you ever tell me Kabehl was like that?" Sinkua asked.

"I don't know. It never seemed like much of an issue, what with his being dead and all," Eytea shrugged, already lost in her work again, "Why haven't you told me what happened between you and your father after he killed your mother? What made you stay with him, and why did you finally decide to leave?"

Now there were questions he couldn't answer. His reason for leaving was obvious to himself, but he feared speaking it to her would ruin what friendship they had. Furthermore, even after all he had given to the uprising of Parliamentary ArcNos, he still lived with the worry that they might reject him as a traitor and an outsider were they to learn of his lineage. After all, he was the one who endangered human foreign aid with his slapdash exploitation of the Wartime Passage Act, and he had proposed the assault on the capitol which left two hundred of their own citizens dead. It was foolish to think they wouldn't be suspicious of him if they learned he was CreSam's biological son, especially after how long he had kept it a secret.

His reason for staying with his mother's killer couldn't be voiced for the mere fact that it seemed not to exist. Half his life thus far had been spent asking himself that question. He had wished for an escape every day after the bullet ripped through his mother's skull, but it took almost five years and the threat of enlistment for him to finally take action. Looking back, it felt like he only needed to open the door and walk away all along. But he never did, and this was the man it had made him, paranoid and secretive.

In the midst of sifting through paperwork, most of which he'd already addressed that morning, CreSam was jolted by a knock at the door.

"What do you want, Malia? I'm busy!" he growled.

"It's not Malia, sir," a petite female voice called back sheepishly, "It's the mail lady."

"What? Oh, right. Mail," CreSam muttered as he pressed a button under his desk, "Come in. Give us our mail. Have a cup of coffee. Whatever."

The mail lady hastily wedged her cart through the opening door the moment it was wide enough to fit. Being a bit wide at the hips, she turned sideways and slipped through behind it. CreSam remotely shut the door behind her.

"Looks like nothing out of the ordinary today, sir," she commented, trying small talk to ease her frazzled nerves.

"We don't need your analysis, Miss Whatever Your Name Is," he dismissed.

"There's one here from the Haprianite Coastal Patrol though. I wonder what that's all about," she added, accidentally consumed by curiosity.

He glared at her silently, his eyes simultaneously freezing her conviction and burning through her façade of a calm demeanor. She cautiously set his mail upon his desk, laying it lightly as though it might otherwise detonate, and slowly backed toward the door.

"But I suppose I should go wonder somewhere else," she sheepishly continued, "and keep it to myself."

"Are you going to have a cup of coffee or not?"

"Wait. You offered me a cup of coffee?"

"Yes, we told you to come in and have a cup."

Strange as it was that CreSam was referring to himself in the plural, a cup of the coffee reserved for his office was more than worth ignoring such bizarre behavior. It was likely a symptom of the ego that came with his status, anyway. Scarcely pulling her eyes from him, she sidled to the pot and poured herself a cup. CreSam urged her to sit before him. Even stranger behavior was his being so cordial, but to deny him would have been vastly disrespectful. He watched her closely, urging her suspicion toward paranoia. She sniffed the coffee then, pleased with the smell, took a small sip.

"How do you feel?" CreSam asked.

"Nervous. Wondering why you keep staring at me like that."

"You don't feel, perhaps um, dead...ish?"

"Deadish? You mean... do I feel like I'm dying?"

"Why are you asking me how you feel?"

"Did... Did you just use me to check if someone poisoned your coffee?"

"Well, if I checked it myself, I might die. What good would it do me to know my coffee is poisoned if I'm dead? Besides, where would they go without me?"

"Why would...? How would... ? Ah, forget it."

"Now be gone from here," CreSam urged, "Leave the coffee."

Once the door had shut behind her, he opened the letter from the Haprianite Coastal Patrol. Though he avoided showing it before such a peon of a guest, he was equally curious about their reason to write him. Shortly into the letter, he found that it was regarding the fleets he had deployed but not in the manner he assumed. Apparently, a few patrol ships came upon a skirmish in international waters, just beyond their zone of jurisdiction. Something had triggered infighting among some three scores of Imperial ArcNosian ships.

The Fleet Admiral went on to confess with great contrition that they were unable to pull any survivors from the wreckage. Furthermore, he explained that they lacked the firepower and overall influence to interfere and stop the civil battle before the fleet had all but annihilated itself. On something of a brighter side, they were able to salvage much of the equipment on the ships.

The letter closed with an invitation to come retrieve said equipment but not without a hitch, of course. A thus far indeterminate price was to be placed on the salvaged goods, and the Fleet Admiral proposed a meeting to negotiate the terms of their safe return. His language implied that he thought it a trade or perhaps payment for saving the goods, but a single warning illuminated his true intentions.

He alluded to the alleged treaty between the two nations. Reminding CreSam of the economic and military assaults that followed ArcNos's two attempts to invade, he warned that much of what had been recovered were munitions and heavy artillery, all of which were still operational. It wasn't a trade or a recovery fee that they wanted. It was a ransom.

In a huff, he grabbed the intercom microphone and angrily ordered every officer of the Platinum Hall into his office, omitting only SenRas. Moments later, Kabehl and Amirione entered together. Minutes passed, yet no one else followed.

"Where are the rest of you?" CreSam demanded to know.

"EshCal is still at sea, and you kicked Malia out of the Hall for some reason or another," Kabehl explained.

"You didn't call for SenRas, but he's still on probation," Amirione added with a grin.

"What are you talking about? I never kicked Malia out," CreSam countered, "And it's EshCal who's on probation, I'll have you know. As for SenRas, I didn't call for him because he's dead."

"When did this happen?" Kabehl asked, failing to hide his exuberance.

"Haprianite Coastal Patrol found his fleet in ruins. Nobody survived."

"CreSam, SenRas wasn't leading that fleet," Amirione explained, "EshCal was."

"Aha! Of course you would say that. You want me to think I've lost a Brigadier instead of just a Colonel. You want me to feel starved and weakened so I'll relinquish control to you, don't you!?" CreSam spouted.

"You don't get it, do you?" Amirione countered, contrition growing in his voice, "Brigadier EshCal is dead."

"Because you killed her!" CreSam shouted, "She was next in line after me, so you thought that maybe if she were out of the way, you'd be next. I know what you're doing, and I won't stand for it anymore."

"Do you now?" Kabehl challenged, "Bold words from a whelp such as yourself. If not for us, you'd still be a miserable pituitary freak of a nobody. Keep in mind who you're striving to appease."

"And you keep in mind who you work for!" CreSam bellowed as he rose from his seat, towering over them, "Enough of your conspiracies and schemes to usurp my dominion. Get out of my office. Get out of the Hall. And get the fuck out of my head!"

"I advise you to realize that if you kick us out of your circle, you'll have no council remaining," Kabehl pointed out, "And you risk losing the protection of the Avatars of Fate."

"I've got the only council I need right here," CreSam enigmatically insisted, "What makes you think we need the protection of a couple of egotistical chronic failures?"

Amirione and Kabehl hesitantly surrendered their keys to the Platinum Hall and mumbled between themselves as they made for the exit. CreSam's finger twitched over the button, impatiently waiting for them to step clear of the door.

"I hope you realize what a risk you're taking by banishing them," CreSam told himself in a foreign voice.

"Don't be ridiculous. They're only in his way."

"Nonsense. They're the reason we have this great office."

"Is that all you care about? This office?"

"Nobody asked you!"

"We need to kill them. That's what you should have done."

"Never mind her, CreSam. She gets moody if she doesn't have her way."

"Don't talk that way about her! She's right, he should have killed them."

"But as far as we know, there is no way to kill them. One survived a broken neck, and the other a bullet to the head."

"Wait, who survived a broken neck?" CreSam asked.

"Kabehl did. His family snapped his neck, but obviously he's still alive."

"Well, we certainly can't make amends with them now. They'd bend us over the table."

"Of course you'd say that. Now that we've burned all bridges with them, we have no choice but to kill them."

"You're the pussy shit who thinks we should have just let things be."

"We had a good thing going there!"

"Would you just shut up and help us think of a way to kill them!"

"Maybe they'll only die if we kill them simultaneously. They could be one person in two bodies."

"That's the most ridiculous thing you've ever said."

"The secret obviously lies with the third Avatar. Malia holds the key to killing those two."

"No, that's not it. He searched her inside and out, and all he got was sweaty."

"When did this happen?" CreSam interjected in his own voice.

"Little over a decade ago."

"Okay, enough about his exploits. Can we get back to the matter at hand?"

"Look, those two are unnatural anomalies born from an organization of similar freaks. If we want to be rid of them, there's only one way. Kill the original, and the offspring all die."

"We don't even know who the original is. His search in Tanelen turned up nothing."

"But he didn't have us with him. Besides, it's either that or wait here until they kill him or convince him to kill himself."

"I'm going to kill myself?"

"Not if we have anything to say about it."

"Frankly, I don't care if he dies or not. He's only holding me back."

"If they kill him, we won't be spared either. They'll rip us away one by one until all that's left is the shell that he once was."

"Well aren't you the melodramatic one today."

"Enough of this bickering. We need to prepare for our return visit to Tanelen."

"But we can't leave now. There's unfinished business to tend to."

"Fair enough. We can't have those two scurrying about unreined in our absence. Besides, there's still the issue of those mole people down in the Subtransit."

"Get them out of the way, and Amirione and Kabehl will have nobody to feed our empire to. Lucky for us, I've already devised a plan for such. Break for lunch, and we'll discuss it after."

Spril rode along the empty walkway, guided by the faint track lights perforating the ceiling. Save for those, the only light to penetrate the passageway was the headlight on his motorcycle. The soft electric hum filled the darkness, but it faded into obscurity as he neared civilization yet again. He clicked the headlight off as he returned to the bright lights of the underground city. Deftly, he swerved around pedestrians and children with their games, slowing as he came into more populated areas. The other members of Parliament were already waiting inside when he pulled up to the meeting hall. He brushed some dust off of the word carved in the door as he entered.

One week had passed since EshCal dropped in with twelve hundred traitorous imperial soldiers. While the decision to allow them permanent refuge was still under consideration, a divided Parliament had agreed to let them stay in the area Sinkua suggested until a verdict was reached. Having worked the most closely with her until the infestation, Spril was assigned the duty of assessing her behavior. Their underground outpost complete, this was the day he would decide their fate.

"So then, what's your verdict?" Phylus asked as Spril found a seat.

"I'd say we can trust them. It's a strange and unexpected turn of events, but nothing tipped me off."

"Then so be it. They're permitted to stay, but I want you to keep a close eye on them," Phylus ordered before any opposition could be presented, "That artillery could either be a blessing or a curse for us."

"Speaking of which, our theory about perpendicular barricades was a bust," MalVek admitted, "but if we can overlap a parallel barricade with a reversed polarity, they might mute one another. We'll be testing it this evening."

"What do you mean by reversed polarity?" Galo asked.

"Those barriers work with monopolar electromagnetism, as opposed to the more commonly occurring dipolar kind. That's why people and objects can pass through in one direction but not the other. If we were to make two barriers, one which allows passage to the east and one to the west, and overlap them, they might neutralize one another."

"Like positive and negative electrical currents," Yrlis added.

"Not exactly, but the principles are similar," NalSet confirmed, "It all means nothing until we test it, though. Our understanding of monopoles is limited, so our theories are more like hunches."

"How do you plan to test it?" Spril asked, "Sounds like it might be hazardous to try it out in your shop."

"You're right about that. The perpendicular barricades did nothing of significance," MalVek answered, "but overlapping parallels might forcibly deflect one another. So, we're going to test it directly on the imperial perimeter."

"We recently finished restoring Biroe's car into a fully operational vehicle, even improved the top speed to one hundred fifty kilometers per hour, on paper," NalSet added, "We've installed small barricade towers in the back, affording protection against attacks from the rear. All we need to do is slowly back it into the barrier around the capitol. Of course, if it works, the team assigned to destroy the generator will need to proceed on foot."

A cacophonous rumbling from above resonated throughout the meeting hall, bringing the conversation and to an abrupt halt. Drinks rattled against the table, and expressions of bewilderment were exchanged. An earthquake would have been the most logical explanation were it not for the fact that the nearest fault line was some sixty kilometers to the southwest. IlcBei snatched the pad of paper from the middle of the table, scribbled a note stating that she was leaving to check the monitors, and dismissed herself.

The moment she left, it became abundantly clear that the rumbling came from several sources acting as one, rather than from a single origin. The sound grew louder as she neared the Epsilon boarding dock. It wasn't until the staircase was in sight that the answer was laid out before her.

Children peered up the stairs curiously, rubbernecking to see who was being so noisy up top. Her vantage point not being particularly suitable for spying, she could only see the bottoms of tires zipping by near the top of the stairs. The street was swarming with motorcycles. She ran for the children as she called out to them.

With a thunderous cackling, bullets rained down upon them, ripping through their small bodies with streaks of smoldering blood trailing behind. IlcBei screamed in horror, her cries echoing wide to alert others of the macabre spectacle. Juvenile bodies collapsed atop one another, shattered and ruined by incendiary bullets. The other children, those spared from the morbid shooting gallery, scrambled in search of protection and consolation. IlcBei rounded them up and led them back to the meeting hall.

"Oh, this can't be good," Sinkua worried, rising to his feet as IlcBei returned with dozens of children in tow.

"Motorcycle cavalry," she trembled, "Huge swarm of them. Gunned down children. Just for looking."

Mixed feelings of terror and rage flooded the room, radiating from everybody within.

"I'm going back to the outskirts to get EshCal. She's our best hope of countering this," Spril announced, "IlcBei, go to the monitoring room and assess how big of a swarm we're dealing with here. Take Sinkua and Biroe with you."

"Why us?" Biroe opposed, reasonably fearing for his life.

"Between his skills as a tactician and your propensity for numbers, you two might be able to start laying some groundwork while I'm gone. The rest of you stay here unless Sinkua orders otherwise."

Seconds later, Spril was back on his bike, ripping down the corridor with expertise. Biroe switched his chair to manual controls so Sinkua could push him to the Epsilon boarding dock. IlcBei trailed behind, her older and stockier body unable to match Sinkua's longer more urgent strides. The others stayed in the meeting room with the children, the rest of whom were sent to join them, trying to keep them calm as they mentally readied themselves for what might become their last stand.

When Sinkua, Biroe, and IlcBei exited the train, they were greeted by one of the Subtransit switchboard operators. She had been assigned to work the security room in IlcBei's absence.

"Oh good, you're here. I was just about to go looking for you."

"It's about the motorcycles, isn't it?" IlcBei asked.

"It's worse than you think. Come look."

The four of them packed into the office, the floor space being particularly limited by Biroe's wheelchair. Sinkua sat on a table to give IlcBei and the operator more room to stand. Every screen was filled with hordes of soldiers on motorcycles, some riding alone and others in pairs, rushing past the hacked security cameras. The sentries were nowhere to be found, not even the destroyed and deactivated ones. Scarcely a scrap of them could be seen through the hordes.

"What do you suppose brought this on?" Biroe asked.

"If I had to guess, I would say the news of losing twenty thousand soldiers and sixty ships pushed them over the edge," Sinkua postulated, "and that's not counting what may have happened to the other two fleets."

"We weren't responsible for that though, not directly."

"Scarcely an issue. They're at war with us, so we're assumed to be behind any counterstrike. Besides, they've undoubtedly become frustrated with our snuffing their every attempt to get one over on us," he explained, his eyes darting among the screens, "So now, they're throwing everything they've got into either flushing us out or suffocating us, figuratively speaking."

"Wait, so you think this is an act of desperation?" IlcBei asked with a sliver of optimism.

"Exactly. Even though there are clearly several thousand of them, all we need to do is make one break in the chain and it will all come undone," Sinkua insisted, his voice trailing off as his focus settled on one specific screen.

Though the swarms of automotive cavalry were continuously dense on all other screens, on this certain one, the numbers were slowly dwindling. Sinkua studied it closely, all the while watching the time in the corner of his eye. For one brief and fleeting moment, the screen cleared and remained empty for perhaps a minute.

"Somebody write this down," he urged while the screen was still empty, "We have a clear spot from 09:42:17 to…"

"09:42:17, got it," the operator confirmed.

"09:43:25," he ended, which was confirmed yet again.

"One minute and eight seconds of clear space," Biroe reiterated, "What do we plan on doing with that?"

Sinkua fell into a contemplative silence, examining the motions of the swarm as it moved through the screens. He looked closely to discern any distinguishing characteristics of the riders, be they in their uniforms, stature, or simply the way their bikes moved. When he reached something resembling a conclusion, he broke the silence.

"As much as I'd love to merely set a trap there, it won't do us much good," he admitted, "There are at least five separate teams. Setting a trap will only stop one of them, and we can't guarantee that the rest will spread to fill in the empty space."

"Maybe we could look for breaks in the other groups or find a way to put them all together," Biroe suggested off the top of his head.

"I had the latter in mind. If we can get your car up to the surface in a back alley, we can inject ourselves into the herd. They're sure to break pattern to give chase," Sinkua explained, "That way, we can redirect them until all or most of them have merged into one."

"With those new modifications, we'll be safe from their gunfire," Biroe reminded, "That's reassuring."

"Fantastic timing, indeed," Sinkua agreed, "This just leaves the matter of when to enter, how to round them up, where to lead them, and what to lead them into. You know, the easy part."

Adorning the wall was a large map of the streets, easily two meters along each edge. While the names of buildings and businesses had long since become inapplicable, the arrangement of roads remained the same. The monitors had been labeled by street name and block number, making for easy correlation.

At Sinkua's urging, all four of them watched different sets of screens, looking to follow the movements of each group. Their goal was to trace the path of each one with no regard for chronology quite yet. Unfortunately, given their massive population, trailing them was perhaps an impossible task by such means. It appeared that segments of them were breaking off and rejoining.

Sinkua's attention slowly waned from the external task at hand. In the back of his mind, he was formulating a plan and, more importantly, a way to piece together the finer details thereof. Specific tasks were being considered, as were the ideal candidates for each one.

The door swung open, startling them from the trances into which they had fallen. A couple of hours had passed, and that one screen had only cleared a second time. Spril stood in the open doorway with EshCal a few steps behind and still straddling his bike.

"Come up with anything yet?" he asked.

"I'm on to something, but I'm still trying to work out the details."

"From what I could hear up top, it sounds like an act of desperation," EshCal noted, "So if we can set up an ambush outside of the city and close it in on them, they should fall quickly."

"I was thinking more along the lines of bringing them to the ambush," Sinkua insisted.

"They'll divert themselves when they see it coming though."

"That's why we need to keep them from seeing it coming," he countered, "By the way, are the others joining us, or will we need to go back to the meeting hall?"

"They should be arriving on the next train through here. Why don't you tell us what you've come up with while we wait?"

Absent any sense of timing or direction, his plan was more of an idea at this point. Still, Spril and EshCal listened intently, EshCal restraining any urge to preemptively criticize a strategy still in its infancy. The ambush itself was going to be the easy part, but getting them there would prove to be simultaneously meticulous and frenetic. Sinkua's plan had promise but, as he acknowledged, would need to be outlined in the finest detail and enacted with comparable precision. The slightest misstep could have ruined the whole of it.

The three of them exchanged proposals as to who would be optimal for each task, both in the planning and execution stages. Despite his youth and absolute lack of formal military experience, EshCal was developing a sense of respect for Sinkua's tactical prowess. It was becoming apparent why Spril deemed him a worthy successor, witnessing his mind in action after having seen him in battle. As initial disagreements were settled, the next train pulled up and deposited the other members of Parliament.

"Okay, everybody gather round," Spril ordered, herding them all toward the security office, "Sinkua is going to go over the situation, the plan, and the role that each of us will play."

Sinkua looked away for a moment as he ordered his thoughts. As he played his monologue in his mind, he found it accompanied by fleeting glimpses of an otherwise inaccessible past. This side of him, born of nature and shaped by nurture, reminded him of the father he once knew, a respectful and honorable man. When his internal monologue came to an end, it was punctuated by the memory of how they left Berinin on the day Galo was born, the day that man began to die. Dismissing it as a burden for another day, he faced the waiting crowd.

"We have at least five separate motorcycle cavalry groups patrolling up top. They appear to be splitting and rejoining periodically, but I'm not certain yet. What we do know, however, is that they're covering every stretch of road covered by our security system, but with one exception. Every hour and forty-two minutes, a small stretch clears out for a minute and eight seconds," Sinkua began, "That will be where we enter the mix. We Hybrids will ride in the back of Biroe's restored car, protected by the monopole shield. Biroe will drive, and Phylus will ride up front, thinning the herd with whatever guns we can fit. We will then lead that particular group off of their set path, eventually merging it with another, and so on until we have all or most of them trailing us. Meanwhile, Spril and EshCal will set up an ambush, equipped with the artillery brought by EshCal as well as MalVek and NalSet's siege machines. The car will serve as bait to lure them into it."

"Where do you need each of us, then?" Eytea asked.

"First thing we need to do is determine how fast they're traveling, but we don't have a reliable scale to work with."

"I can determine velocity from tread marks," Farim boasted, "How sharp of an image can we get on those screens?"

"They'll zoom in up to sixteen times before losing quality," NalSet answered.

"That'll work."

"Okay, so we've got that covered," Sinkua acknowledged, "IlcBei is getting us a schedule for the trains up top as well as a map of the tracks to lie over the street map inside the security office. One of her employees and Biroe are inside studying the movements of the swarms. Yrlis, I want you to relieve him. He needs to be well-rested going into this. Uulan, I'd like you to assist as well. Don't concern yourselves with timing, just driving patterns. When you've got that down, Farim will integrate her estimates on speed and use those to map out their locations on a minute to minute basis. I'll use that to draw out the best path for rounding them up. MalVek, how are those blueprints looking?"

"Good enough to work with. How many would you like?"

"As many as you can build. Vielle, recruit whatever help you can find. I'm assigning EshCal's troops to arranging the artillery machines for launch to the surface, so leave them out. Galo, gather lumber and whatever other materials they need from the hardware store," Sinkua ordered, radiating the confidence of a seasoned commander, "Take my bank card, just in case."

"What will you have me do?" Eytea asked, feeling dejected for having not been assigned a preparatory task thus far.

"You can help me map out our route," Sinkua offered, "And there's just one more thing. Do you two have a crossbow or a harpoon gun, anything of that sort?"

"Seems like we might have an old harpoon gun lying around the shop somewhere. Why?" MalVek answered.

"I need to you affix a spider mine to the tip of the harpoon," Sinkua requested, "and of course, it needs to still fly straight."

"I think we can manage that," NalSet boasted, "Counterweight on the rear, spring-loaded mount on the tip. Shouldn't be difficult."

"Sounds great. Now, everybody go to," Sinkua ordered, scattering the group into their assigned tasks, "EshCal, Spril will relay the launch coordinates to you once we've worked them out."

Biroe headed back to AlsRim's deli when Yrlis offered to relieve him. Not wanting to feel like she was in the way, the switchboard operator excused herself as Uulan entered to help Yrlis. Farim waited inside with them, aiding their efforts as she waited for a clear view of the tread marks.

NalSet and MalVek returned to their shop, the former to work on refitting the harpoon gun and the latter to comb through the siege machine blueprints. Spril joined them to determine a target ratio for construction, independent of EshCal's artillery. Phylus took a trip to the sporting goods store to scour the hunting section for firearms.

IlcBei dismissed herself to run to the nearest general store. There she hoped to find a train schedule and map, one which could be scaled up and superimposed onto the street map inside the security office. Meanwhile, Galo and Vielle traveled back toward the Epsilon boarding dock, where Vielle would begin her recruiting efforts and Galo would continue on to the hardware store.

Sinkua and Eytea waited outside of the security office for the three inside to emerge with the figures. They sat together on the smooth concrete, Sinkua mentally tracing possible routes and pitfalls upon it while Eytea tried to follow his thoughts in his luminescent eyes. While everyone else had been assigned their tasks, hers was to wait in nervous anticipation.

"Are you sure this is going to work?" she asked, visibly worried for both their lives.

"Only in theory," Sinkua blurted, realizing his error a moment too late, "but I'm confident enough of our abilities that I'm sure we can make it work."

"That's all I needed to hear. By the way, you never said why you want the two of us plus Galo and Vielle in the back of the car. Is it so we can help Phylus thin them out?"

"Partially, but there are bigger reasons for us to be there," Sinkua explained, "We have duties suited to our capabilities. Which reminds me, can Vielle drive a motorcycle?"

"It didn't occur to you to ask her?"

"Not until now, no. I thought I'd seen her drive Spril's, but I wasn't sure."

"She's not as good as Spril, but yes, she can drive a motorcycle."

"Well, he can't take her place. She's the only one that can do this."

"Why do I get the feeling this is going to be even more dangerous than you've let on?"

"There's a great deal of risk involved in breaking an unstoppable force."

Chapter 36

Galo and a handful of volunteer workers rolled yet another trebuchet to join the rest along the wall. It stood proudly among dozens of other such siege machines, including spring catapults, lance launchers, and hwachas. The load arms of the trebuchets could scarcely fit under the ceiling, giving the collection the look of a towering forest from within. A truck approached, hauling another load of lumber. After finding Vielle had recruited some three dozen laborers, Galo had judged it wiser to have additional supplies delivered at regular intervals rather than fetch them himself.

"We'll just need one more delivery after this," Galo called to the driver and passenger, "That ought to be plenty."

Ever the isolationist, NalSet stayed inside the lab, working with considerably more delicate materials. He took tentative plans into the development of specialized munitions, including a set of sound-dampened spider mines. Silencing the blast would be all but impossible, but redirecting the emanation thereof showed promise. Considerably more delicate in its construction was the ammunition for many of the machines.

The black powder for the hwachas had to be measured with great meticulosity, and while the electronic scale ensured such accuracy, NalSet felt uncomfortable trusting such matters to amateurs. Virtually anything within a certain range of sizes could be used as ammunition for the trebuchets and spring catapults, though. While they mostly used stones and scrap metal, he and his brother had opted to make household incendiaries using tennis balls and matchsticks as well. While he portioned the black powder for each of the hwacha missiles, a machine of slapdash assembly chopped the heads from matchsticks by the carton.

A visitor knocked twice, and NalSet pitched a still hollow tennis ball at the door. As it bounced back to him, the visitor knocked once more and walked away. NalSet smirked slightly, as the delivery worker from the sporting goods store had recalled his system to avoid interruptions. That spark of happiness was fleeting though, as it reminded him of the arduous task still ahead. The tennis balls needed to be loaded manually, which meant either learning to trust the strangers outside or slapping together a machine to load them without detonation.

"Last shipment of lumber is on its way," MalVek announced as he peeked inside.

"Sounds good. Could you bring that crate in here?" NalSet asked.

"Sure, no problem," he agreed as he hoisted the crate up to his chest, "This the last one?"

"Yup. Now there's just the problem of packing the tennis balls."

"We'll have the workers help with that."

"You'd have to be crazy to trust them with this stuff. One mistake could set the whole shop ablaze."

"You got an idea for how we can finish in time otherwise?"

"I wasn't aware we were on the clock."

"We left the security station almost four hours ago. Sinkua and Eytea have probably come up with a route by now."

Sinkua listened intently, absorbing what of it he could as Farim explained her series of calculations in extensive detail. While she was able to determine straightaway speeds from the tread marks on the screen, speeds on turns and slopes could only be derived through calculated estimates. Using an old protractor she found stashed in one of the office drawers, Eytea measured the angle of each bend and marked the calculated velocity of the cavalry from a chart Farim provided.

Having something of a propensity for numbers, even if it paled in comparison to Biroe's, Yrlis assisted with the more complicated areas as Sinkua plotted each fleet's front position at intervals of five seconds. Every timestamp was stated relative to the point when that opening formed. Before they'd even finished, his contribution to this particular effort began to feel quite robotic, and he was already sketching potential paths in his mind.

The start was the easy part, since all but one option had been eliminated. Complications arose as they reached the first intersection though and were compounded further by whatever roads they did or did not take. Using light pencil strokes, he dotted out potential paths in the same five second intervals. Slowed by its own density, the motorcycle cavalry moved slightly slower than the top speed of their vehicle. Not only did this mean the same estimates could be used in mapping turns and such, but they could also cut ahead of the swarm if the need arose.

Eytea stood behind him, silently studying the map along with his errors, even the ones he failed to notice and the ones he falsely identified as such. Her eyes darted back and forth as she envisioned possible routes, sometimes playing out scenarios of key moments in her mind's eye. Boldly, she reached over his shoulder and began to trace a path with her finger. Sinkua leaned aside and watched her fingertip graze along the wax paper overlay. She had obviously been learning from his pitfalls as she avoided his problem areas quite deliberately. In the middle of her route though, he grabbed her hand.

"See that station over there?" he asked, pointing to a circled area, "We need to get closer to it without wandering around too much."

"I thought the bridge was the priority, though."

"The bridge is pointless without the station."

Eytea stepped back and let him return to his work, somewhat embarrassed by her error. She thought herself foolish for assuming the order of the landmarks to have been arbitrary, even if he had not yet explained the purpose of each one. He reasoned that it would be moot to concern themselves with those details before they knew if the framework of the plan was even possible.

Minutes ticked away into hours as Sinkua diminished the virtually limitless possibilities via penciled trial and error. Eytea occasionally imposed herself to finger a route in search of approval. Each of them failed time and again, though with each one, the recurrence of specific failure points became increasingly uncommon. Eventually, every new idea fell apart at a new point.

"Hold on, I think I've got something," Sinkua announced, his eyes zipping along the map.

Recalling the nature of every previous failure, he isolated what may have been the only path to come anywhere near accomplishing his goal. He confidently dotted the route with strong pencil marks, circling various landmarks, such as merger points, deployment spots, and places to break ahead of the stampede. Finding herself well in tune with his mental machinations on this project, Eytea interjected whenever he appeared to have lost his train of thought, filling the gaps with her suggestions.

"I think this is going to do it," he asserted as he scanned their completed work, "Uulan, take the next train back to MalVek and NalSet's lab. Tell them to get the car in position. Yrlis, go to the outpost and tell them to follow the tracks ten kilometers north-northwest of the Psi boarding dock. Our next shot to deploy is in one hour and thirty-four minutes."

SenRas untucked his shirt and tried to stretch the fabric over his gun holster. As far as he was concerned, carrying the vintage pistol was the most secure way to transport it, but the task of concealing it had complicated matters. As his frustration swelled nearly to the point of surrendering to the need to keep it in a bag, XalRut set a garment over his shoulders. He looked down to see another remnant of an era long past. Sliding his arms into the sleeves of his old brown suede leather coat, he was pleasantly surprised to find that it still fit nearly forty years later, but that paled next to the surprise of XalRut having kept it.

"You left this with me that night," she reminded him, stirring up antique memories.

"I remember. I couldn't afford a gift, so I gave you my favorite coat instead."

"Even after what you did, I held on to it. I guess some part of me hoped that, if you wouldn't come back for her, you'd return to fetch it, and I could at least see you again."

"And now look at what our decisions have wrought. I came back on her behalf, and you're sending me off with the same coat."

"Don't get the wrong idea," XalRut insisted as she brushed the cobwebs from under the sleeves, "I've grown rather fond of this old rag."

"I'll try to bring it back in one piece."

He coiled his manriki and stuffed it in the left inner pocket, leaving one link hooked over the top. XalRut checked the safety cap on the syringe, its chamber filled with clear liquid speckled with suspended black flakes, and slid it into the opposite pocket.

"Are you sure that stuff will work?" SenRas asked.

"As sure as I can be," she assured him, "Do you have the right kind of powder."

"After what we went through to find that vintage stuff, you really think I'd forget it?"

"Fair enough, but I'd blame myself if you forgot and I didn't ask."

"Well, looks like I've got everything I'll need," SenRas concluded, "I suppose this is farewell."

"For now," XalRut added, "Come back when it's over."

"I'll be on the next boat to Quarun."

"And I'll leave the porch light on for you."

What MalVek and NalSet assembled from the remains of Biroe's car was something far beyond restoration. It defied the very concept of upgrade to project itself as the mechanical image of rebirth. The panels had been reinforced with armor plating. Mounted upon the rear bumper was a pair of scaled down monopolar barrier towers, powered by a generator integrated into the motor. A backup power source was hidden in a considerably less accessible compartment. Four seats had been reduced to two, leaving ample room for Phylus to store his new gun collection and for the four Hybrids to wait their turn to deploy from the rear.

The engineer brothers strategically positioned explosives in a geometric pattern on the ceiling. The reborn car sat on a platform with each corner attached to a vertical pulley. Biroe and Phylus sat in the front of the car, a cigarette hanging from Phylus's lips with most of a pack waiting in his shirt pocket, and Sinkua, Eytea, Galo, and Vielle sat anxiously in the rear. The explosives were detonated, inviting the fading daylight into the Subtransit, and four teams of volunteers hoisted the car to the surface.

Two minutes until entry. Biroe eased off the brakes and rolled off of the platform, which the teams lowered back into the Subtransit. MalVek and NalSet headed for the nearest boarding dock to catch a train to Psi. Phylus loaded the first firearm, a rifle with long range and low power.

"Are you clear on the directions?" Sinkua asked.

"That depends. How precisely do they need to be followed?" Biroe returned.

"Enough to hit the circled points at the intervals I wrote down. If you need to improvise, go ahead."

"Then I'm clear," he confirmed as he checked his watch, "One minute to go. We're rolling out."

He eased onto the accelerator, creeping toward the edge of the alley. For all their noise, the motorcycle cavalry had failed to notice that a car had appeared as though by some twist in the fabric of space. The predicted clearing came after a brief moment of thinning, offering their only opportunity to infiltrate for nearly another two hours. Biroe dismissed caution and fear as he stomped the accelerator and tore into the break.

The thunder of their motors surrounded the car, threatening to swallow it into a cacophonous tomb. Foremost riders on the trailing splinter swarm raised their weapons and fired shots at the bastard invader. From inside, the passengers watched with relief as the bullets ricocheted off of the electromagnetic barricade.

Vielle helped Phylus load more guns as the reality of the situation materialized in the form of scores upon scores of automotive cavalry at their rear. Eytea kept her head down, hiding from the pursuers, and anxiously clutched Sinkua's hand while Biroe ripped around corners unyieldingly. To his joy, the brothers had integrated a counterweight system into the frame which virtually eliminated the risk of tipping on high speed turns.

Phylus aimed his shotgun straight along the middle of the car. That first bullet pressed into the glass, cracking it in a spider web pattern before carving a hole through it. It cut through the barrier, accelerated by the monopolar electromagnetism, and ripped through the visor and skull of an unfortunate rider. Three more shots followed along with three more dead riders. Their comrades broke formation to swerve around their fallen bikes.

Sinkua punched the damaged rear window, shattering what remained of the glass and spraying it over the asphalt. With his other hand, he pitched a formidable ball of flame into the angered horde. Clouds of engine fumes were sparked for moment, the sudden whorl of fire frightening riders to the point of lost balance. Biroe widened the gap as he took another hard turn and merged a second fleet into the chase.

Galo positioned himself at the rear of the car as Sinkua scooted aside. He rested his right fist upon his left shoulder, holding his wrist as his Serpent Bracer pulsated with that familiar cool blue tone. With a bellow that echoed even over the rumbling of two conjoined swarms, he swept his arm and launched a bladed arc of ice. It carved into a handful of infantry personnel, collapsing them into piles of blood and oil in the midst of their comrades. More wrecks followed as the falling bikes effected collateral damage. Phylus picked off a few stragglers from the front seat.

"Vielle, it's almost time. Eytea, get in position to cover," Sinkua ordered.

Eytea sat up and leveled her halberd with the tip of the spear puncturing the barricade. A yellow milystic glow radiated and pulsated from the head. Vielle perched upon the rear hatch, her nerves fraught with anxiety and her mind and heart running circles of fear and bitterness around each other. With her cat-o'-nine-tails bound to her back, a thick vine emerged slowly from each of her wrists, snaking around her hands. Biroe decelerated slightly to narrow the gap.

"Now!" Sinkua shouted.

Vielle shot the twin vines at the nearest soldier in the pursuing double swarm. They coiled around the handlebars, constricting like a pair of boas. With her eyes and teeth clenched, she simultaneously hopped off the edge and retracted the vines. Thanks largely to her petite frame, she was launched at the lassoed motorcycle, her body feeling unbound by the fetters of spatial physics as the wind rushed around her. Cracks of thunder sounded from left and right as Eytea rewarded the blind arrogance of potential assailants with bolts of lightning born from the spearhead of her halberd.

The swelling grumble of the motorcycle grown to a deafening roar, Vielle opened her eyes and swung her legs forth. Both feet crashed devastatingly into the dumbfounded rider, knocking him from his seat and helplessly into the stampede. Eytea charged his airborne body with a fatal jolt, killing him before he hit the pavement.

Vielle landed on the open seat and quickly spun around. The asphalt scraping her knee through its denim armor, she deftly pivoted and cut into the nearest alley. Phylus defiantly protruded his torso from his window and unloaded a high caliber shotgun into the crowd, destroying any hopes of pursuit whether by bike or bullet.

Biroe took another hard corner, leading the two merged fleets even farther off course. Another two blocks passed, and a third group entered the mix. The flurry of infantry was becoming too dense for individual maneuverability. This made fantastic sport for Phylus and Eytea as they took turns picking off imperialist troops with bullets and bolts. Having learned the technique through observation, Galo loaded the remainder of the unused armory along with a few Phylus had already unloaded once before.

Remains of urban development began to thin. Sinkua tapped Eytea's shoulder, interrupting what had become more of a game to her than serious combat. He pointed to the bridge on the northern horizon as it came into fleeting view through alleys and cross streets. In the same manner as Vielle, she perched herself upon the hatch.

Lacking the space to do so within the window frame, Eytea spread her wings as she leapt from the back of the car. She dropped slightly before catching a draft and swooping over the triple cavalry fleet. From her overhead vantage point, she dispatched another handful with a series of lightning bolts. Respecting the urgency of the situation, she veered to the north and soared toward the bridge.

As detailed as the analysis of the riding patterns had been, they had not been able to allow for interruptions in formation as soldiers were felled from atop their automotive mounts. Still, Biroe's sharp mind was able to compensate, and thanks to a series of improvised corrections, he lured a fourth fleet into the mix at the expected point.

Galo mounted his glaive atop the rear hatch, the blade penetrating the barricade, and launched a series of icy spears into the crowd. Biroe accelerated for about a minute, opening a large gap behind them. Galo sprayed the pavement with a powerful jet of water from the tip of his glaive, freezing it as it settled. A layer of ice on the road was hazardous enough, but in his haste, he had left it rough and riddled with crystalline stalagmites. Experiences soldiers lost all hope of control as they slid across the ice, many suffering slashed tires as well.

Sinkua hurled a massive stream of fire into the patch of ice, bringing it to a rapid boil. Blinded by the thick cloud of steam, those who followed were helpless to evade the fallen. Galo and Sinkua leaned against opposite walls as Phylus aimed a rifle through the back and unloaded it into the panicked mass.

"Galo, are you ready to thin the herd?" Sinkua asked as he patted his Hybrid brethren on the shoulder.

"Looks to be a fine time for it," Galo agreed.

Galo opened the rear hatch and crouched upon it, his face within centimeters of the barricade. Bullets almost appeared to ricochet off of his body as frustrated soldiers hoped to best the technology of their masters. Gripping his glaive in his right hand, he leapt through the barricade. Phylus leaned partially out his window and picked off those with aspirations to be international assassins.

Galo tucked his limbs as he enclosing himself in a thick layer of ice. His body hit the pavement hard, bouncing and rolling but protected by his crystal armor. Melting the armor over his joints, he got to his feet in the midst of the quadruple fleet, soldiers veering to dodge him out of fear and bewilderment. As a swarm of cavalry enveloped his body, he swung his glaive in a full circle, ripping through their armor and flesh.

"Two minutes 'til the last checkpoint," Biroe announced, "Say, what do we do if the girls didn't hit their marks?"

"That won't happen," Sinkua objected, watching Galo fade into the distance, "Just keep driving and we'll take care of the rest."

After a couple of hard turns, they hit the final straightaway toward the last checkpoint. The dilapidated urban development faded and eventually tapered off into open plains. Phylus withdrew the modified harpoon gun from behind his seat. Sinkua crouched upon the open rear hatch, watching with defiance and hubris as bullets appeared to bounce off of his scarred face. Biroe pounded the accelerator, widening the gap between them and the four merged cavalry units persistently trailing them.

Vielle carved through alleys on her freshly stolen imperial motorcycle. Though the fleet was far behind, she periodically glanced over her shoulder out of fear of pursuit. As urgent as her duty was, she hadn't anticipated the anxiety of traveling alone in such a place without Phylus or Eytea to protect her.

She slowed to swerve toward the wall, idling as she neared the edge of the maze of alleys. The next turn took her back into the depths, and she accelerated once again. In the midst of it all, she found an old railroad maintenance station, abandoned like all the others outside of the fences. She ducked her head as she plowed through the broken front door, spraying splinters over the unkempt tile floor. Scarcely decelerating, she rode through to the control room and pulled the designated lever.

At what she felt to be a safe distance, Eytea swooped up to the top of one of the few remaining tall buildings with an image of structural integrity. From her advantageous perch, she surveyed the terrain, checking for potential obstacles between herself and the tracks. The freight train reached the switch point and veered off its scheduled course. Vielle had been successful.

Eytea leapt from the roof and spread her wings, catching the updraft around the building. As she came near the railroad tracks, the backwind created by the momentum of the train was too great to fly against, and she latched onto the side of a car, just two short of the locomotive.

With a white knuckle grip on the bracket of the cylindrical tank, she eased her way toward the front. When she reached the car directly behind the locomotive, the unsuspecting engineer came into view. Just as expected, his left fist held a lever, which looked as though it would spring forth if released. IlcBei was right about the dead man's brake.

Tightly clutching the door frame with one hand, she leaned in with her halberd in the other. Before the engineer could begin to make sense of the appearance of a young woman, much less one with purple wings, she plunged the halberd through his left arm and into his thigh. His femoral artery severed, he was dead within a matter of seconds, and his left arm being impaled kept his hand from falling away from the brake lever. Eytea looked back toward the city and, as she saw the car reach the final straightaway, swooped away from the doomed train.

His body protected by an icy armor of his own design, Galo bounded against the oncoming quadruple fleet of cavalry units. Several expertly timed swings of his glaive annihilated swerving soldiers, their collapsing motorcycles compounding the swarm's fatal troubles. Once there was ample space between himself and the car, he turned and ran alongside the troops instead.

With a hard stomp, Biroe pressed the accelerator against the floorboard. The dry squall tossed Sinkua's hair about as he crouched stoically upon the rear hatch. From the north, the freight train barreled along with a corpse in the engineer's seat. The ground beyond the tracks spewed geysers of soil and concrete.

Twenty meters shy of the tracks, Sinkua leapt high from the hatch. A dense cloud of smoke obstructed the cavalry's view of him as he set hard upon the asphalt, falling into a crouch. The car briefly went airborne as Biroe crossed the tracks at top speed. A moment later, the train passed with a deafening cacophony resonating from the tracks. Phylus tried to level the harpoon gun but found that its length made such a task impossible within the confines of the vehicle.

Dirt and pebbles spraying up around the tires, Phylus opened the door and stood with one foot on the seat and the other on the window frame. He perched the modified harpoon gun on his raised knee. Biroe slammed the brake and pulled hard into a fish tail, pointing Phylus at the passing train. His aim never wavering, he took the shot with confidence.

The harpoon screamed through the air as soldiers emerged on manual elevators. A testament to Phylus's marksmanship, the prongs of the spider mine bored into the curved surface of the tank, and as a testament to NalSet's craftsmanship, the harpoon passed through the mounting brace and pressed the detonator.

The initial blast ripped through the metallic husk like a fist through paper. Flammable chemicals sprayed from the wound and were immediately set ablaze by the directional explosion. The fire spread rapidly through the contents of the tank until the sudden spike of heat and pressure fragmented the tank into shrapnel.

At the command and direction of a Spril and EshCal, several groups of traitorous soldiers hoisted artillery weapons and siege machines up to the surface. Those already topside moved them into predetermined positions. Masked by the smoldering of the obliterated train car and empowered by their numbers, they quickly arranged an assault on the remainder of the oncoming fleet.

Vielle shredded across the unkempt grass, leaving a high wake of neglected soil in her path. She pumped her fist as the tank car was shredded in a fiery blast, punctuating what she had feared to perhaps be an operation dependent on impossible precision. As inspiring a victory as it was though, she knew this to be only the first of two phases. She dropped into a low crouch and gunned the accelerator, clods of grass and soil caking on her jeans as she rushed to the assault point.

When she reached the road, she paused to catch her breath. The massive plumes of smoke erupting from the remains of the tank were undeniably awe inspiring. She looked to the sky and continued on her journey, reaching the bike's top speed within seconds. A cluster of small explosives rained down upon the imperial cavalry gathered near the ruined train. As she neared the crowd, the echoes of those blasts melded into a single resonant howling, carving through the wind.

A vast shadow was cast over her as Eytea swooped down and snatched her under the arms, lifting her from the bike. Keeping a great deal of its momentum, the motorcycle toppled and slid into the unsuspecting gathering. Eytea carried Vielle, by far a light enough passenger, through the slowly dissipating black plume, and the two of them settled behind the car.

Galo walked among piles of corpses mounted on motorcycles, fallen but still running. Off in the distance, he watched with amazement as Biroe cleared the tracks within moments of the train's passing, serving as the ultimate testament to his brother's talent for strategizing. Unfortunately, even for legs as developed as his, the action was still a long ways off, and he knew it rude to keep them waiting.

Nervously, he erected one of the running bikes. Despite his fear, it did not take off and pull his unwitting body alongside. He brashly shoved the disemboweled body from its motorized mount and took its place. From the position of the last rider's hands, he identified the brake and accelerator to the best of his ability and cut an unsteady path toward the rapidly developing ambush.

Sinkua cleared the smoke screen to present himself to the cavalry as the instrument of their destruction. Staying in a low crouch, he raised his arms and suspended the massive firestorm. Charred sheets of metal rained upon ominously teetering train cars.

He swept his arm forth as he erected himself, and the firestorm spiraled overhead and swirled down upon the oncoming cavalry. Bodies were scorched within their armor. Weapons detonated under the intense heat. Exposed behind incinerated clothing, flesh was melted against charred remnants of motorcycles. Those saved from the flames inevitably entered a chokingly macabre mausoleum of imperial soldiers.

As the smoke cleared and the rest of the pursuing cavalry began to find their way around the pile of scorched corpses, Sinkua turned and sprinted to the smoldering remains of the train car. He leapt atop the mounting frame and ran through the flames and thick black smoke. Safe on the other side, he watched as the cavalry came to a halt within a few meters of the tracks. There they watched in anticipation, seemingly oblivious to what developments awaited them beyond the wall of smoke.

Sinkua ran to the car and stood watch as more and more cavalry troops poured in, waiting for the smoke to fade in apparent hopes of continuing to pursue the insurgents that had taken so many of their own. He pointed to a pair of soldiers poised to operate a lance launcher. Satisfied with the density of their presence, he pointed with his other hand to the middle of the congregation.

"Fire!" he bellowed with the air and confidence of a seasoned field commander.

The two soldiers took aim at the designated area and fired the massive harpoon into the whirling wall of black smoke. In mid flight, most of the harpoon broke into clusters as though it was shattered by wind resistance. Those clusters pierced dozens of holes through the smoke and rained down upon the congregation like angry hail, exploding on impact. Another followed shortly thereafter, the two series of small explosions sparking residual exhaust fumes around the idle motorcycles.

Within moments thereafter, Eytea and Vielle joined the ambush in tandem. Galo followed within seconds, walking with a somewhat bowlegged gait as he topped the smoldering wreckage. Sinkua took his place atop the car, his hand raised. The smoke dissipated, revealing dozens of siege machines to the automotive cavalry. Those were speckled among an array of roughly two hundred cannons as well as some twelve hundred formerly imperial soldiers, who were joined by hundreds of parliamentary troops and volunteers.

Lance launchers were loaded with cluster harpoons. Hwacha chambers were lined with meticulously crafted wooden rockets. Tension catapults and trebuchets were packed with sacks of discount munitions, the latter designed to automatically reload and launch ten to twelve times. Each artillery cannon was accompanied by a crate full of cannonballs.

Sinkua silently pulled his hand down to his side. As an image of rehearsed unison, soldiers and civilians unleashed scores of payloads. Munitions covering a vast technological spread pummeled the sky, appearing to hang for a split second at the zenith of their trajectory. In a fiery symphony, they screamed down upon the cavalry, rending flesh and sinew from bone and scorching the remains. The trebuchets continued to fling payloads into the conflagrating mausoleum.

Vielle ran to a nearby sapling, one of a small handful clinging to life in that neglected field. She placed her ear to its dying trunk and covered the other. From within came a soft distant rumbling, reminiscent of combustion engines echoing between high walls.

"More are coming," she informed Eytea.

Eytea took to the sky for a better view. Just as Vielle had relayed to her from the tree, the remaining two fleets were converging and heading toward the site of the ambush.

"Backup!" she shouted, pointing to the approaching swarm.

Everyone responsible for such tasks scrambled to reload their siege machines and artillery cannons. No hope remained for the soldiers who had fallen into the trap. For those riding into the orchestra of their comrades' downfall, what they lacked in relative numbers they covered with the gift of foresight, and Spril knew this to be so.

"Half of you, about face!" he ordered, "Get ready for a pincer assault!"

Scores of machines were turned about to face away from the smoldering wreckage, the final array alternating forward and backward. Eytea called down to Spril, who announced to the troops when the oncoming second wave had split into two splinters, one continuing west and another heading southwest. A deep silence consumed them as they waited for the next wave to arrive. The collective sound of their engines rolled like a slow thunder as the westbound splinter neared the crash site.

"They're almost here," Eytea announced as she dropped to Sinkua's side.

"Westbound backup is almost here," Sinkua called back to Spril and EshCal.

"East facing team, on the ready!" EshCal ordered in a genuinely authoritative tone.

Her soldiers reloaded their cannons and double-checked their positions and angles. Sinkua withdrew his morningstar, gripping it tightly as he unraveled the chain. The swell of engines grew louder as he watched them round the bend into the final straightaway out of the city. He jumped from the roof of the car and landed next to Galo, who held his glaive in a defensive crouch. The slow thunder of the oncoming cavalry swelled to a massive roar.

"Fire!" Spril and EshCal shouted together.

Infantry mounted atop motorcycles ramped over the wreckage, presumably using their fallen comrades, by the dozens. Cannons blazed as their payloads were launched into the formations of airborne bikes, shattering both humans and machines in flight. Imperial soldiers were robbed of their final breaths as munitions to the chest strangled them from their lungs. As bountiful as the cannon fire was though, several cavalry troops penetrated the defensive wall.

Phylus picked off a handful with one of the last usable rifles, but a canopy of motorcycles still hung overhead with more yet to come. The imperialist traitors readied their own weapons, many wielding both a gun and a melee armament. Spril and EshCal ran to the east to meet the first wave. MalVek followed with his sledgehammer, and Farim trailed behind with her modified canoe oar.

In full sprint, MalVek propped his foot in the open window of the car and, with his momentum for leverage, he sprang up onto the roof. After one more step, he bounded off the other side, swinging his hammer high. His arms and sledgehammer were knocked back by the countering force, but the bike he struck was stalled and crashed to the ground. With vengeful swiftness, Galo skewered the rider with his frigid glaive.

Like a deadly rain, they fell from the sky with guns firing into the organized assault. One by one they were felled by blades, cudgels, and bullets, the siege machines having become useless in such tight quarters. Still, their bullets managed to reach a fair number of their traitors as well as a few Subtransit volunteers. At Spril's command, the east facing team turned to the west. The stench of blood mixed with that of the smoldering wreckage grew chokingly dense.

Fearing the ramifications of an oncoming episode, Sinkua injected his spare shot of anticoagulant into the back of his neck. With the head of his morningstar blazing, he knocked riders from their mechanical mounts as they were unfortunate enough to land within his reach. In the back of his mind, he analyzed their landing and firing patterns far too deeply for his conscious mind to comprehend. As though he was predicting the future, he frequently evaded certain death with a fireball hurled over his shoulder or a swing of his morningstar redirected to a potential assassin.

Eytea kept her targets at bay primarily with lightning strikes from the tip of her halberd. With their sheer numbers though, she knew that relying on that method alone would soon exhaust her. She took to the sky instead, darting about erratically. Handfuls of the imperial soldiers tried to take aim at her only to be slain while distracted. At a safe distance, Eytea smote soldiers one by one with precision strikes. Periodically, she swooped down into the fray like a peregrine, skewering bodies with momentum so great as to lift their bodies for but a second as she turned upward.

Galo flowed through the crowd with his notoriously graceful integration of Tide Dancing and martial arts. He pivoted expertly around mounted marksmen to stab them through the backs. His footwork distracted soldiers as they tried to anticipate his next move, only for him to dispatch them with any number of techniques. Some were pulled from the mounts by acrobatic means and met their demise at the end of an icy glaive or with a crushed windpipe. Others had their throats sliced while more still were pinned under their own motorcycles.

Her timing almost comparable to Sinkua's despite operating on conscious analysis, Vielle disarmed one soldier after another as they landed. Their guns were bound with milystic vines and ripped from their hands in a moment of weakness effected by their bewilderment. Though their armor protected them from the cracks of her cat-o'-nine-tails, save for those to the neck, she circumvented such defenses by constricting limbs and necks to the point of rupturing blood vessels and cracking bones.

Whenever the opportunity presented itself, Phylus snatched a gun as his daughter pulled it from a soldier's hands. Too panicked to aim properly and being inexperienced with firearms of that power, he quickly unloaded each clip into assault.

MalVek barreled through the crowd, bludgeoning mounted soldiers without the slightest cringe at the sounds of their screams and shattering bones. Farim followed a few steps behind, cracking skulls and slashing necks with the flat and bladed sides of her oar head. The two worked symbiotically, each compensating for the other's shortcoming both in their bodies and in their weapons.

EshCal zipped through the crowd, her epee whisking across the air and through armor and flesh. Blood trailed artfully from the tip as she moved from one target to the next, leaving wounds so fine, her victims didn't bleed until she had sliced her next one. Confident of her precision though, she continued to move with no concern for or belief in the possibility of failure.

Spril wove his quarterstaff between arms and guns, separating the two with a swift twist and following with all manner of strikes to vital regions. At the sound of soldiers coming within his extended reach, he snapped the staff back to knock firearms from hands and bodies from mounts. Continuously demonstrating a mastery of his weapon of choice, he repeatedly looked soldiers square in the eye as he disarmed them faster than their fingers could embrace the trigger.

Though the handful of them at the front of this last line of defense managed to evade death, others toward the back were far less fortunate. Bullets ripped and blasted through Subtransit citizens and imperialist traitors without prejudice, leaving their bodies scattered about the field and many machines unattended. Despite the casualties however, they kept hacking away at the assault as it came from the east.

As those numbers began to dwindle, Eytea spotted the next wave closing in from the west. Judging by the timing, she supposed they thought more would have penetrated their defenses and lived long enough to prove influential. She called down a warning and gave an estimated distance.

EshCal gave an order for the remaining troops to split their duties between holding off the westbound assault and preparing for the eastbound one. Even though their numbers had slipped, the task of reloading every cannon and siege machine was far from too great for half of those who remained. They rolled cannonballs into place, drew back the loaded scoops of tension cannons, hitched the next payloads onto trebuchets, mounted cluster harpoons in lance launchers, and plugged rockets with previously entwined wicks into hwacha chambers. Meanwhile, their comrades of mixed political origin continued to stave off the oncoming assailants from the east.

The other half of the pincer closed in, nearing the range of the trebuchets. Unfortunately, the sounds of battle and preparation had grown so loud as to drown out commands shouted from across the battlefield. Instead, MalVek took it upon himself to initiate the counterassault in his own manner.

He broke away from the fighting on the east end and sprinted toward the west. He flung his hammer at an unattended trebuchet, and its head snagged the rope binding the counterweight, snapping it from its hook. One by one, sacks of discount munitions were hurled into the coming fleet. Others joined in, their numbers growing exponentially until all machines were launching their payloads into the fleet by the time the first trebuchet had exhausted its temporary automation.

As the ammunition was exhausted, the prior roar of engines faded to a dull stagnant growl. Bodies and bikes were scorched and crushed, the sheer heat and pressure fusing mechanical components and melting flesh to metal. Those defending the east end slowed their efforts as the incoming assault dwindled to nothing. Farim felled one final victim and stopped with the others, listening for any signs of life as the dust settled.

"Is it… Is it over?" Vielle asked, breaking the vocal silence.

Eytea took to the sky for a better view. From there, she surveyed the environs, scrutinizing any areas where survivors may have been lying in wait. No movement came from any of them. She dropped to the ground and nodded affirmatively.

"Huzzah!" Spril shouted with his quarterstaff held high.

The survivors raised their fists and weapons and returned the call, bursting into a celebratory uproar. Joined by a landmark victory over a common enemy, Parliamentary ArcNosians and traitorous Imperialist ArcNosians stripped themselves of political alignments and exchanged congratulatory gestures. Just a short time earlier, they had recognized the forces turning them against one another and instead turned on those forces and those who chose to embrace them. The offensive lines were devastatingly crippled, and the opportunity to strike at the heart was imminent.

Lord CreSam's reign was soon to end.

Chapter 37

SenRas shuffled down the ramp with the other ferry passengers, his coat wrapped tightly to shield his body from the harsh winds of the Frigid. What had attracted any of those tourists to such an hellacious wasteland was anybody's guess, but it was improbable that they had any part in the civil war. They all appeared so oblivious, but perhaps they came to watch the country fall apart as the ultimate act of bastardly rubbernecking.

Mostly, he looked straight ahead as he walked, but he occasionally darted a suspicious eye toward nearby passengers. Simply not being alone was unnerving enough, but in such mass, it was all the worse. He glimpsed biceps whenever the opportunity presented itself, which was unfortunately scarce because of the weather. The idea that they were privy to his scheme was virtually impossible and still only probable if XalRut was an informant. If she was, she was unmarked.

He had left his car parked near the docks, knowing it would be easier to stay hidden without it. As he buckled his seatbelt with one hand, with the other he shuffled through his selection of music. He inserted a disc of classic ArcNosian music from about two decades ago. It was some of the last domestic music produced before he put CreSam in the path of the Avatars of Fate, thus triggering the machinations leading to this localized apocalypse.

The sun was low in the western sky. He slipped his sunglasses on as he pulled out of the parking lot. For fear of accidentally breaking it, he pulled the syringe from his coat pocket and set it on the passenger's seat.

The streets of the coastal town had long been riddled with dirt caked in blood and oil. Today though, hundreds of pairs of tire tracks ran through this layer of scum, none with any trace of tread. He rolled down the window and breathed deeply of the cold air. The heavy scents of cast iron and black powder were unmistakable.

"How did they get cannons?" he asked himself as he put the window up, "And who brought them all out here?"

SenRas pushed the accelerator, swerving around potholes and pits in the road. Faint lights rose from the holes in the street, up from the Subtransit. It seemed the Parliamentary ArcNosians had expanded their occupation.

As he returned to the outskirts of the capitol, he was greeted by scraps of felled sentries scattered upon the road. Stomping the accelerator, he swerved onto the sidewalk to avoid them, taking out a couple of disregarded lamp posts on the way. Another pile followed a couple of blocks later, then another and another, the last being two collapsed atop one another.

"This is certainly curious," he muttered to himself, "First the cannons, now it appears that not one sentry has survived."

If the two events were connected, they had done a fine job of retrieving the cannonballs. But the only reason to do that would be to hide the fact that they stole them, and if they were that thorough, they would have also covered the tire tracks. As he drove through one pile of wreckage after another, he caught sight of something of an explanation. The head of one lay in the middle of the road with another one's chained spike driven through it. Somehow, they had been turned on one another.

Toward the imperial capitol, the twisted scenery went from the aftermath of mechanical mayhem to absolute morbidity. Imperial motorcycles in utter disrepair were strewn about, each one accompanied by a rider who had met a more grisly death than the last. Bodies were scorched, impaled, lacerated, exsanguinated through the forehead, and electrocuted. They had been crushed under their bikes, fused to them, and run down by their comrades. Among the mess of tracks, a pair ran in a straight line through them all. Someone in a car had either chased them or been chased through the city. Regardless of the arrangement, it was apparent enough who emerged victorious.

When he reached the border of the imperial capitol, he came upon yet another unpleasant surprise. The fence was now accompanied by barricade generators. He scanned his card to open the solid fence, but that still left the problem of the electromagnetic one. Frustrated, he threw the car in reverse and backed up several meters. Once it was back in drive, he stomped the accelerator to the floor. Strangely, the barricade offered no resistance.

"Vestigial barrier?" he asked nobody, "Or maybe it just shut off to let me through."

With the sun disappearing behind the horizon, civilians were filing out of the parking lots and into the streets, heading home from another day as cogs in the machine. The sky was ablaze in a pinkish orange hue accompanied by scores of headlights along the ground, all reflecting off the unsettlingly pristine buildings.

The music disc reached its end as he pulled into the parking lot. He shoved the syringe back into his pocket and wove through the swarm of departing administrative staff. A handful of them welcomed him back while most simply nodded, perhaps unaware of his long absence or even who he was. Communication between departments had long been on a need to know basis with CreSam and his Avatar lackeys deciding who needed to know, but words always found a way to spread.

Alone in the elevator, he nervously checked the pistol. It was loaded with a single bullet and, smelling it again just to be certain, vintage gun powder. As the elevator reached the forty-eighth floor, he returned it to its holster and hid it under his coat.

The Platinum Hall was suspiciously silent and nearly pitch black, aside from the sliver of light piercing the crack at the bottom of CreSam's double doors. With the only switch being near that door, he stepped lightly and slowly while his eyes grew accustomed to the darkness. As he passed each office, he peeked through the window. Not only were they all unoccupied, only one was still equipped for any immediate use. Kabehl, Amirione, and Malia were all gone, leaving only EshCal. Even his own office had been stripped.

At the end of the hall, he turned on the lights and looked back over his shoulder. No one else was around. As he desperately tried to swallow the heavy lump in his throat, he opened the door to CreSam's office.

Rather than finding the psychologically rabid tyrant he expected, CreSam lay atop his desk staring at the ceiling. His chest bounced with his heavy rapid breathing, and his wide eyes were dry and reddened from refusal to blink. SenRas approached cautiously.

"The world is ending," CreSam gasped, "Look at you, back from the dead to drag us into the abyss."

"I'm not dead, CreSam. I never have been."

"Of course you would say such a thing, but for what we've done, I suppose it's only fitting that you'd be the one to ferry us into the ether."

"I'm not here to take you away," SenRas explained, "I'm here to save you."

"Save us? It's too late to save us," CreSam argued enigmatically, "The world is falling apart, and we're to blame. There's naught to do now but wait."

"As long as you're alive, it's never too late. Listen to me. Who put you in this position?"

"I can't…"

"Who coaxed you into working with the Avatars of Fate and siphoning funds from every federal program to fuel the war machine? Who empowered your body and destroyed your mind?" SenRas instigated.

"What's happening?" CreSam gasped with a trembling voice.

"Who taught you to kill your friends, your neighbors, your comrades? Who put the gun in your hand and turned you on your mission partner?" SenRas continued, his voice growing louder.

"Del… DelRol?"

"Who drove you to murder your wife!?" SenRas shouted, standing over CreSam.

CreSam's eyes widened as he sat up in the middle of the desk. Though he could not recall ever having a wife, the paranoia, hallucinations, scrambled memories, conflicting accounts, and the destruction of the outside world all made sense now. They never worked for him. He worked for them, and they had made him their slave, exploiting him as a scapegoat while they shredded ArcNos asunder. They controlled him and silenced in a labyrinth of his own disjointed mind.

"It was him. He set this into motion. He created this monster," CreSam grumbled.

"Say his name!"

"Kabehl," CreSam bitterly muttered.

"And so shall he face retribution," SenRas snarled as he handed CreSam the pistol.

"No. No, this won't work. They tell me he's died before. He'll only come back."

"Do you trust me?"

"As much as I can trust anybody."

"Then believe in me and page Kabehl. I'll tell you when to pull the trigger."

CreSam grabbed the microphone and ordered Kabehl to his office. SenRas returned to the hall and ran to the other end, where he waited with his index finger hooked through his manriki.

Kabehl opened the door and looked around before entering. From well beyond his peripheral vision, SenRas watched him generate a broad sword from his weapon simulator. As the door closed, he lunged from the corner and kicked Kabehl firmly in the kidney with an aggressive bellow. Kabehl called out in pain, whipping about to find who had assaulted him.

"Son of a bitch! Why do you keep getting in the way?" he shouted as he swung his sword with enraged clumsiness.

SenRas snapped the manriki from his pocket and caught the other end in his free hand, stopping the blade with the taut chain. With a hard twist, he jerked the sword from Kabehl's hands. The simulator rolled across the floor as the solidified holographic blade dissolved.

"Now, you know I can't simply stand by and let you have your way with my country, not after what you've done," SenRas calmly explained.

"Not that you could ever do anything to stop us. You're only a nuisance, and that's all you'll ever be," Kabehl hissed, "A decrepit fucking nuisance!"

Kabehl threw a punch only to find his fist caught in the old Colonel's grip. SenRas snatched Kabehl's wrist and whipped his arm around behind his back, pulling it up into a hammer lock. With his free hand, he pummeled the base of his spine.

"Don't ever call me decrepit, you pathetic sack of rubbish," SenRas grumbled in his ear, "You think I'm just a nuisance, a little thorn in your side? You have no idea the sort of agony I can inflict upon you, boy."

"Have you forgotten? I can't be killed. You can abuse my body all you want, but you can never destroy me."

"True enough, but I know somebody who can," SenRas agreed, "CreSam! He's here!"

Kabehl looked ahead fearfully as the double doors swung open violently. There stood CreSam, his chest heaving with heavy breath. He barreled down the hall with the momentum of an infuriated bull. As Kabehl struggled to break free, SenRas withdrew the syringe and slammed the needle into his neck. Kabehl cringed as the harsh fluid raped his blood stream.

"What did you do to me?"

"I mortalized you," SenRas answered stoically as he shattered the purged chamber upon the marble tiles.

He released Kabehl's fist, shoved him forward, and stepped aside. About a meter away, CreSam leapt and, with agility uncharacteristic to his stature, pounded both booted feet against Kabehl's chest, bludgeoning the air from his lungs and knocking him back against the door. CreSam landed on his feet and, never speaking a word, repeatedly buried his fists in Kabehl's gut. All the rage born from years of lies and manipulation were condensed into a single moment, arisen after a long forcible repression. Kabehl vomited until his mouth was flooded with a sickly mixture of bile and blood. Unable to support his own weight, he collapsed to his knees. SenRas reached out and touched CreSam's shoulder, and he stopped the brutal assault.

"It's time."

CreSam drew the pistol and pressed the barrel against Kabehl's forehead. From the depths of his disjointed memory, a similar image flickered, one of a missed opportunity as he leveled a barrel to Amirione's head. Within that memory came another one, all the more faint, as he recalled the words he spoke. They made little sense, but he found himself parroting those words, updated for accuracy.

"Ten years ago, I took the life of a loved one in identical manner," CreSam muttered flatly, "Don't think you're so fucking special that I can't take yours, boy."

He pulled the trigger and put a bullet through Kabehl's head. As the lifeless tyrant collapsed in a pool of blood and cranial debris, a harsh scent filled the air. The smell of death had become so common as to be tolerable, but this was an entirely different sort of harsh. The distantly familiar smell of vintage gun powder flooded CreSam's olfactory. The shroud collapsed, and his mind was bombarded with a faded memory too painful to face yet too urgent to ignore. Over and over in his mind's eye, he watched as the woman he once loved, the woman who loved him, fell dead at the end of his gun barrel.

"You see her, don't you?" SenRas asked calmly, "Who else do you see?"

"A child. By the door," CreSam gasped, holding his head, "My... my son?"

"Yes. MeiLom."

"MeiLom... What have I done? What became of him?"

"He was declared legally dead, but I hear he still lives. It's not too late to find him and make things right."

"As long as I reign under the eye of the Avatars of Fate, I cannot go in search of him," CreSam regretfully countered, "We need to end this war first. Could you bring Brigadier Elite Spril to me?"

"Sir, Spril died two years ago."

"I'm quite certain that he did not. I saw to it that this was so."

"No matter, he's not the one you want anyway," SenRas diverted, not wanting to argue convoluted memories, "There's someone among them who can end this war and will lead you to MeiLom."

"Who might that be?"

"Sinkua."

"In that case, fetch me Sinkua, please. I'll stay here and compile the necessary documents."

The walls of NieRie's Bakery resonated with classic ArcNosian music playing on the surround sound speaker system. Down the way at AlsRim's delicatessen, the same music could be heard, as could be at the bar where Biroe had celebrated his escape from the fetters of imperialism. Nearly a week had passed since the landmark victory at the railroad crossing, and the celebration had yet to stop.

Some drank themselves into a stupor, most of them confining themselves to the bar, as their war stories devolved into hilarious falsifications. They would pass out, wake up a few hours later, and, after a breakfast of pain killers and bagels, return to the party. For their sake, serving alcohol was still restricted to certain times despite the celebration spanning several days without interruption.

The tables in NieRie's Bakery had been cleared out, save for the booths lining the wall, to make room for party games and exuberant dancing. At widely popular demand initiated by Sinkua, Galo demonstrated the styles of the Masnethegean Tide Dancers. He invited Vielle to join him and taught her a few basic steps as well.

AlsRim's deli was considerably less lively than the bakery or the bar. Folks went there to escape the stench of alcohol and get a heartier meal than pastries and small toasted sandwiches could provide. They served party platters and massive sandwiches, some as long as three meters, for celebrating patrons to share.

Off in the outskirts, EshCal and her troops hosted their own celebration. As a show of camaraderie, they invited anybody who wished to join them to do so without announcement or question. That courtesy was reciprocated and accepted at both sides, but it still remained that the locals were heavily in the majority on either side. Spril spent a good deal of time on the outskirts though, somewhat to the chagrin of Yrlis, catching up with EshCal and ironing out old differences.

Late in the evening, the door to NieRie's Bakery slowly opened. A few scattered patrons gave a glance but hardly paid attention to who had arrived. The visitor peeked in and looked around for a moment before finally slipping in with his head down. Sinkua sat in a booth, snacking on an orange scone and watching Galo teach Vielle how to dance like his people. Eytea sat on the table with her legs tucked in.

For all the music and excitement, neither of them noticed the outsider approaching.

"Excuse me. Sinkua?" he called out over the noise.

"SenRas?" Sinkua asked, startled by the announcement, "What are you doing here?"

"Looking for you. Can you come outside with me?"

"Sure, just let me finish my scone."

"Fair enough. Bring Eytea, too."

Sinkua and Eytea both nodded to him, Sinkua because his mouth was full and Eytea out of shy puzzlement. They watched SenRas weave through the crowd and leave the bakery before either of them spoke again.

"What was that all about?" Eytea asked.

"I have no idea why he wants to see me," he half lied, "but I would suppose he wants to see you about Kabehl."

"I can't imagine an imperial Colonel having any news I'd like to hear about that old bastard."

"He may be an imperialist, but he hates the Avatars of Fate. He tried to frame EshCal for sabotage, under the impression that she was training to join their ranks," Sinkua explained, realizing he wasn't making a particularly good case for either of them, "He also tried to save Gijin from Amirione and scared him out of facing Galo and me. At first, we thought he was protecting Amirione, but we've come to have our doubts."

"I see, I think," Eytea somewhat agreed, "So, he thought EshCal was an Avatar of Fate?"

"In training, yes."

"So he tried to frame her?"

"Right. He sabotaged the cannons on the ship that Galo sank shortly before we got here and tried to make it look like EshCal was responsible," he tried to explain, "She worked closely with Amirione, so I suppose that was as near as he could safely get to directly undermining them."

"But she's not an Avatar of Fate, is she?"

"No, but he believed her to be," he confirmed, "which makes me wonder why she associated so closely with him."

"It's a puzzler, especially having proven her stance against them," she agreed, "unless she's really dedicated to her façade."

Sinkua raised his eyebrows at that thought and, as he stuffed the last bite of scone in his mouth, pushed out of the booth and headed for the door. Eytea followed close behind with her wings tucked in.

"Oh good, I was beginning to worry you'd blown me off," SenRas greeted as the door shut behind them.

"You're a suspicious man, SenRas," Sinkua reminded, "but given your suspension, I figure we'll hear you out. Speaking of which, it's been about two months now, hasn't it?"

"I just got back today, but greetings will have to wait," he urged, "CreSam wishes to speak with you immediately."

"Just me? For what reason?"

"He's had a change of heart and wishes to bring the war to an end."

"Really now?" Sinkua responded with wide eyes and a rapidly elevating mood, "Did he ask for me specifically?"

"He asked for Spril, but I explained that he's dead and suggested you instead."

"Spril's still alive, actually. He's in charge of our military," Eytea countered.

"Just when I thought things couldn't get any stranger. No matter, you need to be the one to see him."

"If it'll help, I'll come along."

"It isn't just that. I told him you could help him find his son, MeiLom," SenRas explained with a suspiciously knowing glance.

"I heard he'd forgotten he ever had a son," Sinkua countered dubiously.

"He did, but I was able to jog his memory. That's where you come into the picture, Eytea. Kabehl is dead, this time for good."

"What?! But how?" Eytea remarked, simultaneously ecstatic and offended.

"I injected magnetized iron filings suspended in dopamine into his blood stream. The iron accumulated on the microchip and shorted it out, and the dopamine accelerated the process by elevating his heart rate," SenRas elucidated, "Then CreSam put a bullet in his head."

"Son of a bitch. EshCal promised I'd be the one to kill him once someone found a way," Eytea argued, "but thank you for ridding me of him anyway, I suppose."

"You and CreSam assassinated Kabehl?" Sinkua interjected, "Sounds like you really are serious about breaking away from them and ending this war."

"Wait, EshCal told you that? Why were you making deals with EshCal?"

"She had a change of heart while out at sea, turned against her fleet, and defected from the empire," Eytea recounted, "She and her troops live off in the outskirts. They even helped us hold off and destroy a recent imperial assault."

"Sounds like I was wrong about her. Guess I owe her an apology."

"Our suspicions about her haven't been entirely silenced, to be honest," Eytea admitted.

"What about Amirione?" Sinkua asked epiphanously, "Is he still alive?"

"For the time being, yes."

"Assuming he knows what you've done to Kabehl, it's safe to assume he has his sights set on any of us," Sinkua explained, "We'll need to send someone in after him."

"You're thinking of sending EshCal to prove herself, aren't you?" Eytea asked.

"I am, and just in case we're wrong to believe in her, we'll send Spril in with her."

"Do you really think he can take both of them on?" SenRas asked.

"You have a bad habit of underestimating him," Sinkua answered with a smirk, "I'll go to the outskirts to find him."

"Thank you. I'll wait here," SenRas agreed.

"Hey, would you mind taking me with you?" Eytea requested, "I'd like to see Kabehl's lifeless corpse myself."

"You want to unload a few thousand volts into him for good measure, don't you?"

"I just want to be certain."

"Sure, I'll humor you."

Possibilities scrambled throughout Sinkua's mind as he rode the Subtransit train to the old outskirts in search of Spril and EshCal. It seemed SenRas may have realized his identity as MeiLom, but the fact that he never let on was all the stranger. CreSam's sudden change of heart seemed rather suspicious as well but not entirely impossible. If he had truly forgotten about him, perhaps more of his memory had been compromised.

Of course, if recovering those memories turned him against the Avatars of Fate, that summoned the question of why he associated with them in the first place. Sinkua considered that it may have merely seemed like a good idea at the time, up until it spiraled out of control. Another part of him, nagging from deep within his subconscience, whispered of the possibility that CreSam's involvement may have secretly been nobler than any outsider could suspect. He never was the intellectual sort though, far from the kind of person Sinkua would think capable of infiltration and espionage.

When he stepped off of the train, he was greeted heartily, having achieved meteoric popularity among the soldiers. Upon hearing Sinkua's name called out by more than a handful of exuberant soldiers, Spril wove through the crowd to meet him. EshCal followed after breaking away from a conversation.

"Hey, what brings you out here?" Spril welcomed, "Looks like you've got something important on your mind."

"CreSam is ready to end it," Sinkua spat.

"Oh wow, that counterassault was more effective than we thought!" EshCal remarked.

"Wait, so he's just going to surrender?" Spril pried, "That doesn't sound like him."

"Well, apparently, most of this was the doing of the Avatars of Fate," Sinkua explained, "I don't mean to say they controlled everything, but they did something with his mind to make him easier to manipulate. SenRas helped him recover some old memories, and now he wants to meet with me to discuss the terms of end war."

"He was becoming increasingly wont to irrationality before I left," EshCal supported, "and I suppose asking you to come is a sign that his mind is coming back together. After all, you were the one to issue the declaration of war, were you not?"

"I was, but SenRas said he originally asked for Spril."

"So then he asked for you instead, since SenRas was under the impression that I'd been killed? Sounds like we should both go, then."

"No, I think he wants to see me alone. SenRas believes I know something about the whereabouts of his missing son."

"The one who disappeared five years ago?" EshCal asked, "Do you know anything about him?"

"I might," Sinkua nervously shrugged, "Besides, there's a more pressing matter I need you two to cover. SenRas and CreSam killed Kabehl."

"How did they manage that?" EshCal pried.

"Some sort of injection, something about a high heart rate and magnets. I'm fuzzy on the details. Anyway, that means Amirione is sure to have his sights set on CreSam, which would really ruin our chances of ending this at all peacefully. I need the two of you to hunt him down and cover us."

"You have an ulterior motive, don't you?" EshCal asked dubiously, watching his eyes throughout his explanation.

"Well, yes. I want to send you in so you can prove outright that you're no longer affiliated with the Avatars of Fate, and just in case you're pulling an extraordinarily dedicated infiltration, I need to send Spril in to dispatch the both of you."

"I'm not sure which is more insulting, the fact that you don't trust me, or that you think Spril could take me out even with Amirione on my side."

"Well, let's just say I've got less confidence in Spril's ability to kill the both of you than I do in your combined ability to assassinate Amirione," Sinkua reasoned, "and I'm still sending him out there. Anyway, let's head back."

"Fair enough. I've been looking forward to the chance to kill that bastard for two years now," EshCal agreed.

"I'll take my motorcycle. You wanna ride on the back?" Spril offered.

"Sure, sounds fun. We'll meet you back over there, okay Sinkua?"

"I'll have SenRas lead you into the city."

On the ride back into town, Sinkua contemplated the weight he had just placed on Spril and EshCal. The idea that EshCal would turn on him was only a remote possibility but a possibility nonetheless, and such a turn of events would place him in mortal peril. On the other hand, he was asking EshCal to murder her former partner. Granted, she spoke of having wished to do so for quite some time, but saying and doing were two words separated by a vast chasm. When he reached the Epsilon boarding dock, Spril and EshCal were already waiting for him, but SenRas and Eytea were nowhere in sight.

"They're already upstairs," Spril preemptively answered, "waiting in SenRas's car. Come on."

"Does anybody else know we're doing this?" Sinkua asked as he jogged to the stairs.

"We told everybody in Parliament, plus a few others. They understood the importance of our going alone," Spril confirmed, "I was surprised Galo didn't insist on going with you."

"He understands how important this is to me."

Sinkua ran urgently up the stairs while Spril skillfully navigated the bike up alongside him. Not having much to grip aside from Spril's waist, EshCal clutched the railing instead. Even the imperial motorcycle cavalry hadn't been trained to do such things. Once Sinkua reached the top, SenRas leaned across the seat and unlocked the door for him.

"Let's go end this stupid war," SenRas urged.

"Sounds like a fantastic idea."

SenRas swallowed anxiously several times as he drove, his eyes darting about. It seemed more like he had something to say than something to hide though. After several minutes, he finally spoke.

"So, what's with all the dead soldiers, anyway?"

"CreSam tried to choke us out by flooding the streets with motorcycle cavalries," Sinkua recounted, "but we threw a real bitch of a wrench in the works when we led them out of town and blew up a train car in their path."

"You kids have got some real guts," SenRas complimented, shaking his head in reasonable disbelief, "Sounds like the sort of ingenuity and courage that Brigadier General Elite HarEin loved to see in his troops."

Sinkua had a retrospective epiphany as they passed through the open gate without resistance. They didn't need countering electromagnetic barricades or underground tunnels to launch an infiltration. It turned out they could have stolen an access card from one of the soldiers that attacked them after they deployed the tracking pigeons. This was no time for regret though, but a part of him wished such a thought had occurred to any of them in lieu of thousands more lives being lost. Of course, that could also have presented the opportunity to simple assassinate CreSam while he was still psychologically unstable, before he was willing to treat.

SenRas pointed out Sinkua and CreSam's meeting site to Spril and EshCal.

They stopped momentarily to search for the most likely sniping point. The building directly across the street was the most obvious spot, but finding the occupied window was a considerably more difficult task. EshCal insisted she'd learned enough about his hunting style to know on which floor he'd post, within a margin of error of one floor. Pleased enough with her reasoning, Spril swerved toward the eerily pristine tower.

Sinkua stepped out of the car as SenRas brought it to a halt, his stomach turning somersaults at the end of an esophagus riddled with lumps. With fearful tears in her eyes, Eytea sprang from the car and threw her arms around his neck, clutching him tightly. Sinkua wrapped his arms around her waist and held her reassuringly close.

"What's wrong?" he asked.

"I have a terrible feeling about this. I don't want you to go," she answered shakily.

"I don't want you to worry, but I also can't pass up on this. Trust me. I'll be fine."

"Why can't I come with you?"

"The man was out of his mind up until this evening. There's no telling what he'll do if I bring someone with me uninvited."

"I hate when you get chauvinistic like this."

"It's not chauvinism. This is just a very personal matter for me. I'll explain when it's over."

"I guess that's fair," Eytea reluctantly agreed, "but after I make sure Kabehl is well and truly dead, I'm going to look out for any sign of danger and come after you if I feel like I need to. I don't care how personal it is."

"Fair enough."

The two of them unwrapped their arms from each other's bodies, and Eytea returned to the car. SenRas shot her a quick smile and continued for a couple more blocks to what he knew would soon be his former work place, a building Eytea recognized from their infiltration.

"Kabehl's body is up on the forty-eighth floor," SenRas directed, "but we might have to take the stairs. All this time working here, and I still don't know if the elevators are operational this time of night."

"I'm not too keen on elevators," Eytea noted, "The only time I ever rode in one, it led to some rather unpleasant events."

Sinkua walked alongside the building in search of the entrance. The only one he could find on that particular side, the one facing the tower where Amirione was likely posted, was at the bottom of a flight of concrete stairs. If CreSam suspected an assassination attempt, hosting the meeting in the basement of a nondescript locale was a reasonable precaution. The notion that Amirione had learned of the venue was not beyond possibility. It seemed the Avatars of Fate had ears and eyes everywhere.

His heart furiously pummeled his ribs as he opened the door into a silent and substantially illuminated corridor. Out of habit, he reached for his morningstar, only to remember that he had left it at home. Through confidence he was beginning to regret, he had opted to leave it behind, fearing that coming armed may have offended CreSam with his still recovering psyche. Honoring Gijin's words from the day he bestowed it upon him, he brought his dagger, tucked into his belt and hidden under his shirt.

As he passed an intersection, he was startled by the abrupt sound of combat boots clomping against the floor. Before he could assess the situation, they were upon him. The first snatched his necklace and ripped it from his neck, briefly choking him before the chain gave way. He spun around to snatch it back, but the soldier kept a tight grip on the newly pilfered jewelry. Sinkua grabbed his hand and slammed it against the wall. Still he didn't let up. Sinkua repeated, cracking the wall and the soldier's knuckles, until he finally let the necklace fall to the ground, unable to bend his fingers around it any longer. With a fine ruby particulate dusting the underside of his fingernails, Sinkua reached down to retrieve his relic, only to realize that the soldier had been a deterrent. A heavy bludgeon came down hard upon the back of his head, dropping him to the floor as his peripheral vision blackened at the edges and spiraled inward to nothingness.

EshCal led Spril through what appeared to be an empty building. No trace of interior light could be seen from the main corridor when they reached the floor where EshCal suspected they would find Amirione. Further confirming their solitude, the door to the hall nearest the street was locked electronically.

"Well, if he was here, the window would be broken," Spril guessed, "Up a floor or down?"

"I don't know about that. He might have a way of getting past this lock," EshCal disagreed, "but we'll check the other two floors before we go breaking in. Downstairs first."

One floor down, they found that Spril's deduction had been correct, as was EshCal's assessment of Amirione's hunting style. The window in the door had been shattered inward with traces of blood speckled on the jagged shards.

EshCal reached through to open the door from the inside, careful not to scrape her arm on the bloodied glass. Beyond that door stood the man whose death they had both sought for two years. The day had finally come for Spril to avenge his own death, just as Sinkua had suggested in the Tournament of Duelers. Alongside him walked the woman who tried to be the one to take his life in Amirione's place, now seeking her own enigmatic brand of retribution.

A single door was slightly ajar, the dim light of a desk lamp outlining the inside of the frame. EshCal pointed to herself, then into the room. She then pointed to Spril and into the room at a sharp angle, past the hinges on the door frame and toward the corner. Spril nodded in agreement, and EshCal slowly pushed the door open.

Inside, Amirione crouched by the window behind a mounted sniper rifle. He glanced back, taking a moment to acknowledge the absurdity of somebody finding him in such an isolated spot. EshCal spotted a look of regret in his eyes, perhaps at keeping a light on, before he realized who had come to visit.

"EshCal?" he greeted, "I heard your fleet sank itself out near Haprian. I thought you had died with them."

"Oh sweetie, you know I couldn't leave without having given you a proper farewell," EshCal assured him as she sauntered across the room, her hips leading his eyes, "We parted on such bitter terms."

"As soon as I'm done here, we'll address that," Amirione insisted.

"Whatever it is, I'm sure it can wait," EshCal argued impatiently, "Whoever it is, you must expect them to hold still for a while. Otherwise, you'd get in closer for an easier shot."

"You know me far too well," Amirione agreed with a sly smile as he eschewed his duties and walked away from the window.

"Baby, you have no idea."

EshCal pointed to the desk chair, urging Amirione to fetch it. He grinned in anticipation of what this order surely implied. Excitedly, he sat in the chair and rolled it to the front of the desk. EshCal placed her hands gently on his shoulders, followed by one foot on either side of his.

She eased in closer, slowly moving her taut belly toward his face. Sultrily, she slipped down to his lap, the warmth of her breasts washing over his face as they came within a hair's breadth of grazing it. Firmly pressed on his lap, she artfully swiveled her hips as she ran her fingers through his hair. Leaning in, she breathed heavily on his neck.

"Tell me one thing," she breathily whispered in his ear.

"Anything," he offered, overwhelmed with lust.

"Do you believe in ghosts?" she asked firmly.

Sooner than he could process the question, she exploited his lustful vulnerability. In one hand, she clutched his kidney, paralyzing him in agonizing pain, and in the other, she tightly gripped his throat. She pushed his head back, showing him the upside down image of the ghost he never knew he feared.

"A wise young man once told me, 'Sometimes, great people get to avenge their own death,'" Spril alluded with his quarterstaff laying across his shoulders, "Looks like he was right."

Spril whipped the staff around to his front, holding it over his head as high as the ceiling would allow. Amirione's eyes widened with a fear that Spril craved and thrived upon. With a look of rage and raw determination, he swung the staff down with devastating force. Though the staff shattered and splintered against Amirione's reinforced skull, the impact snapped his neck against the back of the chair, severing his spinal cord. EshCal backed off of his lap as paralysis set in.

"Wh-why?" he gasped through the excruciating pain throbbing in his neck.

"You really don't remember?" she asked as she placed the tip of her epee against his chest, "You poor bastard. Fine, I'll explain. Two years ago, this man who just jacked up your spine was going to face off against your Lord CreSam for reign over the ArcNosian military and government. I, just a Colonel at the time, offered CreSam my assistance and thus the upper hand. He rejected my offer, but you came along behind me and muscled your way in. That was my inside ticket to the top of this man's game of a military, and you took it from me."

"B-but he…" he tried to counter as Spril moved around to his front

"Don't try to throw CreSam under the bus, too," EshCal countered, slowly puncturing his flesh, "He rejected one offer, but when you placed yourself as his personal mercenary and bodyguard, you ruined any chance I had to do as such. So, I spent the next two years seducing my way into your trust and the elite inner circle by extension, all so some day, I could do this to you."

She looked stoically into his trembling eyes as she drove the epee between his armored ribs, through his heart, and out his back. Spril and she watched the color fade from his face as the life left his eyes. She yanked the bloodied epee from his silenced chest, and he collapsed out of the chair and into a heap of himself on the floor.

"Come on," she urged, "Let's go find the others."

Sinkua awoke to the unsettling feeling of blood trickling over his eyelids. He blinked a few times to clear them, not yet taking any particular notice of his environs. When he tried to reach for his face, he found his hands were tied behind his back. At this realization accompanied by the feeling of ropes digging into his wrists, his consciousness returned abruptly.

"About time you woke up," announced a voice that filled the room as somebody wiped the blood from his face, "Now, we can get on with this."

Sinkua looked up to find himself standing bound before six riflemen, all stripped of any indication of name or rank. SenRas's words had been only bait. The peaceful ending he'd been promised was but a trap with his death surely to serve as an instrument of the forced surrender of Parliamentary ArcNos. His necklace hung tauntingly next to a mirror behind the firing squad. A light flicked on to show CreSam watching from behind a two-way mirror.

"Sinkua," he called through the speakers mounted in the upper corners, "You stand before this firing squad under punishment of the crime of kidnapping and mortally endangering a nuclear relative of a federal executive. Have you any final words before we end your wretched life?"

"You wish to punish the man responsible for your son's disappearance?" Sinkua snarled, rubbing the ruby particulate between his fingers, "Turn these guns around and destroy yourself just as you destroyed your son the day you took his mother from him."

"Take aim! Hold steady!" CreSam ordered, his voice trembling slightly, "Fire!"

Sinkua snapped the singed ropes and dropped to one knee, flinging ashes as he threw his arms out. The bullets exploded against the pillar, boring most of the way through it. Armed with only a single bullet each, the firing squad scattered as the post collapsed forth and crashed through the two-way mirror. CreSam fled with fear and rage in his eyes.

Sinkua ran up the fallen post, snatching his necklace on the way, and leapt through the open frame. That familiar life-affirming warmth rushed through his body as he clasped it around his neck. For good measure, he turned and set the room ablaze with the swipe of his hand before giving chase.

CreSam's heavy footfalls and breaths echoed through the otherwise empty halls. Sinkua navigated the maze of corridors, slowly closing in on him. All the while, his own breath grew increasingly ragged, and his pulse accelerated painfully. A blinding orange light flooded the halls with a chokingly dense smoke. His eyes flared as he charged through flames of his own creation. In the corner of his eye, he spotted CreSam passing down a parallel path. He swerved and headed down the adjoining hall to catch him.

Sinkua continued past that hall and on to the next one. There, he circled around to get ahead of CreSam. Catching him by surprise, he burst in front of him, his body illuminated by the flames, and leapt forth with a vicious bellow echoing through the deafening crackle of the inferno. CreSam froze with shock as an ancient memory flickered in his conscience, instigated by this young man he had labeled as his enemy. Those shimmering green eyes pierced through the fiery glow and into the catacombs of his mind. A single word, a name, escaped his mouth.

"MeiLom!" he gasped with wide eyes.

Sinkua's body collided forcibly with his, dropping him to the searing tile floor. Sinkua pinned him to the floor and drew his dagger, ready to line the blade with what drove him to fight. Upon hearing him speak that name though, he hesitated.

"Wh-what did you just call me?" he asked.

"MeiLom," CreSam repeated, "It's you, isn't it?"

"Yes," Sinkua confirmed, swallowing the lump in his throat, "I am the son you lost when you murdered my mother and killed when you thought your vie for power more important than any acknowledgement of your broken family."

"BeiLou… She was such a beautiful person," CreSam sighed, "but what became of you, of us, I never wished for that."

"What do you mean?" Sinkua asked, crouching beside him.

"One of you had to die. I don't remember any of the details behind it, but I chose to kill her and let you live," CreSam explained, "I can't recall if she ever knew, but she died so that you could live."

"And you never told me any of this?"

"You were too young, MeiLom."

"What, you thought I couldn't handle it? You'd be surprised what you can take after living through what I saw that day," Sinkua countered as the flames closed around them, "And it's Sinkua now."

"Fine, you were too young, Sinkua," CreSam agreed with regret in his eyes, "but it wasn't for lack of maturity. I had to wait until you could enlist. Only then would it be safe to fill you in, because then I could protect you until you were strong enough to protect yourself."

"Protect me? It was your bastardization of HarEin's military that I needed protection from."

"Only after what became of it over the years that followed. I always suspected the Avatars of Fate knew my cooperation came with ulterior motives, and though I'll always regret it, I couldn't even tell my own son what I was doing. If they found out that you knew, they would have tortured you for information and killed you once they had their fill. Alone, I was relatively safe, what with their having a use for me."

"You began as an enemy of the Avatars of Fate and now wish to reclaim your stance against them?" Sinkua asked as he rose to his feet, extending his hand toward CreSam, "In that case, treat with Parliamentary ArcNos and come back to the Subtransit with me."

"The first is already being done as we speak," CreSam agreed, "but I can't accompany you to the Subtransit, nor can I join your ranks."

"Why not?" Sinkua argued in frustration, "I'm offering you a shot at redemption! Prove yourself as their enemy! Show me that you're the father I believed in!"

"You can believe in me now more than ever. The Avatars of Fate control Imperial ArcNos through me. My body is chained by unfathomable tracking methods, some of which I'm sure have been documenting every word of this."

"And you knew this all along?"

"Yes. If I go with you, they'll remain in the shadows, using me to find you and your friends and systematically killing us off from the relative safety of darkness," CreSam continued as scorched fragments of the ceiling collapsed around them, "but if I die here tonight and restore parliamentary control, they'll be forced to come into the light to intervene."

"Sinkua!" Eytea shouted from down the hall, running through the flames with a wing over her mouth and nose.

"Eytea, what are you doing here?" Sinkua called back.

"I came to get you, you big idiot!"

"Both of you, get out of here," CreSam urged, slouching against the wall.

"Not until you agree to come with us, CreSam," Sinkua insisted, "You still have a name to make for yourself."

"Are you out of your mind?" Eytea snapped.

"He's not with the Avatars anymore. He never really was," Sinkua shouted over the sound of collapsing infrastructure, "They stunted his mind to keep him under control. Now that he's off their leash, I'm giving him the chance to prove himself."

"Not everybody deserves a second chance."

"You don't know the situation like I do."

"Eytea!" CreSam beckoned, "Take my son and get out of here."

"Your son?!"

"Now do you understand?" Sinkua asked.

"I have too many questions to let you die now," Eytea answered, tenaciously clutching his hand.

"CreSam, you'd better come find us if you live," Sinkua demanded.

"Just go. I'll be right behind you."

"That's a lie, and you know it," Sinkua countered, "but a pleasant one, for a change."

Smoldering ashes rained upon them as they sprinted through the flames, her hand in his passing Sinkua's protection from their burning heat through Eytea's body. The walls cracked around them, their infrastructure compromised by the inferno. Atop weakened support, the ceiling fractured and crumbled.

Never releasing each other's hand, they wove around fallen debris and dodged more as it plummeted. Sinkua peered ahead and recoiled in horror at the sight of a large air conditioning unit losing its grip on the ceiling. He rushed forth and grabbed Eytea around the waist, tackling her to the floor and rolling with her past the air conditioner as it crashed to the floor.

She lay on her back with Sinkua over her on his hands and knees, his hands upon her shoulders. Before he could move aside, a large chunk of the ceiling, loosed by the fallen air conditioner, collapsed upon his spine. His eyes grew wide as he cried out in pain. More followed, fragments of scorched stone and singed wood raining down upon him. Flames fanned outward from his back with every strike as he gritted his teeth and obstinately held his position. Desperately trying to hide the excruciating pain, he stared down into Eytea's tearful eyes as he took every debilitating blow to keep even a scrap from falling upon her.

"Go!" he urged in a split second between strikes.

"I can't!" she objected, tears welling in her eyes, "I can't leave you here like this!"

"I'm just as much to blame for what happened," Sinkua insisted, "but I can't die knowing that you went with me."

"So you would have me let you die?"

"You deserve to live. I don't."

She looked up, deep into Sinkua's eyes, and past him through the hole in the ceiling. Beyond holes in several more ceilings, she could see a faint glimmer of moonlight shining softly around another air conditioning unit. Hearing faint footsteps, her eyes shot to the side. She wrapped her legs around his waist and, after slipping out of his wavering pin, her arms around his upper torso.

"I don't want to let go," she spoke in his ear.

"Eytea…"

Her eyes darted between the holes through to the roof and back down the hall they had come through. The air conditioner broke away from the highest ceiling, ripping a hole and welcoming the moonlight. She breathed heavily, her breasts pushing against Sinkua's comparably heaving chest, and tightened her grip on him as the lifeless appliance plummeted toward them. She whispered three final words to him.

"I love you."

At full sprint, CreSam slammed into their side, knocking them out of the path of the appliance and putting himself in their place. Eytea rolled across the floor, holding fast to Sinkua's body as his consciousness faded. Freeing her hand briefly, she pressed it against the tile floor and launched their bodies upward in tandem with a powerful blast of electricity. Just before the air conditioner crashed down upon CreSam and crushed his body, Eytea exhaled a nigh inaudible gratitude as she spread her wings and carried Sinkua's unconscious body over the wreckage. Straining to maintain her initial burst of momentum, she flew him up through the holes to the roof.

Spril and EshCal watched from the sidewalk across the street as the fire devoured the building from within, each feeling more helpless than the other to rescue Sinkua from the structure collapsing upon him. The seconds ticked by, slowly choking away any fading sign of hope. As it seemed inevitable that they would need to go home without him, and worse still, inform Eytea of his death, a winged figure high above caught their eyes.

"Is that what I think it is?" EshCal remarked.

"It is!" Spril confirmed as the figure descended along the wall, "It's Eytea, and she has Sinkua."

"I didn't even know she was in there."

"Neither did I."

Eytea landed in the middle of the street and collapsed with pained fatigue. She lay panting across Sinkua, who remained unconscious. Spril rushed to her and offered his hand.

"I can't," she gasped, "He's alive, just not conscious."

"Where did SenRas go?" EshCal asked, "I didn't see his car."

"Back to Subtransit," Eytea whispered hoarsely, her eyelids fluttering, "Papers for Phylus."

Her eyelids flickered a few more times until, unable to grasp consciousness any longer, she succumbed to exhaustion and fainted atop Sinkua. Spril shook her by the shoulder. Unable to rouse her, he checked her pulse and, just to confirm her word, Sinkua's as well.

"We need to get them to a hospital," Spril insisted.

"The hospitals here won't treat them."

"Then we'll take them back to the Subtransit. Grab a body and help me hot-wire a car."

His consciousness slowly returning, Sinkua rose to his feet and assessed his immediate surroundings. Eytea lay by his feet, her body disconcertingly still. He placed two fingers on the side of her neck. Though he waited several painful seconds, he could feel no pulse. Tears welling in his eyes, he backed hastily away from her.

The lifeless streets were lined with burning buildings, the fire he sparked in the execution chamber having apparently spread while he was out. A series of massive potholes occurring at regular intervals captivated his focus. His eyes followed them further up the street until he reached their end, and there he found their cause. That familiar mechanized colossus marched along, raining devastation in its wake.

"You!" Sinkua shouted.

"Sinkua!" the resonating voice bellowed back as it turned about.

"You took my family. You took my country," he called back, barreling up the street, "And now you took Eytea!"

From far behind, he could vaguely hear her call out his name. He initially disregarded it as an artifact of remorse, but in spite of his momentum, Eytea's voice grew louder and more distinct. As it did so, the monolithic sentry dissolved in a flood of light, the luminous particles rising into the sky. Though he still couldn't see her, her voice became ever louder. Buildings swallowed their fires and reshaped themselves into prior structures. She called his name as though she stood beside him. The street smoothed, repairing itself to a freshly paved state. The particles born from the sentry's dissipation scattered and illuminated the sky, swallowing the darkness of night. Her voice swelled to an urging shout.

His eyes flickered open yet again, this time to see Eytea's smiling face.

"Eytea? You're alive?"

"As are you," she confirmed, kissing him on the cheek, "You were just having a nightmare, but it's about time you showed some signs of life."

"What exactly happened?"

"When you had me pinned, an air conditioner was about to fall on us. CreSam knocked us out of the way, and it fell on him instead. I'm sorry," Eytea apologized, "That was when you began to lose consciousness. I flew us out and fainted in the street. Spril and EshCal stole a car to bring us back here."

"Oh wow. Thank you," Sinkua nodded, desperately trying to grasp the weight of it all with his wavering consciousness, "Are they still here? I'd like to thank them, too."

"No, they went home once we were both stabilized," she answered, "four days ago."

"I've been unconscious for four days?"

"Now do you see why I was starting to worry?"

"And you've been waiting here the whole time?"

"Well, I don't wanna brag, but I could've gone home after the first day," she teased, "But what good would that be if you can't come, too?"

"Thank you again," he repeated as he sat up and reciprocated the kiss on the cheek.

"Ah, I see our patient finally came to," called a voice from the door.

"Oh hey," Eytea answered, "Yeah, he just woke up a few minutes ago."

"That's fantastic. Welcome back, Sinkua," the nurse greeted, "I'll go get your lunch. There's also someone here to see you, been coming every day since the morning after you checked in. Would you like me to get him?"

"Would you, please? Whoever it is, he shouldn't be kept waiting so many times," Sinkua insisted.

The nurse left and, after a few long minutes, returned with a bowl of beef stew and a glass of milk atop a plastic tray. Despite all the guesses in his mind, behind her followed someone he'd somehow failed to consider.

"Sinkua, glad to see you've pulled through," SenRas greeted as he pulled up a chair beside his bed.

"I certainly wasn't expecting you. What with how that nurse spoke of you, I thought you'd be Galo. Where is he, anyhow?"

"I'll get to that, but first the more personal news. Eytea told me of your medical situation. I asked one of the medical examiners to take a bone marrow sample during the autopsy, but the search party couldn't find his body, just some gnarled scraps of skin and some blood. Not enough to get more than a few conclusive tests, but it would have been moot anyway."

"Well, thanks for trying," Sinkua sighed.

"As for Galo, he and the rest of Parliament are topside along with hundreds of others from both sides, tearing down the fence around the old capitol," SenRas explained, "As his last official order of business, he scribed a bill ordering that in the event of his death, the empire be dismantled and Parliamentary control restored with the highest ranking current or former military officer taking up the duties of Brigadier General Elite."

"Wait, we won? Unconditional surrender?"

"That's right. The details of leadership are still being ironed out, but the former order is being restored as we speak."

"So, highest ranking officer? That puts EshCal in charge, right?"

"I thought so, too, but among the papers was Spril's military personnel death certificate. It wasn't even notarized. His military service paperwork was intact as well."

"Does that put him in charge, then?"

"As the only Brigadier Elite, yes it does."

"That's fantastic, but in retrospect, it only complicates things further. It means CreSam knew Spril was alive, perhaps even that he was responsible for such."

"It's certainly something to think about," SenRas agreed, "He also willed his old house to MeiLom, but I couldn't find the deed to bring to you."

"I guess this means you know my secret," Sinkua accepted.

"Honestly, I knew before your father did."

"Is that why you had the change of heart?"

"Not entirely. Allow me to explain," SenRas began, "When he killed your mother, I was still his commanding officer. He was distraught with anxiety, but he still pushed forward. I followed him on his rise to power, always staying nearby to make sure he never lost sight of what he had done. Nine years later, the attack on Masnethege was to set his final atonement into motion. The plan was for Gijin to condemn ArcNos and consequently turn the rest of Ouristihra against us, destroying him and the Avatars of Fate."

"I guess Amirione ruined that idea."

"He did, but you and Galo did a fine job working in Gijin's stead. Still, you had to be treated as the enemy, a job that became all the easier for CreSam as he lost his mind and any recollection of you as his son. Honestly, whether either of you lived or died was of no consequence to me up until I realized who you were. CreSam was slipping beyond salvation or even atonement, so knowing that you may have been his only hope, I took it upon myself to see to it that you both lived to see the chance."

"All this time," Sinkua sighed, "you were trying to save us both from ourselves and each other? I don't even know what to say."

"After what I'd done, I owed BeiLou at least that much."

"After what you'd done? How did you know my mother?"

"Technically, I didn't," SenRas sorrowfully confessed, "I was, well, am a friend of her mother."

Sinkua fell silent, letting this information settle into his thoughts. As he tried to process this bombardment of life-altering news, he calmed his nerves with the warmth of fresh stew running down this throat. Feeling his vitality creeping back, he turned to Eytea.

"So, what would your mother say to your staying here?" he offered, "That house is far too big for me to live in it alone."

"I don't think she's as ready to let go as she lets on," Eytea answered with a wide smile and beaming eyes, "but I'm sure she'd just love to have you come home with me."

"You think so?"

"I know so, almost as much as I would," she flirted.

"Almost, huh?"

He grabbed the front of her shirt and pulled her closer. She leaned in and kissed him softly on the lips. After a few seconds together in mental solitude, she pulled away with a soft gasp.

"Okay, maybe not almost," Eytea corrected.

"Good, because I'm really not that attracted to your mother," Sinkua joked, "but I'd love to go home to Ferya with you."

Epilogue

"I'm going north to file a report. What's your mission status?"

"The infiltration was a success. They've suspected nothing."

"Fantastic. What of your other objective?"

"The Document is in my possession."

"Well done. I'll come by to retrieve it before I leave."

"I formally request that you take me with you."

"You know I can't do that."

"My mission is over."

"For now, but we can't risk their seeing you in the presence of The Omnimath."

"How long have you known about this?"

"You were told of the arrangement ahead of time."

"I think I've earned a little lenience. Don't you?"

"If you'd like, I can append a message in your stead."

"That'll have to do, I suppose."

"Go on then, what would you like to tell him?"

"… I want to see my daughter."

About the Author

Meticulous to the point of obsession and ambitious to the point of anxiety, E. A. Setser is a career author and publisher trapped in a day jobber's body. He holds a degree in accounting, which has nothing to do with his job in the commercial graphics industry, but it probably helps with being the founder of Social Detriment Publishing. Maybe.

Originally from Tennessee, E. A. and his wife Celia and son Tavin have been working to escape The Bible Belt. They have now made it to Lawrenceburg, IN.

Merch: https://www.zazzle.com/social_detriment
Twitter: https://twitter.com/EASetser
Facebook: www.facebook.com/SocialDetriment
Amazon: www.amazon.com/author/easetser

www.ingramcontent.com/pod-product-compliance
Lightning Source LLC
Chambersburg PA
CBHW060816120726
47909CB00006B/1944